Praise for Penny Vincenzi:

'Big books with intimate storylines are Penny Vincenzi's speciality. However, with *The Best of Times* she has shifted her speciality into a whole new league . . . The novel isn't just a simple story of triumphing over tragedy, it's more a personal, intimate exploration of goodness and doing the right thing at the right time. It is also a reminder of how fleeting and fragile life can be – but how, amazingly, love and lasting happiness can be just around that dangerous corner' *Mirror*

'Astute Vincenzi is at her absolute best when describing the mores, manners and manors of the affluent middle classes . . . Classic Vincenzi' *Daily Mail*

'There's one name that continues to reign supreme, Penny Vincenzi' *Glamour*

'The literary equivalent of a huge box of hand-made chocolate truffles – a total indulgence' *Woman & Home*

'Seductively readable . . . I carried on reading late into the night' *The Times*

'Penny Vincenzi dazzlingly combines the old-fashioned virtues of gripping storytelling with the up-to-the-minute contemporary feel for emotional depth and insight . . . Reading her is an addictive experience' Elizabeth Buchan

'Marvellously engrossing . . . perfect for curling up with on a rainy day. Or any day for that matter' Barbara Taylor Bradford

'Highly addictive. Don't even think of opening unless you've got a lazy weekend to fill' *Daily Telegraph*

'Pick a location where you can be comfortable sitting still for hours . . . once you start reading, you're not going to want to move yourself . . . Totally compelling *****' *Heat*

By Penny Vincenzi

Old Sins
Wicked Pleasures
An Outrageous Affair
Another Woman
Forbidden Places
The Dilemma
Windfall
Almost A Crime
No Angel
Something Dangerous
Into Temptation
Sheer Abandon
An Absolute Scandal
The Best of Times

Christine Palmer

Penny Vincenzi

the best
of times

$\mathcal{R}$
headline
review

First published in 2009
by HEADLINE REVIEW
An imprint of HEADLINE PUBLISHING GROUP

First published in paperback in 2010
by HEADLINE REVIEW

1

Cataloguing in Publication Data is available from the British Library

ISBN 978 0 7553 2089 9 (B-format)
ISBN 978 0 7553 5817 5 (A-format)

Typeset in New Caledonia by Avon DataSet Ltd,
Bidford-on-Avon, Warwickshire

Printed and bound in Great Britain by
Clays Ltd, St Ives plc

HEADLINE PUBLISHING GROUP
An Hachette UK Company
338 Euston Road
London NW1 3BH

www.headline.co.uk
www.hachette.co.uk

For Emily and Claudia, with much love. For saving the plot, the book and their mother's sanity.

Acknowledgements

Some very big and heartfelt thank-yous are due over this book.

First, and very very importantly, to Inspector David Toms-Sheridan of the Traffic Operational Command Unit, who fielded my endless cretinous questions, endured countless plot swerves, and offered his own ingenious take on things to more than one of my dilemmas. And who gave me an enormous amount of valuable police time. I hope no crime went unpunished as a result.

The other person without whom I literally could not have written the book is Aimée di Marco, who not only instructed me most painstakingly on life in an A&E department, but recreated for me with extraordinary vividness the hour on hour progress of a major emergency, the structure of the medical teams, the necessary medical and surgical procedures and the ongoing care of the victims. Her patients are assuredly very fortunate.

And then, Simon Lesley gave me a wonderfully vivid insight into the trials and tribulations of a lorry driver's life.

Many many thanks-yous to Liz Trubridge, TV and film producer extraordinaire, for guiding me through the minefield that is filming a TV series.

I owe much gratitude to Minna and Peveril Bruce, who not only gave me a crash course on farming, but into the complex procedures of mounting a music festival.

Graham Marchant supplied some highly crucial know-how on the mechanics of the E-type Jaguar.

Anna Dudley gave me a wonderfully vivid and witty picture of life as a theatrical agent.

Stuart Greaney conducted a brilliant one-to-one teach-in for me on life as a Management Consultant.

And Sue Stapely who once again beat a path to the doors of her endless contacts to assist me in providing extra background knowledge on all manner of things, and who supplied a fair old bit of info herself... One day I shall find something she doesn't know about; but I haven't managed it yet.

Other important credits: Robert Brown of Corker Binning and Mark Haslam of BCL Burton Copeland for invaluable legal input; more medical help – in the literary sense! – from Roger Freeman (psychiatry), Ursula Lloyd (gynaecology), and David Ward (cardiology); Jessica Sedler for a most evocative picture of auditions; Simon Cornish for his encyclopaedic knowledge of fine eateries and drinkeries; and Sarah Pearce for her insider knowledge of London's coolest and chic-est hangouts.

At Headline, my truly wonderful publishers, so many thanks to Harrie Evans for patient, painstaking, and inspiring editing, and for making it all a lot more fun; Georgina Moore for telling the world about the book, with her unique never-say-die enthusiasm; Jo Liddiard for an inspired marketing campaign; James Horobin for seeing the book into the shops with such gusto and determination, Peter Newsom for sending it winging around the world. And to Nick Venables for a breathtakingly beautiful cover design. Finally, to Kerr Macrae, for his perceptive and all-seeing eye.

Gratitude in spades to Clare Alexander, my wonderfully imaginative, caring and calming super-agent.

To my other two daughters, Polly and Sophie, for their astonishingly ongoing interest, encouragement and support: never taken for granted.

And as always my husband Paul who, on being told in hysterical tones one Sunday morning when I was about two thirds of the way through that I absolutely couldn't finish the book, it was completely impossible, said kindly, but very firmly, 'I'm afraid you've got to.'

It was not the first crisis he has defused; I doubt it will be the last.

Characters

Jonathan Gilliatt, *a gynaecologist and obstetrician*
Laura Gilliatt, *his wife*
Charlie, Daisy and Lily, *their children*
Mark and Serena Edwards, *friends of the Gilliatts*

Linda Di-Marcello, *a theatrical agent*
Francis Carr, *Linda's business partner and good friend*
Georgia Linley, *a young actress*
Michael Linley, *Georgia's brother, a successful lawyer*
Bea Linley, *Georgia's mother*

Barney Fraser, *a banker in the City*
Amanda Baring, *his fiancée*
Toby Weston, *his best friend*
Tamara Richmond, *Toby's fiancée*
Carol Weston, *Toby's mother*
Ray Weston, *Toby's father*
Gerald Richmond, *Tamara's father*

Mary Bristow, *a widow*
Donald Bristow, *her late husband*
Russell Mackenzie, *her old wartime flame*
Douglas Bristow, *her son*
Christine, *her daughter*
Gerry, *Christine's husband*
Timothy, *Mary's grandson*
Colin Sharp, *Mary's driver*

Emma King, *a doctor at St Mark's Hospital*
Luke Spencer, *Emma's boyfriend*

Alex Pritchard, *an A&E consultant*
Adam and Amy, *his children*
Mark Collins, *an orthopaedic registrar*
James Osborne, *a neurosurgeon*

Patrick Connell, *a lorry driver*
Maeve Connell, *his wife*
Liam, Callum and Ciaran, *their children*

Abi Scott, *a photographer's assistant*

William Grainger, *a farmer*
Barbara Grainger, *his mother*
Peter Grainger, *his father*

Rick Harwood, *the driver of the white van*
Dianne Harwood, *his wife*
Jack Bryant, *the driver of the E-type*

Shaun, *a Cub Scout and crash victim*

Sergeant Freeman, *the officer in charge of the crash
  investigation*
Constable Rowe, *his right-hand man*

Merlin Gerard, *the second assistant director on* Moving Away
Bryn Merrick, *the director on* Moving Away
Jaz, *a friend of Merlin's*
Ticky, *an actress*
Anna, *an actress and friend of Georgia's*
Lila, *Anna's daughter*
Sue Riley, *the casting director on* Moving Away

Michael Andrews, *a coroner*
Susan Andrews, *his wife*

It was the best of times, it was the worst of times . . . it was the spring of hope, it was the winter of despair, we had everything before us, we had nothing before us, we were all going direct to Heaven, we were all going direct the other way.

A Tale of Two Cities, Charles Dickens

Prologue

A time near to now

It happened just before 4 p.m. on Friday, 22 August, after a brief thunderstorm. The end-of-week traffic had packed the M4 in both directions, heavy enough to hold cars in the fast lane just within the speed limit, light enough to keep all three lanes moving. Viewed on the CCTV cameras, everything looked orderly and under control.

At one minute to four, a lorry travelling eastwards towards London appeared to swerve suddenly, and then accelerated towards the central reservation, cutting through it with lethal force; and then turned in on itself, its trailer twisting and half rearing before falling on to its side, slithering along the road into the oncoming traffic and finally coming to a halt just short of the hard shoulder. Where it burst open, not only the doors, but the roof and sides, discharging its burden of freezers, fridges, washing machines, dryers, some tossed into the air with the force, some skidding and sliding along the motorway, a great tide of deadly flotsam, hitting cars and coaches in its path.

A mini-bus driving westwards in the fast lane became impacted in the undercarriage of the lorry; a Golf GTi immediately behind it swung sideways and rammed into one of the lorry's wheels. A vast unyielding dam of vehicles braking, swerving, skidding, was formed: growing by the moment.

Back on the eastbound side of the carriageway, the cars

immediately behind the lorry smashed into it and one another; one hit the central reservation so hard it became embedded in it, and the dozen or so after that, with an advantage of perhaps two or three seconds' warning, crashed into one another relentlessly but comparatively harmlessly, like bumper cars in a fairground.

The freezers and refrigerators continued on their journey, more slowly now, but still with lethal effect; one car hitting them head-on made a 180-degree turn, and was struck by an oncoming motorbike; another shot sideways and hit the central reservation.

Up and down on the road, then, stillness formed and a strange semi-silence overtook the scene, engines stopped, horns hushed . . . but soon to be replaced by other hideous sounds, of human screaming and canine barking, and through it all the absolutely incongruous noise of music from car radios.

And then a mass of mobiles, in hands that were able to hold them, called the police, the ambulance service, called home. And even as they did so, the chaos spread out its great tentacles, reaching far, far down the road in both directions so that hundreds were unable to escape from it.

Within the space of perhaps thirty or forty seconds, chance – that absolutely irresistible force – had taken its capricious hold on the time and the place. It had disrupted the present, distorted the future, replaced order with chaos, confidence with fear and control with impotence. Lives were ended for some, changed for ever for others; and a most powerful game of Consequences was set in train.

Part One
Before

Chapter 1

Laura Gilliatt often said – while reaching for the nearest bit of wood, or tapping her own lovely head, for she was deeply superstitious – that her life was simply too good to be true. And the casual observer – or indeed quite a beady-eyed one – would have been hardpressed not to agree with her. Married to a husband she adored, Jonathan Gilliatt, the distinguished gynaecologist and obstetrician, and with three extremely attractive and charming children, with a career of her own as an interior designer, just demanding enough to save her from any possible boredom, but not so much that she could not set it aside when required, by any domestic crisis large or small, such as the necessity to attend an important dinner or conference with her husband or the sickbed or nativity play of one of her children.

The family owned two beautiful houses: one on the River Thames at Chiswick and a second in the Dordogne area of France; they also had a timeshare in a ski chalet in Méribel. Jonathan earned a great deal of money from his private practice at Princess Anne's, an extremely expensive hospital for women just off Harley Street, but he was also a highly respected NHS consultant, heading up the obstetric unit at St Andrew's, Bayswater. He was passionately opposed to the modern trend for elective caesarians, both in his private practice and the NHS; in his opinion they were a direct result of the compensation culture and therefore of the workings of the devil. Babies were meant to be pushed gently into the world by their mothers, he said, not yanked abruptly out in the more brutal environment of the operating theatre. This put him on the receiving line of a great deal of criticism from certain feminist branches of the media.

The beady-eyed observer would also have noted that he was deeply in love with his wife, while also enjoying the adoration of his patients; and that his son Charlie and his daughters Daisy and Lily – his two little flowers as he called them – all thought he was completely wonderful.

In his wife he had an absolute treasure, as he often told not only her but the world in general; for as well as being beautiful, Laura was sunny-natured and sweet-tempered, and indeed, this same observer studying her quite intently as she went through her days, raising her family, running her business, entertaining her friends, would have found it hard to catch her in any worse humour than mild irritation or even raising her voice. If this did happen, it was usually prompted by some bad behaviour on the part of her children, such as Charlie, who was eleven, sneaking into the loo with his Nintendo when he had had his hour's ration for the day, or Lily and Daisy, who were nine and seven, persuading the au pair, Helga, that their mother had agreed that they could watch *High School Musical* for the umpteenth time until well after they were supposed to be in bed.

They were all too young to be committing any more heinous crimes; it would have seemed safe to conclude, given their hugely privileged upbringing, that it was fairly unlikely that they ever would.

The Gilliatts had been married for thirteen years: 'Lucky, lucky years,' Jonathan had said, presenting Laura with a Tiffany Eternity ring on the morning of their anniversary. 'I know it's not a special anniversary, darling, but you deserve it, and it comes with all my love.'

Laura was so overcome with emotion that she burst into

tears and then smiled through them as she looked at the lovely thing on her finger; and after that, having consulted the clock on their bedroom fireplace, decided she should express her gratitude to Jonathan, not only for the ring but the thirteen happy years, in a rather practical way – with the result that she got seriously behind in her school-run schedule and all three children were clearly going to be late.

'And I don't have a very seemly excuse,' she wailed to Jonathan, leaning out of the window of the Range Rover to kiss him goodbye. 'Whatever can I say?'

'Say your husband got held up.'

'Don't be filthy.'

Laura had been nineteen and still a virgin when she had met Jonathan – 'probably the last in London,' she said. This was not due to any particular moral rectitude, but because until him, she had honestly never fancied anyone enough to want to go to bed with them. She fancied Jonathan quite enough, however, and found the whole experience 'absolutely lovely', as she told him. They were married a year later.

'I do hope I'm going to cope with being Mrs Gilliatt – quite an important career,' she said just a little anxiously, a few days before the wedding, and: 'Of course you will,' he told her. 'You fit the job description perfectly. And you'll grow into it beautifully.'

As indeed she had, taking her duties very seriously. She loved cooking and entertaining, and had discovered a certain flair for interior design. When they had been married a year, and their own lovely house was finished to both their satisfaction, she asked Jonathan if he would mind if she took a course and perhaps dabbled in it professionally.

'Of course not, darling – lovely idea. As long as you can do it from home and can cope with any problems on your own. I don't want to come second to any difficult clients.'

Laura promised him he wouldn't, and he never had. And neither, as the babies arrived, in neat, two-yearly intervals, did they. For many years, until Daisy was at school, she simply devoted herself to them, and was perfectly happy. She did have to work quite hard at reassuring Jonathan that he still came first in her life, and was slightly surprised at his impatience and near-jealousy created by the demands of the children; she had imagined he was rather more mature than that. Clearly her mother had been right, she reflected, and all men were children at heart. For the first few years therefore, she employed a full-time nanny, for the demands of Jonathan's professional life on her time were considerable, and he liked her to be totally available to him.

But when Daisy went to school, Laura began quite tentatively to work – small things, finding new curtains for one house, revamping a bathroom for another – and found she loved it 'in spite of the clients'. She had a particular flair for colour, for using the unexpected, and it was for that she was beginning to earn a small reputation. But it all remained little more than a hobby, very much what she did in her spare time: which was not actually in very large supply.

But that was how Jonathan liked it; and therefore she liked it too.

Spring that year had been especially lovely; it arrived early and stayed late, perfect green and gold days, so that as early as April, Laura was setting the outside table for lunch every Saturday and Sunday, and as May wore on, she and Jonathan would eat dinner outside as well, and watch the soft dusk settle over the garden, and listen to the sounds of the river in the background – the hooting of tugs, the partying pleasure boats, the occasional rush of water as a police launch sped along, the raw cries of the gulls.

'How lucky we are,' she said more than once, maybe more than a hundred times, smiling at Jonathan across the table: and he would raise his glass to her and reach for her hand and tell her he loved her.

But now it was midsummer and this being England, the rain had arrived: day after relentless day it fell from dark grey skies. Barbecues and summer parties were being cancelled, floaty summer dresses put away (and jeans and wellies pulled resentfully out of cupboards), the shops were holding what they called End of Season Sales and there was a stampede for flights to Majorca and Ibiza, for restorative weeks and even long weekends in the sun.

For the Gilliatts, there was no such stampede. Laura was packing, as she did every year, for their annual pilgrimage to the lovely golden-stoned farmhouse in the Dordogne, near Sarlat, where the sun would shine down unstintingly on them, heating the water in the pool, ripening the green-gages in their garden and the grapes on the verandah-vine, and warming the stones on the terrace so that the lizards might siesta in the afternoons along with their landlords.

'And thank goodness for it,' she said. 'Poor Serena is so dreading the holidays, keeping the boys amused all those weeks – well, months really . . .'

Jonathan said just slightly shortly that he had thought the Edwardses were off to some five-star hotel in Nice, not to mention the ten days they would spend with the Gilliatts on the way down. Laura said well, that was true, but it still only added up to just over three weeks and that left six or even seven in London.

Jonathan said that most of his NHS patients would not regard that as too much of a hardship, given the three and a half weeks of luxury sunshine. He was less fond of Mark and Serena Edwards than Laura was. Mark was a Public Relations consultant for a big City firm, buffed over-smooth by years of networking and contacting and charming, and Serena was Laura's best friend and, in Jonathan's view, made Laura the repository of just too many confidences and secrets. But they were, officially at least, the Gilliatts' best friends, and Serena and Laura nurtured many a fantasy about (amongst other things) the weddings of Tim and Jack Edwards to Lily and Daisy Gilliatt.

Jonathan was not able, of course, to spend nine weeks in the Dordogne; he took as much of his annual leave as he could and for the rest of the time flew out each Friday afternoon to Toulouse and back each Monday, or if he could juggle sufficiently with his clinics, even Tuesday morning.

They all missed him, of course, but there was still so much to do, swimming, cycling, shopping in the endless markets, and meeting and visiting and entertaining all the countless other English families in the vicinity, that they were almost surprised to find him joining them once more for supper in the thick, sweet-scented air.

And so, as she read reports of what appeared to be almost continuous rain in England, and indeed listened to friends in England complaining about it, and telling her how lucky she was not to be there, Laura savoured the long golden days even more than usual, and even more than usual counted her own multiple blessings.

Linda Di-Marcello was aware that she also was fairly fortunate; which meant that, given her line of work, she was doing very well indeed. Linda ran a theatrical agency, and as she often said, her own role was a complex one. She was, in almost equal parts, nanny, therapist and hustler. It was both exhausting and stressful, and she threatened repeatedly to give it up and do something quite different. 'Something really undemanding, like brain surgery,' she would say with a grin. But she knew she never would; she loved it all too much.

Her name, which everyone assumed she must have

made up, but which in fact she owed to her first husband, was well known in London. The agency's name was actually Di-Marcello & Carr; Francis Carr was her 'non-sleeping partner' as he put it, a gay banker who adored her, had faith in her, and had put up the money for the agency in return for 'absolutely no involvement and forty per cent of the profits'. So far it had worked very well.

She was thirty-six, an acknowledged beauty, with dark red hair, dark brown eyes and a deep, Marlene Dietrich-style voice, and she had been to drama school herself, before deciding she couldn't hack the long slog into stardom or more likely non-stardom, and that she rather liked the idea of agenting. She had had the agency for what felt alternately a very long and a very short five years; before that she had worked for several of the established organisations, before setting out on her own. And she had proved to have a talent for it; she could look at an apparently plain, shy girl and see her shining on the screen; at a charmless, ungracious lout and know he could play Noël Coward.

She didn't have many big stars on her books – yet. She had Thea Campbell, who had just won a BAFTA for her Jo in the new BBC version of *Little Women*, and Dougal Hargreaves, who had just been cast as the grown-up Billy in the sequel to *Billy Elliot*, and three or four more who were almost as successful, but she had a big battery of middle-rankers, mostly picked out by herself from the drama schools, almost all of whom were carving out good careers for themselves. But it wasn't easy. Her younger clients particularly found it hard to face reality; they were inevitably disappointed with the slow progress, and while most of them coped with it well, did part-time jobs in bars and restaurants or worked for pocket money as runners for the TV companies, a handful were trouble, emotionally needy, impatient, and at worst disparaging of the work Linda could get them.

'You know,' she said irritably to Francis Carr, over one of their frequent dinners, which were closer to therapy sessions for her than a business progress report, 'I long to tell these kids that what they possess is actually quite an ordinary talent. Specially the dancers, but the actors too. Thousands and thousands of young people can do what they do and do it superbly well; they need an awful lot of luck and star quality to stand out. And most of them don't have those things. They're an ungrateful bunch on the whole, you know. Nothing ever's good enough for them.'

Francis said that the same could be said of his clients, who never felt their money was invested quite well enough or that he gave any of them quite enough of his attention. 'It's human nature, Linda, a fact of working life.'

'I guess. I don't suppose many of your clients have temper tantrums in your office though.'

'You'd be surprised. They come pretty close to it sometimes.'

'Well, OK. I'm obviously making a big fuss about nothing. And when somebody does take off and I know I've been a key part of that, it's still a great feeling.'

'I'm sure. Had anyone taking off recently?'

'Not exactly. It's all been a bit run of the mill this summer – *if* you can call it summer. That's probably what's getting to me.'

'I don't think so,' he said, with a grin. 'You're always complaining about it.'

'Am I? God, how depressing for you. Sorry, Francis. I'll try and be a bit more positive in future.'

Linda lived in a mansion apartment block just off Baker Street; her flat was large and luxurious, expensively furnished in a mix of antique and contemporary, and absolutely immaculate. Her office – a sleek modern suite near Charlotte Street – was equally so. Linda was a perfectionist – in every aspect of her life. Obsessively tidy, awesomely efficient and possessed of a grinding ambition and determination, she was, by any standards, a hugely successful woman. And yet, she quite often felt, in spite of the professional success, that she was actually a failure.

She was lonely: and however much she told herself that she had a far better life now, happily single rather than unhappily married, she didn't really believe it. No amount of self-indulgence, of looking at the rows of designer clothes she was able to buy, and the treasures she was able to fill her flat with – the expensive furniture, her collections of Art Deco figures and lamps, her growing gallery of modern paintings – properly made up for it. She would have given all of it – well, most of it, anyway, plus the fact that she could do whatever she liked, whenever she liked – in order not to be alone, and not to be lonely. She had girlfriends who genuinely didn't seem to mind, who revelled in their single condition. Linda did mind and she didn't revel in it. She did have a social life – by most people's standards a glamorous one. But it wasn't quite the sort she wanted. Of course, singledom was perfectly respectable these days. It had to be, with so many women on their own. And *Sex and the City* had actually made it fashionable, which helped.

It had its own pleasures and conventions, its own codes. Nobody had to sit at home staring at the cat any more; you could lift the phone, call girlfriends or manfriends, propose any kind of outing, spend your own money, organise your own time. During the week it was fine, she often worked late, and there were theatres and film screenings to go to; and she did plan her weekends carefully, making sure they were fully booked weeks or even months ahead. She did a lot of quick trips – flips as she called them – to Paris, Milan, Rome, usually with one of her single girlfriends, to visit galleries and shop; she was a member of various theatrical and musical associations, a Friend of Covent Garden, of Sadler's Wells and the RSC. It would certainly take a fairly remarkable man to deliver so indulgent a lifestyle.

But – it wasn't actually what she wanted: it was cool and demanding, and somehow self-conscious, when she yearned for warmth and ease. The closest she got to that these days was with Francis.

What she hated and was almost afraid of were solitary weekends, and she struggled desperately to avoid them. Friday was a particularly bad night to be on your own, or even out with a girlfriend, with London packed as it was with the partying young. And from there it was downhill all the way; she tended to sink into a mist of negativism round about teatime on Saturday, developing into a full-blown depression roughly two hours later, and would then sit in front of the TV, determined not to give in and go to bed, drinking rather too much wine, and wondering if perhaps she should have given Mr Di-Marcello another chance instead of throwing him out of the house at the discovery of his first affair.

But she knew, deep down, that she had done the right thing. That was the point, it would only have been the first one – he was about as monogamous as a tom cat. But the divorce had hurt horribly, a misery arguably greater even than that caused by the affair; and had been followed by a second bad relationship, with another charmer, another philanderer, who had been seeing another girl almost before he had moved into Linda's apartment. She had an eye for a rotter, Linda often thought gloomily. She didn't exactly want domesticity, she didn't want children, and she certainly didn't want to take on a man with a ready-made family as so many of her friends seemed to be doing; but she did want someone to share things with, pleasures and anxieties, jokes and conversations – and, of course, her bed.

She did share her bed, from time to time, with men she fancied, who made her laugh, who interested and intrigued her, but no one since The Charmer (she tried not to refer to him, even in her painful memories, by his name, finding it easier to consign him to her mental dustbin that way) had quite qualified as candidates for fulltime life-sharing.

Nor did she meet that many; the world she moved in contained an exceptionally large number of gay men, and still more addicts of one kind or another: 'The London branch of the AA is incredibly A-list,' as a young actress had astutely remarked, and indeed, the meetings were regarded as an excellent opportunity for networking.

'I want a solicitor,' she wailed to her friends. 'I want a bank manager, I want an accountant,' and they would tell her that she wanted no such thing, and of course they were right in one way and quite wrong in another, for what were accountants and bank managers and solicitors but synonyms for reliable and sensible and loyal?

The fact was, she no longer felt free; she felt lonely and insecure. What was the matter with her? Why couldn't she form good relationships, or even if she could, then give them lasting power?

Was it such a big ask? Not just to fall but be *in love*? Whole-heartedly, wondrously, thunderously, orgasmically *in love*? It did seem to be. She really couldn't see how it was ever going to happen again.

'Only five weeks to the wedding. I just can't believe it!'

Barney Fraser looked at his fiancée, in all her prettiness and sweetness, and sighed. 'I think I can,' he said, and he could hear his own voice, just slightly heavy, belying his smile.

'Barney! That doesn't sound very positive. Aren't you looking forward to it?'

'Yes,' he said quickly. 'Yes, of course I am.'

'It's the speech, isn't it? But you'll be fine, I know you will. It's such a huge responsibility, but think how good you were at your parents' anniversary party. Totally brilliant. I was so proud of you.'

'Well . . .'

15

'Barney, you were. Honestly.'

'Well, thank you,' he said carefully, grateful for her support, 'and I expect you're right. It is a big worry.'

'Of course it is. But unnecessary. It's all going to be wonderful – if it stops raining, that is. Pity it's not September, that's usually more reliable, much better than the summer actually. Wouldn't you say?'

'What? I mean no. I mean—'

'Barney, you're not listening to me. Are you?'

'Sorry, Amanda. I was . . . well, I was thinking about something else. I'm very sorry.' Actually he *was* thinking about the wedding; he thought about it more and more. Well, not the wedding. More the marriage.

'Thinking about what?'

'Oh, just work. Sorry. More wine?'

'Yes, please.'

He grinned at her and refilled her glass; there was nothing he could really say about his misgivings over the wedding. It was too late and it wouldn't help. It wasn't his own wedding, for God's sake, that he had misgivings about. It was Toby's, and Toby was old enough, surely, to look after himself.

Amanda was so thrilled at being chief bridesmaid; the bride was one of her very best friends. And when she and Barney got married the following spring, Tamara would be her chief bridesmaid, or best woman or whatever they decided to call her. And Toby would be Barney's best man.

Toby wasn't just one of Barney's best friends, he was absolutely his best friend. They were as close as two people could be, had been ever since prep school when they had lain in their small beds the first night, side by side, each smiling gallantly, refusing to admit either of them felt remotely homesick. It had helped so much, in those early days, the friendship, as much as the pretending did. Once you gave in to the tears, allowed yourself to think properly about home and your mother and all that, you'd had it

16

really. And the friendship had never faltered – intensified, Barney always thought, by the fact they were both only children, and having no siblings at home to play with, were soon spending time with one another in the holidays as well as the term.

They had stayed cheerfully together right through prep school and then into leaving Harrow; then after the separation of university, Toby at Durham, Barney at Bristol, there was the delight of discovering that they were both applying for jobs in the City where they managed to end up not at the same investment bank, that would have been too much of a cliché, but at closely neighbouring establishments, either side of Bishopsgate.

Toby was just the best: clever, funny, cool and plain old-fashioned nice. Barney didn't like to think of their friendship in terms of love, since that was corny and slushy and anyway, these days if you said you were terribly fond of another bloke, people presumed you were gay. But he did love Toby; and admired him and enjoyed his company more than that of anyone else in the world – except Amanda, obviously. Not that you could compare how you felt for your best friend and your fiancée: it was totally different. What was great was that despite their both being engaged and setting up home and all that sort of thing, they were still able to see an enormous amount of one another. Were still really close. And while being Toby's best man was clearly inevitable, just as Toby would be his, it was still a great honour and Barney had been extremely chuffed about it.

And the two girls were great friends, both worked in the City as well. It was very neat: Amanda in Human Resources at Toby's bank, Tamara on the French desk at Barney's. There was no reason why they should not all remain friends for the rest of their lives.

It was just that . . . well, it was just that Barney thought – no, it was stronger than that, he *knew* – that Tamara

17

wasn't good enough for Toby. He'd struggled not to think that, but she just wasn't. OK, she was gorgeous and sexy and clever, and their flat in Limehouse was absolutely sensational, totally minimal, more to Barney's taste if he was honest than the small house he and Amanda had bought in Clapham. It didn't matter at all to him really, but it was a bit too fussy, full of clever ideas that Amanda had found in the house magazines and copied, without considering whether it all worked together properly. But still, it was great and she was great and he loved her, of course, and not having much of a visual sense himself, he just accepted it all. There were more important things in life than décor.

Amanda was solid gold, through and through. Tamara, he felt, was composed of some rather questionable nickel, under her lovely skin. She was selfish, she was spoiled – first by her doting parents, and now, of course, by Toby – extremely possessive, dismissive of Toby's feelings and given to putting him down, albeit with her rather sparky humour, when it suited her. Amanda would never do that; she not only thought Barney was wonderful, she showed it; she told him and everyone else so repeatedly, it could be a bit embarrassing sometimes, actually, but – well, she was great and he really loved her. Toby really loved Tamara too, and he seemed unaware of any shortcomings she might have; he occasionally said that he had to get back early or Tamara would want to know the reason why, or that he would be in trouble for this, that or the other, but it was very much tongue in cheek, and he had certainly been an angel over the build-up to the wedding, agreeing to everything she wanted, even their honeymoon in the Maldives when Barney knew that sort of place bored him and he would have loved to do something less conventional like travelling across India by train, which he had always longed to do. But, 'It's her wedding,' he would say easily, apparently unaware of the irony of it, that it was his too. His loyalty to her was intense – a bit too intense, Barney thought sometimes, whenever he criticised her, however lightly.

So most of the time he played along to the fantasy that she was perfect and that Toby was just the luckiest guy in the world.

And with the stag do – a long weekend in New York – only a fortnight away, it was really much too late to do or say anything about it at all.

He just remained uneasy about it; and couldn't discuss it with anyone. Not even Amanda. Actually, least of all with Amanda. That was a bit worrying too.

Chapter 2

She'd done it now – there could be no turning back. Mary took a deep breath, stepped away from the letterbox and walked home again through the pouring rain, hoping and praying that she had done the right thing. In four or five days, the letter would arrive in New York, at Russell Mackenzie's undoubtedly grand apartment, bearing the news that yes, she thought it would be lovely if he came to England and they met once again, after all these long, long years apart.

Of course it might ruin everything, ruin over sixty years of friendship, and replace happy old memories with awkward new ones. She could only hope not. And she really didn't think so.

Sixty-three years since they'd said goodbye, she and Russell; she'd stood in his arms at Liverpool Street Station, surrounded by dozens of other couples, the girls all crying, the soldiers in their uniforms holding them close, but she'd known she hurt the most; it was almost unbearable, and when finally she had to let him go, it was like a physical agony, as if some part of her had been wrenched off. And she'd stood watching him walk down the platform, then climb into the train, waving to her one last time . . . and she'd gone home and run up to her room, and cried all night and wanted to die. Literally. She had loved him so much and he had loved her too. She knew he had. It wasn't just that he'd told her so, he'd demonstrated it over and over again. Well, he'd asked her to marry him, for goodness' sake! But she hadn't accepted; it had been too frightening, too unimaginable, to go away, all those miles away from everyone she knew and loved. And anyway, she was spoken for, engaged, even if she didn't have a ring on her finger; she was engaged to Donald, sweet gentle Donald, who was coming home to her, to make her his wife.

These days it would have been different, of course; no girl would remain loyal to a man when she thought she might be in love with another, just because she had promised. And to be fair, she knew at least two girls who had ditched their English fiancés and gone off as GI brides, sailed 3,000 miles to marry the dashing Yanks who brought them nylons and took them out for fancy meals and told them of the wondrous places they would be living in, big houses with swimming pools and two cars in the garage. It hadn't always turned out like that, of course; she had heard that Dottie Bradshaw for one had been met at the docks in New York by her handsome soldier lover and taken to a rotten little house in some godforsaken suburb where she had to live with her mother-in-law as well as him, and not a Cadillac in sight.

She had been so surprised when Russell continued to write to her; she had thought their romance would be over, a closed book, with *The End* written in curly writing as she waved him off on the train, but he had done so almost as soon as he arrived back in the States. *I want us still to be friends, Mary*, he wrote. *I can't face life totally without you, even if I can't be with you.*

She had agreed to that, of course: what harm in letters? Nobody could object to that, think it was wrong. And the letters had flown backwards and forwards across the Atlantic ever since.

He had sent pictures, first of himself and his very grand-looking parents and their very grand-looking house, and later, as time passed and wounds healed and lives inevitably progressed, of his bride, Nancy; and she had written of her

21

marriage to Donald and sent pictures of the two of them on their wedding day, and of the little house they had bought in Croydon. And later still, they exchanged news and photographs of their babies, her two and Russell's three, and sent Christmas and birthday cards to one another. Donald had never known; she hadn't deliberately kept it from him, of course, but she had seen no reason to tell him either. He wouldn't have believed that Russell had only been a friend, and he would have been quite right not to believe it either.

The letters arrived about once a month, usually after Donald had gone to work. If one did happen to arrive on a Saturday, and he saw it, she would say it was from her American penfriend. Which was true, she told herself. He was. In a way. Russell's stories of grand houses and Cadillacs and swimming pools were clearly true; his parents were rich, with an apartment in New York and a house in somewhere called Southampton. It didn't seem too much like the Southampton Mary knew; it was full of big houses and people played polo there and sailed on the ocean in their yachts. He and Nancy spent every weekend at the Southampton house, and when his parents died, he inherited it.

It had been a happy marriage, as far as Mary could make out; as hers to Donald had been. But Nancy had died when she was only fifty-two, of cancer, and Russell had married again, to a woman called Margaret. Mary had been very upset about that, she wasn't sure why, and absurdly comforted when Russell told her it was only so the children had a mother figure.

Donald had died on his seventy-fifth birthday, had had a heart attack while the house was full of his beloved family; Mary honestly believed he went perfectly happy. It had been a peaceful, uneventful marriage, full of tenderness. Donald had been a wonderful husband; he had never made much money, had worked away happily at his job in an insurance company and had no ambitions to change it.

As long as he could come home every night to Mary and the children, he said, and knew he could pay all the bills, he was content. He loved birds and birdwatching and went off with a friend every other Sunday – 'I wouldn't leave you every Sunday, Mary, it wouldn't be right' – and would come back full of excitement and stories of birds spotted through the binoculars she had given him on their tenth wedding anniversary, his Box Brownie camera full of photographs. She had never wanted to go with him, even when the children were grown up. She didn't really like birds, found them disturbing. And besides, she relished the peace. Those Sunday afternoons were when she wrote to Russell.

She had kept all his letters, and photographs, safely hidden in her underwear drawer tucked in empty packets of sanitary towels; she knew Donald would no more look in there than fly to the moon. And every so often, she would get them out and relive it all, the wonderful passionate romance that had led to a lifetime of secret happiness.

And then last year, Russell had written to tell her that Margaret had died. *She was a very loving wife and mother and I hope I made her happy*, he said. *And now we are both alone, and I wonder how you would feel if at last we were reunited? I've been thinking of making a trip to England and we could meet.*

He had been over occasionally on business, she knew that, but they had never met. It would have been unthinkable. Just the same, she often thought how odd it was that from time to time they had only been a few hundred miles apart, rather than thousands – and yet still really no nearer.

Mary's initial reaction had been one of panic. What would he think, confronted by the extremely ordinary old lady she had become? He was so clearly used to sophistication, to a great deal of money, to fine birds in very fine feathers; she was indeed his 'little London sparrow',

23

the name he had given her all those years ago. And all right, she lived in a very nice little house now, on the outskirts of Bristol, where she and Donald had moved when he had retired, to be near their beloved daughter Christine and her family, and she had a few nice clothes, and she was lucky, because she had kept her figure. So many of her friends had let themselves go, but she was still slim, so if she did get dressed up she looked all right; but her very best outfits came from Debenhams, the everyday ones from Marks & Spencer, her hair was grey, of course, and a rather dull grey at that, not the dazzling white she had hoped to inherit from her mother, and she had very little to talk about. Her most exciting outings were to the cinema, and they were precious few, or playing whist or canasta with her friends. And although she tried to keep up with the news, she found it all very confusing, specially with foreign affairs, was never quite sure which side who was on; and then Russell spent a lot of his life at things called 'benefits', which seemed to cover all sorts of exciting events, theatrical, musical, even sporting. Whatever would they talk about?

But he had ignored her excuses and protests, rejected her argument that they might spoil everything if they met again now – *what's to spoil? Only memories and no one can hurt them* – and gradually persuaded her that a rendezvous would be at worst very interesting and fun and *at best wonderful*.

I want to see you again, my very dear little Sparrow. Fate has kept us apart, let's see if we can't cheat her while there is still time.

It hadn't been fate at all, as far as Mary could see; it had been her own implacable resolve and just possibly cowardice, but gradually she came round, not to his view exactly, but to feeling that she would greatly regret it for whatever was left of her life, if she refused.

And so she had written to tell him so, saying that he

should go ahead and make the arrangement for his visit, 'ideally at the end of August'.

Which was only a few weeks away.

On that same rainy morning, Linda received a phone call from an independent production company; they were casting a new six-parter for Channel 4, a family-based psychological thriller.

'Very meaty, very raw. We need a young black girl. Must be pretty, and cool as well, properly streetwise. First casting in three or four weeks' time. If you've got anyone, email a CV and some shots.'

Linda did have someone, and she sent her details over straight away.

She'd had Georgia Linley on her books for just over a year and she was beginning to think it was a year too many. OK, she was gorgeous-looking and very, very talented; she'd picked her out from a large cast at an end-of-year production at her drama school, the only one of the cast she'd seriously considered and they'd all been pretty good, put her through her paces and taken her on. Since then it had been an uphill struggle. Georgia had not only been something of a star at college, and hated the crashdown into bit parts and commercials, she was also extremely impatient and volatile; had Linda realised exactly how much, she might not have taken her on in the first place. After every failed audition, she would turn up at the agency and weep endlessly, bewailing her own lack of talent combined with her own bad luck and Linda's inability to help her or even understand the idiocy and blindness of the casting director she had just been to see. Initially, Linda was patient, as she was very fond of Georgia, but a year on and she actually dreaded her phone calls.

A very nice steady boyfriend had seemed to calm her for a while; Linda had prayed for the relationship to continue, but was hardly surprised when it ended. James was charming and very good looking, but he was, not to put too fine a point on it, dull, an accountant with rather predictable ambitions. He had adored Georgia and would do anything to please her. The combination of all these factors rendered him a lot less suitable than he might have seemed.

Of course Georgia had problems – 'issues' as the dreadful expression went; about her colour, about the fact that she was adopted, about her hugely successful, brilliant brother. But as Linda had tried to persuade her many times, none of those things were exactly professional drawbacks.

'There are dozens of successful black actors these days.'

'Oh really? Like who?'

Well, there was Adrian Lester and there was Sophie Okonedo and Chiwetel Ejiofor . . . and after that the list tailed to a halt. Dancers, yes, singers, yes, but not actors; she had tried to persuade Georgia to go for some chorus parts in musicals, but she wouldn't hear of it.

'I'm a lousy dancer, Linda, and you know it.'

'Georgia, you're not lousy. Maybe not Covent Garden standard, but extremely good, and you've got an excellent singing voice, and it'd be great experience. You'd almost certainly have got a part in *Chicago*, or that revival of *Hair* or—'

'Which folded after about three days. Great. Anyway, I don't want to be a dancer. I want to act. OK?'

'OK. But I'm trying very hard for you, Georgia. I don't do miracles. You'll just have to be patient.'

'I'll try. I'm sorry.' And she'd give Linda the heartbreaking smile that was her speciality, and leave.

She still lived at home, in Cardiff, with her adoptive white parents. Linda had met them. Her father was a lecturer at Cardiff University, her mother a social worker – charming, slightly hippie middle-class folk – unsure how to manage the ambitions of the beautiful and brilliant cuckoos in their nest. Their other child, Michael, also black, blacker than Georgia, who was actually mixed race – a fact which added to her neuroses – was five years older than Georgia. A barrister, he was doing well in a London Chambers; he had gone to Cambridge from his Cardiff comprehensive, was acknowledged as extraordinarily clever.

He had been adopted by the Linleys when mixed-race adoptions were still – just – acceptable; had it not been for him, they would probably not have been allowed to adopt Georgia. And while the children had been little it had been such a success; they had seemed happy, secure, well adjusted. As for the most part, Michael still was. There had been no point at which he could have claimed his colour had put a brake on his success; it probably even helped as political correctness smoothed his path at certain interviews, both at universities and in the legal world.

'Which I'm not too happy with actually,' he had told Linda cheerfully, 'it's so bloody patronising. But hey, I've made it, so who cares how? Only me. And I can live with it.'

He was a rather self-satisfied and arrogant young man.

Georgia was neither of those things, and was the more attractive for it.

Well, maybe this production would be her big chance, Linda thought, although, much more likely, it would not. She decided not to tell Georgia about it yet; she couldn't face her unbearable disappointment if the production company never even wanted to see her.

People – non-medical people, that was – always reacted in the same way when they heard what Emma did. 'You don't look like a doctor,' they said, in slightly accusatory tones. She would ask them politely what they thought a doctor did look like, but of course she knew perfectly well what they meant: most doctors were not blue-eyed and blond and pretty, with long and extremely good legs. And although she liked looking the way she did, she had learned quite early on in her career that she might have been taken more seriously, had her appearance been more on the earnest side. As a houseman, she had started to wear longer skirts, tied her hair back in a ponytail, and didn't wear much make-up; and now that she was a Senior House Officer and worked in A&E, she wore the compulsory uniform of regulation scrubs. But she sometimes thought she still looked more like a nurse in a *Carry On* film than the consultant obstetrician she was planning to become.

Emma's official title was now Dr King, and she was working at St Mark's, Swindon, the new state-of-the-art hospital opened by the Health Secretary earlier that year. She knew she was very lucky to be there; it was not only superbly designed and multiple-disciplined, with extremely high-calibre staff, it was just near enough to London, where she had first trained, to see her friends. So many people had been shunted up North, a couple even to Scotland, or to mediocre hospitals, which of course somebody had to go to, but when you had got a really good degree, as she had – a First from Cambridge – you didn't want it frittered away.

She was really enjoying A&E. It was a funny thing to enjoy, she could see that – but apart from obstetrics it was her favourite department so far. It was so different every day; there was always something happening, and yes, you did have to cope with some awful things from time to time, major motor crashes, and heart-attacks, and terrible domestic accidents, burns and scalds, but a lot of the time it was quite mundane. And the whole A&E experience was very bonding, somehow. You shared so much, day after day, you worked together, sometimes under huge pressure, sometimes the reverse, but it had a culture and a language all of its own, and you made really good friends there, lasting relationships. And you felt you really were doing something, making people better, mending them there and then, which sounded a bit sentimental if you tried to put it into words, but it was the reason she had gone into medicine, for God's sake, and it was far more satisfying than orthopaedics, for example, seeing people with terribly painful hips and backs and knowing it would be months before anyone could do anything for them at all, and then it wouldn't be you.

She had spent three of the statutory four months now in A&E as SHO, and was rather dreading moving on. Especially as her next department would be dermatology, which didn't appeal to her at all. She had even considered, very briefly, becoming an A&E consultant, like Alex Pritchard, her present boss, but he had told her it was a mug's game and that she'd never make any money.

'Money isn't everything though, is it?' Emma had said.

'Perhaps you could try telling my wife that,' he'd said, and scowled and walked away; she never knew whether he was going to scowl or smile at her. He was a great untidy bear of a man, with a shock of black hair and beetling eyebrows to match, and very deepset brown eyes that peered lugubriously out at the world. Emma adored him, even while being rather frightened of him; there were more scowls than smiles at the moment, as he was reputedly going through a very unpleasant divorce. But he was immensely supportive of her, praised her good work while not hesitating to criticise the bad, and when she diagnosed someone with IBS and sent them home and they came back in twenty-four hours with an acute appendicitis, he told her he had done exactly the same thing when he had been a junior surgeon.

'You just have to remember, everyone makes mistakes. The only thing is, doctors bury theirs,' he said cheerfully as he found her sobbing in the sluice, 'and that woman is far from being buried. Although with her weight and her diet she probably soon will be. Now dry your eyes and we'll go and see her and her appalling husband together . . .'

But obstetrics had remained her first love, and from the following summer, she would start applying for a registrarship.

Emma was twenty-eight, and as well as her exceptional looks was possessed of an extremely happy, outgoing personality. Everyone loved her; had she not had a considerable capacity for self-deprecation, and a slight tendency towards haplessness, she might have been regarded as oversweetened. She had grown up in Colchester where her father worked for a finance company and her mother was a secretary at the junior school that Emma and her brother and sister had all attended, before going on to the local comprehensive. It had been a very happy childhood, Emma often said, lots of fun, treats and friends, 'but Dad was very ambitious for us, quite old-fashioned. We were all encouraged to work hard and aim high.'

Which Emma, by far the cleverest of the three, was certainly doing: a Cambridge place followed by a Cambridge First, and in a subject acknowledged as very tough, was about as high as anyone could have hoped for. Her career thus far had been fairly exemplary; moreover, she had never thought for more than five minutes that she might have preferred to do something else. She loved medicine; it was as simple as that. She enjoyed every day, found the life hugely satisfying and absorbing, and remained extremely ambitious.

Emma looked at her watch: three o'clock. It was a Friday and it seemed to be going on for ever. She was on the 8 a.m. to 6 p.m. shift, and it had actually been one of the slow days. She felt tired too and her head ached. She'd been out very late last night; she should know better than to go out on a Thursday, but a couple of friends from Cambridge had turned up on the A&E doorstep and asked her to go out, and she really couldn't say no. Although she could have said no to the third and fourth Appletini, which was currrently her favourite cocktail. She wasn't very good at refusing cocktails.

Anyway, all being well, tonight she could go to bed early and tomorrow, she was going to London to meet her boyfriend. She'd only been going out with him for three months, and he was the first boyfriend she had had who wasn't a medic. She'd met him in a bar in London; she'd been with a crowd of friends from Uni and one of them, a lawyer, had worked with him briefly. His name was Luke Spencer and he worked for a management consultancy called Pullman. Emma wasn't very clear what management consultants actually did, even after Luke had spent a considerable amount of time explaining it to her. She knew that when a company was in trouble, or less profitable than it would like, the directors often called in management consultants who would then – for a fee – solve all its problems.

That was Luke's version. Her father's was rather more cynical: 'They ask to borrow your watch and then tell you the time.'

Luke's working life could not have been more different from Emma's; she sometimes felt, listening to him, that he never actually did anything, just went to meetings and made presentations. Clearly she must be wrong about this, since he earned what seemed to her an enormous amount of money and worked tremendously long days, almost as long as hers, but then while she went home exhausted and slumped in front of the television, Luke and his colleagues went out for dinner at expensive restaurants like the Gordon Ramsays and Petrus, and then on to extremely trendy clubs like Bungalow 8 and Boujis and Mahiki. Occasionally Emma and other WAGS, as Luke insisted on calling them rather to her irritation, were invited along on these evenings; the first time Luke had taken her to Boujis, Emma had practically burst with excitement, half expecting to see Prince Harry every time she turned round. How Luke and his friends got on the guest-list there she couldn't imagine.

The other thing that seemed to be extremely important if you were a management consultant was knowing the jargon: Luke was always throwing around phrases like 'blue sky thinking' and 'shifting the spend' and putting something 'in the car park' – which didn't mean your car, but an idea or a concept.

She liked being with Luke; he was cool and fun and funny, and he was certainly different from any medic she had ever known. He threw his money around, which was rather nice, hardly ever expected her to pay for herself, and he wore really nice clothes, dark suits and pink shirts and silk ties done in really big loose knots. He took all that very seriously too. He wouldn't be in his suit today, she reflected, because it was Friday which was dress-down day and the blokes all wore chinos or even jeans. Not any old jeans obviously, not Gap or Levi's, but Ralph Lauren or Dolce & Gabbana; and then shirts open at the neck and brown brogues. Dressing down or indeed up on any day was not something that figured large in Emma's life; with the new bare below the elbows rule, anything went really. She secretly missed her white coat: lots of people did.

She wasn't at all sure if she was actually in love with Luke, although she had decided she would like to be, and she was even less sure if he was in love with her; but it was very early days, too early to be even thinking about it, although she couldn't help it, which was obviously significant. But they had a lot of fun together and she always looked forward enormously to seeing him. He was very sweet, and always tried to take her somewhere really nice, which made a change from medics who thought sitting in the pub together was a great night out. The other thing that she liked and that had surprised her was how much he respected her work.

'It must be absolutely terrifying,' he said, more than once, 'life and death in your hands. And surgery: cutting people open, how scary is that?'

She said it wasn't that scary. 'What, not even the first time?' he'd asked, and she explained that you arrived at the first time so slowly and so well supervised, first assisting and then working together with the surgeon, that you were hardly aware it was the first time at all.

They were going to have quite a bit of time together, thirty-six hours, not just Saturday night, but the whole of Sunday and Sunday night as well, as she didn't have to be back at the hospital till ten on Monday morning. Whole weekends off were very rare, especially for SHOs working in a busy A&E. So she'd be able to stay in his flat, which was a really cool studio apartment in Shad Thames, for two nights, and obviously that meant they'd be having sex, quite a lot of sex.

Luke was good at sex – inventive and very energetic, but also surprisingly considerate and anxious to please. He was full of surprises, Emma thought, smiling to herself as she looked at the text he'd sent her that morning: *Hi babe. Really looking 4ward 2 2moro. I mean really. Got some news. Take care Luke xxx.*

It wasn't romantic, as messages went, but it was sweet. *He* was sweet. Which was probably the last adjective he'd have wanted for himself, but it was true. She wondered what the news was: probably something to do with work. It usually was. And probably something she wouldn't understand. She spent quite a lot of time pretending to understand things Luke told her; he didn't seem to notice.

Anyway, only three more hours; the time was going very slowly. There'd been a few kids with broken bones, a couple of concussions – well, it was the middle of the school holidays – and a boy of seventeen with severe stomach pains. It turned out he'd drunk two bottles of vodka, three of wine and a great many beers over the past twenty-four hours, celebrating his A-level results, and seemed surprised there could have been a connection. And then there were a few of the regulars. All A&E departments have them, Alex Pritchard had explained to Emma on her first day: the Worried Well, as they were known, who came in literally hundreds of times, over and over again, with the same pains in their legs or their arms, the same breathlessness, the same agonising headaches. Most of those were seen by the resident GP in A&E, who knew them and dispatched them fairly kindly. Emma felt initially that she would dispatch them rather more unkindly, seeing as they were wasting NHS time and resources, but she was told that medicine wasn't like that.

'Especially not these days,' Pritchard said. 'They'd be suing us, given half the chance. Bloody nonsense,' he added. It had been one of his scowling days. Which were preferable in a way to the more cheerful ones, which were liable to switch at a moment's notice.

Anyway, she might not look like a doctor, Emma thought, but she was certainly beginning to feel like one. And even sound like one at times, or so Luke had told her, last time he'd had a bad hangover, and she'd been very brisk indeed about the folly of his own personal cure, that of the hair of the dog.

'You've poisoned yourself, Luke, and swallowing more of it isn't going to do any good at all. It's such nonsense and it's so obvious. The only cure is time, and lots of water for the dehydration.'

He hadn't liked that at all; knowing things, being right about them, was his department.

'If I want a medical opinion, I'll get it for myself when I'm ready,' he said in a rare demonstration of ill humour. 'I don't want it doled out in my own home, thank you very much, Emma.'

And he poured himself a large Bloody Mary and proceeded to drink it with his breakfast eggs and bacon.

Alex Pritchard, who adored Emma, and had never met Luke but had heard more than he would have wished about him, and referred to him privately as 'the oik', would have interpreted this as proof, were it needed, of his extremely inferior intelligence.

Chapter 3

Despite the fact that it was eleven-thirty, Georgia was fast asleep when her mobile rang; she surfaced reluctantly, thinking it would be her mum, making sure she didn't stay in bed all day. Which had actually been her plan. It was her day off from waitressing in a Cardiff wine bar, and she was seriously tired. So tired, in fact, that she had cried when she had finally got into bed the night before, so tired that lying down didn't seem relief enough. Georgia was much given to such exaggeration.

'Yes?' she said irritably, rubbing her eyes, pushing her wild hair out of the way.

'It's Linda. Listen, I've got a casting for you.'

'Yeah?' She was awake instantly. 'What?'

'It's a big chance, Georgia – if it happens. Channel 4, post-watershed thriller. Now listen . . .'

Georgia listened, her skin crawling with excitement. It was an amazingly big chance – for both of them. She could see that very clearly.

What neither of them could possibly have suspected was that it would also change both their lives, for ever.

The thing most occupying Laura's time and attention as the long summer holidays drew near to their close was Jonathan's surprise birthday party; he was forty in early October and had said several times that he didn't want any big festivities.

'In the first place, I'll feel more like mourning than

celebrating and in the second I find those Big Birthday parties awfully self-conscious. And then everyone knows exactly how old you are for ever more; so no, darling, let's just have a lovely family evening. Much easier for you too – no stress, all right?'

Laura agreed with her fingers only slightly crossed behind her back, for what she had decided on and indeed planned, was very close to a family evening: just a dozen or so couples, their very best friends, and the children, of course. She was sure Jonathan would enjoy that and would actually have regretted not having a party of any kind; and so far the preparations were going rather well. Before their return from France, she had already organised caterers, a new, young company who guaranteed to supply only very pretty waiters and waitresses; Serena Edwards had been enrolled as her helpmeet with the flowers and decorations, and Mark, Serena's husband, was compiling a playlist and organising and storing the wine. Everyone invited could come, and Mark and Serena had also been enrolled as decoys, and had invited them both for a drink before dispatching them home again for dinner with the family.

Laura had bought an extremely pretty – and expensive – new dress from Alberta Ferretti for herself, and for the girls, frocks from Fenwicks in cream lace; all the children were in on the secret and thought it was tremendously exciting.

Would she recognise him? Well, of course she would, Mary thought. From the pictures. Only people did look different from their photographs and Russell had clearly selected his with great care over the years. He had been very vain even then, she thought, smiling at the memory, always carefully combing his hair into place, and checking his cap was on right, and his nails were always immaculately manicured and buffed. Not very English really. That sort of thing was rather frowned on in England; it raised all sorts of questions about masculinity. Men should be men, and manly, and their nails should be of no interest. She had once heard her father talking to one of his brothers about the fairies in the Army and been surprised, imagining he'd been referring to the winged variety. Later, as she learned the true facts of life, she'd smiled at her own innocence. But there was no way Russell had been a fairy. She could personally vouch for that. Oh, it was so long ago. Sixty-three years . . .

And now, the day was nearly here; only two and a half weeks to go. And after they had met at Heathrow – and for some reason she had insisted on that, it was neutral territory – they would travel together to London, where he had booked rooms at the Dorchester – *two rooms, dearest Mary. Have no fear, I know what a nice girl you are* – for two days, while they got to know one another again – *And after that if you really don't like me you can go home to Bristol and I shall go home to New York and no harm done.*

She still thought much harm might be done, but she was too excited to care.

She had told no one. She didn't want to be teased about it, or regarded as a foolish old lady (which she could see she probably was); she had simply told her daughter Christine, and a couple of friends, that she was going to London to meet an old friend she'd known in the war. Which was absolutely true.

But she had bought a couple of very nice outfits from Jaeger – Jaeger, her! The girl had been so helpful, had picked out a navy knitted suit with white trimmings and a very simple long-sleeved black dress; and then, greatly daring, she had asked Karen, the only young stylist at her hairdressing salon, if anything could be done to make her hair look a bit more interesting.

'Well, we can't do much about the colour, my love,' Karen had said, studying Mary intently in the mirror, her own magenta-and-white-striped fringe falling into her eye, 'although we could put a rinse on, make it a bit blonder-looking. Or some lowlights,' she added, rising to the challenge. 'And I do think you could wear it a bit smoother. We could blow-dry it straighter – not much, don't look so scared. More like this,' she said, putting a photograph of Honor Blackman in the current *Hello!* in front of Mary. 'Quite gentle and soft, just not so wavy.'

Mary heard herself agreeing to this; after all, Honor Blackman was almost as old as she was.

'You going to meet someone special then when you go away?' Karen asked, as she started leafing through the magazine for more inspiration.

'Oh no, of course not,' said Mary. 'Just an old friend, but she's rather – rather smart, you know?'

'Mary, you'll look smart as anything when I've finished with you,' said Karen. 'Now let me gown you up and we'll start with the colour. Very gently, then if you like it, we can push it a bit. When's the trip?'

'Oh, not for another two weeks,' Mary said.

'Well, that's perfect. We can sort something out, see how you like it and then work on it, keep improving it.'

'And if I don't?'

'If you don't, you can go back to your own style, no problem . . .'

'Bless her,' she said later, smiling after Mary as she walked out after the first session. 'That took real courage, but you know what? She looks five years younger already!'

They had met on a bus, Mary and Russell; he was on a forty-eight-hour pass and wanted to take a look at the much-vaunted Westminster Abbey, *Where England's Kings and greatest men are buried* it said in his booklet. The booklet he had had in the breast pocket of his immaculately pressed uniform and which he showed her later, much later, as they sat in a pub, having a quick drink before Russell escorted her home.

Instructions for American servicemen in Britain, 1942 it was called, and issued by the United States War Department; all servicemen had been given a copy on departing for Europe. It had produced a lot of cynical comment on the troopship, with its warning that Hitler's propaganda chiefs saw as their major duty, *to separate Britain and America and spread distrust between them. If he can do that* (the booklet went sternly on) *his chance of winning might return.*

To this end, there were many and disparate warnings: not to use American slang, lest offence might be given: *Bloody is one of their worst swearwords* or to say *I look like a bum – that means that you look like your own backside*; not to show off or brag: *American wages and American soldiers' pay are the highest in the world and the British 'Tommy' is apt to be specially touchy about the difference between his wages and ours.* And that the British had *age not size – they don't have the biggest of many things, as we do.*

It had warned too of warm beer, and of making fun of British accents, but most relevantly, to Russell, of the British reserve. Soldiers should not invade people's privacy, which they valued very highly; and they should certainly not expect any English person on a bus or train to strike up a conversation with them.

Russell had started his journey that day in Oxford Circus – why it was called that he couldn't begin to think – and the bus made its way down Regent Street, stopping halfway. Several people got on, and when Russell realised a girl was standing up next to him, he scrambled to his feet, doffed his cap and said, 'Do sit down, ma'am.' The girl had smiled at him – she was very pretty, small and neat, with brown curly hair and big blue eyes – and thanked him, then promptly immersed herself in a letter she pulled out of her pocket. Trying hard not to think that an American girl would have asked him where he was going, pointing out landmarks, especially to someone clearly a stranger to her city, Russell stood, swaying gently with the bus and trying not to feel homesick, and when a light pretty voice said, 'How do you like London?' he assumed the remark could not possibly have been addressed to him, and ignored it.

The bus had stopped again at Piccadilly Circus. 'See that?' said one old man to another, sitting side by side, pointing out of the window. 'They took Eros away. Case Jerry 'it 'im.'

'Good riddance to 'im, I'd say,' said a woman sitting behind, and they all cackled with laughter.

The bus continued round Trafalgar Square and Russell craned his neck to see Nelson's column: he wondered if Jerry might not hit that as well. They turned up Whitehall. About halfway along, a great wall of sandbags stood at what one of the old men obligingly informed the entire bus was the entrance to Downing Street. 'Keeping Mr Churchill safe, please God.' There was a general murmur of agreement.

Everyone seemed very cheerful. Looking not just at his fellow passengers, but the people in the street, briskly striding men, pretty girls with peroxided hair, Russell thought how amazing it was, given that 60,000 British civilians had already been killed in this war and London was being pounded nightly by bombs, that the city could look so normal. OK, a bit shabby and unpainted, as the well-thumbed booklet had warned, and everyone was carrying the ubiquitous gas mask in its case, but on this lovely clear spring day there was a palpable optimism in the air.

The bus stopped and the woman conductor shouted, 'Westminster Abbey!' Russell was on the pavement before he realised that the girl he had given his seat to had got out too and was looking at him with amusement in her blue eyes.

'Are you going into the Abbey?' she asked.

'Yes, ma'am.'

'You know,' she said, 'we do speak to strangers. Sometimes. When they're very kind and give us seats on the bus, for instance. I bet you've been told we never speak to anyone.'

'We were, ma'am, yes.'

'Well, we do. As you can see. Or rather hear. Now, that's the Abbey to your left – see? And behind you, the Houses of Parliament. All right? The Abbey's very beautiful. Now have a good time, Mr – Mr . . .'

'Mackenzie. Thank you, ma'am. Thank you very much.'

The conversation, her amusement at what he had been told about her countrymen, had made them friends, in some odd way. It suddenly seemed less impertinent to ask her if she was in a great hurry, and she said not a great hurry, no, and he said if she had just a few minutes, maybe she could come into the Abbey with him, show him the really important things, like where the Kings and Queens were crowned.

She said she did have a few minutes, and together they entered the vast space – not a lot vaster, it seemed to him, than St John the Divine on Fifth Avenue, but then St John the Divine had never seen a coronation. Or indeed stood for a thousand years.

She showed him the high altar, she showed him where Poets' Corner was, she pointed out the famous coronation stone under the coronation chair, and then directed him to the vaults where he could see the tombs of the famous, going right back to 1066. 'I've never been down there myself, but I'd love to go,' she said. 'You know Shakespeare is buried here, and Samuel Johnson and Chaucer—'

'Chaucer? You're kidding me.'

She giggled again, her big blue eyes dancing. 'I never thought anyone actually said that.'

'What?'

' "You're kidding me". It's like we're supposed to say, "Damn fine show" and "cheers, old chap". I've never heard anyone saying that either, but maybe they do.'

'Maybe,' he said. He felt slightly bewildered by her now, almost bewitched.

'Now look, I really have to go. I work in a bank just along the road, and I'll be late.'

'What time do you finish?' he risked asking. She didn't seem to mind.

'At five. But then I really do have to be getting home, because of the blackout and the bombs and so on.'

'Yes, of course. Well, maybe another time, Miss – Miss . . .'

'Miss Jennings. Mary Jennings. Yes. Another time.'

And then because he knew it was now or never, that he wouldn't find her again, hadn't got another forty-eight-hour leave for ages, he said, 'If you'd accompany me around all those people's graves for half an hour or so, I could see you home. Through the blackout. If that would help.'

'You couldn't, Mr Mackenzie. I live a long way out of London. Place called Ealing. You'd never find your way back again.'

'I could,' he said, stung. 'Of course I could. I found my way here from the States, didn't I?'

'I rather thought the United States Army did that for you. Sorry, I don't mean to sound rude. Where are you stationed?'

'In Middlesex.' He divided the two words, made it sound faintly erotic. 'Northolt. Base there.'

'Well, goodness me. That's not too far away from Ealing, as a matter of fact. Few more stops on the Tube.'

'Well, what do you know?'

'Goodness, there you go again,' she said, giggling.

'What do you mean?'

'Saying "what do you know?" It's so funny to hear it.'

'I don't see why,' he said, a little stiffly now.

'Oh, I'm sorry. Only because it's such a cliché somehow. I didn't mean to sound rude, to offend you.'

'That's OK. But maybe in the cause of further cementing Anglo-American relations, you could agree to meet me. Just for half an hour.'

'Maybe I could. In the cause of Anglo-American relations.' She smiled back at him. 'All right. I'll meet you here at ten past five. And it doesn't get dark till almost seven now so I'll be all right. Anyway, better go now. Bye!'

And she was gone, with a quick sweet smile, half-running, her brown curls flying in the spring breeze.

And so it began: their romance. Which now, most wonderfully it seemed, just might not be over . . .

Patrick Connell was tired and fed up. He'd stopped for a break on the motorway, and was drinking some filthy coffee: why couldn't someone provide some decent stuff for lorry drivers? They'd make a fortune. He'd been driving for what seemed like for ever and he was still several hours from home, and at this rate, he might have to spend a second night in the cab, in some noisy pull-in, with lorries arriving all night through so he'd hardly sleep.

Life on the road wasn't a lot of fun these days, and you didn't make the money either – £500 top whack. You were only allowed to work forty-eight hours a week, and that included rest periods and traffic jams. The European drivers worked much longer hours, non-stop round the clock some of them, but you couldn't get away with it if you were UK based; you could lose your licence if you were caught. And the traffic just got worse and worse . . .

And so did the sleep problem.

It was turning into a nightmare; a waking nightmare. It started earlier and earlier in the day, a dreadful heavy sleepiness that he knew made him a danger. Even when he slept quite well and set out early, it could catch him, halfway through the morning; he would feel his head beginning its inexorable slide into confusion, force himself to concentrate, turn up the radio, eat sweets . . . but nothing really licked it.

It worried him a lot, so much so that he'd gone to the doctor the week before – without telling Maeve, of course, she was such a worrier – to see if he could give him anything for it. The doctor had been sympathetic, but refused: 'If I give you pep pills, Mr Connell, you'll only get a kick-back later, won't be able to sleep that night – and that won't help you, will it? Sounds like you need to change your job, do something quite different. Have you thought about that?'

With which unhelpful advice Patrick had found himself dismissed; he had continued to take his Pro Plus and drink Red Bull and eat jelly babies and struggle on somehow. Everyone thought lorry drivers could do whatever speed they liked, and everyone was wrong. The lorry itself saw to that; a governor in the fuel pump that allowed exactly the amount of fuel through to do the legal 56 mph and no more. Some of the foreign drivers removed the fuse, or adjusted the pump, but Patrick wouldn't have dreamed of doing that. Not worth it. You got caught, you lost your licence. And anyway, then there was the tachograph fixed in your cab: that told it all, how many hours you'd done, how long you'd stopped, and whether you'd speeded at all. So you literally got stuck in some godawful place, unable to leave because your hours were up. And they could be up simply because of being stuck in traffic, not because you'd made any progress.

What he longed for more than anything right this minute was a shower and a shave and a change of clothes. Life on the road didn't do a lot for your personal hygiene. On the English roads, anyway. It was better in Europe. Like the food. And the coffee . . .

Chapter 4

'What a perfect summer it's been,' said Jonathan, smiling at Laura, raising his glass of Sauvignon to her.

'Yes,' she said, 'indeed it has. And it's even nice here now, for our return.'

'I thought maybe in future we could spend Easter in France as well as the summer,' he said. 'What would you think about that?'

'Well, yes, that would be lovely, except . . .'

'Except what?'

'The thing is, the children are growing up so fast, they've got lives of their own now and they want to be with their friends.'

'They can be with their friends the rest of the year,' he said, sounding mildly irritable.

'I know, but . . .' Her voice tailed off. How to explain that a remote, albeit beautiful farmhouse for weeks at a time wasn't going to be quite enough for children approaching adolescence. She'd hoped Jonathan would realise that for himself, but he didn't seem to.

He had a very strong controlling streak: everything had to be done his way, in accordance with his vision of their lives, and she could see that already Charlie was beginning to kick against it, to argue with his father and not always want to fit in with his plans. And of course the two girls, while wonderfully sweet and biddable at the moment, would inevitably reach the same point. But it hadn't happened yet, and Laura was quite adept at ignoring difficulties. She had even considered having another baby, in order to ensure that at least some of the family remained small and compliant, but of course babies weren't that compliant and Jonathan found them difficult anyway. Probably best to enjoy the near-perfection of the present.

'Oh, now I hope this is all right, darling,' he said. 'I'm going to have to be away next Thursday night. Big conference in Birmingham – old medical student chum's gone over into the pharmaceutical business. He seemed to think if I spoke he'd get a better attendance rate.'

'Well, of course he would,' she said, topping up his glass, smiling at him. 'You're such a draw at these things, such a big name. I was so proud of you at that conference in Boston. That was fun, I loved being there with you. I'd like to do more of that. Maybe I should come next week . . .'

'Oh, darling, I'd love that, of course, but I hardly think Birmingham could compare with Boston. Not worth you packing your bag even.'

'I wouldn't mind,' she said. 'If you'd like me to come.'

'No, darling, don't even think about it. You have enough to do next week, what with getting the children fitted up for school and seeing that mad woman in Wiltshire about doing her house up for Christmas. What an absurd idea! Paying someone to put up a few garlands and fairy lights . . .'

'Jonathan,' said Laura, almost hurt, 'not everyone has the time to do it for themselves. Or the – well, the ideas. That's what I'm for.'

'Of course. I'm sorry, sweetheart, stupid of me.And you'll make it look so lovely. Do you have any ideas about it yet? I'd love to hear them, you know I would . . .'

He did that sometimes, professed interest in what she did. It was only professing, he didn't really care if the Wiltshire house was decked out with barbed wire; but it was very sweet. He was very sweet . . . She was very, very lucky.

Georgia had got the script and knew virtually every word of every part already. She had a near-photographic memory; that was supposed to be a help for an actor, but it could be a drawback too as you knew what everyone else was supposed to be saying, and there was a temptation to prompt them, especially in rehearsal.

Linda was right; this was a fantastic part. The series was a thriller: about a young black girl whose grandmother vanished without trace from the family home. She could have just wandered off, she could have met with an accident, she could have been murdered. The grand-daughter, Rose, was very close to her grandmother, angry at the way her dad belittled and bullied her, convinced he had something to do with her disappearance. The more she read it, the more excited about it Georgia became. She could see how much she could do with it, really develop the character as she went along; she couldn't think of anything else.

The first audition was a week on Friday; it was at the casting director's office, and there would be loads of girls there, trooping in and out, anything up to twenty or even thirty. Tough as that was, Georgia didn't mind the first audition as much as the later ones; it was less tense, the chance of getting the part rather remote, it was possible to relax just slightly. But it was still hideous.

The first thing that always struck her was how many girls there were, all looking rather like her. Which was logical, but always seemed surprising. And her next reaction was invariably that they were all much prettier than her.

Then there were all the awkward little conversations, the longest with the girl immediately ahead – *oh hi, how are you, what have you been doing, love the dress/boots/ hair* . . . And then the long wait while the girl did her bit; and came out smiling, or looking really tense. And then they called you in and it began. At this stage, it was usually just you and the casting director, who would read a scene with you. With the camcorder running, of course. And then you waited – and waited. The first recall came quite quickly, maybe within a day or two; if it didn't, forget it. Tell yourself you hadn't wanted it anyway. And if it did come, that audition was much scarier. You knew they liked you – the pressure was on. The director would probably be there. And there were still five or seven, or even eight of you. All, it seemed, prettier than you, better actors than you. You just felt sick for days and days, waiting. And quite often, for a big part, like this one, there was a third call, with the choice whittled down to maybe two of you. That was really agony.

But it would all be worth it, if she got this part. She'd be on her way, at last. And Linda did seem to think she had a real chance.

'You can act. You look perfect. And you've certainly got plenty of attitude, which is what they're looking for. D'you want to come up the night before and stay with me?'

'No,' Georgia said quickly. 'No, it's really kind, but I'll get the coach from Cardiff first thing. Thanks anyway.'

She didn't like staying with Linda; she was nice – in fact, Georgia was really fond of her – but it was like being with your headmistress, uncomfortable, on show. And her flat was so bloody perfect she was scared to move in case she made it untidy or knocked something over. If an audition was in the morning, she did put up with it, but this wasn't till 3.30, she could get to London in loads of time.

'Fine,' said Linda. 'As long as you're not late.'

'As if! Do you really think I'm in with a chance?'

'I really think so, yes, but there are lots of other girls. What do you think of the script?'

'I think it's great.'

'Me too. And directed by Bryn Merrick. It should be superb.'

It was all absolutely amazing really. She might actually be getting a part, in a brilliant, high-profile Channel 4 series, directed by one of the most award-winning people in the business. She might. And she'd be living in London again properly, like when she'd been at drama school, not just coming up for a few days here and there, for auditions or filming bit parts. She really missed London; she'd loved it, it had felt like home straight away, which had surprised her because everyone said she'd feel lonely and friendless. She liked everything about it, the noise and the rush and the shops and the bars and the feeling that you really were in the heart of things, and she didn't even mind the bad things, the litter and the dirt and the way you could wait what seemed like hours for a bus or a Tube and the fact that, compared to Cardiff, people were quite unfriendly: it was all part of the chaotic charm. The worst thing was the awful cost of everything . . . which would be a factor if she got this part. How would she afford anywhere to live? She'd run up huge debts as a student, wasn't even beginning to pay that off . . . well, maybe she'd earn loads of dosh. Time enough to sort that out if she got the part. If . . . Her head seemed to take off when she thought about it.

Georgia went back to her lines.

'Not long now, Toby,' said Barney.

'No. Absolutely not.'

There was a silence. The stag weekend had been a great success: they'd done all the touristy things in New York – the Empire State, the Circle Line Tour, shopped in Abercrombie & Fitch; and gone to loads of the clubs as well. It was generally agreed they weren't as good as the London ones, but fun just the same. Barney had managed to organise a Marilyn Monroe stripogram for Toby, and they'd got some pretty good pictures of the two of them together – only Toby had got into one hell of a sweat over that and made them all swear that Tamara would never find out or see the pictures.

The general feeling about that was that Tamara should ease up a bit, and that being with strippers was what blokes did on their stag weekends; however, easing up was not Tamara's thing, she'd called Toby at least a dozen times each day over the three days. If Amanda had done that, Barney thought, he'd have had a few firm words – but then Amanda wouldn't have.

Tamara's hen weekend didn't sound exactly great. Amanda was very loyal about it, but even she admitted that an alcohol-free weekend at a spa retreat near Madrid, however wonderful the treatments, and however grand the clientèle, ran out of fun. Several of the girls suggested at least one trip into town, maybe for a meal or a bit of clubbing, but Tamara had said slightly coolly that of course they should do whatever they liked, but for her the concept of the whole weekend had been a luxurious detox and she didn't want to undo all the benefits for one night of what, after all, they did all the time in London. A couple of rebels (who had not included Amanda) had gone out, but had become definitely personae non gratae as a result.

And as the date of the wedding drew nearer she had become increasingly possessive of Toby, disturbing client evenings with endless phone calls, relentlessly emailing him about the arrangements, and even arriving at his desk in the middle of the morning with a handful of ties for his consideration.

Amanda had struggled to explain this to Barney. 'I know it's all a bit much and she seems so cool and self-contained, but she's secretly actually a mass of insecurities, especially at the moment. She's absolutely terrified something's going to go wrong, and she only feels better when Toby's with her.'

Barney didn't trust himself to speak.

51

Emma wasn't sure how she felt about Luke's news. Which was that he was going to Milan for six months. Seconded – that was the word – to some car manufacturers called Becella. 'They are the greatest cars in the world, you know. I'd have one while I was there.'

'Goodness.'

'Yeah. It really is a fantastic opportunity, Emma. I'm well chuffed.'

It went on: how great it would look on his CV, how big a hike in salary he would get, what a cool apartment he would have, how he was going over in a couple of weeks to meet the team, how Pullmans were sending him on an intensive Italian course – 'My degree is Business Studies with French, but I've got an A-level in Italian. They seem to think that's going to be enough, but I'm well rusty.' Finally he sat back and smiled at her and said, 'What do you think?'

It sounded great, yes, she said, really wonderful, congratulations – while wondering if he was getting around to saying he thought they should finish it, stop seeing each other now, before he left – and then he said he knew she'd be pleased, and of course there'd be loads of trips back home: 'Every other weekend, actually, or they're pretty good about flying people out. So you could come over whenever you wanted.'

Not finished then, which made smiling and seeming pleased easier: but how often did she have a whole weekend in which to go to Milan, for God's sake? She'd thought at last she'd found the perfect boyfriend, settled in London, always around, and now he was going off for at least six months. It was . . . well, not very nice. But no worse than that. Which probably meant she wasn't in love with him. She wasn't sure how she felt about that, either . . .

* * *

It had been a particularly happy weekend. The whole family said so. Jonathan had been relaxed and not even on call which meant Laura could relax too, and he had offered each of the children a treat of their choice at breakfast. He did that occasionally; loved the conspicuous spoiling and role-playing of Perfect Father.

'But it has to be in London, no point struggling out, as the roads'll be jammed. London's great in August. My treat is going to be—'

'You're not a child,' said Daisy.

'I'm still allowed a treat. It's a ride on the Eye, so we can have a look at everything. We haven't been on it for ages. Any objections?'

'We'll never get on,' said Laura.

'Don't be negative, darling. Anyway, we will. I've bought tickets.'

'Oh how exciting. When for?'

'Tomorrow morning. Eleven o'clock. And they're VIP tickets, so absolutely no queuing.'

'Jonathan, you're so thoughtful. And so extravagant.'

'You're worth it, all of you. Now then, what would Mummy's treat be?'

'Um – a picnic. Which I didn't have to prepare. In . . . let me see, Kew Gardens.'

'That's easy. We'll make the picnic, won't we, kids? Lunchtime today, Laura?'

'Yes, please.'

They had their picnic. Lily's wish was a rowboat on the river – and then they all went for supper on the terrace at Brown's in Richmond, watching the sun set on the water.

'It's so lovely,' said Daisy. 'It's all so lovely and I feel so happy, I don't really want a treat.'

'That's very sweet, darling,' said Laura, 'and very grown up of you. But how about you and I go shopping, just for a little while, in Covent Garden tomorrow, after the Eye? We could get one of those lockets you liked so much, from that

53

jewellery stall. You too, Lily, if you want to come. Otherwise, Daddy can take you and Charlie to watch the buskers. Or on the roundabout.'

'I'll come,' said Lily.

Charlie's wish was a ride on the bungee jumpers, just beside the Eye, and after their ride they watched him soaring skywards, laughing, his skinny legs pretending to run, his fair hair shining in the sun, while they drank hot chocolate with whipped cream on top.

And then, after the shopping excursion, they went home for lunch in the garden, cold chicken salad and strawberry meringues, and then for a walk along the river, all holding hands.

I'm so happy, Laura thought, so happy and lucky. I wish these years could last for ever . . .

Chapter 5

This was even worse, Patrick thought, than the week before. He had left London on Wednesday morning and now it was Thursday afternoon, and the night drive he had planned to get him home for Friday morning had been scuppered by a five-hour queue at the warehouse for loading up and a stroppy manager, with the words they all dreaded: 'We're closing, mate.'

Useless to argue, although Patrick tried to point out that it was only four-thirty, with half an hour to closing. The man was unmoved. 'I can't get all that on board in half an hour, come back in the morning.'

He'd already done a big drive from London to Southampton (where he picked up a load) to St Austell in Cornwall (to deliver it), and now he was stuck in Exeter. A long way from London, a long way from home. He was very tired; he contemplated parking somewhere illegal, a quiet layby off a minor road if he could find one, but it wasn't worth it, not really. The police were along in no time, banging on your window, waking you up, telling you to move on. Even if you said your hours were up, they didn't care: you had to do what they said. They didn't like lorry drivers.

Well, nothing else for it, he'd just have to bite the bullet, and call Maeve, and then get some food and start looking for somewhere to spend the night.

And – wouldn't you just know it – the weather was getting hotter and hotter.

This time tomorrow, Mary thought, she would be with Russell. She felt alternately terribly excited and terribly nervous. At this moment, the excitement was winning. Her greatest fear – that they would be complete strangers, with nothing to say to one another – seemed suddenly unlikely. It wasn't as if they hadn't been in contact all these years; they had continued to amuse and interest one another through their letters. And how odd that was, she thought, their two lives and lifestyles being so utterly different – but then they always had been; there had been nothing actually in common, unless you counted the war. Which had of course bound people very tightly together, by its shared ideals and hopes, dangers and fears, its requirements for courage and self-sacrifice, its absolute faith in the rightness of its cause. Russell and she, growing up thousands of miles apart, in totally different cultures, had found one another through that war and their respective roles in it, found one another and loved one another; at no other time and in no other way could such a meeting and consequent relationship have taken place. And it was one of the things that had convinced Mary that their lives together could not be shared, knowing that when the war was gone, much of the structure of their relationship would be gone too, the differences between them increased a thousand-fold.

But now – well now, they had their past to bind them; the wonderful bridge standing between any two people, however different, who have raised children, seen grandchildren born, partners die, lost the strength and physical beauty of their youth, faced old age and loneliness, and sharing, inevitably, the broader ideals of love, of loyalty and family, and wishing to pass the importance of those things on to the generations that followed them, their own small piece of immortality.

All these things Mary thought that night, as she lay in bed, unable to sleep, and looking forward to tomorrow.

What *was* she doing here, Georgia wondered. She must be absolutely mad. Out clubbing in Bath, with Esme and Esme's up-himself boyfriend, drinking cocktails that she couldn't afford, when she should be at home in bed in Cardiff, her alarm set for seven, giving her plenty of time to get to the coach station and take the ten o'clock to London. Shit shit shit. It had seemed such a good idea at the time – an evening with Esme in her parents' house. She'd even thought she might run through some of her scenes with Esme, it would help with the awful nerves – and then she could get the coach in the morning from Bath. Her mother hadn't tried to stop her, just told her to be sensible and not miss the coach – as if she would – and then she'd arrived and Esme was all stressed out because of the boyfriend, who she thought was about to dump her, and Georgia couldn't even begin to talk about the audition, let alone her part, just had to try to be sympathetic, so that when he called and asked Esme to meet him in town at some bar or other, and Esme had acted like it was God Himself, and insisted Georgia went too – 'Honestly, Georgia, it'll only be for an hour or so, then we can come back and you can get to bed. I can't go alone, I just can't, I'll feel such a dickhead.' So she had gone, and how stupid had that been? Because now it was almost two, and no prospect of leaving, and she had no money for a cab and the boyfriend kept saying he'd get them home.

She should have stayed with James the accountant, Georgia thought wretchedly; she could have rung James even now and he would have driven over from Cardiff to rescue her without hesitating . . . which of course was exactly why she wasn't still with him. On the other hand . . . well, it was no use even thinking about that one. What would Linda say, if she knew? The chance of her life and she was risking throwing it all away. She'd just have to get up early somehow, take some money out of the hole in the wall (she'd been going to borrow some from her mum, and then hadn't dared ask under the circumstances), and then sleep on the coach. She'd drink loads of water from now on, and anyway, none of them had any money left for cocktails, thank goodness, and just demand they left. Only – God, where was Esme now? She'd been on the dance floor a minute ago, with Thingy's tongue down her throat, and now she'd vanished, must have gone outside . . . oh God, oh God, what was she doing here, why had she come?

'God, it's hot.' Toby pushed his damp hair back off his forehead. 'Might take a dip. Fancy one, Barney?'

'Sounds good.'

They were in the garden of Toby's parents' house; Toby had asked Barney to stay there with him the night before the wedding on Friday. 'Stop me running away,' he said with a grin. But there had been something in his voice, a slight catch; Barney had been trying not to worry about it.

He'd been a bit odd all evening; quiet, edgy, jumping whenever the phone rang. He'd twice left the room to take calls on his mobile. 'Tamara,' he'd said both times when he came back.

Carol Weston had served a delicious dinner for the four of them – poached salmon followed by raspberries and cream – which they had eaten outside, burning copious candles to keep the insects at bay. Ray Weston had served some very nice chilled Muscadet, and proposed the toast to 'The perfect couple. That's you and Toby, Barney,' he said, smiling, and they had sat there, chatting easily until it was dark, reminiscing over that first day when they had left Toby, and Anne and John Fraser had left Barney, 'white as sheets, you both were' in the great hall at Toddingham Prep: and all the long years and football and cricket matches and skiing holidays – for the two families had become friends, not just the boys – and speech days and graduations, and even early girlfriends since; but then Toby became increasingly silent, almost morose, and in the end Carol and Ray went to bed, with strict instructions to them both from Carol not to be late.

'We don't want any hitches tomorrow, any hungover grooms.'

'Oh, for Christ's sake!' Toby said, and there was an edge to his voice that was unmistakable and then swiftly, apologetically, 'Sorry, Mum. But do give me a bit of credit.'

'All right, Toby.' She was clearly surprised.

'We'll just have a couple of quiet ones and then bed, Barney, eh?'

'Why not?'

They climbed out of the pool – they had swum naked, unable to find the energy in the heat even to fetch swimming trunks from the house – pulled on shorts and T-shirts and sat, briefly cool, on the terrace at the back of the house.

'Quiet one then?' Toby said and, 'Yeah, great,' said Barney. He'd expected Toby to fetch more wine, was a little alarmed when he saw him come out of the house with a bottle of whisky and some tumblers.

'Tobes! You heard what your mum said.'

'Oh, don't you start. Everyone seems to regard me as some sort of irresponsible moron.'

'OK, OK. But – you're all right, are you?'

'Of course I'm bloody well all right. But there's no nightcap like Scotch. Neat Scotch. Want some?'

Barney nodded.

'That's better,' Toby said, taking a large gulp, then leaning back in his chair, studying his glass.

'Better? You're not nervous, are you?'

'Well, a bit. Inevitable really, I guess. Lesser men than me have run away.' He smiled at Barney.

'Tobes. You wouldn't.'

'Of course not. What, from a girl like Tamara? God, I'm lucky. So lucky.'

As long as he thought so, Barney told himself firmly, that was all that mattered. A second whisky followed the first; they discussed the arrangements for the morning.

'Got the ring?'

'I've got the ring.'

'Got your speech?'

'Got my speech.'

'Better be a good one.'

'I've done my best.'

'Good man.'

A silence; then Toby said, quite suddenly, 'I've – well, I've got a bit of a problem, Barney. Actually. Been a bit of an idiot.'

'Sorry?'

'I said I've been an idiot.'

'How? In what way?'

'I – oh shit, I should have told you ages ago. Well, weeks ago, anyway.'

He was sweating, Barney realised; and staring into the darkness, his hands twisting.

'Toby, what is it? What have you done?'

'I've – well, I've made a complete fool of myself. With some girl.'

Barney could not have been more astonished – or more shocked – if Toby had told him he was absconding with millions from the bank. He stared at him in total silence for a moment, then said, 'Fuck.'

'Well, yes. I got incredibly drunk one night, with some friends round here. It was a stag night actually – no one you know. Just a local lad. His dad's got a smallholding the other side of the A46 and we used to shoot rabbits together, that sort of thing. Anyway, we went to a club near Ciren, and this girl was there. On a hen night. She lives in the next village actually. Dead sexy, works for some local builder, you know the sort of thing.'

'Think so,' said Barney. He was feeling rather sick.

'Anyway I – well, I screwed her.'

'Oh, what!'

'Yeah. 'Fraid so. I gave her a lift home, in a cab. Well, it seemed a good idea at the time. When we got back to her place, she said why didn't I come in for a nightcap, her parents were away for the night, and one thing led to another.'

'Toby, you lunatic.'

'I know, I know. Anyway, I felt pretty bad in the morning, hoped she'd see it my way, just a bit of fooling around – she didn't.'

'Oh Tobes—'

'She knew where I lived, or rather where my parents lived, became a complete pest, always calling me, at work as well as on my mobile, actually turned up here once or twice. I tried to get rid of her, but it didn't work. She got quite unpleasant, started accusing me of treating her like a tart. Anyway, next thing is, last week she calls, says she's pregnant.'

'Shit.'

'I tried to call her bluff, but – well, unfortunately, I, well, I left all that sort of thing to her. She said she was on the pill . . .'

'You idiot,' said Barney. 'You total, total idiot.'

'Yeah, well, thanks.'

'Well, you are.'

'I know. I KNOW. I can't explain it. I've never done anything like that before. Ever. You'd know if I had. No secrets from you, Barney. No excuses. I suppose it was a combination of last fling time, nerves about – well, about getting married, being married . . .'

'You mean to Tamara?' said Barney quietly.

'Yes. I mean, I do love her . . .'

61

'Course.'

'But she's quite high maintenance. Bit of a daunting prospect. Anyway, that's not an excuse. I don't have one. It was an appalling thing to do. I know that.'

'So, what's happened?' It seemed best to stick to practicalities.

'I told her to have a test, all that sort of thing. She said she had, and it was positive.'

'Yeah, well, she would, wouldn't she?'

'I – I suppose so. Yes. Anyway, she'd gone all quiet and I thought it was OK, but she called me tonight.'

'Tonight!'

'Yeah. That was what all those calls were. She wants some money. So she can have a termination.'

'Toby, you don't have to have money for that these days. You just go to a clinic, and—'

'She doesn't want to do that. She wants to have it done properly, as she puts it. At a private hospital.'

'Well, tell her she can't.'

'Barney, I'm in no position to talk to her like that. I haven't behaved exactly well. Even if none of it's true, I daren't risk it and call her bluff. You know what Tamara's like.'

'Well . . . yes, I do. But—'

'Anyway, she wants a grand.'

'Blimey.'

'Yes, I know. Moreover, she wants it tomorrow. Tomorrow morning. In cash.'

Barney was still struggling to take it all in. He felt sick, oddly scared himself. 'You can't give in to that sort of thing,' he said finally.

'I have to. Otherwise she's threatened to come to the church. She says she knows where the wedding is and when, and I guess she would, it's local knowledge. It wouldn't look good if she turned up at my "smart society wedding", as she called it, would it?'

'No,' said Barney, after a pause. 'I mean, penny to a pound she's not pregnant, nor would she turn up, but – no, it wouldn't be great.'

'So – I've got to give her a grand in the morning. In cash. Which I don't happen to have about me. Do you?'

'Nope. Got about a hundred, but—'

'I'll have to go to a bank, get it out. The most I can get on my card is four hundred quid.'

'I can get that too. Look—'

'No, no, Barney, it's my problem. And then I'll have to take it to her.'

'Where does she work?'

'No, to her parents' house. It's quite near – fifteen, twenty minutes away.'

'You do realise it may not stop at this, don't you? That's the whole thing about blackmail.'

'Yeah, course. But at least whatever she does next, I'll be married, the wedding'll be safely over and Tamara won't have to be confronted by it – literally. I'll deal with it somehow. Anyway, I've got a feeling it'll be OK. I think she'll back off. Meanwhile – busy morning.'

'Yeah. Well, look, surely I can deal with that for you. I can get the money and take it to her.'

'No, that's just too complicated. I'll do it. I've worked it out, I should be back here by ten-thirty, eleven at the latest. Then I'll just change and we can go. We might be a bit late for the ushers' lunch, but that won't matter.'

'We need to leave by eleven, really, for that, mate.'

'Then we'll have to drive faster. Oh God. What a total fucking idiot I've been. I still can't believe it. Let's have another of those, Barney. Then we'd better turn in. Busy day tomorrow.'

He nodded at the whisky bottle. Barney poured the drinks out, his hand shaking slightly, wondering how he could possibly have got Toby so wrong. Reliable, sensible, straight-as-a-die Toby. He'd have trusted him with his life, always regarded himself as the slightly wild card. And now . . .

Waking in the night, mulling over the whole thing again, he realised it hadn't even occurred to him to feel any outrage on Tamara's behalf.

Laura was just drifting off to sleep, her bedroom windows wide open, the muslin curtains hanging absolutely still – oh, for just the tiniest breeze – when the phone rang.

'Darling?'

'Oh, Jonathan – hello. How did it go?'

'Pretty well, I think. Yes. Jack seemed pleased.'

'I bet he was. I bet you were wonderful.'

'Hardly. Anyway, you're all right, are you?'

'I'm absolutely fine, darling. Just a bit hot. But we've had a nice day. Got all the uniforms, which was a bit stressful, but then I took them out to supper.'

'Where? No, let me guess. TGI's.'

'Correct.'

'God, I don't know how you can face those places.'

'Well, the children love them. And I love the children.'

'So do I. But – well, you're a saint. They're lucky to have you. *I'm* lucky to have you.'

'And I'm lucky to have *you*.'

'Well, as long as everything's OK. I just wanted to check. Lily had a tummy-ache this morning.'

'It wasn't serious. You're so sweet, Jonathan.'

'Good. Well – night, darling. I'll be home tomorrow around six, six-thirty. Going straight up to Princess Anne's from here, but I'll call you first thing.'

'Fine. Love you.'

'Love you too.'

That was done, then: very unlikely now that she would call him again.

Jonathan parked his car and walked into the foyer of the

Bristol Meridien, so nicely anonymous, so filled with pleasurable associations.

He checked in and went up to his room, had scarcely pushed the door open when she walked out to greet him, stark naked, holding out a glass of champagne.

'You're very late,' she said. 'What kept you?'

Chapter 6

When all else failed, Georgia prayed. Not because she believed in God (not that she didn't exactly either) but because He did seem, on the whole, to be very good about listening to her and letting her have what she wanted. Which meant, she supposed, that she really ought to believe in Him a bit more: and be a bit more grateful.

Well, if He answered this particular prayer in an even half-positive manner, she promised both herself and Him that she would make a much greater effort, not just to believe in Him, but to behave in a way more appropriate to the belief. Because He most definitely would deserve it.

What she was going to ask of Him today, she thought, taking up her praying position (standing, eyes screwed up, fists clenched in absolute concentration) was not really that difficult to grant. She wanted a car – a car driven by someone else, on its way to London and with a spare seat. And since she was standing just above the approach road to the M4, it would not be a miracle on the scale of the loaves and fishes, or even of walking on water. All God had to do, in fact, was point her out, perhaps nudge the driver into thinking a bit of company would not go amiss, and He'd be free to get on with whatever other tasks were on His mind.

After half an hour, her arm aching now, her bare legs covered in dust and a very persistent piece of grit in one eye, it began to seem that God had better things to do that morning.

At this rate she just wasn't going to make it. She had to be at the audition by three; it was already twelve, and her father always said you had to allow two and a half hours minimum from the Severn Bridge. And that was when you knew exactly where you were going. She had to find some obscure place in the middle of London, and then get herself tarted up, change her top at least and get some slap on, before she could present herself to the snooty cow – they were always snooty – in reception. She was almost thinking of giving up. Of going home again, telling her mother she'd been right and that she had indeed missed not just the early coach but the later one and that it was absolutely her own fault. Only it wouldn't be that easy to get home again; she'd need another lift just to get back to Cardiff. There were no National Express bus stops anywhere near, for God's sake, so she might as well carry on, get to London anyway.

God, she was so stupid. Why hadn't she stayed safely at home in Cardiff and gone to bed early, so she'd have heard her phone when it went off? Only of course she wouldn't have had to, her mother would have made sure she was awake and driven her to the coach station in plenty of time. But it had been nearly three when they got home and her phone had been practically dead and it had failed totally to wake her until almost nine. Esme's mum had been very sympathetic, but she had to get off to work, she said, and anyway, she didn't have a car. Georgia had gone out in a panic to find a cash machine to pay for a seat on the next coach, only it spat her card out, and she couldn't get any money. Her only hope now was the train, but that was terribly expensive; she'd gone back to Esme's in tears, ready to beg some money from her, but she didn't have any either; she'd hoped the boyfriend who'd stayed over might lend her the money, he seemed quite well off, but he was clearly tight, as well as a complete wanker. In the end, he did offer to take her to the M4 in his car, which hardly looked to Georgia capable of getting to the end of the street, and drop her there so she could hitch a lift.

And here she was, on the side of the road, praying . . .

Maeve Connell had also been calling upon the Almighty that day; not for help, but to be her witness in an ultimatum to her husband.

'I swear before God, Patrick Connell, you don't get home in time for my mother's birthday dinner and it's the last meal that'll be cooked for you in this house. Because I'll have gone, left you for good. I'm sick of it, sick to the death of looking after the kids alone, and sleeping alone, and coping alone, and I don't want to hear any excuses about how we'll soon have a great house and a fine car, because right now we have a rotten house and a car that's about to roll over and die. So is that clear, Patrick, because if it isn't I'll say it all again, just so there's no doubt in your mind whatsoever.'

Patrick had told her it was quite clear, and that of course he'd be back in Kilburn, and in good time for the birthday dinner. 'And I have a great gift for your mother as well, just wait till you see it. So kiss the boys for me and tell them I'll see them tonight. Now I have to go, or I'll get pulled over for using the phone and then I'll never arrive in time. Bye, darling. See you later.'

He snapped off his mobile, pulled over into the middle lane and moved up to the 56 mph that was his top speed. The only problem would be keeping awake, specially if Maeve's mother started yakking about the old days in Dublin. He was dead tired. But he should be home by seven at this rate. If only it wasn't quite so hot . . .

Georgia looked at her watch again: twelve-fifteen now. It was hopeless, completely hopeless. She suddenly felt very bleak; this mega-important audition and she'd just thrown it away and some other nicely organised, self-controlled girl would get the part. And Georgia had no one, absolutely no one, to blame but herself. Which didn't make her feel any better. And as for what Linda would say, it just didn't bear thinking about. She'd probably tell her she wouldn't be her agent any more. She'd threatened it often enough.

She gave up praying, gave up smiling at every car that came along, gave up hope; sank onto the grass verge by the layby, buried her head in her arms and started to cry.

Rick Harwood was in a foul mood. He was quite often in a foul mood, but this was five-star quality.

He was supposed to be getting home early, he'd got up at bloody dawn to finish a job in Stroud. Some silly cow had decided at the beginning of the week she wanted the fence he'd put up for her painted white instead of stained brown, and it had meant an extra day and a half's work. He wouldn't have minded so much – it was all work, after all, all money – but she liked to chat and it was well boring, mostly about her husband who was away 'on business, in Japan actually' and his views on life in general and how he liked his garden to look in particular. When she was through with that, she moved on to her children, who were all very musical, especially her eldest who played with the Gloucester Youth Orchestra, 'clarinet, mostly classical, but he's very good at jazz as well, as a matter of fact,' and then her daughter who played the violin and was auditioning for some college of music. Did he want to hear this, Rick thought, slapping white paint on the fence and responding only in grunts to discourage her, like a hole in the head he did; might have been all right if she'd been good looking but she was one of those earnest, rather pale women who went on and on about her carbon footprint. Which didn't quite go with business trips to Japan, Rick thought, but they no doubt paid for the music lessons and the large 4x4 parked in the drive.

Anyway, he'd finished that morning in record time, mostly because she'd gone to Waitrose in Cirencester – 'I know it's a bit of a trek, and terribly wrong of me, environmentally, but it's just so much better quality' – and he was just waiting for her to get back, to hand her the invoice, when his boss phoned and said he wanted him to pick up a load of timber from a yard just outside Stroud and drop it off with him before the end of the day.

Since the boss lived outside Marlow and Rick lived in Reading, this was not too great an imposition, but the yard had been closed when he got there. A bit of paper was pinned on the door saying *Back by 1.30* but it was nearer two when the owner arrived.

'Sorry, mate, got caught up with something.'

'Yeah, well,' Rick said, his face assuming the expression that sent his wife diving quite literally for cover, 'some of us like to get home before midnight, specially on a Friday, OK? Let's have it, PDQ.'

There was still some wood from the last job lying around in the bottom of his van; the man suggested he cleared it out before putting his new timber in.

'Yeah, well, I'll leave it with you then – you can dispose of it for me.'

'Oh no,' said the man, looking at the assortment of dusty, split planks, some of them still stuck with rusty nails. 'You dispose of your own rubbish, mate. Not my problem. Sign here, please.'

Swearing under his breath, Rick signed, and then found that the back doors of the van no longer shut properly.

'This is all I need. Got any rope? I'll have to tie the fucking doors together.'

'You ought to tie those old planks down, mate, not have them rattling around like that.'

'Look,' said Rick, 'when I need your advice, I'll ask for it. Right now I don't, all right?'

And he pulled out of the yard, with Rudi, the black

German shepherd dog who was his constant companion, on the passenger seat. He turned along the A46 in the direction of the M4, cursing the heat, his own misfortune in not having a van with aircon and the fact that his windscreen wash was almost empty.

And that he couldn't now be in Reading much before four.

It was no good, Patrick decided, he needed a coffee. And some water. And a pee, come to think of it. There was no way he could drive all the way to London without stopping. He was still in good time to be able to wish his mother-in-law a happy birthday and give her the watch he'd bought her, and then maybe as a reward for such extremely good behaviour, he and Maeve would have their own private celebration behind their bedroom door. It was overdue, that was for sure.

Smiling to himself at the prospect, Patrick swung off the motorway at the turn-off to the A46 and turned back across it towards the lorry drivers' pull-in.

He saw her as he stood in the queue at the tea-stall; she was only a few yards away, her face tear-streaked, clutching a mug of tea, wiping her nose on the back of her hand. Gorgeous she was, black, no more than twenty, wearing a very short denim skirt and then those funny boots they all seemed to like, sheepskin, not ideal for a hot August day, but then that was fashion for you. She was small and quite thin, but she had very good boobs, nicely emphasised by a pink low-cut T-shirt; her bare arms bore a large number of silver bangles, and her wild black hair was pulled back to one side into a ponytail.

She saw him looking at her and glanced away; he picked up his own tea and a couple of bottles of water and went over to her.

'Not a serious problem, I hope?'

'Who said there was a problem at all?' she said.

'Well, you're crying, for a start.'

'I'm not.'

'I must have been imagining it then. But you seem to be on your own. And this isn't the sort of place I imagine you'd be meeting your friends.'

'Well, you imagine wrong. I'm just waiting for someone.'

'That's all right then,' he said, and smiled at her. He took a slug of one of the bottles of water he'd bought – God, he'd needed that, the temperature must be nearing ninety now – and held out another to her. 'Want some?'

'No, thanks,' she said, looking at it longingly. 'I'm fine.'

'Go on. Do you good.'

'Well . . .' She hesitated. 'Thank you. Just a sip.'

'Take the whole thing,' he said. 'I can get some more.'

'Oh, OK. That's very kind of you.'

Her voice was surprisingly posh; he was surprised. Then he chided himself for being classist or racist or whatever such a reaction might be labelled. Soon, he reflected, you wouldn't be able to say anything at all without upsetting someone.

'Your friend late then?'

'My friend?'

'Well, yes, the one you're waiting for.'

'I'm not—' she said, and then stopped, smiled at him reluctantly. 'I'm not waiting for anyone really. I'm just hoping to get a lift back to Cardiff. You're not – not going that way?'

'No, sorry, my love. Going to London.'

'Oh God,' she said, and her huge eyes filled with tears again. 'If only I'd met you just half an hour earlier.'

'And why is that particularly?'

'I was trying to get there. That's all.'

'Any particular reason?'

'Well, yes. Yes, I had an appointment.'

'Important, was it?'

'Terribly,' she said, and started to cry in earnest again.

'Come on,' he said, sitting down on a bench and indicating to her to join him. 'Tell me all about it.'

'Linda, I've got Georgia on line three.'

'Oh, God,' said Linda, looking at the phone, dreading picking it up. Georgia was most unlikely, she knew, to be calling to tell her that she was on the coach and it was approaching London and she'd be in Soho well ahead of schedule. Or that she'd been running over her lines in the coach and was word-perfect. Or to ask Linda how she was, or to discuss the weather . . .

'Georgia,' she said, picking it up finally. 'What is it? Are you in London yet?' A silence; she felt a rage rising. 'You'd bloody well better be. You can't mess this one up. Where are you, for Christ's sake?'

'Linda, don't be angry – please, please don't. I've – well, I've had a difficult day so far and—'

'I don't want to hear about it. Any of it. Simply tell me where you are.'

'Well . . .' a hesitation, then, and she could hear Georgia jumping into the freezing deep water of disgrace '. . . I'm on the M4.'

'The M4! God in heaven, whereabouts on the M4?'

'Almost in Gloucestershire. The Bath turn-off.'

'Georgia,' said Linda, trying to keep her voice under control, 'I don't know that I can even bear to continue talking to you. Do you know what you've just done? Thrown away a chance, a good chance I might say, of a part, a large part in a new Channel Four series. Gold-dust comes cheaper than that. I worked so hard to get you that audition. I lied, I practically bribed, I begged – and what do you do? You shit on me from a great height. You're a stupid, arrogant, pathetic little girl. Well, that's the end of your acting career, I would say. Opportunities like that don't come along exactly frequently. What am I going to tell them? I hope you realise this damages me and my reputation as much as it does yours. Rather more so, actually, since you don't have one. Now get off this line and out of my life.'

'Linda, please. Please listen to me! I'm so, so sorry. I know everything you say is true, and I don't deserve any more of your help or kindness. But it really wasn't my fault. Really. I was staying with a friend in Bath and—'

'I don't want to hear this. I don't want to hear anything.'

'But isn't there anything you could tell them, that will just make them wait a couple of hours for me? Aren't they seeing lots of girls? Couldn't you ask if I could be last? I know I can be there by five-thirty . . .'

There was a long silence, then Linda said, 'I very much doubt if they'll buy it. Why should they? And yes, they're seeing at least a dozen girls today. They're hardly going to give preference to one who can't get sufficiently off her arse to arrive on time.'

'I know.' The voice was very humble. 'I know. But isn't it worth just trying?'

'I don't know, Georgia. I don't know if I want to confront them even.'

'But you've got to anyway. I mean, you'd have to tell them I'm not coming. Wouldn't it be better for both of us if you told them I had a tummy bug or something. Please, please try?'

Another silence, then Linda said, 'Well I'll consider it. Are you on your mobile?'

'Um no, someone else's. Mine has just died.'

'Oh, for Christ's sake. Give me the number. And if you don't hear from me, don't be surprised.'

'No, no, all right. Thank you, Linda. Thank you so, so much.'

Georgia switched off the mobile and handed it back to Patrick rather shakily. 'I think she's going to try. You were right, it was worth calling her. So – can we go, please? I mean, will you take me? I'd be grateful for the rest of my life . . .'

He had to finish it: absolutely had to. It just couldn't go on, his luck couldn't hold. He told himself so a dozen times a day, of course – and he meant it. For the sake of a few dizzy days and nights of novelty, the absolute adrenaline rush of danger, he was at serious risk of losing everything he had.

He looked across at her, as they drove along, this raw, sexy, not even very beautiful young thing, nearly a decade younger than Laura, and saw his life, its perfect edifice, being rocked to its foundations. He flinched from his own stupidity, his greedy recklessness; and yet even now, as she looked at him, in that literally shocking, absolutely confident way, he wanted her more than he ever, these days, wanted anything.

It wasn't even as if there was anything wrong with his marriage. Laura was the perfect wife, caring, loving, beautiful. Everyone told him so, everyone told him how lucky he was – and he was. Of course. It was just that, well, it was all a bit predictable. Their conversations, their social lives, their family lives, their sex lives. Especially their sex lives. He supposed that was what had actually led him into this heady, dangerous situation. Laura had a rather earnest approach to sex. She knew it was important, she wanted to please him, she claimed he pleased her, she never refused him; but she never initiated it, never suggested anything, never wanted it moved out of the bedroom. He felt every time that she had ticked the experience off, seen yet another duty done and was now moving on to the next thing: be it the school-run, the weekly menu list, honing plans for the holidays, planning the next dinner-party. Which had been the charm of Abi, of course; with her demands, her inventiveness, her risk-taking. Sex was at the centre of her.

And what kind of bastard set those things before love, before loyalty, before family happiness?

His sort of bastard, it seemed.

He had never thought of himself as a bastard, had quite liked himself, in fact. He did all the right things, including a job that actually did some good. He wasn't a banker, for instance, or a corporate lawyer – and he was generous and thoughtful, good to his children, a loyal friend, a pillar of the community indeed.

But Abi, or rather knowing Abi, had changed all that. He knew now that he was rotten to his core, not in the least like his carefully constructed image: he was a liar and a cheat and a philanderer, and he didn't deserve the glorious wife he had been given. Initially he had tried to excuse himself, to tell himself it was only a one-night stand, or at the very most, the briefest fling, purely sex, that it would revitalise his marriage, make him more aware of the treasure he possessed.

But Abi was more than that, more than a fling; he felt increasingly addicted to her. He had never met anyone remotely like her – which explained, he recognised, her fascination for him. She removed him from the gilt-edged tedium of his successful career and perfect marriage.

She seemed to be completely amoral; she had lost count, she once told him, of how many men she had slept with. She drank too much, she did a lot of drugs. She was the sort of woman that he despised and disliked and what he was doing with her, he had no real idea; except that he was having fantastic sex. And more important than that even, finding a huge and dangerous excitement in his life. He had met her only two months before, when he had been (genuinely) at a medical conference; he was asked to speak at them frequently, possessing as he did all the requisite qualities – eloquence, charm, and a hugely successful career. The conference, organised by one of the big pharmaceutical companies, had wanted some photographs taken of the speakers and people at the dinner. The photographer had been an annoying little chap with a nasal whine, but his assistant, following him around dutifully with a notebook to record the names of subjects and a second camera, had been – well, she had been amazing. She was dark, tall and very skinny with incredible legs; her long hair was pulled back in a half-undone ponytail, her black silky dress was extremely short, and although quite high-necked, clung to a bra-less bosom. Jonathan could see it was bra-less because her nipples stood out so clearly. She wore very high-heeled black boots with silver heels, very large silver earrings and quite a lot of make-up, particularly on her eyes, which were huge and dark, and her lips, which were full and sensual.

As she bent down to speak to Jonathan, her perfume, rich and raw, surrounded him, confusing him.

'Sorry about this,' she said, 'but it's my job. Do you mind telling me how you spell Gilliatt?'

He spelled it for her, smiling. 'Don't apologise. You make a nice change from all the other obstetricians.'

'Good.' She smiled back at him, stood up and walked away.

He sat and stared after her, suddenly unable to think about anything else. The soles and heels of her boots were metallic, he realised: they gave her whole outfit a slightly decadent air. She walked – how did she walk? Rhythmically, leaning back just a little, her hips thrust forward. It was a master class in visual temptation.

Jonathan stabbed his fork into his extremely rubbery meat and tried to concentrate on what the male midwife next to him was saying. Something about encouraging what he called 'his mothers' to scream, in order to release their primitive instincts; after five minutes Jonathan felt he would like to release his own.

He looked wildly for the girl; she seemed to have disappeared. Then, as dessert was served he saw her again, working another table in the far corner of the room. He excused himself from the male midwife (now waxing lyrical about womb music) and headed for the Gents; on his way back he spotted her and went over to her.

'Hello again.'

'Hello, Mr Gilliatt.' She had a very slow smile; it was extraordinarily seductive.

'I wondered if you had a business card. I – well, I speak at a lot of these conferences and very often they want pictures for the local press and so on. It's always useful to have a name up one's sleeve.'

'Yes, of course. Well, that's great. I'm supposed to hand them out, so you've just won me some brownie points from my boss. But you don't know if we're any good.'

'Oh, I'm sure you are,' he said. What was the matter with him? He felt about sixteen again, gauche, foolish.

'Well, you'll see how this lot looks, I suppose,' she said.

'Yes, indeed. And – and then decide.'

'Fine. Well, here it is. That's his number and this is mine. Abi's my name. Abi Scott.'

'Thank you very much, Abi. Nice to have met you. Maybe we'll meet again.'

'Maybe,' she said. With another slow smile.

He went back to the table and engaged very cheerfully in a heated debate on induction; fingering Abi's card and telling himself that he would pass it to his secretary at Princess Anne's next day.

He stayed the night at the hotel; he had strange feverish dreams and woke to an appalling headache. He drank two cups of strong coffee and then rang Laura; she always rang first thing when they were apart. He showered and dressed and started packing up his things. He scooped up Abi Scott's card, along with his keys and his wallet which were lying on the bedside table, stared at it for a moment, then sat down again and before he could think at all, rang her number.

They had an absurd conversation, both of them knowing exactly what it was actually about, while dissembling furiously.

He'd like a copy of a couple of the pictures for his wife (important to get that in – *why, Gilliatt, why?*) – could she perhaps email them to him? She could do better than that, she said. They had prints ready and she could drop them off at the hotel, it was only round the corner from her office. That would be extremely kind; she should get reception to call him down. Yes, she could be over in half an hour, he was probably in a hurry to get away.

She was waiting in the foyer when he came down, leaning on the reception desk, fiddling with a long strand of her dark hair. She was wearing the tightest jeans he'd ever seen, they were like denim tights, for God's sake, with the same silver-soled boots worn over them, and a black leather jacket. Her make-up was just as heavy, and her perfume hit him with a thud as he neared her, held out his hand.

'Good morning.'

'Good morning,' she said. 'Nice to see you again, Mr Gilliatt. You know, I never understand all these titles. Why aren't you Dr Gilliatt?'

'Because I'm a surgeon,' he said.

'But most men aren't surgeons, and most of them are called Mr.'

'It's all to do with when surgeons were barbers. It's very complicated.'

'I can tell.' Her eyes moved over his face, rested briefly on his mouth. She smiled again, and the invitation in the smile was unmistakable.

'Maybe I could buy you a coffee,' he said, the words apparently leaving his mouth entirely unpremeditated, unplanned. 'To thank you for bringing the pictures. And I'll try and explain.'

'Yeah, that'd be great.'

'So,' he said, as they settled at a table. 'Do you live in Bristol?'

'I do, yes. But I come from Devon. Born in Plymouth.'

'Oh really? How interesting. I come from Devon, too. I was born in Exeter.' God, he must sound ridiculous to her. Pathetic.

'Yeah? Posh, Exeter, isn't it? Lot posher than Plymouth anyway.'

'I wouldn't know. So, what were you doing before you worked for Mr . . .'

'. . . Levine. Stripping,' she said briefly.

'Really?' He could hear himself, struggling to sound unsurprised, unshocked.

She laughed out loud. 'Not really. Although it wasn't a hundred miles from that. I was an underwear model. Worked for some cruddy local photographer who special-ised in it. Publicity, you know. Shots appeared in the local paper sometimes, if I was lucky. It meant having represen-tatives from the manufacturers at the sessions. They liked to adjust the bras, that sort of thing. It was gross. What I do now is quite civilised.'

'Yes, I see.' There was a silence, then he said, 'Well, I should be getting along really. Back to London. Back to the real world.'

'OK,' was all she said.

Right, Gilliatt. It's still OK. You're still safe. Go and have a cold shower and get off to London. But—

'I'll be down here again in a couple of weeks – another conference, in Bath. Staying here though. Maybe we could have a drink?'

'Yeah,' she said, with that slow, watchful smile. 'Yeah, that'd be great.'

That had been two months ago; since then, he had thought about her obsessively, all the time. She invaded his work, his dreams, his every waking moment. He longed to be with her, and not just for sex. He found her intriguing, almost frightening, so unlike was she to anyone he had ever known. She excited him, she shocked him, and while he did not imagine himself remotely in love with her, he was certainly in her thrall. He was aware of the dangers of her, and each time he met her he promised it would be the last; but then, as he was leaving, the prospect of his life without her – bland, level, respectably safe – literally horrified him. It was as if she had bewitched him, a wicked, beautiful, powerful creature, and he could not break away.

She made him run appalling risks; she would stop suddenly as they walked through a dark street, force him into a doorway, pull him into her; she brought cocaine to the hotel rooms where they met, and made a great play of laying out the lines while the room service meals or drinks were wheeled in; she called him on his mobile when she knew he was at home, claiming to be a patient, refusing to get off the line until he had made some arrangement to see her.

The terror of it all made his adrenaline run high; the comedown was fearful. She had become his personal, addictive drug. He needed her more and more.

But the fear had perversely given him courage; he was resolved that this was the last time, had begun to try and tell her so as they ate breakfast in bed at the hotel, this final morning. It had all been wonderful, he said, really wonderful, but perhaps the time had come to . . .

'To what?' she asked, looking at him sideways, picking up a croissant, dipping it in her coffee.

'Well, to draw a line.'

'What sort of a line? I'm afraid we used all mine last night.'

'Abi, please don't be difficult. I think you know what I mean.'

'Er, no.'

'Of course you do. We have to finish this.'

'What on earth for?' she said, her large dark eyes

puzzled. 'When we're having such a great time? What would be the point? Or did I miss something last night? Were you trying to get away from me, escape into another room or—'

'Of course I wasn't trying to get away from you. Don't be ridiculous.'

'Well then, sorry, Jonathan, but I don't get it. Now come on, let's get rid of this tray and have one last glorious fuck. Then I'll leave you in peace. For now. Oh no, not quite. I forgot, I want a lift to London. Presume that's OK?'

'Of course it's not OK,' he said, irritation finally surfacing. 'I can't possibly drive you into London.'

'Why not?'

'Well – because – because someone might see me – us. You know the rules.'

'Oh, yes, the rules. I stay on my patch, you come and visit it when you can. It's all right, Jonathan, don't look so frightened, I'm not proposing a visit to your very lovely home in Chiswick. I want to do some shopping, meet up with a girlfriend, maybe go to a movie.'

'Oh, right,' he said, relief seeping in. 'Maybe I could drop you at the station.'

'I don't like trains. And I don't really think it's very likely that out of the millions of people in London this afternoon, we're going to be spotted by one of your admittedly large number of chums. No, I'd prefer you to drop me off. Harley Street would be fine.'

'Abi, I am not taking you to Harley Street!'

'Why not? I like it there. I've been there before, remember?'

He did remember, remembered her coming to his rooms, claiming she was a patient, pulling him into her on the examination bed; he still felt sick, just thinking about it. Sick and – amazing.

'You can't come today. Someone might recognise you.'

82

'Yes, and think, There's that nice patient of Mr Gilliatt's again.'

'Abi, *no*.' He took a deep breath. 'And I really do want to talk.'

'We can talk in the car. Waste of time talking now.'

She turned him on his back, began toying with his cock with her tongue. He struggled briefly, then gave himself up to the pleasure of her. It would be the last time . . . He would take her to London and they would talk in the car. He would retreat from the madness and rebuild his life. It would be difficult and he would miss what she did for him, but a few weeks from now it would seem like a dream. A disturbing, dangerous dream. And it would be over, with no great harm done – to him, or Laura or the children or his marriage . . .

The possibility of his harming Abi never occurred to him. And if it had, he would have dismissed it utterly. She really was not his concern.

Chapter 7

Linda had made the phone call. It hurt her to do it, she didn't feel Georgia deserved such consideration, but she could also see that if she got the part, then they would both benefit.

She told the casting director that Georgia had been up all night with food poisoning, but that she was struggling up to London, just the same. She had left late, however, and there was no way she'd be there by three. It would probably in fact be more like five. The casting director said that since Georgia would hardly be at her best, and as they were seeing three more girls next day, then she could come along in the morning at ten-thirty. 'I wouldn't normally be so lenient,' she said, 'but she does look so exactly right and you're not often wrong, Linda.'

Linda thanked her not too effusively – she didn't want to appear grovelling – and tried to ring Georgia back on the number she had given her. It was on message; Linda said could Georgia ring her immediately and get to her office in London as fast as possible. That way she could keep her literally under lock and key until she delivered her personally to the audition in the morning.

She had planned a quiet evening with Francis, who had promised to take her to the new Woody Allen movie; he'd just have to join her and Georgia for supper instead. It really was the last thing she wanted, and he'd be cross, but . . .

* * *

'So is it films you're looking to get into?'

She was a nice kid, Patrick thought, very appreciative, sitting up there beside him, enjoying the view as she put it, doling out his sandwiches and his jelly babies, his chosen sweets on the road, so sweet your blood-sugar level – and thus your concentration – went up just looking at them.

'It's what everyone wants, actually,' said Georgia. 'Actors might say they just want to play *Hamlet* at the National, that they'd turn down anything vulgar and commercial, but that's just total jealousy. Really and truly, they all want to be big names in films and TV. Rich and famous, that's the dream.'

'Well, I'll look forward to your first première,' said Patrick, grinning at her.

'I'll certainly invite you. I'd never have made it, if it wasn't for you.'

'I've enjoyed the company,' he added, 'and that's the truth. But we're not there yet. Mind if I put the radio on?'

'Course not. I think I'll just try the agency once more.'

But the number was engaged.

It was eleven-thirty and Toby had still not returned.

What the fuck was he doing, Barney wondered, pacing the house desperately. Where was he? How could he be this stupid?

They'd all had breakfast together. Toby had said it was important to appear normal and anyway, there was no point getting to the bank before it opened at nine-thirty. After which, he set off, telling his parents some cock and bull story – or so it seemed to Barney – about having to collect some currency from the bank.

'But Toby, no one gets currency from the bank any more. That's what plastic's for,' his father said.

'Not in the Maldives, no cash machines where we're going.'

85

'You really should have done it yesterday,' said his mother. 'It seems awfully silly to go off this morning. Maybe Barney could go for you?'

'No, no, I have to sign for it. And I couldn't do it yesterday – I told you, it wasn't ready.'

'Did you, darling?'

'Yes, of course I did. Honestly, Mother, you don't listen to a word I say.'

'I did rather have my mind on other matters.'

'Well, exactly. I can fill the car up at the same time. I meant to do it yesterday, but I forgot.' Toby had always got himself – and very often both of them – out of scrapes at school by lying; Barney had always been awed by how accomplished at it he was. 'Sorry, sir,' he'd say if they were late for Prep because they'd been dawdling, 'I dropped my locker key coming back from cricket, I was looking for it everywhere, but Fraser had picked it up, came to find me and give it me' or 'I was sick after tea, sir, feeling really rotten, Fraser thought I should go to Matron, but we couldn't find her, anyway, I feel fine now, sorry, sir'. By the time they got to Harrow, he had honed these early skills and could fabricate more complex reasons for late arrival back from town or an overdue essay, usually involving a chain of events difficult to check, an over-crowded – and therefore missed – bus, a mislaid mobile phone, a computer glitch that had destroyed some notes. It was very rare for him not to get away with things: in no small part because he was a succesful boy, very good at games and bright with it, and the staff therefore liked him and were inclined to believe him anyway. Barney, hope-lessly honest and anyway less ingenious, was far more likely to get into trouble.

The Westons finally left at about ten-thirty; they had a couple of things to pick up on the way, they said, before meeting their friends.

'I don't like going before Toby's got back,' said Carol. 'It worries me. What on earth can he be doing all this time? He said he'd be back in about half an hour.'

'Carol, it's fine,' said Barney. 'He just called, said he had to wait a bit for the money, but he's on his way back now. Don't worry, I'll get him to the church on time!'

'Oh, all right. But will you call me when you leave, Barney? I'll worry otherwise.'

'Sure.'

It was twelve before Toby got back.

'Barney, I'm so sorry. She wasn't there – no one was. She made me go to her office.'

'Couldn't you have left it at the house?'

'No, she said she wanted it in her hands. And actually I wanted it in her hands too. No misunderstanding. Even then, I had to wait there for about ten minutes as well. Then she insisted on counting it . . .'

'Yeah, all right, all right. Go and get changed, for Christ's sake. We're supposed to be having lunch with the ushers at one.'

'Well, we'll have to cut it. Barney, the wedding's not till four-thirty. We'll be fine.'

'OK,' Barney sighed reluctantly. 'I'll call them. Now please. Hurry up!'

Toby, clearly shaken, seemed incapable of hurrying. He was a long time in the shower, was fumbling with his tie, then couldn't find the Paul Smith socks he had bought, the only ones fine enough to make his new, stiff, bridegroom shoes comfortable.

'Tobes, mate, we've got to go. Please – we're not just going down the road, you know. I'd better drive – you look bloody awful.'

'Yes, OK, OK. Oh – shit. I still haven't filled the car up!'

'For Christ's sake! You said—'

'I know what I said! Not exactly easy, what I just had to do.'

He sounded quite aggrieved; it annoyed Barney. Then

he thought Toby had been through more stress over the past twenty-four hours than most people did in a year, self-inflicted or not. And had plenty more to come. Best thing was to keep him calm, not argue.

'Well, come on. Let's go. Back way?'

'No, I think because of the petrol, it'd be easier to nip along the M4. It's only one junction, and we can fill up at the service station.'

'But it's Friday. The motorways might be crowded. Do we really have to get fuel?'

'We really have to. The tank's bloody nearly empty.'

'I wish you'd fucking told me last night.'

'Sorry, mate. Anyway, we'll be heading towards London, not out of it. It'll be fine. Much quicker than all those country lanes. We could just as easily get stuck behind a tractor . . .'

Barney was about to say that you could always get round a tractor if it was absolutely necessary, but Toby suddenly said he needed the lavatory. He disappeared for almost five minutes, then came out looking very shaken.

'Sorry, Barney. Just been sick. Nerves, I suppose. Still don't feel great. In fact . . .' He disappeared again.

Well, at least there'd be plenty of lavatories at the service station. Barney went out to Toby's silver BMW to load it up with top hats, tailcoats, Toby's suitcase and some bottles of water. And stood in the drive waiting as patiently as he could for Toby to emerge. It was already past one.

Georgia had discovered a message from Linda on Patrick's phone. She looked at him, smiling radiantly.

'She doesn't exactly say it's all right, but she still wants me to get to London, so I think it must be, don't you?'

Patrick said carefully that he wouldn't really know; life with Maeve and her sisters had taught him never to commit himself to anything, not even an opinion.

'So tell me about yourself,' he said. And she did.

How she had wanted to be an actor all her life; how she had been the star of all the school productions, especially as Juliet. 'Some of those bitches there said, "Oh, you can't have a black Juliet", but our drama teacher was a complete legend, and she said of course you could, it was no more strange than all those white actors playing Othello. And how she had then won a place in Manchester at NAD, as she called her drama school – The National Academy of Drama – and done really well there and how she had been spotted by Linda at the end-of-term performance.

'I'd like to be able to say the rest is history,' she said, biting into an apple. 'That's what they say in stories about famous people and their breaks, isn't it, but I can't. Haven't done anything really yet. If I get this thing today . . . well, it's my big chance, it really is.'

She told him she'd been adopted. 'My birth mother was only fourteen when I was born, and she couldn't keep me, so Mum and Dad took me on. They're very, very good, gave me a really happy childhood. I felt really safe and loved, had lots of nice things, went to a good school, you know? I think I was a bit of a disappointment to them though. It's my brother they're really proud of. He's well brilliant, a barrister. Being an actor can't compare with that.'

'I don't know,' said Patrick. 'There're different ways of feeling proud. If you were to get this part, they'd be proud, I'd have certainly thought.'

'Yes, they probably would be, but it's still not quite what they'd have wanted. My mum dreamed of me being a teacher. God, I couldn't do that. No patience. Not with little kids anyway.'

Patrick agreed that you did indeed need a lot of patience with little kids. 'I have three boys all under eight, and life isn't exactly peaceful.'

'I bet it's not. Your wife must get quite tired. What's her name?'

'Maeve.'

'Maeve, that's pretty. Does she work at all?'

'What, with three kids? She does not, although nothing makes her more annoyed than when people ask her that. "What do you think I do all day?" she says. "My nails?"'

'Oh yes, sorry. Stupid of me. I should know, I get all that sort of shit as well.'

'What sort of shit would that be?' asked Patrick, amused.

'Oh, you know, people saying things like, "How lovely for you, to live in Roath Park." That's the really middle-class bit of Cardiff where our house is. Or, "Wasn't it lucky for you that Chris and Bea adopted you?" What they mean is, how lovely for you to have been adopted by white middle-class people, instead of being dragged up by your black birth mother. Well, it is in a way, but it's bloody hard as well.'

'And why should that be?'

'Well, if you're black, or mixed race, you're black,' said Georgia slowly, 'and it feels odd to be all the time with white people. You have no idea what it was like, as I got to four or five, to go to a kids' party and be the only black face there. You feel – I don't know – terribly on your own. And a bit bewildered. As if you shouldn't be there, not really. Can you imagine that?'

'I think I can, yes.'

'Thing is, you're only there because your own mum and your real family have failed you, and someone's conscience meant you got rescued. And you feel you ought to be grateful all the time and you really resent that. It got better as I grew up, because Cardiff's a pretty mixed community and there were lots of black and Asian kids in my school, so I began to feel more normal. But then I thought, Well, what does that say for my relationship with my mum and dad, if I don't feel good with the people they know and like?'

'Did you ever go and find your birth mother?'

'Yes,' said Georgia flatly. 'But it didn't work.'

'And did that upset you?'

'Yes, it did at first. Then I just sort of pushed her back where she'd been all my life. Nowhere.' She looked at Patrick and smiled. 'I never usually talk about all this stuff. Not till I've known someone for ages, and not always then. You must have some kind of magic, makes people talk.'

'I'm just naturally nosy, I suppose. We're doing well, you know, Georgia. You'll be there by five, the rate we're going. Here, your phone's charged. Best take it, don't want you leaving it behind. Oh Jesus, these people . . .'

A van had cut them up, overtaking from the inside. Patrick had to brake quite sharply.

'That was hideous,' said Georgia, adding, 'white van driver, are they really all bad?'

'Not all, just most.'

Something had fallen on the floor. Georgia bent down to pick it up; it was a small box.

'What's this?'

'Oh, now take a look, I'd be glad of a woman's opinion. It's a present for my mother-in-law, for her birthday. Her fiftieth. We're having a bit of a celebration tonight – it's one of the reasons I have to press on.'

Georgia opened the box; it contained a very pretty watch, on a silver bracelet.

'It's lovely, Patrick. I do like watches. My last boyfriend had bought me a beautiful one the very night I decided to dump him. I had to make him take it back, and it nearly killed me.'

'Why did you dump him? Or is that just one nosy question too many?'

'No. He was just – boring. Nice, what my mum calls charming, really, really good looking. But so boring.'

'Well, that is not a good basis for a relationship,' said Patrick firmly. 'You did the right thing. Even if you did have to give up the watch.'

'You think so?'

'Of course. Maeve and I now, we drive one another mad sometimes, but we're never bored. Now just keep hold of that watch, would you. I should have stowed it away a bit better than that.'

'I'll put it into my bag, it'll be safe there, and I'll give it to you when I get out.'

'Fine. Don't go running off with it, will you?'

'Don't be silly, of course I won't.'

'Oh Jesus. Oh, dear sweet Christ, it's the fucking police. Right behind us. Jesus, that's all we need.' Barney pulled over, guided by the relentless blue light onto the hard shoulder, and wound down the window. *Stay calm, Fraser, that's all you have to do*. Actually, he thought he might throw up.

'Afternoon, sir.'

'Good afternoon, officer.'

'Perhaps you'd be kind enough to get out of the car, sir. Do you have any idea of the speed you were doing then?'

'Er, not quite. No.'

'Hundred and seven, sir. Little above the speed limit.'

'Yes, yes. I'm sorry, officer. I – well, I was in rather a hurry.'

'I could see that.' A half-smile crossed the man's face. It wasn't a very kind smile. 'Going to a wedding, are you?'

'Er, yes. Yes, I am. I'm the best man. My friend here is the bridegroom.' Surely they'd get some points for sympathy.

'You should have set off a bit sooner, sir, I would say.'

'Yes. Yes of course. You're absolutely right.' He must be careful, not sound like a caricature of the upper-class twit. That wouldn't help at all.

'Could I see your licence, sir?'

'Yes, of course. Toby, could you give it to me, please? It's in my wallet – I put it in the glove compartment.'

He passed it over; the cop looked at it carefully.

'So you are Barnaby John Fraser? This is your licence? And it's your own car?'

'No, it belongs to Toby here. Mr Weston.'

'But clearly you are insured to drive it, sir. I'll just take down the details. I see you live in London.'

'Yes, that's correct. But we were staying with Mr Weston's parents in Elcombe.'

'And the wedding is?'

'In Marlborough. Well, just outside.'

'So why did you come up to the motorway, sir? Seeing as Elcombe is on the south side as well.'

'We thought, with the roads all pretty winding and narrow, the motorway would be a better bet.' He knew why the cop was keeping him talking, so he could smell his breath, see if he'd been drinking.

'Well, you could have made a mistake there, sir. Now I'm afraid I shall have to breathalyse you.'

'But I haven't had anything to drink!'

'Regulations, sir. We have to do it. Won't take long.' And then, as Barney handed him back the tube, 'What time is the wedding, sir?'

'Four-thirty.'

'In Marlborough? If you don't mind my saying, sir, that is cutting it a little bit fine.'

'Yes, I know.'

'Have you warned them, let them know?'

'Er, no. I had hoped to be there in time.' *And might have been, without you doing this to me, you bastard.*

'Well, it looks a bit unlikely now, I'm afraid, sir. Let's see . . . Right, there is no alcohol registered.'

'I did—' He stopped. No point . . . arguing.

'You'd better be on your way then. Good luck. You will be hearing from us, of course.'

'Yes, of course.'

'Enjoy your day, sir. What's left of it.'

'Yes. Thank you.' He felt them watching him as he got

back into the car. Turned the key in the ignition, released the handbrake . . . the man walked back towards him. Now what? Now fucking what?

'Keep it down, sir, won't you. Don't want two endorsements in one afternoon.'

They'd be watching them, Barney thought. Even though they were going ahead, he couldn't risk overtaking them. Buggers. Total buggers. God, the petrol was low. Well, they were nearly at the service station. And it was still only just after three. OK, ten past. Should still be all right. All the same . . .

'Think we should call someone?' Toby said suddenly.

''Fraid so, mate, yeah. Who though? Tamara? Her ma?'

'Jesus, no.' Toby turned white. 'Whoever you called about the lunch.'

'Pete. Well, you'd better do it. Get it over.'

'OK. Christ, I'm sweating. Wish it wasn't so bloody hot. Jesus, and now it's going to rain, that's all we need. Shit, Barney, how did this bloody well happen? Fine best man you've turned out to be.'

He'd thought Toby was joking and then realised he wasn't. Not entirely.

Just after three, Jack Bryant pulled onto the motorway. He'd been looking forward to today for some time; he was driving up to Scotland for a bit of grouse shooting with some chums, which would be great fun, and moreover, he was able to drive up in the E-type. She really needed a good run.

The E-type was his pride and joy: bright red, with not a scratch on her – well, not any more there wasn't – soft top, the works. She went like the bloody wind too, 120 mph easy, not that you could do that often these days. When she'd been new, everything had been rather different, of course; all you had to do was keep an eye out for the law and then, providing the roads were empty enough, you could put your foot down. Not these bloody cameras everywhere.

He'd bought her after his last divorce, three years ago. Cost him quite a lot of money, but he'd always wanted one, and after the handout he'd had to give his ex-wife, he felt he deserved something for himself.

Hard to believe he and the car were roughly the same age – well, he was a good bit older truth to tell, and when she was in her heyday in the sixties, he'd been a little boy. But old enough to admire the first one he'd ever seen.

Jack had fallen on slightly hard times; he'd made a fair bit of money out of the first property boom, but not really sufficient to keep him for the rest of his life, or support his ambition to lead the life of a country gentleman. He wasn't a country gentleman, of course; he was a grammar-school boy made good, but he had a lot of friends who were, and in the good years had entertained them to country-house weekends at his home in Somerset, where the food and the wine and the shooting had been good enough for him to stack up credits for years to come. Now the country house had gone and he lived rather more modestly in Fulham, but was to be found most weekends in the country; he was useful, as a single, socially acceptable man always is, and besides, it was impossible not to like him, he was so good-natured, so energetic, such a fund of good stories.

To the more socially distinguished of his friends, he tended to be known – albeit kindly – as 'poor old Jack', and it was in this persona that he was off to the grouse moors. But he would give value in return for his stay, and take back with him a stash of new stories to hawk around the dinner-parties in London.

'Bagged six hundred birds last week,' he'd say, 'staying with old Hugh Argyll. Got into trouble for over-tipping the keeper – gave him eighty quid, but he worked terribly hard, over and above. Earned it, I thought, but they don't even stick to the golden rule up there, I can tell you. Very

Scottish.' Thus branding himself at once as knowing what was what, i.e. how much to tip a keeper, and a generous chap, and not averse to a bit of landed-gentry gossip.

He had actually been in Bristol for a couple of days staying with friends, hence his presence on the M4 that afternoon. And while there, had had the E-type overhauled by a very good mechanic he knew, and then had given her the final once-over himself. Well, you couldn't be too careful, with these old ladies, and it was a long way up to Scotland.

Mary was feeling a bit sleepy. It was the heat, and the fact that she'd been awake most of the night. She might have a little nap, she decided. It couldn't do any harm and it would make the journey seem shorter.

She had already taken off her jacket – the Jaeger one – and had it folded neatly on the seat beside her. She had planned to wear a brooch Russell had given her, all those years ago, also carefully hidden in the sanitary towel packet, but at the last minute had put it in her handbag. The clasp was a bit dodgy – hardly surprising, given its great age – and she thought she could pin it on at the airport. The driver would tell her when they were nearly there, so that she could comb her hair and so on; not that there wouldn't be lots of time when they arrived. The plane wasn't due till six, and the taxi company had advised allowing an extra hour just in case. Mary had allowed an extra two.

'So, how are we doing?' she asked.

'Fine, love.' Her driver, who had told her to call him Colin, was very nice, she thought. Nice and patient. And middle-aged, so almost certainly a better driver. It would have been awful if he'd been one of those tough young ones, with a shaven head. 'An hour and a half at the most from here. Even if the traffic snarls up a bit nearer London.'

'Is that likely?' said Mary anxiously.

'If I knew that, my love, I'd be a rich man. That's what every motorist wants to know, how the traffic is going to be, whether there'll be an accident, that sort of thing.'

'An accident! Oh dear, I hadn't thought of that.'

'Look, Mrs Bristow, we're in the inside lane, as you requested, doing a nice steady sixty-five. Not much chance of an accident happening to us.'

'No, but it's the other people, isn't it?' That's what Donald had always said. It wasn't you, it was the other fellow; you saw so much bad driving on the motorways. Cars speeding, sitting too close behind other cars, motorbikes weaving in and out of the traffic . . .

'Look, even if there was an accident,' said Colin patiently, 'the speed I'm going and us being right next to the hard shoulder, there'd be no way it would affect us.'

'Do you think so?'

'I know so, my love. Look, why don't you have a little sleep? We'll be there then before you know it. You use that little cushion I gave you, make yourself comfortable, and I'll wake you about ten minutes before we get to Heathrow. How's that?'

'What a good idea,' said Mary, and settled herself peacefully in the corner. It had got very dark suddenly. Maybe it was going to rain; it was close enough for thunder. He was right, her nice driver: they would indeed be there before she knew it. And then she'd see Russell, and . . . and . . .

Mary drifted into sleep, smiling.

Thank Christ for that, Colin Sharp thought; put his foot down hard, and pulled over into the middle lane.

'Maybe we'd better have that chat now?' said Abi as they swung onto the M4.

'Maybe we should.'

They were in his new car, a Saab. He had only had it a

week, was still not entirely comfortable with it. The car itself was fine, went like the wind, but the sound system was slightly faulty, kept fading without warning, and the handsfree phone didn't work at all. These modern cars were too clever by half, in his opinion; you couldn't begin to fathom anything out by looking under the bonnet.

Abi was delighted with it. 'It'll be so cool, driving in that. I want everyone to look at me.'

'Well, I don't,' said Jonathan shortly.

She had turned on Radio One, very loudly. He turned it down; she turned it up again.

'Abi, I can't think against that sort of noise, let alone talk.'

'You're showing your age, Jonathan.' But she turned it off.

'Traffic's not too bad,' she said conversationally. She picked up his phone, from where it was lying on the dashboard, and started fiddling with it.

'Abi, put that back.'

'Why? I was going to take a photograph of you.'

'I'd rather you didn't.'

'But you look so sweet. All stern and distant. So different from an hour ago. There, that's great. Now I want to check if you got that text I sent you.'

'What text?'

'While you were in the shower. Yes, here it is, you can look at it later. It's a very nice text.'

'Abi, put that back, please. Now.'

'OK,' she shrugged. 'Anyway, you wanted to talk. So you start.'

'All right.' He took a deep breath. 'Abi, I think it's time we stopped this.'

'Stopped what?'

'You know perfectly well what. Our – this – this relationship.'

'Why?' The question sounded very aggressive.

'Well, I think it's run its course. I've been feeling

increasingly unhappy about it. It's been – well, it's been great – *you've* been great – but I think we should say goodbye before we regret it.'

'I'm not regretting it, Jonathan. I don't think you were either, a couple of hours ago.'

'Abi, look, you don't understand.'

'I think I do,' she said, and her dark eyes were very hard. 'I think I understand perfectly. You've had your fun and now you're getting windy. The excitement isn't quite enough any more. Well, I think that's pathetic.'

'I . .' He decided not to appear too hostile. 'I'm sorry, Abi.'

'So I'm supposed to let you just walk away into the sunset, am I? Quietly like a good girl. Just because you're feeling a bit flakey.'

'Well, you can't have imagined there was any kind of future in it.'

'I might have done,' she said. 'You came on pretty strong to me. As I recall.'

'You didn't exactly hold back yourself either. As I recall.'

She was silent. Then she said, and her voice was very tense, very angry, 'You've got a fucking nerve, Jonathan Gilliatt. For weeks I've been providing sex on demand—'

'I seem to remember you doing quite a lot of the demanding.'

She ignored this. 'Now I've just to fuck off, leave you to go back to perfect little wifey, pretend I was never there. Well, I just might not do that, Jonathan. Might not let you treat me like a bit of shit that got under your shoe. Sorry, but none of this strikes me as quite fair.'

She was right: given how zealously he had pursued her, it wasn't fair.

'Well, I'm sorry. But Abi, you must see, it can't go on for ever. It's not realistic.'

'But I don't see, no. And what if *I'd* prefer it to continue? Had you thought of that?'

He felt a stab of absolute panic; thought he might throw up there and then, in the car.

'You hadn't, had you? You thought because I was easy meat, what I felt or thought didn't matter. You thought I'd do what you said, that I'd just go quietly, say, "Yes, Jonathan, no, Jonathan, three bags full, Jonathan, goodbye and amen and oh yes, thank you very much for spending so much time with me." Well, I'm not going to. I don't see why I should. Actually.'

He glanced at her; she was white, her features taut with rage.

'Are you saying you want money or something? Because if you do—'

'No, I don't want any fucking money. That's a filthy thing to say! What do you think I am, Jonathan?'

'I don't know,' he said, his voice deep with misery. 'I don't know what you are.'

'You're scared, aren't you, now? That I'm going to turn into some kind of bunny boiler?'

'No,' he said, realising this was exactly what he was afraid of. 'Of course not.' And then, looking at the clock on the dashboard, 'This traffic's horribly heavy. I'm going to be late. We need some fuel too. I'll have to call, we'll go to the next service station.'

'Who are you going to call – your wife?'

'No, my rooms in Harley Street. I told you, for God's sake, I've got a clinic at four.'

'Yes, all right, all right.'

He pulled in at the service station; while he filled the car, he also called Princess Anne's. His secretary sounded brisk. 'You have quite a big clinic, Mr Gilliatt. Do you want me to ask people to wait, or shall I just reschedule?'

'Get them to wait if they will. I should be there by four-thirty – five at the latest. I'm so sorry.'

He was sure they wouldn't wait; all those pampered yummy mummies-to-be, they always had something pressing to do, found themselves profoundly busy.

'Oh, and Mr Gilliatt, your wife called. Asked if I'd heard from you. Apparently she's called you a couple of times. Shall I call her, explain or—'

'Yes, that'd be great, Jane. Hard for me to talk, my car phone isn't working properly. Thanks.'

His head was throbbing, his neck oddly rigid. He felt strange, confused. The conversation with Abi had scared him, and at the same time had thrown all his emotions into sharp focus: the longing to finish it, to be safe again – and, absurdly, the misery of losing her.

She got out of the car as he approached it.

'Where are you going?' he asked.

'To the toilet. That OK? Or do I have to get permission?'

'Abi, I'm in a desperate hurry.'

'Well, so am I. To get to the toilet.'

He felt like hitting her. 'Why couldn't you have gone before? While I was filling up the car?'

'I didn't want to then.'

'Oh, for Christ's sake. Well, get a move on.'

'Can I have some money?'

'What on earth for?'

'I want some cigarettes.'

'You're not smoking in the car.'

'I will if I want to. God, you're a tyrant, aren't you? Does Laura do everything you say? I bet she does. I bet she—'

'Abi, stop this. For the love of God.' A car hooted at them from behind. 'Look, I'll move over there. Just don't be long, please.'

'OK. I'll do my best.'

She was over five minutes; he sat there fuming, half-tempted to drive off and leave her. But he was scared of what she might do. He was scared of what she might do anyway.

Might be an idea to call Laura, in case she called him.

101

He dialled the house; it went straight to answerphone. The same happened with her mobile.

'Laura, darling, it's me. Just to let you know I'm on my way, bit late. Don't call me, will you. The handsfree's not working properly, so I won't be able to answer. I'll call you when I can.'

He saw Abi coming back, her face stormy, obviously gearing up for a fight. This was a ghastly situation; he simply hadn't dreamed she'd react like this.

Chapter 8

Mary woke up feeling uncomfortable. She couldn't quite establish the cause of the discomfort straight away, for she also had a slightly stiff neck, in spite of Colin's pillow. Then she realised it was her bladder. It wasn't strong at the best of times, and when she was under stress, distinctly weak. She would never get to Heathrow without going to the toilet; she'd have to ask Colin to stop at the next service station, and hope he wouldn't mind. Men did mind that sort of thing; even Donald had got irritated when she was constantly asking him to stop on journeys. But she was paying Colin, she told herself, and quite a lot of money too; he would have no business being irritated. She was sure Russell would have said that. She had a quick worry about whether Russell would get irritated with her constant need for the toilet – it was not the sort of thing that had been a problem when they had been together before – and then after another few minutes, she took a deep breath and said, 'Colin, I wonder if you'd mind very much pulling in at the next service station? I need to go to the Ladies.'

Colin said he wouldn't mind at all and in fact he could do with a break himself. He'd got through his bottle of water already and they were only about halfway there.

'It's this heat,' he said. 'All right if we just go to the fuel section? Takes so long if you have to park up in Services.'

'Of course. And I'll get you the water, Colin. Unless you want to – to get out yourself, that is.'

'No, Mary, that's fine. Bladder of steel I've got, if you'll excuse my French. Yes, if you would, a couple of bottles and maybe some chewing gum? I like to chew when I'm driving – it helps my concentration.'

Mary hoped that didn't mean his concentration was flagging. She'd seen some very alarming driving that day: cars speeding, motorbikes weaving in and out of the traffic, lorries sitting horribly close behind cars – all with foreign numberplates, she noticed, and just now, a white van sitting on their tail, flashing furiously into Colin's mirror before suddenly accelerating into a very small space alongside them and then shooting into the outside lane against a background of furious hooting.

'What very unpleasant behaviour,' she said.

'Shocking,' said Colin.

'My husband always said that bad driving was really little more than bad manners. Would you agree with that, Colin?'

'I certainly would. Right, here we are, Mary. Doesn't look too busy, considering; shouldn't hold us up much.'

'I do hope not,' said Mary humbly.

'So, what do these things do for you then?' asked Georgia, helping herself to a handful of jelly babies.

'A lot,' said Patrick briefly. 'Wreck my teeth. Make me feel sick. Keep me awake, mostly.'

'How? I'd have thought coffee would be better.'

'I'm practically immune to coffee, Georgia. These are the thing, pure sugar. Don't you eat them all now.'

'I won't.'

'In fact, I'm surprised to see you eating sweets at all. You're so extremely skinny.'

'I know, I'm incredibly lucky. I just don't seem to put on weight. Other girls are really jealous of me. They have to work at it – hardly eat at all, some of them, exist on cigarettes and lettuce.'

'That doesn't sound terribly healthy. Well, I suppose the lettuce is all right.'

'Patrick, they are so unhealthy. I would say at least half the girls in the business have an eating disorder. It comes from people – casting directors and agents and so on – going on and on at you: "You must keep the weight down, you've put on some weight." The camera puts at least seven pounds on you, you see, and . . .'

'What does that mean?'

'Makes you look seven pounds fatter,' said Georgia patiently, 'and it's kind of a vicious circle. If everyone else weighed eight stone or whatever, that'd be fine, but since they don't, you stick out like a sore, very fat thumb if you're not careful. The dancers have it worst. One of my best friends is a dancer and she says she gets so hungry, with all the practising and training, sometimes she can hardly bear it. And maybe then she gives in and eats, and then she feels so scared, she has to get rid of it.'

'And how does she do that?'

'Well, if she's in time, she makes herself sick, if not she takes a ton of laxatives.'

'Dear God,' said Patrick. 'That is one of the saddest things I heard in a long time.'

'I know. It is very awful. So you see how lucky I am.'

'I do indeed.'

She was silent for a while, munching the sweets; then she said, 'So is tiredness a real problem in your job?'

'Sometimes. We're always tired. You don't get much sleep during the week. But, tired is all right, it's the sleepiness that really gets you. It's like a monster, a sticky monster, smothering you in the head.'

'Doesn't something like Red Bull help?'

'A bit. But there's really only one thing to do – stop, get out, walk around. It's the terrible monotony, that's what does it. Everything narrows down to the black road and the white lines.'

'Bit like hypnosis.'

'It is indeed. I've often thought that myself. You keep talking now, ward the monster off for me. The sun doesn't help.'

'OK. You can see a lot from up here, can't you? It's amazing, almost like flying.'

'It is. And you can see a lot of what's going on in the other vehicles as well, as you pass them. I find that the greatest temptation, to peer into people's cars and their lives.'

'Well, why don't you?'

'Because I'm busy keeping my eye on the road, that's why.'

'Well, I'll do it for you for now. Wow, he's a bit of all right, that guy there – look. Sorry Patrick, that's not helpful. Rewind. Here comes a guy in an Alfa, really, really fit. God, he's looking at himself in the mirror, how gross! I cannot bear vain men.'

'I'd have thought there'd be plenty in your chosen profession.'

'There are. One of the downsides. Oh, now here comes a coach driver up beside us. He looks well bored, all those old grannies sleeping. Suppose they've been on some tour or other. Now that old bloke, he ought to be in the coach with them – looks too old to be driving himself. He's going *sooo* slowly, I guess that must be as dangerous as speeding, and – oh God, that looks like a real nightmare! Poor bloke.'

'Who's that then?' asked Patrick.

'A bridegroom. All done up in his monkey suit, well-fancy waistcoat and so on, top hat on the back seat, and another beside him – best man, I expect. They look well stressed. Late, I suppose. Too much booze last night probably. God, how awful. Late for your own wedding. Hope the cops don't stop them. How are we doing?'

'Pretty well. Reckon you might make it yet.'

❅ ❅ ❅

'Thank Christ. Began to worry we'd get stuck high and dry on the motorway next. Don't think that'd go down too well. Shit. Bit of a queue.'

'Mate, it's Friday afternoon. I did warn you.'

'Yes, OK. Give me a break. I need the toilet, can you do the petrol?'

'Sure. How're you feeling?'

'Oh, you know. Not great. But I'll make out. Could do without this gut rot, though.'

Barney resisted the temptation to point out it was stress rotting Toby's guts, not some malign fate. He still felt very shocked and confused by Toby's revelations; combined with the nightmare of being so late, he was finding everything almost surreal. Toby, on the other hand, seemed much better – more normal; it was as if having dealt with the situation as best he could, he could set it all aside and return to his role as model bridgroom. He didn't seem the Toby Barney knew any more; it was almost scary.

Barney filled up the car and then thought that he might at least take a look at the tyres. He'd felt the car pulling a bit. The way they were driving, they needed twenty-twenty wheels.

'For God's sake, what are you doing now?' Toby had reappeared.

'I want to check the tyres,' said Barney. 'The front offside's a tad soft.'

'Shit, Barney, do we have to?'

'Yeah, we do. Look, you go and pay – and get some more water, will you? Time you've done that, I'll be through.'

'OK.' Toby went back into the building. He grabbed two bottles of water, and found himself behind an old lady in the queue. She was fumbling in her bag for something – her purse, he supposed. There were three people in front of her – Jesus, this was taking for ever. He looked at his watch. It was OK. It was fine. Hours yet. Well, an hour . . .

As he stood there, trying to keep calm, his phone rang.
'Toby Weston.'

'Where are you, you little shit?'

He knew that voice. Too well. It was Tamara's father, George Richmond, who doted on his daughter to an absurd degree, who clearly considered Toby to be a most unworthy contender for her hand.

'I'm – we're just on the motorway now, George. Should be with you quite soon.'

'Quite soon! God give me strength. And what the fuck are you doing on the motorway? Why aren't you at the ushers' lunch?'

'Well, I . . . change of plan, George. Sorry, I did phone Pete, you obviously didn't get the message. Be there in no time. Just filled up, want to check the tyre pressures.' He shouldn't have said that. He really shouldn't.

'The tyre pressures! What the fuck are you doing, checking tyre pressures an hour before your wedding, for Christ's sake!'

'Yes, George, I know, but one's a bit down . . .'

'Look, you just forget the fucking tyres and get over here, right now. This is the biggest day of my daughter's life and I'm not having it wrecked for her. She thinks you're practically at the church and you tell me you're on the motorway checking your tyre pressures. What's the matter with you? Now you listen to me. I don't care if the tyre's right down on its rim, you just fucking well get here, you understand?' The phone went dead.

Toby looked at the queue of people in front of him, now down to two, one nice-looking girl and the old lady, and said, easing his way forward, 'Look, can I go first? Do you mind? It's an emergency, I must get away.'

The girl stood aside at once; the old lady gave him the sort of look that he could remember his grandmother giving him when he was naughty and said, 'I do mind, yes, as a matter of fact. We're all trying to get somewhere important, and I have a plane to meet. You must wait your turn, like everyone else. I'm sorry.' And then spent an inordinate amount of time counting out the exact money for her purchases.

The other queues were all longer; Toby just had to wait.

Mary felt mildly remorseful, watching him haring towards a car parked up by the airline. And more so when she realised he was wearing the striped trousers and braces of a wedding guest. That hadn't actually been very kind of her, and neither was it in character. She would have been very cross if she'd seen anyone treating her grandson Timothy like that. But he had been rather arrogant, the young man. If he'd asked nicely she might have felt differently. Although . . . she knew why she'd reacted like that really. It was because she was on edge herself, anxious about meeting Russell, how it was going to be, whether it had been such a good idea, after all.

She got back into the car, gave Colin his chewing gum and water, and settled back into her seat.

'Now you will be careful, Colin, won't you? There was a woman in the queue talking about an AA report. Apparently the traffic is exceptionally thick.'

Which meant, Colin thought with a sigh, confinement to the inside lane for the rest of the trip.

'Barney, come on, come on, we have to get the fuck out of here. Just get in, for God's sake. I'll drive.' Toby threw himself into the driving seat, slammed the door.

'But . . .'

'I said get in. Look, I'm off. You can stay here if you want to.'

Barney got in, telling himself you could only die once. And sending up the closest thing he knew to a prayer that it wouldn't be today.

❖ ❖ ❖

109

In about an hour's time, Tamara thought, fiddling with one of the roses in her hair, she'd be Mrs Toby Weston. Tamara Weston. It was a good name. A very good name. She'd tried it, of course: signing it, saying it, thinking it a lot. And the fact that both their Christian names began with T was great. It looked wonderful on invitations, Toby and Tamara.

She took a last look at herself in the mirror; she was glad she'd insisted on this quiet five minutes alone. Everyone was so excited, her mother particularly, she'd worn them all out this morning. And her sister; she'd been unable to eat her breakfast, said she felt sick. Tamara had felt fine, and eaten quite a good breakfast. Well, she knew lunch would be out of the question, and she'd need something inside her. Nanny had always said that. Dear Nanny. How pleased she'd been when Tamara had told her. It was a pity she couldn't come to the wedding; she would have loved it. But she was getting so old now, and she couldn't wear proper shoes, she'd have been a bit of an embarrassment and she'd have had to be explained to people. Which would be a bit heavy on your wedding day. Tamara had felt guilty not inviting her, but she'd written to explain that there simply wouldn't be room and promising to send her some cake and go and see her with the photographs. That would do, surely. Her mother said she'd felt very bad, but then Nanny had worked for her family as well, had practically brought her up. But . . . well, if you asked everyone you wanted, the guest-list would just get totally out of hand. It had got pretty out of hand anyway, a hundred more than the original top limit. Her father had been rather alarmed, but she'd told him it would be worth it when he took her down the aisle. And Toby had chipped in with the money for the champagne, which was jolly nice of him; he'd said to her quietly that he would have liked to do more, but she'd said no, no, that wouldn't be right, her father would be embarrassed. And

110

she'd paid for her own wedding dress, for God's sake. She'd done her bit.

It was the most lovely dress: Vera Wang certainly knew what brides were about. Very, very simple, heavy white satin, strapless, with a tiny bolero for the ceremony. She did look very beautiful; she stood there, enjoying the fact. Tall and slender – so slender, worth all that hunger – and tanned, her brown eyes looking absolutely huge, her dark hair piled up and the real white roses in it, and then the veil, the long long veil. She couldn't wait for Toby to see her, and on an impulse, she picked up her phone and took a picture of herself in the long mirror. She could show him later, when they were finally alone; it would be days before any of the official pictures arrived. She was glad she'd insisted on having the photographer there right through the day. Those ones he'd taken after breakfast in the rose garden might be a bit corny, but they'd be lovely, and the ones in the long mirror too, as her veil had been put on. Toby would love them. They could have some framed and they could go up in the flat: more original than actual wedding pictures.

Dear Toby; he'd be there now, down at the church, waiting for her with Barney and the ushers. She looked at her phone and suddenly wanted to hear his voice: to tell him how excited she was, to hear him saying he loved her. She picked it up, pressed his number, waited as it rang. Only he didn't answer it; in fact, there was the answering service cutting in.

Hi, this is Toby Weston. Sorry I can't get to the phone right now, but if you leave a message . . .

'Toby, I don't know what you're doing, but I'll forgive you this once. This is just to say I can't wait to see you. I'm sure you look incredibly handsome. Only about half an hour to go. Don't expect me to be on time, will you? Bye, Tobes. See you there. Lots of love.'

✤ ✤ ✤

Laura frowned when she heard Jonathan's message. It was all very well, him telling her not to call in that rather high-handed way, but she needed to know when he would be back. The people next door had suggested supper in the garden. He did obsess over the mobile business; he could surely take a quick call, it would be over in a second. She'd give him another fifteen minutes, and then . . .

This was just about the quietest day she could remember, Emma thought; it would have made a very boring episode of *Casualty*. A couple of fractures, a minor heatstroke, very few Worried Well even; they were probably all on holiday, bothering the local GPs. If this went on, she might even get away on time tonight – she was on the eight till six shift – go up on the train to see Luke instead of in the morning as planned. That'd be really good. He said he'd got something important to talk to her about; she didn't allow herself even to speculate what it might be. Certainly not the sort of 'important' that involved the future, that sort of thing. They didn't have enough of a relationship for that. But still, she was clearly sufficiently important to him to make him want to discuss whatever it was. That was good. Anyway, she'd definitely be with him tomorrow. She'd know then. Probably something more to do with Milan.

She was sitting at the doctor's station reading *Hello!* when the triage nurse summoned her.

'Emma, a child's just been admitted with a very nastily cut foot – stepped on a broken bottle in a stream, apparently. Could you come as soon as you're clear here? She's bleeding rather badly.'

She dealt with the child's foot, and with a woman who had crashed her pushbike into a wall and had broken her wrist. 'I don't know how I came to do it,' she kept saying. 'I was being ever so careful.'

Emma could see exactly how she came to do it; she stank of alcohol. Why did people think it was safe to cycle while they were drunk? Mad. Working in A&E did give you a rather warped view of human nature. She sent the woman off to X-ray, where there was, she knew, a long wait; and then, as the department continued to be so unusually empty and quiet, she returned to the doctor's station and her copy of *Hello!*.

'Give me some more of those jelly babies, would you?'

Georgia looked at Patrick; his eyes were fixed on the road, oddly unblinking. Was he sleepy? She felt sleepy herself, thundering along, the road shimmering in the heat haze. Somehow the unaltering speed increased the tedium enormously; it was as if they were on some vast conveyor belt, alongside dozens more vehicles. What had Patrick said about the white lines? Oh yes, it was as if they were moving, not you, coming towards you interminably, hypnotically; and now – or was it her imagination – it was getting darker.

'We're running into a storm,' Patrick said, wide awake suddenly. 'Dear God, will you look at that!'

And, in an odd yellow blackness, great sheets of rain came beating down on the road, turning it to glass, and then, seeming to wrap around them, crash after crash of thunder; and then the rain turned to hail, the stones hitting the windscreen, vying with the thunder for noise, whiting out the road markings.

Everything had slowed, everything had half-vanished, vanished into the darkness and the water; they seemed alone and oddly lost. She looked anxiously at Patrick, and his face was tense, his hands on the steering wheel white-knuckled. All she could see of the approaching cars was their headlights, some on full beam, an endless procession, and in front of them nothing but spray, thick impenetrable spray, only half-pierced by the long red line of the brake-lights.

And then it was over, as fast as it had begun; they ran out

of it into brilliant sunshine, a still wet road, but the thunder gone, and the sky a sweet clear blue.

'Wow,' she said. 'That was kind of scary.'

'So . . .' said Abi. She was leaning back in her seat, looking across at him. They had driven through the storm, through the darkness of the thunder and the hail, and the sun was shining again. 'So . . . what do you want me to do?'

Relief flooded him. She was going to be all right, after all; she was going to let him go. She'd just been making a point.

'Well, nothing, I suppose. Just – just . . .'

'Go quietly. Is that it?'

'Yes. If you put it like that.'

'I can't think of any other way *to* put it, Jonathan. You want out. If I don't, that's my problem. You have a marriage to look after. And I only have me. Poor little old me.' She sighed.

He looked at her and felt a pang of remorse and irritation in equal proportions. He hadn't behaved entirely well, he could see that. But she was hardly in a vulnerable position. She was financially self-sufficient, she had a flat, she had a good job, a car, she was young, sexy, tough . . . she didn't exactly need him. As Laura did.

'Abi, I'm sorry. I shall miss you, but I don't really have any alternative. Our relationship can't go anywhere. And it's very wrong. You must see that.'

'Well, why start it then?' Her voice was ugly, harsh. 'Why chase me all over the conference hall, call me, send me flowers, invite me for dinner? For fuck's sake, Jonathan, what's changed? What wasn't wrong then?'

'I . . .' He felt very tired suddenly, unable to deal with her arguments. The late night, the drive down from Birmingham, the lack of sleep, the stress of the journey, the shock of the storm: it all combined to confuse him. He slowed the car down.

114

'What are you doing?'

'Moving into the slow lane.'

'Why?'

'Because I want to,' he said wearily. He moved behind a red E-type – lovely old car, he thought, surprised that he could notice it even, given his turmoil – then eased himself into a large space in the slow lane in front of an old Skoda.

'You know it's bloody unfair,' she said, lighting a cigarette.

'Abi, I said not in the car.'

'Yes, I know you did. It's all totally unfair, Jonathan. What do you think I am, some kind of automaton? Oh, I can do big words too when I want to. Didn't you ever think of me when all this was going on? That I might have taken what you were doing just a little bit seriously? When you sent me flowers and bought me expensive dinners and hotel rooms and the odd bit of trinket? Did you see doing all that as a substitute for just paying for me, the price of the sex?'

'Don't be ridiculous. You know perfectly well I'm very . . .' careful, Jonathan, don't start claiming affection, could be dangerous '. . . very concerned for you.'

'Oh really? Well, I don't think I do know that, actually. I think that because you're rich and successful and you've got a wife who believes every single fucking lie you tell her, you can spend nights away in pricy hotels, get your sexual pleasure that way, rather than a quick screw with a tart. Well, it sucks, Jonathan. It's filthy and I think you shouldn't be allowed to get away with it.'

He felt a rush of sheer bowel-churning panic.

'I think your wife ought to know what a complete slob she's married to. I think you should have to deal with that *and* her. And I think maybe I should tell her.'

'Abi, don't be absurd. What good would that do?'

'Quite a lot – in the long run. Not to you, or to me, but

to her and any other poor bitch who you might fancy fucking in the future.'

'You wouldn't dare.'

'Of course I'd dare! What have I got to lose? Nothing. Nothing at all.'

'But – but . . .' He found he was pleading with her, realised that the balance of control had suddenly shifted, that she held it absolutely. 'But Abi, you couldn't do that. You'd hurt her so much.'

'No, Jonathan, it's *you* who's hurt her. Not me.'

'Right, well the storm's over. Didn't like that.' Georgia had resumed her task of keeping Patrick entertained. 'How sweet, there's a dear little old lady, sleeping like a baby down there, in the back of that minicab. Wonder where she's going? And – oh, now that's a lovely car.'

'Which one would that be?'

'There, the red one – look, straight in front of us. It's vintage, isn't it?'

'Oh, now I see, yes, it's an old E-type. Beautiful cars. I've dreamed of having one of those myself, as a matter of fact. Hardly practical for a family man though.'

'If I get to be famous and rich, Patrick, I'll buy you one. To say thank you for getting me to the audition today, the one that's going to start it all.'

'Well, that'd be very nice,' said Patrick. 'Anyway, he's leaving us now – look at the acceleration on that thing, will you?'

Jonathan's mobile rang sharply. He shouldn't, he was driving, but he was in the slow lane . . . He picked it up, looked at it. It was Laura. Without thinking, absolutely conditioned to the handsfree situation of being able to answer the phone anywhere on a journey, wanting only to reassure her and to somehow be safe with her, he pressed the button.

'Hello, darling—'

'*Darling!*' Abi was shouting now, her face ugly with rage. 'How can you do that, you rotten bastard! How can you talk like that? Give me that phone . . .'

'Hello! Hello, Jonathan, is that you?' Laura's voice was faint, crackly. 'Jonathan, what's—'

The traffic was very thick; a huge lorry was alongside them, travelling at the same speed as they, the red car in front pulling ahead now . . . so nice, that old Jag, he'd love something like that . . . the car behind was too close on their tail really – all of them part of a great orderly mass of power, riding the highway in the dazzling sun. He took it in, in some strange detachment, trying to think, absurdly, what to say. And then . . .

'Jonathan, be careful, look out! The lorry – what's happening to it?'

'Patrick, look out, look out! What's happening – what is it? Be careful, look out . . . oh God . . .'

'Shit! Fuck! Jesus Christ!'

'Toby, stop, hold it – for Christ's sake, hold it!'

Part Two
The Accident

Chapter 9

William Grainger always said his life was totally changed in one moment. The moment when he stood, awestruck, in the field high above the side of the motorway looking down onto it; he'd gone out to check on the heifers they'd moved that morning from the field on the other side of the farm. Usually they were untroubled by the traffic, occasionally they became nervous.

This lot seemed untroubled. They walked over to him with their swinging walk, hoping he was food; when they realised he was not, that he brought nothing for them, they stopped, and turned away, an untidy, disappointed, good-natured crowd. One of them had lifted her tail and dis-charged a mass of cowshit on his boots; a protest perhaps, he'd thought, cursing her, pushing his feet through the dry grass to try and get rid of the worst. And then, as he looked down at the road, shimmering in the heat haze, the air brilliantly clear again after the brief thunderstorm, he saw it and knew even as he watched that he would never forget it.

It all happened in a sickening slow motion: a lorry heading towards London suddenly swerving sharply to the right, cutting across the fast lane and then failing to stop, bursting through the central reservation, its trailer sinking onto its side like some great dying beast, and then discharging the deadly flotsam of its load, whatever it was, he couldn't really see, tossed into the air to continue on its journey into the advancing traffic. A mini-bus travelling westwards in the fast lane became impacted in the undercarriage of the lorry; and a black Golf immediately behind that swung sideways and rammed into one of the lorry's wheels. A silver BMW behind the lorry, apparently out of control, spinning, twisting, across the road, came finally to rest, rammed into the car in front of it. Cars began to swerve and skid into one another, like bumper cars in a fairground; one hit the central reservation, another made a small odd leap and landed on the hard shoulder; it all went on, seemingly unstoppable and in both directions.

William stood, frozen with horror now, hearing the scene as well as watching it; the dreadful noise, blaring horns and crunching metal and raw, terrible shouting and screaming, and aware too of the hideously dangerous smell of burning rubber. He could see the vast white cubes, whatever they were, that made up the lorry's load, continuing on their journey driven by the fearsome force of momentum; one car hitting them head on made a 180-degree turn and was struck by an oncoming motorbike, another shot sideways and skidded into the barrier, then rose like a rearing horse and hung on to it, defying gravity, but apparently unharmed.

Instinct told him to go down to the road; common sense told him not to. He could be no use, would add to the chaos; he reached in the pocket of his jeans for his mobile, remembered he had left it in the tractor on the other side of the fence and started to run, waving his arms at the scene first in a futile gesture, as if they would have understood what he was going to do.

Chapter 10

For just a second, Jonathan was tempted to drive on, remove himself from the horror and the carnage, get to London swiftly and safely, rid himself of Abi. And no one would know. If he went on, he had a chance of disentangling his life; if he stayed, he had none.

He chose to have none: he stopped the car and left his former life for ever.

Abi was sitting staring at him, ashen-pale, her brown eyes wide with shock. She was absolutely silent and so was he; the only sound was her breathing, heavier, faster than usual.

She reached out her hand to him and, 'Don't touch me,' he said, without knowing quite why. 'Leave me alone. Stay away.'

He had to think: to try to recall the events of the last – what? Five, ten, twenty seconds? He looked at his watch: two minutes past four. How long had it taken, that blur of sights and sounds and sensations? What precisely had occurred to bring him to where he now was, his car parked askew on the hard shoulder but, amazingly, unharmed? He shook his head, trying to shift memory into focus. He knew what had preceded it, preceded the blur: could recall with absolute clarity the phone ringing, answering it, and then a lorry swerving suddenly, swinging wildly to its right for no apparent reason, and then instead of straightening again, crashing blindly on at an angle of forty-five degrees across the central reservation, causing cars on the other side of the road to react crazily, swerving wildly about, and then somehow slamming to a stop on the hard shoulder, the chaos over, the engine stilled.

The car immediately ahead of him was driving steadily on as if nothing had happened; other cars, coming from behind him, were slewing into one another, gradually coming to a halt. Jonathan sat, fighting for breath, leaning on the steering wheel, recovering from the shock, the road ahead emptied now as the traffic went on forwards, vanishing into the haze of the heat, now and again a dash of brake-lights, but no one stopping; a great self-focussed cavalcade, caught up in the doctrine of the motorway, of pushing on, of getting there, of never looking back, not getting involved, leaving him behind: and he would have given in that moment all he had to be one of them, blessedly blindly unaware of – what?

Of what lay behind him – but it had to be confronted.

He looked, slowly and very fearfully, in the rearview mirror and saw it, about fifty metres behind him, saw it all: the lorry, gone through the barrier, the trailer lying on its side, saw the great wheels facing him, saw the fearsome mass of the load, thrown into the road, and then the westbound traffic, swerving, skidding, riding into chaos.

He opened the door, slowly and very cautiously, started to get out, and then found his legs wouldn't hold him, he felt sick and dizzy and sat down again, his head dropped weakly onto the steering wheel.

He looked at Abi; she was green-white, staring at him, her eyes huge with fright, an ugly gash on the side of her head. 'What happened?' she said. 'I don't understand.'

'I'm not sure,' he said. 'I couldn't see, the lorry seemed to lose control . . .' His voice tailed away.

She got out, looked back at the lorry. 'Jonathan, it's awful. It's gone right through the barrier. And all those white things, what are they?'

'Its load, I suppose. Container burst.'

'But how, why—'

'Oh, for fuck's sake,' he said. 'I don't know. Your head all right?'

She felt the gash, looked at the blood on her hand. 'Yes, I think so. I've got some tissues somewhere, I'll just—'

'Give me my mobile, quickly.'

'I can't find it – I dropped it.'

'Well, give me yours then.' He took it, dialled 999. Asked for police, and gave them the whereabouts.

'Yes, thank you, we've got that one,' the voice said. 'Several people called it in. The emergency services will be there in ten minutes.'

Jonathan looked at the great mass of traffic gathering, stretching in both directions. 'I hope so,' he said. 'It's pretty bad.' And then watched disbelieving, as first one car, then another and then another, moved onto the westbound hard shoulder, accelerating and driving away.

'Stupid fucking bastards,' he said, and then got out of the car and began to walk slowly, compelled almost against his will, towards the lorry.

It was a hideous sight. A mini-bus had gone straight into it, under its wheels, and had crumpled up like so much paper, and from it he could hear the hideous sound of children screaming. A Golf – if only it had been a Merc or a Volvo – desperate to avoid it, had first turned, then skidded 180 degrees into the traffic in the middle lane. Another car, a blue Ford, had managed to miss it, but had driven into the barrier and swung round before it stopped, facing the wrong way. A youngish man, little more than a boy, was climbing out of it, shaking his head as if to rid it of what he had just seen and done; his windscreen was shattered, and blood was running down his face.

Jonathan realised the Golf's engine was still running; turning it off seemed suddenly the most urgent thing. He scrambled over the barrier, ran to the car. The window had shattered with the impact, as had the windscreen. Jonathan looked down and into it: at a girl, or all he could see of her, a mass of long blond hair and blood, a bare brown arm, with a white watch – odd how one noticed these things – flung out towards the windscreen as if warding it off; and yes, the engine still switched on. Jonathan reached in, turned the key, and then very gently lifted the arm, felt for the pulse. And found nothing.

He straightened up and found himself staring into the eyes, the shocked puzzled eyes, of the Ford driver; and simply nodded at him, confirming the girl's death, unable to speak.

'Oh God,' said the boy, staring round him, at the chaos and the carnage. 'What did it? How did it happen?'

'Christ knows. You OK?'

'Seem to be. Yeah. Can't think how. Arm hurts a bit.'

Jonathan looked at his arm; it was hanging oddly.

'Looks like it's broken. I'll check it later.'

They stood there for a moment, looking up at the lorry from the driver's side; the cab was, astonishingly, intact. They walked round it; and as they reached the nearside, they saw the door was open, and a young black girl was standing on the step. She stared at them for a moment, her expression totally blank, and then jumped to the ground.

'You OK?' asked Jonathan, and then: 'You weren't in there, were you?'

She stared at them both, then shook her head, turned her back on them and vomited rather neatly onto the road.

She was very young, and very pretty, Jonathan noticed; after a moment she walked, slowly but quite steadily, towards the hard shoulder, where she sat down and put her head in her arms.

'Shocked,' said Jonathan, 'but she seems OK. Extraordinary.'

'She can't have been in there, can she? Or climbed up to have a look?'

'God knows. Can't imagine it. But – funny thing, human behaviour. I'll check her later. Look – I'm going up into the cab. Make sure the engine's turned off there. It could explode any moment.'

Strangely, he didn't feel frightened, wasn't aware of being brave; just knew it had to be done.

Constable Robbie Macyntyre had been dreading his first big crash. He just didn't know how he would deal with it. He wasn't exactly squeamish, and of course they had had it spelled out to them in training that things like severed limbs and worse were inevitable. And he'd seen plenty of dead bodies already, doing his training on the beat. It wasn't that, more the thought of people in terrible pain, crying out, begging for help; again in training they were told that they were fine, the 'screamers' as they were called – at least they were alive. Robbie wasn't sure he would be able to take that attitude. Well, he was about to find out.

The first calls had come in five minutes ago; hundreds more would follow. Already two cars had left the depot, and he was in the third, with his colleague Greg Dixon. Robbie was intensely grateful that this was not Greg's first big crash – or even his hundred and first. 'Been doing this for ten years,' he'd said to Robbie when he joined the unit. 'Got pretty bloody used to it. Bloody being the word, if you get my meaning.'

Robbie had asked if he actually enjoyed it. 'Not exactly enjoy,' Greg said with a half-smile, 'but unlike a lot of policing, you have a chance of preventing deaths before they happen. Someone's been murdered, all you can do is find the killer; someone setting out as a potential murderer – which all fast drivers are, think about it – can be stopped.'

As far as they had been able to establish, the congestion on the road was already severe in both directions; not only had the lorry jack-knifed and gone through the crash barrier, a mini-bus in the fast lane travelling west had hit it head on. Not much hope for the poor bastard driving that then; they crumbled like cardboard, the old ones, and this was apparently a V reg. The lorry had been a new one, and with a full load; the westbound carriageway was completely blocked, and the eastbound one was clogged by vehicles behind the crash and some of the lorry's load ahead of it.

The main priority now, apart from clearing a way for the emergency services to get through, was to garner information and communicate it to the control room; how many casualties, how many ambulances would be required, whether the fire brigade would be needed to cut people out.

Robbie kept remembering his Superintendent's words: 'Gridlock on the motorway takes seconds; you'll have a mile tailback inside a minute.'

He supposed it wasn't surprising. Whenever he'd been out with the patrol, hauled people over and stood there with them, out of the car, he'd been awed by this immense noise and force pounding past. You weren't so aware of it, distanced from it in your own car, of the thousands of tons of metal, travelling at high speed; it was a sobering experience. His boss said that every learner driver should be compelled to stand on the hard shoulder or on one of the bridges for half an hour, reckoned it might scare them into keeping their speed down a bit. He was also of the opinion that a film of a serious crash, gore and all, should be obligatory viewing for new drivers. Robbie actually agreed with him, but of course it would never happen. There'd be outcries about danger and offended sensibilities, and possibly even a breach of human rights, the way things were going.

One of the main problems subsequent to a crash, he'd been told – although it didn't sound as if it would be relevant today – was rubbernecking. 'You can get an incident on one carriageway and the traffic comes to a standstill on the other,' Greg Dixon said, 'just because people slow down, even crash into the car in front at times, just to have a gawp. Good old Joe Public.'

He didn't take a very rosy view of Joe Public; Robbie was swiftly coming to realise why.

Jonathan slithered down from the lorry's cab; the young Ford driver was still there.

'OK?' he asked.

'Yes, the engine was off. Hell of a mess up there. Windscreen's shattered, blood everywhere. Poor bugger driving it's not too good though.'

'I bet he's not. Is he – alive?'

'Yeah, just. Maybe not for long.'

'Should we get him out?'

'Christ, no. In any case, we couldn't.' He glanced over at the hard shoulder. 'That girl all right?'

'She's disappeared,' said the young man. 'God knows where. She was still sitting on the hard shoulder last time I looked. Nobody with her. But she's not there now.'

'Odd,' said Jonathan. 'Wandered down the road, I suppose. She seemed very shocked. Oh well. She'll turn up again, I expect. She's the least of our worries, I have to say. Shit. That was bad in there.'

A man was walking towards them, holding a small boy by the hand. He was crying and saying, 'Mummy, Mummy . . .'

'Is he all right?' Jonathan asked.

'*He's* all right,' said the man, and he spoke so casually it was as if he was discussing the weather. 'His mother's not though.' He nodded in the direction of a large black car; its windscreen was shattered and there was a woman lying on the road; she had clearly come through the windscreen. 'She'd just undone her belt, just for a second,' the man said, 'to give the little fellow a drink. And she – she . . .' He shook his head, turned away from them.

'I'm a doctor,' said Jonathan gently. 'Would you like me

to come and see her?' He could tell it was futile; but it needed to be done.

The man nodded. 'If you wouldn't mind.'

He turned, Jonathan followed. The man with the broken arm looked after them.

'Poor bugger,' he said. 'Poor, poor bugger.'

Emma had just finished eating a rather dodgy BLT when the news came through. Of a major crash on the M4, with a jack-knifed lorry, a crushed mini-bus, the road blocked in both directions, almost certain fatalities. And by some grisly coincidence, there was a second accident further down the road: a continental truck with a blow-out had slewed across the exit road of the next junction. Nobody was hurt there, but there was a mass of traffic behind it, which meant that the obvious route for the emergency services to the crash, travelling the wrong way up the motorway, was temporarily at least out of the question.

She took a last gulp of equally dodgy coffee, and half-ran into A&E, thinking that she was the only surgeon on duty there that day, and hoping she'd be able to cope. She put in the trauma calls, the special unmistakable bleep, summoning people to A&E, removing them from their day-to-day work and rosters; she would need, she reckoned, an orthopod, a cardio-thoracic surgeon, two general surgeons, two anaesthetists, a general surgical registrar, and ATL – hospital shorthand for Advanced Trauma and Life Support. Plus at least ten nurses. It sounded like a lot of people, but they were all going to be needed.

They stood together in A&E, a group of people – some of whom knew one another only slightly, working as they did in totally different departments of the hospital, others who were in daily contact. There was a minute of formalities, of handshaking, name-giving – a parody, Emma always thought, of arriving at a drinks party.

Alex Pritchard appeared; ten minutes earlier he'd waved to her across reception, off on a clear weekend.

'Thought I'd better come back,' he said. 'See if I could be useful.'

'That's great,' she said. 'Thank you. It's very good of you.' She knew this wasn't quite true; a herd of wild horses wouldn't have kept Alex from a major incident like this one. It was why he did the job he did, why he had never moved on from A&E.

Apart from the surgical registrar and Alex, there was just one other familiar face: Mark Collins, a young orthopaedic registrar she'd worked with a few months earlier on a ghastly multiple motorbike crash. He had been great then, calm and tireless; and no doubt would be again.

'Hi,' she said.

'Hi, Emma. This sounds like a big one. Worse than the bikers, I fear. OK – who's going to be team leader?'

That had surprised Emma too, on her first big incident, with its connotations – again – of parties, games of charades. Somehow she'd thought everyone would just know what to do. But it was essential, she had discovered, to establish a chain of control, for order and swift delegation, and to cut through the chaos and any panic; the first thing ambulance crews always asked on arrival was, 'Who's team leader?'

'You, Alex?' she said now to Pritchard.

'OK. All right with everyone? What news, Emma?'

'Well, it's pretty bad. Jack-knifed lorry, trailer on its side, driver trapped, several cars, mini-bus – three lanes blocked, in both directions, several fatalities. And someone just rang to say people are driving down the hard shoulder in the westward direction, so the road could be impassable pretty soon.'

'People are just great, aren't they? Is the driver of the truck alive?'

'So far. Amazingly, there's a doctor right on the scene.

131

He rang to report that the bloke was completely trapped, steering column embedded in his chest, just about conscious, pulse very weak, but definitely alive.'

'Fire service on its way? Sounds like he'll need cutting out.'

'Sure. But— Excuse me.' Her phone had rung – it was the first of the ambulances. 'Hi. Yes. We have a full team ready. Good luck.'

'This is a bloody nightmare.' Greg Dixon slowed the patrol car to a near-halt; stationary traffic filled all three lanes and much of the hard shoulder as well. People were getting out of their cars, standing on the roofs, shouting at one another, staring into the distance.

'Look at that, those bloody idiots. How are we supposed to get through? How's an ambulance, the fire brigade, to get where they're needed? People could be dying unnecessarily half a mile down the road, for want of a way through. Get on to the control room, Robbie, say we need a couple of off-road vehicles. And yes, we could try approaching from the other direction, of course, but apparently some ruddy continental artic's just had a blow-out and slewed right across the exit road, so no one can get on or off. Now that is shit bad luck. We can either go back and come down the eastbound carriageway the wrong way – probably best to tell the ambulances to do that – or we could cut across those fields. Meanwhile we'll just have to start working our way through this, car by car. Start by ordering those idiots back into their vehicles, tell them it isn't a bloody picnic.'

'Or move the barrier?' suggested Robbie. 'If we can get across to it, go down the wrong way till we get there?'

'We could try that, yeah. Nothing's coming through so it's obviously completely blocked at the scene. Christ, what a mess. Haven't seen one as bad as this for a long time.'

* * *

Jonathan had turned his attention to the mini-bus; the driver's door was jammed shut but the one at the rear opened fairly easily. There were eight small boys inside, all seeming to be miraculously unhurt, but the driver was dead. He was about to climb in, when he heard Abi's voice. 'Jonathan, what can I do?'

She was still white, but very calm; he felt a reluctant thud of admiration for her.

'Help me get these chaps out. They're all fine, I think. Don't look at the front.'

She did what she was told; undid their seat belts, took their small hands, led them, talking encouragingly, shepherding them past the worst of it, trying to distract them from the girl in the Golf. They were dazed, obedient with shock, all white-faced and shaking, many of them weeping, but all astonishingly uninjured.

There was another man in the van, neatly strapped into his seat, as the boys had all been; he was staring in front of him, also unhurt, but apparently reluctant to leave the van. Jonathan urged him out onto the grass verge, where he sat down obediently, then buried his head in his arms. Post traumatic shock, Jonathan decided, and felt at once sympathy and a totally unreasonable irritability. He could have done with some help with these poor little buggers, from someone who knew them; and he clearly wasn't going to get it.

'Tobes,' said Barney. 'Tobes, are you OK?'

It had seemed horribly, unbearably noisy, horns going, brakes screaming, glass breaking; now it seemed equally horribly quiet. The BMW was listing over, half-embedded in the car in front of it, a Volvo estate, but at least safely on the hard shoulder . . . the journey from the outside lane to there, that terrifying interminable journey, was over. But – how? Had it been their fault? Please God, not that, not their fault.

He felt odd, disoriented; his ears seemed to be blocked, sound muffled. He shook his head and looked sideways out of the window, the fog of shock clearing, and saw a surreal landscape of cars – many, like them, come to rest against fridges and washing machines, others at a right angle to the crash barrier, some facing completely the wrong way. At first, as he looked, the landscape was quite still; then like some gradually speeded-up film it came to life as people began to climb out of cars, peer into others, clearly fearful of what they might see; talked on their mobiles, approached one another, united as survivors, members of a blessedly elite club.

And then he realised that there had been no answer from Toby; not even a groan or a grunt, and turned very slowly to look at him, frightened beyond anything. He was lying over the steering wheel, one arm holding it, his face turned to Barney; apart from a flow of blood down his face from a head wound, so normal did he look, so almost alert, that Barney half-expected him to grin, reach out an arm and punch him on the shoulder, say 'Hi'; but he didn't. He just stayed there, silent, utterly still. And then Barney realised that there was a far worse injury to Toby than his head; the car below the steering wheel was crumpled, collapsed inwards, and Toby's right leg below the knee was trapped within it. There was a great deal of blood flowing from it.

Panic gripped Barney; he felt sick and breathless. Then, clumsy with terror, he reached for Toby's wrist, pushed up the new white cuff, felt for his pulse. And for an age he sat there, looking at him, just waiting for something to happen, for him to move, make a noise, groan even, for Christ's sake. But – there was nothing.

'Oh Tobes,' he said aloud now, his thumb moving first gently, then desperately, up and down Toby's wrist. 'Tobes, don't, please, you can't. Shit, where is it – oh God . . .'

And then, moved beyond anything, he started to weep.

'There you are,' Jonathan said to the last little boy, settling him on the grass verge. 'You're fine, I promise. What's your name?'

'Shaun,' he said, and then, 'I'm ever so thirsty.'

'I'll get you . . .' Jonathan began, before realising that he couldn't get him a drink; he and Abi between them had finished the one bottle of water he'd had in the car. And Christ, it was hot; he could have done with another litre of the stuff himself.

'I'll see what I can do,' he said, reflecting with a sort of detached surprise on the fact that here, on a three-lane motorway in the twenty-first century in one of the most highly developed countries in the world, a thirsty child in blistering heat could not have a drink, and probably would not be able to for some considerable time. He felt very isolated, far from real life, the life he knew, filled with order.

He could hear a phone ringing somewhere, and wondered where it was; by the time he'd realised it was his own, it had stopped. He was obviously not functioning as well as he might be; he'd better be careful.

Abi had disappeared; he looked around for her, saw her scrambling over the barrier. He called her name; she turned and scowled at him then continued down the bank, out of sight. Where was the silly bitch going? What was she doing?

He looked rather vaguely for the other girl, the one in the cab; there was no sign of her either. Maybe Abi had seen her, maybe that was where she was going. He looked at the missed call register; it had been Laura. Again. She must be very worried; but he couldn't ring her back yet, he didn't have the strength either to talk to her, or even begin to think about what he might say. The extent of his own predicament was beginning to hit him: being on the wrong motorway, in very much the wrong company. How was he going to explain that, for Christ's sake? But he was unable even to think about it yet.

Another child had taken up Shaun's plea. 'Please, sir, I'm thirsty too,' and then another. God. Poor little buggers.

'Did any of you have drinks in rucksacks, anything like that?'

A couple nodded.

'Where are they then?'

'On the rack. In the bus,' said one of them.

Jonathan took a deep breath and walked back towards the van. Getting back into it would not be the best experience, even for a doctor, whose sensitivities over such matters were supposed to be blunted. But of course there were no rucksacks on the rack; they had all shot forward, and left the van, via the shattered window. No drinks to be had there then.

His phone rang again. 'Police,' said the voice. 'We're approaching you now, getting the cars moved over. Probably about half a mile from you. From your description, it sounds like the truck driver'll need cutting free. Would you confirm that, sir?'

'Absolutely, yes,' said Jonathan. 'You'll never get him out alive without.'

'Thanks very much. We'll be there as soon as we can.'

Abi had reappeared.

'Where the fuck have you been?'

'I needed to pee,' she said. 'So terribly sorry, Jonathan. And don't talk to me like that. None of this is my fault.'

'I hope you're not implying it's mine.'

'Well, you were on the phone,' she said. 'The police might not like that. If they knew.'

'Oh, for fuck's sake,' he said. But he suddenly felt extremely sick.

'Oh Mary, you are even more beautiful than I remembered . . .' Russell was bending down to kiss her now, and then he took her hand and kissed that too, and then, 'Come along,' he said, 'let's go,' and then everyone in the airport was shouting, shouting really loudly, and she could hear horns hooting and radios playing and wondered how that could be, inside the building; and then someone hit her really hard in the back, and someone else said the 's' word and Mary opened her eyes and they weren't in the airport at all. She was sitting in the car still, and there was a very bad pain in her head, and a worse one in her neck; so bad, she groaned aloud as she tried to move.

She hadn't gone to sleep again, surely? She tried to sit up and bit her lip with the pain, then saw Colin turning round, his face white, but apparently perfectly all right; and then she looked out of the window and saw a scene of unimaginable chaos, right across to the other side of the motorway, cars shunted into one another, people walking and even running about, and huge white objects, dozens of them, all over the road. And as she turned round with huge and painful difficulty, she saw a car – a large red car – half-embedded in the back of them.

Colin opened the door, climbed out and walked round to it; she heard him say, 'Jesus!' and then, 'Jesus Christ!' and then, 'You all right, mate?' And then saw him come to the front of the car and lean onto the bonnet, shaking his head, his eyes closed.

Emma turned back to the group. 'Apparently the road on the westward side is completely blocked now. Some moron on the hard shoulder has broken down, way ahead, and the police cars can't get through at all at the moment. It's going to be tough. And our doctor says the lorry driver is in a bad way, that it's a neuro job, in his opinion. He's impaled on the steering column, pulse fairly steady, bit slow, about fifty. Injuries mainly internal, he says, no visible haemorrhage, severe bruising on the left temple, almost certainly concussed.'

'What sort of doctor is he?' asked Alex tetchily. 'I hope he knows what he's talking about.'

'He seems to,' said Mark Collins, 'and as he's all we've got there at the moment, I think we should give him some credence. Pretty bloody brave as well, climbed into the cab, checked that the engine was off.'

'Yes, all right, all right. Sounds like the fire service then, and how are they going to get through, for Christ's sake? Poor bastard'll need fluids, morphine, and it's going to take so bloody long. Westbound's completely blocked and they need to clear a fair bit of garbage on the east side as well – chaos for up to three hundred metres, apparently.'

'We should get HEMS on the case,' said Mark Collins. 'Best thing altogether, from the sound of it.'

HEMS – the Helicopter Emergency Service – were called out far more than Emma would have expected, not just to bad traffic accidents, but to people stranded while climbing, and sailing. Their rescues were hugely dramatic, like a TV programme. She had a secret yearning to be able to join them one day; she was afraid it was unlikely.

The phone rang again. Alex answered it.

'The doctor's called back. He says there's a young girl in a GTi dead – and so is the driver of the mini-bus, plus one other woman. There're a load of kids on board.'

'Any of them dead?'

'Nope.'

Emma still hadn't adjusted to the phlegmatic reaction to all this, to death and disaster, nor to the dark humour, although she knew that got them through. She fought down a rush of sorrow for the girl in the GTi and tried to concentrate on what Alex was saying to the police.

'OK, we'll get a second team out. We've asked for the brigade to approach the scene down the eastbound carriageway, fast as they can. Perhaps you'd be good enough to be ready for them, accompany them over to the lorry. Any more fatalities? Right. Yes, of course. And we'll send some water with the ambulances. What about casualties the other side? Any there, as far as you can see? Fine. Well, let us know.'

William Grainger had returned to the vantage point at the top of his field, having called the police. As it turned out, they'd had dozens of calls before his. He couldn't do anything else really, couldn't ignore what was going on down there, get on with fixing the roof of the barn, or bring the first lot of cows in for milking, or indeed any of the things that had seemed so important an hour ago. There might be something he could do when the police and ambulances arrived – although at the moment there seemed little chance of that. On the great curve of road stretching away from him towards London, the traffic was solid, all three lanes and the hard shoulder motionless; cars that had tried to escape, via the hard shoulder, were at a complete standstill as well. And serve them right, William thought. What kind of selfish idiot would block that, the route so essential to the emergency services? And in front of the crash, on the London-bound road, an eerie emptiness, a road devoid of cars but strewn with strange white rectangles. And even as he watched it, a procession came in sight: a number of breakdown trucks, preceded by police cars, and followed by ambulances. They had obviously closed the road altogether from the next junction, reversed the normal flow of traffic.

His phone rang. 'Mr Grainger? Police here.'

'Hello,' said William uncertainly.

The voice was impatient and calm at the same time. 'Where are you now? As related to the accident.'

'Top of the field, looking down, where I was when it happened.'

'How's it looking, from where you are?'

'Pretty bad,' said William.

'Many people walking about?'

'Yeah, quite a lot now. But it's hard to tell. I'm at least a hundred and fifty metres away from it.'

'How would you feel about a helicopter landing in that field? An air ambulance?'

'Well, the cows wouldn't like it,' said William. 'I'd have to get them moved. Otherwise, it's fine, of course. Just let me know.'

'OK. Could we ask you to move them anyway, as a precaution? Straight away, if you'd be so kind.'

William said he would; and thought how displeased the cows would be, having just got settled in their new field.

'OK, thanks. Might make a bit of a mess.'

'That's perfectly all right,' said William. He switched off his phone, looked down at the chaos, increasing now, further back, in the road, perhaps two, three hundred metres or so away, as more and more people left their cars, some on mobiles, shouting into them, some with dogs on leads, barking furiously, others with small children, many of them crying, carrying them to the grass verge, all talking to one another.

But the scene immediately below him was more complex: a confusing mass of cars and debris, people wandering rather dazedly about, some moving more purposefully. It was all rather surreal, not like real life at all.

Far, far away now he could hear the wail of more police cars and ambulances; better get the cows shifted fast. Thank God, just thank God his parents were away. His mother would be preparing a field hospital, half-enjoying it, and his father probably right down there, trying to direct the traffic.

Greg Dixon and Robbie had been halted 200 metres from the pile-up by the great stash of traffic.

'Bloody hell,' said Dixon, edging the car forward, his hand on the horn, switching on the alarm and the blue light. 'This is a nightmare. Why don't people use their brains, for Christ's sake! Look at those two, just standing there talking – Jesus!' He opened the window, leaned out and shouted at two men standing by their cars just ahead of him, one on the outside lane, one in the middle, chatting. 'Get back in your cars, both of you, please! Move them over, for Christ's sake. And then stay in them. This isn't a bloody picnic. You're putting lives in danger.'

'Bullies, the police are,' said one of the men to his wife, inching his Mercedes forwards, towards the inside lane. And, 'Do be careful,' she said. 'You're going to scrape the side of the car. I said careful . . .'

'Stupid cow,' said Dixon. 'Sometimes I despair for the human race.'

Chapter 11

Maeve looked at the clock: twenty to five already. If Patrick was doing as well as he'd said, he'd be on the outskirts of London by now. Certainly well clear of Reading. Which meant about an hour and a half – with luck – to Kilburn. She was looking forward to seeing him; it had been a tough week. The littlest lad, Ciaran, had had some ear infection, been crying with the pain, and the oldest had got into a fight at school. She'd actually had to go up to see his teacher. It was times like this she longed for a proper husband, as she thought of it: one who was there to help out, to give moral support, talk to teachers, sort out the children. Liam was only seven, but he knew it was his dad who told him what was what, his dad he was wary of, his dad he obeyed. He was a good little chap, but he was cheeky and argumentative, he needed constant discipline, and Patrick being away most of every week just couldn't provide it.

'I'm sorry, sweetheart,' he would say whenever she complained, 'but I can't help it. It's the name of the game. Things have changed even in the last five years. It's a much more difficult business than it was. I do my best.'

'I know you do,' Maeve said, 'but it's very lonely, Patrick, I tell you that.'

'And so it is on the road, Maeve. Very lonely.'

She knew that was true, and she also knew that Patrick would never cheat on her, like so many of the drivers did.

And their wives cheated too. Lorry driving as a profession was not good for marriages.

'But ours will survive,' Patrick often said, 'because I love you so indecently much.'

That was one of his favourite expressions: it always made her smile. And she loved him back, however cross with him she became sometimes. They had a great life together – when they were together. But that just wasn't enough.

Now might she ring him? See where he was? Maybe she'd wait till five. Then he'd have a real idea how he was doing . . .

'No, he's alive.'

Barney had never heard anything as wonderful as those words: spoken by this really great bloke, who'd put his head in the window as Barney sat there, helplessly still holding Toby's wrist. He'd said he was a doctor, and could he help.

'But he's in a lot of trouble from that leg, I'd say, possibly his pelvis as well, and he's probably concussed. The head wound looks nasty too, he's losing a lot of blood from that. But—'

'Shit,' Toby said suddenly. 'Fuck. Holy shit.'

'There you are. Very much alive. He should be OK. I've certainly seen worse.'

'You OK, Tobes?' said Barney.

'It hurts,' Toby said. 'My leg hurts.' And then, after a pause, 'You all right?'

'I'm fine.'

'What happened?'

'Lorry went out of control. We hit another car.'

'Oh, I see.' His eyes had closed again, at what clearly seemed to him an acceptable explanation; he appeared to have drifted away again.

'What should we do?' Barney was trying not to panic, but

it was difficult. 'What can I do? Can you do anything, if you're a doctor? And would it be better if we got him out? He might be cooler. After that rain specially.'

'My dear chap –' for the first time that terrible day, Jonathan managed to smile – 'I don't actually carry spare blood around. Or sutures. Perhaps I should. No, the best thing is to get him into hospital. And we shouldn't move him, and it certainly isn't cooler outside, unfortunately.'

'So – I can't help?'

'We can try and stop that leg bleeding. Tie something round it, make a tourniquet. Got anything we can use?'

'My shirt?' suggested Barney, pulling off his wedding waistcoat, ripping off the shirt.

'Good man. Now if we can just tear it into strips – that's the way, and then I can . . . yes, pass it to me. There – sorry, old chap,' he said as Toby yelled in pain. 'Now what you can do is keep an eye on his pulse. It should be about sixty a minute. If it starts to drop dramatically, just come and find me. I won't be far away. Try to keep him awake, distract him if you can from the pain – it's obviously pretty bad. Just keep talking to him, tell him medical help's on its way.'

'But how do we get the medical help?' asked Barney, his voice desperate. 'Seems pretty hopeless to me. The traffic's totally solid, and those things – look like fridges and freezers—'

'They are fridges and freezers. Came out of the lorry. But they're going to clear them. Emergency vehicles are on their way and the ambulances are being diverted down this side of the motorway. Should be here quite soon, from a large and very good new hospital, I know that for a fact, near Swindon.'

'So – so could you make sure they deal with Toby first?'

'I can't possibly do that. It's not my decision. But I will point out to them that he has serious injuries and probably needs blood urgently.'

'And – you really think we should stay here, in the car? Not get him out on the grass, or on a blanket?'

'Absolutely not. It's impossible to say if there are any internal injuries, but he needs properly assessing before he's moved.'

'Why do you think the airbag didn't work? Neither of them did.'

'No idea. Maybe because of the angle the car was struck. Anyway, it would be very unwise to move him.' He smiled almost cheerfully at Barney. 'Jonathan Gilliatt. Nice to have met you, albeit under rather unhappy circumstances.' He paused. 'From the look of you, I'd say you were on the way to a wedding.'

'Yeah,' said Barney and then, indicating Toby, 'his.'

'Oh Christ. Christ, I'm sorry.'

'Yeah. Bit harsh, isn't it?'

'Very harsh. Jesus.' Jonathan was silent for a moment, visibly moved by this, staring into the chaos; then he seemed to pull himself together and said, his voice much heavier suddenly, 'Look, I'll come back and check on you a bit later if I can.' His phone rang. 'Hello? Oh, good. Great. Look, we have a rather seriously injured man in a car over on the eastbound side, up against the safety barrier, just short of the truck. Car embedded in another. Pulse not bad, sixty or so, but he's probably concussed, and with a very nasty leg injury. I've put a tourniquet on, but he'll need blood urgently, so if you can get that message through to someone – thanks. Silver BMW – er, hang on a minute.' He passed the phone to Barney. 'They want the registration number.'

'It's TTW 06,' Barney said.

Toby had been so chuffed with that numberplate, Barney thought – TTW for Toby and Tamara Weston, 06 for the year they met . . .

'I'm going a bit further down the line now,' Gilliatt said. 'See if there's anything else I can do.' He put the mobile back in his pocket, smiled at Barney. 'They should be here pretty soon. You heard what I said to them. Just let me know if they don't find you, OK? Give me your phone and I'll put my number in it for you.'

'Thanks.' What an amazingly nice bloke, Barney thought; and how lucky he'd been there.

Jonathan was just setting off back through the chaos when a wild-eyed man grabbed his shoulder from behind.

'I believe you're a doctor.'

'I am, yes.'

'It's my wife. Could you have a look at her? Please?'

'Sure.'

'She's in the car, just here.'

It was a Volvo, actually the one the wedding boys had struck from the rear. He looked in the window of the BMW as he passed; Barney gave him a feeble smile.

'OK?'

'Hope so.'

'It's my wife,' said the man. 'She's – well she's pregnant. She's having stomach pains and I'm terrified she's going into labour.'

'How pregnant?'

'Seven months. Well, seven and a half.'

'OK. Let's have a look at her.'

The girl was doubled up over her stomach in the front seat; her face contorted with pain. Jonathan waited, saw the pain clearly pass, saw her relax.

'Hello,' he said, 'I'm a doctor. An obstetrician, actually. So you've come to the right place.'

She tried to smile.

'How long have you been having the contractions?'

'Oh, about . . . I don't know. Fifteen, twenty minutes.'

'But they're quite strong?'

'Yes.'

'And how often?'

146

'Every few minutes.'

'Can I feel your tummy? Just put the seat back, that's right. Lean back, try to relax. Now then . . .'

As he felt her abdomen the girl gasped, bit her lip, threw her head back. No doubt about it. She was in labour.

'Look,' he said gently, picking up her wrist, taking her pulse, 'I do think that yes, you are in labour. Brought on by the shock, I expect.'

'And the blow from behind, surely,' said the man. 'It was incredibly hard, as the other car hit us.'

'I'm sure. Your necks are OK, are they? No whiplash?'

'No, thank God. Enough to worry about without that.'

'Indeed. Well, look. There's not a lot I can do, obviously. The contractions are frequent, but they're quite short, I don't think she's going to give birth imminently. But—'

'Oh God!' The girl started to cry. 'This is so scary. It hurts so much and it's much too early, I – oh God . . .' Another contraction hit her; she groaned loudly.

'Let me get in beside her,' said Jonathan. He sat in the driving seat, waited for the pain to pass, then he took the girl's hand and started talking to her very gently.

'Now look, I can't do much, but there's plenty you can do for yourself. The first thing is to try and relax. I know it's easy for me to say, but it really will help. Have you been to ante-natal classes, done any breathing techniques?'

'Yes, but—'

'Well, do them. For all you're worth. It will help you and help your baby. Now, let's get you more comfortable, before you have another contraction. That seat go any lower?'

'Yes, I think so,' said the man.

'Good. I'd say get in the back, but it's taken a bit of a hammering. The next thing is, seven and a half months isn't so terribly premature. Providing we can get you to hospital, the baby will have an extremely good chance. Promise. Now ambulances are coming, and I'll ring ahead and tell them about you. They can have an obstetric team ready. Oh, here comes another one,' he said, seeing the girl tense, her eyes widen with fear. 'Do your breathing! Go on, that's it. Nice and slow. Better?'

She nodded feebly.

'Good girl. Now you just keep that up. And I'll come back in a little while, check on you. And if you start to feel you want to push, just ring me. I'll give my number to your husband. I'll be with you straight away. Here,' he reached for the man's phone. 'Now you just concentrate on what I've told you, and it's my opinion you'll have that baby in a nice delivery room at the hospital. OK?'

'OK,' said the girl. She looked much calmer.

'Good girl.' Jonathan smiled at her, got out of the car. 'Try not to worry too much. Tough little things, babies. I should know.'

The helicopter was approaching; William could hear it although he couldn't see it. He was standing at the top of the field, ready to wave at it, as the police had asked him to do, hoping there was sufficient area free of trees for it to land. As long as it stayed right at the top it'd be fine, but then it would be that much further from the road. Well, presumably this wasn't the first time it had done this. Probably used to such situations.

There was progress in the scene below him. Unbelievably, a police car was easing its way along, cutting through the apparently solid traffic. Only about 100 yards until they reached the lorry now, and he could hear a second car as well; presumably once they'd cleared a path, others could follow.

William looked at his watch: five-fifteen. That poor bloke in the cab was probably dead by now, if he hadn't been killed when he'd crashed. And the mini-bus behind, half-buried in it – no one could have survived that, surely. All he could see on the other side was a sort of pattern, made up of huge white blocks – the lorry's load, he supposed. Several cars appeared to be crushed against them, but there was more activity over there, people walking about; he thought how thirsty they must be, and decided that once the helicopter was landed and he'd shown them the way down, he'd get down there himself, take some water.

He could see the helicopter approaching now, see the trees bending in its path, could actually feel the cold, shuddering wind of the blades. William stood up and waved both arms furiously; the helicopter began to circle its way down towards him, then dropped dramatically onto the top of the field. The blades slowed; a man got out, waved at William, was followed by another. William ran over to them.

'Hi!' he said.

'Hi. Thanks for this. Couldn't have managed without you. The fire brigade should be here soon, they're being sent down the carriageway from the other direction as soon as the road's sufficiently clear. We're almost certainly going to need them. Now we may be on your land for some time – that OK with you?'

'Fine,' said William.

'We'll get down there, see what's what. Thanks again for your help.'

'Can I go down, with some water maybe? People are going to be terribly thirsty, I thought. This heat . . .'

'Good idea. But stay on the verge, and don't get in the way of the emergency vehicles.'

'Of course I won't,' said William. What did they think he was – some kind of an idiot? People did seem to have a very low opinion of farmers' intelligence. It was hugely irritating.

Luke decided to give Emma a call, find out what time she might be with him in the morning. Or if there was a chance she might get off early tonight. It did occasionally happen, people switched rotas. He called the switchboard at St Mark's; the phone rang for what seemed like for ever. God, you'd be dead long before you'd get through, if it was an emergency. He thought that every time he called her.

'St Mark's Hospital Swindon.'

'A and E, please. The doctor's station.'

'Hold on . . . that number is engaged. Can you hold?'

'Yes, OK.'

He waited; quite a long time. Then a man answered. 'Yes?'

'Oh, hi. Could I speak to Dr King, please? Dr Emma King.'

'I'm afraid she's extremely busy. Big emergency just coming in.'

'OK, mate,' said Luke cheerfully. 'Ask her to ring me when she's through, OK? It's Luke, tell her.'

Alex Pritchard frowned into the phone; he didn't like being called 'mate' by someone who was clearly only just out of short trousers, nor did he like the clear assumption that a big emergency would be over in a matter of minutes or so.

'She could be some time, I'm afraid,' he said, 'but I will pass the message on, of course.'

'Great,' said Luke. 'She's got the number. It's about tomorrow, tell her.'

'I think,' Pritchard said, in tones that would have frozen hell over, 'perhaps you should call back later. I too am very busy.'

'Cool,' said Luke, only very slightly taken aback. 'What would later be?'

'I really couldn't say. Try in a couple of hours.'

'Fine. Will do. Thanks for your trouble. Cheers then.'

Alex put the phone down and sighed. What was she doing with that idiot? He simply didn't understand it.

'What do you mean, he's not coming? Of course he's coming! He can't not come, it's – well, it's – of course he'll come! Just got held up. That's all.'

'Tamara,' said her father, 'he's not coming. He's got caught up in some ghastly crash on the M4. Barney just phoned.'

'Barney! Well, Barney's an idiot – he couldn't drive his way out of a paper bag. Let me have your phone, Daddy, let me call him back. There must be some way he could come, cut across country or something . . .' Her voice rose towards hysteria. 'We can keep the church for a couple of hours, just do everything later. Yes, that'll be all right, that's what we should do.'

'No, my darling, it won't be all right. I'm terribly, terribly sorry, but it won't. Toby's . . . well, Toby's been hurt.'

'Hurt? What sort of hurt? I don't understand.'

'Quite – quite badly hurt, I'm afraid. A doctor's made some kind of an assessment. He's concussed, and one of his legs is injured, and there's a possibility he's got some internal injuries as well. Apparently the car hit a load of freezers or something. Barney wasn't making a lot of sense.'

'Freezers! Oh, now I know it's a joke. Some stupid joke. Barney's always making them. How could a car hit a freezer? It's ridiculous. It's his idea of a really good excuse, I expect. Here, give me your phone.'

'Tamara, it's not a joke,' said her mother, 'or an excuse. Toby's badly hurt, and they're waiting for an ambulance now, to take him to hospital.'

'No,' said Tamara, staring at her, tears rising now in her huge eyes, pushing back her veil, biting her fist. 'No, that's impossible. He was fine this morning, fine early this

151

afternoon, even. Barney must have made a mistake, he's — oh God.'

And she sat down on the front pew in the little church, all bedecked with white roses, empty now of guests, who were all standing awkwardly outside, buried her head in her hands and began to sob, quite loudly, while her parents looked helplessly on. And the vicar, the only other person there, standing quietly at the altar, asking for God's help both to comfort her and to save the life of her young fiancé who was clearly in grave danger of losing it, looked at this beautiful girl, her veiled head drooped in despair, her bouquet flung onto the church floor, cheated of the greatest day in her life, and thought it was a very long time since he had seen anything quite so poignantly sad.

'Excuse me. Someone said you were a doctor?'

'Yes,' said Jonathan shortly. 'I am.'

'My girlfriend's just . . . well, she keeps being terribly sick. She's in a dreadful state. I wonder if you could—'

'I understand you're a doctor.'

'Yes, that's correct, but—'

'A lady here, we're rather afraid she's having a heart attack. She has angina, I wonder if you could—'

'Are you the doctor?'

'I'm a doctor. Yes.'

'My wife's cut her head very badly. I can't stop it bleeding, and I wonder if you could take a look at it?'

Jesus, Jonathan thought, exhausted now, desperate for some reprieve, what would they all have done if he hadn't been there?

'Miss, miss! Can you help me, miss?'

Abi looked down at the ragged group of little boys that Jonathan had led so patiently, one by one, from the mini-bus. She had been wandering about between the cars, dazed with shock, hardly looking in them for fear of what she might see. For the most part, there was nothing too dreadful, the majority of people were just shocked or cut and bruised. A few had nasty-looking lacerations, and one man had a broken shoulder, or so his wife thought, another a badly cut head. And some were completely unhurt, pacing up and down, making mobile phone calls. A lot of babies were crying, and small children clinging to their parents' hands; older ones were wandering about and then being recalled to their cars, being threatened with every kind of punishment if they didn't stay where they were told.

The heat was awful, the sun relentless; and the air close and stifling. There was an odd smell, at once sickly and sour. They might not have been outside at all, and indeed the air itself was cloudy with traffic fumes. Several people were walking dogs up and down, dogs that were clearly suffering in the heat. One man had shouted that there was a little water in the ditch at the side of the road, over the fence, 'But very little, mud really, mostly dried up.' A couple of dogs had been taken down there; one of them had run away and its owner was distraught.

Jonathan was temporarily nowhere to be seen. Abi felt terribly sick; she would have given anything for a drink of water herself, but felt if anyone should be thirsty, if anyone should suffer – she should.

She tried to smile at the little boy. 'What's the matter?'

His eyes were big and scared as he looked at her. 'I think I'm going to have an asthma attack, miss,' he said, 'and I haven't got no inhaler with me.'

'Where is it then?' asked Abi. It was a stupid question, she knew, but she only felt capable of stupid questions; any capacity for rational intelligent thought had left her.

'It was in me—' He paused, clearly breathless. 'In me rucksack, miss.'

'Oh.'

'And I'm ever so thirsty, miss.'

'Me too, miss,' said the boy next to him and then another and another.

'Well, look,' said Abi, 'I haven't got any water, I'm afraid. But I can go and ask in some of the other cars. A few people seem to have bottles. Now you, Master Asthma . . .'

The little boy managed to smile at her. 'Yes, miss?'

'I can't do anything about your inhaler yet. I'm sorry. But when Jon— the doctor comes back next time – he's the man who got you out of the bus – I'll see if he might have one.'

'All right, miss. But me chest feels well tight. I'm scared, miss, really scared. I get it really bad, sometimes have to go to hospital.' And he burst into tears.

'Don't be scared,' Abi said, and she sat down beside him, put her arms round him. 'Very soon now the ambulances will be here and they'll have inhalers, I'm sure. So you've just got to hang on a bit longer. What's your name?'

'Shaun, miss.'

'Right, Shaun. Well, do you know, when I was your age, I had asthma. If I got an attack and I didn't have my inhaler, I used to do breathing exercises.'

'Did you, miss?'

'Yes. Shall we try? Not too deep, just nice even shallow breaths. That's right. I'll do it with you. While I'm counting. Ready . . .'

Shaun, his large blue eyes fixed trustingly on her, obeyed. After about ten breaths he said, sounding more breathless still, 'It's not helping, miss. I'm that wheezy.' And he started to cry again.

'Oh God.' Abi looked round. This horrible air wouldn't be helping. Maybe she should try and move them all, up into the field beyond the fence. She saw Jonathan walking towards them, waved at him to come over.

'You haven't got an inhaler with you, have you? For asthma?'

'No, of course not,' he said tersely. 'Why should I?'

'Well, you're a doctor, you might have one.'

'Jesus,' he said. 'I've just been asked if I have a stethoscope. Someone else seemed to think I could set their arm. Now you want an inhaler. I'm not a walking pharmacy.'

'No, of course not. But Shaun here – Shaun says he's getting an asthma attack and I wondered . . . I just thought you might . . .'

'Well, you thought wrong,' he said. 'And I have more serious concerns than a bloody asthma attack. The driver's bleeding to death in that truck, and the bloody medics – oh, here they are, thank Christ. This way, please, quickly!'

'I can't help it, miss,' said Shaun tearfully. 'Why was he cross with me?'

'He's just very worried,' said Abi, looking after Jonathan as he directed the ambulancemen towards the truck. 'He's not cross.'

'My mum always says that about my dad, when he gets cross,' said another of the little boys. 'Says he's upset, not to take no notice.'

There was a general chorus of recognition at this scenario. Abi looked at them and smiled for the first time. Distracting them was clearly the best thing she could do; it would help them all, even Shaun. Especially Shaun.

'Why don't you all tell me your names?' she said. 'One by one. Not surnames, just first names. I'm called Abi.'

'What, like the church, miss?'

'A bit. Spelled different. Short for Abigail.'

'That's a nice name,' said Shaun carefully. His breathing was very quick and shallow, and speaking was clearly difficult, but he seemed calmer.

'Thanks, Shaun. Yes, I like it. But everyone calls me Abi. Right, let's hear it from the rest of you.'

They all told her their names, then where they lived, what they liked doing, what their mums were called. Almost cheerful. And then –

'I'm so thirsty, miss, I got to have a drink. Can you get us one, miss?'

The others all joined in. A couple were crying, saying they'd never felt so thirsty, not never. Abi felt like crying herself. Had any of this been Jonathan's fault? He'd been on the phone – had he lost control? They were right at the very front of the crash, after all. Had she distracted him? Yes, OK, the lorry had skidded violently, or seemed to, but how much after that was avoidable? Probably nothing, but if it was . . . *Abi, don't, don't go there, it's the way to madness, it had been an accident, that was all, a terrible, awful accident. Concentrate on what you can do. Like water, water* . . . How on earth was she going to find some water?

William was working his way down the field, skirting round a small spinney of young trees, carrying his containers, when he saw her: a young black girl, very pretty, with wild dark hair, stumbling along just above the ditch. She was crying silently.

'Hello,' he said. 'What's wrong? Can I help? Are you involved in the crash? Is someone with you hurt?'

She stared at him, her Bambi-sized dark eyes filled with panic; then she shook her head and moved on, trying to run away from him through the long, uneven grass.

'Look,' called William. 'I want to help – I live just up the hill.'

She turned then and said, 'No, no, I'm fine, thanks.' She had a pretty voice, light, slightly husky.

'You sure? Because—'

'I'm quite sure,' she said. 'Yes. But thank you.' And she moved on again, making clear the encounter was over.

William shrugged and continued on his journey. She

seemed all right; not hurt anyway. He could see more pressing claims on his attention. Odd though, but then this was a very odd day.

The little boys' distress and thirst was growing. Abi began to feel panicky, but she mustn't panic: it would be fatal, it would spread. She saw a woman walking towards her with a spaniel, and pointed him out to the boys by way of distraction; they crowded round, stroking him, asking the woman what his name was.

'Jasper.'

'That's me brother's name,' said Shaun. 'My mum's boyfriend says it's a poof's name.'

'Oh really?' said Abi, smiling at the woman. She didn't smile back; indeed, she glared at Shaun. Maybe she felt Jasper's sexual identity was under threat. Dog owners were inclined to be potty, in Abi's experience.

'I don't suppose you've got any water?' she said 'By any amazing chance?'

'If I had any I'd give it to this poor fellow,' the woman said firmly. 'He's beside himself. We're going to try in the woods.'

'OK,' said Abi carefully. 'Fine.' She walked back up the road a bit; a man was just draining a very small bottle of Evian. 'I don't suppose you've got any more of that?' she said.

'Sorry, no. I gave my son all but a few drops, we just don't have any more. I'm hoping the police might help.'

'OK,' said Abi again. She went back to the boys, sat down with them again. 'Sorry. Not yet.'

'But I need a drink!' One of the biggest boys was getting angry now. 'I really really need one. I'll die if I don't. We all will.'

'No, you won't,' said Abi. 'Of course you won't. People can live for quite a long time without water, you'd be surprised. However thirsty you are.'

157

'But miss . . .'

How on earth could she get them a drink? How could normal life have disappeared so swiftly?

And then: 'Need any help?' said a voice. And like some kind of divine visitation came a man, a young man, very tanned, with brown rather shaggy hair, wearing baggy – and filthy – jeans, a check shirt that had clearly left the shop many years earlier, and some very heavy dusty boots. And he was carrying – yes, he was actually carrying – two very large plastic containers . . . filled with –

'Oh my God,' said Abi. 'Water! How amazing. Can't be true.'

'It certainly is. Was last time I looked, anyway.' He grinned at her; the widest, sweetest grin she had ever seen. She smiled back.

'And,' he said, 'I've even got some paper cups. Here, kids. Watch out! One at a time, or you'll have it over. That's better.' He held out a cup to Abi. 'You want some?'

'No, no,' she said. 'These really need it.'

'So do you, by the look of you, if you don't mind my saying. That's a horrible cut on your head. How did you do that?'

'Oh,' she said. 'Oh, I hit it as we stopped. It was pretty sudden.'

'Yeah? It looks pretty nasty. Here, take a cup. Let me . . .'

'Thanks so much. And I might take another over to Jonathan – he's a doctor – he's over there, see, by the BMW.'

'Could I have some of that? For the dog, he's desperate. I've got a container – here, look.'

It was the woman Abi had approached earlier; the dog would drink half the water, she thought, looking at it panting furiously.

'Oh no, I don't think so,' said the young man. 'There's a lot of people here in terrible need. Sorry about the dog, but he'll be OK. Get him into the shade, I would. Hello, young chap,' he said to a toddler, clinging to his father's hand. 'Need some water? Here we are.'

He stood there, on the roadside, doling out his precious water, cup by cup, firmly refusing second comers.

'I'll get some more in a minute. Just for now, I think it's got to be one cup per person. Not fair otherwise. The only person who can have two is Shaun here, because he's not very well.'

'Where did you come from then?' said Abi, looking at him in a kind of wonder. It was like that miracle, she thought, the one about the five loaves and two fishes or was it the other way round, feeding five hundred . . .

'I live in a farm, just behind the hill there. The chopper's on our land. I saw it happen, actually.'

'Oh – really?'

'Yes.' His voice was very quiet, rather slow, surprisingly posh. You didn't expect farmers to be posh. 'I was standing up there with the cows, had just moved them, and there it was, everything breaking up. Or seeming to be.'

'Yes? So what happened exactly? Do you think?'

'Well, the lorry just swerved, really hard, and went through the barrier. No apparent reason. Straight through, slewed across. And then the load just . . . well, it was as if it had burst, came out of the doors at the back, the sides, out the top even. Did you see any of it?'

'No, not really,' said Abi. 'I – we – were just ahead of it all.'

'Scary, isn't it? Terrible things accidents. One minute everything's perfectly fine, under control, the next . . . well, it's not. Lives ruined, all these people hurt through no fault of their own. Through nobody's fault really.'

'Yes. Terrible.' She smiled at him, and sipped the water, the cool, wonderful water. She ought to get some to Jonathan really.

* * *

It was horrible, this waiting; you felt so impotent. And the longer the ambulances took to get through, the greater the danger to the injured.

Alex looked over at Emma; she was very pale.

She saw he was watching her, turned away, walked over to the water fountain. He followed her.

'You OK?'

She was surprised, the last person she'd have expected to notice her. She managed to smile at him. 'Yes, of course.'

'Good. Shouldn't be long now. Couple on their way back apparently. Funny time this, isn't it? Waiting. I always get a bit panicky.'

'You do!'

'Yes, I do. After all these years.'

'I always think it's a bit like – well, did you see *Atonement*?'

'I did, but – oh I know what you mean. When they were waiting for the injured to arrive from Dunkirk. Yes. Don't think this'll be quite that bad, though. Oh God, Emma, I'm sorry – I forgot. Someone called Luke phoned.'

'Oh, don't worry,' said Emma, 'it's fine. It honestly doesn't matter.'

She smiled at him: a sudden, much happier smile. She obviously really liked the oik, thought Alex. How extraordinary.

Linda was trying to get hold of Francis on one line, to break the news that they would be sharing their evening with Georgia, when he called from his mobile on the other.

'Hi, Linda. You OK?'

'Fine.'

'Look, I'm really sorry but I'm going to have to take a rain check on this evening.'

'That's a shame, but why?'

'VBC' (short for Very Big Client, as he called them, along with various other shorthands, like VTL – Very

Tedious Lunch) – 'VBC lives in Chippenham, and the M4 is closed both ways, apparently. Anyway, I have to look after him, take him out for a meal, check him into a hotel, just nanny him along. Sorry, Linda.'

'No, it's fine,' said Linda, suppressing the stab of irritation that Francis's dutiful client care always aroused in her. 'God, I hope Georgia's all right. She's on the M4. Hitched a lift in a lorry.'

'Wouldn't know. Not sure where the hold-up is, even. But on that Wiltshire–Gloucestershire stretch somewhere.'

'I'd better call her,' said Linda. 'Enjoy your evening.' And she put the phone down and called Georgia's number.

Hi, said her husky little voice, *this is Georgia. Leave your name and number and I'll get back to you as soon as I can. Thanks for calling.*

'Hi, Georgia. This is Linda. Give me a call, will you, when you get this. I'm worried about you. Apparently there's some problem on the M4 – the road's closed. Speak soon.'

Mary looked across at Colin; he was sitting on the bonnet of the car, lighting yet another cigarette. That was his sixth since the accident; she'd been counting. Not that it mattered and it was probably helping him, but she wished she could do something that would make herself feel better. She felt terrible – sick and exhausted, and her neck and her head hurt. Colin had found her some paracetamol, but they hadn't really taken the edge off the pain.

The people in the car behind, who had rammed into her, were being very kind too. The driver, a man, had sprained his wrist very badly, but apart from that, they were unhurt. No doubt because their car was a Volvo; you couldn't beat a Volvo – built like tanks as they were. Gerry, her son-in-law, always had them, said they were worth their weight in gold and it seemed they were.

A middle-aged couple, Janet and John Smith – 'No one

will believe those could be our real names,' said Janet, smiling – they were on their way to the Cotswolds for a few days' break, meeting two friends in Cirencester. 'Look how lucky we've been,' Janet said. 'We could have been a few cars further forward, and it would have been curtains. It frightens you, just thinking about it, doesn't it? Fate, chance – you're at their mercy, aren't you?'

They had produced a rug from the car, some picnic chairs and a Thermos, sat Mary down, given her a cup of tea. Which had been very welcome, but if she'd thought a bit longer, she would have refused it. It had gone straight through her . . .

They had agreed, all four of them, that they were in for a long wait. There were seriously injured people who must have first claim on the ambulances and paramedics. Which of course was right, but . . .

She looked at her watch; nearly five. Just an hour until Russell's plane landed. Obviously she couldn't possibly get there now. What would he think? What could she do? *Keep calm, Mary, keep calm.*

She was desperate now to go to the lavatory, but of course there was no opportunity. There were a few trees at the bottom of the bank, but hardly enough to conceal her. She wondered if she could enlist Janet Smith's help, ask her to hold up the blanket, perhaps – but decided she didn't know her well enough. And John Smith would be able to see her . . . What could she do? She'd just have to try not to think about it. After all, she hadn't had anything to drink except the tea, since her lunchtime glass of water, had carefully refused Colin's offer that she might share his.

Her bladder stabbed at her; it was agony. And something else stabbed at her; the squeezing pressure on her chest that signalled an attack of angina.

She felt absolutely terrified suddenly. For there was something else in the boot of the car, something fundamentally important to her – her nitrate spray. She took it everywhere with her in case of an angina attack, and always, always had it in her handbag. Only the bag, a new one, bought for the occasion, along with the Jaeger suit, was rather slim and elegant, and she hadn't wanted to overload it. How could she have done something so stupid and so dangerous?

Mary began to cry.

Chapter 12

'Please! Please let me go with him. I don't want to leave him, it's important he shouldn't be alone.'

'He won't be alone, sir. He'll have us with him. And an officer of the law.' The man grinned at Barney. 'But come on then.' He paused. 'You haven't got another shirt in your car, I suppose, sir?'

'No, not actually,' said Barney, realising suddenly how ghastly he must look, naked to the waist, braces flapping about, his upper body and probably his face covered in blood. Toby's blood.

'Right then. Get in the back.'

It seemed like a very long journey; it actually took about eight minutes. They were thrown about rather; Barney felt violently sick by the time they arrived, and kept thinking Toby must be suffering horribly. But he seemed to have moved into an almost dreamlike state; he was conscious, but silent and very pale. He was lying under a blanket, strapped onto a bed. One of the two paramedics had put a drip into his hand. 'Just fluids for now,' he said to Barney. 'They'll give him blood as soon as we get there. This'll make it easier, and much quicker.'

'How do you think – well, how is he?'

'I really couldn't say, I'm afraid. He's obviously lost a lot of blood. He'll be assessed when we get there, they'll tell you as soon as they can. Oh, here we go, siren on, must be a red light. Hold on tight, sir, that's the way.'

* * *

'Oh God,' said Janet. 'She looks terrible. Mary, are you in pain, my dear? Is it your neck? What can we do?'

'Yes,' said Mary, whispering through clenched teeth. 'I am in pain. I have angina, Janet, and I need my nitrate spray.'

'Yes, of course. Tell me where it is and I'll get it.'

'But you can't. It's somewhere in there.' She nodded at the two impacted cars. 'Impossible.'

'Well, we can try,' said Janet briskly.

'I'll go,' said Colin hastily. 'You stay there and relax, Mary. I'll get your stuff out in no time.'

Five minutes later he returned. Mary was biting her lip, breathing fast, her eyes large and frightened.

'I'm sorry, it seems totally impossible. Your bonnet,' he said to Janet, 'and my boot really are totally fused. Dear oh dear. Let's see – I could put in a call for an ambulance. I mean, they're presumably coming in force, and if we tell them one is needed down here . . .'

'Good idea,' said Janet. 'Mary, what is it, dear? Try to be calm, you'll make everything so much worse.'

'I need the toilet,' Mary whispered, and then moments later, flushed with misery, 'I've wet myself, Janet. I'm so sorry, so very sorry. How dreadful . . .'

'Never mind,' said Janet tenderly, putting her arm round her. 'It doesn't matter, it really doesn't. Please don't get upset about it.'

'I can't help it,' said Mary and then, overcome with pain and misery, she started to weep again.

'I'll call the ambulance service,' said Colin. 'Make sure one comes down here. Easier said than done, in all this, but—'

'They'll get here,' said John, wincing at the pain from his wrist. 'It's what they're trained to do.'

Patrick wasn't answering his phone. Funny. Maybe he'd left it in the cab while he went for a pee or something. He did that sometimes, it drove her completely mad. Maeve wondered if the traffic was specially bad, and turned over from Magic, which was her favourite, to Radio 2. She hated the music, but they had the best traffic reports; that woman, Sally Traffic she called herself, she was great. People phoned in from all over the country, telling her of hold-ups and so on. She'd be coming on any minute now, after – or was it before? – the five o'clock news. If there was a bad hold-up coming into London, she'd certainly be getting reports of it.

'Maeve! You there?' Her mother let herself into the house.

'Oh, yes, hello, Mum. You're early.'

'Yes, well, I got out of the hairdresser's in record time, so I thought I might as well come over. You all right, darlin'?'

'I'm fine, thanks. Never better. Well, a bit tired – you know. So what's new?'

'Yes, you look a bit tired. Sit down, love, have a cup of tea. Here, I'll make it.'

'Thanks.'

Her mother filled the kettle, carried it over to the hob. 'It's terribly hot out there. Shocking. Over ninety, they're saying. It's this climate change, I suppose, it's—'

'Mum, shush a minute. I want to hear the traffic report. I can't get hold of Patrick and—'

Sally Traffic's kindly tones cut into the room. 'We're just getting news from Bob on the Chippenham stretch of the M4. There's absolute gridlock there in both directions, so avoid going onto the road at all if you possibly can. We'll bring you more news as it comes in.'

Well, that explained it. Although he should have been an awful lot further on than Chippenham by now. Unless he'd been lying to her about his progress, of course. It wouldn't have been the first time.

This was all she needed, him being late tonight: after he'd promised. Well, she'd have plenty to say to him when he did walk through the door . . .

* * *

Gradually order was being restored. Two fire crews were still working on their grim tasks; the second lorry, blocking the exit road, had been righted, and most of the casualties had been driven away in ambulances. Constable Robbie Macyntyre followed Greg Dixon respectfully about as he strode amongst the wreckage on the motorway, alternately talking into his radio, informing the AA and the RAC and local radio stations, taking witnesses' names and addresses, waving their cars over for inspection, and talking to the people who were stranded.

Mostly they wanted to know when they might get away; whether they could move their cars, whether the police could help with water, and as the time wore on, food. Robbie felt extremely sorry for some of them, even those who were unhurt, clearly anxious that they were missing appointments, or worse, that their babies or small children were suffering in the heat. Several people's mobiles were running down; they found this very distressing, even if they had phoned their families several times to reassure them. Clearly the mobile was the new security blanket. One woman started shouting at them, demanding water, but on the whole they were pretty calm and cooperative. Greg was calm too; reassuring them that it shouldn't be too much longer now before they could start clearing the cars, directing them to the police car that had arrived with a huge supply of water, and offering the use of his and Robbie's mobiles where essential.

Their task now that the worst was over – although the poor sod in the lorry was still being cut free, the air ambulance still waiting – was to keep the scene as far as possible intact, until the investigation unit arrived. They had found witnesses, taken their names and addresses, but still no one could leave. Measurements and photographs had to be taken, a plan of the scene, complete with details of the debris, the exact location and direction of skid marks: only when that was completed would they begin to get the cars out. Fortunately, the road into London was more or less clear now: free of traffic, and the lorry's load, but two lanes were still being used for the emergency services. There were a few cars on the hard shoulder, the doctor's – great bloke he was, fantastic help – and a rather nice middle-aged couple who'd walked back about 200 yards – the only ones who had, incredible it was really – to see if they could do anything, only then the woman had become very upset by the horror of the scene and they'd gone back to their car to wait for someone to tell them what to do.

There'd been another drama with some girl who'd gone into labour. Robbie had been told to stay with her and the husband until they were safely on their way. He hadn't liked that too much. She'd been in considerable pain, lying back in the seat, alternately moaning and panting like a dog.

Her husband, who was sitting beside her, told Robbie to be quiet when he expressed concern. 'Don't interrupt,' he said. 'She's doing her breathing exercises, she needs to concentrate.'

'It's quite bad,' she said suddenly, pausing in her panting. 'What's happening? Why isn't the ambulance coming?'

'It's coming now.' Robbie managed a smile. 'Should be here in five minutes.'

'I don't want to have it here,' she said, gripping her husband's hand, 'I'm so scared.'

'No need for that,' Robbie said, hoping it was true. 'And listen – yes, I can hear it now, here comes an ambulance. I'll just flag it down, make sure it stops. Over here, quickly, please!' he called to the two paramedics. 'The lady's here, in this car.'

As he said afterwards to his girlfriend, he'd never been so terrified in his entire life, not even when that young thug came at him with his knife. 'Thought she was going to have it then and there.'

The girlfriend said briskly that policemen were always delivering babies. There'd been a story in the *Daily Mail* only last week, and she was sure he'd have been perfectly all right. Robbie was sure he wouldn't.

'Jonathan? Thank God – at last! Wherever are you? Where have you been?' Laura's voice was unusually harsh; he winced at the thought of how much harsher it would become.

'I'm on the M4, darling. Sorry not to have got in touch before.'

'The M4? What on earth are you doing on the M4? I thought you were coming down from Birmingham. Everyone's been so worried. I rang the clinic, obviously, but they hadn't heard from you since early afternoon, and then when I did ring you, you know, this afternoon . . .'

'Yes,' said Jonathan shortly.

'Well, I heard your voice and then it was just – just an awful noise and then nothing. Are you saying that wasn't you?'

'Laura, it wasn't quite the time for chatting. I did tell you not to call anyway. You know the handsfree isn't working, it's bloody dangerous.'

There was a silence; he could hear her digesting this, taking his hostility on board, being puzzled by it. And hurt. Then she said, 'I'm very sorry. It's just I was worried about you.'

'Yes, of course. Sorry.'

'So what have you been doing?'

'There's been a very bad crash on the motorway,' said Jonathan, struggling to keep his voice level, finding it hard to believe that she didn't know. 'Really bad. I got caught up in it. A lorry driver went through the barrier. At least three people were killed, I'm afraid.'

'Oh my God, how ghastly. Are you all right?'

'Yes, I'm fine. But I've been doing what I could. Obviously.'

'Yes, of course. I understand. But – well, I wish you'd phoned, darling, I've been so worried.'

'I'm sorry. Somehow, with all that's been going on, I didn't think of it.'

'But I've called you twice more. Didn't you get the messages?'

'Laura, I've been pretty preoccupied. There were a lot of badly injured people, one chap practically bleeding to death, an old lady having a suspected heart attack, I really didn't have time to chat.'

'No, of course not.' He could hear her even now, being perfect, struggling not to sound irritable. 'How horrible for you, darling. I'm so sorry. You must be exhausted. When do you think you might get away?'

'I don't know,' said Jonathan. 'Fairly soon now, I think. Most of the casualties are on their way to hospital, although the poor bugger in the lorry is still being cut out by the fire brigade.'

'Poor man. Is he alive?'

'Yes, he is. Just.'

'Do you know what happened? Were you near him when he went through?'

'Pretty near,' said Jonathan, 'yes. It's all a bit of a blur. The lorry just seemed to lose control. Look, sorry, darling, got to go. The police are waiting to speak to me.'

'Why?'

'They're getting witnesses' statements.'

'But I thought you said you didn't see—'

'Laura, I was there! Very near the lorry. Of course they want a statement from me!'

'Yes, yes, of course. Sorry, darling. Look – ring me when you get away. Love you.'

Laura felt distressed when she put down the phone. Too distressed, in fact, to wonder exactly why he'd been on the M4. He was clearly traumatised; and it was terrifying to think he'd been that near to a fatal accident. Supposing he'd been behind the lorry instead of ahead of it, he could have been killed. These things were so arbitrary. Life was so arbitrary . . .

Charlie appeared in the doorway. 'Hi, Mum. When's supper?'

'Oh, I think I'd better feed you and the girls quite soon. I was hoping Daddy would be home early, but he's been involved in a crash on the M4 and—'

'A crash!' Charlie went white. 'Is he all right? What happened?'

'Darling, he's fine. Sorry, that was stupid of me. He's just got held up and he's been helping the injured and so on, as far as I can make out. He was very near the crash.'

'God. Poor Dad. Scary. What happened?'

'Apparently a lorry went through the central reservation. He'll tell us all about it when he gets home.'

'Poor old Dad,' said Charlie again. 'Lucky for all those people he was there, that he could help.'

'Indeed. He's such a good person, your dad.'

'Certainly is,' said Charlie.

'Come with me! Please! You gotta come with me.' Shaun gripped Abi's hand. He was still wheezing, fighting for breath.

She looked at the ambulance driver. 'Can I?'

'Yeah, suppose so. Might be a long wait the other end, though. Come on now, mate,' he said to Shaun. 'You're not trying. Use that inhaler properly – deep breaths, that's right.'

'I'll help him,' said Abi, 'if you let me come. I used to be asthmatic. And he's very upset, he's had a terrible day.'

'Yeah, course he has. Well, if you really want to come, you can. But like I say, we could be talking hours. After we've got to the hospital, that is.'

'I don't mind how long it takes. I really don't. And his

171

mum'll come sooner or later.' She meant it; she had to do something useful. She would sit with Shaun right through the weekend if it was necessary.

'Well, OK. We're going to take the other little chap as well, the one with the suspected broken wrist. The others are being taken by the Highways people, I gather, also to St Mark's, and their parents will collect them from there. They've all been notified.'

The other man in charge of the boys had already gone to St Mark's; he'd remained very shocked, staring silently ahead of him, shaking violently from time to time. He had a very bad cut on his head and a suspected concussion. Abi and William had liaised over the welfare of the childen; he would wait with them until they had all been taken safely away.

'OK,' she said now. 'Well, William, this looks like goodbye. Thanks for everything. You've been great.'

'It was nothing. Wish I could have done more. Bye, Shaun.'

'Can't he come too?' Shaun said, and William grinned and said he'd got to get back to the farm.

'Lot of cows need milking.'

'Doesn't anyone help you?' asked Abi curiously.

'Well we've got a herdsman, but he's off now. And my dad, it's his farm really, he's away. First holiday for five years, supposed to mark his retirement. That'll be the day.' He smiled again; but his voice was slightly barbed.

'Oh really?'

'Yeah, really. Well – good luck. How're you going to get home?'

'Oh, I'll manage. Don't worry about me. Bye, William. Thanks again. Come on, Shaun – in we go.'

William watched her as she climbed into the back of the ambulance; the last he saw of her were her amazing legs in those silver high-heeled boots. Extraordinary to wear them on a day as hot as this . . .

'Right,' he said, sitting down in the grass again, next to the other boys, 'we've just got to wait now. Shouldn't be too long. Anyone know any more good songs?'

It wasn't until all the boys had been driven safely off by the Highways Agency that he found Abi's mobile in the pocket of his jeans, and remembered her asking him to take it while she led the boys one by one down the bank to pee.

Chapter 13

The afternoon had blurred into the evening; time had become irrelevant. Emma supposed she felt tired, supposed she felt upset even; but she was not actually aware of it. She worked like an automaton, on what were often quite menial tasks, conscious only of the superb organisation that was directing everyone's efforts. If Alex had told her to clean all the toilets she would have done it without question.

Six beds had been set up in Resusc, each a separate trauma station, with its relevant medical staff, this one for chest injuries, that one for orthopaedics, and another for lacerations, each with its own supply of monitors, blood, oxygen and small trolleys supplied with catheters, IV equipment, chest drains. Ambulances arrived, people were brought in, were assessed and directed to the relevant station; and then on to theatre and where necessary Intensive Care. This being a new hospital, all such essential places were on the same floor and sufficient of them; what on earth would this have been like, Emma wondered, in some inefficient place where the lifts creaked up and down and there was a queue for theatres.

For much of the time she moved from station to station, seeing patients, trying to reassure them, administering painkillers, putting in canulas and then intravenous drips and blood, taking blood tests, listening to chests, organising X-rays. Again, no one had to be moved anywhere; the X-rays were portable, brought up to the beds, the machines moving round the patients, Dalek-like; many people had fractures, and the simpler ones she set herself, having checked with the orthopaedic registrar – wonderful, calm, even funny Mark Collins – and she sewed up lacerations too, and butterfly-clipped minor head wounds.

In the middle of the crisis, as she stood momentarily unemployed, waiting for an X-ray, a lad was brought in from the town centre, with bad stab wounds. Emma took him for a CT scan. The wounds turned out to be only to his muscles, and to ease the chaos, she took him to theatre to stitch them up. He was upset, as much by the scene around him in A&E as his own problems. 'Don't you fret,' Emma said, smiling at him. 'This is a quiet night: you should see us when we're busy.' She connected the anaesthetic to the canula.

'You don't look like a doctor,' were his last words before he lost consciousness.

Many of the cases were fairly mundane – broken ribs, fractured wrists; some more serious, mostly head injuries. There was a girl in premature labour – she was seven and a half months, so there was much room for optimism as Emma told her, holding her hand, timing her contractions as they waited for a midwife to collect her, checking there was someone still spare to set up an epidural, soothing the wild-eyed husband.

Emma was spared almost entirely her greatest dread, badly injured children; for the most part they had survived in the astonishing security of their safety seats. One small boy had a concussion, another a broken leg, a very young baby was badly dehydrated – her mother had been knocked unconscious and was unable to feed her – but for the most part, they grinned at Emma cheerfully as she checked bumps and bruises, enjoying the excitement and drama, intrigued by her stethoscope, asking her endless questions.

A middle-aged man in considerable pain and having

trouble breathing was frantic that his wife should not be contacted. 'She has a heart condition, I don't want her panicking.' He proved to have several fractured ribs, one of which had punctured his lung and caused a pneumothorax. 'Nothing we can't fix pretty quickly. You can go home tomorrow, tell your wife you've got in a fight,' said Emma cheerfully, setting up a chest drain.

'Oh, bless you,' he said, patting her hand, and then, 'You don't look like a doctor, you know.'

'I do know,' she said.

One case was particularly poignant: a young man was stretchered in, covered in blood, his equally blood-soaked friend walking beside him.

'They were on their way to the injured guy's wedding,' Mark told her when she met him outside theatre. 'How cruel is that?'

'Very cruel. Bad as he looks?'

'Not sure. Head injury fairly superficial. I was afraid he might have a subdural haematoma, but no, we've done a CT scan. Horrible mess that leg, though – tibia and fibula fractured, lost about two pints of blood. Which is fine, he's young and fit, but we're not sure yet if we can fix the leg. Going to try and pin it, but it's extremely complex . . .'

Russell looked at his watch; he kept looking at it, willing it to stay still, stop making it later, stop Mary failing him. But it was moving relentlessly on, ignoring his bewilderment, and his unhappiness: seven-forty-five it said now. He'd been dreading that: a whole sixty minutes passing, making her a whole sixty minutes late. Surely she'd have got a message to him, if she'd been held up somewhere. Surely it couldn't be that difficult . . .

He'd come through to Arrivals at a half-run, he'd been so excited, his heart thudding, pulling his flight bag behind him. The rest of his luggage had been FedExed to the hotel. Although he'd instructed her to wait at the Hertz desk, he'd still wondered if she mightn't walk over to where everyone else was waiting, leaning on the barrier. He scanned the row of people – scruffy for the most part, generally young, lots of children, sitting on their fathers' shoulders, pulling on their mothers' hands, people holding banners saying things like *Welcome Home Mum*, and the rows of dark-suited drivers, with their signs neatly filled with people's names. He had been met all over the world by such people; automatically he scanned the boards now . . . But there was no neat, smiling white-haired lady, waving as she had been in the wildest of his wildest dreams, calling out, 'Russell! Over here!'

Just – strangers. Looking at him blankly as he walked past them, disappointed he was not who they wanted him to be. Well, it would have been horrible for Mary to be standing there, being jostled about, pushed out of the way. How sensible of her to have realised that, to have done exactly what he said. He could see the Hertz desk now; reassuringly unmissable, with three young people, two men and a girl standing talking to people. No doubt she was there. He couldn't see her yet, but of course she was tiny: anyone standing in front of her would have blocked her from view. He hurried on, bumping into people, irritating them.

'Watch what you're doing, Grandad,' said some surly youth; he hoped fervently no one had spoken to Mary like that.

Right; he was ten yards away now – any minute he'd see her. She didn't seem to be standing in front of the desk; maybe she'd taken his advice and asked for a chair, sat down. She'd warned him she'd probably be early, so she'd be tired by now. But – tired or not, she wasn't there. Russell felt a great lurch of disappointment, closed his eyes for a couple of seconds, unwilling to trust them, then opened them again, thinking that this time she'd be there, holding out her hand to him, as excited as he was. But – she wasn't.

Well, she would be. Any minute. She would appear, as breathless as he had been, hurrying through the crowds; maybe she'd been held up in traffic, or maybe – yes, that seemed quite likely – maybe she'd popped into the rest room. The toilet, as they called it here. If she'd been waiting a little while, it might have become quite necessary; she wasn't young, just as he was not, she would be sharing the same frailties. That was probably the explanation. He stood by the desk, his eyes scanning the crowd, waiting patiently for her return.

After five minutes it began to seem a less likely explanation, although there might have been a long queue, and then perhaps she'd been doing her hair, powdering her nose, wanting to look her best for him as he had for her. But after another five, that seemed unlikely too.

He turned to the young man on the desk. 'Hi,' he said.

'Good afternoon, sir.'

'I – I'd arranged to meet someone here. A lady. She – well, she seems not to be here just yet. I wonder if she had announced herself to you, as I told her to do if I was late.'

'Well, let's see.' The young man's voice had been carefully coached into faux concern. He pressed a few keys on his computer. 'What would the name have been, sir?'

'Mrs Bristow. Mrs Mary Bristow.'

'Mrs Bristow . . . Let me see – no, there's nothing from a Mrs Bristow. What was the first name again, sir?'

'Mary,' said Russell, 'but she wouldn't have given that. She—'

'Mary. No, no Marys either. Nothing, sir. I'm so sorry. But you're very welcome to wait here, sir. I'm sure she won't be long. As you can see, it's very busy. And I believe the traffic out of London is terrible.'

'She wasn't coming out of London,' said Russell, and he

could hear the sadness in his own voice. 'She was coming up from Bristol.'

Mary had written that in her last letter: that although she'd be in a car, there'd be no risk of bad hold-ups, because she'd be travelling against the traffic. *And I shall allow lots of time, Russell, you can be sure of that. Was I ever late for you?*

And she wasn't; somehow she had always been on time, working her way briskly across London, hopping from bus to bus, often walking if the traffic was bad. Well, she had been once, terribly late, two and a half hours, but she had turned up safely just the same, had run into the bar where he'd agreed to meet her, flushed and flustered. 'The siren went off, and I had to go down to the Tube and wait for the All-Clear. I'm so sorry.'

It had been his last night before being moved to a new base; he wouldn't be able to stay long, he had warned her, but she'd said she'd get away from work early especially. 'I might not see you again for a long time, and I don't want to waste our last evening together, not seeing you.'

It had been quite early, long before the dangerous night-time pounding, a series of doodlebugs released across London. Everyone hated doodlebugs; they first roared then spluttered overhead like so many monstrous motor-bikes, and it was only when the noise stopped that you knew you were for it, that they were about to drop . . .

'I'm so, so glad you were still here,' she said, smiling as he kissed her, and he said of course he was still there, he'd have waited for her all night if needs be, risked getting into every kind of trouble.

As he would now. And this had only been an hour . . .

The lorry driver had been brought in by helicopter, Alex told Emma, the last casualty to arrive, and had been taken straight to theatre. His chances were not rated very high.

She had expected him to be old, but he was in his early thirties, with a young family.

'He fielded most of the steering column,' said Alex. 'Poor chap. You name it, he's got it – fractured ribs and sternum, tension pneumothorax, contusions of his heart, and then a few more minor things . . .' he grinned at her, 'like a . . . ruptured spleen, some liver injury. They've worked wonders on him though. He's very much alive. At the moment. Amazing the punishment the human body can take.'

'Any spinal injuries?'

'Not established yet. Poor bugger. Wife's on the way apparently.'

'I hope someone's with her,' said Emma. 'She'll be terrified,' and then suddenly found she had to sit down. 'God,' she said, 'it's ten o'clock. How did that happen?'

'Tired?'

'A bit. Any idea at all yet what caused this?'

'Not yet. Police doing their work right this minute, no doubt. But the lorry was at the front of it all, went through the barrier. Could have been him – fell asleep, skidded, whatever.'

'Well, if it was, he's been well punished for it,' said Emma soberly.

Abi and Shaun were still waiting in A&E. They'd arrived almost two hours ago; there'd been some trouble contacting Shaun's mother. Shaun couldn't remember her mobile number, the landline wasn't answered for about half an hour, and then she had to arrange transport from Reading. Abi was beginning to feel as if they might be there for ever.

It had still been light when they'd arrived; now it was dark. The ambulance ride had been horrible; they'd been really thrown about. Shaun had been sick twice and Abi felt more than once she was pretty close to it. What it would be like to be in one if you were actually ill, she didn't like to think.

The relief therefore of reaching St Mark's was intense. It was a vast, pristine building, gleaming in the evening sun, only four storeys high but with wide curving steps leading up to two sets of sliding doors, a mass of glass and steel fronting, and a forest of signs directing people to A&E, Outpatients, Obstetrics and Gynaecology, the Day Unit and a lot more in what appeared to Abi to be virtually another language. The ambulance had parked outside the A&E department, 200 metres or so to the right of the main entrance. Abi felt suddenly nervous. What on earth might be going on in there? Maybe they could wait outside. She felt she had seen enough blood and guts for one day – literally.

It was very noisy, with ambulance sirens cutting end-lessly through the air, and a lot of shouting. Ambulances were pulling up constantly, porters running out with wheeled stretchers, nurses following them, some patients being lifted out of the ambulances and eased onto the stretchers, some put into wheelchairs, others rather dazedly walking in, leaning on the nurses' arms. But it was a clearly directed chaos, there was a smooth transition from outside inwards, no one hesitating, no one asking where they should go. It was impressive.

'Right, my love, follow me. Let's get you registered.'

Abi took a deep breath and braced herself for a scene like something out of *ER*. But inside it more closely resembled Waterloo Station in the rush hour than *ER*; a huge room, with a large raised desk by the entrance with three women sitting at it, and an electronic sign that said *Welcome to St Mark's. Approximate waiting time from arrival is now 3 hours 15 minutes. We are very busy, due to a major incident. Minor problems should come back tomorrow.* No one seemed to be availing themselves of this advice. People were crammed onto chairs, standing three-deep at the desk, pestering any nurse reckless enough to appear for information. Children were crying, running about, being shouted at; mobiles were ringing constantly, despite stern written instructions not to use them, and the three women on the desk were astonishingly calm as they fielded questions, issued instructions (mostly to sit down and wait), put out calls for people to go for assessment and handed out admission forms to newcomers.

A coffee machine set against the wall had a large piece of paper stuck on it saying *Broken* and a water machine was completely out of cups. A small corner with a low green fence round it, marked *Children's Play Area*, was empty of both children and toys; there were several battered model animals and Thomas the Tank Engines being fought over in various parts of the room.

Bureaucracy took over. Abi was handed a form to fill in and had to leave most of it blank, having no idea who Shaun's next-of-kin was, apart from it being clearly his mother, nor his address, nor even his religion. She elicited as much information from the still wheezing Shaun as she could, but it was patchy; the woman at the desk sighed as she looked through it, told Abi she'd have to wait. Since they'd have had to wait if the form had been filled in fully and in triplicate, Abi couldn't quite see the point in this remark, but she sat down obediently with Shaun – having taken him, wildly protesting, into the Ladies when he wanted to pee – and played Hangman and Join the Dots with him until he slumped into an exhausted stupor. Thanks to his treatment in the ambulance, his condition was no longer regarded as urgent.

A white-faced young woman next to her, with a small girl on her lap, sat staring at the door; she looked as if she was about to cry. Abi smiled at her.

'You OK?' she asked.

'Not really, no. I'm worried out of my wits. My other little girl's out there somewhere with her dad; she's been hurt and they're waiting for an ambulance.'

'I'm sorry,' said Abi. 'Is she badly injured?'

'Not according to him,' said the girl. 'He wouldn't know bad if it hit him in the eye. Stupid bugger.' It was clear her daughter's father was not an object of great affection. 'He says it's just a banged head, but that could be anything, couldn't it? He'd been to collect her from her nan's, they were late leaving. I said to him, if he'd been on time for once in his life, she'd be home tucked up safely in bed by now, but no, he had to go and check on a job he was doing first.'

'That's the thing about accidents though, isn't it?' said Abi. 'It's all bits of chance and fate, muddled up together. I'm sure she won't be long, there are so many ambulances out there, and they've cleared a way right through the traffic.'

'Yeah? You see much of it then?'

'No, not really,' said Abi. 'I've been looking after this little boy and his friends. They are Cubs; off on a week's camping, weren't you, Shaun? But honestly, all the seriously hurt people were collected hours ago. I'm sure your daughter's fine and they'll be here soon.'

'I bloody well hope so,' said the woman. 'There'll be trouble if they're not.'

And trouble if they are, Abi thought; she didn't rate the young father's chances.

A man with his arm in a makeshift sling was sitting staring into space, grey-faced, in a chair opposite Abi. He started chatting to her, clearly glad of the distraction, told her about some woman who'd lost her dog in the chaos.

'Oh no!' said Abi. 'How awful.'

'Yeah, well, she certainly thought so. I should think the whole of the M4 heard her. She was crying, calling its name. Bella it was. Golden retriever.'

'Oh dear, poor Bella. So . . . what happened to you?'

'Oh, my car hit one of the fridges. Front's pretty well stove in. The wife's coming to get me, but we live in

Manchester, so it's a bit of a way.' He shifted, winced. 'I'll be glad to get this set.'

A nurse appeared, called out, 'Brian Timpson!'

He stood up. 'Well, nice talking to you. See you later.'

Almost immediately his place was taken by a hard-faced young man, carrying a notebook; he'd been talking to several people, she'd noticed, some of whom had been more receptive than others. She wondered vaguely if he was an ambulance chaser, a representative of one of the new breed of insurance companies who offered impossible compensation to victims on a no-win no-fee basis, and thought he'd better not come anywhere near her if he knew what was good for him, when he said, 'Hi. Bob Mason, *Daily Sketch*. Wonder if you'd mind if I chatted to you for a bit. You were out there in the crash, I take it.'

Rage shot through Abi; this was even worse than insurance.

'I was,' she said coldly, 'and I'd mind very much if you chatted to me. Actually. Just piss off, will you? I'm surprised they let you in in the first place.'

'OK, OK,' he said. 'Sorry to have troubled you.'

He stood up, walked towards the toilet and disappeared; she watched him, wondering if he would actually sink low enough to try and get a story there, and decided he would. She had a very poor opinion of the press.

The department was emptier now, but people were still waiting in various stages of impatience and resignation. Abi was too exhausted to feel anything at all. Every so often she wondered vaguely what Jonathan was doing, what complex lies he might be telling Laura; that was as far as her curiosity, or indeed her emotions, extended towards him. He seemed to belong in an entirely different point in her life, another time, another place; the accident had, in some strange way, restructured everything.

She was just considering moving into a corner seat, where she might be able to doze at least, only it would mean waking Shaun, when a young man, looking deeply distressed, walked dazedly in, slumped down in the chair next to her and put his head in his hands. He was naked from the waist up and his trousers were held up with red braces. Poor bloke had obviously had a very tough time. She debated saying something to him, then decided not; she could scarcely believe it when the reporter sat down on his other side and said, 'Hi. Bob Mason, *Daily Sketch*. Mind if I talk to you? I'm just—'

The man lifted his head out of his hands – he looked half-dead himself, Abi thought – stared at him for moment, then he said, 'Yes, I bloody well do.'

'OK, mate. That's fine. Sorry to have troubled you.'

'Yeah, well,' said the young man. His voice was aggressive. Abi caught his eye and half-smiled at him.

'Parasites,' she said, as Mason walked away. 'They shouldn't be allowed in.'

He said nothing, stood up still looking dazed, walked over to the water store, which someone had attended to, and filled a cup of water for himself.

As he stood drinking it, a nurse appeared in the doorway. 'Mr Fraser?' she said. 'The doctor will talk to you now.'

Mr Fraser half-ran out of the room.

'Such a sad story,' said a middle-aged woman, across the room. 'He was on his way to be best man at a wedding. The bridegroom's been very badly hurt.'

'God,' said Abi, 'that's so terrible.' She felt freshly shocked. Fate was certainly having a field day.

Linda was beginning to feel extremely worried. Something quite serious must have happened to Georgia. She'd been so upbeat, so confident of being on her way, so grateful to Linda for re-scheduling her audition. And suddenly, she appeared to have vanished. Linda had tried ringing her again twice, and her phone was still on message. That was unlike her too. Georgia never missed an opportunity to chatter. She must have left her phone somewhere – maybe when she and the lorry driver were having tea together en route. Or was she still stuck in that jam on the M4 that Francis had told her about? No, that was impossible – it was well into the evening now. But if she was . . . then Linda told herself to stop fussing. Georgia was more than capable of looking after herself. And she didn't have to be anywhere until the morning; there was plenty of time. *Get a life, Linda, for God's sake.*

She tried Georgia's phone just once more and then started clearing her desk preparatory to leaving it. Linda could no more have left an uncleared desk than she would have left home in a crumpled skirt or shoes in need of heeling. But Georgia was still not picking up.

'Want a ciggy?' Josie said.

Maeve nodded feebly. She had hardly spoken since they left London, had sat silent and oddly still.

'Help yourself. Lighter in my bag as well.'

Maeve lit the cigarette with a shaking hand. It was years since she'd smoked, but it had seemed a good idea suddenly. She dragged on it and promptly felt sick, opened the window, retching, hating the feel of the hot dead air.

'Sorry, Josie. Not used to them these days. You want it?'

'Yeah, thanks. You OK, darlin'?'

'No. Not really.' For the first time, Maeve began to cry. 'I'm afraid, Josie, I'm terribly afraid. He must have been driving too fast. And he was tired. He'd come up from Cornwall yesterday, slept in the cab.'

'I thought they couldn't drive too fast, thought it was all controlled by the engine, or something.'

'Yes, that is true. But maybe he was going too fast for how tired he was. Maybe he went to sleep at the wheel. It's the great nightmare that, Josie. Oh God. And then I . . . I . . .' she fumbled in her bag for a tissue, 'I tell him to get on home quickly, it being my mother's birthday and all, that he'll be in trouble if he doesn't. Suppose he needed a rest? Suppose he didn't dare take one? That'd be my fault then, wouldn't it? My fault, all these people injured, and some dead as well. Patrick horribly hurt, they said he lost six pints of blood by the time they got him out. Josie, six pints! You only have eight, don't you? Great big man like him, with only two pints of blood left . . .'

'Yes, but they'll be putting more into him,' said Josie, exhaling hard, filling the car with smoke, stroking Maeve's thigh comfortingly. 'He'll be there now at the hospital, being taken care of, and they work such wonders these days, don't they?'

'I suppose so. I don't know. Oh Josie,' she said, wiping her swollen eyes, 'if only I hadn't nagged at him to get home early. If only I'd just let him be . . .'

Abi was half-asleep, her head lolling onto Shaun's, when she was jerked awake by a voice saying, 'Shaun! Shaun, where are you?' and he sat up, rubbing his eyes, and then shot off in the direction of a pallid, overweight young woman, yelling, 'Mum, Mum!' and pushed himself into her slightly reluctant arms. She was accompanied by two other small children and an equally overweight older woman, who Abi assumed was her mother. They all came over to Abi, who started to tell Shaun's mother how brave he'd been and how proud of him she should be.

The woman stared at her rather blankly and then said: 'You're all right, are you?' to Shaun, interrupting the little speech.

'I think he's OK,' Abi said rather tentatively. 'He had an asthma attack, as I expect you know, but he's been checked over by the doctor here and given some Ventolin on a nebuliser, and all he needs now is you, I should think.'

'Yeah, well thanks. Who can I ask about him?' The girl sounded hostile.

'Well, I'm not sure,' Abi said. 'They're pretty busy here,

as you can see. I suppose the women over there on the desk would be best. But a doctor did return him to me, saying he was fine—'

'Yeah, well I want to hear it from them,' she said. 'What's he doing with you anyway?' She sounded suspicious, as if Abi had kidnapped Shaun rather than looked after him.

'I was involved in the crash,' Abi said, struggling to sound patient. 'I was with a friend and we weren't hurt, and so he got the boys out of the mini-bus and left me in charge of them while he went to see if there was anything else he could do. And then when the ambulance came for – for your little boy, he wanted me to go with him. So I did. We'd become friends by then, hadn't we, Shaun?'

Shaun nodded, tentatively putting out his hand again, into hers.

'Oh yeah. Well, thanks anyway.' His mother spoke grudgingly, looking Abi up and down, clearly taking in her tight trousers and her spike-heeled boots. 'Give over, Shaun, don't hang on to me like that, I can't hardly breathe.'

Abi felt a rush of rage. 'He's had a horrible time, you know,' she said firmly, 'really horrible. The driver of the mini-bus was . . . well, he didn't survive. I think Shaun needs lots of reassurance, you know?'

'I don't know what it's got to do with you,' said the woman. 'You're not a doctor, are you, or one of those therapists.'

'No, but—'

'Mum, it was horrible,' Shaun said. 'Mr Douglas – he was killed, he was all covered with blood and—'

'I don't really want to hear,' said the girl. 'Just try not to think about it, Shaun, that's the best thing. Come on, say goodbye to the lady and let's go and try to find a doctor, make sure you're all right. Bye,' she added rather tersely to Abi, and then, when Shaun started clinging to her and crying, and Abi hugged him back, 'I said come on, Shaun, leave the lady now.'

'Bye, Abi,' Shaun said, a filthy hand wiping over his filthier face. 'Thanks for looking after me and the singing. I liked the singing.'

'Singing!' said the girl as they moved off. 'What on earth you been singing for? Whose daft idea was that? Come on, and you, Mum, over here.'

Shaun was led away, and Abi wearily walked over to the desk.

'Any chance of a taxi to the nearest station, would you think?' she asked.

'You could try,' said one of the women, 'but I don't rate your chances.' She handed Abi a few cards; Abi rummaged in her bag for her phone. It wasn't there.

'How are you feeling now?' The nurse smiled into Mary's eyes. 'Bit better?'

'Yes. A little. Very tired, that's the worst thing. So tired.'

'Well, that's quite usual, considering what you've been through. Are you comfortable now? They'll be taking you to theatre in a minute.'

'Theatre? I don't need surgery, I haven't been injured.'

'Of course not, dear. But they're going to have a look at that heart of yours, it's not working too well just at the moment.'

'It's only my angina,' said Mary fretfully. 'I've had it for years. The nitrate spray works wonders, I'll soon be right as rain.'

'Well, Mr Phillips wants to be quite sure. He might want to do some more tests.'

'Who's Mr Phillips? And what isn't he sure about?'

'He's one of the cardiologists. He'll be along in a minute, and you can ask him yourself.'

'Honestly,' said Mary, 'I'm fine. I keep telling you. And I have to get out of here, I'm so worried.'

'Now why are you worried? Your family have been notified, they're all fine and they're on their way.'

'No, not my family. I was meant to be meeting an old friend at the airport, and – oh dear, he'll still be waiting. Can we get a message to him somehow, please?'

'I'm sure we can. Do you have a number for him – a mobile perhaps?'

'No, I don't,' said Mary, and she started to cry. 'I lost it in the crash. I was supposed to be meeting him at the Hertz desk at Heathrow – do you know it?'

'Not personally, my dear, no. And then where were you going? Home?'

'No, no, to a hotel. The Dorchester. In Mayfair.'

'Well, maybe we could call there.'

'Oh,' said Mary. She hadn't thought of that. 'Oh, that would be very kind. Would you?'

'Of course. Straight away. Now you must try to keep calm, Mary, or your blood pressure will go up at this rate.'

'I can't keep calm. Please, please help me. It's so important.'

'I will, my dear, I promise. Now look, you lie back, try and have a little rest. Just until Mr Phillips comes.' She bustled away; and Mary relaxed a little.

Unfortunately, as the nurse reached the nursing station a new patient arrived from theatre; she had lost a lot of blood and needed various drips set up, after which yet another elderly lady was brought straight up from A&E, deeply distressed. Mary's call was first postponed and then forgotten.

An hour later, and Russell was growing increasingly desperate. He asked a Hertz girl now if she was quite sure there'd been no call for him; she smiled her brilliant, slightly patronising smile and said she was quite sure.

'And no lady came here, asking for me? My name is Russell Mackenzie.'

'I don't think so, no.'

'Could you just check again, then? There could have been a changeover of staff, the message could have been mislaid.'

'Of course.'

He watched her as she rummaged under the desk, spoke to her colleagues; saw her whisper to one of them, indicating him, smiling behind her hand. How dare she? How dare she find his anxiety funny?

He glared at her as she came back.

'I'm sorry, Mr Mackenzie, no. I could put out a call for her though. Would you like me to do that? There might just have been a confusion about the meeting place. I could ask her to make her way here, if you like.'

'That would be very kind,' said Russell, crushing a violent irritation at this second implication of confusion. 'Better not change the meeting place though, just in case she doesn't hear it.'

And he listened, full of new hope, as a Mrs Mary Bristow was told to go to the Hertz desk in Arrivals as soon as possible, where Mr Russell Mackenzie was waiting for her. Only to feel the hope ebbing away as ten, fifteen, twenty minutes passed, with not a sign of Mary.

But he continued to wait. Even though he knew it was probably fruitless. It was almost three hours now, and she would surely have got a message to him somehow. She'd got his mobile number, although of course it was very complicated, he'd tried to explain that she'd have to use the International Code, and he could tell from her reply she was going to find it terribly difficult. But – she'd surely manage if she had to. And he had to keep faith somehow. Supposing she did appear, even now, his Mary, his little London sparrow, anxious, breathless, finally arrived, how could he not be there for her, how could he fail her? Three hours was nothing; not when he'd been waiting sixty years . . .

'Emma, why don't you go home? Everyone's done, either on the wards or in ITU.'

'I can't go home. Not yet. I'm worried about that boy who was stabbed. I feel responsible for him.'

'But he's on a ward now and there are other people to look after him.'

'I know, Alex, but I feel he's my patient. He told me I made him feel better.'

Alex thought that Emma would have made any male feel better, but he didn't say so. She was in no mood for flirtatious chatter.

'Well, all right – go up and check on the ward. I bet he's asleep. And then go home. OK?'

'Yes, OK,' she sighed, 'but then I wanted to check on the baby as well. The prem one, caught in the crash – you know. See if it was all right.'

'I should just call up to the ward. They'll tell you.'

She ignored this; made her way to the surgical ward via maternity. The baby was a lusty four-pound boy, in an incubator, but the prognosis was excellent.

The father was sitting by his wife's bed, holding her hand; she was asleep.

'Thank you so much,' he said, smiling up at Emma. 'You really helped her down there. I'm so grateful.'

'It was nothing. I'm sorry I couldn't have stayed with her longer – obstetrics is my specialty. Or will be. But I'm on A and E at the moment, and there was rather a lot to do.'

'Yeah, we felt bad in a way, so many people in such terrible trouble. All we were doing was having a baby.'

'You can't do anything much more important than that,' said Emma. 'I think so, anyway. Well, take care of them both.'

'I will.'

* * *

As she walked towards the surgical ward, she saw a young man and a middle-aged couple standing in the corridor. They all looked very distressed.

'Hi,' she said. 'Can I help? Are you looking for someone?'

'Our son,' said the woman. 'He was in the M4 accident today, you know . . .'

'I do know,' said Emma. 'I work in A and E.'

'Oh my goodness. Well, perhaps you even looked after him, so you may know what's happened to him. We were told he'd been taken to theatre, but that was hours ago, and now we've been sent up here. Oh dear . . .'

She started to cry; Emma put her hand on her arm. 'Tell me his name, and I'll see what I can find out for you. Everyone's been so busy today.'

'Of course. We appreciate that,' said the man. 'Weston's his name, Toby Weston.'

'Right. Look, there's a waiting room down there, it's got a coffee machine which might just be working, and you'll be more comfortable. I'll get back to you as soon as I possibly can, hopefully in a few minutes.'

The ward sister was very brisk; she was clearly exhausted.

'He's only just been brought here, he's been up in Recovery . . . He's holding his own, that's all I can say. No chest injuries and his neck's OK. CT scan showed that. And quite a mild concussion, but that leg is a mess. They've done what they can, with an external fixator, but the main danger of course is infection – I don't need to tell you that. He's on a morphine drip, pretty out of it, poor lad. Tell them his condition's serious but stable, that's always a good one. Don't want to get their hopes up too much, don't want to scare them. Oh, and your stab victim's going to be fine. He's asleep. Nice boy, just walking home from the pub, apparently.'

'I know,' said Emma. 'He kept crying and saying he

didn't start it. Thanks, Sister. I'm going home now, but I'll tell the Westons what you said. Can they see him? They seem very sensible.'

'I'd rather not just yet. Maybe in an hour or so, for a few minutes. Better warn them about the fixator. Can look a bit scary.'

'Yes, OK. And tell Darren – that's the boy – that I came to see him, will you? I promised I would.'

'I will if I remember,' said Sister wearily.

The young man was standing in the doorway of the waiting room when Emma went back; he was rather curiously dressed, she thought, in slightly baggy striped trousers with braces hanging down and a T-shirt. He was white-faced and looked completely wiped out.

'Hi,' he said. 'Is there any news?'

'Well, he's stable. Serious, but stable.'

'Is that good news? I never know with you lot.' He tried to smile.

'It's good-ish. If he's stable then he's coping. But he's still quite ill. He's only just down from Recovery. Were you there in the crash?'

'I was in the car with him,' he said. 'We were going to his wedding.'

'His wedding!' said Emma, and she felt quite sick at the thought. 'That was you, was it? I'd heard about that. How awful. I'm so sorry.' So that explained the striped trousers. They were part of his monkey suit.

'Yes. Look, I'd better go and tell his parents. They're in a terrible state.'

'I'll come and tell them if you like,' she said. 'People always prefer to hear from doctors direct.'

She went in, smiling her professional smile. 'Hello again. Well, the news isn't too bad. Your son is seriously ill, he lost a lot of blood, and the wound to his leg is quite extensive – but he is stable.'

'Oh thank God,' said the man. He blew his nose rather

hard. 'There you are, darling, what did I tell you?'

'Can we see him?' asked Mrs Weston.

'Not quite yet. He's only been back on the ward about half an hour. Sister says she'd rather you waited for another hour or so. Then you can see him, but only for a few minutes. And he may not be properly awake even then. Oh, and I should warn you, they've fixed his leg with an external fixator: that's a sort of cage-like frame outside the leg, with pins going through to the bone. It may look a bit alarming, but don't worry.'

'We don't mind,' said Mrs Weston, wiping her eyes. 'We don't mind anything. We just want to see him. Thank you so much, er . . .'

'Dr King,' said Emma.

'You don't look old enough to be a doctor,' said Mr Weston.

Emma smiled at him determinedly; that was the variation on not looking like one. It usually came from older men.

''Fraid I am,' she said. 'Anyway, I'm leaving now. I'm off duty tomorrow, but I'll be back on Sunday and I'll see how he is then. Try not to worry. It sounds like he should be OK.'

'Thank you so much,' said Mrs Weston.

'I think I might come down with you,' said the young man, 'if that's all right. I could do with a bit of fresh air. I won't be long,' he said to the Westons.

'You take your time, Barney. We're not going anywhere.'

'What I could really do with,' he said to Emma, once they were in the lift, 'is a fag. I expect you think that's terrible.'

'Of course I don't. I smoke myself occasionally. When I'm out.'

'Yeah?' He grinned at her.

'Yeah. I know it's appalling, but—'

'Is it really appalling?'

'Well yes, it really is. I mean, I'm a doctor, I should know better. Yet here I am, asking for cancer, heart disease, emphysema, and that's just for starters.'

'I plan to give up one day. Very soon.'

'Great. Right now I should think you need one.'

'Jesus, I do. Sorry!'

'So what happened? Or don't you want to talk about it?'

'I don't have that clear an idea,' he said. 'This lorry suddenly swerved in front of us. Went right through the barrier. And we – we had a blow-out, I think – trying to stop. And then – well then it's all a bit of a blur. We finished up embedded in another car – an estate. It sliced right through the window, don't know why I didn't catch it as well. I – oh shit, sorry.' His voice quavered; he dashed his hand across his eyes. It was pretty bloody scary. The whole thing.

They had reached the ground floor; she ushered him to the main door, where he stood leaning against the glass, taking deep breaths.

'It must have been hideous,' she said.

'Yeah, it was.'

'Look – sit down here for a bit. You're obviously pretty shattered.'

'Yeah. I feel a bit – sick actually. Sorry. I—' He bolted for some bushes, was gone for a while, came back looking shame-faced.

'I'm so sorry,' he said, sinking down beside her on the steps. 'Not very cool.'

'Don't be silly. I'll get you some water – stay there.'

When she came back, he still had his head in his hands.

'Thanks,' he said, taking the cup from her. 'You're very kind.'

'All part of the service. You should go home,' she said, 'you're all in. Is anyone here with you?'

'Yup. The Westons – Toby's parents, I'm going back with them.' He held out a pack of Marlboro Lights to Emma. 'Want one?'

'No, thanks. I'd get the sack, if they caught me smoking in this.'

'What – your uniform? What happened to the white coats?'

'Oh, some initiative got rid of them. Don't ask me which. Bare below the elbows is the rule now. I'm sorry actually, I rather liked my white coat. Made me feel like a grown-up.'

'You look quite grown up to me,' he said. 'What sort of a doctor are you then?'

'I'm going to be a surgeon, I hope. An obstetric surgeon.'

'Sounds very impressive. Did you see Tobes when he arrived?'

'I did, yes, but only very briefly. It's been a nightmare day.'

'I bet.' He held out his hand. 'Barney Fraser.'

'Hi, Barney. Were you going to be the best man?'

'Yup. I was.'

'That is so hard. How's the bride? How's she coping?'

'Pretty badly, I think,' said Barney. His tone was dismissive. Emma looked at him sharply. Not a lot of love lost there.

'Have you spoken to her? Is she coming to the hospital?'

'In the morning. She's too upset to come tonight, apparently.' More dismissive still.

'Right. Well, I'd better go. I'm quite tired.'

'I bet you are. Thanks so much, Dr King.'

'Emma. Actually. Bye then, Barney. Good luck. And – I know it's nothing to do with me, but you should take it easy for a couple of days. You've had an awful shock. Don't expect to just feel fine because it's over.'

'Oh, I'm all right. But thanks.'

Thinking about him as she drove her car out of the hospital, she reflected that he was really rather good looking, with his spiky brown hair and hazel eyes with darker flecks in them and that gorgeous smile. There was something incredibly charming about him. She wondered if he had a girlfriend and then mentally slapped herself. *You've got a perfectly good boyfriend of your own, Emma. Get a grip.*

Linda was just going to bed, had already tidied her perfectly tidy living room, made herself some camomile tea and sorted out her clothes for the next day, when she decided she couldn't ignore the fact any longer that Georgia might have been caught up in the crash. Yes, if she'd been hurt her mother would have been informed, but then her mother would surely have contacted Linda. She knew she was coming up for an important audition, and unless Georgia had been very seriously injured – and some people had, of course – she would have let Linda know.

With some reluctance and a strong feeling of dread, she called the Linley household, bracing herself for the worst.

'Bea, I'm sorry to call so late. Linda Di-Marcello here. I wonder . . . if you've heard from Georgia.'

'Oh, hello Linda.' Bea sounded slightly surprised. 'Yes, she's arrived home safely. Bit weary – and very disappointed she didn't get the part, of course. But I've told her there's always another time, and I'm sure you'd say the same. She's asleep, but I'll tell her you called. It's very kind of you, thank you so much.'

Georgia was lying under the covers, her pillow over her face to smother the sound of her weeping. It was a terrible thing she'd done: so terrible. And how was she ever going to put it right?

Part Three
Next

Chapter 14

'Where are you going now?'

Laura tried to keep the exasperation out of her voice, but it was difficult. She felt extremely exasperated: on the verge of anger. Jonathan had hardly spoken to her since he had come in, just before nine the night before. He had walked in, white-faced, his eyes dark with exhaustion, dropped his overnight bag on the hall floor and stood there, as if he didn't know where he was.

'Hello,' he said rather vaguely. 'Sorry to be so late.'

'Don't apologise, Jonathan. Come in and sit down, tell me all about it. What would you like – tea, Scotch, water . . .'

'Water'd be great. Thanks, darling. But could you bring it through to the study? I really need to check my emails.'

'What – now?' she asked, surprise making her stupid.

'Yes, now,' he said. 'It's important. I've been out all day, no one could get hold of me, and I don't know what's been going on at the clinic, or the hospital.'

'But I want to know all about it, what happened.'

'Laura, I really don't want to talk about it. Not yet anyway. I'm all in.'

His voice shook slightly; she told herself he had had a day of such horror that few people would be able even to imagine it, and that she must be patient.

She walked into the kitchen, where Charlie was watching *The Simpsons*.

'Charlie! Why aren't you in the playroom?'

'I was worried about Dad. I wanted to see him the minute he got in.'

'He's just got in,' said Laura briefly.

'Yeah? Cool! Where is he?'

'He's in his study.'

'His study! What – he went straight in there, didn't even come to say hello?'

'That's right,' said Laura. 'Charlie, he's very tired, probably can't cope with any of us. Bit shocked even. He must have had a hell of a day.'

'Yeah, but—'

'Well, I'm sure he'll be in soon. He wants some water.' She took a bottle from the fridge.

'Can I take it? Then at least I can say hello to him.'

'No, I don't think so,' said Laura.

'But Mum . . .'

'Charlie, I said no. All right?'

He stared at her. She was never impatient like that.

'It's cool, I only asked. He's OK, is he?'

'He's fine, yes. Just – exhausted.'

'Well, when he does come out, tell him to come and see me. I'll be up in the playroom. Trouble is the girls are watching some stupid Bratz DVD.'

'They should be in bed,' said Laura. 'I'll be right up to tell them so.'

She walked into the study; Jonathan was sitting staring blankly out of the window. It was still just light, but the sun was sinking, a great red ball etched out of the brilliant turquoise sky.

'Lovely sunset,' she said, setting the water down.

'What? Thanks, darling.'

'I said lovely sunset.'

'Yes, very lovely. I'll be finished soon, Laura. I'll come and find you, all right?'

'All right. I'll be in the kitchen, waiting to have supper with you.'

'Darling, I don't want any supper. I still feel sick.'

'But Jonathan, you haven't eaten – or have you? Did you get something at the hospital?'

'What hospital?' He was looking at her blankly now.

'The hospital handling the casualties.'

'What on earth makes you think I'd go there?'

'Well, I just thought you might. As you'd been helping the – the crash victims.'

'Christ no. Plenty of people to do that, once they got there.'

'I see. So what have you been doing all this time then?'

'All what time?'

'Jonathan, it's almost nine. You called me at five, five-thirty. Said the ambulances were coming. Did you stay on after that, helping there? Or were you talking to the police or something?'

'Laura, what is this, an inquisition? I finally got under way at about seven. They had to check my car—'

'Your car? Why?'

'Oh, to make sure it's mechanically sound, brakes OK and so on. Apparently it's standard procedure these days, if you're involved in a crash.'

'I thought you weren't involved?'

'Laura, I was there, for Christ's sake! Look, I wasn't about to argue with the police. And then the traffic was still appalling. It's two hours under good conditions. And I gave some bloke a lift. Young chap, got caught in it all, desperate to get to London, almost in tears, missed some crucial meeting. I dropped him off in the Cromwell Road. There were a lot of people like that, lives just thrown into the air. Thanks for the water. I'll see you later.'

'I'll have some supper then if you don't mind. I've made some pasta.'

'Of course I don't mind. I'll be in later.'

But he wasn't. At ten-thirty he was still in the study. She

knocked rather nervously; he was sitting staring at his laptop screen.

'Are you nearly through? I'd like to go to bed soon.'

'Well, go to bed. Don't wait for me, darling. I'll be up pretty soon.'

'What on earth for? I want to be with you, I'd rather wait.'

'I'd rather you didn't. Look, you just go ahead. I'll be a while yet.'

'All right.'

And finally, at eleven, she had gone up to bed on her own and stayed awake a long time, watching some stupid old film, thinking that at any moment he'd appear, saying, 'Sorry, darling, sorry sorry sorry', as he so often did when he knew he'd kept her waiting. But at midnight he had still not appeared and she finally fell asleep.

And now here he was, wearing his cycling clothes, for heaven's sake, at seven in the morning.

'I'm going for a bike ride,' he said in answer to her question. 'To try and clear my head. I've got my morning round to do at the clinic. I'll see you after that.'

'Breakfast?'

'I still don't feel very hungry.'

'Jonathan, you must eat.'

'I'm not one of the children, Laura. I can decide for myself when I need food.'

'Oh, please yourself,' she said, allowing irritation to break through for the first time. 'And don't forget we're going to lunch with the Edwardses.'

'The Edwardses? What for?'

'What for? Jonathan, what's the matter with you? They've asked us, that's what for. They're having a barbecue.'

'I really don't think I could face a barbecue today,' he said. 'I feel absolutely shattered. I've got a clinic to do, and it's going to be bloody hot again.'

'Well, I think you're going to have to face it,' she said. 'It's Serena's birthday. There are several couples going and—'

'If there are several couples, would it really matter if I wasn't there?'

'Yes, it would. She's my best friend and she'd be very hurt. The children are coming, their children will be there.'

She couldn't help it; she felt her temper rising. 'Oh, just go out on your bloody bike. I'll see you later.'

'OK,' he said, and he was gone.

'He's being really weird,' said Charlie. He had come down the stairs and heard most of the conversation.

'Just a bit.'

'D'you think he's getting Alzheimer's?'

The absurdity of the question made Laura smile. 'No, darling, of course I don't.'

'OK. Just wondered.'

She went into the kitchen with Charlie and started doing the scrambled eggs he loved. She felt confused and upset. She needed to talk to Jonathan, needed him to tell her about it; she also needed to know why he had been on the M4 and not the M40. She tried to crush the notion that he was avoiding her because he didn't want to tell her.

Russell woke horribly early; he hurt all over. Not just his heart, which felt physically sore, but his head, his stomach, his limbs. It was as if he had been beaten up. He got up, walked over to the window and opened the curtains. It was going to be another lovely day. At a little after five, it was almost light, the sun was shearing through the trees, the sky was the just slightly hazy blue that speaks of staying power. Russell sighed heavily and turned away; he would have looked for rain, for greyness, for cold – the weather of disappointment.

What had happened to Mary? How could she have failed him like this? Why hadn't she somehow got a message to him? He had told her where they would be staying: at the Dorchester, the American home from home. Even if she hadn't been able to send a message to him at the airport, she could surely have rung there.

It had suddenly occurred to him as he waited in his growing misery at the airport, that of course that was what she would have done – phoned the hotel. So much easier than contacting the Hertz desk at the airport, or his mobile. It was a flash of pure joy, and he had rung them immediately; just speaking to them had made him feel better, to be receiving courtesy and consideration rather than disdain.

'Ah, Mr Mackenzie, how nice to hear from you. We were a little anxious, since you have been so long – your luggage arrived hours ago . . . We are so looking forward to seeing you again. Your usual room is waiting . . . A pleasure, Mr Mackenzie.'

But then came the same cold disappointment: there had been no message yet, nothing from Mary at all.

And after another hour, he had gone out heavily to the forecourt and into the limo that had been waiting ever since he had landed, and was driven to London. And as they drew nearer to the hotel he became hopeful again, for perhaps she would be there, waiting for him, and they could have dinner together and she would explain what had happened and then they would plan what they were going to do the next day and the next, and possibly even the rest of their lives.

He had arrived at the desk breathless, looking round wildly in reception on his way, half-expecting to see her there, small and neat and smiling; only to be told that no, so sorry, there was no message still, and no one had arrived asking for him either. And after walking all around the ground floor, checking the bars and the restaurant – for how could they be sure she hadn't arrived unannounced, and had just gone in and settled herself down to wait – he had gone up to his room and ordered a Martini and then another and sat in a chair, staring at the telephone, and after a while he began to weep, as he had not since he had been a young GI leaving England on his way home at the end of the war, sitting in the lavatory on the troop train, thinking of Mary and wondering how he was going to get through the next eighty years or whatever without her.

And then, slowly but very surely, he started to get cross.

Russell was a very nice person – kind, caring, and for the most part thoughtful. But he was rich and successful; and like many rich and successful people, he was spoiled. All his life, from his earliest childhood, he had had everything he wanted: the toys, the outings, the fun. And, as he grew up, the girls. His natural self-confidence, combined with considerable charm and good looks, brought girls, notionally at least, to his door. Plus of course his ability to take them to the best seats in theatres, the best tables in restaurants, invitations to the best parties. Girls loved him: and admired, flattered and didn't argue with him. It was all extremely easy.

He had always known he would take his place in the upper echelons of the family textile company; his father had wanted him there, could appreciate his considerable abilities. He had never had to struggle for anything.

And then he had met Mary, the second in a series of shocks to his system, the first being the danger and discomfort of war and the discipline of the Army. Mary was not like any girl he had met before, in that she was quite hard to impress. It was one of the things that made her special. She did fall in love with him, and at first sight, as she often said: but she was quite critical too, didn't like the way he snapped his fingers at barmen and waiters and shouted at taxi drivers, and he did have a tendency to look down on the less educated or successful. And they had quite a dust-up one evening, as she put it, when he was quite rude about Marilyn, her best friend, remarking to

Mary that someone really should tell her that her hair looked as if she had dyed it herself in the kitchen.

'Which she probably did,' Mary had said with some asperity, 'not being able to afford the sort of hairdresser you'd consider suitable. Marilyn is a kind and good person, and a very loyal friend, and if you criticise her, you criticise me.' Upon which she had marched out of the bar and had stood at the bus stop refusing to speak to Russell until he first apologised and then agreed that they should go out with Marilyn and her boyfriend in a foursome. He had heard himself, to his own considerable astonishment, rather meekly going along with all this. Meekness was not something that came easily to Russell.

Losing Mary had been the worst and greatest shock of his life; but once he had begun to recover from that and was returned to the world he knew, that of money and worldly success, he forgot any lessons he might have learned from her. He worked hard, to be sure, but for considerable rewards. He lived in both style and comfort, first one wife and then another ran his home and did what they were told, his children were brought up in awe of him, and his reputation as one of New York's more generous philanthropists assured him of further admiration. And now, in the senior department, as he called it, of a gilded life, he was rarely crossed, never criticised, and had his every demand almost instantly met.

He was finding the present situation extremely difficult. Whatever it was that had happened to Mary, this was the twenty-first century, for heaven's sake! Even if she was unwell, she could have rung the hotel, or got word to him somehow. Or somebody could. It showed a lack of consideration as well as courtesy: he was hardly likely to shrug off her non-appearance. He had gone to enormous trouble to make everything perfect for her; had anticipated her every need, answered her every question in advance. She could surely have shown him a little consideration in return, anticipated his anxiety, eased any of his feverish imaginings. And if there was a real problem, something serious, then surely her family would have contacted him. He had given her all the numbers, the hotel, his mobile . . .

Sorrow turned to self-pity turned to resentment turned to outrage. Mary had, not to put too fine a point on it, stood him up.

And now the damn sun had the nerve to shine . . .

'Mrs Connell, are you all right?'

Maeve struggled to sit up; she had been asleep on the sofa in the High Dependency Unit corridor. A doctor – she knew he was a doctor from his name badge – was looking down at her; he had a lot of dark hair and very kind dark eyes. He looked about forty-five, possibly more; that was reassuring. Maeve felt that doctors should be old – certainly well into middle age.

'Yes, I'm fine,' she said. 'Thank you.'

'I'm Dr Pritchard, the A and E consultant. I admitted your husband last night. Specialist doctors and surgeons have been looking after him, but I wanted to come and see how he was doing, say hello. And to see how you were.'

'Never mind how I am,' said Maeve, 'what about Patrick?'

Dr Pritchard was silent. That's it, she thought. He's died, he's gone, and they've sent this man with the kind eyes to tell me. He's probably the person they always send.

'He's died, hasn't he?' she said.

But, 'No, he's holding on. It's amazing, but he is. He must be very strong, Mrs Connell.'

'I suppose he is, yes. I don't know why, since all he ever does is sit in that cab.'

'But he is still dangerously ill, I'm afraid. There were abdominal and chest injuries, his spleen is ruptured, we've had to remove one of his kidneys and part of his large intestine. None of which is necessarily fatal: clearly far from it.' He smiled at her.

'Is that all?'

'Well, he'd lost a lot of blood, of course, but that's fairly easily dealt with. He also had some injury to his heart – contusions, we call them, that is blood collecting in a sac round it – but we put a needle in and drained it.'

'Is he conscious?'

'Semi, I'd say. Just as well for him. Actually we decided to keep him asleep last night, to make sure he was stable. There are a lot of drugs going round his system. He has a tube in his throat and he's on a ventilator; it's doing his breathing for him.'

'It sounds so dreadful,' she whispered.

'I know. But we would hope to extubate him quite soon now.'

'What does that mean?'

'Turn off the anaesthetic drugs, and wean him off the ventilator. Take out the tube. He'll start to breathe on his own and wake up. Of course, he'll be given plenty of painkillers. He'll be pretty out of it for a day or two.'

'Can I – that is, when can I – see him?'

'Oh, pretty soon, I'd have thought. But you have to be prepared for a shock, Mrs Connell. His face and hands are cut, although not as badly as I might have expected, given the windscreen was shattered, so that's something. His head is swollen and a bit out of shape and there are all these tubes coming in and out of him. Not the prettiest sight, I'm afraid. And he'll be very confused, but he'll want to talk – people always do.'

'You're very kind,' said Maeve, and she meant it. People said the NHS was falling apart these days, but as far as she could see, it was absolutely wonderful. Fancy a busy doctor finding the time to talk to her like this . . .

❖   ❖   ❖

Time was actually not a problem for Alex Pritchard that day. He could, indeed should, have been at home – he was not officially on duty, but he had come in partly to check on the condition of the more serious victims of the crash, partly to get out of the house. He had looked back on it, standing there in the sun, the lovely big Edwardian house where he and Samantha had lived for sixteen years and raised two children, and felt at one and the same time sad and outraged that he was about to lose it. It was to be sold, and the proceeds were to buy another more than adequate house as far as he could see for Sam and the children, and a rather inadequate flat for him. He was to lose the children he loved so much, apart from every other weekend, he was to lose quite a large proportion of his income, he was going to be extremely lonely, and all so that Sam could pursue her own life and her own new relationship. It was desperately unfair – and OK, he hadn't been the greatest husband, he'd been bad tempered and difficult, and absent a lot of the time, and not the greatest father either, and yes, Sam had had to bear the brunt of the whole domestic thing, running the house, caring for the children, going to parents' evenings and nativity plays on her own, all that stuff – but did he really deserve this exile? To this dreadful new country, where he had had to learn a dreadful new language of custody and maintenance and adultery and decrees both nisi and absolute, and a new set of customs, of coldness and hostility, of distortion of facts and perversion of memory, of the fading of loyalty and denial of truth.

And yes, he had had an affair, albeit a brief one, born of retaliation rather than desire, and how happy for Sam that he had, for her lawyer had been able to add it to the sins of omission and absenteeism that had lost him his family.

It was doomed to failure from the beginning, his marriage, he could see that now; to the lovely Sam, ten years younger than him, with her social ambition and her need for admiration. She had never understood the whole medical thing, the claims of the job, the loyalty to the patients, and never bothered to try either; being the wife of a doctor was akin to being the wife of a soldier, you took the life on with all its pressures and trials, you bonded with the other wives, and you tried your damnedest not to complain. Sam had signed up to none of that; and all their rows had started from that point.

Why was he always late? Why did a crisis at the hospital take precedence over a dinner-party? Why should she give up her time and energy to hospital causes? Why then was she so happy with the lifestyle his large salary brought her? Why couldn't she say just for once that she was proud of him and what he did? Even if she didn't mean it. She had been in every sense a disappointment; he had been beguiled by her, had thought he was marrying a princess, when beneath her lovely face and body and her protestations of adoration was a self-seeking Ugly Sister.

Well, he had learned his lesson and very painfully; and if he ever had another relationship it would be with someone who understood his career and the life it led him into, someone who was not concerned with her own life and her own ambitions. Only he never would have another relationship; he would never have the stomach for it.

He looked back on Mrs Connell as he walked away, being ushered into HDU by a nurse, and wondered how on earth she was going to cope with what lay ahead of her. For he had not told her – how could he, it was too soon, the extent of the damage too uncertain – that there was possible damage to Patrick's spinal cord. It was more than possible that he would be paralysed, a helpless cripple, wheelchair-bound – and how would she care for him, in addition to three young children?

212

Dianne Harwood looked across the breakfast table at her husband. 'This sounds like an awful pile-up yesterday, Rick. On the M4. Didn't you see anything of it at all?'

'No. Why should I have?'

'Because you were on the bloody road, that's why. Around the same time. Four o'clock, it says here.'

'Course I wasn't. I was delivering the stuff to the boss in Marlow by four.'

'Oh, OK. What if you'd been a bit later, though. Doesn't bear thinking about.'

'Yeah, well I wasn't.'

'Says here a lorry went right through the central reservation. So random, isn't it?'

'Yeah, suppose so.'

'There were two chaps right behind, on their way to a wedding. The bridegroom it was, he's in hospital. Isn't that sad?'

'What – sad he missed his wedding? Could've been a blessed relief.'

'You're such a charmer, you know that? And then the lorry driver, he's in Intensive Care, still unconscious he was, last night. At least three dead, it says, and loads of serious injuries. It's enough to make you think you'll never get in a car again.'

'Yeah, well some of us have to.'

'I know, babe, I know. Part of why your job's so stressful, isn't it? Was the traffic very heavy then, when you was driving up?'

'Not specially, no. Oh, I don't know. Can we stop this, Dianne, talk about something a bit more cheerful?'

'Tamara, are you ready, darling? Daddy's got the car at the front of the house.'

'Yes, coming, Mummy, just finding my shoes.'

They had to be the right shoes, it seemed important.

Wearing the right clothes altogether was important. Toby was probably a bit down in the dumps today, and it would cheer him up to see her looking really great. A lot of girls might not have bothered about it, specially having been robbed of their wedding day, but Tamara was not being beaten by a little something like that. There would be another wedding day, and they could start planning it that very morning. She was taking her diary with her, so that they could choose another date at least.

She felt extremely proud of herself, being so strong about the whole thing. She could think of at least half a dozen friends who would have been completely destroyed by it. Of course, she had been dreadfully upset yesterday, and worried about him, and there was no way she could have gone to the hospital last night, she'd looked appalling, her eyes all piggy and her skin blotchy with crying, and she'd felt competely and utterly drained by it. Even though the wonderful phone call had come through from Carol Weston, saying that Toby was going to be all right, she had still felt really sick and faint. Her mother had asked her if she wanted to go over to St Mark's in Swindon, but she'd said she couldn't possibly, and anyway, Carol had said that Toby was completely out of it, heavily drugged, so there wouldn't have been any point.

But today – well, today was quite different. She felt really refreshed, and able to cope with it all.

Her parents had been fantastic, had said she mustn't worry about the reception or the food being wasted, which actually she hadn't given a thought to, and who would have done? It had been a bit horrid waking up and looking out on the marquee, but they were taking it away today, thank goodness, and by the time they got back from the hospital everything would be more or less restored to normal. And – *look on the bright side, Tamara* – you'll have a wedding still to plan and look forward to, when it would have been all over. That was a pretty fantastic thought. She'd always been good at looking on the bright side. Toby too, it was one of the reasons she loved him so much. She finally settled on a pair of white patent high-heeled mules, which went with the red shift she had decided to wear – it was one of Toby's favourites, he said she was his own personal Lady in Red in it – and ran downstairs barefoot, holding them in her hand.

'Darling!' her mother said. 'You look lovely.'

'Yes, well, I thought I should put on a good show for Toby. Cheer him up. I owe him that, don't you think?'

'I do, darling. Although you mustn't expect too much. The ward sister – I didn't think NHS hospitals had sisters any more – said he was still pretty confused and in quite a lot of pain.'

'Well, I expect he is, poor darling. But that doesn't mean I can't cheer him up. And hopefully we can find out when he'll be coming out of there. I mean, NHS hospitals don't keep people in for longer than they can possibly help these days, do they? He'll probably be home by Monday. He could come and stay here, that'd be fun . . .'

'Hi,' she said, smiling at the nurse standing at the entrance to Toby's ward. 'I'm Tamara Richmond. I've come to see Toby Weston. Is that OK? Which bed is he in? If you just show me, I'll be fine.'

The nurse didn't like her; she could tell that straight away. She looked her up and down as if she was some kind of alien and then said, 'If you wait there, I'll just go and see. He's not very well this morning, I'm afraid.'

Silly cow; of course he wouldn't be very well. He'd been in a major car crash, lost lots of blood. Talk about an understatement . . .

The nurse came back.

'I've just asked Sister. She says you can see him, but only for a few minutes. If you just follow me . . .'

❀ ❀ ❀

'It was so awful,' she said later, sobbing in her father's arms in the car park. 'I thought he'd be sitting up in his pyjamas, you know, and I could give him the strawberries and everything, and he was just lying there, looking all pinched and white, and there were lots of drips and things, and one of them was blood, and goodness knows what the others all were, and then he had this cage thing over his leg, with sort of pins going through his skin, it made me feel quite sick actually, and he turned his head just very slowly and said my name, but he could hardly get that out, and he tried to smile, Daddy, but he couldn't quite manage it, and then his eyes closed again, and he tried to give me his hand but it sort of flopped before it reached me. And I said hello and tried to give him a kiss, but I couldn't get at him properly with all the tubes and stuff, and it was so upsetting I just started to cry. And then some beastly nurse said if I'd like to wait outside, the doctor was coming to see him and I said couldn't I stay and she said no, she didn't think that was a very good idea, that's the NHS for you, treating everyone like idiots, and I had to wait outside for ages and then when the doctor came out I nabbed him, said how was Toby and he said not very well, but he'd be back in a couple of hours and he'd have a better idea then. He seemed to think I could just wait. So I went back to Toby and he just seemed to be totally out of it, and I tried to hold his hand again and he said, "Sorry, darling", and just seemed to drift off again. And then the nurse came back and said she was sorry, but that was enough for now, and if I liked I could come back this afternoon. I'm just so disappointed and upset, Daddy, and so worried. He's obviously much worse than anyone was letting on last night.'

'Oh darling, try not to worry too much.' Gerald Richmond passed her his handkerchief. 'Come on, blow your nose. You've been so brave up to now, you've just got to keep it up a bit longer. Shall we go and have a nice lunch somewhere, maybe in Marlborough, and then come back this afternoon? Would you like that?'

'Yes. No. Oh, I don't know. I mean, honestly, Daddy, if you'd seen him, you'd have wondered if there was any point my visiting. It was quite scary. He hardly seemed to be there.'

'Well, if the nurse told you to go back and the doctor's been to see him, I'd have thought it was worth it. I'll come with you, if you like. Just to hold your hand. As Toby can't.' He smiled at her. 'Come on, poppet, dry your eyes. We'll go to the Bear, have a really good lunch, and then come back and see how he is. I'm sure he'll pick up very quickly – he's young and very fit.'

'Yes, all right. Thanks, Daddy, I expect you're right. Oh, now look at me,' she said, half-laughing as she studied herself in the mirror. 'My mascara's all run, and I don't have any make-up with me. Maybe we could buy some stuff in Marlborough after we've had lunch.'

'Of course we can. You're being very brave, darling. I'm so proud of you.'

'Thanks, Daddy. I don't feel very brave. Oh, it's all so sad. Pretty cruel, fate, isn't it? Why did it have to happen yesterday? And to me?'

Chapter 15

Abi was in the gym; she felt absolutely dreadful, sick and exhausted, aching in every limb – and seriously stressed. Not helped by the minor – but unsettling – problem of having lost her mobile phone. She'd rung it repeatedly, in the hope someone would have it and answer it, but it remained stubbornly switched off. Clearly she needed to speak to Jonathan; the police had told her they would want a statement from her, as she had been in the forefront of the crash, and she presumed they had said the same thing to him.

The thought most frightening her was an odd, almost shadowy anxiety that she had in some way contributed to the accident. She kept telling herself that was impossible. The only thing she could remember clearly was the lorry suddenly veering away from them towards the middle of the road. It had all been such total chaos. But, as she had pointed out to Jonathan, he had been on the phone – and she had been shouting at him, swearing at him even – she'd provided a pretty serious distraction. Suppose Jonathan had swerved, made the lorry swerve too? It didn't bear thinking about. And because they'd been right at the front, they'd surely be required to recount very precisely what they had seen. And if all she could tell them was that it was a blur, that she couldn't really remember, they wouldn't be very impressed. They might even think she was covering something up.

She presumed Jonathan would require her to go along

with whatever story he planned to tell Laura: the reasons for being on the wrong motorway, and her presence in the car. It was extremely unlikely, she felt sure, to be the bald truth; and that shifted the balance of power between them just a little. Yesterday, Laura could have been kept in ignorance of Abi's existence – unless Abi herself confronted her with it. Today, she almost certainly could not. It would emerge that Jonathan had not been alone in the car, it would emerge during police questioning, and he would somehow have to explain who she was and what she was doing there. So if he wanted her to go along with any lie he might concoct, she held quite a few more cards than she had done; and that was actually rather pleasing.

Abi was not vindictive; in spite of her threat to Jonathan of confronting Laura, she had no real intention of doing so. Rather perversely, she was actually on Laura's side. She didn't admire her, indeed she viewed her – and other wives like her – with something near to contempt: for their dependency, their willingness to do what they were told and be what they were bidden. She viewed their naïvete in trusting their husbands, their blindness to the dangers of their situations, with scorn, and their unquestioning acceptance of their financial dependence, and their somehow inferior status, with disdain.

Kept women, Abi regarded them as – lacking in courage, personal ambition and indeed, self-worth. She had no desire to join their ranks; she would not consider moving into a large house, wearing expensive clothes and driving a flashy car if it was not due at least in some large part to her own efforts. She wanted her own stake in life; not one bought by simpering at dinner-parties and providing sex when required.

Just the same, she felt that while they paid what seemed to her a monstrous price, these women did deserve better than being cheated on. She despised Jonathan for what he was doing to Laura: he was the real wrongdoer in her eyes, the villain of the piece, playing with Laura's happiness and love, and that of his children, like some sleek, greedy animal, taking what he wanted wherever and whenever he could find it. And it was he, not Laura, who deserved to be punished for it.

But to punish Jonathan would be to punish Laura too; and not to be contemplated in the normal run of things. This run, however, was not normal; it was extraordinary, and as a result of it Jonathan could find himself threatened – not by a malign mistress, as he might have envisaged, but a malign fate, which he would certainly have not.

And she really couldn't help enjoying that prospect just a little.

'How're you feeling, mate?' Barney smiled determinedly at Toby. He was half-asleep; in fact Barney had asked the nurse if it was really all right to talk to him.

'Yes, should be,' she said. 'He's very drowsy, it's the morphine, but it'll do him good to have a visit. Just a few minutes though. His parents were here earlier, and his fiancée, so he is tired.'

Barney returned to the bed; and after a few minutes Toby did open his eyes with an obvious effort and said, 'Cheers, Barney,' and managed a rather feeble smile.

'You doing OK? They treating you all right?'

'Yes, course. They're great. I'm fine, be out of here in a day or two, I expect.' He closed his eyes again, grimaced, tried to shift his position. 'Christ, this leg hurts.'

'The nurse said you were on morphine, thought that'd fix it.'

'I am. Big disappointment. Helps, I suppose, I certainly know when it's wearing off, but it still doesn't kill it. I've got a sort of pump thing, so I can give it to myself, but it knows when you've had enough, so you can't OD – unfortunately.' He tried to smile again.

'I hear you've had lots of visitors,' said Barney.

'Yeah, Mum and Dad. And Tamara, of course. She's been such a brick.'

'A brick?'

'Yeah, so good about cancelling the wedding. Didn't complain at all.'

'Really?'

'Yeah. She wanted to set another date, brought her diary, but I just wasn't up to it. She seemed a bit disappointed about that, but – maybe tomorrow.'

'Well, no rush eh?'

'No. But it would make her feel better, she said.'

The thought of Tamara pestering Toby in his hospital bed about another date for the wedding made Barney feel slightly sick.

'How's the food?' he said after a pause.

'Don't know. I'm just getting stuff through these things.' He indicated the various drips and lines. 'So – pretty tasteless really.'

'Amanda sent some grapes. Here. But if you can't eat them . . .'

'Thanks. How is Amanda?'

'She's fine,' said Barney. 'She says she'll come in with me tomorrow if you like, if you don't have too many visitors.'

'Yeah, course. Give her my love.' His eyes closed; he was clearly exhausted. And he was certainly in no condition to talk about the things that were worrying Barney. He patted Toby on the hand, told him he'd be back later and went down to the main entrance, where Amanda was waiting for him.

'How is he? Can I come up and see him?'

'Best not. He's in a lot of pain. Poor old Tobes.'

'Oh dear,' said Amanda. 'It's just so, so sad. And so unfair.' Her blue eyes filled with tears; Barney put his arm round her.

'He'll be all right,' he said. 'Promise. Come on, let's start driving back, maybe have something to eat on the way?'

He took her hand; as they started going down the steps, Emma came running up them. She recognised Barney and smiled.

'Hi. Nice to see you. How's the patient today? I haven't been up there yet, but I was planning to check.'

'Oh, you know. Not too good. Seems in a lot of pain.'

'Try not to worry,' she said. 'He should be fine. It's almost the worst day, this. Lot of trauma – medical trauma, I mean – swelling, bruising coming out.' She smiled at Amanda, held out her hand. 'I'm Emma King, one of the A and E doctors. I met your – Mr Fraser – on Friday night, when he was leaving your friend's ward.' She stopped uncertainly.

'I heard you'd all been wonderful,' said Amanda, taking the hand. 'Thank you so much. I'm Amanda, Barney's fiancée.'

'Well, you know. We do our best.'

And they stood there in the sunlight, shaking hands: two pretty girls with blond hair and blue eyes, worlds apart in education, class, lifestyle and aspiration, slightly wary of one another without having the faintest idea why.

There was a silence, then Emma said, 'Well, I mustn't hold you up. And I will go and see – Toby, was it? As soon as I can. I'm supposed to be off-duty today, but . . .'

'Yes, Toby, that's right,' said Barney. 'Do you really think he's going to be OK?'

'Without having seen him I can't say, obviously. And I'm not his doctor. But I can't see why not. Try not to worry. Bye now.'

'Bye,' said Amanda. 'Come on, Barney, we must go too.'

So he did have a girlfriend, Emma thought, looking after them as they walked towards the cars – and what a suitable one. And she had a boyfriend: didn't she? So why was she even concerned about Barney? She wasn't. She so wasn't. And she was really late. She must go.

Mary sat in her bed in the cardiac ward, feeling physically better, but increasingly agitated about Russell, begging to be allowed to go home. They kept saying no, that she had to stay another forty-eight hours, that Mr Phillips was very pleased with her, but still wanted to keep an eye on her.

She'd had what they told her was a small heart attack and they had advised a cardiac catheterisation. Mr Phillips, the cardiac consultant, had told her there was a narrowing in the artery, that had been treated by inserting a small balloon and there was now nothing to worry about. It had sounded rather alarming – they had gone into her heart through an artery in her leg – but although she was a bit sore she felt fine.

'So why can't I go home?' she asked, and they said, well, she was in her eighties, it had all been a considerable trauma for her and she needed to be kept under observation. And indeed to rest.

The last thing Mary felt she could do was rest; in her wilder moments, she felt like rushing out of the hospital, in her dressing-gown if necessary, hiring another taxi and directing it to the Dorchester Hotel herself. She supposed that once Russell had received the message sent by the nurse, he would simply wait until she got in touch with him herself. Just the same, she needed to know that he had got it; and she could only do that by telephoning his hotel. But she didn't have the number: that was also in her address book in her attaché case. How stupid, how terribly stupid of her that had been. Well, she could find out the number from Directory Enquiries.

'Can I get up, go down the corridor?' she asked the nurse. 'I want to use the telephone.' She was told perhaps tomorrow, not today. 'But we can bring the phone to you, Mary, that's no problem.'

'Oh, would you, dear? That's very kind. Thank you so much.'

And all might yet have been well, had not Mary's daughter Christine and her husband, Gerry, arrived at that very moment. There was much embracing and kissing and, 'There now,' the nurse said, 'they'll make your phone call for you, Mary, I'm sure.'

'What phone call is that, Mum?' asked Christine, setting down the cyclamen plant she had brought.

'Oh, to a friend of mine. It's not very important.' She still couldn't face telling Christine about Russell; down to earth, sturdily conventional Christine, certainly not if everything was going to go wrong now. She'd look even more foolish.

'That nurse seemed to think it was.'

'No, she didn't, dear. Don't worry – I can do it when you've gone.'

And she submitted to an inquisition about the crash and her role in it that was so long and detailed that she became exhausted; one of the nurses noticed and said that she thought Christine and Gerry should leave her to rest. After which she was finally able to make her phone call – only to be told that Mr Mackenzie had checked out of the Dorchester a couple of hours earlier.

Jonathan had got extremely drunk at the barbecue. He was surprised by how drunk he was. He hadn't actually consumed that much – a couple of beers, two or three glasses of wine – but by the time everyone was on the tiramasu and the pavlova and the homemade sorbet, he could hardly stand. Correction: he couldn't stand. He staggered over to the table where the children were hurling the sorbet at one another, sank down, and rested his head on his arms, realising he was experiencing the almost forgotten sensation of what he had called in his youth 'the whirly pits' – the nauseous dizziness, the heaving of the ground, and the general sense of absolute physical misery.

It was Charlie who noticed, Charlie who put his arm round his shoulders, asked him if he was OK, Charlie who brought him the bottle of mineral water that he forced into himself before knowing the absolute humiliation of throwing up on the path as he ran desperately for the lavatory.

'Darling! Oh darling, how awful . . .' Laura's face and voice showed nothing but concern. 'You poor, poor thing, let me help you. Serena, I'm so sorry, I think it's delayed reaction from yesterday. It must have been such a horrible experience for him, and the heat, of course – he really doesn't do heat very well.'

And grateful for the excuse, dimly aware that Mark Edwards was hosing down the path even as Laura helped him into the house, terrified he was going to vomit again, he bolted into the Edwardses' cloakroom and sat there for a long time, holding his head and wondering how on earth he was going to get through the next days and weeks – and possibly even years.

For the dawning of the day had made him realise that he was in an appalling mess. To start with, he was going to have to explain to Laura why he had been on the M4 at all, rather than the M40, and moreover with a woman, a young and attractive one – for whose presence he would have to provide an acceptable explanation.

There was also the uncomfortable fact that at the time of the crash, he had been on the phone, as Abi had already reminded him, and the police might very well take the view that that made him at the very least not entirely blameless, and that they should investigate his version of events rather more closely than they might have done. Of course it had not been dangerous, not in the least, and the moment he had realised the trouble they were in, he had quite literally dropped the phone – but then again, they might not accept his word for that. And maybe – just maybe – it had made him more culpable, had meant his reactions were not as sharp as they should have been. Maybe he'd swerved into the lorry.

Forcing himself to relive the whole thing in painstaking detail, over and over again, he had decided that that, at least, was not even remotely possible; but the police might well not agree. And there would be a lot of close questioning: of Abi as well. He was, in fact, in what was known as a terrible bind.

William was having a difficult day. Another one. The cowman, returned from his day off, had pointed out a couple of cows looking out of sorts. 'Could be bluetongue, let's hope not.'

William agreed they should hope; it was not in the language of farming, with its day-on-day routine of problems, some of them huge – like foot and mouth or TB – some smaller – like mastitis, or the delivery of a sickly calf – to express emotion verbally. When they had had to slaughter their entire herd in 2001, because of foot and mouth, he and his father had agreed that it had been a rough day; when later, he had seen his father, tears rolling down his face, standing in the empty milking parlour, he had clapped his arm round his shoulders and said, 'All right, Dad?' and his father had cleared his throat and said, 'Bad business this, William,' and they had both known exactly how rotten the other felt and seen no need or indeed future in talking about it. If the cows had blue-tongue, it would be pretty disastrous, not least because there was not the same level of financial compensation from the government; but they would survive. They would survive because there was no alternative. All their money, their assets, their entire future was invested in these acres of Gloucestershire. They might own the land, two thousand acres of it, they might be rich on paper, but it was of arguable value to them if farming as an industry failed. The land was unsaleable for any other purpose, unless you counted the government's apparent ambition to turn the countryside in its entirety into some kind of cosy theme park. The only option was to make it work somehow.

And right at the moment, the news was not all bad; farming was having one of its rare ups rather than downs. The price of milk had risen, along with everything else, there were reports of a coming food crisis, of a world shortage of wheat and rice, a higher demand for dairy products, which was improving the outrageous, profit-leeching price of milk – and food prices too were higher than they had been for years. But costs were still great, the price of fuel was eye-watering, and the farm overdraft was still way over the agreed limit.

The argument about bio-fuel crops raged too; hard to plan when any day there could be some completely new set of regulations, and no doubt these would change and change again before anything was finally agreed.

And then they were under siege from the Greens, constantly and rigorously inspected by people who seemed to know almost nothing about the realities of farming, but who would ruthlessly cut subsidies if a new and entirely necessary building entailed cutting down trees or cropping hedges. The government urged them all to diversify; which William was absolutely in favour of, except that diversification inevitably led to more people, more construction, more waste products, more traffic, more noise. Which led to more complaints from the Greens.

And then his parents were very opposed to change. His proposal to jack up the commercial shoot business had fallen on very stony ground; his father loathed seeing what he called the City Boys tramping over his land, in charge of guns many of them were scarcely qualified to use. It was a miracle, he said, none had been injured. And then just before lunch today, hours before he'd been expecting them, his parents had arrived back from their holiday and his father had been heavily critical about the state of the yard and the fact that the cows had not been moved to the other field, despite his instructions; and his mother was full of complaints about the state of the house.

William explained about the crash and the helicopter in the field, which his father had seemed to find rather unsatisfactory, and said he'd move the cows that afternoon. He even managed to apologise to his mother for the mess she had returned to, which he did have to admit was rather bad; washing up piled in the sink, dirty clothes overflowing in the basket, wet washing smelling from not being hung out. But then, when had he had time for all that? He'd been out on the farm from six every day, grabbed some increasingly stale bread and cheese at lunchtime and come in at dusk, to feed himself on some tins from the store cupboard.

'Sorry, Mother. Just been a bit busy.'

'I don't know what you're going to do when I retire,' his father said, as he had at least fifty-two times a year for the past five years. William longed to tell him that his life would be a great deal easier if he could run the farm on his own, using his methods, streamlining costs as he saw fit, instead of it being one huge unworkable compromise. But as far as he could see, his father would never retire; he was sixty-two now, and the farm was still his whole life. There was nothing else that held any interest for him, certainly not the pretty village house that he had bought for himself and his wife nearly three years ago and which had been empty ever since, or a series of trips designed to try to fill their lives, the first of which had clearly been a failure. He knew he should have a serious confrontation with his father on the subject of modernisation, but he was very fond of him, and shrank from pointing out the unpleasant fact that he was growing old and out of touch. William was a gentle creature, hated conflict: and in any case, he knew he wouldn't win.

Time, he told himself without quite believing it, would solve the problem, along with the related one of his living at the age of thirty-four in his parents' house, his domestic life entirely in the care of his mother. It had its bright side, obviously – there was always a meal on the table, and his washing done, but on the other hand, he found being told still to hang up his coat and take his boots off and clean up the bathroom after himself quite trying. He should be married by now, he knew, and he really wished he was, but somehow he'd never found anyone who both knew about farming and who he fancied; and who would put up with living in a house where time had stood more or less still since the 1950s.

And besides, he didn't really have the time to find her . . .

And all through this long, predictably difficult day, he kept returning to the one before. He kept seeing it all, again and again, almost detachedly now, something on television or a film, or even a radio play, for the noises had been as vivid and horrifying as the sights. He remembered feeling the same way about the events of 9/11. He had sat watching the screen, fascinated as much as appalled and actually thinking what a fantastic film it was, how brilliant a notion. But it had been real, of course: and yesterday had been real, the deaths and the pain and the grief and the moment-by-moment awareness of seeing lives wrecked and ruined. He had seen so much and yet so little of the actual crash; from his grandstand view had focused on the lorry, but that had been all. With a gun to his head he could have told no more details, no possible further causes; the police would be requiring a statement, he knew – he was a key witness, given his viewpoint – but he feared he would be a disappointment to them. He felt increasingly distressed by some memories, all still so vivid, the girl in the Golf lifted tenderly out as if that was important, the hideous sight inside the mini-bus; the young father weeping over his dead wife; and comforted by others, by his ability to provide a safe landing for the helicopter, the astonishing gratitude of people when he gave them the water, the easing of the misery of the small boys and the sudden relationship formed with that girl, that tough, brave girl, so gentle with the little boys . . .

He was just washing his hands in the kitchen before sitting down to the scratch meal his mother had organised and which was a great deal better than anything he had eaten for a week, when he saw her mobile lying on the windowsill by the sink; he had left it there the night before, intending to do something about it, but then had gone to sleep in front of the TV and forgotten all about it. He couldn't just keep it; it was probably important to her, and she certainly wouldn't be able to come and get it, she had no real idea where he lived after all, or even what his name was, apart from William. Probably the best thing was to trawl through the numbers, see if he could find one he could ring. Most of the names meant nothing to him; he had looked for 'Mum' and 'Dad' and even 'work' and 'office' and found nothing. And then he saw 'Jonathan' and remembered that was the name of the chap she'd been with. It was a start anyway.

He walked over to the back door and stood looking at the yard, thinking about Abi as he called the number; her amazing legs and her huge dark eyes with all those eyelashes – bit like the cows' eyelashes, he thought, that long and curly – and her dark hair, hanging down her back. She'd been nice, really nice, and very, very sexy; not the sort of girl who'd find him interesting though, and hardly likely to fit into his life.

A woman's voice answered the phone: a pretty, light voice. 'Hello?'

'Oh, good afternoon,' William said. 'I'm very sorry to bother you, but I think you might know someone called Abi . . .'

Chapter 16

Luke was waiting for Emma in the Butler's Wharf Chophouse, just below Tower Bridge. She was late. Unlike her, that – very unlike her. He'd tried her mobile, but it seemed to be dead. He hoped she was OK.

She'd been a bit funny when he'd told her about Milan. He'd been surprised; he'd thought she'd see it as an opportunity, lots of girls would, having a boyfriend working in Milan, with all-expenses-paid trips over there whenever she fancied them. Milan was one of the shopping capitals of the world, for God's sake.

Of course she'd miss him, and he'd miss her. But it was such a brilliant opportunity for him. Look so good on the CV. And there were things like Real Milan and a very cool flat and the car, of course. It wasn't as if they were married or anything, they'd only been together for a few weeks. Well, a couple of months now . . . But then they didn't see that much of each other anyway, with her always being on duty or on call or whatever.

Tricky, women were: even the really cool ones like Emma. But he was planning to make her feel really good later, with what he'd bought her. There was no way she wouldn't be pleased with that . . .

He ordered another Americano, went over and got a paper from the rack by the door. It was the *Daily Mail*; one of his favourites. They told it like it was, the *Mail*, none of this pussyfooting about, being politically correct. If they reckoned some problem was down to too much immigration, or lack of discipline in schools or insufficient funding for the troops, they said so. That bloke Littlejohn, he didn't mince words; Luke would like to shake him by the hand.

The front-page news was rather boring: Afghanistan. Luke had a bit of trouble with foreign affairs. He turned to the inside page and saw a bird's-eye view picture of a pile-up on the motorway. He was about to give that a miss too when he read *almost all the casualties were taken to St Mark's, the new state-of-the-art hospital in Swindon, where medical staff worked tirelessly through the night . . .*

'Blimey,' said Luke, and he started to read intently. It sounded pretty shocking. Lorry through the central reservation, spilled load, at least three dead and many more injured; an elderly widow with a heart attack, a five-mile tailback, a mother-to-be in labour . . .

'Hi, Luke.'

It was Emma – smiling, but pale and tired-looking. She was wearing jeans and a T-shirt, her blond hair scooped rather untidily back, and had no make-up on. It was all rather unlike her, she usually made more effort. Still . . .

'Hi, babe.' He kissed her. 'Come and sit down.'

'Thanks. I'll have one of those, please.' She indicated the coffee.

'I've just been reading about the crash. So that's why you didn't ring me again last night. It was obviously a big one.'

'Yes, it's in lots of the papers.'

'Says here it was the worst this summer. God, Emma . . .' He sat looking at her in silence; she smiled.

'You look rather – impressed.'

'I feel it. Definitely. Yeah. My little Emma, involved in a thing like that. Were you actually, you know, doing things? Operating and so on.'

'Well, of course I was,' she said, taking a large gulp of

coffee. 'What did you think I was doing, reading a magazine?'

'No,' he said. 'No, course not. It just sounds – so bad.'

'It was so bad. It was awful. Lots of casualties, loads of injuries, people's lives wrecked for ever.'

'You know,' he said, 'I often think that, about crashes. Someone takes his eye off the road, just for a second and – that's it. Bloody terrifying.'

'It is. Anyway, sorry not to have rung you.'

'That's all right, babe, I can see why now. You OK?'

'Yes, course. Bit tired.'

'Yeah,' he said. 'You look tired.'

'Thanks,' she said briskly. 'That's exactly what I need to hear.'

'But, you do. You can't help it. I'm sorry for you.'

'Well, good.' She looked at him and the great blue eyes filled with tears; she dashed them away, smiled determinedly at him. 'Sorry. Got to me a bit.'

'Poor you. You always say it doesn't – that it's important you don't let it.'

'Well, I might say that, but I couldn't quite manage it last night. You know, I might like a drink.'

'Course. What d'you fancy?'

'Oh, glass of white wine. I'll just go to the loo. See you in a bit.'

Luke looked after her thoughtfully; she seemed in a very odd state.

'Tell you what,' he said when she came back, 'why don't you go back to the flat, have a kip before tonight. I've got us a table at Alain Ducasse at the Dorchester.' He paused, clearly expecting a reaction; he quite often did that and quite often Emma had no idea why. She did what she always did then, and said, 'Goodness, Luke, that's so amazing.'

'Oh well, you know, just knew the right name . . . Anyway, you want to be able to enjoy that, and I've got something to do this afternoon, thought we could do it together, but I can manage.'

Emma stared at him. Such thoughtfulness was not quite his style. Then she leaned forward and kissed him.

'Oh, Luke,' she said, 'you're so sweet. And you're right, I am very tired. That'd be lovely. I'd really appreciate it. Thank you.'

Talking to Abi had beome a priority – before the police started taking statements. It was no use denying she was in the car, that would be stupid. She'd been there, she'd been seen with him, talking to him, by a dozen or more people, probably been seen getting out of the car even.

But they had to get their story straight. Why they'd been together, and on the M4, what they'd seen, how they thought it might have happened. And Laura was going to have to know: important the story was watertight for her too. He'd been working on it. Abi was just a colleague, from the conference, he'd never met her before, just giving her a lift to – where? Maybe not London, maybe just Reading, somewhere like that.

The last time he'd seen her she'd still been sitting with the little boys. Then she'd vanished. He hadn't really cared – then. He just wanted her removed from anywhere near him, from breathing the same air as him. The same polluted, stinking, hot air. Later he'd begun to worry; wonder who she might have talked to, what she might have said. He'd tried to raise her the night before, had walked down the road away from the house, praying Laura wouldn't see him; it was a risk, he knew, but an essential one. There had been no reply, her phone was clearly switched off. He didn't leave a message: too risky. And again this morning, while he'd been out on his bike; still no reply. It was now 6 p.m. and he was beginning to feel frantic; he had her work number, but she was hardly likely to be there.

Maybe he should email her. She had a laptop in that scruffy little flat of hers, supplied by the office as there was so much weekend work, but someone other than her might see it. Someone like her housemate, Sylvie; he'd met her once, hadn't taken to her at all. She'd looked at him as if she knew precisely what he and Abi were about to be doing. He wouldn't trust her an inch. Just the same, he had to talk to Abi soon . . .

Patrick always said afterwards that the worst thing in a way was not knowing what he could and couldn't remember. Going through the barrier, certainly; calling on God to keep the trailer from jack-knifing – He'd failed him there all right – and then a swirling mass of pain and fear, and a complete inability to move. Something had trapped him, he seemed to be in some kind of a vice, and every time he struggled to get out of it, the pain got worse, like a great beast tearing at him; after a while it seemed better to stay in the vice without struggling. And then, after a long time, there seemed to be people with him, one trying to get at his hand, saying, 'This'll help you, mate, just hold on,' and wondering how his hand could be of any use when his whole body had been rendered useless. And then he had swum off somewhere, where the pain was removed from him, although he could still feel it in some strange way; and then there was a long blank when nothing seemed to happen at all. He remembered some angel smiling down at him, holding his hand, an angel with long blond hair and huge blue eyes; in fact he'd been afraid he'd died, and gone to heaven, and asked her where he was. She'd said he was just going into theatre and he'd wondered why on earth anyone should think he was up to watching a play in the state he was in; after that he couldn't remember anything much at all, and he certainly couldn't have told you how much time had passed, but he seemed to be surfacing somehow into something very uncomfortable – and then as he opened his eyes to see what it looked like, there was Maeve, smiling at him.

'Sweet Jesus,' she said, and, 'No, no, darling,' he said, 'not Jesus, no – it's me, Patrick.' Maeve then burst into tears and Patrick said it was a fine thing that she didn't prefer her own husband, even with all his faults, to Jesus, and then he felt completely exhausted and went back to sleep for quite a long time.

Luke walked down to Tower Bridge Road and hailed a cab. 'Tiffany, Bond Street,' he said. The cabbie grinned at him, as he paid him off.

'Who's the lucky girl then?' he said.

Luke hoped very much that Emma would think she was lucky, would be pleased with what he was going to buy her. He'd studied the catalogue online, settled on something, and then he had thought he and Emma could go and purchase it together that afternoon. And if she didn't like it, then he'd get something else. But having studied it for real, on his own, he couldn't believe she wouldn't absolutely love it.

Russell sat in the lobby at the Dorchester, waiting for his car to arrive. He could hardly believe this was happening, that instead of being in London with Mary, as they had planned, revisiting old half-remembered places, lunching with Mary, then driving out to Bray for dinner at the Waterside Inn with Mary – God, he must cancel the table, it had been booked for weeks, they wouldn't be pleased – he was going back to New York without her. He felt wounded as well as angry, and he wanted the safety and reassurance of home. The more he thought about Mary and what might or might not have happened to her, the more he felt convinced that she had just not tried hard enough to contact him – and that hurt.

He had thought he would stay a day or so in London, looking up old friends, seeing business associates, but that would possibly entail painful explanations as to why he was there, and he simply couldn't face it. He stayed at the Dorchester until lunchtime, still hoping she would contact him, had called her home, several times, but there had been no reply. He left a couple of messages, giving his mobile number, but his phone remained stubbornly silent.

They had brought him *The Times* with his breakfast, but after he had read the front and the City pages, he phoned down and demanded the *Wall Street Journal*. It was the only paper he ever read. The young man who brought it asked him if he would like him to switch the television on, but Russell told him sharply that if he wanted to watch it, he was quite capable of switching it on himself. He hated the way the young patronised their elders over anything to do with technology, assuming they couldn't possibly deal with it.

Russell was an enthusiastic user of technology – of his laptop, his iPod and his iPhone, and he had a state-of-the-art sound system in his apartment. Unlike most of his fellow Americans, however, he was not a television watcher; he hated its banality, its obsession with trivia. He preferred the radio and most of all he loved the BBC World Service. He and Mary had discovered that they both listened to it when they couldn't sleep, and although their nights only partly overlapped, he still liked to think of her lying there, listening to the same voices, the same news reports. It brought her closer . . .

Well, he had obviously been keener on that closeness than she had. Looking at her last letter, combing it for clues, he found largely imaginary ones. *I am really excited, but naturally very nervous, I am sure you can understand that* . . . Clearly the nerves had got the better of her. *Let's hope that nothing will keep us apart* . . . why should it, unless she was half-expecting not to make their meeting. *I do hope reality will not be a nasty shock!* . . . In spite of the exclamation mark, she was clearly genuinely concerned that they would not live up to their youthful selves.

'Your car is here, Mr Mackenzie; and your flight confirmed, leaving at four-thirty.'

He looked at his watch; it was almost one. Very early he'd be, too early indeed, but he was used to that. He was obsessive about time. Mary had always been very punctual too. *Stop thinking about her, Mackenzie, you just lost her for the second time.* Once to another man, and now probably to some misguided sense of loyalty to him.

The journey, once they were on the M4 extension was swift. 'Bit different from yesterday, sir,' the driver said. 'Shocking, this road – in both directions. Traffic held up for hours, it was. I gave up, just went home. There was no way you could get through.'

'Really?' said Russell, getting his iPod out of his attaché case and rather ostentatiously fitting the speakers into his ears. He had no intention of getting involved in a conversation about traffic, for God's sake.

He checked in, went to duty free and bought himself a couple more books and then moved up to the First Class lounge. The girl at the desk smiled at him.

'Nice to see you again, Mr Mackenzie. Do go through. One of the stewards will fetch you a drink.'

'I'll have a coffee. I'm going to check on my emails.'

'Certainly, Mr Mackenzie.'

He walked through the seating area, passing the TV screens on his way. As he did so, he half-heard something about an accident the day before and that someone or other was still in Intensive Care. Ignoring it, he moved into the computer area and called up his emails. There were three: two from his secretary, one from a colleague. He'd tried very hard to persuade Mary to have email, but she'd resisted. 'I like getting letters,' she said, 'and if it's urgent you can telephone me.'

A steward appeared with a tray. 'Your coffee, Mr Mackenzie. And there's a thirty-minute delay on your flight, I'm sorry.'

An hour passed while he wrote emails and looked at the online edition of the *Journal*; then he decided to get a whisky. That might help. He walked out to the bar; they had only one whisky, and that was a blend.

'I'm not drinking that rubbish,' he said. 'I want a single malt. What is this – Economy or something?'

'I'm sorry, sir, I could try—'

'No, no, just give me a Club Soda.'

He went and sat down near the screens, so that he could see the latest on his flight. No further delays; they should be in the air in thirty minutes. And he could shake the soil of bloody England off his feet. He should never have come back, never.

He couldn't settle now to his book; he picked up a paper that was lying on the table in front of him, flicked through it. Usual Saturday rubbish, too many articles, not enough news; there was something about gridlock on motorways: that was what he liked about the *Journal*, it was just about the stuff that mattered. He threw it down again, pulled one of the new books he had bought out of his flight bag. Patricia Cornwell, now she knew how to tell a good story . . . Mary didn't like her. The only crime novels she enjoyed were by Agatha Christie.

Not too much gore, she had written. *Why make life more unpleasant than it need be?* Why indeed, Mary?

The flight was called. He walked to the departure bay slowly; there seemed to be yet another delay of some kind.

'For God's sake, what is the matter with this airline?'

'Sorry, Mr Mackenzie. If you just wait over there, shouldn't be more than a few minutes.'

He sat down, sighed heavily. This was what he hated most about flying, sitting helplessly, life at least temporarily out of his control.

The man sitting next to him was reading a newspaper; he had it fully open, knocked Russell's arm as he tried to fold it over.

'Sorry, mate.'

Russell looked at him coldly; he was blasted if he was going to say it was all right. It wasn't.

The man turned to his companion, a pasty overweight creature in a tracksuit.

'Shocking thing, that crash yesterday,' he said. 'Thank God we wasn't trying to get a flight last night. Says here there was a jam for seven miles, both directions. Hundreds of people missed their planes.'

She leaned over to look at the paper. 'Look at that,' she said. 'What a mess. Blimey. Three people killed . . . oh, and that is so sad, someone lost their dog.'

Russell glared at them both and stood up. All anyone seemed to be interested in today were car crashes.

'Would Rows A to G please commence boarding immediately. First and Club Class passengers may also board at their convenience.'

Better check his phone for the last time; not that there was anyone he wanted to hear from.

There was one message on it. Left that day, half an hour earlier. A number he didn't recognise.

Hello, is that Mr Mackenzie? It was an English voice. *Mr Mackenzie, you don't know me, but you left a message on my mother's answering machine. Mrs Mary Bristow. I'm afraid she's in hospital – she was involved in a traffic accident yesterday. We only heard ourselves quite late last night. Anyway, if you want to ring me back, my number is . . .*

A series of clicks went off in Russell's brain. *Hold-ups for miles in both directions . . . serious traffic accident . . .*

in Intensive Care . . . hundreds missed their flights . . .

'Oh, no!' he said aloud. 'Oh God, no.'

So there had been a reason: a perfectly good reason. And he had been too blind, too self-centred to try to find it. And Mary, his little Mary, was lying in a hospital, possibly dangerously ill.

Russell stood up, half-ran to the desk. 'I'm not going,' he said. 'You can check me off that flight. I have to stay.'

'But Mr Mackenzie, we can't—'

'You can and you will,' he said, 'and quickly, if you please. I'm in one hell of a hurry.'

Georgia was pushing some cold chicken round her plate when the phone rang. Her mother answered it.

'Hello? Oh, hello, Linda. Fine, thank you. Yes, she's here. I'll get her to the phone.'

Georgia made frantic *no* faces at her mother; she took no notice.

'Georgia, it's Linda. She wants to talk to you.'

'I – I can't.' She really couldn't sit here, with her mother listening, having the sort of conversation that Linda would insist on.

'Georgia, come along, dear. She's ringing from London.'

Bea Linley was of the generation and mindset that still worried about the cost of long-distance calls.

'Mum, I said I can't talk to her.'

'Well, you must. I've said you're here, so it would look very rude – and anyway, she might have news of that part. Maybe you passed your audition after all, you never know.'

'Look, I'll ring her back on my mobile. In a minute. She won't mind.'

'Well . . .'

'Please see she does,' said Linda, when this was relayed to her. 'It's important.'

'Yes, of course I will. I'm so sorry.' Bea put the phone down, glared at Georgia. 'Linda works so hard on your behalf, she deserves better than that. Now go and ring her back at once. I'm ashamed of you, I really am.'

'Oh stop it.' Georgia was half-shouting, her eyes filled with tears. 'I told you I didn't want to talk to anyone. I just want to be left alone!' And she walked out of the room, slamming the door after her.

Abi's flat was in Montpelier, a rather unlovely part of Bristol; she'd bought it eighteen months earlier, on the strength of her new job. She loved it; it was in a small purpose-built block, had two bedrooms – the smaller of which was let to her best friend Sylvie, to help pay the mortgage – a very cool galley kitchen with white cupboards and black work surfaces, a living room with floor-to-ceiling windows and a bathroom which, as Sylvie said, was too small to swing a kitten in, and certainly could not accommodate a bath, but which served its purpose perfectly adequately.

Abi was intensely proud of her flat. She still, a year later, would stand smiling in the hallway when she got home, finding it hard to believe that she actually owned a property. It was certainly more than her mother ever had. She had furnished it slowly, through the year, refusing to put any old rubbish in it that she didn't like; the Bristol branch of Ikea had served her well. The room she was most proud of was the living room, with its white blinds, white carpet – no one was allowed in with their shoes on, Jonathan hadn't liked that at all, on his one visit – and two black corner sofas. She'd talked a photographer mate into giving her a very nice set of black and white prints of pictures he'd taken in New York, and had them framed cut price by one of the suppliers at work; it all looked seriously classy. Her latest acquisition was a plasma TV, not too huge – it would spoil the black and white decor, she thought – but big enough to feel you weren't missing anything watching a film on DVD rather than in the cinema.

She was actually sitting and watching *Notting Hill* for the umpteenth time, having got back from the gym exhausted but feeling slightly better and wondering if she could face any lunch, when she decided to ring her phone just once more.

'Hello,' said a voice.

'Oh,' she said, and she was so pleased to hear it that she almost burst into tears. 'Oh my God, it's William, isn't it?'

'Yes, it is. And that's Abi? I was hoping you'd ring.'

'So – you've got my phone?'

'Yes, it's here, quite safe. You gave it to me to hold yesterday. I'd put it down and forgotten all about it. I've only just switched it on.'

'Fantastic. Thanks a lot. I was beginning to give up hope, thought I must have dropped it on the road or something. It was such a terrible day, and—'

'Certainly was. How are you feeling?'

'Oh, you know. Bit out of it. Look – could I come and get it, do you think? I'm really missing it.'

'I think I ought to bring it back to you, actually. Given that I walked off with it.'

'No, you didn't. I walked off without it. Anyway, I haven't got anything to do this afternoon and you probably have.'

'Well, just a bit.'

'Tell me where you are, and I'll drive over.'

'Hello, Linda.'

'Hello, Georgia. How are you?'

'OK. Why shouldn't I be?'

'Well, I could be forgiven for wondering, don't you think? First I have to change the time of your audition, then I wait for hours for you to arrive, and you don't return any of my calls. Then I hear that you're back at home and you've told your mother you didn't get the part. What's going on?'

'Nothing's going on.'

'So why didn't you go to the audition?'

A silence, then: 'I just lost my nerve. I was scared, OK? Really scared. I'm sorry, Linda. Very sorry.'

'What were you scared of? You've done auditions before.'

'Yes, I know I have. And I know they're bloody scary, OK? I got stage fright.'

'They're very disappointed. They really thought you'd be ideal.'

'Yeah? Well, they'll have to get over it.'

'That is an extraordinarily stupid attitude, Georgia. Not the way to get on.'

'Maybe I don't want to get on.'

'In that case, you won't be needing me any longer.' Linda struggled to keep her temper. 'This kind of thing does me no good at all. I mean that, Georgia. If you're not worried about your future, I'm certainly worried about mine.'

'Yes.' The voice had changed, become more subdued. 'Yes, I know. I'm sorry, Linda.'

'Well, look. When you feel ready to talk about it some more, call me.'

'Yes, OK.'

Another silence. It was tempting to just put the phone down, but Linda was fond enough of Georgia and worried enough about her not to.

'There were several articles in the papers today about the crash on the M4,' she said.

Georgia swallowed. 'Oh really?'

'Yes. It sounded very bad. Several people were killed, and some poor lorry driver is in Intensive Care.'

'Oh. Yes, I see.' A silence. 'But – is he all right? Did it say?' Her voice shook slightly.

'He's alive. But not very well.'

'Did it – did it give his name?'

'No, they never do until they're sure the close relatives have been informed. Why?'

'Oh, no reason,' Georgia said uncertainly. 'Did it – did it say what caused the crash?'

'No. The police are still investigating it. So – you didn't see anything of it at all, then?'

'No. No, of course I didn't. I told you I didn't. Why are you asking me all this? Just leave me alone, Linda, will you? Please!'

It hadn't been easy to find Paget's Farm; William's directions had been a bit random, she was hopeless at reading maps and because she didn't have a proper address for him she couldn't use her Satnav. In the end, Abi found herself driving through the scene of the accident and then turning back on herself, via the next junction. That had been hideous. The crash barrier was still broken, the central reservation ploughed up; there were areas taped off on both sides of the road, a lane closed, police cars parked on the hard shoulder and several men, two in uniform, studying photographs. A sense of déjà vu flooded Abi; she went back there, in that moment, to the noise and the chaos, the broken cars, the crumpled mini-bus, people shouting and groaning, children crying. It carried the memory, that stretch of road, across time and physical fact, rather as a battlefield does.

When she reached the turn-off, she pulled onto the grass verge at the top of it, and sat there, her arms resting on her steering-wheel, her head buried in them, wondering how she was going to live with that memory for the rest of her life.

There was a sharp tap on her window; she looked up and saw a policeman staring in at her and thought, Shit, they've recognised me, the girl shouting at the man with the phone, distracting him, making him skid; and she opened the window, looked up at him with absolute dread, expecting accusation, arrest even. But, 'You all right, madam?' he said, and, 'Yes, thank you,' she replied, hardly able to get the words out for the terror in her throat. 'Just feeling a bit queasy. It's the heat, I expect,' and was amazed to find she could actually move her face into something resembling a smile.

'Shouldn't really stop here, you know,' he said. 'Move on as soon as you feel you can. Need any medical help?'

'Oh, no, thank you, I'm fine really. Like I say, it's the heat, that's all.'

She drove on, missed the turning William had instructed her to take, and found herself in a village, where she stopped an old chap who was wandering down the street looking at the paper. He was able to direct her, with amazing ease, to the Graingers' farm. 'Paget's is just after the church, take a left, looks like a track and go up to the end and there it'll be straight in front of you.'

And there indeed it was, settled just slightly down from the track, quite a big square-ish house, with a yard to the left of it and several cars parked, most of them old, including a totally dilapidated pick-up truck, one newish-looking Land Rover and a couple of tractors. Abi parked her car next to the Land Rover and knocked on the door.

William was in the milking parlour, his mother said, adding graciously that Abi could wait if she liked, or go up there; she didn't know how long he'd be. As Abi hadn't the faintest idea where the milking parlour was, or indeed what it was – it sounded like something in a cartoon, with all the cows lounging around on sofas – she decided on the waiting.

She'd dressed quite carefully for the occasion in jeans and a T-shirt and some new red Converse trainers; she didn't want William to think she was some towny airhead, tottering through his farmyard in three-inch heels. She smiled at Mrs Grainger, who managed what might have passed for a smile in return, something rather pinched and brief; she was not in the least what Abi would have expected William's mother to be like, not a cosy lady in a cotton pinny, making bread, but a rather smart, upper-crust woman with grey, well-cut hair, wearing dated but clearly expensive trousers, a check shirt and a pair of brown leather loafers.

'Would you like to sit down?' she said.

'Yes, thank you, that would be very nice,' said Abi carefully.

'Come through to the drawing room.' She led Abi down the hall and into a rather dark room, lined with books and paintings, and gestured towards a sofa. 'Do sit down. Can I offer you something, a sherry perhaps?'

Abi shook her head. 'No, I'm fine, thanks. I'll just wait.'

'Yes, well as I say, he could be back in ten minutes, it could be an hour. My husband is over there with him.'

Abi couldn't quite see the relevance of this, but she smiled politely and sat down where she was told. She folded her hands in her lap in what she hoped was a ladylike manner and smiled apologetically at Mrs Grainger.

'I'm so sorry if I'm being a nuisance,' she said.

'You're not, of course. But you must excuse me. We've been away and there's rather a lot to do.'

When she had gone, Abi stood up and wandered round the room; the walls were covered in extremely old and faded brocade paper, the carpet was not a proper fitted one, but a sort of very large rug, set down on flagstones, and threadbare in places. What looked like the remnants of about a hundred fires, a vast heap of ash and burned-out logs, lay in the grate, and there were no curtains at the rather tall windows, just wooden shutters.

The furniture was very old and seemed to Abi rather mismatched: a round polished table in quite a light colour, and then a chest so dark it was almost black. There were two deeply comfortable-looking armchairs but the sofa was stiff and button-backed. Several portraits hung on the walls, mostly of men and clearly going back a century or two, although there were two of women, both pretty, one in a low-waisted narrow ankle-length dress, and one in what looked like an elaborate nightie. The one in the nightie was painted against a rather romantic parkland background, the other was standing in front of a fireplace – the fireplace in this very room, Abi realised. She wondered if they were William's ancestors. Somehow the sweet-faced, untidy bloke she had met yesterday didn't seem to fit in here.

She looked out of the window now; as far as she could see were fields, and hills and trees. She wondered if it all belonged to the Graingers and decided if it did, they must be very rich. If her boss knew, he'd be having kittens; he was always saying they should try getting in with the hunt ball lot.

She sat down again and started flicking through some copies of *Country Life* magazine lying on a table; they amused her for about five minutes at most, and then she put them down and went back to the window. There was nothing else to read, except some books. Abi was not much into books, and certainly not ones entitled *Famous Horses of the British Turf*, or *The Stud Book*. There were literally dozens of them, going right back to the nineteenth century.

After about twenty minutes, she got very bored, and purely by way of a diversion, decided to go in search of a loo. As she crossed the hall, looking tentatively at the doors, Mrs Grainger appeared.

'Can I help you?' she said.

'I was wondering if I could use your toilet,' said Abi apologetically. A slightly pained expression settled on Mrs Grainger's face.

'Of course. Follow me.'

She led the way upstairs and across a landing, then: 'The lavatory is there,' she said, pointing down a corridor and emphasising the word rather pointedly. Silly cow, Abi thought. The walls of the loo were covered with photographs of Mrs Grainger and a man who was clearly Mr Grainger, and occasionally of William, presenting cups to people holding cows – very large cows, maybe they were bulls – or equally massive pigs, and occasionally standing by horses.

There was even a press cutting, which had been framed, showing the Graingers standing at the front of their house surrounded by a pack of hounds and some huntsmen on horseback, Mrs Grainger holding a silver tray covered with small glasses, offering it up to one of the riders. *The Hon Mrs Peter Grainger serves punch at the Boxing Day Meet at Paget's Farm* the caption read. Abi felt reluctantly impressed. She'd not met many Hons.

Back downstairs, as she crossed the hall again, William appeared. He was filthy – his face grimy and sweat-studded, his hair awry with shoots of grass in it, and as an extra accessory, an enormous cobweb slung from one of his ears to his shoulder. Abi smiled and then, as she studied him, giggled slightly.

'Hello,' he said. 'Sorry, I didn't realise you'd arrived.' And then, as she continued to smile at him, he added, 'What's so funny?'

'Oh, nothing. Sorry. You've got . . . Here, let me.' She stepped forward, reached up and pulled the cobweb from his ear. As she did so, Mrs Grainger appeared again; from her expression, a casual observer might have assumed she had caught Abi flashing her breasts at her son.

'Ah,' she said, 'you found the lavatory.'

'Yes, it was – it was very nice, thank you,' Abi said – and then, aware of how absurd she must sound, she giggled again. This was turning into a farce.

'Well, it's very good to see you,' William said, smiling his amazing, life-changing smile.

Abi smiled back and thought how wonderful it was to see him, and then – driven by some compulsion entirely outside her control – she reached forward and kissed him on the cheek.

'I'm not sure my mother knew what to make of that,' he said, handing Abi the large gin and tonic she had asked for in the pub. 'You kissing me.'

'Yes, I'm sorry,' she said, 'really sorry, William. I don't quite know what came over me. It's been such a sh— horrible day, two days, and then suddenly there you were and everything seemed so much better and I just wanted to let you know that. Sorry.'

'No, no, don't apologise,' he said. 'It's fine – doesn't matter if she liked it or not. I certainly did.' He indicated the drink. 'That all right for you? Got enough ice?'

'Oh yes, thank you. Plenty. It's very nice.'

'Good.' He took several large gulps of beer and then set the glass down again. 'That's better. Bad day for me too. Lost a calf this afternoon.'

'Oh no,' said Abi. 'Where? Should we go and look for it?' and then felt stupid when he said, half-laughing, 'Not lost like that. She was born dead – breech, got the cord round her neck. Dad and I were tugging for over an hour, but she came out limp as you like, and we couldn't get more than two breaths out of her. Heifer calf too, much more of a loss.'

'Oh, I'm sorry,' said Abi.

'Yeah, well, it happens. Then we couldn't get the old tractor started. That's how I got so filthy, rummaging in the barn for a jump lead – and Dad, he tends to take it out on me, that sort of thing.'

'Yes, I see.'

'So it was really good to find you there and to have something to take my mind off all that stuff. How were my directions?'

'Rubbish,' she said, grinning and then, rummaging for her cigarettes: 'Could we go outside? I really need one of these.'

'Course. Want another drink?'

'Oh, no thank you. I have to drive back. I'll be causing another—'

'Another what?'

'Accident. I felt really, really bad on the road again down there. I—'

'I know what you mean. Bit heavy, wasn't it? Come on, let's go outside. Want some orange juice or something?'

He came out with the orange juice, and another pint for himself; she smoked a cigarette and then another.

'Sure you won't have one?'

'No,' he said. 'I never got the hang of them. I did try to like them once, when I was at college, but they just made me feel sick.'

'Oh I see,' she said. 'And where was college?'

'Cirencester,' he said, clearly expecting her to know what Cirencester was, and even half-surprised she had asked. 'I went there straight from school.'

'And where was school?'

'Eton,' he said, with much the same intonation. Abi decided it was time to go.

As she dropped him off at the bottom of the track, he said, 'Thanks for coming. Very good of you. I should have come to meet you halfway. It's terrible when you lose your phone, isn't it? I'm always doing it, and I don't suppose mine's nearly as important as yours. I did ring a number on yours, by the way, but whoever answered it wasn't very helpful.'

'And who was that?' asked Abi, thinking she must reprimand Sylvie, or whoever it was he had spoken to, for not telling her.

'Oh – that chap you were at the crash with. Jonathan. I

scrolled through looking for a name I might recognise, and saw his.'

The evening seemed to have got even hotter.

'And?'

'Well, I didn't get him, I got a woman. His wife maybe? I tried to explain, said I'd been at the crash, and that you'd given it to me while you saw to some kids. I asked her if her husband was a doctor, just to satisfy myself I'd got the right bloke. Anyway, she just rang off – very abrupt she was.'

'Oh, really?' said Abi. 'I wonder why . . .'

Chapter 17

Jonathan was drifting in and out of a painful, dehydrated sleep when Laura came in and sat down on the bed.

'How are you, darling?'

'Oh, bit better. I'm so sorry, Laura. Embarrassing you like that.'

'It's all right. You've had such a terrible time. I just felt very sorry for you.'

'Oh, darling.' He reached out, took her hand. 'I'm so lucky to have you.'

'I'm glad you think so.' She drew her hand away after a moment, pushed her hair back. Her voice was as sweet as usual, but there was something odd about it. He couldn't quite work out what.

'Would you like anything? Some more water, camomile tea, something like that?'

Jonathan shuddered. Apart from an automatic distaste for anything as close to a folk remedy as camomile tea, he could only contemplate water.

'Water, please. With ice in.'

She came back with a big jug, set it down, smiled at him again.

'Kids all right? Not too ashamed of their father?'

'Don't think so. You mustn't worry about it.'

'Well, it was pretty – unattractive.'

She was silent, then shrugged. She didn't often shrug; it was distant, cool – unlike her. A tiny spiral of something – not fear, more unease – began to work its way into

Jonathan's stomach. He shifted in the bed.

'Jonathan,' she said after a pause, 'can you tell me just one thing?'

'Yes, of course.'

'I still don't understand why you were on the M4, not the M40.'

'Oh,' he said, and was astonished at the ease with which the lie came out. 'Cutting down there can actually be quite a good idea on a Friday afternoon. Rather than sticking on the M40, which is a horrible road – I hate it. Always get a build-up of traffic towards the M25. So it didn't seem as silly as it sounds.'

'It actually does sound quite silly,' she said. She had a strand of hair she was winding round her finger, round and round, endlessly, her eyes fixed on his face. It was disconcerting; he felt the spiral move again.

'I know. And of course it was a big mistake. As it turned out.'

'Yes. It certainly was. But – all's well that ends well, I suppose. For you anyway. I'll leave you in peace, darling. See you later.'

She left the room, closed the door behind her. Jonathan sat sipping the water. He suddenly felt very frightened indeed. He absolutely must speak to Abi, and as soon as possible.

'Jonathan?'

'Oh, hi.' That was all. No 'How are you?' No 'Are you all right?'

'Jonathan, we need to talk.'

'It's good to hear from you, but I'm a bit tied up at the moment. I'll call you back later. Everything OK with you?'

Obviously *she* was there; there or near. Abi couldn't believe how calm and normal he sounded. Well, he was a devious bugger. They wouldn't be in this situation otherwise.

'Yes, fine,' she said, 'but—'

'Terrific. I'll speak to you first thing in the morning if that's all right with you? Or later this evening, maybe?'

'Either.'

'Right, I'll see what I can do. We can discuss the prognosis then.'

'The what?'

'Yes, absolutely. Well, thanks for ringing. Bye now.'

It was clearly not the occasion to tell him that William had spoken to Laura. Pity. For all sorts of reasons. Not least that she was really rather looking forward to it.

'Mrs Connell? Hello. Your husband is doing very well, you know. Very well indeed, holding his own magnificently.' It was Dr Pritchard again. Maeve managed somehow to smile at him. 'Now, Staff Nurse says she thinks you should go home for twenty-four hours and I agree with her. You look completely exhausted. He'll be fine, I promise. He's in very good hands, you know.'

'Yes, of course,' said Maeve, 'I do know that. But—'

'Got a car here?'

'No. My friend brought me in yesterday and she's gone home now, obviously. My mother's coming tomorrow, so I could maybe go home with her.'

'How about the train?'

She hesitated, and then started to cry. She hadn't cried before, not once, but somehow these minor problems of getting home, not being able to afford the train, seemed to be defeating her.

'The thing is, I haven't got – got much money – on me. That is . . .'

He looked at her in silence for a moment, as if he was absorbing all these things without having to be told, and then said, 'Mrs Connell – Maeve – do you mind if I call you Maeve?'

She shook her head helplessly.

256

'Maeve, I've got to pop out for half an hour, go into town, so I'll take you to the station if you like. And if you're short of cash, I can lend you twenty quid, if that would help.'

'I couldn't possibly.'

'Now why ever not? You're not going to do a runner with it, are you? You can pay me back tomorrow or whenever it is you next see me. Come on now, dry your eyes and I'll be back for you in about ten minutes. Don't argue – I insist. And don't worry about your husband. He's not very well, of course, but he's more or less off the danger list and it's safe for you to take a breather.'

Jack Bryant settled into a wonderfully comfortable, battered old chair in what Hughie Argyll called his study, but which would have contained most of his Fulham flat. It was a glorious evening; the view of the moors was ravishing, the colours just turning autumnal. He was clearly in for a very good few days.

'Another gin?' Hughie picked up the bottle, waved it at him. He was one of Jack's oldest friends; they'd had a hell of a time together in the sixties, Annabel's and a different dolly bird every night, and he'd taught Jack to shoot as well. Good chap.

Jack grinned, held out his glass. 'Yes, thanks.'

'You must be tired. Hell of a drive, even in that car of yours.'

'It was fine. Enjoyed it. Lovely to give the old girl a bit of a run. And of course I stopped in York last night.'

'Yes. Well, lovely to have you here. I think I can promise you some good sport tomorrow. We got three hundred today.'

'Fantastic. Can't wait.'

'You didn't get caught up in that crash yesterday then, on the M4? We thought it might have delayed you.'

'No, bloody lucky. Must have missed it by inches.'

'Really?'

'Yes. I read it was at four p.m. I can't have been clear of that spot by more than five minutes. If that.'

'Christ. You must have a guardian angel of some sort.'

'Doubt it. Anything angelic gave up on me years ago, as you know. But it sounds ghastly.'

'You didn't even see anything of it?'

'No, nothing.'

'Good. Well, I'll leave you to get settled in. Expect you'd like a bath before dinner. No rush, down here for drinks at seven-thirty. Margo's dying to see you.'

Luke grinned at Emma. 'You look great, babe. I really like the dress.'

She'd known he would; it was black, low-cut, very short, not a lot of it at all really. What she thought of as a bloke's dress. They were in another cab now, on their way to the restaurant. Her sleep had done her good, she felt relaxed and happy. And pretty sexy too, actually.

He gave her a kiss; he was wearing a great shirt, collarless linen, blue and white stripes, a beige linen suit and those new-style trainers. He was so cool; and really really good looking. And so sweet.

A uniformed doorman was standing outside the Dorchester. He whisked open the taxi door, stood respectfully aside while they got out. 'Good evening, madam, good evening, sir.'

Now this was what posh places should be like, Emma thought. Those cool bars were all very well, but if you were going to spend loads of money, you surely wanted a bit of service. She smiled happily at Luke, allowed the doorman to usher them through the revolving door, stood looking round the lobby. It looked wonderfully luxurious, huge urns of flowers, deep sofas, smiling staff everywhere.

'The restaurant, please,' Luke was saying. 'Alain Ducasse.'

'Certainly, sir. This way, please.'

'Luke!' hissed Emma. 'I just want to go to the loo, OK?' She had a rather weak bladder; it alternately amused and irritated Luke. Tonight was definitely irritation.

'Sorry. You go on. I'll follow in a minute.'

'Oh, OK. Yes. Good idea.'

She went into the Ladies, which was extremely luxurious. A woman was waiting by the basin when she came out, holding a towel. She stood patiently while Emma washed her hands, then handed it to her; and then took it and threw it into a basket. Clearly in Dorchester country, you didn't do much for yourself. Emma half-expected her to come and help her comb her hair and put her lip gloss on for her.

She walked back into the lobby, looked around for someone to tell her where the restaurant was, and then heard – or thought she heard – the words 'St Mark's Hospital, Swindon', spoken in an American accent.

She must have imagined it. Must have. She must relax, stop obsessing over the day before.

But then: 'Yes. On – let me see – yes, Agatha Ward. Can you confirm they'll arrive first thing in the morning? I'll wait.'

No, this was for real.

He stood there, tapping his fingers on the concierge's desk; a tall white-haired man, with Paul Newman blue eyes and a neat white moustache, clearly quite elderly, but standing ramrod straight and wearing a suit that looked as if it had only just left the tailor's.

The girl at the desk looked up at him from her phone. 'Yes, that's all fine, Mr Mackenzie.'

'Good, good. And I'll want a car to take me there, to visit my friend, first thing. As early as possible. I'd like to be there by . . . let me see, nine o'clock.'

This was too much for Emma; she walked over to the desk.

'Do forgive me for interfering,' she said, 'but I couldn't help hearing what you said, and it's the most amazing coincidence. I'm a doctor at St Mark's. I'm really sorry, but you won't be allowed in at nine. Ten-thirty is the earliest, and it really isn't the nicest place to be hanging around.'

The man looked at her; at first she thought he was going to be cross. Then he smiled, a slow, sweet smile.

'That is so extremely good of you,' he said, 'and I will indeed forgive you for interfering. Thank you so much. Make that an hour and a half later then,' he said to the desk and then, turning away, taking Emma's arm, he said, 'I wonder if you'd be kind enough to give me news of a patient there. A Mrs Mary Bristow. She was involved in the crash on the freeway yesterday.'

Clearly he moved in a world where hospitals were small and exclusive, Emma thought, and where any doctor would recognise any patient's name.

'I'm sorry,' she said, 'but there are around fifteen hundred patients in St Mark's at any given time.'

'Fifteen hundred! My God!'

'Yes, it's a very big hospital. But a very good one. I was on duty in A and E yesterday, when people were arriving. I'm afraid I don't remember a Mrs Bristow. Was she an elderly lady?'

'A little elderly,' he said with another sweet smile. 'May I say, incidentally, you don't look old enough to be a doctor.'

Emma smiled back. 'Well, trust me, I am. Anyway, I assume, since you're going to see her tomorrow, that Mrs Bristow isn't too seriously ill?'

'Well, you know, I don't believe so. They didn't tell me much, when I phoned, except that she was comfortable.'

'And that you could go and see her?'

'Oh yes. And her daughter, I spoke to her, she said she didn't seem too bad. But I don't suppose you could get any more details for me? Now, I mean. I really am most concerned.'

'Well . . .' Emma hesitated, then thought that really he was extremely charming and it would be nice to help him. 'I – I'll see what I can do. Only – well, I'm supposed to be having dinner with my boyfriend.'

'Oh, my dear young lady, the last thing I would want to do is stand in the path of true love. Forget it, I'm sure she's absolutely fine.'

'No, no, it's perfectly all right. I'll just go and tell him, and then I'll call them, OK? Could you possibly show me the way to the restaurant,' she said to the girl behind the desk. 'Oh no, it's all right, here's my boyfriend now.'

Luke was put out and more so when Emma said she'd be five more minutes. Even when she explained.

'I didn't realise you were on call,' he said irritably.

'Luke . . .'

The old gentleman stepped forward, held out his hand to Luke. 'Russell Mackenzie. I am so very sorry to intrude on your evening, but I am extremely worried about a friend in hospital and this enchanting young lady of yours has offered to help.'

'Fine,' said Luke, slightly grudgingly. 'I'll be at the table, Emma.'

'Oh dear,' said Russell Mackenzie. 'I'm afraid he's a little annoyed.'

'He'll get over it,' said Emma. 'He's very good-natured. Now then, let's see what we can do. I can't promise anything, but . . .'

Five minutes later she smiled at Russell. 'She's fine. Well, much much better. She has angina, apparently –'

'Yes, she does.'

'– and had an attack at the scene of the crash. They did an exploratory investigation under anaesthetic, put a catheter into her heart. They thought she'd probably had a minor heart attack, but she's doing well now. And yes, you can see her tomorrow.'

'I cannot thank you enough,' said Russell, 'and now

261

you'd better get along to that young man of yours. That fortunate young man.'

'OK,' said Jonathan, 'this is what we say. I've got it all worked out. Our relationship is purely professional, you're just a colleague.'

'A colleague? How could I be a colleague? I'm not a doctor.' She was standing at her bedroom window, looking out; she saw Sylvie coming along the street, went over and shut the door, stood leaning against it in case she came in.

'Of course you're not a doctor. Don't be ridiculous. You take photographs at conferences. Or rather your boss does. So you were there at the conference in Birmingham. You came up by train from Bristol that morning.'

'Jonathan, one tiny problem. They can check that.'

'Why the fuck should they want to check it? There's no reason for them not to believe us, it's got nothing to do with the accident. All they'll want to know is what we saw, and not why we were there together. It's irrelevant. Just keep telling them that. I was giving you a lift to London, or maybe not London, possibly Reading – what do you think?'

'Whatever,' said Abi. She felt close to tears, without being sure why.

'OK, Reading then. Don't forget.'

'What was I going to Reading for?'

'Well, to visit friends. For the weekend.'

'Jonathan, this is getting so complicated. Do we have to do this? You don't think it might be better to tell the truth?'

'Abi, no. For Christ's sake. Do you want to—' He stopped suddenly.

'Do I want to what, Jonathan? Oh, I get it. This is about your marriage, isn't it? About being caught with your pants down – literally.'

'I – to a degree, yes. Of course. I don't want Laura hurt.'

'Maybe you should have thought of that earlier.'

'Oh Christ.' She could almost hear him struggling to

keep calm. 'Abi, please – look, we're far more likely to get into trouble over this if there was any indication that we were having an affair.'

'I don't see why we should get into trouble at all. We weren't doing anything wrong – except that you were on the phone, of course.' She couldn't resist that.

'Yes – well, hopefully that won't come to light.' His voice was very cold. 'I would say there's no need to actually mention it. Unless they ask, of course. Would you agree with me?'

'You mean will I go along with you on it? I'm not sure. Why should I lie to the police on your behalf?'

'I'm not asking you to lie, simply not to mention it.' She didn't answer. She could almost hear him sweating. It was very, very pleasant.

'Abi?' he said.

'Yes?'

'Can I have your agreement to that?'

'Let's see what happens, shall we?'

'No. I need to know that you agree.'

'I don't see why. If they ask, they ask. Look, you were in no way responsible for that crash, Jonathan. We both saw what happened. The lorry went into a skid, it couldn't stop, went through the barrier.'

'Of course.'

'Well then. We just happened to be there. We didn't hit anything. Or cause anyone to hit anything.'

'No. We didn't.'

'And then you did your Dr Wonderful act. What's for them to be suspicious about?'

'Nothing. It's just that . . . well, it is a bit of a blur, and I can't help feeling anxious about it, I'm not sure why. I'm glad you don't.'

'No,' she said, aware that she was not being strictly truthful, 'I don't. And I really don't like the idea of lying to the police.'

There was a very long silence; then he said, 'I need you to do this, Abi.'

'So you said. I, on the other hand, don't need to do it. Funny, that.'

Another shorter silence. She'd got him now, got him shitting himself.

Then: 'Abi, I think you do need to do it. Actually.'

'Oh, why?'

'Because I don't think you'd want the police to know about your little habit, do you?'

She felt the floor literally heave under her. She closed her eyes, put her hand out to steady herself. He couldn't have said that; he couldn't.

'What?' she said, and the voice wasn't hers; it was weak and shaky.

'You heard. You love your bit of – what do you call it – charlie? Don't you, Abi? It is an offence to possess it, as I'm sure you know. And if they think you might be passing it on, making money, that's still more of an offence. A woman at the hospital was arrested last week; they found a nice little hoard in her flat – reckoned all her jewellery and most of her furniture had been bought with the proceeds.'

Abi struggled to stay calm. It was very difficult. She had a friend who'd got caught with drugs in her flat; she'd received a suspended sentence and a big fine. She'd lose her job, she might even go to prison, she—

'I can't believe you're saying this,' she said, amazed that her voice sounded so steady; 'or thinking it even. Anyway, I seem to remember you enjoying the odd snort.'

'You might have trouble proving that. You provided it – rather visibly, I seem to remember, on one or two occasions. And who do you think they'd believe, you or me?'

She threw her head back, stared at the ceiling, tears stinging her eyes – as much from shock as fear. This was a man who'd told her he cared about her, who'd sought her out, said she was one of the best things in his life . . .

'Don't worry, Abi. Of course I won't say anything to the police. Or to your boss.'

'My boss! For fuck's sake, do you think he'd care?' *He might though, he might.*

'As long as you do what I ask. All right? Just stick to the story. It won't be difficult, clever girl like you.'

'Screw you, Jonathan Gilliatt. Screw you to hell.'

'So – does that mean I have your agreement?'

She thought – wildly, fearfully. He had her; he really did. Even if the police didn't believe him, they would check her out, her friends, work, Sylvie, everyone.

'Yes, you do,' she said, 'Fuck you.'

'Right. Good. Well, that's that, I think. The less we communicate, the better at the moment. Don't ring me, for Christ's sake.'

'No,' she said. 'Don't worry, I won't.'

'Good. And don't forget: keep it simple.'

She cut him off. Bastard. Absolute bastard. How did people get to be like that? How could she have been taken in by him?

Abi suddenly felt very sick; she made the bathroom just in time. Afterwards she stood in the shower for what felt like hours, came out and lay down on the bed. And then went into the kitchen, pulled a bottle of wine out of the fridge. She'd downed one glass, was pouring another when Sylvie wandered in, wearing nothing but a thong. For some reason, it irritated Abi.

'You shouldn't wander round like that,' she said.

Sylvie stared at her. 'Why on earth not?'

'The perve across the street might see you, that's why not.'

Sylvie shrugged. 'So? Wouldn't be the first time. What's the matter with you, Abi?'

'Nothing,' said Abi. 'Nothing at all.'

'You look awful.'

'Thanks.'

'No, you do. You're not in the club, are you?'

'Of course I'm not,' said Abi irritably. And then, 'Sylvie, you don't ever keep any stuff here, do you?'

'What? What kind of a moron do you think I am? Course I don't. Why?'

'Never do, that's all.'

'Abi, what is this? Someone coming on to you?'

'Course not. I was just checking, that's all. It *is* my flat. I need to know these things. Anyway, I'm going to bed.'

Lying there, watching some talent show on the TV, trying to calm her whirling, heaving fear, she thought there was no way she was going to tell Jonathan now that William had called and spoken to Laura. Let him dig his own grave on that one. Funny that Laura hadn't mentioned it yet. She was obviously cooler than Abi had realised. Waiting for Jonathan to trip himself up. Clever really. Very clever. Perhaps she had misjudged her.

'I'm sorry, Luke. Oh my goodness.'

'Yeah, well, I thought it'd be nice.'

On the table, in an ice-bucket, stood a bottle of champagne. Emma's heart began to thump. What was this all about, for goodness' sake? What had he arranged? Surely, surely not. But then . . . *Emma, don't even go there. There is no way Luke is going to propose.*

They'd only been going out for three months and he was much too cool, much too concerned with his career, and his image and . . . well, everything really. He hadn't even said the L word yet. He just wanted them to have a really good evening, no more than that.

'Cheers,' she said, raising her glass to him. 'This is lovely. Thank you – and sorry about the hold-up.'

'No worries. Champagne all right?'

'It's gorgeous – just what I needed. Oh, and the sleep, of

course. That was so thoughtful of you, Luke. Bless you. I was terribly tired. Bit of a day yesterday, as you gathered.'

'Mine too, babe. Bit of a week, you could say. Talk about tough. Three presentations, visit from on high, lot of schmoozing . . .'

'Poor you. It sounds dreadful. Specially the schmoozing.' She smiled at him. She loved to tease him about the hardships of his job.

'Yeah, well, someone has to do it.' He grinned back at her; he didn't mind the teasing either. He was so good-natured. The perfect boyfriend. She was lucky to have him. Very lucky.

She ordered melon and parma ham and then cold poached salmon. It was too hot to get excited about food.

Luke looked disappointed. 'You should be more adventurous, Emma. This is a real cutting-edge menu. We ate here the other night. How about the tuna tartare? Or the duck with truffles?'

'Oh, sorry. Maybe the tuna then. Thank you.'

'And a little white wine for Madame? I've ordered a white burgundy. Think you'll like it. Bit pricy, but . . .'

'How pricy?'

'Emma, a lady should never ask the cost of her dinner . . . Oh, all right.'

She knew he was dying to tell her. 'So?'

'Eighty-five quid.'

'Eighty-five . . . Luke, that's terrible. I mean, very extravagant. People live on less than that for a week.'

'OK, OK, don't go all socialist on me. I get enough of that from Dad. It won't help some old granny, us drinking cheap rubbish. Just enjoy, OK?'

She sipped the wine.

'Isn't it great? Had that the other night as well.'

'Yes, it's wonderful.' She actually couldn't taste much difference from the £4.99 Chardy she bought in Tesco; in fact, she thought she might actually prefer the Tesco.

267

'Anyway, Emma . . .'

What was coming? She took a large gulp of the wine, although she was sure it should go down in small, appreciative sips.

Their food arrived; there was a lot of fussing with the pepper pot, and some parmesan shavings for Luke's *bresaola*.

Then he said, 'Thing is, Emma, there's something really important I want to say.'

'Yes, Luke?' She took another mouthful of the wine. She'd be drunk in no time at this rate.

'I haven't said it before, because I wasn't sure. I've never said it to anyone, matter of fact . . .'

She put her fork down. This needed her full attention.

'I – I love you, babe. I really do.'

'Oh, Luke.' She felt tears in her eyes; joyful, wonderful tears.

'Hey,' he said. 'The idea was to make you happy.'

'Sorry. I am. Terribly.' She hoped her mascara wasn't running.

'It's taken me a while to realise, but I was talking to Mum the other night, and . . .'

He was worryingly devoted to his mum; any girlfriend was in danger of taking second place.

'Yes?'

'And she said it was obvious to her – she'd never heard me talk like that before, and she said I should tell you.'

Good old Mum; if she'd walked in then Emma would have hugged her. She must stop thinking harsh things about her.

'Oh, Luke.'

'Yeah. So . . . well, that's about it, really.'

She was silent; realised he was looking slightly embarrassed, less his usual confident self.

'That's wonderful,' she said. 'Really wonderful.'

'Good. Now there is something else.' He raised his fingers, signalled to the waiter. 'Could you bring that package over now, please? The one I asked you to keep at the desk?'

'Certainly, sir.'

She sat in an agony of suspense. Package? What would be in a package? Surely not that. Not yet, not . . .

The waiter put the package down in front of Luke; it was blue, that glorious, soft turquoise blue, with that wonderful, wonderful white ribbon – Tiffany! What came from Tiffany? Well lots of things, but—

Luke handed it to her. 'Go on,' he said. 'Open it.'

Her hands shaking, she untied the bow. Inside the wrapping was a box. A quite small box. With another white ribbon.

'This is like Pass the Parcel,' she said. She undid the second bow; took the lid off the box, pulled out the small blue pouch. What was it? What could it be, if not—

'Oh Luke, that's so lovely! Oh, my God!' She was fighting to keep her voice enthusiastic, not to betray the disappointment that was there. *Emma, Emma, he loves you, that's enough, anything else would be too much now, don't be ridiculous, and how could any girl be disappointed, getting a gold Paloma Picasso heart on a chain, and not just plain gold, but the one with a diamond set in it. God, it must have cost a fortune; he must really really care about me. Never mind it's not a ring, it's absolutely gorgeous.*

'I love it,' she said, leaning over to kiss him. 'I really love it. Thank you *so* much, Luke. Here, help me put it on.'

'Good,' he said, and he sounded very smug, 'I thought you'd like it. Now you have to wear that all the time, Emma, OK? So you think of me all the time. Even when I'm away.'

'Of course I will,' she said, and she was crying now. 'I promise, Luke, I really do. I couldn't bear to take it off anyway, not ever. Oh dear, I must go to the loo again. My make-up'll be all smudgy and—'

It wasn't until she had repaired her make-up, put on some more perfume, combed her hair and admired the necklace, that she realised she hadn't told Luke that she loved him too. Well, there'd be plenty of time for that later. Maybe when they were in bed . . .

Chapter 18

By Saturday evening Mary had begun to despair of ever hearing from Russell again as the hours went by with no word, no message of any sort. She found it extremely painful that he had apparently made no effort to find her; it displayed a lack of true devotion. She found herself comparing his behaviour rather unfavourably with what Donald's would have been: he would have walked to the ends of the earth, she was certain, turning up every single stone in his path, before giving up on her. And the crash had been in all the papers, you had only to turn on the news on that first morning to see graphic pictures of the pile-up, the lorry straddling the motorway, the ambulances and police cars and the helicopter. There had even been several references to the hospital; how could Russell have missed all that?

Whatever the reason, it was a crushing disappointment. Instead of spending a joyful weekend with her long-lost sweetheart, she was spending a miserable one with a lot of sick people and some well-meaning but distinctly tiresome nurses.

She had cried more than once, when she was sure no one would be aware of it. She knew crying in hospital was never a good idea, as it brought with it dire prognostications about sending your blood pressure up, and thus delaying your departure. But she just couldn't help it: she seemed to have run out of courage.

And then it all began to go right.

The rather plain nurse had come over to her bed with the message at six o'clock. 'From a gentleman, Mary, he sounded like an American.'

'Yes?' she had said, staring at the girl. How could she ever have thought she was plain? She looked almost unbearably beautiful.

'He said to give you his special love. He was called – let me see, don't want to get it wrong, do we? – Oh yes, Mr Mackenzie. That mean anything to you?'

'Oh yes,' said Mary, 'oh my goodness, it does.'

'He said he's coming to see you in the morning. He wanted to come this evening, but I told him you were tired, that you'd had your procedure, and he said he'd be here first thing.'

And Mary had flown up into some unreachable, untouchable place of happiness and felt she would never, ever come down again.

And then, on Sunday morning, the flowers arrived – a vast bouquet of red roses.

'My word,' the nurse said, 'St Valentine's Day's come late this year. I don't know what I'm going to put them in, Mary. I haven't got a vase big enough for half of them.'

'You don't have to,' said Mary. 'Look, they're in water already. Can I have the card, please, Nurse?'

For my beloved Little Sparrow, it said. *Get very well, very soon. My love, Russell.*

Mary burst into tears.

She sat waiting for him, feeling rather queenlike in her high bed – while not looking remotely queenlike; she was sure, in fact, her hair looked dreadful, the flatteringly bouffant shape Karen had bestowed upon it hopelessly squashed and flat. But she had done her best with her make-up and had been allowed to have a shower, only of course her lovely Revlon body lotion had been crushed along with everything else in the boot of the car. She was completely unable to eat any breakfast; just as she had been unable to sleep.

And then – first the message, then the flowers and then – there he was, walking across the ward, smiling, his brilliant blue eyes fixed on her, and he really didn't look so very different, still so handsome and so slim and tall, and the years rolled away and they were young again, standing together in Parliament Square and she had known she was falling in love; and it was all she could do not to leap out of bed and run into his arms.

Only it wasn't necessary, for he half-ran to her instead, with little quick steps, and when he reached her, he took her hand and kissed it, and she simply felt warm and safe and absolutely happy. This was love, then, as they had known it all those years ago; and they might be a little older now, might have lived between them for a great deal more than a hundred years, might have known sorrow and separation, and then new love and happiness with others, and new sorrow too; but their love for one another, steely and strong, had lived on, just as sweet, just as joyous, and being old and physically frail had absolutely nothing to do with it. And how would you explain that to a young person, she thought, noticing that the nurses were watching them, smiling, wondering, she had no doubt, what on earth they were doing, those two old people, holding hands, both of them crying, behaving like foolish young things. But we are foolish young things, in some ways, she would have told them, had they asked, for they had missed out on a lifetime together, she and Russell; their relationship was still young and tender, even if they were not, and they had much to do, in whatever time was left to them, to nurture it and allow it to come into its own.

The police, or rather the CIU – the Collision Information Unit – called Jonathan on Sunday to discuss when they might talk to him. He'd been told he'd be hearing from them; they were interviewing every witness, and he was a key one. Just the same, it was still a shock, still far from welcome. It meant the matter of Abi being in his car would now have to be confronted. The lies would have to begin. Hopefully Laura wouldn't have to hear them, but . . .

'Just a quick call, Mr Gilliatt, to arrange a time; the sooner the better while it's all still fresh in your mind.'

'Yes, of course. Although I should tell you, a lot of it is rather a blur.'

'That's all right, sir. Most people say that. Just tell us what you can and we'll worry about the rest.'

'Very well. How long might it take? Just so I can plan it, you know.'

'About two hours.'

That had sounded like a long time. He felt a bit sick. He'd expected half an hour, twenty minutes even. How could it take two hours?

'Well, that's fine. But I wonder – could it be in the evening? I'm a surgeon, I have a lot of patients.'

They'd settled finally on Tuesday evening, at six-thirty.

He'd slept horribly badly again, and he was sitting in the conservatory just before supper, trying to read the Sunday papers – he dreaded mealtimes, every mouthful had to be forced down – when Laura walked in with a bottle of white wine and a bowl of olives.

Her voice was at its sweetest; the coolness of the past twenty-four hours or so seemed to have passed.

'I thought we'd earned this,' she said, smiling at him. 'I know I certainly have. Bit of a day, with the children and so on.'

'Yes. I'm sorry, darling, I've been no use to you at all. I'm feeling much better now – I'll be back on course tomorrow.'

'Good. I'll look forward to that.'

'Um . . .' This was it, he had to do it, had to broach the

274

subject of the police interview. 'Just one thing, darling. The police are coming here on Tuesday evening, about six-thirty, to talk to me about the accident. Presume you'll be around?'

'Are they? I'd like to sit in on it, if you don't mind.'

A thud of fear hit him; he tried to ignore it.

'Well, darling, I don't mind, of course. But they might feel differently. Protocol and all that.'

'I can't see why. Anyway, if they don't want me there, they can tell me and I'll go away. Obviously.'

'All right.'

'When you say "talk to you", what exactly does that mean?'

'Well, I don't know any more than you do really, but I presume they're gathering evidence.'

'Evidence?'

'Yes – about how it happened. What I saw.'

'Yes, I see. And how *do* you think it happened?'

The cool tone had returned; he felt uncomfortable.

'Well, it's so hard to say. Everything seemed so . . . so calm, everyone was driving in a very orderly way, no one was speeding. And then suddenly, out of the blue, for no apparent reason, this lorry swerved and I suppose skidded, and went through the barrier. It had just rained, of course, and—'

'Yes, I see. So where were you in all this? In front of him, at his side . . .'

'Laura, what is this – a rehearsal for Tuesday?'

'Don't be ridiculous. I could have lost you, it's terribly frightening – of course I want to know everything!'

'Sorry, yes, of course you do. Well, I was more or less beside the lorry, on the inside lane. There was an old car immediately in front of me, which presumably just drove on – anyway, he disappeared – and in front of the lorry a sports car of some kind, not sure what it was – an E-type, I think – that disappeared too. There really was no apparent reason for the lorry to do what it did. I thought he might have had a blow-out but I looked at his tyres and they were all intact. Anway, incredibly lucky, considering, and given that there were fridges and freezers literally flying through the air, I found myself – and that was what it was like, finding myself, I certainly don't remember getting there – stopped at an angle on the hard shoulder, about a hundred yards ahead of him. It was all bloody scary.'

'Of course. Terrifying. And then you involved yourself, helping all those people. That was so good of you, Jonathan. They were lucky you were there.'

'Well, you know. One does one's bit. I think I helped, yes. Hope so. Er, Laura . . . ?'

'Yes, darling?' She was smiling again. 'More wine?'

'Yes, please.'

She refilled his glass. Her own was still almost untouched.

'Thank you, darling. Look, there is one thing . . .'

He stopped.

She leaned forward encouragingly. 'Go on.'

'Yes. Well, I hadn't told you before – silly really, so unimportant, but it might come out in this interview thing.'

'And what's that?'

'Well, I wasn't alone in the car.' He found he was sweating, his hands felt clammy.

'Oh really? Had you given someone a lift?'

'Sort of, yes. Someone I met at the conference. A woman – very nice. Needed a lift to Reading, had a problem with her car' – he must remember to tell Abi that. God, it was getting so complicated.

'That was kind of you. Maybe another reason to cut down to the M4. If she had to get to Reading.'

'No, no, I wouldn't have changed my plans for something like that. No, I mentioned that I'd decided to go that way, at the end of the morning session, and she asked me if I could give her a lift.'

'I see. She was a doctor, was she?'

'No, she worked for the PR company who were covering the conference. She – assists a photographer, gets everyone's names and details, that sort of thing.'

'Oh, I see. For the trade press, I suppose.'

'Possibly. Anyway, it's just that she was in the car, and of course when the police were taking names and addresses, they took hers, so – yes, she's bound to be mentioned. I just thought I should tell you, so you wouldn't be surprised, that's all. Especially if you're going to be sitting in on the interview. Which I would love, actually. I've just been thinking about it – it would help, not the nicest thing to have to recall in great detail.'

'No. Well, that's very considerate of you, darling. Thank you for telling me.' She leaned back in her chair, took a sip of wine, smiled at him very sweetly. He allowed himself to relax just slightly. She seemed to have accepted it all right. Silly to have worried, really – why shouldn't she?

'Tell me, Jonathan. Would that have been – Abi – by any chance? Was that this woman's name?'

It would have helped if he hadn't spilled his wine, put his glass down on the tray just a little too quickly and caught the edge of the olive dish, so that it tipped over and discharged its contents.

He was very aware of Laura watching him while he mopped rather ineffectually at the tray with his handkerchief and the paper napkins she had brought out, that new, slightly distant expression on her face. Finally he refilled his glass and then sat back in his chair and managed to smile at her.

'Sorry, darling. What a mess.'

'You could say that,' she said, and there was an edge to her voice that was unmissable.

'Anyway – yes, Abi, that was her name. Abi Scott. How did you know that?'

'A very nice young man rang up, said he'd been there on Friday, and that this Abi had given him her phone to look after – I'm not sure why. She went off without it, and yours was one of the names on it, so he rang.'

'Really?'

'Yes. He said none of the other names meant anything to him, but he did recognise yours because she'd been with you, had mentioned you. He was very charming, and very diffident about bothering me and so on.'

'I see. Well, that was nice of him. When did he call?'

'Yesterday afternoon, while you were asleep.'

'You should have told me.'

'Oh darling, I didn't want to wake you up. And then I forgot. Till now.' She smiled again; the smile sickly-sweet now. 'The only thing I wondered, Jonathan, was why your name is in her phone? Since you'd only just met her.'

'Oh,' he said, thinking fast. 'Well, I was moving around from car to car, and she was doing other things; we didn't want to lose contact with one another, so I put my number in her phone. I actually –' thank God he remembered that – 'did the same for several people – a girl who'd gone into premature labour, which reminds me, I must call the hospital, see if the baby's all right – and a nice young chap, best man to the bridegroom, the one whose leg was crushed . . .'

'Yes, yes, you told me.'

'It was very chaotic. I don't think you realise quite how much. It was the best way to cope with it.'

'I see,' she said, and then with a half-sigh, 'Oh Jonathan, this had better be true. Otherwise, I can't quite think what I might do. Except that I'd want to be sure you wouldn't like it.' And she got up and stalked out of the conservatory; when he followed her a few minutes later she was nowhere to be seen.

Charlie was in the kitchen. 'Mum said to tell you she's

going to bed, doesn't feel too good. I'm just making her a cup of tea.'

'Oh, I'll take it up,' said Jonathan.

'Well, actually, Dad,' he looked slightly embarrassed, 'she said to tell you not to go up, that she was going to just try and go to sleep. Sorry.'

'That's OK,' said Jonathan. 'Thanks for helping.'

He left it at that; making a fuss in front of Charlie wasn't going to help at all.

William couldn't stop thinking about Abi. It wasn't just that she was the sexiest girl he'd ever met, or even the most interesting. That went without saying. It was that she was so nice to be with. Easy to talk to. She'd been so interested in everything he'd said about the farm and its problems. It had been quite funny, actually, when she'd suggested they went and looked for the lost calf.

She'd said, as so many people did, that she'd thought farming would be hard work, but really rewarding. Which it was, of course, although probably not in quite the way she imagined. The rewards came in the recognition of his good fortune, in working in such a beautiful place – people always seemed surprised when he said that, probably thought he was too thick to appreciate it – and in doing something he believed in and that for the most part he enjoyed. Of course a lot of it was tough, the days were unbelievably long in the summer, and cold and dirty in the winter, and the amount of paperwork these days would drive anyone insane. He would have added to the credit balance working for himself, but he didn't – he still worked for, rather than with, his father. Peter Grainger would obviously see that differently.

But Abi – she was really interesting. She'd been so great at the crash: fantastic with all those kids. She didn't look like a girl who'd be good with kids, but she was. And then going off in the ambulance with the little one with asthma. Not everyone would have done that.

His mother had been predictably snooty about her. 'What an unusual young woman,' she'd said. That was how Barbara Grainger described anyone she didn't like, or considered beneath her. Which covered most people really. She was a terrible snob. There were lots of good things about his mother too, of course: she was clever and very generous – it was her money that kept the farm going, or helped to keep it going, and he had never ever heard her allude to that – and she was extremely hardworking, slaved doing the food for shoots and so on, and very loyal to her husband, never criticised him for the ongoing financial failure of the farm over the years. William often wished that she would. It would provide an opportunity for him to put forward his own ideas, suggest new methods, different approaches, investments even; but it was two against one, two against him. Which was one of the many reasons he wished he could find someone to marry, so he'd feel part of a team, his own team, not a kind of understudy.

His brother Martin, who had never shown the slightest interest in the farm, and was a very successful lawyer in London, was always telling him he should stand up to them, claim his share, insist on doing things his way; but it was easy for Martin. In the first place he didn't have to live with the conflict that would create, and in the second he was extremely thick-skinned, aggressive as William could never be. He often sat at the dinner table when he came down to the farm for a weekend, expressing his opinion on things he actually knew very little about, telling his father he should move into the twenty-first century, take a more commercial approach, and William would sit and wince, while actually wishing he could be a bit more like that himself.

His father would get annoyed and argue with him, but his mother never seemed to mind; Martin was, without a shadow of doubt, her favourite. He was the youngest, that had a lot to do with it, but also he had rarity value; he wasn't there every day as William was, of as much interest as the kitchen table or the tractor.

Barbara had never got on very well with her daughter either. Alison was a cold creature, had married a rich Scottish landowner and become rather estranged from her parents. William had actually been quite sorry for his mother when Alison had had her first baby, and not invited her mother up to visit for over two months. On the other hand, Barbara had been so delighted by Alison's marrying into the McKinlay family that she didn't greatly care what happened after that. Which left Alison and her mother quits, in William's opinion.

Anyway, there could be no doubt that she had disliked Abi; found it impossible to communicate with her. Neither of which greatly worried William, and he decided as he worked that afternoon on a fence that the helicopter had damaged as it landed, that he really would like to see Abi again. Although quite what the point of such a meeting would be, he wasn't really sure. She was hardly farmer's wife material. But . . .

Chapter 19

Linda's initial reaction was to say no; she didn't want to risk her reputation again. She'd found the whole business extremely painful professionally, and Georgia simply didn't deserve it. But after two double espressos, she decided that Georgia was still her client and that she owed it to her – professionally – to put the proposal to her. She was amazed the production company had come back to her at all; the other girls must have been of a very low standard. Or Georgia must be exceptionally right for the part. Probably a bit of both.

She called Georgia's mobile; it was switched off. Not even taking messages. She tried the landline. Bea Linley answered.

'Oh – Linda. Hello. Nice to hear from you.' She sounded flustered. 'Georgia's – well, she's gone out.'

'OK.' Linda could hear the controlled exasperation in her own voice. 'Ask her to call me, would you, Bea. As soon as she gets in. It's important.'

'Yes, of course. Is it about that part? Are they reconsidering her?'

'Something like that.'

'Oh Linda, that's wonderful. She's been so upset, ever since she got back. Won't eat, keeps crying, just stays in her room . . .'

'But she's gone out now?' said Linda crisply.

'That's right, yes. I'll get her to call you the minute she comes in. Thank you, Linda. She's a very lucky girl.'

'She certainly is,' said Linda. 'Very lucky indeed. Bye, Bea.'

She decided to give Georgia an hour, then she'd call the production company, say the girl wasn't going to audition for them. It really would be the end of her professionally; no one would ever take her seriously again.

'Mum! I can't!'

'You can and you will,' said Bea, 'immediately.'

'I'm not going to.'

Bea didn't easily lose her temper; long years of being a social worker had taught her resilience and extreme patience. She lost it now.

'Georgia, I think it's time you took a hard look at yourself. You're not a child, you're twenty-two years old. Your father and I have been very patient, we've supported you in every sense of the word all your life, never put any sort of time limit on it, and you've taken that completely for granted, our faith in you as well as the practical help. And now, with what sounds like a real chance of actually getting a part, you just turn your back on it without a word of explanation to me, or to Linda. It's absolutely dreadful and I feel quite ashamed of you. Now I'm going out to work – it's clearly escaped your notice that most of us have to do that – and when I get back, I want to know that you've arranged to go for this audition, or you can forget the whole wretched acting nonsense and go and find yourself a proper job. Your time's up, Georgia. It's your decision.'

Barney was sitting at his desk, going through the motions, trying to pretend it was any old Monday, when the police phoned. They would like to interview him about the crash they said: when would he be available?

'Oh, whenever it suits you,' Barney said, fighting down the stifling fear that seemed quite literally to slither up from his stomach and take possession of his head several times each day.

'Obviously you're in your office now, sir, so perhaps we could see you this evening?'

'Er – yes, this evening's fine.' Best to get it over with. 'Where did you have in mind?'

'We could call round to your home, if that suited you. More pleasant than at a police station, but it's up to you.'

'No, home sounds good. Around seven? Er, can you give me an idea of the sort of things you'll be asking so that I can be prepared – brush up on my memory a bit?'

'Oh, we're just looking to get all the information we can, sir. Everything you can remember of the crash. It will be a cognitive interview, that is to say we'll run through what happened, in as much detail as you can give us, so that we can begin to build up a picture of what happened. Probably best not to think too much beforehand, just answer the questions as we ask them. It was only a couple of days ago, so hopefully it's still pretty vivid in your mind.'

'It certainly is,' said Barney soberly.

'Good. You are, of course, a prime witness. Now, if you could just give me your home address . . . ah, Clapham, very nice. Now there will be two of us. I'm Sergeant Freeman and I shall be accompanied by Constable Rowe.'

'Very good, Sergeant. Thank you.' He called Amanda, told her they were coming.

'Am I allowed to be there too? Give you a bit of moral support?'

'Why should I need moral support?' Barney demanded. He felt edgy already. He felt edgy all the time. Not sleeping properly. It was hideous. He should have taken a couple of days off, as Amanda had suggested. And that doctor, Emma whatever her name was, as well. It was just that work, having something else to think about, had seemed a good idea.

'Simply because it might not be the nicest experience for you, reliving it. Look, I'll wait till they get there and then if they say no, I'll go away. I think that's the best plan.'

Amanda was the sweetest girl, but she was very stubborn. Once she had decided on a course of action that she thought right, there was no shifting her.

Barney was feeling very odd altogether. He was terribly worried about Toby, of course; not just his physical condition, which seemed pretty bad, but what he was supposed to do about everything. Like that girl. Did she know about the crash? And if she did, might she turn up at the Westons' house, or even the hospital, wanting news of Toby? He decided that was pretty unlikely. Hopefully she'd got what she wanted and that would be the end of it. It was just that only he knew about her, and with Toby in this half-baked state, Barney felt he had to carry the can for anything that happened. Suppose Tamara got to hear of her somehow? It was possible. The girl was obviously trouble in a big way.

He hadn't yet got over the shock of Toby's behaviour: that he had been capable of such a thing. He had thought he knew him so well; suddenly he didn't know him at all. It was rather like discovering that the sweet-natured Labrador whom everyone in the family adored and trusted had suddenly savaged a child. It was pretty hard to cope with.

And then there was the business of the tyre. OK, they hadn't caused the accident, but they had had a blow-out. And driven into the car in front and caused the girl to go into labour. Not to mention causing the damage to their own car and consequently Toby's leg. It seemed very possible to Barney that the soft tyre could have contributed – or even caused that. He should have insisted on checking it, made Toby wait somehow. Was he supposed to mention the tyre to the police? It wouldn't look very good. He really needed to discuss it with Toby: who was in no state to discuss anything with anybody. Well, maybe it wouldn't even come up.

He was also having trouble sleeping; having feverish dreams and waking, sweating, several times each night, with a terrible sense of fear. And he couldn't stop thinking about the girl who'd had the baby; OK, it had turned out all right, but it might not have done. God, he felt a mess . . .

Maeve was sitting in the corridor, waiting to go into HDU to see Patrick, when she saw Dr Pritchard coming towards her.

'Oh, Dr Pritchard, good morning,' she said, scarlet with embarrassment. 'I'm so sorry not to have paid back your money. How dreadful, when you've been so kind. I have it here – I simply forgot.'

'Mrs Connell – Maeve – please don't worry, I'd completely forgotten about it. There's no rush. Look, I wonder if we could have a little chat. Come into the patients' room, would you? I don't suppose your mother is here?'

'No, she's not. She's looking after the boys.'

'Oh, of course. Stupid of me. Look . . . just wait a moment, I'll be back.'

She waited, terrified, worrying what he might be about to tell her, that Patrick was worse, perhaps, or . . .

'Maeve, this is Sister Wales. Sister Jo Wales. She's been helping to look after Patrick.'

'Oh! I'm delighted to meet you.' Maeve managed to smile at Jo Wales.

'Hello, Mrs Connell. We haven't met before. I've been off-duty this weekend.' She was a very pretty blond girl, tall and slim and very well-spoken; Maeve took all this in, while waiting to hear the news, the terrible news that Patrick had died. Or was going to die.

'Mrs Connell,' she said, 'your husband is better today. Much stronger.'

Maeve said nothing; a great 'but' hung in the air, dark and threatening.

Dr Pritchard spoke the but. 'But, I'm afraid there are some anxieties over his condition.'

'But you said he's getting stronger?'

'Indeed he is. But I'm afraid he sustained some damage to his spinal cord. In the crash. It was very difficult to assess the extent of it before today. But now we are worried because he says he can't feel his legs too well. This could – only could, mind – indicate some permanent nerve damage. Of course it's early days and things might change, he's very poorly still and a little confused, but . . .'

'So,' she hardly dared ask the question, 'so what does that mean?'

'A few more days may change the outlook considerably, but what it could mean is that he is paralysed. From the waist down.'

'Oh God!' The room seemed to swim round Maeve. She felt very sick. She looked desperately at Dr Pritchard, her eyes boring into him, as if she could change what he was saying simply by the sheer force of will; and then suddenly she slumped in her chair.

'Maeve!' It was Jo Wales. 'Here, put your head between your knees. That's right. Take some nice deep breaths. That's better. Dr Pritchard, get her some water, would you? No, don't sit up yet. Have a drink, little sips. There, there, don't cry . . .'

But Maeve did cry, loud, heavy sobs, rather as the boys did when they were upset or frightened; she felt consumed by grief, by fear and above anything else, a sense of complete outrage.

'Sue? Hello again. This is Linda Di-Marcello here. Look – about Georgia Linley. I've had a call from her and she is very much better. She says she could definitely come up and do an audition tomorrow. So – over to you. Any time.

What? Yes, I'm sure that would be fine. Thank you so much, Sue. Please tell Bryn I do appreciate his patience. We both realise how lucky Georgia is to get another chance. What? No, I'll accompany her myself. Don't worry, I won't let her get away again.'

She had no idea how she was going to get through it. But anything was better than being alone in her room just thinking about it. Being alone with the memory. And the terror. She must just get on with it. Stop hiding, running away. And nobody knew what she had done, after all. She hadn't thought of that in her initial blind panic. Except Patrick, of course. Patrick who had been so kind to her.

And it looked like he was getting better, according to the papers.

Just take it a day at a time, Georgia. One day and then the next. And then, one day, possibly quite soon even, she would go and see Patrick in the hospital. She would. She really would. But not today. Or tomorrow. It was going to be quite hard enough, just getting up to London and doing the audition. After that she'd see. Take one day at a time. That was what she had to do. One day at a time.

Mary was trying to concentrate on the book Christine had brought in for her, the new Danielle Steel, her favourite. She always felt she was getting a glimpse into the kind of life Russell led in America, all those rich glamorous people, but she couldn't stop thinking about the lorry driver, who was, she knew, somewhere in the hospital, dangerously ill: the nurses had told her he had sustained the most dreadful injuries . . . There was quite a lot in the papers even today about the horrors of the crash, about how several people had been killed and how the lorry driver was not expected to live; it made her even more aware of how fortunate she had been, how nearly she could have died.

Police are conducting a full investigation into the cause

of the crash. The death toll from such accidents continues to rise; one of the more horrific statistics of our time is that every minute of every day a child dies or is seriously injured in a road accident somewhere in the world; and that the annual death toll is 1.2 million. And yet people continue to drink and drive, use mobile phones, and take their eyes off the road while looking for sweets, CDs, or even turning round to check their children. Another very frequent cause is going to sleep at the wheel: tiredness is as dangerous as alcohol especially to long-distance drivers.

Suppose he had gone to sleep? The paper hadn't actually spelled it out, but it did make you wonder. You saw them thundering up and down the motorway endlessly; rather as if they were on some kind of conveyor belt. Poor man, how dreadful that would be: knowing you had caused all those deaths, just because you were tired and had lost concentration for a few seconds.

She suddenly felt very restless; she had been stuck in this ward for too long. Hospital was such a strange shadowy echo of real life. It did such a funny thing to time for a start, dulled it, so that morning merged into afternoon and then evening, without anything really happening or changing at all. Clocks meant less than whether Doctor had done his round, or the morning drink had arrived, or visitors had started to trickle in.

And then you had very little control over anything; you just had to wait until the next event. And you felt yourself changing too, becoming more passive, less questioning. If a nurse said you had to go for an X-ray, or she was going to take some blood, or gave you a heap of pills, you didn't ask her why, or what for, or what they were, you just obeyed her. If a doctor told you you were doing well and you still felt terrible, you didn't argue. If the food was awful you didn't complain and if your bedtime drink came two hours before you would even think about going to sleep, you drank it.

Mary could see how people became institutionalised. It required a huge effort to go against the hospital current, to disobey, to argue, to question: much easier just to drift along with it. Well, it had only been four days, but she'd give a lot to get out of it for a few minutes. She longed to go for a little walk, just round the hospital, and wondered if they'd let her. Probably not. Best not to ask perhaps: just slip out while no one was looking. They were terribly busy. She could just say, if they asked, that she was going to the day room to watch TV.

She told the lady in the next bed she'd be back in ten minutes, put on her dressing-gown and slippers, and walked rather purposefully past the nursing station. There was nobody there.

Feeling rather as if she'd escaped from prison, Mary set out along the corridor and made for the lift. She had no idea where she was going: just to be out of the ward was pleasure enough. The lift was full of people. They all seemed to be going to the ground floor; Mary thought she might as well go there too. She might even get a whiff of fresh air: that would be wonderful.

She was tempted to actually go outside, but that really did seem rather reckless. She wandered round the foyer for a bit, looking at all the fortunate people who could go out into the street at will, without getting permission or signing forms, and then saw a Costa Coffee outlet; it looked rather cheerful and normal. There were several people in dressing-gowns, sitting chatting to one another and even to other people who had obviously come to see them; she was tempted to go in, but there wasn't anything she fancied. Hospital air killed the appetite. She decided to go back to the lift, and on her way passed a sign to ICU; she knew what that meant – Intensive Care Unit. Presumably that was where the lorry driver lay, poor man. As she stood there, a young woman, looking absolutely exhausted, walked towards her, her eyes blank and unseeing, and then passed on and into the café, where she sat down at one of the tables, slumped over her handbag.

Without stopping to think, Mary followed and sat down opposite her.

'Hello,' she said, and smiled at her encouragingly. 'You can tell me to go away if you want, but you look to me as if you could do with some company.'

The woman stared at her; then shook her head.

'Can I get you a cup of tea then?'

'No – that is – yes. Thank you. Good and strong. With sugar.' She was obviously far too weary to wonder why a strange old lady in a dressing-gown might be bothering with her.

Mary went over to the counter, paid for the cup of water and tea bag that passes in such places for a cup of tea and carried it over to the table, together with several mini-cartons of milk and packs of sugar.

'There you are. I should leave the bag in for a bit longer.'

'Thank you for that. I will.' She looked at Mary then managed a very faint smile. 'Are you a patient here then?'

'I am indeed. Only until the end of the week, thank God. Then I'm going home.'

'Well, you're a lucky woman.' She had an Irish accent; she was rather pretty, Mary thought, in spite of the exhaustion. She dunked the tea bag up and down in the cup, then fished it out and added the milk.

'That's grand. Thank you.'

'That's all right. Now you don't have to talk, you look terribly tired.'

'I am. I feel I've been here for ever. My – my husband's in Intensive Care.'

'Oh, how terribly worrying for you. Has he had surgery?'

'He has indeed. A great deal. But that's only the beginning.' She started to cry, then looked back at Mary and said, 'I'm sorry.'

'Don't be silly,' said Mary, rummaging in her handbag for

a clean tissue, and then, very gently, 'Do you want to tell me about it?'

'Mr Fraser? Sergeant Freeman, CIU. And this is Constable Rowe.'

'How do you do,' said Barney. 'Come into the sitting room. This way. Ah, now this is my fiancée, Amanda Baring.'

'How do you do, Sergeant,' said Amanda. 'I was wondering, is there any reason why I shouldn't sit in on the interview? I wasn't there, at the accident, but I thought it would be nicer for Barney – Mr Fraser – if I was with him while you talk to him. I promise not to interrupt or anything, but . . .'

She smiled at Sergeant Freeman, who smiled slightly foolishly back.

'No, that's perfectly all right,' he said. 'If that's what you both want.'

'It is. Thank you. Now, can I get you a cup of tea?'

'That would be very welcome,' said Sergeant Freeman.

'Certainly would,' said Constable Rowe.

They were an odd pair, Barney thought. Freeman was thin, almost gaunt, looked as if he hardly ever went outside. Rowe was plump and rosy, and looked like an Enid Blyton policeman. A notional helmet sat on his head. They settled side by side on the sofa, and Freeman took out a large pad of paper and a pencil. Barney half-expected him to lick it.

Amanda came in with the tray of tea and some biscuits, and there was a few minutes of chatter about the heat and the odd weather generally and maybe it was climate change. 'Although I don't think so,' said Constable Rowe. 'These patterns come and go, always have done. I think it's a lot of nonsense myself, put about by the politicians . . .'

Sergeant Freeman gave him a look that would have refrozen the ice cap, and said they had better start.

'Now as I told you, this is what we call a cognitive

interview, sir, based on your recall. I shall simply ask you what happened and make notes, and then go through the facts again, just to make sure everything's clear, possibly making more notes. At the end we'll complete a statement, incorporating all the information, which you can then approve and sign.'

No wonder it was going to take two hours.

'That sounds pretty straightforward. Ask away,' said Barney.

'But before we start, sir, how is Mr Weston?'

'Not very well, I'm afraid. A bit better in himself today, but his leg was very badly mashed up.'

'I'm very sorry to hear that, sir.'

'Thank you.'

'Now I realise he was driving, but it's your recollection, your interpretation of events that's important.'

They began with the basics, name, address, profession, when and why he had been on the M4 that afternoon.

'The wedding was at four-thirty, which would mean, if you'll forgive the observation, that leaving when you did, you were cutting things a bit fine.'

'Yes, it was rather late,' said Barney.

'Any particular reason?'

'Er, yes. Mr Weston was feeling unwell.'

'In what way, sir?'

'Well, he had a stomach upset.'

'Yes, I see. Would that be a euphemism for a hangover, sir? Forgive the assumption, but—'

'No,' said Barney firmly, 'it wouldn't. He did have a few drinks the night before – wine with dinner and so on – but I do assure you, as we didn't leave until almost two o'clock the following day, he would have been absolutely fine. No, he was extremely sick, several times during the morning.'

'And could you tell us exactly how much he drank, sir? Very important, as I'm sure you'll appreciate.'

'Well, not really no.' Barney fought down his irritation; he hadn't expected this. 'I suppose, maybe half a bottle of wine with dinner, certainly no more, and a couple of glasses of whisky afterwards.'

'Were you also drinking, sir?'

'Well yes, I kept him company. We weren't going anywhere, so . . .'

'Indeed not. So what else did you do in the evening? After dinner?'

'Oh, we swam in the pool. Talked. Played some music. You know the sort of thing.'

'Unfortunately, Mr Fraser, I've never been privileged to be a best man. Anyway, let's get on to the journey. Why did you choose the M4 route? Bit of a long way round, isn't it?'

'Longer, but quicker,' said Barney. 'The other way involves endless back roads and narrow lanes. And we needed to get some petrol. We thought it would be easier to go to the service station, fill up there.'

'Given that you were already late, was that absolutely necessary?'

'Yes. The tank was practically dry.'

'Forgive me for saying so, sir, but I'd have thought that would be part of the best man's duties, to get that sort of thing done the day before.'

'I assumed Toby would have done it. He'd been at the house all the day before.' Barney felt edgy suddenly and under threat. What was this, a post mortem on his performance as best man? 'But I should have checked, you're right. Er – is that really relevant?'

'Probably not, sir, no. Now, his parents, as I understand it, were at the house? When did they leave?'

'Oh, about ten-thirty, eleven. They were having lunch with friends in Marlborough.'

'Weren't they worried about their son's condition?'

'We managed to keep it from them. Yes, they would have been very worried.'

'I see. And when you left the house, who was driving the car?'

'I was.'

'So, you stopped at the service station and filled up the tank. Did anything of note happen on your way there?'

'Yes,' said Barney reluctantly. 'We were stopped by the police.'

'For speeding?'

'Yes. And of course that made us later. Much later.'

'Presumably you were breathalysed then, sir?'

'Yes, of course.' He was beginning to feel beleaguered. 'And it was absolutely fine.'

'Right. Well, we can check on that, of course. May I ask what speed you were travelling when you were stopped?'

'Er . . . a hundred and seven,' Barney said sheepishly, with an apologetic look at Amanda.

'A little over the speed limit, sir. Well, we don't need to waste time on that now.' Sergeant Freeman made a separate note. 'And then you proceeded on your way, to the service station?'

'Yes, that's right.'

'More slowly, perhaps?'

'Much more slowly, yes. We couldn't risk getting stopped again.'

'It must have been getting late by then?'

'It was. It was half-past three.'

'And you filled up with fuel. Anything else?'

This was it. No need to mention it though. Completely irrelevant. Red herring.

'No, nothing else.'

'You didn't need oil, or windscreen wash?'

'No, we didn't. And then we went on our way.'

'And were you still driving?'

'Well – no,' said Barney. 'Toby took over.'

'Why was that?'

'He just wanted to. I think he felt less stressed if he was behind the wheel.'

'Right. Were you aware of any other cars at this point, or indeed earlier, driving erratically ahead, overtaking you?'

'Yes, there was one,' said Barney slowly, 'and I noticed it only because I thought how unfair it was. It was a white van and he was going like the clappers – tailgating, flashing, weaving in and out of the traffic, really behaving extremely dangerously. He certainly deserved to be stopped. As much if not more than we did.'

'I see. I don't suppose you were aware of any markings on the van, any name of the firm?'

'No. Sorry.'

'That's all right. Someone else might have seen it. Now tell me what happened next. Take your time.'

'We were just driving along in the outside lane,' said Barney. 'The traffic was quite heavy, and everyone was driving very steadily. There'd just been a storm, it had hailed and so on, and the road was still wet. Anyway, quite suddenly it seemed, the lorry just lost control.'

'Which lorry would that have been, sir?'

'Oh – well, the one in the crash.' Did he have to explain every single thing?

'You were beside it? Behind it?'

'Behind it, but in the outside lane. There was a Volvo Estate in front of us, more or less level with it. Anyway, he veered over to the right, towards the central reservation, and just – well went through it. Stopped finally on the westbound side, jack-knifed, total chaos. Anyway, Toby slammed on the brakes, obviously, but we had a blow-out. I've never known anything like it; it's never happened to me before. It was absolutely terrifying. The car was all over the place, it was as if the steering just didn't work. Or the brakes. We seemed to be swinging about on the road, and then somehow, Toby got it back under control and it – well, it went into the Volvo. Which had managed to stop. It was so odd – it seemed to happen so slowly, as if we had all the time in the world. I know people always say that. So weird.'

'Indeed. Now, as you say, you weren't speeding at all. We checked your engine control unit of course. Were you aware of hitting anything, however small, that could have caused the blow-out?'

'What – like a sharp stone, you mean, something like that?'

'Something like that, yes.'

'No,' said Barney, 'not consciously. But there could very easily have been something – I suppose.'

'Again, Forensics are doing a full report on your car, and they may come up with something. Of the tyre being cut in some way.'

'But surely, the tyre was in bits. How could they see anything at all?'

'You'd be surprised what they can see, sir. Anyway, you impacted with the Volvo. Then what happened?'

'Again it all seemed to happen so slowly. We just went on and on into its rear. We hit it on Toby's side. It crushed the bonnet and drove the steering column down into his leg, as far as I could make out. He was bloody lucky it wasn't worse, I suppose.'

'Indeed, sir. Are you all right?'

'Yes. Yes, thanks.' But he wasn't; he could feel his eyes filling with tears. He pulled his handkerchief out of his pocket, blew his nose. Amanda came over to him and took his hand. He looked at Freeman. 'Sorry. All a bit vivid.'

'I'm sure. That's perfectly all right, sir. Anyway, I'm going to go over this with you now, and then prepare a statement, and you can sign it if you're happy with it. Shouldn't take too long.'

Going over it meant a gruelling trawl through the whole thing again: when he had first become aware of the lorry, if he could pinpoint where the white van had been, its condition, whether the lorry might have been speeding, how much the storm might have slowed them down, how wet the road had been. It seemed quite literally endless.

'God,' said Amanda, when they'd gone, 'you poor darling. Let me get you a beer. They're very thorough, aren't they? All those questions about how much you'd drunk, who was driving. You don't think Toby was over the limit, do you?'

'Absolutely not,' said Barney impatiently. He felt completely exhausted, drained of emotion, and the last thing he wanted was further questioning. 'He'd had the same as me, I swear to you, really not much at all, and it was fifteen, sixteen hours later, for God's sake, and when I was breathalysed, when they stopped us, I was fine.'

'Yes, of course. But a hundred and seven, honestly, Barney, so dangerous.'

'Yes, all right. I know. We were in a hurry, for God's sake.'

Amanda handed him a can of beer, sat down next to him and took his hand again. 'OK?'

'Yeah. Thanks.'

Then she said, 'Barney . . .'

'Yes?'

'There's one thing I still don't understand. Haven't from the beginning. I mean, why did you leave so late? It does seem awfully stupid.'

'I told you. Tobes was in a bad way. Throwing up all over the place.'

'Oh yes, I see,' said Amanda. But she didn't sound altogether convinced.

'Nice young chap,' said Constable Rowe as they drove through the crowded streets of Clapham. 'And what bad luck. As for the bridegroom, imagine missing your own wedding like that.'

Sergeant Freeman said he knew several people who might have wished to miss their own weddings, and that they should examine the CCTV footage at the service stations as soon as possible.

'With what in mind exactly?'

'To make sure everything happened exactly as he said.'

'But what might he not have done?'

'I don't know at this stage. But the devil is in the detail in this game, Rowe. And it's the detail we have to concern ourselves with.'

'You don't think he was to blame for the crash?'

'I don't think anything, Rowe. That's not our job. Our job is to get the facts. No more or less than that. I've told you that before.'

'Yes, I know you have,' said Rowe soberly.

Chapter 20

'Shit,' said Jonathan aloud, and his eyes filled unaccountably with tears. He was sitting at his desk in his tiny room at St Andrew's, ostensibly going through his notes for the next patient. The day had seemed interminable, everything everyone said to him meaningless. He was aware of having asked one woman the same question twice, of telling another quite sharply that she was overweight and it wouldn't do the baby any good; and was also very conscious of the raised eyebrows and looks exchanged between the nurses and midwives.

He must speak to Abi before the police interview, absolutely must – they might be interviewing her first – but it was just so difficult to find the opportunity. And every time he did manage to call her, her phone was stubbornly on message.

And he really needed to know what Laura was going to do or say during the interview; even the mildest indication that she was suspicious of the relationship might lead to further questioning. And then there was the small matter of the phone call . . .

He went out into the hospital grounds, armed with his mobile, and dialled Abi's number. 'Abi, it's Jonathan. Please call me. There are various things we need to discuss most urgently. Any time in the next three or four hours.'

He realised he didn't even know if the police had been on to her yet. Christ, it was getting worse by the minute.

❖   ❖   ❖

Abi knew Jonathan wanted to contact her; indeed, she was enjoying the knowledge. Or rather she was enjoying not responding to his calls. It was her only revenge; and it was quite sweet. She liked the thought of him sweating, fearful of what she might say to the police, fearful of what she might yet say to Laura. It served him right. God, he was a bastard, blackmailing her like that.

It was only when the police rang and said they would like to interview her about the crash, that she decided, in her own interest, she had better let him off the hook. She was eating a sandwich at her desk when the call came through; it rather destroyed her appetite.

His voice was terse, impatient. 'I wish you'd got back to me sooner. You must have heard my messages.'

'You're not the only busy person in the world, Jonathan. I have a life too, you know. I can't just take phone calls in the middle of jobs. I realise they're not as important, my jobs, as chatting up mothers-to-be, but—'

'Oh, just stop it,' he said. 'Look, have the police been on to you?'

'Yes, they have, as a matter of fact. They're coming to see me on Thursday.'

'Right. Well, there's one new thing for you to remember. You had a problem with your car, that's why you didn't have it with you at the conference. Can you remember that?'

'I'll try.'

'Abi, please, for God's sake, this isn't some silly game, it's very important.'

'What, so Laura doesn't find out about me, do you mean?'

'That she doesn't know the truth about you, yes. She's insisting on sitting in on the interview; it's essential we get the details right.'

'You know, I still don't see why the police should care about what you get up to outside the marital bedroom.'

'That's not the point.'

'Why isn't it?'

'Oh, for Christ's sake! Look, you've got it all, haven't you? The lift to Reading, the car, all that stuff. And it's probably best not to mention the phone call. Which wasn't a phone call, in the strict sense of the word, as you very well know. I answered it and then threw the bloody thing on the floor.'

'Is there anything else you'd like me to say? Like you weren't there at all, I just happened to be driving your car . . .'

'Don't be so bloody ridiculous!'

'Lying to the police is a crime, you know, Jonathan. It's called perverting the course of justice.'

'How do you know that?'

'You think I'm so stupid, don't you? I looked it up on the internet. You're inciting me to commit a crime. And actually committing one yourself. That's called blackmail.'

There was a silence, then he said, 'I think you're in danger of making a very big mistake, Abi. I could, if required, get witnesses, you know. Employees at hotels for a start. I seem to remember you rather enjoyed impressing them with your little demos.'

She felt sick again. Very sick.

His voice changed. 'Look, Abi, I'm not asking you to cover up some crime. As you say, we didn't do any harm. I just – well, I just don't want Laura hurt.'

'What an incredibly touching statement. If you don't want her hurt, you should keep it in your trousers a bit more. Poor bloody woman, being married to a shit like you.'

'Abi, please. This isn't getting us anywhere. Look, I've got to go. Is this going to be all right? Are you clear about what you're going to say?'

'Yes, all right, Jonathan,' she said. 'I've got it.' And then, because she couldn't resist it, she added, 'I think.'

Two could play at this game.

＊ ＊ ＊

How was she doing this, Georgia wondered, when she'd spent the past three days crying and quite literally wishing she was dead. She'd been in bits only half an hour earlier, holding Linda's hand, shaking with nerves and feeling terribly sick. And now, suddenly, she felt fine – cool, self-confident and upbeat.

It was always like that; all actors knew about Dr Stage. Dr Stage could mend a sprained ankle so its owner could dance, could heal laryngitis so a voice could fill a theatre; he could cure migraine, gastric flu and asthma, staunch tears and heal grief, summon strength and banish pain. Not for ever, not even for very long, but long enough for the show to go on. And he was working very hard on Georgia's behalf at that moment.

She walked into the casting director's room, pushing back her cloud of black hair, smiling radiantly at the people watching her from behind their table. She was surprised – and pleased – there were three of them when she'd been expecting just the casting director. Every moment was important now, she knew; the camcorder was running already, filming the way she looked, moved, talked, smiled.

'Hi, Georgia. I'm Tony, the casting director, this is Bryn, the director, and you know Sue, my assistant.'

'Yes, I do. Hi. Thank you so much for letting me come today. I'm really sorry about last week.'

'That's OK. So – what are you doing at the moment? What have you been up to?'

'Oh, lots of things. Episode of *The Bill*, episode of *Casualty*, two episodes of *Hollyoaks*, bit of modelling to make ends meet.' She grinned at them.

'Who was the modelling for? TV?'

'Yes, one for a car commercial, one for a new chocolate, and a fashion shoot for *Glamour*.'

It didn't add up to a row of beans, and they would know it; the scenes for *The Bill* and *Casualty* had been tiny,

Hollyoaks only a bit bigger; she'd been in a crowd scene in the car commercial, maybe slightly more of a presence selling the chocolates, one of three girls eating as suggestively as the client felt they could get away with. And fashion shoots – she might just as well have not mentioned it. Except that it did mean she looked all right. But they could see that for themselves.

'Oh, and I've done some workshops in Cardiff, and some dance classes too. Just so I don't seize up.' She smiled at them again.

'Very good.' A pause. Then the standard questions they always asked: would she shave her head if she was asked, did she have any tattoos anywhere on her body, would she take all her clothes off, do a nude scene. Georgia told them she'd shave her head and take her clothes off all in one scene if they asked; no tattoos though, so if they were looking for them . . . they laughed. Then there was a silence; they were going to tell her to go away, not bother, she thought, panic rising, but, 'Well, from those scenes we sent you, Georgia, would you like to do Scene Ten, with a bit of a Brummie accent maybe. Sue will read the dad.'

'Sure.' That was lucky: Scene 10 was her favourite. She walked towards Sue, stood with her legs slightly astride, her hands on her hips.

'Dad,' she said, 'can I have a word?'

By the time she finished the scene she felt quite emotional. There was a moment or two's silence while she – and they – returned to real life. She could tell they'd liked it; you could sometimes. They sat looking at her in silence, the casting director smiling. Then he said what they always said, 'That was great.' Even if you fell over or couldn't get a single word out, they said it was great. But the silence had been quite encouraging.

'OK, Georgia,' the director said. 'Now could you do it again, please, without the accent. Just in your normal voice.'

It wasn't quite as good, and she was more nervous, and doing it in her own voice, her middle-class voice, just tinged with Bristol, made it harder to get lost in the part, but they still smiled at her when she'd finished.

'Thank you, Georgia. That was great.' Again. 'Thank you very much. We'll be in touch. Shouldn't be too long. Few days, probably.'

'Fine. Thank you.'

She allowed herself to tell Linda she thought it had gone well; she felt she owed her that. And Linda had been really cool, not reproached her at all, not asked her any more questions about the crash. Not that Georgia would have answered her if she had. Indeed, she didn't think she would be able to. The only way she could cope now was pretending it had never happened. Or rather that she hadn't been there. That seemed to be working quite well.

'Good evening, Dr Gilliatt. Sergeant Freeman, CIU. This is my colleague, Constable Rowe.'

'Ah yes, do come in, Sergeant.' He ushered them into the hall and towards the drawing room. God, it was like the executioner arriving in the cell. 'Can I get you anything – cup of tea, coffee perhaps, cold drink?'

'Tea would be very nice, thank you, Dr Gilliatt.'

'Er – actually it's Mr Gilliatt. Because I'm a surgeon – silly medical distinction.' God, he was blathering. Why on earth do that, make such a stupid point, put their backs up straight away. *Shut up, Gilliatt!*

'Hello.' It was Laura, emerging from the drawing room, smiling, looking very cool and composed, dressed in white linen jeans and a blue shirt. She held out her hand. 'I'm Laura Gilliatt. I'll fetch the tea. It might be nicer in the conservatory – we've got all the blinds closed and the fans going.'

'That sounds ideal, Mrs Gilliatt. Thank you.'

Jonathan sat down facing them, struggling to be calm,

305

fighting a rising panic and a fear that he might actually vomit. Laura came in with the tea-tray, handed round cups and saucers, offered biscuits. They both declined; Rowe clearly reluctantly.

'Right, Mr Gilliatt. Just to start with some background . . .' He'd expected nice easy stuff, like name, address, car registration at that stage, all that sort of thing, but – 'Perhaps first we could establish exactly what you were doing on the M4 that afternoon, sir? Just so we're fully in the picture, you understand?'

Right in the deep end then. He took a steadying breath, smiled at them carefully. He didn't look at Laura; she mustn't think he was anxious. About any of it.

'I was driving back from a pharmaceutical conference. I'd been speaking at a dinner the night before. At the Birmingham International Hotel.'

'So why the M4, sir? Why not the M40? Or did you go somewhere else on the way? Just curious, sir, it doesn't matter, of course.'

'It was Friday afternoon. The M5–M4 route may be longer, but it's often less congested.'

'And you left Birmingham when exactly, sir?'

'Oh, let me see. I suppose late morning.'

'Right. So you cut down onto the M4 and reached it at what time?'

'Well, it must have taken a couple of hours. I'm not absolutely sure.'

'That's perfectly all right. Not important. And then you drove straight on towards London?'

'Yes.'

'Did you stop at all?'

'Yes, for some petrol. At Leigh Delamere.'

'Fine. So that would have been about what time?'

'Well, I suppose about two-thirty.'

'And you were alone, were you? In the car?'

'No.' He felt Laura stiffen, from right across the room. 'I

306

had a young lady with me. Abi Scott. She was at the conference in a business capacity, but she'd been having trouble with her car; she'd come up by train and I offered her a lift to Reading. She was spending the weekend there.'

'I see. Ah yes, Abi Scott.' He consulted some notes. 'We'll be interviewing her as well.'

'I'm sure you will be. Anyway, it was a purely professional relationship. I'd never met her before.'

He was aware of Freeman glancing up for a moment, seeming about to ask something, then returning to his task.

'Right, sir. So were you in a hurry to get to London?'

'A little, yes. I had a clinic at four-thirty at Princess Anne's, the private hospital where I work two days a week.'

'Which is where, sir?'

'Just off Harley Street.'

'So you needed to press on a bit? Especially as you were going to make quite a detour into Reading. To drop off Miss Scott.'

'Well – yes.' He was aware of Laura shifting in her chair, uncrossing and then recrossing her legs.

'I see,' said Freeman. 'Sounds quite a tight time-frame to me. I imagine you were driving fairly fast – in the outside lane, perhaps?'

'Not at all, no. The traffic was very heavy, there were a couple of minor hold-ups . . .'

'So your hunch was a wrong one?'

'I'm sorry?'

'About it being quicker on the M4.'

'Yes, it was a mistake. A bigger one than I knew.' He smiled, at them and then at Laura; her face was expressionless, she didn't smile back.

'So, just before the crash, you were driving along – in which lane, sir?'

'Oh – the inside lane.'

'Why would that have been, sir? If you were short of time?'

'I had a bad headache. I'd had a hard week. The traffic was very heavy in all three lanes, then there'd been a brief thunderstorm, which was disconcerting. The sky got very dark, there was lightning, thunder, torrential rain and then even some hail. A classic summer storm. It was hard to see for a bit, and afterwards there was a lot of water on the road. Very dangerous.'

'And what time was that, would you have said?'

'I'm not really sure. About three forty-five, I suppose.'

'Yes. Well, we can check that. So would you say that it was the storm that decided you to move over?'

'No, it was a number of factors. As I said. Maybe it was the decisive one. Anyway, then the storm was over as fast as it had begun.'

'Right. So at what point were you first aware of the lorry?'

'Oh, I don't know. Around the same time.'

'And were you driving along level with it? Behind it?'

'More or less level. Yes.'

'Any other traffic that you can recall, sir? In your immediate vicinity, that is, just prior to the accident? No bad driving that comes to mind, no vehicle that could have cut across the lorry's path, perhaps?'

What did that mean? Was he suggesting it might have been him? His own fears came back, reinforced by the questioning. Had it been him, confused by the row with Abi, the phone ringing? Had he lost concentration, veered in front of the lorry in some way? No. He hadn't. Surely, *surely* he'd remember if he had. God, it was frightening.

'No,' he said firmly, 'nothing like that. Everyone was driving rather well, as a matter of fact. I do remember a rather fine old E-type in front of the lorry, but he was driving perfectly safely. Pulling ahead steadily, but certainly not speeding.'

'And the vehicle ahead of you?'

'Oh, it was a saloon of some kind. Again, driving very

steadily. The driver stopped and came back after the crash. In fact, he was the only one who did. I suppose everyone else was just too far ahead to take it in. Even in their mirrors.'

'Including the E-type?'

'Yes.'

It went on and on; could he pinpoint where he had first noticed the lorry? Had he been driving erratically, cutting in and out of lanes? Then, suddenly: 'Did you have the radio on, sir?'

Christ. They thought he hadn't been concentrating. He hadn't.

'Yes. Briefly,' he said, 'although not just prior to the crash. Miss Scott had switched it on. A little while before. But I found it distracting, asked her to turn it off again.'

'I see. So you were just talking?'

'Yes. Chatting, you know.' Just chatting. While he tried to end the relationship, while she threatened to go and see Laura . . .

'And I presume you weren't using a phone?'

Shit. Here it came. He managed to prevaricate.

'The in-car system in my car wasn't working properly and I had my ordinary mobile with me. I called my secretary at the clinic, from the service station, to say I might be late.'

'Did anyone call you?'

Jesus. This was getting difficult. Now what did he say?

'I did,' said Laura suddenly.

'At what time would that have been, Mrs Gilliatt?'

They weren't going to like this.

'Oh, I don't know. Two or three times. He just didn't answer. I was frantic with worry. Then finally I got through.'

'And what time was that?'

A long silence. Very long. Her eyes met his very steadily. He remembered an expression about your entrails withering or something. His were doing exactly that.

'It was around four, I think,' she said finally. Reluctantly.

'And what happened?'

'Well, it was answered. He said "Hello, darling".'

'And was that all?'

'Absolutely. There was an awful noise and then it was switched off. Well, it went silent at least.'

'Did you switch it off, Mr Gilliatt?'

'Not consciously. I just flung it down. The lorry was already skidding—'

'Skidding?'

'Well, swerving. Whatever. I was scared by then by what was happening. Switching the bloody phone off was the last thing on my mind. When I got it out of the car, it was certainly off. Maybe Miss Scott did it, I honestly don't know. I keep telling you, it's all a bit confused.'

'Of course.' Sergeant Freeman's voice was soothing. 'It's entirely to be expected. But can we establish that you weren't engaged in conversation on the phone?'

'Yes, we can.' Well, not on the phone, anyway . . .

'Right, sir. Could we perhaps now concentrate on the actual crash? What was the first thing you were aware of, the first sign that something untoward was clearly happening?'

'Well – oh God, I wish I could remember the details. I'd say the first thing I was aware of was the lorry, swerving violently away from us, and I couldn't see why. It was bloody frightening. It seemed to be out of control. I – well, I just put my brakes on and made for the hard shoulder. Managed to stop there. Incredibly lucky. I was the very last car to get through, so to speak, before the road was blocked off.'

'So you stopped?'

'Yes. I was at quite an angle to the barrier. I – well, I just sat there for a moment or two, wondering what the hell had happened. And then I got out, and all the fridges and

310

freezers and so on were spilling all over the place, they were almost the first thing I noticed. Shooting up both sides of the road. It was almost surreal. And I looked back and saw this dreadful sight. The lorry, ploughed across the other side of the road, all this – this stuff – everywhere, and cars just skidding, swerving, driving endlessly into one another.' He paused, smiled feebly across at Laura, then said, 'It was all extremely traumatic.'

'Of course, sir. It must have been dreadful.' Sergeant Freeman waited respectfully for a moment. Then: 'Now – if we can carry on from there, sir. What did you do next?'

Jonathan suddenly had an odd release of tension; he was able to relax, he supposed because now the memories were clear, unconfused. He found he could give a straight-forward account; it was acutely painful, reliving his genuine emotion at the death of the girl in the Golf, the young mother, the carnage of the mini-bus, the horror in the lorry driver's cab . . . but it was easier.

Freeman paused in his note-taking, looked at him and smiled. 'You acted very courageously, sir, by all accounts. Climbing up into the cab, to switch the engine off. Most commendable.'

'I'm sure anyone would have done the same.'

'I'm afraid you're wrong there, sir. Now while we're talking about that point in the events, could we ask you about a girl by the lorry?'

'A girl – what girl?' He stared at him stupidly. Then, 'Good God. I really had forgotten about her! Yes, of course! You know, because she just disappeared, I assumed – well, I imagined, someone was looking after her.'

He was genuinely embarrassed, discomfited, he could see Laura was staring at him. Another mysterious girl. Did this put him in an even worse light? But it was true: with all the stress over Abi, the trauma of the crash, the intensely harrowing nature of the whole affair, he had forgotten what had seemed a very minor incident at the time. The girl had not been injured, she had not been causing anyone any trouble – and she had quietly disappeared. Small wonder then that he had forgotten about her.

Sergeant Freeman obviously agreed. 'That's perfectly all right, sir. You had a great deal on your mind.'

'You could say that. Yes, I was standing with another chap; he wasn't badly hurt, just a broken arm, I think.'

'That's right, sir. Mr Blake, it was him who told us how you climbed up into the lorry. And he said this young lady just appeared, out of the cab.'

'Yes, she did. Well, I assume out of it. She was actually standing on the step – I can't think she'd have climbed in to have a look. She could have been related to the driver in some way, I suppose, or a friend, or she could even have been a hitchhiker. She was obviously very shocked, she vomited, didn't say anything and then just went over to the hard shoulder and sat down on the ground, but she clearly wasn't hurt. I was too concerned about the lorry bursting into flames to pay her much attention, but when I got down on the ground again, she seemed to have disappeared. I intended to have a look for her later, but there were more serious things to worry about. She might have turned up at the hospital, I really have no idea.'

'Could you describe her?'

'Yes, of course. She was very young, pretty, black or certainly dark-skinned. I think she was wearing a dress of some sort, and then a pair of boots. Suede boots with a sort of fur or sheepskin lining. I did notice the boots because it seemed so extraordinary on such a hot day . . .'

'Ugg boots,' said Laura. 'They all wear them, the girls. However hot it is. Our daughters are pestering me for some.'

'Right. That's very interesting. She might well have some valuable information, if we could find her. Thank you, Mr Gilliatt.' And then: 'Now the young lady, sir. Miss Scott.' A

312

pause. Christ. Not again. 'What happened to her? She wasn't hurt, I take it?'

'Well, she did cut her head, on the dashboard, as we braked. It wasn't serious, just a gash. She was fine.'

'Then you drove on to London, I believe?'

'Yes, I did. Eventually. They – your people – had finished the tests on my car and they let me go. I gave a lift to a nice young chap, desperate to get to a meeting. He'd abandoned his car about a mile back, just started walking. He knew he wouldn't make it, of course, and there would be some rather serious repercussions, I gather, but anyway . . .'

'And Miss Scott?'

'She was looking after some small boys – Cubs, I think they were – and she went to the hospital in the ambulance with one of them, who was having an asthma attack.'

'Have you heard from her since?'

'Oh no. Not really. She called, to let me know she's OK. As I said, our relationship was entirely professional.'

'Fine. Well, I think that's all for now, sir. We may have to ask some more questions later.'

They weren't entirely satisfied then; they had their suspicions. 'I really don't think I can possibly tell you anything else. I'm sorry.'

'No, no, sir. It's just that if any other evidence came up, we might want to check it with you. Given that you were at the very front of the crash, one of our prime witnesses so to speak. But – you've been most helpful, sir. Thank you very much.'

When they'd gone, he looked at Laura. 'God. Bit of an ordeal.'

'Indeed,' she said. Her voice was toneless.

'Think I might like a drink. How about you?'

'No, thank you. Sorry if I dropped you in it. With the phone business.'

'That's OK.'

'But I just think it's best to be completely honest.'

'Of course it is. Sure you don't want a drink?'

'Quite sure.' A pause, then: 'I hope you're being completely honest with me, Jonathan.'

'What do you mean?' It was all he could think of to say.

'You know what I mean. About Abi Scott.'

'What about her?'

'Oh Jonathan, please! I'm not a complete cretin. You're somehow on the wrong motorway—'

'Not wrong. Different from what you'd thought.'

'All right, different. With a strange woman.'

'A business colleague.'

'A business colleague. Who you didn't even mention when we spoke earlier.'

'No. I didn't.'

'For whom you were going to make a large detour when you were already late for your clinic. It doesn't add up.'

'Well, it should,' he said, determined not to sound self-righteous. Or even ruffled.

'Really?'

'Really.'

'What does she do, this girl? Tell me again.'

'She works for a commercial photographer, who was at the dinner, taking photographs. She helps him, gets people's names and so on. To send the photos to.'

'Yes, I see.'

'She's very nice,' he added. 'She'd be very amused if she could hear this conversation.' Wouldn't she just?

'I don't see why. Is she married? Living with anyone?'

'Laura, I haven't the faintest idea.'

'Oh really? I'd have thought you would have, all those hours in the car together. She must have told you something about herself.'

'Well, she did say she had a boyfriend. Darling, this isn't like you. Please! Let's go and see the kids, I need a bit of distraction after all that. It wasn't the best hour of my life.'

There was a long silence; then: 'Yes, all right,' she said. 'They're watching TV.'

He followed her through to the den; he felt sick and shaky. Not just because of the police interrogation; or even hers. But because there was a new darkness between them. Created not just by Laura's discovery of Abi's existence, but by her clear unwillingness to accept his explanation. Lovely, lovely, trusting Laura. That was the really disturbing thing.

Chapter 21

It was much more scary, the second recall. All actors knew that far more hung on it. You had more to lose; you were higher up, you had further to fall. The pressure was really on.

Just the same, most of them took some pleasure in the situation. Anyone watching Georgia, as she walked into Linda's office on Friday morning, might have assumed she had been told the part had gone to someone else.

'I don't know if I can face it,' she said. 'I've been feeling so terrible, all the way up on the train. I thought I was going to be sick twice. I spent most of the journey in the loo.'

Linda struggled to keep her voice level. 'Oh, I'm sorry,' she said. Georgia couldn't be pregnant, could she? That would explain a great deal. She tried not to think about it. 'I know how tough it is at this stage. Just the same, you're clearly in with a fighting chance. Try to be positive, darling.'

'I am trying,' said Georgia. 'It's just I'm so tired, I can't sleep for stressing about it – and what if I don't get it, then what? I'm terrified, Linda, absolutely terrified.'

Linda felt a strong desire to slap her. 'Well, you don't have to go,' she said. 'There are three other girls, all still in the race. Just give up now, why don't you?'

Georgia stared at her. 'Of course I'm not going to give up now,' she said, her voice throbbing with outrage. 'That's a ridiculous thing to say.'

'No more ridiculous than you saying you can't face it. Georgia, for God's sake, pull yourself together! You've chosen a career that's full of these situations. If you want a nice easy life, go and work in a shop or something. Now I've got work to do; please excuse me. I'll see you back here after the audition.'

'All right,' said Georgia. 'Sorry.' And then she suddenly sat down in the chair opposite Linda's desk and started to cry.

'Sorry, Linda. I just feel so awful. It's – well, it's everything, really. Not just the part. I'm upset about lots of things at the moment.'

Linda pushed a contract to the back of her desk. There had to be more than this to it. There just had to be.

'Want to tell me what they are?'

'No, I don't think so. Well, not most of them, anyway.'

'It might help. Come on, I'm all yours. You can't go on like this, you'll have a nervous breakdown. What is it?'

Georgia looked at her, and there was something like terror in her great brown eyes. She took a deep breath and then said, 'Well, it's . . . That is . . .'

'Yes?'

'Well, you see, I . . .' And then she drew back, as if from some deep physical danger. Literally shifted her body in the chair. 'No, I'm sorry, Linda, really. I'm being silly. I've just got my period, I feel like shit.'

She wasn't pregnant then. That was something.

'OK. You going to be all right on your own? You know they want a different scene this time, don't you?'

'Yes, of course.'

'Prepared it?'

'Linda!' The tear-stained face pushed itself into a smile. 'What do you think I am?'

'I hope you're a professional actor, who doesn't let her personal problems get in the way of her work. OK?'

'OK. Promise. I'll see you later.'

317

She did seem OK, Linda decided. Just going a bit over the top emotionally. Nothing new there then.

'That looks like a lot of paperwork.' Constable Rowe smiled at Sergeant Freeman; he didn't smile back.

'It is. It's Forensics' report on the crash.'

'Oh yes. I thought you'd read it.'

'I have read it, of course,' said Freeman coldly. 'I like to keep referring back to it. As our investigations go on, certain things fall into place. Or don't.'

'I see.'

No one would ever guess how much Freeman enjoyed his work, Rowe thought; his mood appeared increasingly doomy. He sat in his dingy cream-painted office, his desk piled high with boxes of papers – each one a different case – gazing morosely over a dying plant on the windowsill at the equally dingy view of the police car park and beyond it the backs of some very unlovely houses. Constable Rowe's office, which he shared with two others, was much more cheerful, the walls adorned with girly calendars, the desks with photographs of their families. He couldn't understand why Freeman didn't personalise his a bit more. But then he kept himself to himself, did Sergeant Freeman, wasn't going to share his private life with anybody; even via a few family photographs. He seemed particularly gloomy today; Rowe decided to play safe and confine himself to very simple questions.

'What things don't fall into place then, Sergeant?' he said.

'These bloody planks. Are they relevant? I can't for the life of me think how. But – they could be, I suppose. And the loose wheel nut they found on the road. Where does that fit in?'

'Into someone's wheel, I suppose,' said Rowe cheerfully and then seeing Freeman's expression hastily composed his features and added, 'I've no idea. Sorry.'

'I wasn't expecting you to have the answer, Constable. It was a purely rhetorical question.'

'Yes, of course. But surely, as I said, it came off one of the other vehicles in the collision.'

'No, Rowe, it didn't. We would know that from the examination of those vehicles.'

'Well perhaps it doesn't have anything to do with the accident, then. Maybe it had been in the road a long time.'

'I doubt that very much,' said Freeman grimly, 'and so do Forensics.'

'Oh.'

'The devil's in the detail in this game, Rowe, I've told you before. This is a detail. We just have to find out how important it is.'

'Or how much of the devil is in it, I suppose,' Rowe said thoughtfully.

'Yes, Constable. Precisely.'

At last, Mary was allowed to go home, a whole week after the accident. She'd never have believed she'd have to stay in so long. And even now, they said it was too soon for her to go home and be on her own; she would have to stay with Christine, which, although not ideal, was a lot better than remaining in hospital. And she got on pretty well with Christine, always had, although she sometimes felt rather nervous of her. She was a sturdy woman who had inherited her father's build, rather than her mother's, and his heavy features, rather than Mary's sparkly prettiness.

Christine was wonderfully capable, ran her home along almost military lines, but she was also judgemental, very strict with her family and easily made impatient. Plus she was deeply conventional; a regular churchgoer, on the Parish Council, Chair of the local Women's Institute. Her morals were rigid. So – how would she react to her mother's news?

She had been mildly curious about the mysterious voice

on her mother's answering machine; Mary had told her he was the husband of a very old friend from the war years, and that they had all been planning to meet up together in London. Christine had seemed to accept this; she had been too worried about her mother's health and the drama of the crash to think very much about it all and she was in any case a rather self-centred woman, not given to contemplating the lives of even those quite close to her in any depth. And mercifully Russell had obeyed Mary's instructions not to reveal their situation to anyone.

It seemed to Mary quite likely that Christine would be shocked; and if not shocked, disapproving. It was quite a difficult situation for any daughter, to discover that her mother had been corresponding with a man, of whose existence neither she nor her father had any knowledge, for sixty years. And that the couple had been – finally – reunited. It was a situation that required very delicate handling.

Russell came in to see her every single day, and each meeting had been happier and more wonderful than the last. Any doubts had fled, leaving her at once excited and at peace about him and his part in the rest of her life. They talked and talked, remembering, laughing, reliving, rejoicing. And planning what they might do, where and how they might be together. The only thing that was unthinkable now was not being together. They had had enough of that; more than enough. After sixty years of separation she and Russell were going to be married. Perhaps, they agreed, had they not so nearly missed one another, had Mary not been ill, they might have felt more cautious, have agreed to take it slowly; as it was, with fate giving them a glimpse of what might be, and all too soon, not a day could be wasted. They had been given this priceless treasure, this second life; they must nurture it and honour it and savour the happiness it so clearly contained.

Russell had continued to stay at the Dorchester. Mary

had suggested he move to a hotel nearer Swindon, but he was nervous, it seemed, of anywhere other than the West End of London. He had always been like that, even when he was billeted out in Northolt or wherever; had had this deep conviction that the only proper place to be was an expensive, upper-class one. She had teased him about it a lot; she could see she probably would again.

'So when I'm home in Bristol, will you still insist on staying there?' she had asked, and he had said no, that he was investigating a hotel between Bristol and Bath which sounded pretty decent.

'Only pretty decent, Russell? You sure that's good enough?'

He had been fretting over the hospital too; saying he would rather she was in a private one, but she had told him that was ridiculous, she really was in a very good place. Of course you heard horror stories these days, about dirt and infection, and people being rushed out before they were well enough, but St Mark's didn't seem in the least like that. It was spotless, and the staff had been very firm about when she might be allowed to leave; she was actually very lucky to be there.

They'd had to arrange the times of his visits quite carefully, so that they didn't coincide with Christine's. He said he couldn't see the problem with that, he couldn't wait to meet Mary's children, both of them, but Mary told him she thought it might be a bit of a shock for them, particularly for Christine.

Each day Russell asked her if she had told Christine, and each day she said no, she would tell her when she was home. The semi-public situation of a hospital ward was not suitable for something so important and personal.

But now, they would be alone together all day and every day, for a while; and she could tell Christine all about him. And hopefully, when she came to terms with it, Christine would be really happy for them both. Hopefully . . .

'Abi?' It was William's calm, deep voice. 'It's William here. I've just had the police on the phone – got to give them an interview. Wondered if they'd approached you as well.'

'Hi, William,' said Abi, thinking it would be worth going through any number of police interviews to have William discussing them with her. 'It's great to hear from you. Yes, they have. In fact, it's tonight. I am *so* not looking forward to it.'

'Oh, it'll be all right,' he said easily. 'You were just a witness, that's all, nothing to worry about. All you've got to do is give them a straightforward account of it all.'

'I know, I know, but . . . well, I only have to see a policeman and I feel I've done something wrong.' As she very often had, she thought, and what on earth would William say if he knew about the real her . . . 'When are they seeing you then?'

'Tomorrow morning. I can't say I'm looking forward to it either. My father'll be getting involved probably, telling them the field's been ruined with their helicopter.'

'Well, it probably was. And you could tell them the cows are all having nervous breakdowns as well. Must have been so horrible for them.'

'I hadn't thought of that,' he said, and laughed. 'Yeah. Good idea.'

There was a long silence, then, 'Look, I was wondering,' he said diffidently. 'How would you like to have a drink tomorrow night? We can have a chat, compare notes.'

'That'd be great.' Was this for real? Was he actually asking her out? God . . .

'OK. It's a date. Where should we meet? Bristol, I suppose.'

'Long drive for you though. And then you won't be able to drink much.'

'Oh, don't worry about that. I'm used to it. I'm not a big drinker anyway. Tell me where we can meet. You can show me a few of the bright lights over there – how would that be?'

'Great,' said Abi. 'Yeah. Really great.'

'Good.' He sounded slightly surprised himself. 'And meanwhile, don't worry about the interview. All you've got to do is tell the truth, describe exactly what you saw.' (If only it was as simple as that, if only she hadn't got to lie and lie, and remember so many crucial things.) 'It's no big deal. What about your friend, the doctor? I expect they're seeing him as well.'

'Yes, I believe so,' said Abi, and then automatically, 'He's not a friend, William, just a business connection.'

'Oh, sorry. I thought you were mates.'

'No, not at all. I thought I'd told you, I'd never met him before Friday. He gave me a lift from the conference . . .' This was quite good, she could rehearse her lines.

'Oh, OK.' He sounded slightly bemused, then said, 'Well, it'll be interesting to see what they do want to know. I suppose my having had the bird's-eye view, so to speak, my account will be quite useful to them.'

'Yes, I'm sure it will. Well, good luck to you, William. And thanks so much for calling.'

'That's OK. I'm out on the tractor, good time to talk. And I'll see you tomorrow night.'

She sat thinking about him for a bit after ringing off; sitting there on the tractor, looking brown and so bloody fit, with those lovely kind, sort of hazel-ish eyes . . . Oh God. What was she doing, fancying a farmer of all things? And a posh farmer at that. And what was she doing, seeing him? Where was the sense in that? Ideally, she should be distancing herself from everyone and everything to do with the crash, not going out with them. It was a bit silly. She was bound to give the game away, slip up somehow.

She had been genuinely hurt as well as angered by Jonathan's rejection of her; she had not, of course, ever imagined that their affair had any real future, but somehow

323

he had beguiled her with his generosity, his enjoyment of her company as well as her body, his apparently genuine interest in her, into thinking he did actually care about her as a person. And how stupid had that been? Of course he hadn't. He was like all the rest of them. He had wanted what he could get out of her and beyond that – nothing.

Abi took a very dim view of men; not unnaturally, considering what she had endured at their hands. She was aware of being something of a walking cliché: knocked about by her mother's first boyfriend, after her own father had walked out, seduced by the second, and then forced to listen to his lies that she had seduced him. Which had resulted in her being thrown out of the house at the age of fifteen. After that there had been a long parade of boyfriends, one of whom she had genuinely loved. He was the one who had killed himself. By the time she was twenty-one, Abi had turned into the sort of person she really didn't like – without being able to see what she could have done about it.

She couldn't suddenly become marriage material now: she couldn't wipe out her rather desperate past. No one was going to look after her, she had to do it herself; and part of that seemed to be taking her sexual pleasure where she could, rather as men did. Only it was all right for men. Even married ones like Jonathan. It was all very unfair.

The police were coming to the flat the following night, a mere forty-eight hours after talking to Jonathan, so that the slightest deviation from his version would be very, very noticeable. Why had she let him talk her into this, for God's sake? Why hadn't she just refused, called his bluff, said she was going to tell the truth. She spent half the day standing outside the office, smoking.

The reports in all the Sunday papers had been awful. The lorry driver, who she now knew was called Patrick Connell, was very seriously injured and still in Intensive Care. Toby Weston, the bridegroom (the media had latched onto that story in a big way), was still heavily sedated, his leg with its multiple fractures a grave cause for concern. And there were several photographs of the families of people who had died, and of the blond girl in the Golf, taken on some beach the previous year, laughing, holding the hand of her boyfriend. There were even reports of an old lady who had been unable to get to the airport to meet her childhood sweetheart, but that seemed very unlikely. Probably some hard-nosed reporter had made it up. There were also a lot of annoying stories about Jonathan – his courage and how hard he had worked, how calm he was and how skilful. Although, annoying as they were, they were true. It was one of the reasons she didn't actually want to drop him in the shit. She supposed she did still care about him, just a bit. Which was why the way he was treating her was such a shock.

What was he getting into, William wondered. It was insane, absolutely ridiculous. But then who said relationships had to be sensible? Wasn't that the whole point, that relationships couldn't necessarily be called to order, that an attraction was uncontrollable and could, if followed, lead to some very pleasant chaos. William would have welcomed a bit of chaos into his life just now, his uneventful thirty-four-year-old life; he was too young to be settled into total predictability, too old to have to conform to his parents' lifestyle. He wanted an adventure: and if not an adventure, at least an excursion to adventure's perimeter. And Abi had seemed to be leading him towards one, beckoning him with her long, magenta fingernails, luring him with her dark, knowing eyes. OK, she could clearly be troublesome, but God she was sexy. Everything about her was sexy: her face was sexy, her voice was sexy, her body was sexy, thin and lithe, and yet with those extraordinarily full, high breasts, her walk was sexy – would he ever be able to forget those silver heels – she was a living breathing master class in – well, in sexiness.

So – what was wrong with that? Absolutely nothing at all. In fact, it looked rather the reverse.

William put the tractor into gear and sent it up the hill feeling suddenly pretty bloody good.

Maeve had been sitting with Patrick for some time, and was beginning to think rather longingly of the coffee shop and of what had become her supper, a latte and a cookie. She was thinking also (for the sitting with him had a very tedious aspect) that on her way back she'd pop up and see her new friend Mary.

She was absolutely dreading Mary going home; she had come to depend on her in the past few days. She was so wonderfully comforting and cheering, and filled with common sense; Maeve had even told her about the dreadful possibility of Patrick being paralysed: 'It will be unbearable for him. He's so active, so strong – he loves haring about; he can carry two of the boys and run at the same time. How will he cope with sitting in a chair for the rest of his life?'

'He will because he'll have to,' Mary said. 'You love him so much and he loves you so much and you know, Maeve, it's a wonderful thing, love. They say faith can move mountains, but so to my mind can love. But you don't know, he may recover completely. They can do such wonderful things these days . . .'

Maeve had thought Patrick was getting more 'with it', as she put it, day by day, and he was expected soon to be moved to a normal ward; it might be a long time before he came home, and the very least he had to face was major abdominal surgery, but he was very much alive still, which a week ago had seemed far too much to hope for.

She was saying all this to Patrick, and thinking it would be nice when he started talking a bit more himself, as Dr Pritchard had assured her he would, when he reached out for her hand and squeezed it very tightly, and said, 'Maeve, I'm beginning to remember.'

'Remember what?' she said, and there was a band round her chest as tight as his hand round hers.

'The accident. What happened. How it happened.'

'Yes?'

'It was hot. Terribly hot.'

'Yes, of course it was.'

'The sun was so bright.'

'Yes, I'm sure . . .'

'And I was so tired, Maeve. So tired.'

'Oh, Patrick . . .' She'd been terrified of this: ever since she'd heard about it, certainly since she'd known he was going to live. She wanted to stop him, to shut him up, to keep him – and her – safe from the memories. But . . .

'I was eating jelly babies, you know.'

'Sure, they help.'

'No, they weren't working. I can remember eating them, lots of them, handfuls. I could feel my head going, you know? The fuzzing, I've told you about the fuzzing.'

'Yes, Patrick, you have.'

He had: the feeling that his brain was getting confused, not functioning properly.

'I went to the doctor about it, you know, but he couldn't help.'

'No, I didn't know that.' Had he told her? She couldn't remember.

'That's all I can recall. The fuzzing – and then blankness.'

'Yes, but, Patrick darling, that was when you blacked out. Lost consciousness. Not went to sleep. Went unconscious. Of course you can't remember.'

'Well, I think I can. And what is more, Maeve, I think there was someone else in the cab.'

'Someone else? What on earth do you mean?'

'I don't know. I just seem to remember . . . there was someone else there.'

'But Pat, how could there have been? There was no one with you when they found you. We'd have known if there had been – and where could they have gone?'

'I know. But I still think – oh, I'm so afraid, Maeve. So afraid I must have – gone – gone to sleep . . .'

And then he stopped talking and tears squeezed slowly and painfully from his eyes, rolled down his cheeks, large, childlike tears. And Maeve, still clutching his hand, stroking it, trying to comfort him, thought that if he had gone to sleep, if he had caused that crash, for which he had been punished, and was still being punished so horribly, then she was to blame as well, for hassling him, hurrying him home, when perhaps another hour or two of rest would have made all the difference. All the difference in the world; and for some people indeed, the difference between life and death.

'Dr King? Emma?'

Emma jumped. She had been on her way to the café to grab a coffee and a Coke; she was terribly tired. She turned, looked to see who had called her, and saw Barney Fraser, Toby Weston's friend.

'I thought it was you. How are you?' he asked.

He was looking different, she couldn't think why, then realised he was in his City togs: sharp suit although the jacket was slung over his shoulder, formal shirt, pink check, really suited him, a tie even, albeit hanging loose round his neck.

'Just on my way to the café, get a shot of caffeine before I go back to town,' he went on. 'You?'

'I'm in search of caffeine too.'

'OK. We could go together.'

He smiled at her. God, he had a wonderful smile. God, he was so gorgeous. *Stop it, Emma. He's taken. And so are you . . . now.*

'OK. Mustn't be long though.'

They went into the café. She grabbed a Diet Coke, then joined him at the coffee counter and ordered an Americano.

'Snap. Same as me. I actually wanted a double espresso, but they're not great at coffee speak here.'

"Fraid not.'

'Can you sit down for five minutes? Or do you have to rush back?'

'Well – five minutes.'

'Cool.'

'So, have you been visiting Toby?' she asked.

'Yes, I have.'

'Driven all the way down from London?'

'No, I came on the train. I'm about to call a cab, there's a notice about them in the main reception. How's the service this time of night?'

'Not bad. Not good, either.'

'Oh well. You win some, you lose some. It was a brilliant way of coming down.'

'Yes, it would be.' What on earth were they discussing transport methods for? 'How is Toby?'

She knew he wasn't very well; she'd talked to Mark Collins about him the day before. He had been running recurrent fevers from Sunday night and complaining of feeling generally unwell. His blood pressure was low and today he even seemed confused. 'It points to infection, I'm afraid,' Mark had said. 'Worrying, but not at the moment actually dangerous. We've upped the antibiotics and we're going to take him to theatre tomorrow and do a washout. It's just such a horrible mess, poor chap. So cruel, the whole thing. I mean, the end of this particular road – well you know what it is as well as I do.'

Amputation, Emma thought, wincing: what a terrifying prospect for a young bloke in his thirties. She hoped Barney didn't realise that, at least.

'How is he?' she asked again. As if she didn't know.

'Not great. They did some washout thing today.'

'Well,' she said carefully, 'that should do some good.'

'And if it doesn't, he'll lose the leg, right?'

She was shocked. 'Nobody here told you that, did they?'

'No, no, I rang a mate who's a medic.'

'Oh, I see. Well, without knowing Toby's case . . .'

'Emma, it's OK. I've taken it on board. It's hideous, but—'

'But it really would be a last resort. And I hope he's miles from that. You haven't told his parents this?'

'No, of course I haven't. I'm not a total retard.' He looked slightly put out.

'Sorry. It's just – well, we have to be so careful about that sort of thing.'

'No, it's fine, I haven't told anyone. Except Amanda, that is.'

Amanda. The Sloaney, perfect girlfriend. Correction, the Sloaney, perfect fiancée. He looked very dejected; Emma wondered what on earth she could say. Nothing really.

'How did Toby seem in himself?'

'Oh, bit out of it actually. Didn't say much about it hurting, maybe that's a good sign. Or would it be the drugs?'

'Honestly, probably the drugs.'

'I was afraid you'd say that. When – when will they know if it's worked?'

'Oh, not for several more days. Um, what about his fiancée, has she been down much?'

'I'm not sure. She's still at home with her parents, getting over her cancelled wedding.'

His voice was bitter; Emma looked at him sharply. He interpreted the look, said, 'Sorry, shouldn't have said that.'

'You can say what you like to me, Barney. But – well, it must be pretty awful for her, worrying about Toby, and she wouldn't be human if she wasn't upset about the wedding.'

'Of course.'

'What do you all do?' she asked with a glance at her watch.

'Oh, Tobes and I are those wicked banker people. You know, earn as much as the budget of a small country. If you believe the press, that is.'

He probably wasn't exactly poor though.

'And Amanda, what does she do?'

'She's in HR. In the same bank as Tobes. And Tamara, she's on the French desk at my firm.'

Emma wasn't sure how a bank could have a French desk, but she didn't like to say so.

'Yeah, so it's all a bit incestuous really. Tamara is seriously cool. You should see their apartment – talk about retro.'

'I probably wouldn't appreciate it,' said Emma, laughing. 'I'm still at the furnished flat stage myself, don't really notice what it looks like at all.'

'Yeah? How long will you be here, do you think? Moving on, up to London or whatever?'

'I have no idea where I'll be. But I want, eventually, to go into obstetrics. At the moment I'm just a general surgeon, doing my four-month stint down here, in A and E, which I do love.'

'You're a surgeon?'

'Yes.'

'You mean you actually . . .'

'Cut people up? Yes, I do.' She grinned. 'Don't look so horrified!'

'Not horrified, just seriously impressed. I mean, you don't look old enough to be a doctor at all, and—'

'Oh, don't!' she said. 'If I had a pound for every time I'm told that . . . I think I'll put it on my tombstone: *She Didn't Look Old Enough* . . . Barney, I really must go. It's been lovely talking to you, but God knows what's happening down there.' She nodded in the direction of A&E. 'Look,

I'll pop up and see Toby tomorrow, if you think he'd like that.'

'Emma, anyone out of short trousers would like being visited by you. Actually, even if they were in short trousers.' Barney smiled. 'Thank you so much. You've really cheered me up.'

'It was a pleasure. Honestly.'

She held out her hand; he took it, then rather hesitantly bent down and kissed her cheek.

'Pleasure for me too. Honestly. Thank you again. For all your help, not just this evening.'

And then he was gone, hurrying out of the café, pulling on his jacket.

Emma walked rather slowly back to A&E, then sat down at the doctor's station and said, 'Shit.'

And Barney, settling into the corner of a cab on his way to the station, said, 'Fuck.' For much the same reason.

Chapter 22

It had gone pretty well, Abi thought. They'd questioned her quite closely, but she hadn't let them rattle her.

She'd been pretty stressed by a panic phone call from Jonathan very early that morning, telling her more things that she must and must not say. Like the time they left the conference in Birmingham – that she must be vague, say between eleven-thirty and twelve, that they'd been held up at the service station. And – change of information – he had now told them Laura had called his mobile at four. 'Well, *she* told them, actually. But she said she only heard me saying hello and then it all went blank. That OK?'

She was silent.

'So – is that all right?' he repeated.

'Is what all right?'

'About the phone call, for God's sake!'

'I suppose so. Who do I say it was?'

'You don't have to say anything. Just say it rang and I answered it and hurled it on the floor when the lorry started to swerve. It might not even come up. Did you switch the phone off, incidentally? I didn't and—'

'Yes, I did.'

'Fine. Well, I think that's everything. Bye then.'

She didn't answer. She felt very bleak suddenly, bleak and alone. He hadn't even wished her good luck. Bastard. God, how she hated him. Her earlier sense of still – just – caring about him had vanished.

Anyway, she'd said what he'd told her; about their

relationship, about her car not starting so she'd gone by train to the conference, and then all the stuff about the accident – a relief to be able to relax and just speak the truth for a bit – and then, through slightly gritted teeth, she'd told them how marvellous Jonathan had been afterwards. Which was true as well.

She said they'd hardly spoken since then, just that she'd reassured him that she was safely home . . .

She was actually quite pleased with herself, felt high with relief. And at least it was over. The very worst was over . . .

And now she had her evening with William to look forward to.

'Well, what did you think of that then?' Sergeant Freeman closed his notebook, filed Abi's statement carefully, and turned to Constable Rowe.

'Oh, she seemed rather nice,' said Rowe. 'Attractive girl. Very, very sexy.'

'Indeed. Any man would be tempted by her. Even a man with a beautiful wife. You didn't think her story was in any way suspicious?'

'No, not at all. It tallied exactly with his. With Mr Gilliatt's.'

'So it did. Too exactly, I'd say. Almost word for word, at times. Like them both insisting that they had "a purely professional relationship". Why did they both feel the need to tell us that, do you think? It's not relevant.'

'No, but I suppose in his case, with the wife there . . .'

'Yeah, yeah. But the exact same words? And about her car not starting – she just volunteered that; we didn't ask her, so why tell us? It was all a bit pat. Liars will always say the same thing. Something's starting to smell a bit here, something's not quite right.'

'Yes, but why should they be lying?'

'Well, in his case, it's easy to understand. His whole

marriage hangs on it. For her – well, maybe she's got a bit of a crush on him, thinks if she goes along with him he'll carry on with the relationship. She probably gets some pretty good perks out of it. These girls do, you know – expensive little trips abroad, for instance, staying in the best hotels, jewellery – and so on.'

'You're making her sound like a tart,' said Rowe, surprised to find himself quite indignant on Abi's behalf. 'And anyway, what's it got to do with the crash? Doesn't mean they're guilty of anything else, or lying about anything to do with it.'

'No, of course not. But she may be covering up some other thing that happened. Maybe he was partly to blame. Maybe she was. Maybe he was driving dangerously, not looking what he was doing. Maybe she was distracting him. He was very vague about the crash, given that he was right up there in the forefront. I wouldn't be totally surprised if he slewed out into the road, in front of the lorry, in the absence of any other explanation for it suddenly swerving.'

'The driver could have gone to sleep.'

'True. He could also have had to swerve. People do some funny things on the motorway, Rowe. Very funny. To one another, that is.'

'You mean she could have been kissing him or something?'

'Rather more than kissing,' said Freeman.

Rowe was silent; then he went rather pink. 'You don't mean . . .'

'I leave it to your imagination, Constable. Anyway, we've got his measure now. We can take other things he says with a pinch of salt. As I said, they've obviously liaised over the story. What's he got on her, I wonder, that she's agreed to it? Like I said, she might be in love with him. Or there may be something else she doesn't want us to know about. As the investigation goes on, that could well

335

emerge. We'll just tuck this into our back teeth and keep it there. All right?'

'Yes, all right,' said Constable Rowe.

Sergeant Freeman smiled for the first time that day. 'That's why this game is such fun, in its own peculiar way. I think we have to go back in, ask a few more questions. If there's any chance of their colluding, then they'd be guilty of perverting the course of justice, which I don't need to tell you is a very serious crime indeed. We must take a very close look at the CCTV footage at the service station too, see what we can pick up there. Also her firm, what's it called – oh yes, Conferphoto – check whether they did actually cover this conference. I'm beginning to wonder.'

'Should I check with her firm, or the conference organisers?'

'The organisers, obviously. We don't want her rattled, thinking we're on to her. We don't want to rattle either of them in any way. Just let them go for a bit, see what they get up to. You know what they say, Rowe, give them enough rope and they'll hang themselves.'

'Poor Mr Connell.' Jo Wales walked into the nurses' room on HDU. The police had become very pressing about questioning Patrick, and reluctantly his doctors had agreed. Jo had sat in on the interview and her conviction that it was too soon had strengthened with every moment.

'Did they upset him?' Her colleague Stephanie Hitchens, who had also nursed Patrick, had been equally against the interview.

'Yes, they did. I nearly stopped it twice – sorry, Maria,' she said to the Polish cleaner whose path she was obstructing. 'Carry on. Anyway, he recovered himself each time. So I let them have their fifteen minutes.'

'Are we any the wiser?'

'Not really. He's still going on about remembering

336

getting drowsy, eating his jelly babies – in tears once. That's when I asked them to go, but he said he was all right, wanted to finish.'

'Oh Lord. I really don't think they should have agreed. It's too soon.'

'I know. But they did assure him it was a preliminary chat, that they'd come back for a more detailed one later on, when he was feeling better.'

'And that's supposed to reassure him? For God's sake. Anything else?'

'One thing, yes. He said he thought there might have been someone in the cab with him – was actually beginning to remember something.'

'Really?'

'Yes, and you know I heard him saying that to Mrs Connell too. He was quite emphatic about it then. I just dismissed it at the time.'

'Seems very unlikely. I mean, where could such a person have gone?'

'Well, exactly. But of course the police got very interested in it, started questioning him more closely – he got very upset.'

'Poor Patrick. It's all so cruel. There he is, the sweetest man, having to cope with all this horror. I'll pop along and chat with him for a bit.'

Maria, whose English was much better than most people in the hospital realised, finished her desultory floor-wiping, and set off for the lift, pushing her trolley of cleaning utensils rather fast. That would give her something to tell the journalist who had been pestering her for information for the past few days. And she should get that fifty pounds he had promised her. She parked the trolley in main reception, risking the ire of the admin department, walked quickly across the car park to the dark blue Ford parked in the corner, and climbed into the back seat.

❖ ❖ ❖

William liked Sergeant Freeman; he was so straight-forward, so calmly determined to clarify details. And so reasonable when William said he couldn't remember something, or couldn't be sure about something.

'So, it looked as if the lorry went into a skid?' said Freeman.

'Well, yes. He swerved quite suddenly. Although I don't know what the technical definition of a skid would be.'

'A slide, sir. The wheels sliding along the surface of the road, out of control. But a loss of control can equally be caused by something other than a skid.'

'I would have thought, given the storm and so on, an actual skid was very likely. But I'm not an expert. Your chaps must have examined the road.'

'Indeed they have, sir. So, you saw no apparent reason for this swerve?'

'Not that I could see, no.'

He had apologised from time to time: that he'd had no idea how long after the rain had stopped the crash had happened, or whether the traffic had been travelling faster on the westbound carriageway than the east.

'You must think I'm a pretty useless witness, but I can only tell you what I saw. What I know I saw.'

'Not at all, sir. Conjecture is useless when we're trying to establish facts. Far rather you were honest. Now, I believe that after the chopper had landed, you went down to the road and handed water round. Very good of you, sir.'

'Not at all. It was nice to be able to do something.'

'Any other details, however small, that you noticed on your way down? Anyone walking about on your land, for instance?'

He'd half-forgotten until that moment, so small a part had she played in the day. 'Well, there was someone, as a matter of fact. A girl.'

'A girl? Was she on her own?'

'Yes, very much so. She seemed a bit – out of it actually.

She was just scrambling along through the spinney, as we call it – it's pretty rough underfoot there – looking upset, and I did ask her if she was all right. She said she was, and walked on. She clearly wasn't hurt or anything, and I decided I'd better worry about all the other people. I thought I might see her again, but I never did. I mean, maybe she was just looking for somewhere to pee or something. I don't know.'

'Could you give us any details about this girl? Her age, height, the colour of her hair, or what she was wearing?'

'She was black, with long curly hair. She was pretty, young, and with a nice voice, I did notice that. It was a bit husky. And she was quite well spoken, too.'

They asked him what she was wearing, whether he'd seen her again at the end of the day.

'No, she just vanished. Sorry.'

'That's fine.' Sergeant Freeman gave William one of his rare smiles. 'You've been very helpful, Mr Grainger. Very helpful indeed.'

And then they'd got on to Abi. William told them she'd been helping the little boys from the mini-bus, that she'd organised a sing-song, that she'd gone off with one of them in the ambulance. He also mentioned that she'd been with the doctor, the one who'd been helping at the crash.

'Ah.' Grainger consulted his notes. 'Would that have been Miss Scott?'

'Yes, that's right. Abi Scott.'

'And her relationship with Mr Gilliatt was what, would you say? How would you describe it?'

'Well, it wasn't at all personal, if that's what you mean. They were just colleagues.'

'She told you that, did she?'

'Well, yes. They'd been at a conference of some sort. She seemed to know him moderately well – I mean, she called him Jonathan, rather than Mr Gilliatt, not that that means much, I know.' He grinned suddenly. 'He seemed pretty annoyed with her, actually. Don't know why. Very aggressive attitude. He was even shouting at her at one point. But he was under a lot of strain, poor bloke. He was absolutely marvellous, did so much to help, keeping people calm, telling them what to do.'

'Yes, he seems to have been very helpful,' said Sergeant Freeman. 'And so have you, Mr Grainger. Thank you very much.'

Jack Bryant had had a good week. He'd bagged over one hundred brace of grouse, eaten some excellent meals and furthered his acquaintance with Margo Farthringoe most satisfactorily. She was fifty-one, modestly good looking, extremely sexy and a very good shot. She was also newly separated from Gordon Farthringoe, who was disporting himself around town with a fine example of twenty-two-year-old arm candy.

Jack was loading up the boot of the E-type with as much grouse as he could decently take away with him when he thought he should give the car the onceover. She wasn't as young as she had been and she needed a lot of TLC. Everything seemed fine: except that she seemed to have lost a wheel nut. Bit of a bugger. He had no idea where he might have lost it; decided it would be foolhardy to try to drive all the way back down the M1 without it, and embarked on a quest for a new one. It took most of the day; the border country was not rich in specialist garages. His irritation was considerably eased however by the offer of a further night at the Argylls': and a further foray into the arms of Mrs Farthringoe.

Sue Riley, the casting director, had called Linda.

'Right, Linda, we'd like her, please. She's perfect. It's not just that she really can act, she looks exactly right. And her attitude is great – spunky little thing. Oh, which reminds me, can she swim? Writer's just put in a scene where she falls in the river.'

Linda said yes, Georgia could swim – thinking that if she couldn't, she'd pay personally for a crash course for her – and then said how thrilled she was and how thrilled Georgia would be.

'Great. We'll start drawing up the contract then. We're going into pre-production now, so you won't hear anything much for a couple of weeks. Filming starts late September, early October. We'll try to do all the externals first, while there's still plenty of daylight. Praying for good weather. Anyway, tell her congratulations from us. We're looking forward to working with her.'

'I will. Thanks, Sue. I'm delighted.'

And she was; this was the big one for Georgia, she would be on her way now. Because the series was clearly high quality – she'd been very impressed by the script – it would get plenty of attention from the critics and therefore so would Georgia. Linda felt very happy suddenly; she sat back in her chair, enjoying the pleasure before ringing Georgia, feeling, albeit briefly, her own success, her moment. It didn't happen very often, this happy congruence of opportunity and fulfilment, of demand and supply, but when it did, and for someone new like Georgia, it was infinitely worth all the networking, all the manoeuvring, all the trials-by-ego. Suddenly everything was in focus: no longer an optimistic blur. It was heady stuff.

Linda got up, went over to her fridge and took out one of the mini-bottles of champagne she kept there for such moments. Later she would toast Georgia; right now she was toasting herself.

She poured herself a glass, savoured it for a moment, then lifted the phone and dialled Georgia's mobile number.

'Darling, it's good news.'

'Yeah?' The voice was shaky, breathless. 'Do you mean really good news?'

341

'I mean really good news. Yes, they want you.'

'Oh – God. Oh God, Linda, that is so – so cool.'

Ouch, thought Linda, that word. That inadequate, all-purpose word. Time surely that someone came in with another. However . . .

'I know. It's lovely. Many, many congratulations. I'm totally thrilled. What are you doing now?'

'I'm in Topshop, Oxford Circus, with a friend. I'm staying with her.'

'Well, want to come over, have a glass of bubbly? You can bring the friend, that's fine.'

'Can I? That's really kind, Linda. Let me just ask her.' She could hear the Topshop noise in the background, the thudding music, the voices, could hear Georgia saying, 'I got it, I got it! Yeah yeah, that part . . . yeah, I know . . . want to come and have some champagne with my agent? She's really cool . . . No, go on, I want you to . . .' and then: 'Yeah, Linda, we'd really love that, thanks so much. Can we come over right now? We'll be about thirty minutes.'

'Great. I'll get the glasses out.'

'Cool.'

It really was very cool Linda thought, and decided it was worth sending Francis an email to tell him. He sent one straight back, saying, *Well done. I'm proud of you.* He always reacted like that: as if she was the one who'd got the part. It was very sweet. *He* was very sweet. She didn't know what she'd have done without him. Well, she wouldn't have the agency for a start.

'Hi, it's us.'

'OK, I'll let you in. Push on the door.'

They came in, Georgia alight with excitement and triumph, the friend smiling, slightly shy. She was a rather mousy little thing. Georgia often had such friends; it was a sign of her insecurity, her need to shine.

'Hello,' Linda said. 'Well done, Georgia. I'm very proud of you.'

'Thanks. This is Zoe.'

'Hi, Zoe. OK, here we go. Cork out – wow, that was a noisy one . . .'

They stood there, Linda and Zoe, with glasses raised to Georgia. Georgia hugged them both.

'I so can't believe it. When did you hear?'

'Oh, a few minutes before I rang you. It's very good, Georgia. A great coup.'

'So what's the timing? When do we start shooting?'

'In about a month. They're in pre-production. They plan to start shooting at the end of September. Outside scenes first, Sue said. Oh, and she wanted to know if you could swim. I said you could, obviously. But if you can't . . .'

'Course I can swim. Oh God, it's so exciting. How's the money?'

'The money's not bad, Georgia. We'll discuss it later. You'll have to find somewhere to stay, obviously. But I've got a couple of other girls who are looking for flatshares.'

'That'd be cool. Wow, it's soooo great. Oh Linda, thank you so, so much. I know how hard you've worked for me, and I know I don't deserve it.'

'Well, sometimes you do.'

'I'm so happy I could die. Or fly.'

'Well, don't do either, there's a good girl,' said Linda. 'We need you very much in one piece for the foreseeable future.'

'Don't worry, I'll take huge care of myself. Did they say I needed to lose any weight?'

'No, they didn't,' said Linda. 'Don't even think about it.' She looked at Georgia thoughtfully; they were all obsessed with their weight. Maybe Georgia had been starving herself. That would account for her rather violent mood swings . . .

* * *

Russell was also so happy, as the week drew to an end, that he felt he could die or fly. Seeing Mary again had not been simply wonderful, but reassuring: that she was still the dear, small person he remembered, warm and bright and filled with sense. It had brought back the past, their past, into vivid life, as if the sixty years in between had never been, as if the past had somehow magically become the present.

And the minute they had got over what was surely a very small hurdle, when Mary had told her children, and he had met them, then there would be no stopping them.

William had driven to Bristol to meet Abi in a state of considerable turmoil; he felt anxious and excited in just about equal measure, alternately wishing he had obeyed his innate instinct that he shouldn't see her again, and then wondering why on earth he hadn't invited her out sooner.

She was so bloody sexy, and seemed really nice too, much nicer than you'd have thought a girl like her would be, and seemed to like him too. Of course, a relationship between them was a pretty futile idea; she obviously lived life very much in the fast lane (an unfortunate choice of words, he thought, smiling to himself), and his was pretty much in the slow one. No girl who hadn't been brought up to it could possibly understand or countenance farming, the 24/7 commitment, the back-breaking struggle to make it work with all the official interference, plus the resistance from locals if you even tried to do anything extra. An old friend of William's from Cirencester days had started a venture of Tanks Weekends on his Somerset farm, hugely popular with the corporate entertainment lot, whereby for a fat(ish) fee, groups of men could come and drive tanks over the fields and play soldiers. This had made all the difference between profit and loss on his balance sheet, but local people claimed he was ruining the area, wrecking the environment, and he was about to put his hands up and

344

admit defeat. Then there were the new locals, the city boys who had bought the big houses and some of the land that the farmers couldn't afford to run any more, and played at farming at the weekends. There were a fair number of complaints from them too. 'They like cows, but they like quiet cows that don't smell,' as William's father put it.

Anyway, Abi Scott no doubt would want quiet cows that didn't smell either, and she certainly wouldn't want a boyfriend who smelled of cows quite a lot of the time himself, nor getting those silver-heeled boots muddy.

And as for what his mother would have to say . . . the whole thing was pointless and this must be a one-off meeting, dedicated, as he had said when he called her, to discussing their respective interviews with the police.

But then – he'd walked into the bar she'd suggested, and she had waved at him, come over to meet him, kissed him hello – her perfume was incredibly powerful, musky and sweet – taken his hand and led him back to her table. He had said he mustn't drink, that he had to drive; three beers later, his head was swimming a bit and he was wondering rather anxiously how he was going to get home. Maybe if they had a meal – a large one – and he drank only water he'd sober up sufficiently.

He would not have drunk so much had he not found himself so relaxed; he might have expected to find someone like her hard to talk to, but she was easily chatty and funny, and she had a talent for listening too, asking him endless questions about the farm, about his life, about his parents even, and displaying what seemed a genuine interest in the answers.

And he had slowly become aware that one of her long legs was pressing against his, that she was leaning closer to him, that she was studying his mouth as he talked; the combination of all these things, together with the three beers and the heady cloud of her perfume was making him feel physically dizzy. Surely, surely she couldn't fancy him.

345

Not really. She must be playing games, or practising or something.

God, he was so gorgeous. And sexy too – in the most extraordinary, off-the-wall-type way. No, that wasn't right, he was completely *on* the wall. She would never have believed she would find herself fancying someone like him: so public school, so straight down the line, so old-style polite. He actually came round to push in her chair, for God's sake, stood up when she went to the toilet and again when she came back. OK, Jonathan had been quite courteous. He'd let her go through doors in front of him, and walked on the outside on the rare occasions when they were in the street, but he certainly hadn't treated her like this. It was amazing. She felt like someone completely different. The sort of person who'd grown up used to that sort of thing herself. She supposed she might get fed up with it pretty quickly, that it might even start to annoy her; although why she wasn't sure. Just because it was alien, didn't mean she didn't like it. It was like being stroked, or eating chocolates, or lying in the sun; it was soothing, warming, totally pleasing.

And he was so incredibly good looking. He could have been a model, if he'd wanted. OK, his haircut was a bit dated, but then it suited him. It was great hair. That wonderful rich, conker brown and then sort of blond streaks.

He had no idea how attractive he was. He was a bit like a child, completely unselfconscious about himself; she looked at him now, sitting in the bar, his long legs stretched out in front of him, his shirtsleeves pushed up to the elbows, showing his tanned forearms, covered in thick blond hair – grinning at her, talking about the farm, about how much he loved it in spite of everything, loved being out of doors all the time, about the satisfaction of it, of harvesting the wheat, of rearing healthy animals. She'd argued with him about that, said she couldn't quite see what was so satisfying about that, you reared them and then you killed them as far as she could see, but he said no, no, you were doing something totally positive, giving them a decent life and then providing food for people, good food, not rubbish. That was what beef cattle were for, he said, contributing to the food chain in the best possible way. Of course they had to go off to slaughter, 'But they don't worry about it. You see, they don't know it's coming – it just happens, quite quickly, just one day. It's not like factory chickens: that's a living death, they're wretched all their lives.'

She nodded in what she hoped was a well-informed way.

'My brother's an accountant, one of those City types – now that's an awful existence, pushing non-existent money around, helping rich people stay as rich as they can. It's a mean, selfish little life, that, in my view.'

She was surprised by how articulate he was; somehow she'd always imagined farmers would be the strong, silent type. William talked really well once he got going, and with passion. When he moved on to the supermarkets and how they screwed the farmers into the ground, ruined the small ones, she began to care about them too. Usually she glazed over at such conversations, but she could have sat there for more hours still – mostly just watching him, to be sure – but still enjoying listening to his deep, rich voice – and yes, it was a bit posh and she didn't usually like posh, but it was his. So she liked it.

'Sorry, Abi, you mustn't let me bore you. You probably want to talk about our respective interviews with the police.'

She'd been looking at his feet in their Timberland boots: they were very big feet. Was just letting her mind wander, most pleasurably, on to the myth or otherwise of the big-feet-big-cock theory, thinking how much she'd like to test it . . . maybe not tonight but soon. Please, please let it be soon . . .

'You're not boring me,' she said, 'and I don't want to. Plenty of time for that.'

'Yeah. Fine. Look, I've had far too much to drink. Can we find somewhere to eat and let me buy you dinner? I need to consume about five thousand calories even to start to mop it all up. We could talk about the interviews then, or maybe you've got other plans?'

Abi, reflecting that her other plans would use up a great many calories, said, no, no, she hadn't and dinner would be great.

He suggested Browns; he would know Browns, she thought, it was made for people like him. She didn't often go there, because it was – well, full of people like him. Which tonight seemed pretty good.

'So come on,' he said, when they had ordered a large steak for him and a crab salad for her, downing an enormous glass of water, immediately pouring himself another. 'What about you? Tell me about your job, tell me about your family, tell me what you like doing.'

She had an almost irresistible urge to tell him what she really liked doing and how much she'd like to do it with him; but suppressed it and gave him as sanitised a version as she could of her life, her friends, her job. It was no use pretending she worked for a management consultancy or that her friends ran art galleries, he'd see through that in seconds. But she cut out the lingerie modelling, the drugs, and – obviously – most of her boyfriends. Especially the last one.

'So – no one serious at the moment?'

'No.'

'I can't think why not.'

He looked so genuinely baffled that she wanted to kiss him. She did kiss him. Only on the cheek, but . . .

'What was that for?' he asked, grinning at her.

'For wondering why I hadn't got a serious boyfriend. I wish.'

'But why not? I really can't imagine.'

'Because they're mostly rubbish, that's why. The men I meet. Spoiled. Up themselves. Waste of space.'

'That's pretty damning,' he said, laughing. 'You must have met a particularly bad lot.'

'Not at all. Completely standard. That's how men are these days, you know. They get it all handed to them on a plate. Don't have to work for anything, on a personal level, that is. So why should they bother being nice or – or anything.'

'Oh dear.' He looked less amused now, was staring at her with something close to concern. 'You sound very disillusioned. I feel I should make an apology for my sex.' He poured himself yet another glass of water. 'God, I'll be peeing all the way home. No, seriously. You've obviously been very hurt by – by someone.'

'Yes, lots,' she said, and the person who had hurt her the most and the most recently swam before her eyes, and the magic was gone, albeit briefly, and she felt suddenly and dreadfully sad.

'Well, I'm sorry,' he said. He was clearly much too much of a gentleman to ask her about it; and she could hardly tell him. So they sat in silence for a moment or two, and then he said, 'Look, I should be getting back quite soon. I'll get the bill – and we've still not talked about our interviews. So, how was yours? Was it as awful as you expected?'

'No. No, it was fine. Sergeant Freeman and PC Rowe: what a pair! They were very nice. Much less scary than I expected. Yours?'

'Yes, I agree they are nice chaps. Very thorough. They went into absolutely everything. Who I talked to, all that sort of thing. They even asked about you.'

'Me! What did they ask about me? For heaven's sake!'

'Oh, well I told them how great you were, helping the little boys. How you went to the hospital with one of them. And then they asked me if I knew anything about your relationship with the doctor bloke.'

'My relationship with – but I don't – that is, why should they ask you that?'

'No idea. Well, first they asked what happened to your car, why it wasn't still on the motorway, and I said you'd been with the doctor in his.'

'Yeah?'

'And then they asked me if I knew anything about your relationship with him. I said absolutely nothing, except that it was a professional one, that you'd been at a conference together.'

'Oh. Right.'

'I also said he seemed pretty tense, was shouting at you at one point.'

'Well, he was. Quite true.' Did it matter, them knowing that? Not really. And William had said all the right things, that her relationship with Jonathan was only professional. But – why were they interested? It was a bit worrying.

'Anyway, that was about it really. Ah, here's the bill. No, no, I insist,' as she fumbled for her cards, 'don't be silly. Look, can I drop you anywhere?'

God, he was such a fucking gentleman; most men, after buying you three cocktails and dinner, would expect to be well into your knickers. She seemed to have stopped wishing he wasn't a gentleman . . . she was worrying instead that he didn't want to.

'Well no, it's OK, I'll get a cab.'

'Oh, now that's ridiculous. I'll just drive you home.'

Maybe he did want to. It seemed crazy not to find out.

They went out to the street and as they walked to his car, she put her arm through his, and he looked down at her and smiled in that totally charming way, and then he said, 'Come on, hop in.'

Abi hopped.

It was a ten-minute drive; as they parked outside the block, in her bleak, narrow street, she said, hoping she sounded like the nice girl he seemed to imagine she was, 'Would you like to come in for a coffee?'

'No,' he said, 'I'd love to, but I really mustn't. My ghastly brother's coming down tomorrow.'

'What, the accountant?'

'That's the one. God, I must be boring. Banging on about my family.'

'William,' said Abi, reaching up to kiss his cheek, 'you couldn't ever be boring. I could listen to you all –' she had been going to say 'all night' and amended it hastily to 'all day. Even talking about your cows. Your girls, as you call them.' He did; she had found that unbelievably sweet.

'Really?' She was sure if it had been light, she would have seen him blushing. He did blush, became discomfited quite easily. He wasn't exactly shy, but he was quite bashful. She supposed it was his upbringing. All those years at public school, growing up without women. She wondered if he'd been in love with any of the boys. You heard all that stuff about those schools, but somehow she couldn't imagine William being gay. Even for a few pimply months. He was the most hetero bloke she'd ever known.

The other thing he did was giggle. He had a wonderful laugh, a booming, roaring laugh, but he also, when suddenly amused, giggled, uncontrollably and infectiously.

'So why is he coming – your brother? Family party?' She thought of Mrs Grainger with her tight, cool smile; not a lot of fun partying with her.

'No, no. It's business. Potentially difficult actually. Which is why I want to have a clear head.'

'Why? In what way?'

'Oh Abi, I've bored you enough.'

'No, you haven't. I told you, you couldn't. Come on in and tell me all about it.' She knew Sylvie was out for the night. They'd be quite undisturbed.

He said nothing, just got out of the car, came round and opened the door for her. This was just ridiculous. She felt as if she was in a fifties movie or something. She got out, smiling, trying to be graceful and ladylike, and promptly tripped on a jutting paving stone and fell forwards.

Now if Sylvie had been watching, she would have said it was deliberate. It wasn't. Just the same, his arms went out to catch her and, having caught her, somehow went round her; and she stood there, held by him, looking up at him, and he was looking down at her, and then slowly, rather tentatively, he bent his head and started to kiss her. And having started, continued, and it was the most fantastic kiss, hard and probing and quite slow at the same time; and she felt herself responding in the most unladylike way, meeting his tongue with hers, feeling the kiss working, moving downwards, the sensation warm and invasive, rippling out in a series of ever bigger sensations, and she pushed her hips against him, felt him responding; and then suddenly he drew back, stopped kissing her, just looked down at her, half-smiling, half-embarrassed and said, 'Abi, I'm sorry, I—'

'Sorry?' she said and then in a most unladylike way, 'Fuck sorry, William. Just do it again, or come in or—'

'I mustn't,' he said. 'Honestly, Abi, I'd love to, I really would, but . . .'

'But what?' she said, genuinely puzzled.

'Well – you know. We hardly know each other.' And that made her laugh, rather weakly, leaning against him, and pulling his head down and kissing him, quite differently now, on the cheek, on his nose.

'You really are special,' she said. 'So, so special.'

'Not really,' he said. 'Dead ordinary bloke, I am.'

'No, William, you're not ordinary, not ordinary at all. Promise me one thing: let's do it again, very soon.'

'What – drink and dinner?'

'Yes, if you want. Drink, dinner, kiss and then see what happens next. OK?'

He was silent, looking down at her very seriously, almost

anxiously, and God, she thought, I've gone too far, pushed myself forward, acted like a tart; and then he smiled and said, 'Yeah, well, that'd be great. Absolutely great. I'll ring you, OK?'

'You'd better,' she said, releasing herself from him, grinning at him, walking towards the front door of her block. 'And if you don't, I'll ring you. I haven't been very well brought up, you see. That's what I do, ring blokes I fancy. Night, William, thanks for a great evening.'

'No,' he said. 'No, thank *you*. It's been so great. You're very special too, Abi. I hope you know that.'

And he drove off, slowly, and she stood there, looking after him, and then went inside and got into bed, and lay there wide awake, still excited, still hardly touching reality, wondering how soon she might see him again and whether that time she would be able to persuade him into bed with her. Even though – what was it he'd said? Oh yes, even though they hardly knew one another. Incredible that people still thought like that. Absolutely incredible.

And William drove home, rather slowly, in case he was actually over the limit, playing his favourite Bruce Springsteen CD, and wondering if it was even remotely possible that a girl as sexy and funny and fun as Abi could really enjoy being with him, and whether she'd meant it when she said she'd like to go out with him again.

Chapter 23

Laura wanted to believe Jonathan more than anything on earth. About Abi Scott. Her whole life and happiness hung on it. And indeed, her family's happiness. Because if it wasn't true, if he *had* been having an affair with her – with anyone – then there was no way she could stay with him. She had always felt that trust was synonymous with love, that one couldn't exist without the other. However wonderful Jonathan was, however good their marriage, however perfect their life, if he'd betrayed her, she couldn't possibly go on with it. How could you go to sleep beside a man, wake up with him, live in his house, bring up his children, if he had lied to you, if all those 'I love you's all those 'I couldn't live without you's had been said to someone else.

If he had made love to someone else, known her body intimately, caressed her, entered her, made her come – then how could you possibly stay with him, accept those lies, forgive them – and him? How could your sense of safety and confidence ever return? How would you ever believe him again if he said he was working late, on a business trip, dining with colleagues? Suspicion would poison everything, every smile, every kiss, every caress, would distort pleasure, wreck contentment, ruin memory. That was the worst thing perhaps; that you would remember all the most precious times, the commitment to stay together for ever, the arrival of the babies, the sweetly charged intimacies of marriage, and know it had all been a sham; see it as distorted, ugly, cruelly changed.

She was trying: so hard. To get it back, the happiness and the trust. But until she knew for sure, she was failing. And becoming obsessed with the need to know.

'So how did it go?'

Ah. So now he was jumpy. That was good. Abi smiled complacently into the phone.

'Oh, pretty well. Yes.'

'They accepted your story?'

'Of course. Why shouldn't they have?'

'Abi, you know perfectly well—'

'And as I keep saying, it's got nothing to do with the crash. Who you were with and why.'

He ignored this. 'There were no questions about the phone?'

'No, there weren't actually.'

'Well, good.' She could almost feel his relief, coming down the line. It annoyed her. He was going to be all right, he and his bloody perfect marriage, and she'd had to lie to the police over it. It wasn't fair.

'There was just one thing,' she said. This would be fun.

'What was that?'

'The police interviewed William today.'

'William? Who's William, for Christ's sake?'

'The farmer. You know, who had the helicopter on his land.'

'Oh yes. OK. And?'

'And they discovered he'd been chatting with me at the crash so they were asking him about us. About our relationship.'

'They *what*? Jesus Christ. What sort of questions?'

'Just if he knew what kind of relationship we had. He said we were just colleagues.'

'That's all right, for Christ's sake. That's fine.'

'Yes, I know. But then apparently he told them he'd thought you seemed angry with me, that he'd seen you shouting at me.'

'For fuck's sake, what did he tell them that for?'

'Because you were, I expect.'

'But why did he tell them? What relevance was there to the interview with him?'

'Jonathan, I don't know. They're obviously interested in us, that's the point. Anyway, it's fine, we both told them it was purely professional, so did William. Look, sorry, got to go.'

She cut him off. It was a good moment.

'Now this is interesting,' said Freeman. They were examining CCTV footage. 'Here we have our best man, standing in the queue for the tyre gauge.'

'What's wrong with that?' said Rowe.

'Nothing. It's the responsible thing to do – especially if you're thinking of driving rather fast.'

'So?'

'But the point is, Mr Fraser told us he hadn't done anything at the service station except get fuel.'

'I expect he just forgot.'

'Rowe, you don't forget things like that. Especially when mere minutes later, your tyre bursts and contributes to a major accident. No, this is interesting. I think we should talk to Mr Fraser again. Ask him about it. Or, which might be cleverer, talk to Mr Weston. The bridegroom. Get a separate account.'

'You can't do that yet,' said Rowe. 'He's very unwell. I thought they said he might be having major surgery on Monday.'

'Mr Connell is also very unwell. We learned quite a lot from him.'

'Well, that's true. Although it was pretty muddled, I'd say. All that stuff about feeling sleepy and eating jelly babies. And the second person in the cab.'

'I've told you before, Rowe, the devil's in the detail in this game.' If he said that once more, Rowe thought, he'd thump him. 'The very fact he was talking about jelly babies, not just chocolate, could be important. If he can be precise about his sweets, then we can take more notice of the rest of his testimony.'

'Yes, I suppose so,' said Rowe.

'Now it could be his confusion, this second person in the cab. But put together with what – three reports now about this mysterious girl at the scene of the crash – I think it bears a very close look indeed. She'd have had a very clear overview of what happened, if she was up there. An eye-witness, you might say.' He paused. 'You know, Rowe, I'm wondering if we can get the media interested in this one. We'd get more eye-witnesses to what actually happened. And in particular, who else might have seen this girl, and a second person in the lorry – of course, they are not necessarily one and the same. I think I'll talk to the PR department first thing Monday. See if they can get it on the news.'

'Hardly news,' said Rowe. 'A crash that happened ten days ago.'

'Well, it made national news then. It was the worst crash of the year. And we're appealing for information, for someone to come forward. That intrigues people. It's certainly worth a try. Maybe we can get one of the later slots in the programme, just before they wind up. You must know the sort of thing.'

'What, you mean when they find a duck marching her ducklings down the High Street?'

'A few notches above that,' said Freeman with a sigh, 'but yes, you've got the idea.'

'So – how would we go about it?'

'Oh, we contact one of their researchers, give them the story, make it sound as interesting as we can; after that it's up to them. Bit of a beauty contest, really.'

'I wouldn't have thought Patrick Connell would qualify for that title,' said Rowe, 'or did you have Abi Scott in mind? Very attractive girl, that one.'

'I didn't mean literally a beauty contest,' said Freeman rather coldly. 'It was a figure of speech. Beauty contest, as in one proposition for the programme set against another.' He sometimes doubted if Rowe would ever make Sergeant, let alone Inspector.

'I wonder if they ever found that missing dog,' said Rowe suddenly. 'The golden retriever. That would be the sort of thing they'd like.'

There was a silence, then Freeman said, slightly grudgingly, 'It could be, yes. Why don't you check it out, Constable?'

They had had a case conference on Patrick Connell: James Osborne, who was generally acknowledged to be one of the most brilliant neurosurgeons in the business, Alex Pritchard, John Baker, the physician in charge of his case, and Jo Wales, who was nursing him on a daily basis.

There was clearly a serious problem; Patrick had sustained a thoracic fracture, and apart from the lack of sensation in his legs, he had no control over his bladder or bowels. Osborne, however, was hopeful; he said the spinal cord had not been actually ruptured and in his opinion, Patrick would recover. 'May take months, but I'd put a lot of money on it. Want me to talk to him?'

Alex Pritchard said that perhaps it would be better if he talked to the Connells himself.

'I've got to know them pretty well and Mrs Connell is a bright soul, she'll be perfectly able to understand. And we can discuss how to deal with Connell and his reaction to the news. I would say he's in danger of becoming seriously depressed. He feels a tremendous guilt about the crash and I'm quite worried about him, as it is.'

The alacrity with which everyone agreed to this rather emphasised to Alex what an extremely difficult and unpleasant task he had taken on.

* * *

Mary was laying the table for supper when she heard the phone ringing and Christine answering it. She hoped it wasn't Russell. She still hadn't had the all-important conversation with her daughter.

It was going to be difficult, the conversation: Mary knew it was. Christine would be shocked, suspicious. It was something to be got over as soon as possible. The longer she left it, the worse it would be. Mary worried about it more each day. Especially now that Russell was moving to his new hotel, and would be coming over to see her every day. Which of course she wanted, desperately, but this was a big hurdle to be got over first. She kept opening her mouth to talk to Christine, had even more than once embarked on a conversation that might at least lead up to it – but then something had happened, had interrupted her.

She breathed a sigh of relief when she realised that the call was from Maeve Connell, until she realised that Maeve was crying.

'Mary, I'm so extremely sorry to trouble you, but I so much wanted to talk to you. Is it a bad time?'

'Not at all,' said Mary. 'What is it? Is it bad news about Patrick?'

'I – well, you could say so. Although Dr Pritchard, God bless him, said there was much to be hopeful about. He talked to us together, thank God. I could not have told Patrick myself, I can promise you that, Mary.'

'I'm sure Dr Pritchard realised that,' said Mary.

'Yes. Anyway, there is,' she paused, clearly gathering sufficient courage to continue, 'there is damage to the spinal cord. But apparently the neurosurgeon, Mr Osborne, thinks there is a good chance of recovery, that the damage is more like a very bad bruise caused by – let me get this right, I wrote it down – a fragment of bone rupturing the vertebrae and pushing on the spinal cord. But then he went on to say there were no certainties and that Patrick must realise that. Meanwhile, he has to stay in hospital, of course. I can't possibly look after him, and – and—'

She started to cry again. Mary waited, helpless, wishing beyond anything that she could be with her.

'How did Patrick take it?' she asked finally.

'Very badly. He was quiet for a bit, then he started shouting at Dr Pritchard and Jo Wales, that sweet, lovely Sister who's in charge of the nursing, and telling them to get out, and me too, that he needed to be alone; and then, Mary, he started to cry, like one of the boys it was, just sitting there sobbing, like a great child. It went on and on. And I can't begin to think how to comfort him, or to help him. I don't know what to do.'

And Mary, staring out of the window at the autumn dusk settling on Christine's garden, could very well see why.

Georgia was beginning to feel she had two heads. Or two selves. It was very odd. There was the Georgia who had just got a part in a prestigious TV series, who was feeling rather pleased with herself, who felt life was pretty all right really; and there was the other Georgia, who was scared and miserable and ashamed of herself, who didn't remotely know what to do to make things better. Or rather who did know, but lacked the courage to do it.

Sometimes one Georgia gained control, sometimes the other; and they could switch at a moment's notice. She could be walking through Cardiff, going to meet a friend, listening to her iPod and looking in the windows of Topshop, and without warning the terror would be there, taunting her, the terror and the awful despair. It paralysed her; she would stand still, shaking, feeling she would never move again, trying to dismiss it, to set aside the memories and the guilt, and then she would have to call the friend, plead illness, and go home again, creeping under her duvet, crying, sometimes for hours at a time.

And then, equally without reason, it would go again, and she would find herself able to say, well, was it really so bad, what she had done. Lots of people would have reacted the same way, and no one need ever know, and one day, yes, one day she would go and see Patrick who was, after all, still alive, and say she was sorry. Only she knew she couldn't. She really, really couldn't.

It had been so great, the evening with Abi, such a high, such a laugh. William grinned to himself every time he thought about it. He'd felt so good with her, so easy. She'd really seemed to like him, and he'd certainly known he'd liked her, and for some extraordinary reason, the differences between them just hadn't seemed to matter.

He couldn't help wondering though – no, more than wondering, worrying – that she'd just been faking her interest. Being polite. She couldn't possibly have wanted to talk about cows and milk yields and granaries. God, why had he let himself run on like that, like some demented old bugger with straw in his hair? But then, how could he have talked about the sort of things she would have found interesting? He couldn't. Even if he'd known what they were, which he didn't. He actually was a demented old bugger – OK, maybe a young one – he had no knowledge of the cool, sassy world she obviously lived in. She must regard him as a sort of curiosity, a time and place warp; she possibly had found the evening interesting, but only because it – and he – had been like nothing she had experienced before.

But she'd seemed pretty pleased when he'd kissed her. It had taken him completely by surprise, that. He hadn't intended to; it had just all been a bit much for him, her clinging on to him, when she tripped and so on: and – then she'd said they must meet again. That really was amazing. He was trying to decide how soon he could ring her to fix it, and where they might go, when the phone rang.

It was his brother, asking if he could bring some people down for one of the corporate shoots in the autumn. 'Presumably you could let us have it cheap – free even. I've told them and they all seemed very keen.'

'Well, that's OK,' said William. 'If they're so keen, they can bloody well pay. Or your firm can. It'd be good. I want to build the shoot business up – it costs us a fortune to pay the keeper, keep the birds in good nick and plenty of them, prepare the drives and so on. Do you know what we charge guns now?'

'I think you're going to tell me.'

'Yes, I bloody well am. Thirty pounds a bird, and on a good day we'll bag two hundred and fifty, maybe three hundred birds.'

'Jesus. Sounds like money for old rope to me. Three hundred birds at thirty quid a bird, works out at nine thousand quid. For one day. Blimey.'

'It certainly isn't money for old rope,' said William. 'We have to give them a good lunch, we have to keep the shoot lodge up to scratch, pay people to beat and pick up. Look, the money we earn on the shoots is a crucial part of the farm's budget. Ask Dad.'

'Dad said he thought it would be fine for me to bring some friends down. He said he likes to have family days, that he hates all the corporate stuff.'

'But they're not family, are they? You just said so.'

'Family, colleagues, friends – where do you draw the line?'

'I draw it,' said William firmly, 'where I know the day's a commercial one. Designed to improve business relationships. I'm sorry, Martin, I'm not going to give in on this one.'

'That your last word?'

'Yes.'

The phone went down. Arrogant bugger, William thought. He should try running a business where officialdom constantly interfered, where every new business scheme was blocked and scuppered by a towny government who had no interest in or understanding of the affairs of the countryside, who sent their minions out day by day to nit-pick and interfere . . .

'That all right, William?' His father looked up from the pile of paperwork they addressed themselves to every Sunday evening. 'I told Martin I thought it would be fine, as long as it was only one day.'

'No,' said William. 'It's not all right. And I wish you wouldn't interfere in one of the few areas of this farm that are actually in my control.'

'William, your father's not interfering.' His mother was leafing through cookery books. 'He feels Martin has a right to a day's shooting here with his friends. And I tend to agree with him.'

'Mother, they are not his friends. They're business colleagues. And they're all bloody loaded. And he doesn't have any right. The farm is nothing to do with him – lucky sod. I'm going to the pub.'

'I thought you were going to help with the paperwork, William. There's a lot to do.'

'Fuck the paperwork,' said William, and slammed the door.

He felt demoralised and upset; they all clearly regarded him as a complete pushover. He certainly didn't feel up to ringing Abi; that was probably how she regarded him as well. Once at the pub, he got extremely drunk, so drunk that he had to walk home. That didn't make him feel any better either.

'Wednesday's the big day now,' said Toby. He had rung Barney at work; his voice was painfully cheerful.

'Yeah? For what?' As if he didn't know.

'Oh – this final washout thing. If they don't think it's working, then . . .'

'Then they'll try again,' said Barney. 'Obviously.'

'Mate, they won't,' said Toby.

'Course they will. They're not going to give up on you.'

'No. Just take the leg off. Or some of it.'

'Oh Tobes, of course they're not. Whatever makes you think that?'

'Because the fucking doctor told me so, that's what. He was very nice, very positive, said he was fairly confident that it would be OK, but we had to face the fact that it might not be. I'll have to sign a consent thing apparently, before I go down. Shit, Barney, I'm scared.'

'You'll be all right, Tobes. I know you will.'

'I don't.'

There was a silence, then Barney said, 'So, have you told Tamara?'

'What? Oh no, no. I thought it would upset her too much.'

'Upset her?' Barney had heard of getting red spots in front of your eyes, caused by rage; he actually saw them then. But it would do Toby no good to start railing against Tamara. No good at all. He needed nothing but positive vibes.

'Well, that's very brave of you,' he said carefully. 'Brave and unselfish. What about your parents?'

'No, I haven't told them either. Poor old Mum, she's upset enough as it is.'

'Well . . .' Barney sought wildly for something to say that might help. 'Tell you what, Tobes, would you like me to come down on Wednesday? Be there, when it's done? Not in the operating theatre, of course,' he managed to grin, 'don't think I could cope with that, but I'll spend the time beforehand with you, be there when you come back. With two good legs, obviously.'

There was a silence while Toby digested this, then he said, 'Shit, Barney, you are the best. Would you really? Yeah, that'd be great. They said it'd be the afternoon probably, and I was thinking what a ghastly long day it would be. But you'll be at work—'

'I'll be there. I'll take a sickie. Don't worry about it. I've been through this with you before, don't forget. When you broke your leg at school. Who sat there with you half the evening, in casualty, telling you not to blub? Who played poker with you every day for a week? Who—'

'Yeah, OK, OK. It'd be fantastic, Barney, mate. I'd really appreciate it. Thanks.'

Some time, when Toby felt better, Barney thought, they should discuss the little matter of the tyre. Just so they were singing from the same songsheet. If anyone asked Toby, which they probably wouldn't.

Alex parked his car and looked rather dolefully at the hospital. He had only come in because he couldn't bear to be at home, or what was about to be home no longer, for an offer had been made on the house, and Sam was gloating about it. Saying not only was the price far better than they might have hoped in the present climate, but that the purchasers had no chain; they had sold their own house and could proceed with considerable speed to an exchange.

'Yes, that's all very well, but where do you think we're going to live, in three weeks' time or whatever?' he'd said to her over breakfast and when she'd finished reporting the content of a phone call from the estate agents.

'Well – we can rent. Of course, I'll need a bigger place than you. The children have to have somewhere decent to live. Adam's going into his GCSE course next term, and Amy's in the middle of hers. You don't want their chances scuppered, do you?'

'Of course not. Although I have to say, hustling them out of one house and into another isn't exactly conducive to successful study.'

'Oh for God's sake! You know perfectly well what I mean. This is a fantastic opportunity and we should take it.'

'And what about me? Where am I supposed to go? Perhaps you'd like me to go and live in the hospital?'

He had meant to sound ironic and was astonished when she said, a note of hope in her voice, 'Could you really, Alex? That would certainly be a solution short-term. Easier to find one flat than two.'

That was when he walked out and went to the hospital. It was more distracting than any of the alternatives – far preferable to a game of golf, a lunchtime session in the pub, even a visit to the cinema. That was the worst thing of all, he was discovering; suddenly you were forced to do things on your own, to find pleasure in your own company, to renegotiate the terms of old friendships. And he felt much too tired and cynical for any of it.

'Hello, Alex. Nice surprise – I wasn't expecting you today.'

It was Emma, looking rather tired; she'd been off-duty for the past twenty-four hours. Alex supposed she'd been with the oaf, and tried very hard not to think about what she might have been doing with him.

'Yes, well. Thought I'd pop in, see what was going on.'

'Good idea.'

'You all right?'

'Yes, fine, thanks.'

'Been out enjoying yourself?'

'You could say that. My – my boyfriend took me to the most amazing club called Boujis. I don't suppose you've heard of it – William and Harry go there quite a lot.'

'William and Harry who?' said Alex.

'Alex! William and Harry as in the princes.' She stopped, realising that he wasn't very interested in what she'd been doing, with or without William and Harry.

'I'm a bit late, I'm afraid, sorry,' she said.

'That's all right. Don't worry about it.'

Poor Alex; he looked very down, Emma thought. They all knew about the divorce, knew to be tactful, to ignore his worsening moods, not to comment on unexpected appearances except in the vaguest possible way. And she had heard, on the hospital grapevine, that he was very upset about Patrick Connell and his failure to recover the use of his legs. Of all the misconceptions about the medical profession, perhaps the greatest was that doctors remained detached from their patients and their troubles; she had learned that very early on. However hard you tried, they stayed with you.

'It's pretty quiet,' he said now. 'Hardly worth my coming in.'

'Give it time,' said Emma cheerfully. 'It'll hot up soon.'

'Maybe. My word, there's a nice bit of machinery.'

It was a Porsche, open-topped, dark blue; driven by a girl with a mass of dark hair and wearing a very low-cut top. She parked and got out, looked up at the hospital and almost visibly squared her shoulders; then pulled out a mobile and walked towards the door, talking into it. She was posh, Emma noticed. Very posh. As she reached them, she half-smiled at them. 'Won't be too long,' she was saying. 'Toby's still pretty much out of it. I'll probably be over in about an hour.'

Ah, Emma thought, this must be Toby's fiancée, the one Barney disapproved of so much. She was very beautiful, and she had an amazing figure. Very, very tall, with incredibly long legs, she wore white cropped jeans with a red T-shirt and very high-heeled sandals.

She had stopped now quite near them, pulled out a pack of cigarettes, lit one and inhaled hard. She was obviously bracing herself for the visit. Barney must be wrong, Emma thought, she was clearly upset. And then she heard her say, 'I know, I know. Apparently dear St Barnaby's coming down later. He's always bloody well here. I'm quite lucky to find Toby on his own these days.'

Emma felt so outraged she was tempted to pull the cigarette out of the girl's mouth and tell her that smoking, even in the car park, was not allowed.

Chapter 24

Patrick was in the grip of a horror that had a physical presence, that was invading him just as the pain had done on the day of the accident. Somehow talking to the police had made it worse, had made him more certain that he had gone to sleep; just hearing his own voice, describing it, made it seem impossible that there could be any other explanation. He had killed all those people, ruined all those lives; it was his fault, he had blood on his hands as surely as if he had taken a gun and shot them all.

They'd told him it would come back, his memory, but the more he tried to remember, the more difficult it got; it was like trying to see through a fog that was thickening by the day. Even the other person in the lorry's cab seemed to be disappearing into that fog; it had been a faint sliver of hope, that, but actually, what good could it do, what difference could it make? Even if someone had been there, he had still been at the wheel . . .

The horror never left him; he lay for hours, just wrestling with it, woke to it, slept his drugged sleep with it, dreamed of it. There was no room for anything else – for hope, for calm. And now, added to it, was the news that he was probably going to be paralysed for the rest of his life – although in these first early days, even that had seemed of lesser importance. It was all going to go on until he died; there was no escape anywhere. He reflected on the skill and care that was going into his recovery, or his possible recovery, and there seemed no point, absolutely no point at all in any of it. He wished it would stop altogether; he wished he could stop.

And then in a moment of revelation, it came to him that if he really wanted that, he could have it.

Constable Rowe appeared in Sergeant Freeman's office.

'The *Daily Sketch*'ve been on the phone. Some hack's asked us to comment on a report that there was a second person in the lorry driver's cab, who subsequently vanished.'

'How did that get out?'

'God knows.'

'I hope you haven't been talking, Rowe?'

'Of course I haven't,' said Rowe indignantly.

'Well, I suppose it could help us get the crash back on the TV. Any news there?'

'Yes, there is a bit.' Rowe was looking rather pleased with himself.

'Well, what is it?'

'One of the news programmes is looking into a follow-up story on the crash.'

'Excellent!'

'Yes, they're interested in the mysterious girl. Anyway, they want you to ring them. And what shall I say to the *Sketch*?'

'I'll deal with that,' said Freeman firmly.

'Oh, and by the way,' said Rowe, 'they've found the dog.'

Alex looked in on Patrick; he was sitting staring into space, his expression blank.

'No Maeve today?'

'No, she's not well today. It doesn't matter. I'm all right.'

'How are you feeling?'

'Oh, you know. What you'd expect, really.' He sighed again; he seemed very subdued. Subdued and something else. Almost sullen.

Alex patted his arm. 'Sorry, it must seem like an eternity.'

Patrick shrugged.

'Are you beginning to remember a bit more?'

'No,' Patrick said flatly. 'Nothing. And not being able to remember makes it worse. The worry and so on. What I did that day.'

'Patrick, you must try not to—'

'Blame myself?' He looked angry suddenly. 'Is that what you were going to say? I can't help it! What else could have caused it, all those people injured!'

'Many things or situations could have caused it,' said Alex gently. 'That's why the police are taking such care over their investigations. You may not be able to remember the accident, but others may be piecing together a picture that's quite different from anything you can imagine. What you're suffering from is fairly common, after concussion; has anyone explained it to you?'

Patrick shook his head.

They should have done, Alex thought. It was neglectful not to – it could be a spur to his recovery. He felt a stab of remorse.

'What you've got is called retrograde amnesia, and it means literally not being able to remember an incident or incidents before sustaining the concussion. Sometimes it can take months to recover. It's only just over a week since the accident, and you must try to be patient. Now I know it's easy for me to tell you not to worry, and of course I understand all your concerns. But the best thing you can do is concentrate on getting well. Try to get some rest now. That'll do more for your memory than anything.'

'You look tired, Mum. Why don't you go through and watch TV? Gerry'll help me clear away, won't you?'

'Oh no,' said Mary. Her heart thumped uncomfortably. *Don't start getting upset, Mary, the last thing you want is an angina attack*. 'Look – I'd like to talk to you both about something.'

'Oh, all right.' Christine looked intrigued. 'Gerry, why don't you go and put the kettle on, make us all a cup of tea?'

Mary waited until Gerry came back, then said, 'The thing is, well, look, dears, this may come as a bit of a surprise to you.'

'Mum, nothing you did would surprise me,' said Christine.

'Really, dear?'

'Yes. Look how you went off to Austria last year with Edna, that was pretty wacky, we thought, and your bowls team winning the cup. We imagined you just played bowls for a bit of fun, not training up to championship standard.'

'Well, you know my views about doing something properly, if it's worth doing at all. I brought you up to that, didn't I? Anyway, this is a bit more serious than bowls, or going to Austria.'

'Right. Fire away.'

'Well, you know I was on my way to London last week – the day of the crash? I wasn't entirely honest about the reason.'

Christine was looking anxious. 'It wasn't your heart was it, Mum? You weren't going to see some new specialist?'

'No, dear. I was going to meet someone.'

'Yes, you said. A friend.'

'Indeed. But he was a little more than a friend.'

'He? Mum, what have you been up to?' Christine's eyes were dancing.

'Nothing,' said Mary indignantly. 'Well, not exactly. The person I went to meet was an American gentleman, called Russell Mackenzie.'

'Oh, the one who rang? I did wonder . . .'

'Yes. We met a very long time ago. During the war.'

'The war! What, before you married Dad?'

'Indeed. Anyway, he was a GI and we – well, we became very fond of one another.'

'What, you had an affair, you mean?'

'Certainly not,' said Mary. She could feel herself flushing. 'Not in the way you mean. We didn't do that sort of thing in those days. Well, I didn't anyway.'

'But you were in love with him?'

'Yes,' said Mary. 'Very much.'

'Gosh, how romantic. Weren't you tempted to marry him, go out there after the war, be a GI bride or whatever?'

'No, I wasn't. I had promised to marry your father – we were unofficially engaged. He was in a prisoner-of-war camp. As of course you know.'

'But you still had an affair – all right, a relationship – with this chap?'

'Yes, I did. But he knew there was no future in it, that I was going to marry your father.'

'Yet he carried on chasing you? And you let him?'

'I know it's hard for you to understand, dear, but it was wartime. Things were very different.'

'Of course. Anyway, he went back to the States?'

'Yes, and married someone else in due course and I married your father. But we kept in touch. We wrote regularly, all through the years. We remained very close. In an odd way.'

'How regularly? A few times a year?'

'No,' said Mary. It was best to be truthful. This was too important not to be. 'No, we wrote at least once a month.'

'Once a month! Did Dad know?'

'No, he had no idea. I knew it would upset him. That he wouldn't understand.'

'I'm not sure I do either.' Christine's face was suddenly flushed. 'You're telling me you were so involved with this man that you wrote to him every month for years and years and years, right through your marriage, but it didn't affect your feelings for Dad?'

'Yes, that's right.'

'But Mum, it must have done. I couldn't deceive Gerry like that.'

'It wasn't exactly deceit, dear.'

'Mum, it was. Did he tell his wife? This Russell person?'

'No, he didn't.'

'Well, it sounds pretty odd to me. Pretty unbelievable really – I mean, that all you did was write, if you were so devoted to one another. Did he ever come over? Did you meet him without Dad knowing?'

'No, Christine, I didn't. I wouldn't have done that.'

'Well, go on.' She was looking almost hostile now. 'What happened next in this romantic story?'

'Chris!' Gerry was looking very uncomfortable. 'Don't get upset.'

'Well, I am upset. I suddenly discover there's been another man in my mother's life, and that my father didn't know about him.'

'Not exactly in my life, dear.'

'Oh really? Sounds like it to me. He was important to you, he must have been, otherwise you'd have stopped writing.'

'Yes, but that was all we did. Is that so wrong?'

'Well, not exactly wrong. But think if Dad had found out – wouldn't he have been upset?'

'Yes. Which was why I never told him.'

'Well then. It was wrong. Anyway, go on.'

Mary felt like crying; this was exactly what she had feared.

'Well now, you see, Russell's wife has died, and he's come over to see me and we – well, we still feel very fond of each other.'

Chrstine said nothing. Then: 'Has he been to the hospital?'

'Yes, he has.'

'But you didn't tell me?'

'No, dear.'

'You were obviously feeling guilty about it. That proves it, as far as I'm concerned. He was there, in your marriage to Dad, even if Dad didn't know. I think it's really bad.'

Mary felt her eyes filling with tears; Gerry noticed and said, 'Chris. Easy! Your mum's done nothing wrong.'

'I'm sorry, but that's a matter of opinion. Anyway, what happens next? I hope he's not coming here.'

'Not if you don't want him to.'

'I don't.'

'But I would like you to meet him.'

'I don't want to meet him.'

'But you see, Christine, we are planning to spend a lot of time together. A lot. I know you'd like him if you only met him.'

'I don't want to like him. And what does "a lot" mean? I hope you're not planning to set up house with him or something.'

'Chris!' said Gerry.

Mary met her daughter's eyes steadily. Best to get it over. Since Christine was so upset already, there was no point in holding back. She had hoped to take it gently, to let Chris meet Russell, to get to know him, but . . .

'Actually,' she said, 'we are hoping to – well, to get married. We feel very strongly that we've spent enough time apart.'

'Married!' Christine looked appalled. 'Oh, please, spare me. You've been reading too many Mills and Boon books, Mum. You've not been apart from this man, as you put it, you've been married to Dad. Who you were supposed to love. Poor old Dad, he must be turning in his grave.'

'Chris,' said Gerry, 'I think we've had enough of this conversation. You're really upsetting your mother!'

'Good. She's upset me. And I don't know what Timothy's going to say. Oh, I'm going to go and do the clearing up. I'll see you both in the morning.'

Mary felt dreadful. Russell had been wrong; he'd said Christine would understand, would be happy for her. Now what could she do? It would be difficult even phoning him while she was staying here. Everything was spoiled; she felt guilty and ashamed, instead of happy and excited.

She went to bed and lay thinking about Donald, and acknowledged that he would actually have minded very much if he had known, and feeling, for the very first time, that she had betrayed him.

'I know it's awful of me,' said Tamara, slipping her arm through Barney's as they walked towards the lift, 'but I'm beginning to feel just the tiniest bit selfish about all this. I mean, I haven't said one word to Tobes obviously, and he can't help what's happened, but . . .' Her voice tailed away.

Barney felt a wave of rage so violent he actually wanted to hit her, instead of taking her for a drink, as she had persuaded him to do. She had come back to work at the beginning of the week – 'Well, I was so bored and fed up, working suddenly looked like quite fun by comparison' – and had appeared by his desk after lunch, asking if he wanted to go for a drink after work.

He had suggested Vertigo, with its fabulous views; she had declared it one of her favourite bars, had said she was sure it would make her feel better.

Barney had not the slightest interest in making Tamara feel better, but it was hard to refuse without appearing very aggressive. And so, here he was, up on the forty-second floor of Vertigo with her and faced with at least an hour of her phony distress. Actually the distress was genuine, it was just over the wrong cause.

'Yes,' she said, sipping thoughtfully at her champagne, 'like I was saying, Barney, I just can't help it, I feel really, really bad.'

'About Toby, you mean?'

'Well, yes, obviously, poor angel. And he's being so brave and good, stuck in that awful place. I mean, if it was me I couldn't have stood one day, let alone, what is it – ten? No, more than that now. Just visiting there is bad enough, but staying there . . . ugh!'

'How do you think he's doing?' asked Barney, desperate to postpone the moment when she would clearly expect sympathy. 'With his leg, I mean.'

'Oh darling, I don't know. It's just dragging on and on. The doctors don't seem to know what to think about it. Between you and me I wonder if they know what they're doing, half the time – but Toby seems to think they're marvellous and his parents do too. I'd have insisted he went private, saw some decent consultant, but it's not up to me, of course. Apparently they've made enquiries and been told he couldn't be anywhere better. But surely they could get a second opinion!'

'Yes, that's what he told me on Sunday, how good it was. Amanda and I went down.'

'Barney, you're so sweet and good, to go and see him so often. I can't tell you how much he appreciates it.'

'I feel it's the very least I can do,' said Barney briefly. 'He is my best friend, after all.'

'I know, but it's such a long way.'

'It is, yes. I'm surprised you came back up here actually, Tamara, when you could visit him so easily from your parents' house.'

'Well, as I say, I was getting very depressed. Being there kept me thinking about the wedding, you know? No distraction. It wouldn't be so bad if we'd been able to settle on another date, but we can't even do that.'

He was silent.

'Anyway, he so understands, bless him. That I need to get back to work. And of course, I'll be there every weekend.'

'Right.'

'It's all beginning to hit me now. It was rather awful, you know. Everyone leaving, going back to the house, no one in the marquee, mountains of food, buckets of champagne, the staff having to be sent away. It was just terribly upsetting.'

'Yes, of course,' Barney said. 'Terribly. I'm so – so sorry, Tamara.'

'I know you are. And I wouldn't point the tiniest finger of blame in your direction. Not the tiniest.' There was a silence, then she said suddenly, 'Except – why were you so late, Barney? I'd quite like to know. Seeing it cost me my wedding.'

Barney felt his stomach lurch; he had been half-expecting this, half-expecting an inquisition.

'Tamara, it was the crash that cost you your wedding.'

'No, it wasn't.' Barney looked at her; her dark eyes were very hard in her lovely face. 'It was because you left so late. If you'd left in time, you'd have been there hours before the crash. I mean, you were going to have lunch with the ushers, weren't you?'

'Yes.'

'So?'

'Well, the thing is, Tamara, I . . . he . . . that is . . .'

'Yes? What is the thing, Barney?'

'The thing is, Toby wasn't very well. He kept throwing up. All morning. I actually called the doctor, who gave him a shot to stop it. We couldn't set out before. It was impossible.'

'Oh. Oh, I see. Poor old Tobes. Something he ate, I suppose. Or a bug. I mean, you wouldn't have let him get drunk, obviously, so it wouldn't have been a hangover.'

'No, of course not,' said Barney.

'He didn't actually mention any of that, not about the doctor or anything. Well, thank you for telling me. I feel better now.'

'Good,' said Barney. He found he was sweating. The

377

champagne was wonderfully cold, he drank down half the glass gratefully.

'Obviously I'm not going to raise it with Toby. He's feeling guilty enough, poor darling.'

'*Guilty?*' Barney was genuinely shocked.

'Yes, of course he's feeling guilty! I mean, he shouldn't, and I did tell him that, but he can't help it. I mean, wouldn't you? If it had been yours and Amanda's wedding?'

'I don't think so,' said Barney. 'No.' He couldn't take any more of this. 'Look Tamara, I—' His phone rang. 'Excuse me,' he said with relief, 'it's Amanda. Hi, darling. You all right?'

'I'm fine, Barney. But Carol Weston's been on the phone, wants to talk to you. Some bad news about Toby's leg, I'm afraid. I think she'd like you to ring her. And are you going to be late, because if you are . . .'

'No,' said Barney. 'No, I'm leaving right now.'

Chapter 25

Georgia was sitting in the kitchen in Cardiff, grazing through the newspaper and wondering if she should get a job in a bar for the next two or three weeks until *Moving Away* went into production. (It was one of the good days.) Her mother would appreciate a bit of economic help, and she could certainly do with some clothes. Of course, they didn't like it when you walked out of those jobs just as you were beginning to be useful, but that was their problem. The money they paid didn't exactly buy loyalty.

Maybe she should look in the paper, see what was available, or on the net. She poured herself another cup of coffee and rummaged in the drawer for last week's local freesheet, then got a HobNob out of the tin and turned to the job section. There was quite a lot of bar work, too much indeed to take in properly; she wrote a few details down and then before going to the computer to send some emails, returned to the newspaper. The *Sketch* was such a crummy paper, she thought, then: 'Oh my God!' Georgia felt a clammy sensation in her hands and face, thought she might be about to throw up.

She stood up, her eyes fixed on the paper, then walking very slowly, went upstairs to her room and shut the door, and sat on her bed, staring at the paper as if her life depended on it. And then lay down and pulled her pillows over her face.

The paper fell to the floor; open at a page of minor news items, the largest of which read *Mystery on the Motorway* and continued with a story of a *so far unconfirmed report that the lorry driver who had crashed through a barrier on the M4 the previous week, causing a seven-mile tailback in both directions and killing several people, had spoken of a second and unidentified person in his cab who had subsequently vanished.*

This is the first indication that there might have been a passenger in the cab. The police refuse to confirm or deny it and there have been no further reports. If such a person does exist, then he or she could clearly have valuable information which would go a long way towards establishing the original cause of the crash, something police are very eager to settle.

Although many of the injured are recovering in hospital and some have returned home, there is still anxiety over the fate of Toby Weston, the young bridegroom who sustained serious injuries in the pile-up, and never reached his wedding. The bride-to-be, Tamara Richmond, told our reporter she was 'absolutely distraught with worry'.

The crash, which is still being investigated by the police, was one of the worst for years. There have been several calls recently for lorry drivers' hours to be more strictly regulated. While British drivers for the most part adhere to the rules, drivers from the continent often cover twice as many miles in a week, and break the speed-limit for heavy vehicles. This can lead to acute tiredness and dangerous driving. The lorry driver in question was British.

'Very carefully written,' said Freeman to Rowe, when the *Sketch* article was brought to his attention. 'Plenty of suggestion that the crash was caused by dangerous driving on the part of the driver, without actually saying so. Nothing we could actually object to.'

'It's disgraceful,' said Rowe. 'Hardly going to make the poor sod feel better, is it?'

'No,' said Freeman, 'but it'll probably make the TV people more interested in our case.'

'The PR people were more interested in the dog,' said Rowe.

Patrick had embarked on what he thought of as his project; the end of the horror, the waking from the nightmare. It was so simple, so perfect that he felt – just for a moment – a sense of actual joy. It would free him from himself and what he had done, and free Maeve and the children from him. It might cause a little unhappiness in the first instance, but that would pass; it involved a degree of physical discomfort that turned into pain, and some long, dreadfully wakeful nights, but for such a little while, he could endure it quite easily. It was essential to conceal the pain, and the wakeful nights, vital not to complain. He must not be seen to be suffering more than they would expect; that would result in questioning, examinations, reviews of his drugs.

He had begun immediately, on the day of the police visit – the day when he had realised that his misery and guilt were infinite, would never leave him: he had begun to store up his painkillers and his sedatives. They all came in tablet form now – the drips and lines had been removed – and it wasn't very difficult at all, now that he was in a side ward, to hide them. The nurses brought them in, set them down on his bedside table and, for the most part, left him to take them. If they remained for more than a few minutes, chatting or whatever, he would take them – to allay suspicion – but he grew adept at making excuses: he needed more water, he liked to take them with his meal, he was uncomfortable and needed more pillows. He knew which were the painkillers, and indeed the sedatives, and folded them neatly into tiny packages which he stowed between the pages of the Bible the hospital chaplain had brought him; he continued obediently to swallow the others. He had no idea how many he would need; but he was prescribed so many and his hoard grew so fast that he felt a week's supply would easily suffice. Not to dispatch the old Patrick, to be sure, the strong and vigorous father who could hold all three boys in his arms at once, while they squealed for joy, who could carry in vast loads of shopping for Maeve, who played football every Sunday with his mates and was never out of breath; but this new Patrick, thin and frail, and exhausted by moving from his bed to his chair and back again, with his clean white soft hands and his sickbed pale skin. It could not take so very much to dispose of him.

'Georgia? It's Linda. You OK?'

'Yes. Why shouldn't I be?'

'No reason at all. You sounded a bit odd, that's all. Look, I've had a call from the production coordinator on *Moving Away*. They want you to come up to London on Friday. That OK?'

'What for? I – I – don't know.'

'Well, darling, you'd better know, and pretty sharpish. They still haven't finally cast the grandmother's friend – she's quite key, as you know – and they want you to do a read-through with the two they're down to.'

'Why me?' said Georgia, playing for time. She still felt petrified, only safe when she was bunkered down in the house where no one could see her.

'Georgia, don't be dense. You have several quite emotional scenes with this character. The chemistry between you is important.'

'Oh. Oh, I see. Well, actually I'm not sure if I can do this Friday, Linda. Sorry.'

'How can you not be sure! This is the most important thing in your life at the moment.'

If only it was. If *only* it was.

'So you'd better bloody well do Friday. Friday morning,

first thing. The production offices, in Charlotte Street. They'll pay expenses obviously. Wear something that's pretty much in character. Which I suppose your clothes are anyway.'

'Linda, I really don't think I can—'

'Oh, Georgia, for God's sake, what is the matter with you? You're to be there – OK? It'll be over by midday, they said.'

Georgia felt like crying. Ever since she'd read the item in the paper, she'd been expecting someone to walk up to her and say, 'Oh, you're the girl in the lorry driver's cab, I recognise you.' Which was ridiculous, of course; it was no more likely to happen now than at the beginning. Even so, every time she even thought of it, she felt violently sick, and then she managed to calm herself, to tell herself she was being ridiculous: who could have seen her, right up there? And then she'd think yes, but she'd had to climb up into the cab. That had created a lot of amusement at the pull-in; a lot of cat-calling and whistling and, 'You always were the lucky one, Connell!' Any of those people could recognise her. Any of them. And then there were the people who'd seen her by the lorry, and that farmer dude she'd met in the wood. Any of them, any one of them.

And then she'd tell herself that hardly anyone read the *Sketch*; it was a dying newspaper, and it was such a tiny little story, tucked away on an inside page.

'Sorry, Linda,' she said. 'Of course I'll be there.'

Toby was very low: two days to go. Barney had gone down that evening. He found his friend sitting in bed, pale and morose.

'I'm shit scared,' he said. Tears formed in his eyes, rolled slowly down his face. Barney reached out and gripped his hand.

'Oh God, Barney, what am I going to do? How am I going to face it? It's so fucking unfair.'

'It is, mate. Fucking unfair.'

'Just five more minutes and we'd have been OK.'

'I know, Tobes, I know. I guess that's fate for you.'

'Yeah. We should have left earlier, shouldn't we? Tamara keeps saying that.'

'Oh really?' Cow. Bitch. Total bitch. How helpful. How totally helpful.

'Still, you did your best, I know.'

'Yeah, I did. And Toby, you know – we couldn't have left much earlier.'

'We couldn't?'

'No. Course not.'

'Why?'

'You must remember why. You had to go and see that girl.'

Toby suddenly looked different; wary, almost suspicious. 'Barney, that so didn't happen. You do know that, don't you?'

'Yes. Yes, it's OK, Toby, of course. Don't worry, mate!' He drew his finger across his throat, grinned at him determinedly. 'Your secret's safe with me.'

'It's not funny,' said Toby. 'Not a joke, OK?'

'Yes, OK.'

'Just didn't happen.'

'No, all right.' Barney began to feel mildly resentful. What did Toby think he was going to do – tell Tamara, his parents?

'But Tobes, there is something else.'

'Oh Christ. What?'

'The tyre. You remember?'

'What tyre?'

'The one that blew.'

'Oh yes.'

'Well, I didn't tell the police about it being soft.'

'Was it?'

'You know it was! And we didn't put any air in because you didn't want to wait.'

'Oh – Christ, no. We don't want to tell them that. Start looking for trouble . . .'

'No. Good. Well, I just thought they're bound to interview you when you're out of here. Important we're singing from the same songsheet.'

'Yeah, OK. Pretty obvious, I'd have thought.'

'Right.' He felt almost angry. He'd been making himself sick with worry over this whole business and Toby was treating him with something close to arrogance. Suddenly he couldn't bear it any longer. 'Look, Toby, I must go. Got to get back.'

'Have you?' He didn't sound very interested. 'Yes, OK.'

'But I will be back here on Wednesday. Promise.'

'Yeah, I know. Oh Barney, you're – well, you're all right, you know that?' He seemed to come to himself again, reached across the bed and shook Barney's hand; the sheer stiff-upper-lipness of the gesture made them both grin, slightly embarrassed.

'Right. See you then. You won't be here much longer. We'll have a party, Tobes, biggest fucking party ever, when you get out of here. We'll have you dancing on the tables.'

'I hope so.'

'Course we will. It's a date. Cheers, Tobes. See you.'

'Cheers, Barney.'

Barney felt very upset as he left the hospital, almost physically dizzy at the horror of what might lie ahead, and – he had to be honest with himself – pissed off by Toby's behaviour. Of course he was ill and scared shitless, Barney would have been too, but he didn't have to treat him like some kind of wanker who was going to sell him down the river. He sat down suddenly on the steps, trying to pull himself together, fumbling in his pockets for his cigarettes. And then, 'Barney, isn't it?'

She was standing above him, her huge eyes concerned;

she had no make-up on and looked more absurdly young than ever, he thought, in her doctor kit.

'Oh, hello, Emma.'

'You OK?'

'Yes. No. Well – just left Toby. He's –' no point getting into the other stuff – 'got to have this final washout thing on Wednesday, and they've told him he might lose his leg. Or part of it.'

'Oh Barney, I'm so sorry.' She sat down beside him, her blue eyes full of sympathy.

'Yeah, well. These things happen, I suppose.'

'I'm afraid they do. But it's not certain, is it? They're still hopeful?'

'Toby doesn't seem very hopeful. Anyway,' he said with a deep sigh, 'I'm going to come down again on Wednesday. Be with him. Before and so on. And after.'

'That's great. That'll help him a lot, I know it will.'

'Really?'

'Well, yes. Support – positive support – is really important on these occasions. What about his fiancée?'

'Oh, she doesn't know.' He was unable to disguise the contempt in his voice. 'Toby says it would upset her.'

'I see.'

'I feel like shit,' he said suddenly. Why was he talking to her like this? As if he didn't know.

'I'm sure you do. You're so fond of Toby and—'

'No, no. More than that. I feel awful, a lot of the time. Really bad, you know. About the accident. About us having that blow-out, hitting the other car, that girl and her baby, all those people killed, Toby's leg . . . and look at me, not a scratch. Doesn't seem right.'

'Lots of people feel like that,' she said.

'How do you know?'

'Oh, I don't mean about this particular crash, although I'm sure they do. No, it's the whole thing about – like you say, people dying, you getting off without a scratch.

Survivor guilt it's called: very common. It wasn't your fault, Barney, any of it. You can't start thinking that.'

'I have started thinking it though,' he said. 'I think it all the time. It's horrible.'

'Maybe you should talk to someone about it.'

'I am talking to someone. I'm talking to you.'

'No, I mean someone who could help.' She looked at him, her eyes so full of sympathy and concern that he immediately felt better.

'I'm sorry, Emma. I hate that sort of stuff.'

'What stuff?'

'Oh, you know, counselling – all that crap. I'm fine, honestly.'

'Sure?'

'Yes. I'll just have a fag, that'll cure me.'

She laughed. 'Look, I've got to go now, but I'm here on Wednesday. On duty. Come and find me in A and E while he's in theatre. If I'm not too busy, we could have a coffee or something, pass the time. If that'd be a help at all.'

Barney looked at her; her expression was sweetly earnest. Seemingly unable to help himself, he leaned forward and kissed her on the cheek.

'That is so, so kind of you, Emma,' he said. 'And of course it would be a help. Thank you.'

'It's a date then. Oh dear, I'm late.' She smiled at him, jumped up, half-ran across the car park. Of course. She was off to meet the boyfriend, no doubt. Lucky bastard. Lucky, lucky bastard.

Chapter 26

'There's a letter for you, Mum.' Christine smiled at her briefly, but it was a polite, rather cool smile, the one she had been using ever since Mary had told her about Russell.

Mary didn't know what to do. She had hoped that a day or so would bring her daughter round, get her used to the idea, but it hadn't happened. She was distant with her mother, leaving the room rather than being alone with her, discouraging any conversation more meaningful than what they might have for supper; and Mary of course hadn't been able to see Russell herself. She had been hoping to invite him over to Christine's or, as he had suggested, he would invite them to his hotel for lunch; but there was clearly no question of that. Any mention of him was strictly off-limits.

It was very hard; there he was, a few miles away, not a few thousand, and she was no more able to see him than she had been for the past sixty years. It was like being a teenager with disapproving parents.

She had phoned him next day, when Christine was out, to explain; he had been surprisingly relaxed about it, had said he was sure she'd come round in a day or two; as the two became three and then four, he was growing impatient. And it was so difficult to talk to him at all; she had to wait to use the phone until Christine was out, and once she had come back and found Mary talking to Russell. There had been no doubt it was him on the other end of the phone;

she had said goodbye quickly and rung off, which made her look very guilty.

'I'm sorry, dear,' she had said, and Christine had replied, very coldly, that it was fine, of course, Mary must talk to whoever she liked. Well, only another week, and then she'd be in her own home; and she had booked a cab to take her over to the hotel on Saturday, when Christine would be out for the day and wouldn't know. But the long-term prognosis was not good.

She took the letter from Christine – it was written in that unmistakable American handwriting – and went upstairs with it. That in itself stirred memories: getting Russell's letters and hiding them in her pocket, hurrying upstairs with them, or out to catch the bus to work before her mother could see them, ask her what they were.

He wrote wonderful letters, vivid and passionate; she would read them first in her room, then on the bus, sometimes smiling, sometimes crying, and then at work, and then in the canteen at lunchtime and then, oh then, over and over again in bed at night, falling finally asleep with them under her pillow. She knew them by heart within days; and when she was helping her mother with some particularly boring task, holding the skeins of wool unravelled from half-worn-out garments, while her mother wound them into balls, ready for re-knitting, or 'doing the butter' – the beating of milk into the melted and minute butter ration, so that it went further – or when they were listening to the wireless in a rapidly cooling room, for her mother obeyed to the second the Board of Trade's instruction to turn off the gas fire half an hour before they went up to bed, she would recite the letters in her head, sometimes smiling involuntarily at a particular passage.

And here she was today, she thought, half-amused at the irony, still scuttling upstairs to read a letter unobserved, only now she was hiding it from her daughter rather than her mother.

My darling little Sparrow (the letter began), *How hard this new separation is . . .*

That afternoon, Maeve walked quietly into Patrick's room; he was sitting staring straight ahead of him. He had become very pale and thin in his two weeks' incarceration. His hands particularly seemed to have changed; they were white and soft, an old man's hands, not the sort that could fix anything around the house, that could lift huge heavy weights, that could hold and caress her . . . They lay outside the bedclothes, neatly in front of him, hardly looking alive.

'Hello, love.'

He scarcely looked at her, just sighed and said, 'Hello, Maeve.'

'How are you today?'

'I'm how you'd think,' he said, and his voice was bitter. 'I am sick of being here, in this bed. I'm in pain, I can't sleep, I'm going to be here for the rest of my life, and no doubt people would say I deserved all of that, and I would say it of myself. I'm a murderer, I killed all those people.'

'Patrick, hush.' She went over to the bed, put her arms round him, kissed his cheek. 'You don't know that. You're just allowing yourself to think it. You have to try to keep faith with yourself. Something else might have happened . . .'

He responded not at all, remained sitting stiff and still, staring ahead; great tears formed in his eyes and rolled slowly down his cheeks. Then he said, 'I remember enough to know I was desperate for sleep, tried all the usual tricks, biting my own fists, counting backwards from a thousand . . .'

'You don't remember this other person being there with you yet? It's not clearing at all?'

'No,' he said and his voice was bitter. 'It *isn't* clearing! If anything, it's going further away. I'm beginning to think it was some kind of hallucination, wishful thinking.' He reached for a tissue, blew his nose, wiped his eyes. 'How are the boys?'

'They're fine. They want to come and see you so much. Ciaran has done you a fine picture, look, Callum wants to tell you about his new teacher and Liam says I have to give you fifty kisses. Shall I bring them in tomorrow? Mum says she'll drive us all down.'

'I don't want to see them,' he said.

She stared at him. 'For the love of God why not?'

'I want them to forget about me.'

'Forget about you! And what sort of a child will forget his own father – as fine a one as you? And why should he?'

'If the father is a killer, if he's been responsible for the deaths of many people, he's better forgotten, Maeve. I wish only one thing now, that I had been killed myself, that I had died in that cab.'

'Patrick Connell, will you just shut up now?' The seemingly endless strain and exhaustion finally defeated Maeve; she felt angry with him, angry not for what he had done – or not done – but for his willingness to give in, to turn his back on them all.

'How dare you talk like that, how dare you, when the finest doctors in this hospital have worked so hard to save you, when your own childen cry every night they want to see you so much, when I feel so tired I could just lie down on that floor and sleep for all eternity myself. But I can't, Patrick, because someone has to keep going. Someone has to see after the children, and visit you every day, and work so hard to cheer you.'

He turned his head to look at her, and his expression was quite blank, his eyes dull and disinterested.

'You don't have to come,' he said. 'It would be much better if you didn't.'

Maeve straightened up, looked at him very briefly and then picked up her bag and walked out of the room.

Russell's letter had been to tell Mary that she wasn't to worry about him, they had the rest of their lives together after all, but to concentrate her efforts on making her peace with her daughter.

That really is the most important thing right now. How extraordinary this all is! I've started to worry about my children's reactions as well. Maybe we should run away together to Gretna Green and get married with just a couple of witnesses. I dreamed of doing that occasionally during the war. But it's not what I want, of course: I want all our friends and family there, I want everyone to watch us being married, you becoming Mary Mackenzie. After all these years.

But Mary could see that both their families might find this a little difficult. It wasn't as if they'd been part of one another's circle, a natural relationship growing out of friendship. That was the whole problem. And she was sure Russell's rather grand family would look down on her. What had seemed incredibly romantic and exciting suddenly was turning into a depressing mess.

Barney was trying to distract Toby with Scrabble. Not with one hundred per cent success. Not, if he was honest, with much more than fifty. They'd finished one game; he offered him another.

Toby shook his head. 'Sorry. Bit tired.'

'Yeah, 'spect you are. Well, can't be much longer. Then you'll be able to have a really good sleep.'

Toby didn't even try to smile, just turned his head away and stared out of the window at the teeming rain. Barney sat there, helplessly silent, every word of encouragement and support wrung out of him, praying that they would come and, in the strange parlance of hospitals, 'take Toby down'.

'Toby, hello!' At last: only it wasn't Toby's doctor, or the nurse or even the anaesthetist. It was Emma, smiling that smile of hers, walking towards them, her ponytail bouncing up and down. 'Hi, Barney! How foul is this weather? Anyway, can't stop. I just came to say good luck, Toby. I'm sure it'll be fine.'

Toby managed a half-smile; he was very pale. And who could wonder, Barney thought, looking at him, facing the fact that he might wake up minus a leg or part of it anyway. It didn't bear thinking about; he was sure if it had been him, he would have been blubbing, or throwing up or—

'Right, Toby!' It was one of the ward nurses, also smiling. 'They're almost ready for you. Now let me help you into this,' she put a green surgical gown on the bed, 'and this very fetching stocking. You haven't got any false teeth, have you?'

'No. Probably have a false leg soon though,' said Toby. He tried to smile and failed; his teeth were chattering, he was extremely white. Barney had seen Toby frightened a few times: when they were caught out of bounds at prep school and sent to the Head, when they were going into their first GCSE exam, when they were going to the hospital after Toby had broken his arm, when he was about to make a speech at a friend's wedding. He knew the signs, but he had never seen him as bad as this.

He and Emma looked at each other helplessly as the nurse drew the curtains round Toby, in order to help him change; then both gave equally fatuous smiles at him when the curtains opened again.

'Cool!' said Barney. 'Really suits you.'

'Wait till you get the hat on,' said Emma.

There was a silence, then: 'Very nice of you to come up, Emma,' said Barney. 'Isn't it, Tobes?'

'What? Oh – yeah.'

Another silence. Then: 'Right.' It was the nurse again,

with two orderlies and a trolley. 'Here we are with your personalised transport. We'll just pop you onto this, Toby – careful, boys, that leg's very sore – and take you down to theatre. All right? Feel OK? Oh, how stupid, I've left your watch on.'

'I'll take it,' said Barney, reaching over and unbuckling the watch, wondering if it would be the last time he would see Toby as Toby, for a crippled one was so unthinkably different. He suddenly felt tears at the back of his eyes; blinked furiously, took the watch and put it in his pocket.

'Cheers, mate, I'll be here when you get back. With a big can of beer.'

'You'll do no such thing,' said the nurse, but she was smiling. 'Come on, Toby then, off we go.'

'Oh shit!' Toby suddenly reached over and clasped Barney's hand. 'I don't like this, Barney, I don't like it one bit.'

'Tobes! You'll be fine.'

'Yeah, but what if I'm not? How will I – how can I – Jesus!'

'Come along,' said the nurse. She looked rather tense herself, Barney noted. 'Sooner we go, the sooner you'll be back. And you heard what your friend said; he'll be here, waiting for you.'

'Bye, Tobes,' Barney said, and try as he would, he couldn't get the shake out of his voice. 'See you.'

And then the trolley moved away, out of the ward and Barney was left staring at Emma.

'How long do you think it might be?' he asked.

She hesitated, then met his eyes. 'It will depend. If the news is good, if the leg is healing, he'll be back in an hour or so.'

'And if not?'

'Well . . . longer. Yes. Quite a bit.'

'So, after an hour, it's bad, yeah?'

'It could be. But this isn't an exact science, Barney. You never know, so don't start fretting just because it's,' she looked at her watch, 'let's see, he'll be about fifteen minutes actually going into theatre, being anaesthetised and everything. And then . . . let's say three quarters of an hour, all being well. But then he'll be in Recovery, they won't rush him back up here straight away. I'd say you don't want to begin to worry for two hours. Which is one o'clock. What are you going to do until then?'

'Oh, don't know. Thought I'd go for a drive. Don't want to just sit round waiting.'

'OK. Good idea. You can hardly go for a walk in this rain. Well, look, when you get back, come to A and E, and if I'm not hopelessly busy, I'll ring theatre, get some news for you. OK?'

'OK,' said Barney. He felt too choked even to thank her. 'Yeah, cool. See you, Emma.'

'See you, Barney. And try not to worry. There really is a good chance.'

'Is there?' he said, and he sounded very bitter suddenly. 'I'm not entirely sure you think that – I don't think any of you think that – oh shit. I'm off. See you around one, then.'

'Around one, Barney, yes.'

Barney drove out of the hospital gate and headed, without being sure why, in the direction of Cirencester. He rather liked Ciren, as it was called locally; it was a classic Gloucestershire town, full of golden stone buildings and still relatively unspoiled. He parked in the centre of the town, sat down on a seat and smoked a couple of cigarettes and suddenly found himself consumed with anxiety, a fear that was so physical he actually shook, over what might be happening to Toby right this minute. How would he manage with only half a leg? What would he do, when he couldn't swim or run or play tennis or ski, when he was forced into spectatorhood, sitting eternally on the sidelines, feeling out of everything? How would he be able to cope with the social life of work, the rowdy drinking, the late-night dining, the clubbing, when he had to be helped in and out of places, relying on friends, on kindness, permanently grateful, always different from the rest? How would he live with himself, imperfect and maimed – yes, that was the horrible word for it? Of course they would give him a prosthesis, and people managed wonderfully well with such things, and Toby would try with all the courage he had to do the same. But at the end of the day, he would no longer be the Toby he had been, impatiently fit and fast. He would be a different, less independent creature, robbed of being physically confident and – Barney knew – slightly ashamed of himself. And what of Tamara, what would she make of him? No longer her perfect, wonderfully handsome fiancé, but someone she would certainly see as second-rate, second choice. Oh, she'd make all the right noises, vow faithfulness, loyalty, support. But – give her six months, present her with a different and perfect young man and it was horrible to contemplate how quickly she would back off, making ugly, feeble excuses . . .

Barney wrenched his mind off Tamara, and how she might – or rather would – behave, looked at his watch which had advanced terrifyingly far, and drove very fast back to the hospital.

He was in such a state of terror as he parked his car that he misjudged the size of space available to him and hit the wing mirror of a horribly new-looking Audi TT in the next bay. He thought at first he hadn't done too much damage, but as he got out, he realised the mirror was dangling limply from its moorings, the glass shattered. Barney knew about those Audis; fixing it would cost several hundred pounds. Well, it hardly compared with a shattered leg. He found it hard to care about either the car or its owner. He scribbled a note and left it on the windscreen.

He looked at his watch; one-fifteen. Shit. Toby would probably be out of theatre now. Conscious and needing him. Fine friend he'd turned out to be. He ran across the car park, and then, unable to contemplate hearing the bad news on his own, made for A&E and the company of Emma. It was deserted, apart from a woman with a wailing baby and an elderly man with an arm in a sling. He looked over at the reception desk; there was only one woman on duty and she was chatting to a nurse about some event in the department that had taken place earlier in the day. He walked over and waited politely for what felt like ten minutes; then driven beyond endurance said, 'Excuse me.'

'Yes?' said the woman coldly. The nurse looked him up and down, then said she'd better be getting on and left.

'I wondered if I could see Dr King. Dr Emma King.'

'What would it be concerning?' Why did people in such places always use this extraordinary language? Did they have lessons in reception-speak? For goodness' sake, Barney, concentrate.

'A patient,' he said firmly.

'Which patient?'

'He's called Weston. Toby Weston.'

'Well, there's no one of that name here.'

'No,' said Barney, slightly desperately. 'No, he's on Men's Surgical.'

'Well, that would be the place to see him,' said the woman. 'Surely?' Her tone implied that Barney was clearly in the last stages of dementia.

'But it's not him I want to see. He's in – been to – theatre this morning.'

'Well, that's nothing to do with Dr King. Who told you to ask for her?'

'She did,' said Barney firmly.

'Well, I can't think why.'

'I could explain,' said Barney, 'but . . .' He looked at the clock. Nearly half-one. 'Look,' he said, 'couldn't you just page Dr King or something, and tell her I'm here? She is expecting me.'

'Well, I really don't know,' said the woman. 'I suppose I could try.' She clearly saw this as an extraordinarily difficult task. 'But I can't guarantee she'll see you.'

'She will,' said Barney, 'I swear to you. She's expecting me.'

'Well, I don't know why she wouldn't have mentioned it,' said the woman. 'That's the normal procedure.'

Barney felt himself beginning to sweat. 'Look, could you just page her. Please. It really is very important!'

The woman sighed and started tapping at her computer keys. 'I need the number – King, King . . . there's nothing coming up yet.'

'Emma King,' said Barney. 'Surely you know her? She works here in this department.'

'Well, she may do, but that doesn't mean I know her number. There are a dozen doctors in A and E, we don't just carry their numbers round in our heads, you know.' She returned to her list: more clicking. God, Barney thought, one-thirty . . .

'Barney! Hi.' It was Emma. Barney had never seen her without a lift of his heart; at that moment he felt he could have taken off through the hospital roof. 'I wondered where you were. Come with me. It's fine, Pat, he's a friend.'

'Well, he might have said so in the first place,' said Pat. She glared at Barney. He smiled back.

Emma took him through the doors at the back of the waiting area; and then along a corridor, into a small office.

'Here we are. I'll ring up to Theatre now. Haven't heard anything – I asked them to let me know, but . . .'

'It's twenty to two,' said Barney. 'Doesn't that mean it's bad news?'

'Not really,' said Emma, her face intently sympathetic, 'it could mean anything, the most likely being they forgot. It was the nurses in Recovery I spoke to. They'll have several patients to worry about, it was a long list this morning and if there was a crisis with even one, they're hardly going to remember to call me about another.'

'Yes, I see,' said Barney. Thinking, what if the crisis was Toby?

Emma dialled a number; waited. And waited. Hours seemed to pass. Barney felt he was about to throw up.

'They're obviously frantic,' she said. 'Just not answering. Look, let's go up there. Come on.'

She led the way on what seemed to Barney an endless journey: into lifts, along corridors, through doors, through more doors. Looking at his watch as she stopped in front of a door marked *Medical Personnel only* he was amazed to see it was only five minutes since she'd appeared in A&E.

'Wait there,' she said, and knocked on the door. A nurse dressed in scrubs appeared.

'Yes?' she said.

'Sorry,' said Emma. 'Dr King, from A and E. I wondered if you had any news of a patient. Toby Weston.'

'Oh, him. Not yet, no,' said the nurse. 'You asked for someone to ring, didn't you?'

'Yes, I did.'

'We've been frantic. He's only just out of theatre. Still under. Shouldn't be long. Wait out there,' she glared at Barney. 'I'll give you a shout.'

That was it then: nearly three hours. It must have gone horribly wrong. There could be no other explanation. Toby had lost his leg. And his old life with it. It was so bloody unfair. And if Barney had got him onto that road just a bit earlier, none of it would have happened, they'd never have got into that bloody accident. It was his fault: Tamara had been right about that at least . . .

He looked at Emma; she had blurred, and he realised

he was crying. *Stop it, Fraser, not for you to blub. Get a grip.*

He turned away; felt a hand slide into his. A cool, small hand.

'Don't give up yet. They've been terribly busy,' she said; 'so they might have had to delay the operation.'

'Or they didn't. Or his leg's gone. How could it take this long, Emma, how could it possibly?'

'I don't know,' she said, 'but as I told you, this isn't an exact science. They're not building a car.'

That reminded him. 'Oh shit,' he said, and it seemed so unimportant that he actually smiled. 'I've just driven into a brand new Audi TT in the car park.'

'Yeah? Do much damage?'

'Broke the wing mirror. And the thing that holds it on. Wires dangling, that sort of job.'

'I shouldn't worry. Anyone who can afford a car like that can afford a new mirror.' She grinned at him. 'How's that for looking on the bright side?'

'Like it.'

They were both silent; he realised he was still holding her hand. He looked down at it, and then at her, smiled slightly awkwardly.

'Thank you for doing all this, Emma. It's very good of you.'

'It's my pleasure. Honestly. Well,' she smiled suddenly, that brilliant, light-the-day-up smile, 'I mean I hope it will be.'

She withdrew her hand; they leaned against the window, looking out. They were at the front of the building, above the main entrance. Two ambulances raced in, lights flashing, sirens going; a woman was walking towards the car park, clearly crying; a small boy was being pushed in a wheelchair towards the ramp.

'I don't know how you can stand this,' Barney said, 'it's not a load of fun, your job, is it?'

'Oh, you'd be surprised,' she said. 'Of course there's sadness, awful sadness, but there's such a lot of happiness too. Even in A and E, people come in frightened, in pain, and leave smiling, feeling much better. I would say there are more happy days than sad ones.'

'And what is it you're planning on doing, long-term? Didn't you say babies and stuff?'

'Yes. Now that *is* a happy old business. Bringing babies into the world, nothing like it.'

'I suppose, yes. That doctor at the crash, that great guy who helped so much, he did that, didn't he?'

'Yes, he was a bit of a hero altogether. I Googled him, actually, after reading some of the reports. He's a very smart gynaecologist and obstetrician. Rooms in Harley Street – that sort of thing.'

'Would you like that?'

'What, private practice? No, don't think so. I don't approve of any of that, really.'

'Any of what?' How was he managing this, chatting away, properly interested, when Toby was . . .

'Well, you know. Private medicine, private schools, I think it's all wrong. Sorry, Barney, I guess you went to one. I don't want to sound rude.'

'You don't. And I'm sure you're right – it isn't fair. But . . .' The fear cut into him again; why was he burbling on like this? What was happening to Toby?

'What the fuck are they doing in there?' he said, staring at the door. Emma didn't look at him, he noticed; just went on gazing out of the window. 'If – if they do – you know . . .'

'Amputate?' she said gently. It was somehow good hearing it spoken, confronted like that.

'Yeah. If they do that who'll tell him? The doctor, the nurses?'

'They will,' she said, 'very carefully. They're quite gentle these days. The surgeon in charge of Toby is a friend of mine.'

'*What!* You know the guy who's doing this?'

'Well, yes.'

'Oh, for fuck's sake!' For some reason this made him angry. 'Why the fuck won't he tell you at least? That is so arrogant. What sort of rules do you people live by?'

She stared at him. 'Barney, you don't quite understand. It's—'

'You're too damn right I don't. Here we are, sweating our guts out, no one having the decency to come out of that door and tell us what's happening, and you say the person doing this to Toby is a *friend* of yours. Rum sort of friend, that's all I can say.'

She shrugged, turned away; he had clearly upset her. Well, that was fine. She—

The door opened suddenly, and the nurse came out.

'Dr King,' she said, 'can you come in a minute?'

Well, that was definitely it. He knew now. It was the worst. He felt sick, then as if he might cry again; he turned away from the door, stared down the corridor.

'Barney.'

He turned. Emma was standing looking at him; she was flushed, looked close to tears herself.

'Yeah?' he said, aware he sounded hostile still. And then he realised she was smiling, and yes, almost crying at the same time, and then she said, in a voice that was clearly struggling not to shake, 'Toby's fine. The leg's good, it's beginning to heal. He's only just coming round properly now. Mark, that's the surgeon, says you can see him, just for a moment. Want to come in?'

'Oh shit,' said Barney. 'Oh for fuck's sake. Oh, Emma. Emma, I'm *so* sorry, I didn't mean anything I just said. Here . . .'

And suddenly he was hugging her, and she was smiling up at him and hugging him back, and then she took his hand again and led him through the door and into a small room where Toby lay on a high, hard bed, struggling to smile through the confusion of his anaesthetic.

'Hello, you old fucker,' said Barney. 'You really put us through it this morning, didn't you?' And then he couldn't say any more, because he really did start to cry, tears running down his face; and he realised both Emma and the nurse were smiling at him and he pulled out his handkerchief, blew his nose very hard and said, 'Well done, mate. Bloody well done.'

Chapter 27

Laura was sitting at her desk, planning, just a little reluctantly, the party for Jonathan in two weeks' time.

She had decided that she should go ahead with it, that she had no actual reason not to, that the only positive thing she could do for the time being was behave naturally, and as if she believed Jonathan's story about Abi Scott. There was no future in recrimination, or cross-examination. If Abi was indeed a work colleague, then acting like a jealous neurotic would wreak further damage; she still didn't quite believe it, however desperately she wanted to, but dissembling was clearly the dignified route. Dignity was becoming important. If Abi did indeed prove to be Jonathan's mistress, then she would be in a stronger, more controlling position for having behaved well. And she did actually, in her more lucid moments, feel very sorry for him; he was clearly exhausted, haunted by the crash. It had really hit him very hard. She supposed because of all the might-have-beens and could-have-beens. If they'd been that near the front, it could very easily have been him. That haunted her a bit too.

No, the party would cheer him up. And if she did cancel it, people would talk, might not be satisfied with reports of stress. As far as all their friends were concerned, Jonathan had nothing to be exhausted or wretched about. He had behaved impeccably – and more – at the crash; he had been enormously helpful to the police. He had even, and he made sure everyone knew this, Laura had noted slightly

404

cynically, made several calls to the hospital at Swindon to enquire after the lorry driver's progress and even the young man whose leg had been so badly smashed on the way to his wedding.

So, the party must go ahead: everyone was primed for it, the children were excited, and at least she could wear her lovely new dress.

She called Serena Edwards, her chief conspirator. 'Everything all right for it still?'

'Absolutely. We'll pick you up at six, take you out for a drink – oh, I've even booked a table at the River Café, or rather pretended to – told them to say they're expecting us, should he call.'

'Oh Serena, you are wonderful! And how good of them.'

'Well, we are very regular customers. Like for your birthday dinner.'

'That's true,' said Laura, remembering with a stab of pain the perfection of that evening. Could it really only have been a few months ago? It seemed like a lifetime, just ten friends, sitting there on a magical spring evening, the cake brought in by the waiter, looking round the table at everyone as they sang 'Happy Birthday', across at Jonathan smiling at her, touching the gold charm bracelet from Links he had given her that morning, with a promise to give her a charm every year. 'Until I've bought the shop up. Which should take about a hundred years.'

She had been so happy then, felt so safe . . . She felt tears sting at the back of her eyes, brushed them impatiently away.

'Laura, are you OK? You sound a bit odd.'

'Oh yes. Yes, I'm fine.'

'Is it Jonathan?'

'Well, you know. He's being quite difficult, irritable, can't sleep for reliving the crash.'

'Poor old boy. Well, the party should cheer him up.

Try not to worry. We still on for the Sanctuary on Monday?'

'Yes, course. Bye, Serena.'

Freeman and Rowe had been to interview Mary Bristow that day. Expecting a dotty old lady, they had found themselves confronted by a razor-clear mind, and an extremely lucid account of what she had seen of the accident and indeed the road that day.

'There was some terrible driving. You know, as I lay in hospital, I thought it was rather surprising there weren't more accidents on this scale, with so many cars driving much too fast. People are so aggressive and drive so selfishly. This dreadful habit of sitting close behind other vehicles and flashing at them, it happened to us several times. And the way people drive in and out of the different lanes without signalling, coming up far too close, cutting it much too fine. As my late husband used to say, driving carefully yourself is not enough. "It's not you, it's the other fellow."'

Rowe nodded at her and smiled approvingly. 'How right he was, Mrs Bristow. We often say the same thing ourselves, don't we, Sergeant Freeman?'

'Well, words to that effect certainly,' said Sergeant Freeman. 'Can you remember noticing any particular cases of bad driving, Mrs Bristow?'

'Oh yes, several. Two or three lorries, cutting in and out of the slow lane, moving in front of people. I have to say they were all foreign numberplates. I found that reassuring, in a way. At least our drivers seem to know how to behave.' She smiled at them. 'More cake, either of you?'

'That would be very nice. Thank you, yes,' said Rowe. 'Did you make it yourself, Mrs Bristow?'

'I did indeed. I love baking. It's a very soothing occupation. It certainly calmed my worries about today. Sergeant?'

'Delicious, but no thank you.' Sergeant Freeman waved

the plate away and looked pointedly at Rowe. 'Some of us have to watch our weight. I'm sorry if you were worried about today, Mrs Bristow.'

'Oh well, you know, one wants to help and yet one doesn't want to say anything not strictly accurate. Memory is a very subjective thing, isn't it?'

'True. You'd be surprised how very differently people describe the same event. Any more particular cases of bad driving that you recall?'

'Well, several motorbikes. They should be banned from the public roads in my opinion. And yes, I did notice several white vans – they're supposed to be the worst, aren't they? Anyway, one did particularly strike me: he'd been sitting very close behind us, and then he shot past, and I noticed that he didn't even have his rear doors properly fastened. They were just held together with a bit of rope. It seemed very unwise.'

'I see. Did you notice any writing or anything like that on his van?'

'Not exactly. There were three letters on one of the back doors, obviously part of a name, but not in sequence – if you see what I mean. That is to say, not a complete word or name. The rest had come off. It wasn't at all a well-looked-after vehicle.'

'Can you remember what the letters were?'

'I can, as a matter of fact.'

These old parties: amazing, thought Freeman. He supposed it was surviving the Blitz or something.

'Yes,' she said, 'they were W D T. In that order. I remember because we used to play a game with the children, making up words from car numberplates. I'm sure you know the sort of thing. I mean B and T and W would obviously be Bristow. Although proper names were not allowed, of course.'

'Of course,' said Freeman. He was beginning to feel rather confused himself.

'So yes, I still do it rather automatically. Ah, WDT, I thought, War Department. They loomed rather large in our lives at the time. I don't suppose it's much help, but—'

'It could be a help, Mrs Bristow, certainly. I don't suppose you were playing the same game with the numberplate?'

'Oh – no. I'm so sorry. Not his. Some of the others, but not his.'

'Well, never mind. And at what point in the journey did you see this van? Shortly before the crash?'

'Oh no, it was a good fifteen minutes before. And he was going very fast. He would have been well ahead – unless he stopped, of course, but it was after the service station, I do know that. I can't believe he could have been responsible in any way. The luck of the devil, as my late husband would have said.'

'Right, so you stopped at the service station – that would have been at what time, Mrs Bristow?'

'Oh, about – let me see, three-fifteen. We moved off in less than ten minutes. My driver, and I would like to stress that he drove quite beautifully, in the inside lane at my request, all the way – he needed some chewing gum and I offered to buy it for him as I needed to go to the Ladies.' She hesitated. 'I feel a little guilty now, about something I did.'

'Oh yes? I'm sure it wasn't too bad.'

'Well, I hope not. A young man, who I now know was the poor bridegroom, because he was wearing the striped trousers and so on, asked if he could go ahead of everyone in the queue. I said he should wait his turn, that we were all in a hurry for various reasons. I do hope that didn't affect the course of events at all. It must have delayed him, perhaps made him drive too fast. One is so aware of how tiny things can lead to greater ones. What is that called, something about butterflies?'

'The butterfly effect,' said Rowe, 'and I've never understood it. A butterfly can flap its wings in the jungle somewhere and cause a hurricane three days later . . .'

'Perhaps we should move on,' said Sergeant Freeman. 'Can you give us your account of what you saw of the collision?'

'Well, this is where I really am going to disappoint you. I fell asleep, you see, and woke up as we stopped and the car behind drove into us. It was very shocking, and of course if we hadn't been in the inside lane, it could have been very much more serious . . .'

She was silent for a moment; her eyes filled with tears. She fumbled in her cardigan pocket, produced a lace-edged handkerchief and blew her nose. You didn't often see handkerchiefs like that these days, Freeman thought, it was all tissues. Funny the kinds of things that dated people.

'Take your time,' he said gently. 'Just tell us what you remember.'

'I'm afraid the rest is all rather confused.' But she proceeded to describe the position of her car relative to all the others near her, and to the lorry, and what she had observed.

'Pity all our witnesses aren't that clear in their accounts,' said Rowe, as they drove away.

'True. Those letters might be a help. Bit of a needle in a haystack.'

'Well, we'll have to do some anagrams. I'm not too bad at those myself. I like crosswords.'

'Really.' Freeman gave him the chilly look that Rowe was growing to know rather well. 'You must let me know if you have any brainwaves. Anyway, I'm certainly beginning to want to talk to that van driver. Maybe we could get him mentioned on the TV programme as well.'

* * *

Oh, my God. Oh. My. God.

Just as well He hadn't answered that particular prayer, then. The one about the read-through being cancelled. Or she'd never have set eyes on Him. Not God, but still worthy of a capital letter. The most unbelievably gorgeous bloke she'd ever seen . . .

Who was he? What was he doing here? And he was actually walking towards her, smiling at her, saying, 'Georgia?'

'Yes,' she said and her voice sounded odd, slightly squeaky. She tried again.

'Yes, that's me.' That was better.

'Thought so. I'm Merlin, the second assistant director on *Moving Away*. So we'll be seeing quite a lot of each other, once shooting starts.'

'Great!' Not the cleverest answer, but what could you say in response to the discovery that you'll be working with someone who looked like – well who did he look like? A dollop of Orlando Bloom, a smidgen of Johnny Depp, maybe even a sliver of Pete Doherty at his most savoury. Tall he was, and very thin, with almost black spiky hair, dark brown eyes and a rather narrow face, and really great clothes – tight black jeans and combat boots and a white collarless shirt.

'Great,' she repeated feebly.

'Yeah, it looks like it'll be fun. We're very excited about it. Great cast – including you, of course.'

'Well, I don't know about that.' *Come on, Georgia, say something a bit intelligent. Interesting. Not completely dumb.*

'Oh yes. Casting director's been raving about you.'

'Thank you,' she said, and smiled. He smiled back. He had absolutely perfect teeth. 'I'm pretty excited about it myself, I can tell you,' she told him. 'Still pinching myself about getting it.'

'Me too. I mean *me* getting it. Have you worked with Bryn before?'

'No, never.'

'I have. He's a great director. And he makes it fun too. Where did you train?'

'Oh, NAD.'

'Yeah? I had a friend there.'

He would have done. Probably had girlfriends everywhere, every college, every studio, every port.

'Anyway, come on over, Georgia. Everyone's here.'

He steered her towards a group chatting together like lifelong friends. She recognised some of them: Tony, the casting director, Bryn Merrick the director of course, but not a rather scarily efficient-looking person called Trish, who was the producer. Georgia moved round the group shaking hands, smiling nervously, saying how thrilled she was to be part of the production. She felt very shaky, partly because of being with all these brilliant people, partly because Merlin was touching her. Even if it was only on her shoulder. Well, you had to start somewhere.

'Right, Georgia. A word.' Tony drew her aside. 'We've got two actresses reading for Marjie. Both are very talented, both very suitable – it would be helpful in our decision to see how you relate to each of them. I expect Linda's explained.'

'Yes, she has.'

'So we want you to read the same scene, first with Barbara, who's already here, and then do a bit of improvisation with her . . .'

Georgia took a deep breath and told herself she must stay calm. She always found improvisation the most scary thing of all.

'And then Anna is coming in later. Same thing with her. Oh, and by the way, Davina – you know, she's playing your mum – is coming in around lunchtime. She's got a meeting with the executive producer, and she specially wanted to meet you. So if you can hang around for a while . . .'

'Yes, of course,' said Georgia. 'No problem at all.'

The first read-through was fine; she liked Barbara very much, she was funny and fun, and put her at her ease. But somehow when they did the improvisation – Bryn suggested a scene where they were both remembering Cath, the granny – it became more difficult. Barbara made Georgia feel rather insipid and too low-key for her own part. She did her best, but it was a struggle.

'Marvellous,' said Tony, as they finished. 'Thank you both. God, this is going to be difficult. Barbara, thank you so much for coming in. You like our Rose, then?'

'Very much,' said Barbara. 'We'll have fun, won't we, Rose?'

Georgia said she thought they would and Barbara left.

'Right,' said Sue, 'coffee, I think. Anna's coming in at twelve. Merlin, could you get that organised, darling?'

How wonderful, Georgia thought, to be old enough and sophisticated enough to be able to call everyone 'darling'. Especially Merlin.

Anna didn't look so right, Georgia thought. She was rather beautiful in a hippie sort of way, with silvery-blond wavy hair and intensely blue eyes, and was surely much too young for the part; but she was a marvellous actor. Georgia was amazed at the way she simply put on ten years with the first line she spoke. And she was surprised to find how she could relate to her in the improvisation, far better than with the over-jolly Barbara.

Tony said all the same things again: a lot of marvellouses and thank yous and how difficult it was going to be, making a choice. Anna left. The four of them went into another room and Merlin grinned at Georgia.

'Well done. You were awfully good. Honestly.'

'I don't know about that.'

'No, you were. Tough decision now, I'd say.'

'Yes, I should think so.' Why couldn't she say something witty and incisive, for God's sake?

They all emerged smiling; she was terrified they might ask her which of the two she had felt more comfortable with, but they just told her how well she'd done and thanked her again.

'Now Davina's been held up for a couple of hours, Georgia. It's up to you, of course, but if you'd like to meet her, she'll be here about three. Can you find something to do till then?'

Georgia said she'd go shopping and headed for Topshop. She got back on the dot of three, to be told Davina now wouldn't be there till four.

'Drink?' said Merlin.

'Oh yes, thank you. Diet Coke if you've got one.'

'There's white wine.'

'No, honestly, I'd prefer the Coke.'

'OK,' he said with his amazing smile. 'I'll follow your example.'

Now he'd think she was a killjoy as well as boring.

Merlin was sitting quietly reading; for want of anything better to do, Georgia had followed his example. Every so often he looked up at her and smiled, offered her another Diet Coke, then went back to his book. Georgia felt sure it must be something very intellectual; she was actually reading the latest Sophie Kinsella and had tucked the *Metro* round it, so that Merlin might think it was one of the Booker short list or something.

'Sorry about the wait,' he said suddenly. 'I'm sure if you wanted to go, it'd be fine.'

'Well, do you think I should?'

'No, no, I'm sure she meant it about wanting to meet you. But if you've got something important on, I know she'd understand. She really is great.'

He was rather posh; he sounded as if he'd gone to public

school. But maybe it was just luvvie talk. Again.

'Honestly, it's fine. I don't have anything to do this evening.' She shouldn't have said that; what kind of loser had nothing to do on a Friday night?

'Wish I didn't.'

No doubt he had to go out clubbing with some hot young actress.

'My parents' Silver Wedding party. Three-line whip.'

'Oh really? Where is it?'

'Elena's L'Etoile. They've got the private room upstairs.'

'Oh, great,' she said. Hoping she sounded as if she knew all about the private room at Elena's L'Etoile.

Davina turned up at five when almost everyone had gone home except Merlin. He was clearly an important ingredient in all this, Georgia thought. Davina was an absolutely dazzling black woman, with a huge smile showing big perfect teeth, her fountain of black hair braided.

She kissed Georgia, said how much she was looking forward to being her mum for a bit. 'Bryn says you're a real find,' she added.

'Really?' said Georgia. 'Everyone's been so kind to me today.'

'Well, why shouldn't they be? We're quite a nice lot really, promise. Now do we know who's doing Marjie yet, Merlin?'

Merlin said he didn't.

'Go and find out, darling. I've got my fingers crossed for Anna – she's such fun and such wonderful stories.'

Merlin went off obediently; Georgia smiled at her.

'I love your hair,' she said tentatively into the slightly long silence, and then felt silly, but Davina smiled and said, 'Well, I'm hoping everyone will – it's taken me four days.'

'Do you do it yourself?' Georgia asked.

'Of course. I enjoy it, it's therapy. Hard on the arms, but . . .'

Bryn came into the room. 'Davina, my darling, how totally gorgeous you look. Come on into my office, meet my assistant. I hope you'll be pleased to hear Anna's cast as Marjie. She related very well to Georgia here. Georgia, you were great today.'

'That's marvellous. Georgia, I'd have loved to chat a bit longer, but I've got to go after this. Got a train to catch to Paris.'

Georgia thought how glamorous that sounded, and indeed how wonderful all the rest of the day had been, and then of her own train going to Cardiff: and suddenly felt the nightmare closing in again. She didn't want the day to end, she really didn't.

Merlin said he'd have to fly. 'But thanks so much for coming in today, Georgia, and for being so great. Cheers. Lovely to have met you.'

'Lovely to have met you too. Thanks, Merlin.'

She went down to reception, thinking gloomily about the journey back to Cardiff; and then wondered what Linda was doing and if she'd left the office yet. She might be able to go and see her and tell her about her day. It would keep the enchantment of the day going a bit longer.

Linda was delighted to hear from her; she told her to hurry round to the office and they could have a glass of wine to celebrate what had obviously been a successful day.

Mary was up in her room at six o'clock; she had just had a bath and was lying on her bed in her dressing-gown and slippers, before getting dressed again for supper. She liked to do that; it gave Christine the run of the kitchen, and helped ease the general tension, which was still high. She had spent much of the day reading another letter from Russell, over and over again. It was the most wonderful letter, four pages of it, telling her how much he loved her and was missing her, and how he had been wondering where they should live.

415

It will be difficult deciding; we will both want to be in our own countries. Right now I'm thinking we might split the year and do six months in each, buy two houses. That way we can each see as much or as little of our respective families as we and they wish. Or maybe three months and then a change. You have a rival, I'm afraid: I have fallen in love with Bath and the surrounding countryside, and I know you will love many places in the States.

The thought of having two homes made Mary feel quite dizzy. She thought how unbelievable a young person – her grandson Timothy, for example – would find such plans being made between two eighty year olds. Absurd even. But it wasn't, it was just wonderfully exciting and joyful.

She was just getting the letter out of her bag to read it yet again, when Christine called up the stairs. 'Quick, Mum, they've just trailed an item about the crash.'

'What?' said Mary stupidly. 'What crash?'

'Your crash, of course. Goodness, it must be two weeks ago now. Come on, hurry up or you'll miss it. Or shall I record it for you?'

'Oh no, dear, I'd very much like to watch it. As long as you don't think Gerry would object to my sitting in my dressing-gown and slippers.'

'Of course he won't mind.'

'Good, only your father would never countenance such a thing. He said you let one standard slip and then all the others follow it.'

'Yes, Mum, I know,' said Christine, who had heard this before at least a hundred times. 'But Gerry won't mind. Come on down, and I'll make some tea, shall I? And do be careful on the stairs in those slippers.'

She sounded more her old self; seeing Mary as some sort of elderly child. Well, it was better than being an adulteress . . .

* * *

416

Linda decided to watch the news while she waited for Georgia; she seldom switched the office set on, but it was useful, both for viewing actors' DVDs and watching them on chat shows; and to bridge the gap between the end of work and going out to see some play or other.

She decided she needed a glass of wine; she was just pouring it when a horribly familiar scene presented itself.

The children were all in bed when Maeve arrived home, still deeply upset at Patrick's behaviour. Her mother told her to go and sit down in the front room while she made some tea. She brought it in on a tray, together with some biscuits and the remains of a box of chocolates, and then joined Maeve and suggested they watched TV for a bit.

'Put your feet up, darlin', it'll do you good. This'll soon be over, the News, and then we can watch— Oh, my God! Maeve, do you see what they're doing?'

For there on the screen was some old footage of the crash; the horrible sight of Patrick's lorry, the trailer lying on its side, and the cars scattered about it like toys, and the girl newsreader was saying something about revisiting the scene of the M4 crash and then there was a quick rundown about it, when it had been, how many people had been involved.

'But two weeks later, there is some good news. The lorry driver is recovering well; the baby boy born prematurely – the mother went into labour as she and her husband waited in the tailback – is thriving and is going home this weekend and the famous golden retriever who was lost in the chaos turned up at a farm and has been reunited with her owner. In fact, you can see Bella for yourselves in a couple of minutes, we have her in the studio with one very happy owner. But before we do that, there is one rather more serious matter. The police are still gathering evidence on events leading up to the crash and would be

417

interested in hearing from anyone who may have seen something they feel relevant that afternoon, a car or van possibly driving erratically – or perhaps some debris on the road.'

All calls would be treated as confidential, the reporter went on. They were particularly interested in a young girl who . . .

'Oh my God,' said Maeve. 'Oh my dear Lord!'

'Laura, put the telly on quickly. Channel Eight, the news. Don't ask, just do it.'

'. . . a young black or mixed race girl who was seen by several people at the scene and is thought to have been possibly travelling in the lorry, and who has not yet come forward . . .'

'Hi, Linda, I brought you a bottle of— Oh my God, what's that about? Oh, my God . . .'

'So if you know anything of this girl, or you think you know where she might be, please do get in touch with the police in confidence. They do stress that there is no suggestion of anything suspicious, merely that in a crash as big as this one, there must be no stone left unturned in the subsequent investigation. And now, as promised, we have Bella and her owner, Margaret Ross, from Northamptonshire.'

'Oh, Mother Mary and all the saints!' said Maeve.

'Oh, I do hope Maeve is watching,' said Mary.

'How extraordinary,' said Laura.

Georgia made an odd sound; Linda looked at her. She was standing absolutely rigid, her hand clasped over her mouth.

And then she suddenly sat down, as if her legs wouldn't hold her any longer, her eyes still fixed on the screen.

'Georgia,' said Linda, very gently. 'Georgia, was that you?'

Chapter 28

Looking back on those first few days, at Georgia's ongoing and deep distress, Linda thought it was only surprising that the girl had survived so long and so well. And that she herself might have anticipated some of the later consequences. But she didn't.

The story had come out haltingly, punctuated with much weeping, self-flagellation, and sheer blind terror at what she had done – and concealed – through two long, dreadful weeks.

She had quite simply panicked. Linda had tried to reassure her, to tell her that it was not so unusual, not so dreadful a thing to do. But Georgia would have none of it. 'It was terrible, awful. He'd been so kind to me, and there he was unconscious, with God knows what injuries – and did I try and help? I might have been able to, might have managed to get the ambulance sooner, but – no, I just ran. It was disgusting of me, Linda. I'm so, so ashamed. But somehow, the longer I left it, the worse it seemed, what I'd done. And do you know what my very first thought was? After we'd crashed? That I'd miss the audition. Can you imagine anything as awful as that?'

'You were in shock,' Linda said. 'I keep telling you, it brings about some very strange behaviour.'

She had felt dazed at first, Georgia said, not sure what she was doing. 'I felt very sick, and dizzy. Two men by the lorry asked me if I was all right and I couldn't speak to them; I threw up right there, in front of them, it was horrible. And then I had to sit down for a bit. Everyone was much too busy looking after people who were really hurt to bother about me. After that I climbed over the barrier, by the hard shoulder, and slithered down the bank and started running. All I could think of was getting away. Does that sound crazy?'

Linda shook her head. 'Not at all.'

'There were all these cars crashed into each other, and huge white things everywhere, I didn't know what they were then, but of course they were Patrick's load, fridges and freezers and stuff. I just turned my back on it all, and ran. Towards Cardiff. That was all I wanted, to get home. I found a sort of track thing and followed that, and when I couldn't run any more I walked, on and on. Every yard I went, I felt less frightened, I was further away from it all. I felt – safer. How weird was that? I cut up into that bloke's land, that farmer guy who was just on the TV, and then on to a village and then I hitched a lift in a car going to Bristol.

'The driver said he'd been avoiding the M4, that there'd been a terrible crash, miles and miles of tailback, and I had to pretend to be surprised. Oh, God.'

In Bristol she had eventually managed to get a lift in a lorry going to Cardiff: 'I was scared of being in another one, I thought he might crash too.'

'And – tell me, do you think Patrick went to sleep?'

'To *sleep*?' said Georgia, looking at her, her eyes very wide. 'No, of course he didn't go to sleep. I saw exactly what happened. It wasn't his fault in any way at all. In fact,' she paused, gathered her breath, then said in a desperate tone, 'in fact, if it was anyone's fault, it was probably mine.'

Shaking, clinging to Linda's hand, she rang the programme helpline, who said they'd get the police to call her.

'Pretty soon, they said. Linda, I feel sick. I feel so awful. What will they think of me? What will they do to me? I'm disgusting, I deserve to be put away somewhere. Oh dear. Can I have another cigarette?'

It was a measure of her distress and of Linda's intense sympathy with that distress that she had actually agreed to let her have a cigarette. And not just one, but several, through the long hours that followed the programme. Linda loathed not just smoking, but smokers; it was a crusade with her, had been long before smoking was made illegal. To allow Georgia to smoke in her flat was akin to handing round glasses of wine at an AA meeting.

It was she who took the call; she passed the phone to Georgia. 'It's a Sergeant Freeman.'

'Thanks. Hello? Yes, this is Georgia Linley. Yes, I did. Yes, I think I can help. Linda, they want us to meet them at some police station in the morning. They're going to ring back with the exact address. Is that OK? Yes, that's fine. Thank you. What? No, it's not my mum, it's my agent. No, I'm fine, thank you. I'll be there, in the morning.'

She put the phone down, looked at Linda, her small face somehow gaunt, her dark eyes red with weeping, her small, pretty nose running; she wiped it on the back of her hand. She looked about six.

'You will come with me, won't you?' she said with a tremor in her voice.

Linda held out her arms and said, 'Of course I will. Come here, you.'

And Georgia went to sit next to her on the sofa, resting her head on Linda's shoulder, and said, 'I couldn't do all this without you, you know.'

'Well, I'm glad to have helped.'

'You have. So, so much. You've been great.' Another sniff, then, 'You'd have been a great mum, you know. You really should have, before it was too late.'

'Well, thanks,' said Linda.

* * *

The police were very kind, very gentle with her; steeped in a deep middle-class prejudice against them, Linda was surprised and pleased by how well they handled the whole thing.

Georgia sat, her teeth chattering with fright at first, but still telling her story perfectly lucidly, up to the point of the actual crash.

'We were just going along, very steadily, chatting – you know. Patrick was absolutely fine, not going fast at all, driving really carefully in the middle lane. We'd been through a storm, that was quite scary, it got very dark, and he slowed down a bit, said the water on the road was dangerous after the heat. But the sun was out again, it had stopped raining. And then – suddenly – there was this great crack of noise and we couldn't see. Not at all. It wasn't dark, just everything blurred. It was like being blind. I couldn't think what was happening. It was so, so frightening – the windscreen was impossible to see through. And Patrick slammed on the brakes and then swerved, quite sharply, and he was hooting and shouting—'

'Shouting? What was he shouting?'

'Oh, you know, things like "for the love of God" and "Jesus" – well, he is Irish,' she said with the ghost of a smile. 'And then the lorry just wouldn't stop. It went on and on, it seemed for hours. I couldn't see anything either, except out of the side window, and I could see through that, see we were going completely across the middle of the road, with the traffic on the other side coming towards us. It was weird, it all happened so slowly. And then – we stopped. And I felt a sort of violent lurch, as the trailer went, and there was this horrible noise and . . . oh, dear, sorry.' She started to cry.

'Now, now,' said Sergeant Freeman, 'no need for tears. You've been most helpful, your account is quite invaluable. As I explained to you, with the lorry driver unable to remember anything much, this is the first really lucid account we've had. So – what did you think had happened? To cause it?'

'Well,' she said, blowing her nose on the tissue Linda handed her, 'I did realise then that the windscreen was shattered. There wasn't a hole in it, the glass just had all these weird patterns all over it, making it impossible to see.'

'Something hit it, perhaps?' said Freeman. 'Maybe that was the crack you heard.'

'Yes, I did think that. But what could it have been?'

'That's for us to find out. You can stop worrying about it now.'

'You're being so kind,' she said. 'You must be so shocked at me, by what I did.'

'Miss Linley,' Freeman said, 'if you saw one per cent of what we do, you'd understand that we're not very easily shocked. Isn't that right, Constable?'

'Absolutely right,' said Constable Rowe.

And then, 'You might be shocked at this though,' she said, in a voice so low it was almost inaudible.

'I doubt it. Try us.'

'I think some of it could – could have been my fault.'

'Your fault?' Sergeant Freeman was clearly struggling not to smile.

'Yes, you see, I – well, I dropped a can of drink. As we swerved. On the floor. It was rolling around. I think it might have interfered with Patrick's – Mr Connell's brakes. And if I hadn't done that, maybe he could have stopped. I mean, oh God . . .'

'Miss Linley,' said Sergeant Freeman, 'we will, of course, put this into our report, but I really don't think you should worry about it too much. The brakes in those things are huge, very powerful and power-assisted. One small can of drink rolling around would not, in my opinion, have had the slightest effect. What would you say, Constable?'

Constable Rowe smiled at Georgia and said yes, indeed, he would say the same thing. He found himself very moved by her distress. She hardly looked old enough to be out in the world at all, let alone hitching lifts in lorries.

'Really?' she whispered.

'Really. But of course we could be wrong and as Sergeant Freeman says, it will go into the report. I hope that makes you feel better?'

'It does. A bit.' But she was still looking very uncertain.

'So, you would say the whole accident was caused by this shattering of the windscreen? By Mr Connell being unable to see? Not because of any other cars? Please think very carefully, Miss Linley, it's very important. Very important indeed.'

'Oh, definitely, yes. Suddenly, he had to drive without being able to see. It was like he was blindfolded. That was the only reason. I'm sure. He kept saying, "Dear God", over and over again, and trying to hold the wheel straight. I don't know anything about cars or driving, but I think he probably did skid. The road was wet, there'd been the storm.'

'Yes, of course. Well, that's pretty clear. Now, let's just talk about the other cars, Miss Linley. Did you notice any in particular?'

'Oh, a few. Yes. You notice everything from up there. I was talking to Patrick, describing things to him. He asked me to – said it helped ward off what he called the monster.'

Sergeant Freeman looked up sharply. 'What monster would that be? Did he say?'

'Being sleepy. He said it was like a sticky monster in his head. But,' she looked at them, their faces suddenly more serious, 'but he was not, I swear to you, not remotely near going to sleep. You really do have to believe me.'

'It's all right,' said Freeman, and despite the soothing words, Linda thought that she could detect a slight change in his expression. 'That's absolutely fine. Now, go on, tell us about the other cars.'

'Well, there was a lovely car in front. A sports car, maybe an old one, bright red, amazing. By the time of the actual crash, he'd gone. But he was driving very nicely, if that's what you mean. Not speeding.'

'Right. How far ahead was he, would you say? At the moment of the – when the windscreen went?'

'I'm not sure. Impossible to say. I mean, I could still see him, quite clearly.'

'Could you read the registration number? Was it near enough for you to read it?'

'I don't think so. He was pulling ahead quite fast. I suppose about fifty metres, something like that.'

'Right.' His mood had changed, Linda thought. He was clearly at once excited and relieved by this rush of clear information into what had previously been a very dark confusion. 'What about a blue Saab? Did you notice that?'

'Oh, yes I did, actually. They were beside us, just before it happened. Well, a bit behind – you can't see anything when the car's right beside you – I noticed it in the big mirror and I was interested because it was such a nice car, and there was a man and a woman in it and they seemed to be quarrelling. Anyway, she was waving her arms about and stuff. And then,' she stopped, 'look, I don't want to get anyone into trouble.'

'Don't worry about that. Tell us what you saw.'

'Well, he did seem to be on the phone. On a mobile. But then I heard the crack and Patrick hooting and shouting and – well, I've told you the rest.'

'You have indeed. So there was no question of their driving in any way dangerously? Pulling out in front of the lorry, for instance?'

'No, no, not at all.'

'Right. Well, you've been very helpful, Miss Linley, very

helpful indeed. And try not to worry about that drink can. I really think you can put your mind at rest.'

'Really?'

'Yes. Although, as I said, we will put it into the report, of course. One last thing – did you notice a white van at all, with the back doors just tied shut, on the road that afternoon at any stage?'

'I certainly did, yes. He was driving like a maniac. But he couldn't have had anything to do with it, he passed us doing about ninety ages before the crash.'

'You didn't notice any writing on it? Any logos of any kind?'

'No, I'm sorry. Nothing at all.'

'Was the driver alone in the van?'

'No. Well, he had a big dog sitting beside him.'

'I really cannot tell you how helpful you've been, Miss Linley. You've given us an invaluable account, and the information on the other cars is most useful as well.'

Soon after that, having read her statement and signed it, she was told she was free to go.

'Poor Mr Connell will be pleased, won't he?' said Constable Rowe. 'Suppose you'll be letting him know.'

'Yes, of course.'

'Today?'

'No, Monday morning will do perfectly well. Am I not to be allowed to have a weekend, just for once?'

'Yes, of course you are,' said Constable Rowe hastily, and then added, 'I was wondering: might the windscreen have been shattered by that wheel nut?'

'Very unlikely,' said Freeman. 'Very unlikely indeed.'

'Hi, William. It's Abi.'

'Abi! Oh my God. Yes. Hello?'

'Hello, William. What kind of a reception is that?'

'I – oh, sorry. It's wonderful to hear from you.'

427

'Hope so.' She laughed. That laugh. That – almost – dirty laugh. 'I did warn you, I'd ring if you didn't. Anyway, I thought it might be good if we went out tomorrow night. Had a bite to eat. Or a drink. What do you think?'

Blimey. Was this what girls like her did? Took the initiative, made the running . . .

'Yes, that'd be great. Fantastic. Yeah. Thanks – for thinking of it. Er, tonight'd be better. Well, sooner.'

She laughed again. 'I've got to go out with some mates tonight, William. Sorry, a friend's going to Australia for a year. I'd ask you along, but I don't think you'd enjoy it too much.'

'OK then. Tomorrow it is.'

'Good. I thought I'd come over to you, save you the trek. We could meet in that pub you took me to.'

'Are you sure?'

'Yes, of course I'm sure,' she said, and he could hear her smiling on the other end of the line. 'Don't be ridiculous. Eight-ish?'

'Eight-ish,' he said. 'Yes. Great. Well, thanks for calling.' He rang off and punched the air.

'I told you not to come.'

'Yes, but Patrick, I have the boys here, all of them, longing to see you.'

Patrick looked at Maeve, wall-eyed; it was as if he couldn't see her at all. His whole face was blank, somehow closed in on itself.

'I told you not to bring them either. What's the point?'

'The point is they want to see you. They miss you.'

He was silent. This was scary, she hadn't expected this, had thought – hoped – it had been a passing rejection, part of a bad day, depression at the next round of surgery; this was something much darker, deeper than that.

'So, will I bring them in? Just for a minute or two. And I have some news – some very important—'

'Maeve, I said no.'

'But—'

'And if it's about some tomfool TV programme, I really don't want to hear it. Half the hospital has been trying to tell me. Just leave me be. I'm very tired.'

He turned on his side, away from her, closed his eyes. Maeve looked at him, then very quietly backed out of the room and closed the door. The boys were outside in the corridor, coiled up springs of excitement.

'Can we go in now? Is he still in bed? Can we give him his chocolates?'

'Not just yet,' said Maeve carefully. 'He's not ready, right at the moment. We have to go outside just for a little while.'

'But you promised!'

Maeve looked helplessly over their heads at her mother; hoping she'd read the situation, would be able to help.

She didn't.

'Well now, if he's not ready, boys, he won't be long. Maeve, will we leave you with Patrick, come back in ten minutes or so?'

'Yes – no.' She felt absolutely beaten. In fact, she felt like turning to the wall herself. And she had woken that morning so excited, so sure that if she told him about the programme, the girl seen running away, it would all begin to come back, to make sense; but it seemed she couldn't tell him anything at all; he had cut her off, was wilfully deaf to anything she might say.

The sheer piercing disappointment of it all was too much; she managed to smile at her mother, to tell her to take the boys to the café, said that she would wait up here for a few minutes, then come and find them.

And tell them then that they had been rejected, that their daddy, their beloved, loving, funny, caring, gentle daddy, had somehow turned into a hard, blank-faced stranger who wanted none of them.

❖   ❖   ❖

Patrick experienced an intense stab of remorse as the door closed behind Maeve; he was tempted for a moment to try to call her back. Then he told himself that there was no point; she was far far better off without him, and so were the boys, and in every way. He felt very tired; it had been a long wakeful night without his sleeping pills, and a painful one too. The temptation at one point to raid his hoard, to take at least one of them was intense; then he thought he would simply be prolonging the agony, literally. He had calculated that by tonight he would have enough; he would take them after he had been settled for the night. And then – oblivion. No more remorse, no more pain, no more being a burden on everyone. He was actually looking forward to it; he knew it was a mortal sin, knew he should have absolution, was afraid in his very darkest moments of going to hell. He had thought of asking for the priest, but it seemed dangerous. He might be tempted to confess, or even to talk of his absolute wretchedness, his sense of being abandoned by God, as well as by everyone else, and the hospital priest was a clever, sensitive soul; he might well become aware of Patrick's despair and the danger of it. So he must do it alone; must say his own prayers, ask for God's forgiveness himself, and then – leave. He could manage; he was afraid, but not as afraid as he was of continuing to live with this terrifying misery and guilt.

Alex Pritchard was in his room at the hospital, trying to focus on the latest initiative from the NHS, which was clearly going to entail many extra hours of form filling and provide no benefit to anyone, as far as he could see. Why those bloody people couldn't just leave them to get on with the business of treating the patients in their care, rather than behaving as if they were running a factory or a bank, he really didn't know.

The entire hospital, it seemed, was in a state of acute excitement over some item on the television last night – a story that there had been some girl in the lorry with Patrick Connell. Who had subsequently disappeared. As a result, the hospital had received several calls from reporters, enquiring how Mr Connell was, and whether it might be possible to speak to him, or a member of the medical staff about his recovery, and about the vanished girl. The switchboard had been given strict instructions to say No Comment, which so far had not deterred any of the journalists from continuing to try.

Georgia hadn't realised at first that there was anything in the papers about her. It was only when she and Linda were having lunch that Linda passed her the *Mail*, looking rather grim.

'Sorry, darling. But you ought to see this, I'm afraid.'

It was only a small item on an inside page, mostly conjecture: illustrated by yet another picture of the crash and headed *Mystery Girl of the M4.* But it was enough to upset her considerably; to see her behaviour described for the millions of people who bought the *Daily Mail* to read about. And no doubt, there would be millions of other people, reading it in other papers.

'Oh shit,' she said. 'And I thought the worst was over.'

'Try not to worry too much. It's not that interesting.'

'I can think of lots of people who would think so, if they knew it was me. Like everyone in the new series, for a start. What on earth will they make of me, Linda? They'll be so shocked to find I'm not the nice little girl they thought, just a rotten, cowardly wimp. And they'll realise it was all lies about the audition as well, that I wasn't ill at all. Oh God!'

She started to cry again. And Linda, looking at her, felt very much afraid that she might be right. As for what the press might make of it, if they knew the Mystery Girl was an about-to-be high-profile young actress . . . well, maybe they never would. But Linda was rather familiar with the press; she felt this was a story that might run and run.

'Georgia, darling, don't cry. You've been so brave today.'

'Yeah, and so cowardly for all those other days.'

'You're beginning to put it right. Don't be too hard on yourself.'

'Linda, how can I *not* be hard on myself! Not only do I know I'm a complete coward, half the country knows so too.'

'No, they don't, because they don't know it's you,' said Linda, determinedly positive. 'Don't meet trouble halfway, Georgia. Are you hungry?'

'Not really. You go ahead though. I might have a glass of wine. Oh Linda, thank you so much for all you've done today.'

'Honestly, my love, I'm only glad I've been able to help you. What did your mum say?'

'She was all right about it,' said Georgia, sounding slightly surprised. 'She said she'd thought something was worrying me, but she reckoned I'd tell her when I was ready. I suppose she thought I was pregnant. Why can't mothers raise the bar a bit? They can only think in terms of that, or drugs. Or an eating disorder. It's pathetic.'

Linda said nothing; she wondered if this turned her into some kind of surrogate mother.

'Anyway, she said it was very good I'd been to the police and to thank you for going with me and she'd hear all about it when I got home. Oh, and never to hitch-hike again and how many times had she told me not to.' She grinned weakly.

Linda disappeared into the kitchen, came back with a tray of cheese and biscuits, some fruit, and a bottle of wine.

'What would you have been doing tonight?' asked Georgia.

'Oh, having dinner with a couple of girlfriends. Nothing much. To be honest with you, I get very tired of having dinner with women, and pretending we wouldn't rather be having it with men.'

'Linda, do you really?' This was sufficiently surprising to distract Georgia from her own misery. 'I didn't know that. I thought you had this wonderful, self-sufficient life, that you'd had enough of men.'

'I've had enough of *bad* men. I wouldn't mind a few good 'uns.'

'Oh sorry. I didn't realise.' Her face was concerned; she looked almost embarrassed.

'Why should you?' Linda raised her glass to Georgia. 'Here's to your future.'

'Thank you. I feel a bit like I don't deserve one, you know? Or whether I've even got one any more.'

'Oh, don't be so ridiculous.'

There was a silence, then Georgia said, 'Linda . . . the other thing is, I've been wondering – do you think I ought to go and see Patrick? Or at least get in touch with his wife? I mean, she must be so worried, and wondering who or where the girl – well, me – is. I mean, I so don't want to, but . . . Tell me, what do you think, Linda?'

'I had been thinking about it, to be honest. I think it would be the right thing to do.'

Another silence, then: 'Maybe I will. I'm absolutely shit scared, and he'd be quite within his rights to spit in my face, but I feel he ought to know what I've told the police. He might be feeling terrible, with all these stories in the papers about him going to sleep, don't you think?'

'Pretty terrible, yes. Well, it would be very brave.' She really thought so; in a way, it would take more courage even than going to the police.

'Maybe I'll go to the hospital tomorrow. Linda – would you come with me?'

'Of course I will. Don't be silly. Now come on, drink up, otherwise I'll have much too much of this stuff. I'm incapable of leaving anything in a bottle of wine.'

'It's nice to be able to do something for you,' said Georgia, smiling rather feebly.

'You all right then, Patrick?' Jo Wales smiled at him. She was just going off duty.

'Yes, I'm fine.' His voice was flat, very tired.

'I heard the family came to see you today.'

'They did, yes.'

'And were they pleased to see you?' She knew he hadn't seen them, but she felt a chat might help.

'No. I sent them away.'

'Why did you do that? Your wife said the boys were so excited.'

'Yes, well, I didn't feel up to it. Three of them, it's too many. Maeve should have brought maybe the two older ones. I told her I wasn't ready to see any of them.'

'Oh, I see. Maybe tomorrow, then?'

'No, I don't think so.'

She looked at him thoughtfully. His face was oddly expressionless, his eyes blank.

'Are you feeling OK, Patrick?'

'I'm feeling how you'd think I might be feeling,' he said. It was an aggressive statement, delivered in an aggressive tone. It was unlike him.

'Well – I'm sorry. Is the pain very bad?'

'It's not great.'

'Next week's surgery should help quite a lot, with your tummy. Is that the worst?'

'It hurts everywhere except my legs, and what wouldn't I give to have some pain there as well.'

Jo smiled at him gently, put her hand on his shoulder. 'You will. You must have faith.'

'Faith I've lost, along with everything else.' He stared down at his hands.

'Well, let's see. In time, I promise you, things will be better.' He shrugged.

'Is there anything you'd like to watch on TV tonight? There's quite a lot on, a good film . . .'

434

'No, I don't want to watch anything,' he said. 'I'm very tired. I just want to be quiet, to be left alone.'

'All right. Well, I hope you get a good night, Patrick, at least.' She walked out of his room, stood in the corridor for a moment, then went to find Sister Green, on duty that night on the ward. An extra sleeping pill would probably not be a bad idea. Just for tonight.

Alex didn't want to go home. That fact alone made him feel even more miserable. And angry. It wasn't that he couldn't, but that he didn't want to. Not only had Sam ended their marriage, and seemed intent on winding up their family with extraordinary efficiency, she had virtually rendered him homeless. Well, deprived him of a place he wanted to be, where he was welcome.

Their bedroom had long since ceased to be in any way his, and the small spare room was uncomfortable and unwelcoming. Sam and the children occupied the kitchen and the family room in the evening, and if he walked into it, even the children looked awkward, forced to confront his discomfort. And the drawing room was too formal to relax in. He still had his study, of course; but it was very much a study, occupied with his desk and computer and files and books, not somewhere he could sit back and relax. He had spent quite a lot of time this summer out in the garden, even when it was raining, sitting on the patio, reading and listening to music there, but it was getting cold now, and dark earlier and earlier; he had realised how absurd things had become when he had found himself using a torch to read the paper one evening, as the sky darkened. It was so terribly unfair.

Anyway, he had no stomach for staking any claims over personal space tonight; he would rather stay at the hospital. He'd brought in his pyjamas and wash things. He had a room there, with a bed; he could get some food at the café and then go to bed; read himself into a stupor and hope no major accidents or traumas might disturb him. Anyway, he wasn't even on call; if they did want him, he could tell them to get stuffed. In fact, that was precisely what he would do. He could even drink a glass of wine. Or two. Or even three.

Patrick had asked to be settled for the night early. He said he was very tired; he didn't want to watch television, he just wanted some peace and quiet and to be left on his own. Was that really so much to ask? Sue Brown, the young nurse who was looking after him, wasn't used to him being bad-tempered and was quite upset, but she did what she was told, brought him his hot drink and his drugs, and said if he wanted anything, to ring for her.

'But hopefully you'll have a lovely sleep, Patrick, and feel much better in the morning.'

'Maybe,' said Patrick.

When she had gone, he made his preparations very carefully. He felt calm, but oddly more hopeful. Not frightened at all. He wrote a letter to Maeve, telling her how much he loved her and how this way would be much, much better for both her and the boys. He thanked her for being a wonderful wife and told her that the boys had the best mother in the whole wide world. He signed it, *All my love, my darling Maeve, Patrick.*

He wrote a separate letter to the boys, telling them how much he loved them and how sorry he was to have sent them away that day. *Be good for your mummy. Liam, you will be the man in the family now, so you must look after her. And remember me always, as I used to be, not as I am now. Your very loving daddy.*

Then he wrote another note *To Whom It May Concern,* asking not to be resuscitated if there was any question of it. He was afraid they wouldn't take much notice of that, but he knew you could do that in living wills, and what was this after all, but a living will?

And then he wrote a note to Alex Pritchard, thanking him for all his kindness both to him and to Maeve, and telling him how much he had helped both of them in the first awful, early days. *All doctors should be like you, Dr Pritchard*, he finished, signing it off, *Yours with gratitude, Patrick Connell.* He contemplated asking Dr Pritchard if he could keep an eye on Maeve, try to comfort her, but decided that would be too much to ask.

He propped all the letters up on his bedside unit, and then he felt very sleepy and lay back on his pillows to rest.

The sun was setting by then; he could see the sky from his window. It was ravishing – a stormy red, streaked with black, with great slanting shafts of light pushing through the clouds: a child's Bible sky. He lay there quietly, watching it blaze and fade; and then he reached into his bedside cupboard for his rosary, the rosary that Maeve had insisted on bringing in, and said his prayers. He asked God for His forgiveness for what he was about to do, committing a mortal sin, and he asked Him too to forgive him for the dreadful carnage he had wrought on the motorway. He felt that if God was a good and loving God, He would understand his anguish and find it in His heart to forgive him.

He asked Him to comfort and care for Maeve and the boys; and then he recited to himself the twenty-third psalm. He would indeed be walking through the valley of the shadow of death; he would need God's rod and staff to comfort him. He prayed again that he would not be denied it. And then finally he said a Hail Mary and the Lord's Prayer; and made the sign of the cross.

As he did so he discovered that he was weeping, that his face was wet with his own tears; and discovered too that he was not really surprised. The life which had seemed so promising, so filled with delight and family pleasure and a wife he loved and who loved him, was gone for ever, destroyed not by some malign stroke of fate, but his own carelessness and arrogance. He would not see that life again, it was lost to him; and he did not deserve it. He had caused immense misery to many, many people; he had robbed a child of his mother, a mother of her child. He had read the papers, read the interviews, in spite of the efforts of the hospital staff to keep them from him, and he knew the sense of utter loss and desolation and anger felt by the people whose lives he had destroyed; it seemed absolutely wrong, a reversal of the proper order of things that he should be still alive. He would die, and it would be a reparation of sorts, would perhaps show some of those poor, unhappy people how sorry he was for what he had done to them. He hoped someone would tell them.

And then he sat for a while longer, his head bowed, holding his rosary, reflecting on what he was about to do, and preparing himself for the moment when it became reality.

Chapter 29

He knew he'd never be able to forgive himself. Never. It was so true, what they said. Everyone made mistakes: but doctors bury theirs.

How could it have happened? How could a desperately ill man, confined to his hospital bed and under intensive medical scrutiny, have managed to store up enough drugs to kill himself – and, more importantly, how could he, Alex Pritchard, have failed so totally to recognise the depths of that man's despair! He felt shocked at the failure of the hospital and its systems, and perhaps worst of all, ashamed of himself, that he could have been so bloody obsessed with his own problems that he hadn't noticed what was going on under his own nose.

He'd met Maeve in reception at 3 a.m.; she had come in a car that he had personally arranged and paid for. She was white and wild-eyed.

'Hello, Maeve.'

'Dr Pritchard! It's good to see you. How is he?'

'He's . . .' He hesitated, he didn't want to say too much. 'He's doing OK, we think. There was concern about his kidney, his one remaining one, you know, but it seems to be coping, with the help of the drugs. He's not completely out of the woods yet, but we're hopeful.'

'Oh Dr Pritchard, thank you. Thank you so much.'

'No thanks due to me,' he said, and meant it.

* * *

The alarm had been sounded around 10 p.m. Nurse Sue Brown, checking on her patients just after ten, had found them all peacefully asleep. Even poor Patrick Connell.

The other nurse – there were always two of them – was not at the desk. Sue had settled down to do the reports, and then remembered she'd been instructed by Sister to give Mr Connell an extra sleeping pill that night. Which she had, of course. She'd counted them out very carefully, and had then fetched him some extra water as he'd asked, and when she got back, he'd taken them all. But she wasn't sure what that brought his total dosage to. She'd need his notes to do that; and they were in his room, of course, hung on the bottom of his bed. Just for a moment she was tempted to leave it and fill it in in the morning, when she went off duty. It seemed a terrible shame to risk waking him. But no, it was too important. It had been dinned into them as students that absolutely up-to-date records were crucial. 'You are expendable,' their lecturer had said sternly. 'Should something happen to you, there is always another nurse, but there's not another set of up-to-date records.'

Sister Wales was very nice, and very kind, but she would not tolerate inefficiency of that order, so Sue had got up and walked down the corridor to the small side ward where Patrick Connell lay.

She opened the door very cautiously, terrified she'd wake him. Thunderous snores greeted her. He seemed very firmly asleep. Good. She fished the notes out of the pocket at the bottom of his bed, and was just leaving the room again when she realised he was lying rather oddly. In fact it was less a lie, and more of a slump. A rather uncomfortable-looking slump, indeed almost a collapse, onto his right side. Probably he just needed his pillows adjusting, which she could do, but then that would almost certainly wake him. She moved over to the bed, to see if she could ease him into a more comfortable position without disturbing him too much, and saw the neat pile of notes on his bedside unit. Sweet; he'd obviously been writing them rather than reading.

The top one was addressed to *My boys*. That was good. He'd sent them away today, she'd heard; he was probably telling them how sorry he was and how much he'd like to see them soon. As she leaned over him, starting to ease his pillows into a more supportive position, she knocked the pile of letters onto the floor: she bent down to pick them up from where they had scattered, and saw that one was addressed to Dr Pritchard. That was odd. Why write to one of the doctors, when he could ask to see him? And then she saw another *To Whom It May Concern* and her heart began to beat uncomfortably hard.

She looked at Patrick again, and then reached out for his hand, to take his pulse. It was cold, and the pulse was very slow.

Sue Brown picked up the notes, half-ran from the room, along to the nursing station, and set off the alarm. It was the early hours before it could be pronounced with any degree of certainty that Patrick was going to be all right.

Alex, in HDU, had realised for the first time perhaps how wretched and impotent it was to be on the sidelines there; he thought he would never be impatient with relatives again.

He had sat with Maeve in the relatives' room, fetching her tea which she didn't drink, talking in platitudes, even holding her hand while she wept and berated herself for her part in the accident, for not being more understanding and sensitive to Patrick's depression.

'How could I have got cross with him, Dr Pritchard?' she asked, wiping her eyes. 'Telling him to pull himself together, not to be so selfish. How could I have done that?'

'You've been under a dreadful strain,' Alex said, 'and you've been so brave and loyal. How many people would

have done that awful journey every day, uncomplaining?'
Not for the first time, he reflected on how fortunate, in
some ways, they were, these two, especially Patrick. What
he would have given for a wife like Maeve. Even a little like
Maeve . . .

As the night wore on and the news improved, Maeve fell
into an exhausted sleep, and Alex went briefly back to his
own bed. But he was unable to sleep. How could they help
this poor, wretched man, shift him from his obsession that
the crash had been his fault? How deep must be his
depression, that it had driven him to such an extreme
course of action? Dr Baker was confident that the amnesia
would clear – but how long was it going to take? And
anyway, what might it reveal? That he had indeed gone to
sleep, that it had actually been his fault?

Maeve had told him of Patrick's half-memory of
someone in the cab. 'But he decided he must have
imagined it after all. That's why it was so wonderful, the
report of the young girl at the crash – the one the police
thought might have been in the lorry. I was going to talk to
him about her yesterday, but he was in no mood for it, and
I was too upset. You never know, it might have jogged his
memory a bit further. I know you said we had to be patient,
but how long for, Dr Pritchard, and how long before he
tries to – to do it again . . .'

'We won't let him do it again,' he had said, but the words
sounded hollow.

'And maybe this girl will come forward, do you think
that's much of a possibility?'

'I don't know, Maeve. I wish I did. We shall just have to
hope.'

'We will indeed. And pray. God's been doing not such a
bad job for Patrick so far over this. Maybe He'll carry on a
little longer.'

The sheer perversity of this was almost too much

for Alex, but he managed to smile at her and say he hoped so too, and then went in search of yet more unwanted tea.

The journalist from the *Daily Sketch* was woken by his mobile ringing at 7 a.m. It was Maria, the hospital cleaner. She was talking very quietly and very fast. He had to ask her to repeat herself twice before he worked out what she was saying.

'Mr Connell, he try to kill self. Last night. He all right now. You meet me dinnertime. And bring my money, OK?'

Maureen Hall, the receptionist at the main entrance of St Mark's, took an immediate dislike to Linda. She was so bloody sure of herself, and so la-di-da. Standing there as if she owned the place, in the middle of a busy Sunday afternoon, not an auburn hair out of place, demanding to see Mr Patrick Connell, and looking as if she'd come on pretty strong if anyone told her she couldn't.

Which Maureen was about to do. There had been a huge drama overnight, concerning Mr Connell; the whole hospital knew about it. It might normally have been kept quiet, but thanks to the television programme, Patrick Connell and his case had become famous and the interest in him intense. Every paramedic, every cleaner, every member of the medical staff knew about him; there was absolutely no chance that the discovery that he had taken an overdose and was back in HDU would not be broadcast over the hospital bush telegraph. And it was bound to make the papers. Stories were persistently getting out from somewhere. No one quite knew how Connell had managed to get hold of the drugs; there was talk already of an inquiry and dark mutterings about heads rolling – most unlikely, in Maureen Hall's view; no one's head ever seemed to roll in the NHS.

'I'm sorry,' she said now to Linda. 'You can't see him.

He's in HDU – the High Dependency Unit – and can't have any visitors.'

'In that case, I wonder if I could see the doctor in charge of his case, please?'

'I'm afraid that won't be possible,' said Maureen Hall disdainfully. What did she think this was, a private hospital? Only sort she knew about, probably. 'Our doctors are all very busy, not available for consultation in that way.'

'I see. Well, it is very important that I – this young lady and I – see someone who is caring for him.'

Maureen Hall looked at the young lady; she was very young indeed, and looked terrified, standing behind the woman, chewing her nails.

'The only thing I can suggest is that you talk to the PALS people.'

'And who or what are they?'

'Patient Liaison. They may be able to help you. Would you like to see them?'

'If that really is our only course of action, yes. Please.'

'What name shall I say?'

'Di-Marcello – Linda Di-Marcello.'

'Right.' Maureen tapped on her computer keyboard with her long nails; a silence ensued, then she said, 'I've got a Miss de Marshall here, she wants to see someone about Mr Connell. Mr Patrick Connell. Yes. No, I know that, but she's very insistent. Can she come up, maybe you can explain? Thanks, Chris.'

She turned to Linda. 'You can go and see them now. Second floor. The lift's over there. It's signposted when you get up there. Sorry, madam,' she said with exaggerated politeness to the woman standing behind Linda and Georgia in the queue. 'Sorry to have kept you so long.'

'Cow!' hissed Linda to Georgia. Even that didn't make poor Georgia smile.

* * *

'I can't tell you how important it is that we see the doctor or doctors responsible for Mr Connell,' Linda said. They were now in Patient Liaison. 'There must be someone who would talk to us. I don't think you quite understand. This young lady was with him on the day of the crash. You do know about the crash, don't you, Miss . . . ?'

'Mrs Singh. Yes, of course I do.'

'In that case, you must know how important it is that we should be able to talk to a doctor or someone. If we can't talk to Mr Connell himself.'

'Mr Connell is extremely ill, as I explained to you. It would be quite impossible for you to see him.'

'Yes, but—' Linda stopped. She felt so exasperated that words temporarily deserted her. She looked at Georgia, who had suddenly stopped chewing her nails and looking frightened. And was leaning on the desk, half-shouting at Mrs Singh: 'If he's extremely ill, he needs to know what I can tell him. It's really, really important. It could make him feel much better. Now we're not going to go away,' she stopped suddenly, took a deep breath, then went on, 'we're going to stay here as long as it takes. All night and all of tomorrow, making a nuisance of ourselves. So you really might just as well be helpful, instead of obstructive. I mean, what about his wife? Is she here, could we see her? Or could you tell us where she lives, so that we could talk to her. Just do *something*, for God's sake, instead of just telling us Mr Connell is extremely ill. We know that, we don't need to be told.'

She sat down again, looking pleased with herself; Linda felt like clapping.

'Just a moment, please. I will go and make some enquiries.' Mrs Singh got up and walked out of the room.

Alex had showered and changed his shirt, had what the café rather optimistically called a Danish and some very bitter coffee, and was on his way back to Maeve. Patrick

445

was increasingly alert and increasingly angry apparently; demanding to know why his instructions had been ignored, refusing to see anyone, even Maeve. She would need his support.

He picked up his bleeper, walked through his largely deserted department, informing the staff on reception that he would be back shortly, and made his way to the lifts. There were two people waiting there: a rather glamorous red-haired woman, exactly the type he most disliked, and a very pretty black girl who looked as if she might be about to run away. As they got in, the woman took the girl's hand and held it. The girl half-smiled at her, then resumed her petrified expression. Presumably they were worried about someone up there. He reminded himself that he wasn't going to find relatives tiresome any longer, and managed to smile at them. The woman smiled rather briefly back.

There was one other person in the lift with them: a tall young man with curly brown hair, dressed in jeans and a denim shirt. He wore a very anxious expression and didn't look at any of them, just stared down at his feet.

As the lift stopped, Alex stood back and allowed the two women to get out first. The young man followed, then stood studying a file he was holding, scribbling notes on various pieces of paper and peering out of the window that faced the lift. Obviously something to do with the planning department, Alex thought. Bloody nuisance, all of them.

The two women stood there, looking at all the signs and arrows, clearly puzzled as to where they should go. Slightly to Alex's surprise, Maeve Connell appeared, hurried towards them.

'Hello,' she said to them, 'I'm Mrs Connell. It's so good of you to come. Oh, Dr Pritchard, hello. I'm taking up so much of your precious time. Have you come to see Patrick?'

'No, I've come to see you. And my time isn't very precious today, I told you. I hear there is some good news now – to a degree – of Patrick?'

'You could call it that, I suppose. But he – oh dear, I don't know what to do. Anyway, these two ladies may be able to help.'

She looked anxiously first at Alex, then at them; Linda smiled encouragingly at her. 'Do please go ahead, talk to the doctor. We'll wait.'

She had a nice voice, Alex thought; the only thing he could find to like about her. It was very low and husky, rather – actressy. She was rather actressy altogether.

'No, no,' he said, 'it's fine. Maeve, you talk to the ladies, I'll go back to my room. If you want me, you can get any of the nurses to page me.'

'All right, Dr Pritchard. Thank you so much . . . He is the kindest man on God's earth,' she said, ushering Linda and Georgia along the corridor. 'I don't know what I'd have done without him, these past two weeks.'

'Is he in charge of your husband?' asked Linda.

'Not exactly, no. He's the A and E consultant. But he did admit Patrick, and kept a very close eye for a few days, until . . .'

'So, Mrs Connell . . .' Georgia's voice was tentative as they sat down in the relatives' room. 'How is Patrick?'

'Call me Maeve, please. Well, he was getting better, but of course he has a very long way to go. He's paralysed from the waist down—'

'Paralysed!' Georgia's hand shot to her mouth, her great dark eyes filled with horror. 'Oh no!'

'I'm afraid so. The neurosurgeon is hopeful that it's temporary, but of course it's hard for Patrick to believe that. He's had to have a lot of surgery and will have more. And he's very depressed. He – well, he took an overdose last night.'

'An overdose?' Georgia's voice rose and cracked in an odd way. 'Oh God, oh no, is he—'

'No, he's all right. They found him. In time.'

'Oh, Mrs Connell. Maeve. If only – I mean, if only I'd known.' She was biting her lip, her eyes swimming with tears.

'You couldn't have known. Nobody could. Nobody did.'

'No, but I mean . . . that he was so depressed. Oh, this is awful!'

'Well, he's alive and safe.' Maeve clasped Georgia's hand. 'Maybe you can help. The woman from Patient Liaison said you were with Patrick – was that before the accident?'

'I was in the cab with him when it happened,' Georgia said. 'He gave me a lift, he was terribly kind to me—' she stopped suddenly, as a new agonising anxiety hit her – 'Mrs Connell – Maeve – I do hope you don't think there was anything – that is, that I was – Patrick was—'

Maeve smiled at her: her exhausted face suddenly lightened.

'If you mean did I think you and Patrick might be up to something, well of course I didn't. It never even entered my head. All the years he's been on the road, Patrick has never done anything like that. Used his freedom, as you might say. I trust him totally, Georgia. If he gave you a lift, it was purely because he wanted to help you. He's the kindest man on God's earth, and he's also the loyalest. So don't you go worrying about anything like that.'

'Thank you. I just suddenly thought – anyway, the whole point is, I was there when he crashed.'

'So, did you see what happened?' Maeve asked, so quietly that Georgia could hardly hear her.

'Yes, I did. Everything.'

'Because he is convinced that the accident was his fault. That he went to sleep. That is what is so terrible. That's all he can remember. Being sleepy. Even though most of the reports talk of another car going out of control in front of him.'

'Maeve, I can tell you, with absolute certainty, that he did not go to sleep. No way. We were chatting, he was fine. Right up to the very last moment. I don't know how far all the enquiries have got, or what Patrick or you think, but I can tell you, absolutely for certain, that it wasn't Patrick's fault. Not in the very least.'

'It's me, love – Maeve. How are you feeling now?'

'Dreadful.' And he did look it, back on all the machines, and drips, propped up on high on the HDU bed, grey-white, his skin somehow transparent, his eyes sunken in his thin face. 'I keep telling you, stop coming here! For the love of God, just leave me in peace.'

'I have some news for you, Patrick. Some very important news.'

He shrugged.

'You know you said you thought someone was in the cab with you, just before the crash?'

He shrugged again.

'Well, she's here. She's come to see you. A young girl, name of Georgia.'

'I don't care. I don't want to see anyone. There's no point.'

'Patrick, there *is*! I swear to you. A lot of point. It's going to make all the difference.'

'How could it? Tell me that.'

'Because she says she saw what happened. *That's* the difference.'

'She saw me going to sleep? Is that what she saw?' His voice was dull, heavy.

'No, that's exactly what she *didn't* see. She says— Will you see her, Patrick, please? Just for a moment.'

'Maeve, I'm too tired. Too tired for girls with fairy stories. Why should I believe what she says, that she was

449

there at all? She'd have come before, if it was true. I just wanted an end to it. They've robbed me of that, now leave me be, will you?'

He closed his eyes; Maeve left the room, made her way along to Linda and Georgia.

'He – oh God he says he doesn't want to see you. He says how can he believe you were there . . . Oh, it was good of you to come, both of you, but I'm afraid there was no point. Not with Patrick anyway. Maybe if you talked to the police again.' She looked utterly defeated; her eyes swimming with tears. She tried to smile and failed totally, her mouth trembled and she bit her lip.

'Oh dear, this is dreadful.' Georgia started rummaging in her bag, 'Maeve, do you think this might make a difference? Here.'

She put a small box into Maeve's hand.

'What's that?'

'It's a watch. It was a birthday present for your mother. Patrick showed it to me and then he gave it to me to look after, because it kept falling on the floor. I've been . . . well, I've had it all this time. Oh, I'm so sorry. I feel so dreadful about what I did, so ashamed.'

'Now don't you fret about that,' said Maeve. Georgia suddenly seemed nearer Callum's age. 'It's enough you've come now.'

'Not quite enough, I'm afraid. But – well, let's hope the watch might make him remember a bit more, make him want to talk to me.'

Maeve took the box, opened it; a small watch lay inside. It was very pretty indeed, set in a diamanté bracelet. She sat staring at it for a moment, then said, 'I'll take it in to him. Thank you, Georgia. Thank you so much.'

Five minutes later she came out again, smiling, her small tear-stained face radiant.

'He remembered it,' she said. 'He kept looking at it, and

then he said he'd bought it for my mother. And then he asked me where I'd found it.'

'And?'

'And I said you'd had it. And he said to thank you. For looking after it.'

'And does he . . . does he want to see me?'

'I think he will now. Could you come in with me? Would that be all right?'

'Of course it would,' said Georgia. 'It'd be absolutely all right.'

Alex Pritchard decided to go home. A tedious day with nothing to do in A&E was beginning to look even worse than trying to find a corner he could call his own at home. He'd just go up and make sure Maeve was all right – presumably those women had something to do with it all, but he couldn't imagine what – and then leave.

The corridor was deserted; he went into the relatives' room and found the red-haired woman sitting alone, talking into her mobile. She looked up at him, half-smiled and went on talking.

'Just tell them that you haven't had any formal voice training, but you can sing well enough for the chorus. Yes, I'm pretty sure. You can put them on to me, if you like. Yes, of course. I'll be in the office. Now if you want me again this afternoon, just ring my mobile. Sure. *Ciao.*'

She rang off and was clearly scrolling down her numbers, ready to make another call; it annoyed Alex. There were several notices in the room asking people not to use mobile phones.

'Sorry,' he said, making a conscious effort to sound polite, 'but you really are asked not to do that.'

'Not to do what?'

'Use your mobile on hospital premises.'

'Oh I know,' she said.

'Well then—'

'I also know that it's a load of nonsense.'

'Oh really?'

'Of course. It can't really interfere with equipment, can it? It's just so you don't have patients rabbiting on all day in the wards. Which I completely sympathise with.'

'Oh, you do?'

'Yes.' She smiled at him; she hadn't smiled before. It was a very nice smile, and she had beautiful teeth, he noticed. And very nice eyes, dark brown, unusual with the red hair. Didn't make up for a considerable arrogance though. He didn't smile back.

'I'm afraid you're wrong,' he said. 'If everyone used their mobiles on hospital premises, especially an area like this where we have extremely sensitive equipment, it would be very bad.'

'Really?' She stared at him. 'That's not what I've been told.'

'Then you've been told wrong.'

'OK. But I'm not everybody and this is an important call. I really don't think one phone in use will do much harm.'

'And I do. So please stop using it. Or go outside.'

'I . . .' She stared at him then stood up, switching off her mobile. 'Then I shall go outside. This is a very important call, actually, to Georgia's mother. She wants to know where she is.'

'And Georgia is?'

'The girl who's with me. I'm her agent. Look, we're wasting time. Or rather you're wasting my time. You've made it very clear I mustn't use my phone, so I shall naturally stop. Good afternoon.'

He ignored this and she stalked off down the corridor. He looked after her. She had rather good legs. And an arrogant walk. She was a very arrogant woman altogether. He hoped this would be his last encounter with her.

As he stood there, Maeve and the girl came out of HDU.

452

Maeve's face was literally shining; Georgia was swollen-eyed and tear-stained.

'Oh, Dr Pritchard,' said Maeve, clasping his hand. 'I'm so glad you're here. I hope you haven't been waiting all this time.'

'No, no, I was just coming up to see if you were all right, to say goodbye to you. I really ought to get home. And of course I wanted to hear how Patrick was.'

'He's so much better, so much happier. When I think . . . well, Georgia here really has turned things round. Bless her heart.'

She smiled radiantly at Georgia, who managed a very watery, wobbly smile back.

'Yes, Georgia saw everything that happened, Dr Pritchard. She was up in the cab of the lorry – Patrick was giving her a lift to London. And it wasn't Patrick's fault at all, she says. Something hit the windscreen and shattered it, so he couldn't see. As simple as that. Georgia has told him again and again that he was as good as blinded; there was nothing he could do. Now isn't that the most wonderful news? And he's sitting in there, just – just happy. I don't think he can quite believe it himself.'

'Maeve, I'm so pleased for you. So very pleased. And good for you, Georgia, for coming forward.'

'Not really,' said Georgia. 'I mean I – well, I should have done it earlier.'

'What matters is that you did it at all,' said Maeve. 'When I think of the state Patrick was in . . .'

'Well, exactly,' said Georgia. She blew her nose, tried to smile at Alex. 'I've just been a total wimp right from the beginning. I feel so ashamed of myself. But I have told the police everything now, so maybe . . .'

'Well done,' he said. 'That doesn't sound too wimpish to me. No doubt they'll be along to talk to Patrick again. I'd better warn the PALS people, Maeve. They may well have been on to them already.'

'Thank you, Dr Pritchard. You're very kind.'

'Rubbish. It's lovely to see you looking so much better.'

'Um, do you know where Linda – my agent – went?' asked Georgia, looking around. 'I thought she was going to wait here.'

'Ah,' said Alex looking rather uncomfortable. 'She's gone outside. My fault, I'm afraid. She wanted to make some calls and I – I suggested she did it outside the hospital.'

'Oh. Oh, dear.' The tears welled up again.

Alex felt a stab of irritation, then remembered again his vow about being patient with relatives – it was going to take some doing – and said, 'Look, why don't I take you down to the café, and you can wait there for Miss – Miss . . .'

'Di-Marcello,' said Georgia. 'But she won't know we're there.'

'Yes, she will. I'll tell the people up here to re-direct her when she gets back. Which she will any minute, I'm sure.'

'Oh, OK,' said Georgia, 'that'd be very kind. Sorry,' she added, 'we're taking up a lot of your time.'

Having been annoyed, Alex was disproportionately touched by this. Here was this girl, not much older than his own daughter from the look of her, actually aware that people other than her had pressures on their time. Extraordinary.

'That's perfectly all right,' he said. 'You look as if you could use a stiff espresso.' He guided them towards the lift. 'Now Maeve,' he said, 'I'll wager Patrick wants to see those boys of yours now. Am I right?'

'You are indeed, Dr Pritchard. He said to bring them tomorrow, to take them out of school.'

'Excellent.' He smiled at her.

He was obviously very fond of her, Georgia thought. What an amazingly nice man.

* * *

Linda was walking up the broad hospital steps, finishing a call when she saw him walking down towards her. The doctor, the arrogant, rude doctor. They were all the same. One of her friends had married a surgeon, and then spent the rest of her life being treated, as she put it, like his scrub nurse. She scowled at him, rather exaggeratedly switching her phone off.

'Don't worry,' she said, 'I've finished. I'll just go up and collect Georgia, then we'll be out of your hospital for good.'

'Well, she's not up there any more. She's in the café. That's what I was coming to tell you. I didn't want you to go on a wild-goose chase.'

'Oh.' She stared at him, clearly surprised. 'Well, that's very – very kind of you.'

'No, no. The hospital is vast, you can lose someone very easily.'

'I could always have called her, you know,' said Linda, 'on my mobile. Had you not been around, of course.' She looked at him, and then smiled. 'Sorry. That was a cheap shot. I shouldn't have been using the phone, I do know that. I apologise if I was rude. It's been a bit of a weekend. No excuse, but . . .'

'I can imagine. And I apologise in turn. It's been a bit of a one here too. Complete nightmare.'

'Really?' He looked different suddenly; shaken and less sure of himself. He was actually rather attractive, she thought. In a wild sort of way.

'Yes. I can't go into details, but – well, suffice it to say I haven't had much sleep.'

'Isn't that the norm, in your profession?'

'In my discipline, certainly.'

'Your discipline?'

'Yes, I'm the A and E consultant. Pretty unpredictable lot of patients.'

He had an extraordinary smile; it had a fierce quality. It

completely changed his face. Linda felt slightly disoriented by it.

'Anyway, let me escort you to the café, make sure you and – Georgia, is it? – are safely reunited.'

'Georgia, yes. But I really think I'm capable of finding it on my own. And I'm sure you've got better things to do.'

'Right now, I don't think I have,' he said. 'As a matter of fact.'

Georgia was drinking her coffee, eyeing a newspaper someone had left behind and wondering if she was brave enough to look at it, when a young man in a denim shirt sat down at her table.

'I – wonder if you'd mind if I joined you?'

'What – oh no, course not, go ahead.'

She'd thought he meant just to sit and read or something, but he smiled rather determinedly at her and said, 'I – that is, was it you in the lift an hour or so ago? Going up to HDU?'

'Might have been. I mean, I have been up there, yes.' God. She hoped he wasn't trying to chat her up. She looked at him rather coolly and picked up the newspaper. Anything, even reading a story about a cowardly girl who had run away from a car crash, would be preferable to that. Today at any rate. And that shirt – oh, please! Then – *don't be such a bitch, Georgia*. He was probably a much nicer person than she was. He had quite a sweet face. He was probably worried about someone.

'Do you have a relative up there?' she said.

'No, no. Not up there. You?'

'Oh – no. Just a friend.'

'Not Mr Connell?'

What was this?

'How do you know about Mr Connell?' she asked.

'Oh, most people do. In the hospital.'

'Really? Well, I – I don't.'

'Is that right? I thought I saw you with Mrs Connell.'

'You must have imagined it. Look, who are you? Are you something to do with the hospital? Or—'

'I suppose I'd better come clean,' he said. 'I'm from the *Daily Sketch*.' He held out his hand. 'And you are?'

Georgia stood up. She wasn't prepared at all for what she did next; it was as if she was watching someone else.

'You can just fuck off,' she said, and her voice was very loud, 'fuck right off, away from me, away from the hospital, away from Patrick Connell. You are totally disgusting, you and all the rest of you, writing lies about people, implying things you don't know are even remotely true.'

She half-ran out of the café. All the other customers sat transfixed, staring first after her and then at Mason, who stood up, trying to look as if he was in control of the situation, and then hurried out after her and into the car park where both his car and his laptop were waiting.

Part Four
Moving On

Chapter 30

All she'd done was sigh. And it had been a very small, quiet sigh – she'd thought. That nobody could possibly have heard. But that's what had done it. Had launched her into this totally wrong and wonderfully right thing; where every day, every minute was amazing and shiny, where everyone, however dull or unpleasant, seemed charming and amusing, where every task, however disagreeable or onerous, seemed engaging and fascinating. Where she felt calm and cool one moment, and dizzy and sparkly the next; where she looked in the mirror and smiled at herself, where she relived every conversation, every memory, every confidence, every sweet small discovery until she might have expected them to have become commonplace, and yet still they seemed fresh and important and worthy of further examination still. Where she was, in a word – or rather two – *in love*. Absolutely, unquestioningly, and for the time being at least, most joyfully in love. And able to see that what she had felt for Luke had not been love at all; to be sure, there had been happy occasions, pleasing conversations, good sex – but it had been finite, reasonable, entirely suitable in every way. How she felt about Barney was infinite, unreasonable and entirely unsuitable; and it was the most important and defining thing that had ever happened to her.

He'd said he ought to go that afternoon, once he had seen Toby and knew he was all right. The medical staff had told him that he'd be groggy for a while and would need to rest before going back to the ward, so to be honest, there was no point him staying. And he'd told Emma that he really should get back to London; there was a very important client coming in the next day, demanding to see the whole team, and Barney had work to do before then. Emma found what Barney did as baffling as what Luke did, possibly more so, for he spent his whole life moving money around from country to country, currency to currency, money that nobody ever seemed to see or hold or count or that even paid for anything, virtual money almost; but she nodded and said in what she hoped was an intelligent way, yes, of course, and that she'd keep an eye on Toby but she was sure he'd be fine and probably go home in a few more days. From which viewpoint, one from which she and Barney would never see one another again, everything looked suddenly rather miserable. Which was ridiculous because – he had Amanda and she had Luke.

'Yes, I see,' said Barney, after a pause. 'That's excellent news. Really excellent. Good. Thank you again, Emma. Couldn't have got through the day without you.'

'Of course you could,' she said, smiling, and, 'No,' he said. 'No, I couldn't. Not any of it actually.'

And then, as she stood there, staring at him not smiling any more, he bent and kissed her lightly on the cheek and said, 'Bye then,' and turned away; and that was when she'd sighed. She just couldn't help it, it came out unbidden, unexpected, born of the bleakness of seeing him turn from her; she'd stifled it as best she could, but it had been there just the same, a most determined expression of how she felt – and it was ridiculous, totally ridiculous, and she had so much to do, and she'd promised to call Luke about the weekend . . .

But Barney had clearly heard it and turned back to her, and there was a brief silence, and then he said, 'Emma, could I – that is, well, could I buy you a drink a bit later? Before I go back?'

'A drink?' she'd said, carefully stupid, as if a drink was an alien concept.

'Yes,' he'd said, smiling. 'You know, one of those things, buy it in a bar, bit of alcohol in it, makes you feel good. Just to say thank you, for all your help and support today. And all the other days. I'd like to, very much. But if you're working, of course, or you've got something else on . . .'

'No,' she said, 'no I'm not working. Not after six anyway. And I haven't got anything on. No.'

'Well, that's good,' he said. 'So – does that mean yes? I'm a bit confused.'

'Yes. I mean, it does mean yes. Thank you. That'd be great. Yes.' And wondered if he realised as clearly as she did, what he had asked and what she was saying yes to.

They had a drink, in a pub she had suggested. A nice pub, gastro variety. It was a lovely evening now; they sat outside and chatted. Slightly awkwardly. Quite awkwardly, actually. Both knowing why. She should have said no. She shouldn't have sighed.

After a bit he said he should go; and she said she should go; and they got back into Barney's car and drove back to the hospital, so that Emma could pick up her car.

'Well,' she said, 'that was very nice, Barney. Thank you. And – don't worry about Toby any more.'

And she smiled politely and she certainly didn't sigh. Mistake, the whole going for a drink thing. Big mistake.

Barney remembered the next few moments for the rest of his life. Watching her smile, open the door, swing one long leg out of it. And feeling a rush of sheer and shocking panic. She was going, the moment was passing, the day was over, the excuse almost gone. Well – good. He was engaged, she was probably nearly engaged – what was he doing even thinking what he was thinking?

He put out his hand, onto her arm. Her thin, brown arm. Which was warm and felt – well, felt wonderful. She looked at him, startled; then down at his hand and then back at his face. Her eyes, those huge blue eyes, meeting his. It was fatal, awful.

'Don't go,' he said.

'But Barney . . .'

'Please don't go. I don't want you to go.'

And then, very quietly, 'I don't want to go either.'

He put the car in gear, drove very fast out of the car park, down the road, towards Cirencester. He knew the whole area extremely well. Knew where there were lanes, quiet lanes, with gateways into fields, where you could stop. And park. And turn to someone. And kiss them. Over and over again. And feel them kissing you back.

Later he said, 'I knew, you know. I knew the minute I saw you.'

'Me too. There he is, I thought, there's The One.'

'And then what did you think?'

'I thought, Oh shit. I said, "Oh shit".'

'I thought the same. I thought, There she is. And then I thought, Oh, fuck. I said, "Oh, fuck".'

'Because it's rubbish, isn't it? All that?'

'Course it is.'

'I mean, I've got Luke.'

'And I've got Amanda. I'm engaged to Amanda. Who's—'

'Who's lovely. Beautiful. And so nice, I can tell.'

'Lovely, beautiful and so nice. But I don't seem to love her. Not like I thought I did.'

'And then there's Luke. Who's such a dude and so nice. But I don't seem to love him either. So – what do we do?'

'Explore it a bit,' said Barney. 'We have to, it's the only thing to do.'

They did; they explored one another. But quickly, for there wasn't much time. It couldn't go on, unless they were sure. One long evening, talking talking talking. One long night, making love, hardly sleeping, in Emma's shabby flat. One long day, walking, talking, kissing, worrying; another evening talking and one hurried, wonderfully awful fuck in a room at the hospital.

Like all lovers, they developed jokes, codes, secrets.

'Thanks for calling' meant 'I can't talk now'; 'Maybe tomorrow' meant 'I miss you'; 'My pleasure' meant 'I love you'.

And every time, every meeting led them nearer to being sure: that this relationship was the one that mattered, and the other ones could not go on, and almost equally sure that they wanted to spend the rest of their lives together.

'It's easier for me. I'm not engaged, I don't live with Luke, he'll get over it.'

'And I am engaged, and I do live with Amanda and she'll take a long, long time to get over it.'

'It's so awful. For her.'

'Terribly awful. As she would say.'

'Oh, Barney.'

'Oh, Emma.'

'I love you, Barney.'

'I love you, Emma.'

'It's so awful.'

'And so wonderful.'

'Yes. It is. Really wonderful. Still can't believe it.'

'Oh, I can,' he said, tracing her face gently with his finger, kissing the finger, placing it between her breasts. 'I can believe it very well.'

Spoiled brat this one – bit like his friend. Both of them born with extremely large silver spoons in their mouths. For some reason he liked this one less.

What must it be like, to be one of these people, Freeman thought, looking at the obvious trappings of wealth on display even here, in his hospital cubicle, the laptop, the iPod, the silver-framed photographs by his bed, the huge plate of grapes, the box of chocolates from Fortnum & Mason, the pile of new hardbacks . . .

To know that if you wanted something, you could almost certainly have it; that if you didn't want it you need almost certainly not; to feel that pleasure was your birthright, happiness a given, success taken for granted. To have gone to the best schools, the best universities, to have no doubt travelled widely, to drive the best cars, to wear the best clothes.

It must feel pretty bloody good, he supposed, having known little of any of those things – but then what did it do to you? Did it make you happy? Did it create a conscience? Or did it make you arrogant, ruthless, greedy for more?

A working life in the police force had actually nudged him towards the former view: most criminals, in his experience, had been given too little, had been deprived, emotionally, physically and intellectually. They had been brutalised early, disciplined too late. Their horizons were limited, their ambitions material, their emotions stunted. Relationships were about sex, parenthood about fear. Just the same, the theory didn't always hold good. Life could still deliver surprises.

'Sergeant Freeman, do sit down.' Toby gestured at the chair by his bed.

'Glad you're feeling better, sir. And that your leg is mending.'

'Yes, thank you. You're not as glad as I am. Still bloody painful though, I can tell you. I should be home in another day or two. Thank God. Er . . . I thought there were going to be two of you.'

'There are, sir. Constable Rowe is on his way. Shouldn't be more than a few minutes. He just popped into the shop on the ground floor for some peppermints. Ah, here he is now.'

Rowe arrived; Toby offered them both some grapes and the Fortnum's chocolates. Rowe accepted both; Freeman shook his head.

'Now what can I tell you, Sergeant?'

They went through the formalities, the reasons for choosing the M4, the exact location of the church, the late departure – 'I wasn't too well, seemed to have picked up a stomach bug, kept throwing up. All you need on your wedding day!'

'Not a hangover then, sir? If you'll forgive the question.'

'Lord no, we hardly had anything the night before. Well, Barney had a few, I simply wasn't feeling up to it.'

He was cheerfuly upfront about being stopped by the police. 'Barney was driving, going at a hell of a lick, but then we were very late. I have to say that if we hadn't been stopped, we'd have made it in time. Still, even bridegrooms aren't above the law, I suppose, Sergeant.'

'Indeed not, sir. But you did also have to stop for petrol, I believe?'

'Yes, we did. And I – well I had to go to the loo again.'

'But you didn't need anything else – no oil, nothing like that?'

'No, no, just the fuel.'

'Although the CCTV shows you in a queue for the air line.'

'Ah yes. Yes, we did. That is, we were there.'

'Were you worried about the tyres, sir? Did you have any reason to think they needed checking?'

'No – in fact, they were new tyres. I've got the receipt somewhere – I could certainly find it for you. I was just being careful.'

'Very wise. So you didn't think one might be soft, something like that? Which could of course have contributed to the blow-out.'

'No, nothing like that. As I say, I just thought we should check them.'

'Even though you were so late?'

'Well, yes.'

'I see. Well, we may be mistaken, but again, according to the CCTV, you drove away without doing so.'

He was a good actor; he didn't look remotely rattled.

'Ah. Well, maybe we did.'

'Do you not recall what happened, sir?'

'Well . . . I went in to pay for the fuel, you see. It was all a bit of a blur. We were pretty stressed out, as you can imagine.'

'Indeed. But try to remember, sir, it could be important.'

'Yes, I suppose it could. Yes. Look, I – I don't want to get anyone into trouble.'

'Why should you do that, sir?'

'Well, the thing is, Barney – you know my best man, Barney Fraser?'

'Yes. We have talked to him.'

'And did he explain about what happened?'

'Not as far as I can recall, sir, no.'

'Ah. Well, you see I did want to check the tyres. As I said. But he was so worried about how late we were – well, it was his main duty, after all, to get me to the church on time, all that sort of thing – anyway, he said there wasn't time to check them, that we couldn't wait, that they'd be fine, and he persuaded me to carry on . . .'

'Perhaps you didn't see the latest report from Forensics?' said Constable Rowe as they drove slowly down the lane. 'The one that came in last week, while you were away, about the fragment of tyre with the nail in it?'

'Oh yes,' said Freeman, 'I saw it. Very interesting.'

'But if that was the cause of the blow-out, as Forensics seem to think, what was all that about whether or not he checked the tyre pressures?'

468

'There have to be some perks in this job, Rowe,' said Freeman stolidly, 'and seeing little shits like that squirm is one of them.'

It was a great pity, as Linda Di-Marcello remarked, that Georgia looked like she did and did what she did. The tabloids all tracked her down, the *Daily Sketch* leading the pack, and there were two or three nightmare days when the story ran in most of them. Her hauntingly lovely little face, with its great dark eyes and wayward cloud of hair, sat above the caption *M4 Mystery Girl* or in some cases *M4 Mystery Girl Found* and then informed the reader not only that the mystery girl in the lorry was Georgia Linley from Cardiff, but that she was an actress who had just won a part in a new Channel 4 drama and that she was on her way to her audition in London when the crash occurred.

A couple of the more salacious ones even hinted at Patrick's motives in giving Georgia a lift – and hers in accepting.

There was a quote from Georgia, composed by Linda with damage limitation in mind, saying how sorry she was for any problems she might have caused, that she was unable to answer any questions about the crash because it was still under police investigation, that she had visited Patrick Connell in hospital several times, that he was recovering well, and that his wife and she had become great friends. All of which, as Linda also remarked, was true.

Just the same, it was acutely unpleasant for Georgia; she went home to lick her wounds (and to break the news to her parents who were shocked and supportive in equal measure), but found this was not an ideal place to be either, as she had always been fairly well known locally and now couldn't even go to Tesco without people recognising her. She spent almost a week in her room, refusing to see anyone; it was only when a party of old friends arrived on her doorstep and insisted she came out with them – 'What do you think's going to happen, Georgia – public lynching? Don't be so bloody daft' – that she did indeed brave one of Cardiff's hottest night spots, got extremely drunk and actually managed to have a good time. And began to feel a little better. And, as Linda said, it wasn't that big a story or even that big a deal, and in a day or two she would be very old news.

But she continued to feel ashamed of herself, ashamed and remorseful; and most of all, dreadfully anxious about starting work on *Moving Away* and about how badly the other members of the production team might think of her.

Jonathan still felt he was living in a nightmare.

Even a call from that old goat Freeman, telling him that there was evidence that the crash appeared to have been due in large part to the lorry sustaining a shattered windscreen – why couldn't these people speak proper English – but that they were still gathering evidence, failed to make him feel much better. If they were still gathering evidence, then it could even now be seen as important that he'd been on the phone, and God knew where that could land him.

He woke in the morning, horribly early every day, his head throbbing and with the now familiar sense of dread. He wasn't sure what he dreaded; its very namelessness made it worse. Sometimes it was the police coming back, with more questions; sometimes it was Abi, arriving on the doorstep wanting to talk to Laura; sometimes it was bungling some delivery or other in his growing exhaustion. None of these things had happened and indeed, he told himself, as the days passed into weeks, they were becoming less and less likely. But the dread continued.

He looked back on his old life, years ago as it seemed rather than weeks, with its easy pleasant patterns, with something near disbelief. He was often depressed, frequently nervous; his professional confidence shaken, his smooth charm roughened by weariness and self-doubt.

The whole household seemed on tenterhooks, no one easy, even the children; Charlie was edgy, less trustful, almost wary of him, the little girls awkward and fractious. And for what? Jonathan wondered. Taking their emotional cues from their mother, he supposed, without realising it.

Laura had changed, had moved away from him; she was oddly self-contained, less hostile, but far from warm. They were sharing the marital bed once more; but it was as if she had drawn a barrier down it, holding him from her by sheer force of will. Occasionally he would put out a hand, turn to kiss her; but, 'Goodnight, Jonathan,' she would say, in that new, cool voice, and turn away from him. He felt she was biding her time, waiting for something to happen, she knew not what, only that when it came, she would recognise its significance and therefore know whether or not their marriage was still viable. And he could see that the danger of that something was still extremely real.

Abi had never been so happy. Day after day it went on, like some wonderful long, golden summer. An absurd, sweet happiness, born of this absurd sweet love affair. Absurd and so extremely unsuitable. For both of them . . .

It had begun in earnest, that night in the farm office, adjacent to the lambing shed. Not many people had sex in farm offices, adjacent to a lambing shed. Or not many people she knew anyway. Well, nobody she knew. Maybe they did in the country. Life was certainly different there.

They'd met in the pub and he'd suggested they went to another one, a couple of miles away. 'Too many people here I know.'

'Are you ashamed to be seen with me, William?' she'd asked, and he'd blushed and said, 'Of course not!' in tones of such horror that she'd laughed. 'It's just that we'll be – well, you know – interrupted all the time,' and they had driven to the other one in the Land Rover, and she'd had two vodkas and he'd had two beers and it had straight away begun to get out of hand. Or rather she'd got out of hand. She just couldn't stand it, sitting there, looking at him, with those bloody great feet of his, and his ridiculously sexy mouth – and she'd savoured that mouth, now she knew what it could do – and his eyes moving over her, looking at her cleavage and her legs – she'd worn a dress, she thought it was time he saw her legs – and a bit quiet, not talking so much as usual, grinning slightly foolishly every so often; she'd shifted her chair nearer him, and pushed one of her legs up against his, as much because she wanted to touch him, even through those ridiculous trousers he'd worn – what were they called? Cavalry twill or something, really grossly old-fashioned – and they'd shared two really disgusting sausages, or rather he'd eaten one and three quarters – he'd said he was starving as usual – and she'd had a quarter although she had tucked into his chips and then he'd said would she like another drink, and she'd said, 'No, William, not really, thank you very much,' and he'd looked a bit nonplussed and gone completely silent and she'd said, 'I tell you what I would like, William,' and he'd said, 'What's that?' looking slightly nervous, and she'd said, 'I'd like to go out to the car,' and they'd sat in it and snogged rather deliciously for a while, and then she'd said, after he'd made it clear he wanted what she wanted, every bit as much, possibly even more, 'I'd like to go back to your house. To your room,' and he'd been so horrified that it had been quite funny. It was as if she'd suggested doing it in front of his parents.

'Abi, we can't do that. I'm sorry. We just can't.'

'But why?' she said, 'I don't understand. William, you're thirty something, what are you like?'

'I know that, Abi, of course I do, but – well, you've met my parents, can you really imagine them sitting calmly watching TV if they thought – if they knew – we were . . . Well, it just doesn't happen. It's their house, not mine, and I have to live by their rules. Honestly,' he grinned slightly feebly at her, 'if I tried, I'd be so – so . . . well, I wouldn't be able to do it.'

She decided not to ask him what he'd done in the past, wondering suddenly and slightly wildly if there'd *been* a past, and simply said, 'Well, we have to find somewhere, William. I'm sorry – I'd suggest going back to mine, but I don't think I can wait that long.'

That was when he'd come up with the idea of the office.

It hadn't been too bad, the office. It was away from the house, quite far away – they'd gone in his car down a long track – part of what he called the lambing shed. Which was hardly a shed, but a huge building that could have housed half a dozen families. They went into it; the office was at the far end, a surprisingly clean warm pair of rooms. 'This is my bit, mine and Dad's; the other's for the farm secretary. She—'

'William, I don't want to know about the farm secretary. I'm sure she's very nice, but – oh God, can we just get on with it?'

He started to kiss her; that incredible style of kissing he had, slow and hard and sort of thoughtful; and while he did so, she managed to pull her dress off. All she was wearing under it was a pair of pants.

'Oh shit,' he'd said, setting her away from him slightly, staring at her in a sort of wonder. 'Shit, Abi, this – you're – I . . .'

And then he'd started kissing her breasts, in the same way, and then she'd pushed him down onto a sort of large couch thing, and – well, then it had all been totally incredible. He'd certainly done it before.

It seemed to go on for hours – wonderful, wild, noisy hours – as he worked on her body, made its sensations rise and fall, ease and tauten, as he moved slowly, then fast, then slowly again, pushed her to the edge, then pulled her back, as she felt everything with her head and her heart as well as her body, as he invaded every aspect of her, every

473

capacity for pleasure she had, as she came, yelling with triumph, and then again and then yes, yet again.

They'd fallen asleep after that; hugely wonderfully uncomfortable, on the couch. He'd woken her, kissing her, saying her name, saying, 'Abi, wake up,' sounding so anxious that for a moment she thought maybe the farm secretary had arrived to claim her desk.

But, 'It's half-past five,' he said. 'We start at six, and it's Monday. I thought you'd need to get back.'

'Oh, I do,' she said. 'God, I do,' and she'd stood up, yawning and kissing him alternately, pulling on her dress.

'I'll take you to your car,' he said.

'Can't I have a cup of tea? There's a kettle in there, I saw it, and cups.'

He'd made two cups of tea, obviously very nervous that someone would walk in, and then they'd walked, giggling like naughty children, over to the farmyard and he drove her to the pub and kissed her and waved her goodbye as she drove off into the dusky morning, and the last thing she said was, 'You mind you call me,' and he said, 'I will, I promise.'

And he had. And now, nearly two weeks later, it was – well, it was absolutely great. They alternated between her place and one of the empty holiday cottages on the farm – he said he hadn't thought of them before and they were certainly more comfortable than the farm office. There were three of them, called – rather unimaginatively, Abi thought – Cottage Number One, Cottage Number Two and Cottage Number Three. They were the tenants of Cottage Number One. She didn't mind them being cold or the beds being lumpy, although she did wonder why the grockles, as William called the visitors, didn't expect a higher standard of comfort. Nor did she really mind William's insistence that they only used candles in case his mother or the cowman who lived quite near them noticed the lights on and came to investigate; it seemed rather romantic. They cooked Ready Meals, usually curry, on the time-warp electric stoves, and drank some very indifferent wine – William, unlike Jonathan, had no interest in wine – and then had a lot of wonderful sex. She didn't even mind the drive home at some point in the night; in fact, she rather liked it. The roads were clear and she could play the radio and sing loudly along with it, and think about William and how sweet and funny he was, and how much she loved being with him and not just for the sex. Her only fear, and it was truly dark and dreadful, was that William would find out what she was really like.

Chapter 31

'Patrick, hello. It's me.' Georgia stood in the doorway of his room, holding a rather tacky bunch of flowers – why had she brought flowers, for God's sake? You didn't take men flowers, you took them stuff to eat . . .

'Georgia! Hello, my darling, how are you?'

'I'm fine.'

It was a lie. She didn't feel fine, she felt awful; even now, when she had got the worst of it over, she still felt guilty and so shocked at herself. And looking at poor Patrick, lying there in bed paralysed, trapped in hospital, when she was absolutely all right, able to do whatever she liked, go wherever she wished – it was just terrible. She should at the very least have been lying there too, injured, alongside him.

'Good. And you've brought me flowers. Now isn't that nice? We'll ask the nurse when she comes to bring us a vase. It's very good to see you, love, and I don't know what I was thinking of last time, that I never asked you if you got your part.'

She nodded, fighting back the tears. This was pathetic, it wasn't going to do Patrick any good if she started crying; she was supposed to cheer him up, that was why she'd come. And he was being so brave, patently making such an effort for her . . .

'Yes, Patrick, yes, I did get it.'

'Well, isn't that grand? Tell me all about it, Georgia. I have little enough to occupy my mind lying here. I get so fed up with the TV and I can't abide even looking at the papers.'

Well, that was something. He might have missed all those stories about her running away, leaving him when she could have stayed and comforted him ... She pulled herself together, and gave him as lively an account as she could of the series, of the audition, of the other people on the production.

'There's a lovely woman called Davina, Patrick, she's playing my mother, she's so nice, and then there's this bloke called Merlin. He's one of the director's assistants, he's great fun, and I'm learning so much ...'

She looked at Patrick; his eyes were closed and his head was lolling on his pillow. She had bored him to sleep, rabbiting on about herself and what she was doing.

Georgia slipped very quietly out of the room and went downstairs, blinded by tears. What was she going to do, how was she going to live with herself for the rest of her life, awful, awful person that she was.

She saw a sign to the café and decided to go there, have a Coke or something, try to pull herself together; but sitting here, drinking it, she felt worse if anything, and suddenly it was all too much and she buried her head in her arms and started to cry.

'Are you all right?' It was a very pretty blonde girl, dressed like a doctor, looking down at her concernedly.

'Oh – yes. Yes, I think so. Sorry ...'

'That's all right. I was just getting myself a coffee and I saw you there. Are you worried about someone? Is there anything I can do? I'm a doctor in A and E.'

'Oh, are you?' Georgia wiped her eyes on the back of her hand, managed to stop crying. 'Do you work with Dr Pritchard?'

'I work for Dr Pritchard, yes. Do you know him?'

'I met him when I first came to see Mr Connell. He's a patient here.'

'I know about Mr Connell. And is that who you're here to see now?'

'Yes. I've just been up there.'

'You don't have to worry about him. He's getting better, I do know that. He's doing very well.'

'Oh, but I do have to worry! You don't understand.' Georgia started to cry again helplessly, unable to stop.

The girl held out her hand. 'Why don't you come with me? There's somewhere quiet you can sit, and I might even be able to find Dr Pritchard – get him to reassure you.'

Unable even to think for herself, Georgia nodded, then stood up and followed Emma out of the café, towards A&E.

'Right, apparently Dr Pritchard's busy, I'm afraid, but I've got a few minutes. Do you want to tell me what the matter is?'

'No – well, no, you're much too busy.'

'I just told you I wasn't. Come on, it'll make you feel better. You're obviously in a bit of a state. I'm Emma, by the way, Emma King, and you're . . .'

Emma remembered after a bit; Alex had told her about Georgia, and anyway, she'd read the papers. She was the kid who'd run away, left Patrick in the lorry, taken weeks to come forward. Shocked, no doubt. Poor little thing, it must have been the most horrific experience.

'And I just feel it should be me, up there, lying in bed, not moving. It seems so terrible I got away, scot free.'

'Look,' said Emma gently, 'I think what you're suffering from, Georgia, is something called survivor guilt. I don't usually go for all that jargon, but we see quite a lot of it here. In fact, I know someone else who was in that crash who feels much the same way as you. Not quite so bad, but . . . And it's logical, really. You see Patrick, horribly injured, and wonder why you should have got away without so much as a bump. It's the opposite in a way of what he might be thinking: Why me? You're thinking: Why *not* me? Isn't that right?'

Georgia nodded. 'And thinking that I should have done more to help him.'

'Georgia,' said Emma gently, 'you couldn't have done anything. Not personally. It took hours to cut him out, you know it did.'

'Yes, but I could have stayed with him, held his hand – anything, really.'

'I know, but you didn't, and I daresay it was pretty grim in there. You know, people quite hardened to all this sort of thing, firemen and so on, even they get upset sometimes.'

'Yes, but then I didn't even come forward, as a witness. When it was so important. I mean, he tried to kill himself and I—'

'But you did in the end. And very bravely. Now I know it's easy to talk, but you really mustn't beat yourself up over it quite so much. Try to put it behind you. You're an actress, aren't you? Concentrate on that.'

'I can't, though! I don't feel remotely interested in it. I really don't. I've just got this great new part, it's the chance of a lifetime, people keep saying that and I just don't care. And then it was in all the papers, I don't know if you saw it . . .'

'I might have done.'

'Well, it was. And all the people in the production, they'll all know it was me, and I can't face them . . .'

'They'll know it was you and they'll be sorry for you.' The triage nurse appeared in the doorway, gesticulating at Emma. 'Look, I've got to go, but you can stay here as long as you need. The best thing you can do, if you've got time, is come and see Patrick lots, cheer him up. Not cry all over him.' She grinned at Georgia. 'And when you visit, come and find me. I'm usually here. If I'm too busy I'll say so, but otherwise we can go and have coffee or something. OK?'

❖ ❖ ❖

Later, she told Alex about Georgia.

'Poor little thing. What it must have been like for her, up in that lorry, I daren't think. She's in a terrible state. Her parents should be doing more to help, but maybe they don't realise. Didn't you say she was here with her mother?'

'No, no, not her mother. Her agent. Bit of a toughie.'

'She won't be much help then.'

'Possibly not,' said Alex. 'Look, sorry, Emma, I must go.'

He stalked off; Emma looked after him thoughtfully. She could have sworn he was a bit – what? Embarrassed. Why on earth . . .

Incredibly pushy, what that woman had done. He couldn't quite believe it. Calling the hospital, asking for his secretary, leaving a message and then calling again before he'd even begun to think what to do about it. And then, just – asking him out. No excuses, no 'I wanted to hear more about the Connells' or 'I wondered if Georgia had helped as much as we hoped'. Simply, 'This is Linda Di-Marcello here.'

He'd been completely taken aback, just hearing from her. The last person he'd thought to find on the end of the phone.

'It was very nice meeting you on Sunday. I've been hearing so much about you from Georgia. Well, from Maeve Connell really. And I wondered if you'd like to go to a show one night. I get tickets for pretty well everything, very privileged position. I don't know what sort of thing you like, but there's a new musical previewing, based on *The Canterbury Tales*, supposed to be good, or there's yet another *Macbeth*: take your pick. Oh, and what sounds huge fun at Sadler's Wells if you like dance, sort of flamenco cross tap.'

'Well, I – that's very kind. I'm not – well, I don't like dance. Not too keen on Shakespeare either.'

'Fine. *Canterbury Tales* then. The tickets are for

Saturday week. Any good? And then we could have a meal afterwards.'

'I'm not sure. I'll have to check my rota. Can I – can I get back to you?'

'Of course.' She gave him her office number. He rang off sweating.

It was Francis who'd made her do it. Dared her to do it. She'd been telling him how the day had gone, how difficult Georgia had found it, how sweetly grateful Maeve had been, how much she thought they'd helped. And then threw in a little anecdote about Alex and how they'd had a spat over the phone and then made up in the car park.

'He turned out to be quite sweet. We apologised to each other. Apparently he's going through a hideous divorce, Georgia informed me. She got all the goss from Maeve Connell.'

'Really?'

'Yes. I'd be on the wife's side, I think. He's clearly very arrogant. Sexy though. Nice smile. Which of course aren't enough to keep a marriage together. I should know.'

'Sexy eh? Your type?'

'No, of course not. Well – maybe. Dark and brooding.'

'Maybe you should ask him out.'

'Oh, don't be so ridiculous, Francis!'

'Why is it so ridiculous? Or is this not the woman who sat and moaned through an entire evening that she was lonely and longed for a man?'

'I did nothing of the sort.'

'Yes, you did.'

'Well, not very seriously.'

'I'd say pretty seriously. Actually.' There was a pause, then he said, 'I dare you, Linda.'

'What did you say?'

'I said I dare you. To ask him out. What have you got to lose?'

'My dignity.'

'What's so great about dignity? Doesn't warm the other side of the bed. Go on.'

'No.'

'Look – you ask him out, I'll pay for everything when we go to Bilbao.'

'Really? First class, five star?'

'Yup. Promise.'

She was silent, considering this, then she said, 'All right. You're on.'

'Good. No cheating though. I'll want proof.'

'Francis, I don't do cheating, as the young say. I'll ask him. Is that all I have to do?'

'Well – and take him out if he says yes.'

'He won't say yes.'

It was Amy who'd made him accept. Dared him to accept. He got home that night and found her watching *Sex and the City* instead of doing her homework, and switched the TV off. She glared at him.

'First Mum, now you.'

'Where is Mum?'

'She's gone out.'

'With?'

'Um – with Larry.' She avoided his eyes. She and her brother adored both their parents, patently found the break-up painful, were struggling with conflicting loyalties.

'Oh yeah?'

'Yeah. He looked so ridiculous – he's such a medallion man; they were going to some concert or other. Duran Duran. I mean, please. Good thing you don't go out on dates, Dad.'

'And how do you know I don't?'

'Well, you're too old for a start. I mean you're much older than Mum, aren't you?'

He was stung. 'Not that much. Thanks, Amy.'

'Well, honestly, Dad. As if.'

'Actually,' he said, slightly nettled at being written off so swiftly, pouring himself a Scotch, joining her on the sofa, 'actually and just for your information, I was asked on a date today.'

'You were what!'

'Don't look so horrified. I was.'

'What – an actual date? Not some medical lecture?'

'An actual date.'

'By?'

'By some woman I met.'

'How long have you known her?'

'I don't really. We only met a few days ago.'

'Dad! What's her name? What's she do?'

'Her name is Linda Martello. Something like that. And she's a theatrical agent.'

'God! No kidding. Is she as old as you?'

'No. Not quite.'

'Good looking?'

'Yes, I would say so.'

'And she's asked you out?'

'Yes. To some play and then to dinner.'

'That is so cool. Are you going?'

'No, of course not.'

'Why not?'

'Well, because – because I don't want to. I don't particularly like her. I'd have nothing to say to her.'

Amy sat studying him; then she said, 'I dare you.'

'Sorry?'

'I dare you to go out with her.'

'Amy, of course I'm not going to go out with her!'

'Why not? She sounds really cool. She could be a big help in my career on the stage. And it might be fun. Your life is *so* not fun. I really think you should.'

'Amy—'

'If you don't, I'll tell all my friends.'

'I don't care.'

'OK. I'll tell your secretary. And she'll tell the whole hospital.'

'You wouldn't.'

She laughed. 'No, probably I wouldn't, but I do think you should go. I'd like you to. Go on, Dad, live dangerously.'

They met outside the theatre: arrived at exactly the same time, exactly fifteen minutes before curtain up. Not a lot of time to run out of talk, the awkwardness kept at bay by the various rituals: drink, programmes, settling into seats.

Very good seats. Maybe it was going to be all right.

The musical was terrible. Linda said, as the curtain came down on the first act, that there was no reason they should stay.

'Honestly, I don't mind. I'm not enjoying it, and if you're not either, where's the point?'

He agreed there was none and they went to the restaurant. She had booked it – Joe Allen's, in Covent Garden. Alex, while appalled by the noise, did manage to absorb the fact that it offered the opposite of a romantic atmosphere, so at least she had spared him that. Their table wasn't ready, as they were so early; so they sat at the bar. And tried to talk. It was difficult; they had very little in common, no knowledge of each other's worlds. She told him one of her best friends was married to a surgeon; he told her his daughter wanted to be an actress. There was a silence. She apologised for the play; he said he hoped the management or whoever had given her the tickets wouldn't notice their empty seats. There was another silence.

'So – how many actors and actresses do you have on your books then?' he said.

'Actors.'

'I'm sorry?'

'I said actors. No such thing as actresses any more.'

'Oh really?'

'Yes, it was such a silly distinction, when they both do the same thing. I mean, you don't have doctresses, do you?'

'No, indeed,' he said. 'So – how many actors?' He stressed the second syllable, sounding slightly derisive.

'About two hundred.'

'That sounds like quite a lot.'

'It is quite a lot.'

Another silence; a very long one. Then she suddenly said, 'Look – this was probably a bad idea. This evening. I'm sorry.'

'No, no, not at all. Very nice idea.'

'Same as the musical, really. If you'd rather go, I won't mind. I mean, there doesn't seem a lot of point.'

He looked at her; she really was – what? Not pretty. Features too strong. Beautiful? No, not really. But – arresting. The amazing auburn hair, and the dark eyes. She had a wonderful figure, tall, slim, good bosom, fantastic legs. And very nice clothes. She was wearing a black dress, quite low-cut but not embarrassingly so; and a bright emerald-green shawl. And emerald-green shoes, with very high heels. It was a shame really, that she was so – well, a bit harsh. Very direct, very opinionated. And he hadn't liked being corrected over the actor business.

She looked at him; he really was – what? Not handsome. Features too irregular. But – attractive. Sexy. The wild dark hair, the probing dark eyes. Surprisingly nice clothes: that dark navy jacket – really well cut, and the blue-on-white stripes of the shirt really suited him. Maybe the ex-wife bought them. Or had bought them. Or he'd gone shopping with the daughter. The one who wanted to be an actress. God, he had teenage children. What had she always thought about getting involved with someone with teenage

485

children? Not that she was going to get involved with him. Absolutely not. Arrogant, over-opinionated. And she hadn't liked the way he'd half-mocked her over the actor business.

'Well, look,' he said, 'it's been very nice. Really, I've enjoyed meeting you. I appreciated your asking me out. But – well, I'm on call tomorrow. So maybe not dinner. If it's all the same to you.'

'Absolutely,' she said.

She smiled at him, totally in control. She was a very cool customer. Much too cool for him. And the sum total of her knowledge about the medical world was her best friend marrying a surgeon. Hadn't he sworn never to get involved again with someone who didn't understand the profession? Not that he was going to get involved.

'Well, we've ordered this.' She gestured at the bottle of wine. 'May as well finish it.'

'Good idea.'

She looked at him, as he picked up his glass. What a disaster. Well. She'd done it. Never would again though. Bloody Francis. What a thing to make her do. So not her. Maybe what people expected of single successful women of a certain age, but . . .

Suddenly she wanted to tell him. It wouldn't matter now. They would never meet again. And she didn't want him to think she was what she wasn't.

'I – want to tell you something,' she said.

'Oh yes?'

'Yes. I only – well, I asked you out because I was dared to. It's not the sort of thing I usually do. Honestly. I couldn't have you going away thinking I was some kind of hard-as-nails ball-breaker.'

'You were dared?'

'Yes. 'Fraid so.'

'That's really very funny,' he said, and started to laugh.

She smiled back, half-annoyed. 'Why?'

'Because I was dared to accept. It's not the sort of thing I usually do either.'

'Oh God.' She was laughing now. 'I like that so much. Who dared you?'

'My daughter. She told me I should get a life. Who dared you?'

'My partner. My business partner, that is. He told me more or less the same thing. And I thought, What have I got to lose?'

'I thought the same. And—'

'Miss Di-Marcello, your table is ready.'

'Oh. Oh, but we don't really . . .'

'Oh, come on,' Alex said. 'Let's eat. I dare you.'

Chapter 32

She'd hoped, very much, that things were about to get better. The TV programme had definitely had an effect on Christine; it had made her realise what a lucky escape her mother had had. Seeing the size of the crash – again – realising how easily Mary could have been just a few cars further forward, or even hit by one of the freezers, had sobered her. She was quiet during supper, and when Mary had said goodnight to her later, she had kissed her and said, 'Night, Mum. Thank goodness you were where you were – on the road, I mean.'

Mary felt more cheerful than she had for a week as she got herself ready for bed. She had switched on the radio and turned the light out; she was too tired to read and she liked being lulled to sleep by the well-bred voices of the World Service announcers. But it wasn't quite time for the World Service, and there was a programme on Radio Two about popular music over the past sixty years. Starting inevitably with the war. And equally inevitably with Vera Lynn, singing 'The White Cliffs of Dover'.

The hours she'd spent listening to that song. On her gramophone. The gramophone Russell had bought her, as a parting present. She'd been worried her mother would want to know where it came from and had to invent a woman at work who didn't want it any more.

'But they're expensive things, Mary. I'm surprised she didn't want to sell it.'

'Oh, she's got a lot of money, Mum.'

'Even so. Well, you'd better look after it.'

As if she wouldn't: the very last present Russell ever gave her, before going off to Normandy. He'd given her other, more personal things, like the bluebird brooch – that had been easier to explain; she'd said she'd spotted it in the Red Cross jumble sale, and her mother would never know its eye contained a real diamond. Then of course there were all the usual things that the GIs had been able to afford, that the British troops couldn't, like nylons and perfume. And the gramophone record (together with the sheet music) of Vera Lynn singing what she always thought of as the 'Bluebird song'.

She'd played it over and over and over again, until it had become too scratched to listen to any longer, and of course it was always on the wireless too, the song that had seen so many romances started – and had kept them alive through the long years of separation. Whenever it was played, after the war even, when she was with Donald again, married to Donald, but most of all when she was coping with the unhappiness of saying goodbye to Russell, it was him she thought of; she could almost feel him beside her again, dashing, handsome Russell with his perfect manners, dancing with her – he'd been a wonderful dancer, not born with two left feet like poor Donald. They had foxtrotted and waltzed, him holding her very close and telling her how lovely she was; they had even jitterbugged together in dance halls like the Lyceum and places like the Café Royal, and most wonderfully of all, Mary had thought, at the Royal Opera House, Covent Garden. It had been closed for ballet and opera performances, but, rather surprisingly, was the scene every afternoon for tea dances. They had only gone there once, for Mary was working, but she had been given the afternoon off and met Russell in the Strand, at Lyons Corner House, and they had walked together through Covent Garden Market and gone in the wonderful great doors of the Opera House; she had felt like a queen herself.

She had never gone again, never even thought of going to a performance there in the years since; it was terribly expensive. But every so often when she was near it, in the Strand or on Waterloo Bridge, she would make a detour and stand outside, looking up at it, and the years would roll away and she would feel Russell's hand pulling her up the steps and into the red and gilt foyer, and hear his voice saying, 'Come along, my lovely little Sparrow, come and dance with me . . .'

She lay there in the darkness that night, listening to it and smiling. It seemed a very good sign.

But it wasn't too much of a one; because the very next day, when she said casually at breakfast that Russell had asked if she would like to take Christine and Gerry to his hotel for lunch the next day, so that they could meet, Christine's rather pale face had gone very pink and said she was sorry, but she really didn't feel she could.

'I'm sorry, Mum, I just can't get used to the idea, and I feel – well, let's just say I'd rather not.'

'All right, dear,' said Mary, trying to sound calm, when she actually felt like screaming. 'We'll leave it for a little while longer. Maybe next weekend?'

'Mum,' said Christine, 'you don't understand: I really don't want to meet this man. I'd feel terribly disloyal to Dad. I know you don't see it like that, but I can't help it. You're going home in a few days and then you can see him whenever you want to, but meanwhile, please respect my feelings and just – well, leave me out of it.'

That had been too much for Mary; she had gone up to her room and cried. After a while, there was a knock on the door and Gerry came in. He was clearly very embarrassed.

'I'm sorry, Mary. Very sorry. I think it's – well, very nice, that you've got this – this friend and I can't see Chris's problem. But you know what she's like, terribly stubborn, and she did adore her dad. I'm sure she'll come round.'

'Yes, I hope so,' said Mary. She could have said a lot more, like Christine was spoiling the first real happiness she had known since Donald had died, and that she hoped Gerry didn't think, as Christine clearly did, that she had been conducting an adulterous affair for the past sixty years; but she felt that would be disloyal to Christine and wouldn't help matters at all in the long run.

She blew her nose and thanked Gerry for being so understanding and tried to cheer herself up by the thought that at least she could spend the next day with Russell and that the following week she'd be home and she could see him whenever she liked. But she felt dreadfully sad.

She and Russell didn't have so much time together that they could afford to waste it; every day was precious, to be savoured and treasured. It seemed so harsh that one of the other people she loved best in the world should be so judgemental and unforgiving.

It got better, of course – much better – when she was in her own home, so much prettier than Christine's, with all her little knick-knacks and endless framed family photographs, where she had been now for the past week. Russell came over every day in the car, or he sent the car for her and she was driven over to Bath; his hotel was absolutely beautiful, had once been a very grand country house, and they would wander round the grounds, arm in arm, talking, laughing, remembering one minute, looking forward the next.

And Russell had fallen in love with the beautiful countryside around Bath and the lovely houses that lay within it; and now, he said, he had one to show her, one that he thought she would really like. She had thought he meant something like a National Trust property perhaps, that they could look around and have lunch in.

So she dressed up with particular care, putting on the Jaeger suit, the fateful Jaeger suit; Russell was waiting for her on the doorstep. He got in beside her, said they could have coffee later and told Ted, the driver, to go 'to the house near Tadwick we saw last night', and they drove along in silence for about half an hour, Russell's blue eyes shining as he looked out of the window. Mary could feel his excitement; it was like being with a child on Christmas Eve.

It was a perfect autumn day, golden and cobweb-hung, mists still lying in the small gentle valleys; they were climbing slightly now, and then Russell said, 'Close your eyes.' She did so obediently, felt the car turn off, slow down, stop: 'Open them,' he said, and she did, and saw a narrow lane curving down just a little to the left, with great chestnut trees overhanging it, and at the bottom, there it was: a grey stone house, quite low, just two storeys, with a grey slate roof, tall windows and a wide, white front door, complete with fanlight, and overhung with wisteria. They drove down towards it. Ted pulled up outside the front door, and they got out.

It was very quiet, very still; the only sound wood pigeons, and somewhere behind the house the wonderfully real, reassuring sound of a lawn mower.

'It's lovely,' she said. 'Does it belong to a friend of yours?'

'You could say so. Knock on the door, let's see if we can go in.'

The door had a lion's head knocker; it was so heavy, Mary could hardly lift it. She heard footsteps, heard the door being unbolted, watched it open, found herself looking at a grey-haired woman, wearing a white overall. She smiled at them.

'Good morning, Mr Mackenzie.'

'Good morning, Mrs Salter.'

Not a close friend then, Mary thought.

'This is Mrs Bristow. She'd like to see the house, if that's OK?'

'Of course. Come in, Mrs Bristow.'

The hall was big and square, with a slate floor; a wide curving staircase rose from it, with a tall window on the turn. There was a drawing room, with tall windows and

492

wooden shutters, and a huge stone fireplace with a wonderful-smelling wood fire burning; next to it was a dining room, with another stone fireplace and French windows opening onto a terrace overhung with a rose-bearing pergola; there was a kitchen, with a vast wooden table, and a dark green Aga; nearby was another smaller, very pretty room, lined with books. Upstairs were the bedrooms, one after another – Mary lost count after five; some bigger, some smaller, two bathrooms with large, rather elderly-looking claw-footed baths and two throne-like lavatories, set in mahogany bench seats. After a while Mary ran out of polite appreciative things to say and just smiled. It was an easy house to smile in; it contained an atmosphere of peace and happiness.

Finally, Mrs Salter said she expected they would like some coffee and that now the sun had come out, it might be nicer if they had it in the morning room – this turned out to be the book-lined one. 'And would you like some biscuits or something, Mrs Bristow? I've just made a lemon drizzle cake.'

Mary said coffee would be lovely and there was nothing she liked more than lemon drizzle cake. Russell ushered her into the morning room and she sat down in one of the deep armchairs by the fireplace and looked at him.

'Like it?' he asked.

'I absolutely love it. It's beautiful – the sort of house you see in illustrations in old books. But – whose is it?'

'I'm so glad you feel like that. I thought you probably would, but one can never be sure.' He paused. 'And if you really like it, little Sparrow, then,' he paused, smiled at her, blew her a kiss across the room, 'then it's yours.'

'Is that Emma? *The* Emma? The Doctor King Emma?'

'It is indeed. And is that Barney? *The* Barney? The Banker Barney?'

This was another code; there was another Emma at the

hospital who worked in A&E reception, and The Barney had grown out of that.

'It is indeed. How are you, what have you been doing?'

'Um, let me see. Stitched up a little boy's foot; set an old lady's arm; gave an old man an enema.'

'Did you say an enema?'

'Yes, I said an enema. He came in with terrible tummy pains and a stomach like a football; acute constipation, so we—'

'Yes, all right, all right, too much information. When can I see you?'

'I've got Thursday off. And Friday actually. All day.'

'Friday all day? Jesus. There's a temptation.'

She waited. Then he said, 'OK. I can swing the afternoon.'

'Yes?'

'Yes. I'll be down around – oh, I don't know, two.'

'Call me when you're near.'

'I will. And you think of something we can do . . .'

'Barney! So much.'

'OK, OK. But where to do it?'

'Er – my bed?'

'You're on. Oh God. I mustn't even start thinking about it. Bye, The Emma.'

'Bye, The Barney.'

He phoned at two: 'Guess what!'

'You're not coming,' she said, bracing herself.

'Of course I'm coming. I'm on the train. There in twenty minutes. Can you meet me?'

'Um – not sure if I have the time. I'm rearranging my spice jars.'

'OK. Sounds pretty important.'

'But I'll try to be there.'

He got off the train; his heart literally pounding. Funny how that happened. His heart hadn't pounded – in that way

494

– for years. Probably since he'd had that affair with the girl on holiday, just before he met Amanda. His life had always been amusing, fun, successful; he'd had a few flings, done well at work, earned a lot of money, drunk more than was good for him, bought flats and cars and clothes and gadgets, gone on expensive holidays, decided he was in love with Amanda, asked Amanda to marry him – and seen his life laid out most pleasingly ahead of him, punctuated only by such predictable events as newer and better jobs, more cars, more expensive holidays, and in due course a wedding, a honeymoon, a new and bigger house and of course children.

Emma had not been a predictable event; and had made the rest quite clearly totally unpredictable as well.

'You are extremely inconvenient, you know,' he said to her now, as they sat in her lumpy dishevelled bed, in her dingy, untidy bedroom, having had some extremely wonderful sex, and drinking the champagne he had produced from his laptop bag.

'I'm sorry.'

'That's all right. But there I was, thinking I'd got it all sussed, that I knew where I was going, and how and when, and then along came you, and just blew it all up in the air.'

'Is there anything I can do to make myself less inconvenient?' she asked, smiling. 'Any little thing, you have only to let me know.'

'No, I'm afraid not. It's the fact of you that's inconvenient. Not you. You are – well, you're pretty convenient. In yourself.'

'Yes?'

'Yes! You suit me absolutely perfectly. You couldn't possibly be even point nought nought nought per cent better for me.'

'Nor you for me.'

'You're worth it all,' he said, his face suddenly very serious. 'All the chaos, all the problems we're going to have. In fact, if you were more convenient, I probably wouldn't realise the worth of you nearly so well. I'd just think, Yeah, she's a bit of all right, I'd like a bit of that, and you'd just be easy. Pure pleasure. Which you are of course, anyway, but kind of – well, inconveniently.'

'You're talking nonsense,' she said, smiling and getting out of bed.

'Where are you going?'

'To get some more champagne.'

'But – you'll come back?'

'What do you think?'

'I think you might.' He put out his hand, caught hers, and lay there, looking up at her, his eyes moving from her face to her small breasts and on down to her flat stomach, her mound of surprisingly dark hair – 'But I am a natural blonde,' she had said laughing, the first time he had remarked on it. 'I really am,' and, 'Yeah, yeah, very likely,' he'd said. 'I love you, Emma,' he said now. 'So much.'

'I love you too, Barney. So, so much.'

'Hey, you put an extra *so* in. I noticed.'

'Well, how I feel needs an extra *so*.'

'You mean, you reckon you love me more than I love you? Emma, I love you more than anything I could ever imagine, more than anything else in the world.'

'And I love you more than more than anything else in the world.'

'I like that,' he said, smiling at her, looking like a happy child. 'I like that very much indeed.'

They delighted one another: in every possible way. Each found the way the other looked, smiled, talked and thought absolutely pleasing. They argued, to be sure, quite often, and quite vociferously, about politics, privilege, religion. It was one of their pleasures indeed, shifting – albeit slightly – from long-held perceptions with surprise, acknowledging the other's views with grace. Thus Emma found herself regarding privilege with a little less hostility, Barney as something that should come not as a right but a reward; and Barney would acknowledge that faith could possibly be a force for the good as well as bad, Emma that the dutiful Christianity she had grown up with deserved at least to be asked some questions.

Sex for Emma was different with Barney: moving from pure, heady pleasure to something more thoughtful, more emotionally founded. And she for Barney was an astonishing delight, inventive fun, tireless.

They both closed their minds – with enormous difficulty – to the thought of the other sex, with The Others. It was something that would end: with the resolution of things. Which was drawing nearer, clearer, absolutely inevitable, meeting by meeting, day by day.

And yet was being held off for a little longer, by Barney at least; and with Emma's understanding. He had known Amanda for years, had lived with her for over a year; their backgrounds were identical, they had lived the same sort of lives with the same sort of people, and when they met, had found countless friends in common. It was a charmed, closed circle that Emma found herself confronted by; Amanda was protected not only by her relationship with Barney, but by the conventions and mores of its members. By choosing Emma, Barney would be rejecting not only Amanda, but a large and powerful tribe, a lifetime of comfort within it; it would take great certainty as well as great courage to do so.

He felt in possession of both – but he was still aware of the huge and devastating effect it would have, not only on Amanda, but on his professional status and confidence as well.

It would not be easy: in any way at all.

Chapter 33

'Is that Georgia?'

'Yes, it is.'

'This is Merlin Gerard.'

'Who?'

'Merlin Gerard. Second assistant to Bryn Merrick.'

'Oh Merlin, I'm sorry. Yes, of course, I – I was miles away.' God. How embarrassing. He must think she was totally brain dead. Not used to having to explain who he was like that either. Not to some dumb newcomer who'd never worked on a proper series before. Well, that was a really good start.

'Look, Wardrobe have asked me to get in touch. They want a day with you asap. How are you fixed?'

'Oh – I'm pretty clear. Yes.' If only she could say she was going to Mustique or Mexico or somewhere for a few days. But—

'Well, that's great. They're talking about Monday. Is that OK?'

'Yes, fine.'

'Good. If you could be at the Charlotte Street office at nine-thirty?'

'Yes, nine-thirty's fine.' She'd have to get a very early train. She really must sort out somewhere in London to live.

'I'll tell them. Thanks, Georgia.'

'Um – how was the dinner?'

'The what?'

'Your parents' silver-wedding dinner.'

'Fancy you remembering that! Amazing. I'd practically forgotten it myself.'

He would have done. He'd probably been to Mustique or Mexico himself since then.

'Yes, it was good, thanks. I missed the starter, Pa was pretty annoyed, but Mummy sorted him out.'

Pa. Mummy. What twenty-five year old called his mother Mummy? Posh ones, obviously.

'Anyway, sweet of you to ask. And I'll see you – maybe – next Monday.'

'Might you not be there?' She shouldn't have said that. It sounded soppy.

'Possibly not. We're out looking at houses with the set designer.'

'Houses?'

'Yes. For filming in. We're got a short-list of three, all just in from estate agents.'

'Did you actually find them?' There seemed no end to his talents. And importance.

'No, course not,' he said, sounding amused. 'The location manager does that sort of thing.'

'Oh I see,' she said humbly.

She put the phone down feeling terrible. Not just because she'd been so pathetic with Merlin, but because it was actually going to start happening now. She'd got to face them, start working with them, and they'd all know she was the awful, cowardly, pathetic girl who'd run away from the crash. Leaving the lorry driver close to death. What on earth would they think of her? Not a lot, probably. Every time she thought of it, of how they would view her, she felt sick. They'd probably all been discussing it, calling each other, saying, 'Did you see those stories in the paper, she seemed such a nice girl, butter wouldn't melt in her mouth, and all the time . . .' Oh God.

She'd been to see Patrick twice more, and that lovely

doctor girl Emma was quite right, it did help a bit. She felt she was doing something for him now at least, and he had been so mortified that he'd gone to sleep on her, as he put it. The second time she'd gone, a very nice old lady had arrived; she was called Mary and seemed to know both Patrick and Maeve quite well.

'I was in the crash as well, you see,' she said, 'and I was brought here for a few days. I met Maeve and we became good friends.'

Patrick had gone to sleep again, which made Georgia feel better – at least it wasn't just she who had that effect on him – and she'd suggested to Mary that they went and had a coffee together. Mary had seemed incredibly pleased by this and they'd had a really good chat; she told Georgia that Maeve had told her all about her, and how kind she was being, visiting Patrick, 'and how brave you were, coming forward . . .'

'Hardly brave,' Georgia had said. 'I waited a fortnight.' But Mary said nonsense, it was coming forward at all that mattered and that moreover, it was very nice to see a young person giving up their time to visit someone in hospital.

Georgia had really liked her; she was really pretty, in an old lady sort of way, and very sparkly and seemed really interested in Georgia's acting, which Maeve had also told her about, wanted to know all about the series and how it was going. She obviously had a lot of money; she'd had a huge car and a driver waiting for her and she'd insisted on dropping Georgia off at the station.

'It's been lovely talking to you,' she said, kissing Georgia goodbye. 'I do so enjoy young people. Thank you for your time, my dear.'

She obviously saw shared time as a rare and precious gift – and how sad was that, Georgia thought. She had always enjoyed old people, they seemed much more interesting than a lot of young ones, and one of her friends at school, Mary Patel, had had an amazing grandmother. Georgia could have sat all day listening to Mrs Patel's stories of her life as a young girl in India.

She'd talked to Linda about her worries that the cast would all be shocked by what she'd done; Linda had tried to reassure her with an annoying comment about how the stories would just have become fish and chip wrapping by now. Pretty stupid anyway, Georgia reckoned; who wrapped fish and chips in newspaper these days, for God's sake, and everyone knew that stories lived for ever on the internet – that was where people looked you up. She'd Googled her name a few days ago and was appalled at all the references. Well, she'd just have to tough it out. Somehow. Trouble was, she just didn't feel very tough.

Alex wasn't used to feeling happy. It was like wearing a very unfamiliar style of clothing. He kept checking it out, cautiously, feeling he had no business with it, waiting to find it was a mistake, and each time discovering it wasn't.

They had had such an extremely good time together – in the end. A superb meal – Linda had told him to have a hamburger – 'they're not on the menu, but they're great' – some very good wine; there had been a rather clever pianist playing jazz, and they had talked for hours and hours, until long after midnight.

'Lord,' he said, looking at his watch, 'I'll miss my last train if I'm not careful.'

He didn't, and sat, smiling out of the window, thinking about her, how interesting she was, how many good stories she had to tell – and how clearly popular she was. People kept coming over to the table all evening, greeting her, kissing her, bit over the top some of them, but then so was she – or certainly nearing the top. But it didn't seem to matter, because she was funny about it too. 'He's very sweet, but not quite as sweet as he thinks,' she would say, or, 'She's adorable, but she is also her own greatest fan.' She told him about her work, how alternately glamorous and dreary it was; he told her about his – 'Bit the same, certainly, when it comes to dreary, but it can be hugely rewarding and fascinating too.'

She was engagingly open about her personal life: 'I've been disappointed once too often,' which made him able to be the same: 'I've only been disappointed once, but it's ongoing, and very, very bad.'

He found her attractive; amusing, amused by him, sexually intriguing. It wasn't overt, her sexuality, it was subtle, almost restrained. But it was definitely there.

They parted with a brief, and very social kiss; laughing, she gave him her address, 'So you can fetch up there if you do miss your train. I have a very nice spare room.'

They both knew he would sleep on a park bench rather than do so; but it was a charming gesture, and he hoped charmingly received.

'I'll ring you,' he said, and meant it; and he could see she would want him to.

'I shan't ring you though,' she said, and meant it. 'Not again. Totally over to you.'

He had rung her, the next morning, to thank her; and two mornings later, to invite her to dinner again. She accepted; said it would be lovely. It was ten days later, the first date they could both manage; it was extraordinary too, to have something to look forward to.

It had happened: inevitably. Mrs Grainger had arrived at Cottage Number One, just as Abi had removed every stitch of clothing, apart from her high heels, and was dancing in front of William. Who was sitting on the sofa, wearing a shirt but nothing else – they had actually been playing Abi's version of Strip Jack Naked – and grinning at her happily.

Abi always said later that Mrs Grainger must have known she was going to find her son inside, doing something unsuitable; if she had actually feared intruders or squatters, as she said, she would have brought Mr Grainger, complete with shotgun, with her.

In the event, she simply opened the front door, put all the downstairs lights on and walked into the sitting room; seeing her face (as Abi also said) was almost worth all that followed, the complex mingling of embarrassment, shock and grim disapproval.

'Ah, William,' was all she said; and the worst thing for Abi was his immediate reaction. He went very white, reached for his trousers and started pulling them frantically on. Abi stood staring at him for a moment, before sitting down on the sofa, and pulling her dress around her shoulders, at least covering her breasts, on which Mrs Grainger's attention seemed to be focused.

'I'm sorry, Mother,' said William – what for, for God's sake, Abi wondered. For behaving like a red-blooded man? For having, at the age of thirty-four, a sex life?

'Yes,' Mrs Grainger said, turning her gaze on him now. 'Yes, well, it was rather alarming. Realising there was someone in here. I didn't know what to think. You should have told us you intended to use it.'

Abi giggled; she just couldn't help it. What was he meant to tell them? 'Please, Mother, I intend to use Cottage Number One this evening for some sexual activity. I hope that's all right.' Or words to that effect. Mrs Grainger gave her a very cold look; William a desperate one.

'Sorry,' she said hastily.

'Right. Well, I'll leave you—' She was going to say 'to get on,' Abi thought and almost giggled again. But she didn't.

'Please lock up carefully when you leave.' And she stalked out.

'Oh, Lord,' said William.

'William,' said Abi, for he did seem disproportionately upset, 'William, I know it's embarrassing, but you haven't committed a crime. You're having fun. And at least with a girl. Think if I'd been a boy. Or a cow.'

'Abi, please!' said William. 'It isn't funny.'

'Yes, it is. It's terribly funny.' And then she realised how genuinely anguished he was and sat down, took his hand. 'Come on. What's so bad? The worst is that she's seen me for what she clearly feared I am, no end of a hussy, leading her little boy astray. She'll get over it.'

He shook her hand off. 'No, Abi. You don't understand. She won't. It wasn't very – kind to her.'

'What on earth does that mean? What was unkind? You weren't laughing at her.'

'You were,' he said, very quietly.

She stared at him: silenced with shock. Then she said, 'I can't believe you said that.'

'Sorry. But – but it's true. She would have been very upset by that.'

'Well, she shouldn't have been. What planet is she living on, for God's sake?'

'Abi, please. Don't be so – so harsh.'

'Oh, for God's sake. This is absurd.' She stood up, started dressing, climbing into her pants, slithering into her dress. 'I'm not listening to any more of this rubbish. If anyone's harsh, it's her. And arrogant. Where's her sense of humour? Where are her good manners, for God's sake?'

'Good manners?'

'Yes. What she should have done was apologise for intruding. Not made us both feel like we were in some kind of a porn show.'

'We were, as far as she was concerned,' said William. 'You don't understand.'

'No, I clearly don't. And if this is how your lot behave, I'm glad I'm not one of them.'

'What do you mean, my lot?'

'You posh lot, disappearing up your own arseholes. What about thinking of me, William, how *I* felt – what about defending *me*? I'm not surprised you're still on your own, that's all I can say.' She picked up her bag. 'I'm off. Cheers.

Good luck in the morning. Hope you don't get your bottom smacked. Or maybe that's how she gets her kicks. And you.'

She was crying now, aware that she was beginning to show William the real Abi, not in that moment caring.

'Abi! Don't talk like that, please!'

'I'll talk how I like. You should try doing the same – you might find your life got a bit better.'

And she walked out of the cottage, slamming the door behind her.

Laura had bought Jonathan a really nice birthday present: he collected antique medical instruments, and she had found an old otoscope in a beautiful leather case, lined with blue silk. She gave it to him the night before his birthday, as she always did, it was a family tradition; and he was terribly touched and pleased.

'I'm just thankful you haven't got anything elaborate planned for tomorrow, darling,' he said when he had thanked her, and she had said (while crossing her fingers and touching the bedhead at the same time), no, just dinner with the Edwardses, as she'd told him.

'Pity we can't be with the kids really,' he said. 'I do like them to share in our birthdays.' And she said, yes, but they were having the big family party next day, with her parents, Jonathan's mother, and various cousins, and the children would be very much part of that.

'Not sure I feel quite up to that either,' he said with a grin and then, kissing her very gently, 'I do love you, Laura. You're far too good for me. I couldn't bear any of this without you.'

And somehow the ice that had been holding her heart had softened, and she had returned the kiss, and then he had turned the light out, and his hands had been on her and she hadn't felt anything but tenderness and he was very gentle, very sweetly insistent and she had felt herself moving to and with him; and when she came, trembling with the long, long release, she wept. And heard something from him that was halfway between a sob and a sigh, and realised that there were his tears on her face as well as her own.

Abi had expected William to call. To say he was sorry, that he could see her point of view at least, to say he wanted to see her. But he didn't. Her phone remained stubbornly silent. Maybe he really thought she was the one in the wrong; that his mother had been deeply upset, that Abi had insulted her.

If that was the case, then there really was no future for them. Not that she'd thought they had one; in her wildest moments she hadn't expected to be Mrs William Grainger. But a prolonged love affair – fun, sex, being together – that had looked quite possible.

How could she have got him so wrong? How could he be so totally under the influence of his parents? How could he be such a wimp? It was unbelievable. And then, as the morning wore on, she began to worry: maybe she was more in the wrong than she'd thought. Maybe she *had* behaved badly, hurt William beyond repair. She certainly wasn't worthy of him. Wimp he might be, but he was – well, he was quality. Not rotten, not damaged goods like she was. And she was going to miss him – horribly. Because although she wasn't sure if she actually loved him, she was terribly, terribly fond of him. She loved being with him. And now she'd blown it. Fuck, fuck, fuck.

Jonathan found himself working in the morning of his birthday, at Princess Anne's; he was only on call but at ten o'clock one of his mothers went into premature labour and he had to go in.

'Ladies shouldn't have babies on your birthday, Daddy,' Daisy said indignantly.

'I know, sweetheart, but as you'll find out for yourself

one day, babies don't always arrive very conveniently. I'll try not to be too long.'

'Tell the baby to hurry out.'

'I will.'

'I'd like to have a baby on Daddy's birthday,' said Lily, 'as long as he was there. It would be like a welcome party, wouldn't it?'

'A bit,' said Laura. The girls both giggled.

They were all excited. Once Jonathan and Laura had left for supper with the Edwardses, the children – and Helga – were to move into action: admit the caterers, and the florist, explain where everything had to go, and then receive the guests as they arrived, show them where to hide (in the darkened conservatory). Helga was to telephone at eight and ask Jonathan and Laura to come home, saying that there had been a power cut and she didn't know what to do – thus explaining the unlit house when they arrived.

It was hard to see what might go wrong.

Abi was driving back from Bristol, having thought – mistakenly – that a bit of shopping would cheer her up, when her phone rang. At last! William! It had to be. He'd obviously thought about it and— She pulled into a side road, took the call. Dear William. How sweet he was. And she would be so, so nice about his mother, so apologetic about what she'd said . . .

'Abi? This is Jonathan.'

It was made much worse by his not being William. By being thrown back into a different, uglier life; it really hurt her, shocked her even.

'Yes?'

'I just wanted to make sure you'd heard about the lorry driver.'

'What about the lorry driver?'

'That his windscreen had been shattered. That's why he

veered across the road. So there won't be any charges of any kind.'

'Yes. Yes, the police did tell me.'

'Good. So that draws the line very neatly, I think. It's over. The whole ghastly nightmare.'

'I don't suppose the lorry driver thinks that. Or the man whose wife was killed. That is such a typical thing for you to say. I'm all right, so everything's all right. Pure bloody Jonathan Gilliatt.'

There was a pause; then he said, 'That was an extraordinarily unpleasant remark.'

'Oh really? Maybe you don't inspire pleasant conversation, Jonathan. How's Laura?'

'Laura is fine.'

'Did you ever – ever have to confess about me?'

'That's nothing to do with you.'

'I think it might be, actually,' she said, rage and pain rising up to hit her. Here he was, doing it again, putting her in the box marked *Rubbish* set well apart from his real life, as no doubt he saw it, with his perfect wife and perfect family.

'What on earth do you mean by that?' He sounded wary. Well, good.

'I mean that of course it's to do with me. I'd quite like to know if she ever learned about us. Or if you'd managed to sweep me under the carpet, put me out with the garbage, pretend I'd never existed. I'm not sure why, but it matters to me, where I stand in Laura's life now. Whether I'm the woman her husband fucked, or still the business associate, being given a lift to London.'

'And what's it to you, one way or the other?'

'If you can't see that, Jonathan, then you really are even more stupid than I thought,' she said, finding the view of the quiet suburban street suddenly blurred, wondering why he could still hurt her so much. 'Because she ought to know there's something rotten in her marriage, that it's not quite the perfect thing she imagines – that she's got it, and you, horribly, horribly wrong. Poor cow,' she added almost as an afterthought.

'Abi,' he said, and the venom in his voice quite frightened her, 'you have no right to talk about Laura and my marriage.'

'Well, I think I do, actually. You dragged me into it. I mean, that's what it amounts to. Even you can't see yourself as a free man. You had everything – a perfect bloody life, with a wife and children – and still you chose to fuck around with me. Not my idea, Jonathan. Yours.' Silence. 'And then,' she took a deep breath, 'then you have the fucking nerve to tell me your marriage is nothing to do with me.'

'It isn't,' he said, 'and I cannot see by what perverted logic you can imagine it might be. My marriage is mine, mine and Laura's—'

'And pretty unsatisfactory, I'd say, judging by your behaviour.'

'How dare you say that to me!'

'I dare because it's true.'

'It is *not* true.'

'Well, I think Laura might see it rather differently.'

'Abi,' he said, 'you even think about coming near me and my family, and you'll regret it horribly. I've warned you before and—'

'Of course I'm not coming near you and your family. Why should I?'

'Because you're rotten enough. Disturbed enough even, I'd say. You have considerable problems, Abi. Personality problems. Maybe you should take a look at yourself, rather than throwing accusations at other people. Anyway, I have to go. I had intended to have a perfectly pleasant conversation, reassuring you that you had nothing more to worry about. You've made it very unpleasant, predictably enough. Pity.'

And the phone went dead.

Abi sat there for quite a long time, staring at her phone; she felt no longer angry, just rather tired and drained. And then the pain began. It was awful, the worst she could ever remember. She had never liked herself; in that moment, she loathed herself. She kept hearing Jonathan's voice, telling her she had personality problems, that she was rotten, possibly even disturbed, and she found herself agreeing with him. She was indeed absolutely rotten; she was amoral, promiscuous, dishonest. And all right, he had pursued her, but she had at no time refused him, told him she didn't sleep with married men. She had encouraged him, enjoyed him, despised his wife, dismissed his family. She was a completely worthless person; she had no right to expect decent treatment from anybody.

She managed to find the strength to start her car, and drove home; Sylvie was mercifully out. She poured herself a large glass of wine and lay on her bed drinking it and smoking and thinking about herself. And how she had been conducting a relationship with a man who was quite simply good, transparently nice and kind and honest; how could she have possibly thought that could work? That he could want to be with her if he knew even a little about what she was really like?

She had worked a kind of conjuring act on William; she had managed to distract him from her true self, to deceive him, to create an illusion, to show him something that she was not and never could be. No wonder he hadn't called her; he had seen something of the real Abi last night, as she mocked his mother, argued with the sort of values he had been brought up to, berated him for not descending to her level. She deserved never to see him again. She never would see him again.

She didn't deserve him. She deserved rotten people, rotten like her. Rotten like Jonathan.

She started to think about Jonathan again. She didn't

want to, but she couldn't stop. OK, he'd strung her along very nicely. But – God, she had let him. That was one of the most humiliating things. Allowed herself to believe him, when he told her she was special, hugely intelligent, that he enjoyed her company, quite apart from the sex. Just remembering it now made her want to throw up.

She'd been hurt by a great many men, but Jonathan had won the game easily. He was the most sophisticated of all her lovers by far and the cleverest too; he was like some kind of sleek, wily cat, toying with her, allowing her her illusions and then, with infinite care, clawing them back again.

He had demanded a great deal of her, and not only since the crash; in return he had given her no support, shown her no concern, offered her not a shred of kindness, merely bullied and threatened her. He had pursued her, without any thought for the consequences, for his wife and family or for her; his only concern had been himself. Himself and his dick. He had abandoned her totally, without pity or thought. She could have killed herself for all he would know or care. In fact, that would probably have suited him very well. She hated him, beyond anything.

This was lovely, Laura thought. It was turning into a really happy day. Better, far better than she had hoped. Jonathan had arrived home just after lunch, the baby safely delivered, five pounds, no great problem to spoil his day. He seemed more relaxed than she could remember, laughing with the children at lunch, asking Charlie for a birthday game of chess – 'only you have to let your poor old father win' – showing them his otoscope, explaining how it worked, letting them look into each other's ears. And it was going to get even better this evening.

William had spent a wretched day. He had shot into the kitchen at breakfast-time, grabbed some bacon and a slice of bread and made himself a sandwich, filled a Thermos with coffee and headed out for the furthest point he could: East Wood, a six-acre spinney. He was felling some of the younger trees; it was exhausting and noisy, and made thought fairly impossible. He didn't want to think. It hurt too much.

Abi made her decision almost without realising it. She felt more positive suddenly, and that she needed to see this thing finished. Properly, formally, unarguably finished. What was that stupid word people were always using? Oh yes, closure. That was what she needed, closure. And she needed to see Jonathan for that. Shouting down the phone was not enough, she wanted to confront him, to tell him to his face what a shit he was, what he had done to her. Exactly how much he had hurt her. To point out to him that yes, she might be rotten, but so was he. She wasn't going to let him walk away from her. And she wanted Laura to know it too. Never mind all that sisterly solidarity shit. It was the only thing that would make her feel better. She could hardly feel worse; things certainly couldn't be worse. And after that, she would reassess her life, decide what, if anything, she could do with herself. Maybe she should move to Australia, an old dream of hers. She had lost William, and with him any thought of becoming a better person; there was certainly nothing to keep her here.

She might just drop in on Jonathan this evening, if he was going to be at home.

She looked at her watch; almost six. She picked up her phone and dialled his number. It was on message. His smooth, actor-y tones told her that he couldn't answer her call just at the moment, but that if she left a message he would get back to her as soon as possible.

If it's an obstetric enquiry please call my secretary Mrs Horne, and in an emergency, please ring Princess Anne's, Harley Street, where your call will be dealt with. The numbers are . . .

Abi shut him off. She wasn't going to leave a message; she was sick of leaving messages to which he didn't respond. She wondered idly about ringing Mrs Horne, to whom she had spoken several times before, professing herself a patient. And telling her exactly what a total 100 per cent bastard she worked for. It didn't seem entirely satisfactory, although it could be fun. But the clinic, in bloody Harley Street where he had all those pampered princesses worshipping the ground he walked on, now she might do a little mischief there. He might even be there – she knew he was often on call on Saturdays . . .

She dialled the number, asked to be put through to him. 'I'm so sorry, Mr Gilliatt has left for the day. Can one of the other doctors help you?'

Resisting a temptation to say only if they were up to Mr Gilliatt's standard on text sex, she asked if they knew where he was.

'I'm afraid not. He's not in tomorrow. Perhaps you could ring on Monday?'

As the day wore on, William thought increasingly about Abi. And with increasing remorse. She was right: in a way. His mother had behaved quite – well quite inconsiderately. Unkindly, even. She couldn't really have thought they were burglars or intruders. Burglars and intruders didn't normally light candles. And having discovered it was him, him and a girl, the tactful thing would have been to say something non-committal and quickly withdraw. After all, he wasn't sixteen, he was thirty-four. Did she really think he was going to get married before he had any kind of a relationship?

Yes, perhaps he should have warned her – and his father, of course – that he was using the cottage occasionally; maybe he should have gone further, asked their permission. Except that they would have wanted to know why, and how could he have told them? Not for the first time, William became aware of the absurdity of his domestic sitution; not for the first time did he wonder what on earth he could do about it. And then it came to him, that perhaps he could move into Cottage Number One, or Number Two or Number Three. Make his home there. So that he could claim some independence, privacy, grow up at last. It seemed not unreasonable. He worked on the farm for a very modest income; he could surely claim the cottage as some kind of a perk. If they really kicked up, he could offer to pay them rent. But surely they wouldn't. He would ask them that evening; the thought quite cheered him up.

She decided to ring first. She didn't want to waste a long journey. He didn't know she had the landline number, would probably change it if he did. She'd been keeping it for an important enough occasion. This felt like one.

The phone didn't ring for long; then, 'Hello?' It was a little girl's voice: one of his flowers. God, that always made her want to throw up.

'Is that Daisy? Or Lily?'

'It's Daisy.'

'Hello, Daisy. Is your daddy there?'

'No, he's gone out. But he will be back. Quite soon.'

'Are you sure about that?'

'Yes. Quite sure. It's his birthday. We're doing a surprise party for him. Mummy's bringing him back here at about eight o'clock.'

'Oh really? How lovely. Wish I'd been invited. Well, never mind. Bye, Daisy.'

'Goodbye.'

Such a beautifully expensive, posh little voice. Well, lucky Daisy. She'd been born with a silver spoon in her mouth all right; and it had stayed there, while she was given the best of everything. Like Lily and the beloved Charlie. Jonathan was so proud of Charlie. He never seemed to think she might not want to hear about him. Or about the girls. *So sensitive, aren't you, Jonathan? Such a charmer.*

The more she thought about him, being given this party by his family, a lavish affair, no doubt, no expense spared, the more she wanted to throw up. Or kill him. Or both. There he'd be, smiling that awful smooth smile of his, receiving gifts and kisses and compliments, everyone wishing him well, and no one, no one at all, certainly not Laura, knowing what a complete shit he was. He'd managed to lie his way out of everything: how did he do it, the bastard?

Well, not tonight he wouldn't.

'Sorry, Jonathan,' she said quite cheerfully, as she dressed for the occasion in some new leather jeans and a very low-cut black top – well it was a party, after all – 'but you'd better make the most of the next two hours. Because after that – bingo!'

Not since the Sleeping Beauty's christening was a guest going to wreak so much havoc at a family gathering.

It didn't go terribly well. His parents, still cool with him, said they would of course consider his request, but the cottages were a valuable source of income and they couldn't quite see how he imagined making the money up. William found himelf growing increasingly irritated; he wasn't after all a farm labourer, he was their son. The farm would be his one day, any loss of income incurred now he would have to deal with.

Abi was right, it suddenly seemed to him: they were arrogant, his parents, in their attitude towards him. It was appalling that he should have nowhere he could call his own, other than a bedroom, in their house. The fact that it had never occurred to him to demand such a thing was irrelevant.

He began to feel he owed Abi an apology: on his

mother's behalf as well as his own. Neither of them had been very kind to her that night, very considerate of her feelings. Her initial amusement had been – actually – rather generous. And typical of her. She was generous. And warm and funny and – well, really very kind.

He should tell her so. He went out immediately after supper, drove to the pub and sat in the car park, calling her. He hadn't expected her to be sitting at home, waiting for him, but he did leave a message: saying he was sorry that she had been embarrassed, sorry that he hadn't been more considerate, and asking her to call him. He added that he missed her and really wanted to see her. And then he went into the pub to get drunk and hope for her call.

Christ, what a nightmare. What a complete bloody nightmare. When he'd been hanging on to his sanity – just – getting through it day by agonising day, longing only for peace and quiet, and here he was, confronted by what seemed like a hundred people, all laughing and joking and slapping him on the back, telling him what a great guy he was, and Laura hanging on his arm, kissing him and everyone else, saying wasn't it great everyone had come, wasn't he wonderful, who would have thought he was *so* old . . .

The conversation with Abi had upset him badly; and made him nervous. And somewhere in some deep well-buried place, he felt a stab of something close to remorse. It was true what she'd said; he had instigated their affair. He had turned his back on his perfect wife and his perfect marriage, albeit briefly, walked out of the Garden of Eden for no other reason than that he had felt in need of some new, exotically flavoured fruit. And was Abi really so rotten? Not really. She was a girl on the make, sure; but there were thousands, millions of those. She'd had a raw deal from life; he'd taken advantage of that, used it, enjoyed flattering her, flashing his money around, taking her to expensive hotels, buying her expensive jewellery. It had made him feel good, important even – and in return she had given him the excitement, the sense of sexual self-esteem that Laura had failed to do. Even at the very beginning of their relationship.

Christ, what a mess. And here he was, trapped in this farce of an evening. Which somehow encapsulated his whole life. The fantasy that was marriage to Laura, and the reality that Abi had confronted him with.

It was all he could do not to run away, hide in the garden somewhere; and he didn't even dare get drunk, for fear he'd say something compromising . . .

It was going so well. She was very glad she'd done it. He seemed so pleased, and everyone had really made an effort, looked wonderful, brought amazing presents . . . And the caterers and the very pretty boy waiters they'd brought with them were just great. Mark's music was perfect, the children looked so sweet and so excited, the girls had absolutely gone to town with their acting, rushing out into the hall when they'd arrived, clinging to Jonathan saying they were *so* frightened in the dark – and then the lights had gone on and everyone had sung 'Happy Birthday' and he had looked a bit shocked at first, but now he was just smiling and smiling and kissing her and saying thank you over and over again, and what a star she was . . . Oh, it had most definitely been the right thing to do . . .

No call yet. Well, what could he expect. She would be out somewhere, and in any case would be in no hurry to talk to him. She was probably still very hurt, hurt and upset. It surprised him sometimes how sensitive she actually was; she wasn't really the toughie she seemed.

He'd never forgotten how she'd gone off to the hospital with Shaun that day, for instance. And she was absolutely ridiculous about animals, fussing over a kitten in the street she'd thought had been abandoned, and getting quite worked up when he'd told her he'd just sent a couple of bull calves to the abattoir. Of course, she was a townie. But townie or not, he was terribly fond of her and very upset that he and his mother had made her so unhappy. And he didn't want to lose her. He really didn't.

He texted her, to tell her that she should listen to her messages, in case she hadn't realised there was one; and then in a sudden rash rush of courage, composed another saying *I love you*. He sat looking at it for a while before he sent it, slightly surprised that he could be telling her that, when he had only said it two or maybe three times to any girl before in the whole of his life, and making sure he meant it, and wasn't just trying to make her feel better. But he did mean it, he discovered; he did love her, or was certainly on the edge of loving her, and he desperately didn't want to lose her. He pressed 'send' and then decided to go home before he was too drunk to drive even the half-mile to the farm gates.

Abi reached Chiswick just before nine. She got in a slight tangle, trying to find Chiswick Strand, set as it was rather unexpectedly off a huge roundabout, but by nine-fifteen she was outside the house. The vast, beautiful house, looking over the river, set slightly up and back from the road behind very pretty iron railings. Abi didn't know much about houses but she could see it was old, older than Victorian, very tall; in fact, it seemed to go upwards for ever, but wide too, endless windows, with an in-and-out gravel drive. She wondered briefly why there were no cars in it, except Jonathan's Saab and a Range Rover, and then remembered it was a surprise party, the guests would have been directed to park elsewhere. And indeed, just slightly further down the road was a line of Mercedes and Beamers and a couple of Porsches: clearly Jonathan's friends were not short of a bob or two. Well, they wouldn't be, would they? He wouldn't associate with losers.

She parked her Ford at the end of the queue and patted it.

'Don't you feel intimidated now,' she said to it briskly, and then walked towards the house.

She had wondered how she would get in, whether someone would demand an invitation or something, but the front door was not locked, it pushed open easily. She stood in the hall; it was empty, but she could hear music and people laughing. A large gilt mirror hung on the wall; she went over to it, replenished her lip gloss and her perfume, combed her hair. She wanted to look as good as possible for her entrance.

As she stood there, a little girl appeared behind her: an absurdly beautiful little girl, about eight years old, with long blond curly hair, wearing a white lace-trimmed dress and silver shoes. 'Hello,' she said, 'I'm Lily. Have you come to the party? You're late.'

'I know,' Abi said, smiling at her. 'I'm sorry.'

'That's all right. Don't worry. They're just serving the food now. Do come in,' she added graciously.

'Thank you. I will.'

Abi took a glass of champagne from a tray and stood in the doorway, looking into a huge room, golden it seemed, lit with dozens of candles, and filled with great urns of white flowers. People stood in groups, smiling, beautifully dressed people, holding glasses of champagne, and by the fireplace stood Jonathan, and next to him, leaning against him, smiling up at him, was – well, she supposed it was Laura. Lovely she was, quite small, with a fall of blond hair and dressed in something truly amazing, layers of pale cream chiffon and lace. On the other side of Jonathan were the two almost identical little girls and a boy, Charlie of course, very handsome, with smooth brown hair, dressed in jeans and a blue shirt, already nearly as tall as his mother. It was all unbearably perfect – the light, the music, the display of family togetherness – and Abi really couldn't bear it.

She started to move across the room. Jonathan still hadn't seen her, was holding up his hand, Laura was tapping on her glass, Jonathan was saying, 'This is not a speech, promise, promise,' and everyone laughed and called out, 'Good thing too,' and, 'Why not?' and, 'Better not be' . . .

He saw her then, standing there, an entirely dark presence, in her black clothes, her eyes glittering, infinitely dangerous; and he was so terrified, he literally could neither move nor speak. He saw Laura look at him more sharply, puzzled at his sudden silence, and then follow his gaze towards Abi; felt her stiffen, heard her intake of breath. In his worst, his wildest nightmares, he could not have imagined this, this invasion of his family and his home, and in front of all their friends, this confrontation with the awful ugly truth of her and what he had done. What might she do, or say? How could he stop her?

She stepped forward, right up to him, and said, 'Hello, Jonathan. What a very lovely occasion. I thought I'd add my good wishes to everyone else's. That's what you deserve. Happy birthday,' she added, and leaned up and kissed him on the lips. 'You must be Laura,' she said, turning to her, and she could hear a distinct graciousness in her own voice. 'I'm Abi. I'm not sure if Jonathan's told you about me. I'm so sorry, I can't stop.'

And she turned and walked out again, and he stood staring after her, noticing, absurdly, that she was wearing the same high silver-heeled boots that she had had on, the day of the crash.

Chapter 34

Illogical things, emotions. She would have expected to feel rage, pain, humiliation; but all she felt in those first few minutes was embarrassment. That all their friends should have come with such generosity and genuine good will to Jonathan's party, and then have been forced to witness this extraordinary thing. It seemed so wrong somehow. Rude. Churlish.

In half an hour they were all gone, not mentioning the intruder – for so Abi had seemed – not properly meeting her eyes, just saying they would go and leave them in peace, very sweetly and charmingly to be sure, kissing her, shaking Jonathan rather awkwardly by the hand; he remained standing by the fireplace, hardly moving, his face shocked and white, managing the occasional smile as someone else said cheers, and what a good party, and then the room was empty, the candles and flowers and abandoned champagne glasses the only signs that there had been a party there at all. She found herself worrying then about what everyone might have done next, met up outside perhaps and walked to their cars or taxis, theorising about exactly who Abi was – while obviously having a very clear idea – agreeing to meet in this or that restaurant, a decent distance from the house.

She directed the waiters to clear the room, and then dismissed them, told Helga to start putting away the food, load up the dishwasher.

The children were upset, the girls baffled, Lily in tears of disappointment, Charlie clearly troubled and with at least half an idea of what Abi's visit had all been about. Laura took them up to the playroom, told them not to worry, everything was fine, and she'd be up in a minute to help them get to bed. And then she went back downstairs.

She realised now, of course, that she had never believed any of Jonathan's explanations. From the moment that man, whoever he was, had phoned, asking if Abi was there, she had known. She felt ashamed of allowing herself to pretend. She had let herself down. Been weak, cowardly, feebly female. She should have faced him on that very first explanation, told him not to insult her, instead of playing the sweet, simple, loyal little wife. Well, not any more she wasn't. Rage – and outrage – were growing in her, making her strong.

Jonathan was sitting in a chair now, his eyes fixed on her, watching like a terrified child as she moved around – blowing out candles, collecting the remaining glasses. When finally she had done, and faced him across the room, he said, 'Darling, I'm so sorry – so, so sorry she did that.'

'She!' Laura said. 'Jonathan, she didn't do that. *You* did.'

'But Laura—'

'Just stop it, please. I don't want to hear anything from you. You can do what you like, I really don't care.'

'How – how are the children?' he asked.

'I think they're all right. The girls didn't understand at all, just thought she was another guest, but they're disappointed that the party never really happened. Charlie's clearly got a better idea.'

'Did he say anything?'

'Well, he asked who she was. Of course. They all did.'

'Oh Christ,' he said. 'Dear sweet Christ. What – what did you tell them?'

'I said she was a lady from work who I'd never met – getting rather close to your story, isn't it, Jonathan – and that she had another party to go to, and that was why she couldn't stay. The girls seemed to accept that; Charlie, I'm not so sure. I think he's brooding about it. He's old enough to be able to see that she wasn't too much like all our other friends. In fact, when Daisy said she liked her black trousers, he said he didn't, and he didn't like her much either. But it could have been worse. I suppose.'

He was silent. Then, 'I'm sorry,' he said again.

'For what? Doing it, having the relationship at all? Lying to me? Getting caught? Bad luck, wasn't it, being involved in the crash that day. I wonder if it would still be going on if you hadn't. Well, she's very sexy. I can see that. Which I do realise I'm not.'

'Laura—'

'And probably rather good fun. Wives tend to be dull.'

'Please—'

'And young, of course.'

He was silent.

'I suppose she wasn't the first. Not that it makes much difference.'

'She was the first. I swear. And the last.'

'Yes, well, she's definitely that.'

'Of course.' There was a slight – very slight – look of hope in his eyes. Laura crushed it swiftly.

'Yes. Because that's it, Jonathan. Absolutely it. It's over. Our marriage is over. As of now.'

'Darling, you can't—'

'Don't darling me. And I can. I'm quite a strong person, you know.'

'Yes, I do know. That's why—'

'But I've always said there were two things I wouldn't be able to bear. One was anything bad – really bad – happening to one of the children. The other was you being unfaithful to me.'

'But Laura—'

'I just can't cope with it, Jonathan. It's not the humiliation, although that's quite hard. It's not the pain –

not exactly. It's the death of trust. I'd never be able to believe you again, about anything, and I could never, ever again let you near me. I'd always be wondering if you'd been – been making love to someone else. I mean, how . . .' her voice broke, she hesitated, then went on, 'how long has it been going on? Months? Years?'

'A couple of months. That's all. And I was about to finish it, I swear to you. That's the awful irony of the whole thing. I'd told her in the car that day, that it had to end, that I didn't want to go on with it any more. I'd been regretting it so much, Laura, hating myself for it.'

'Oh really? And what's that supposed to make me feel? Grateful? Reassured?'

'No, of course not. But—'

'I keep thinking back, you know,' she said, 'to all the times you must have been with her. Going to hotels, I presume. Or does she have a little pad somewhere? No, don't answer that – I don't want to know. Ringing me last thing, like you always do, make sure I'm safely settled. Telling me you – you – Oh God, you are disgusting, Jonathan. I wish I need never see you again. I suppose we'll have to have another conversation about what we're going to do but I really don't want to. And all that stuff, lying to the police, in front of me.'

'Laura – darling—'

'*Don't use that word to me!* Don't even imply you care about me. You couldn't. I don't know you at all, do I? Not at all. I thought you were one thing and you're suddenly quite another. After living with you, and – and –' her voice shook then steadied, 'loving you for fourteen years, I find I don't know anything about you. Not really. You've become a stranger. It's very simple and there's nothing more to be said. It's all very sad.'

'But Laura, you can't throw away all those years of happiness and a good marriage because of one – one indiscretion,' he cried.

'It wasn't a good marriage,' she said, 'I know that now. And the happiness wasn't very soundly based. So I can quite easily throw it away, as you call it. I'm going to bed. Good night.'

Abi just could not stop crying. She had started at the Chiswick roundabout, and had finally checked into a motel somewhere near Reading, blinded now by her tears, fearing that she would crash the car. She had had enough of car crashes.

She went into the cell-like room, flung herself down on the bed and cried for quite a lot longer. Her mind, mercifully numb at first, was coming round and confronting her with what she had done. Of all the wicked, awful things in her past, that had undoubtedly been the worst. The cruellest and the worst. Jonathan deserved cruelty but Laura didn't: she had seen how nice she was, it shone out of those big blue eyes and that pretty smiling mouth, as she gazed up at Jonathan. It wasn't her fault that he was such a 100 per cent, A1 shit. She didn't deserve to have her beautiful straight little nose rubbed in it; she should have been left to her illusions.

And Charlie too, that handsome, cool boy: the little girls had been simply baffled but he had been upset, his face crumpling into confusion as he stared up at his father and then back at her, some instinct telling him who she was – what she was.

She had destroyed a whole family that evening; and she should be destroyed herself, punished most horribly for her crime: and it *was* a crime, there could be no doubt of it, worse, far worse than anything Jonathan had done to her.

She was a totally bad person; there was nothing to redeem her.

She lay there fully clothed, staring up at the ceiling, smoking cigarette after cigarette; somewhere towards dawn, she fell into an aching, troubled sleep.

At about the same time, William awoke, his head raging. He reached for his phone, looked at it hopefully: there was no message, no text. Where was she? What was she doing? Was she ill? Had she hurt herself? Surely nobody, however angry or upset they were, could ignore the kind of messages he had been sending. Especially the text. Maybe she hadn't seen them. Unlikely, she was always checking her phone. Perhaps she'd lost it, dropped it somewhere. That would be awful. She wouldn't know he'd been trying to contact her, trying to make amends. He would try just once more, sending a text; he couldn't ring her at this sort of time. If he didn't hear then, he might even go down and see her. He had to make her realise how he felt.

He wrote, rather sadly now, *Abi, please get in touch. I'm sorry and I love you* and sent it; and because he knew he wouldn't be able to go back to sleep, got dressed and walked out to the top of the field where he had first seen the crash that day: and stood looking down and thinking about it, and how it had totally changed his life, and willing his phone to ring.

'Charlie.' Jonathan met his son's eyes across the kitchen table; he was heaping the usual vast amounts of muesli and fruit and yoghurt into his bowl.

'Yes?' His voice was odd, hostile.

'You OK?'

'Sure. Why shouldn't I be?'

'Oh, I don't know. Just checking. I – just wondered if you'd like a game of chess this morning.'

Charlie looked at him very directly, was silent as if considering him rather than the offer, then said, 'No, I don't think so. Thanks. I've got things to do.'

'Oh, OK. Well, maybe later?'

He shrugged. 'Maybe.'

It was a rather frightening conversation. Almost as frightening as the one with Laura the night before.

Abi called at seven, sounding exhausted and ill.

She thanked William for his messages and said it had been lovely to get them; and then said she was very sorry, but she didn't want to see him any more, that it had to be over.

William asked was it about his mother and she said no, it was not about his mother, it was all about her; she really couldn't have any more to do with him, and she wished him well.

'I'm just not your sort of person, William. That's all. I'm so sorry. Goodbye.'

It was a long time since William had cried. The last time had been when his grandfather, whom he had really loved, had died. He had felt then as if a very large and important part of him had gone too. He had the same feeling now; and he stood there, staring down at the place where he had first seen Abi, thinking about her, and how much he did, without doubt, love her, and he began to cry very quietly and bitterly.

Chapter 35

'Oh Georgia, hi! Lovely to see you. Coffee? Merlin's not here, I'm afraid, gone out with Location.'

'Oh, that's all right,' said Georgia. She felt oddly relieved; Merlin was gorgeous, but he took a lot of living up to. Mo, who was the third assistant director, was very undemanding. She was plump and rosy and smiling, and looked more as if she should be working at a nursery school than in an ego-ridden industry like television.

'Now Sasha – she's going to be sorting your costumes out – will be along in about fifteen minutes. I think she's planning on going shopping for most of your stuff, places like Topshop and Zara. You should have a fun day.' She grinned at Georgia. 'You looking forward to all this?'

'Oh – yes, I think so.'

'Only think so? Most girls'd be beside themselves.'

Oh God, now she was already getting it wrong. They'd all think she was seriously up herself. As well as a bitch and a coward.

'Oh no, no, I'm terribly excited. Just – just scared. You know?'

'Really? I'm sure you don't need to be. They all keep saying how great you are.'

'Well, let's hope they're right. If they really are saying that.'

'Look – I didn't make it up, OK?' Mo looked slightly less friendly.

Shit. Shit. This was turning into a disaster and she'd only been here about two minutes.

'No, course not. That's not what I meant. But you know how it is, first big break, you can't quite believe it's true.'

'I know.' Mo smiled at her, the cosy nursery persona returned. 'Anyway, you don't have to worry about a thing. Just enjoy it. Mustn't she, Sasha?'

'Mustn't she what?'

Sasha had walked in. She was seriously stylish. She was wearing a pale pink smock top over a purple sweater, striped tights on endless legs, and pink Converse boots. Her hair was tied up on one side of her head, and fell spikily to her shoulder; her long nails were painted brownish plum, as was her mouth. She wore a purple crocheted bag satchel-style and a great many green bangles adorned her skinny wrists. Georgia was wearing drainpipe jeans and a sweater; she felt she might as well have been in a navy blazer and pleated skirt, so unimaginative did it seem.

'Oh, Mo was just saying I should enjoy today,' she said nervously.

Sasha nodded coolly. 'Well, some of it.' She didn't smile; she was very tall, much taller than Georgia, with a rather beaky nose which she looked down. Georgia felt more uncomfortable every minute.

'I thought we'd start with the shops—'

'Yes, Mo said we probably would.'

'Really? I didn't know you were so well informed about Wardrobe, Mo. Anyway, yes – standard size ten, are you?'

'Well, eight sometimes. Depends on the shops. Ten in Topshop and Primark, maybe eight in Zara.'

'OK. Shoes? I've got a massive amount of shoes.'

'Six.'

'Fine. We don't need to waste time on them. Right – let's go. Or do you want to finish your coffee?'

'Oh no, no,' said Georgia, hastily, putting it down. Finish

a steaming, gorgeous-smelling mug of coffee, the first of the day: who'd ever want that? She followed Sasha out: not daring to look at Mo.

'Oh dear,' Mo said to no one in particular. 'Poor Georgia.'

'Why poor Georgia?' It was Merlin.

'I thought you were out today, Merlin.'

'I will be in a minute. Matt's downstairs, sent me up for his fags. What's the matter with Georgia, then?'

'Sasha doesn't like her.'

'Oh, Lord. Poor love.'

'Exactly. And I think she's quite nervous.'

'Which won't help. Oh well. She'll learn.'

'How's Ticky? Good weekend?'

'Ticky's fantastic. Weekend – not so much so. Give me that coffee, Mo. I could use one.'

William was helping his father deliver a breech calf when he decided to go and see Abi. It was just too important not to. Mobiles and text messages were all very well, but he needed to see her, to watch her face when she told him she didn't want to see him any more, to make sure there was nothing she hadn't told him, that there wasn't an ingredient in her decision that he had missed. He would drive down to Bristol that evening, and if he couldn't get hold of her, he would just wait, outside her flat, until she turned up. He would sit there all night if necessary; she would have to come home sooner or later.

He felt better just for having made the decision, and even found a touch of slightly brutal humour in the situation. It was hardly romantic, standing there, heaving the calf out of its mother, hearing her bellowing with pain, her great eyes rolling: exactly the sort of thing that Abi would find most alien and disagreeable about his life, given her tendency to fret over things like kittens. His father had an expression for sentimental townies: he called them

530

Bambi Lovers. William had an uneasy feeling Abi was a Bambi Lover.

But – such considerations were premature, to put it mildly. He simply needed closure. Or, just possibly, the reverse . . . The calf was out now alive, its mother licking it with her great rough tongue. And it was a heifer.

It seemed a good omen.

Jack Bryant was back in London and feeling rather pleased with life. He had several shooting weekends in his diary, an invitation for Christmas – always a bit of a lottery – in Ireland and, best of all, a very nicely developing relation-ship with Margo Farthringoe, who had proved to be even more fun than he had ever realised. She had just arrived for dinner in the flat – he was putting the finishing touches to his speciality, Beef Wellington, before placing it in the oven – and they were about to settle down to what she called 'some spiced hors-d'oeuvre', along with a bottle of the Bolly she had brought, when the bedside phone rang.

'Mr Bryant? Mr Jack Bryant?'

'Yes, that's me.'

'Sorry to trouble you, Mr Bryant. This is Sergeant Freeman. CIU division, Avon Valley Police.'

Lordy Lordy. He hadn't been driving that fast, surely. He never did these days, and certainly not in the E-type. It was too noticeable.

'Yes, Sergeant. What can I do for you?'

'We're investigating the crash on the M4 last August the twenty-second. Can you confirm you were on the road that day?'

'Let me see – August the twenty-second . . . just hang on a moment, let me look at the diary . . . oh yes. Yes, I can indeed, Sergeant. I was on my way up to Scotland. But I saw nothing of the crash; I was ahead of it.'

'That's fine, sir. And you were driving a red E-type? Registration number JB 246?'

'Yes, I was. But—'

'Very likely nothing to worry about, sir, but we'd like to come and have a chat with you as soon as possible.'

Jack agreed to see them next day; his mind whirling. What the hell had he done? He looked across at Margo, who was waiting expectantly on the other side of the bed.

'What was that about?' she asked.

'No real idea. Police, wanting to know if I was on the M4, day of that pile-up. I was, of course, I was on my way up to Scotland. God. How do they know so much, these days? Bloody police.'

'Don't get me going on that one, darling, they know bloody everything. Cameras everywhere, all that information stored on your credit card. Makes me really angry. We're living in a police state. What happened to habeas corpus, that's what I want to know.'

'Abso-bloody-lutely. What am I supposed to have done?'

'Nothing, I'm sure. Come on. Let's see if we can help you forget about it.'

Georgia sat on the train back to Cardiff, thinking how she really must find somewhere to live in London. Shooting was starting in a matter of weeks; she could hardly commute. But somehow, she still felt so down-hearted, so unsure of herself, that the prospect of looking at a load of grotty bedsits or flatshares seemed impossible. And the day hadn't helped; it had been totally shit, trailing round with the increasingly snooty Sasha. Georgia had started by giving her opinion on the clothes, which ones she thought were cool and would suit her, but had then shut up as she realised they weren't going to agree about any of them, and in fact the worse she thought she looked in something, the more Sasha liked it, saying withering things like, 'You have to look at yourself in character, you know, Georgia. It's Rose we're dressing, not you.' And getting tireder and tireder, finding it impossible to talk, even over the ten-minute sandwich break they took; and then finally, worst of all, finding that her feet might be size six but they were also quite broad; they'd dropped into Sasha's workroom to try some on, and all the shoes she had were very narrow and high-heeled and simply didn't fit her. She felt like one of the Ugly Sisters, trying on pair after pair, and none of them remotely right.

'It's too infuriating,' Sasha said. 'This means another half-day on shoes, and I simply haven't got that sort of time.'

Georgia had been much too demoralised by then to point out that it had been Sasha, not her, who had assumed the shoes would fit her . . .

And then they'd got back to the offices and Merlin had been there, and although he'd been really friendly for about five seconds, he then went into a huddle with Sasha in the corner about locations and how the first assistant didn't seem to have the right idea at all, and Merlin could see Bryn wasn't going to like any of the five shortlisted houses; and then Sasha had said she'd had a shitty day too, and why didn't they go and have a drink. Leaving Georgia alone with Mo, who was very sweet but clearly wasn't going to risk sympathising with her too much when her own job was dependent on pleasing everyone; and then worst of all, Bryn Merrick arrived and was very short with her, just nodded and said, 'Hi,' and asked Mo where the fuck Merlin was and when Mo said she didn't know, he'd glared at Georgia as if it was her fault. 'I seem to be working with a group of total layabouts,' he said, and stalked out again.

Georgia had left then and called Linda, hoping for a bit of encouragement and reassurance, and possible suggestions for who she might share a flat with, but Linda had left early to go to one of the drama school productions.

She decided to cut her losses and go home; feeling like Cinderella limping her way bewilderedly back from the ball.

'Is that The Emma?'

'Yes, it is. And that's The Barney, isn't it?'

'It is. You OK?'

'Very OK.'

'I wondered if you could make an evening this week, by any chance?'

'Thursday evening'd be good. If you can clear it.'

'I can clear it.'

'Fantastic. Where? I can come up to London.'

'Can you really?'

'Yes, of course I can. Where shall I meet you?'

'Oh God. Here comes the hard bit.'

'No use asking me. I don't do London.'

'I know. Well, anywhere's risky, I guess. Nowhere cool, nowhere trendy . . .'

'Specially not on a Thursday. Client night for Luke.'

'Right. Well, tell you what. There's a wonderful old-style hotel called the Stafford. Off Pall Mall. Couldn't be less cool. An entirely safe venue, promise. So meet you there at what – seven? Unfashionably early?'

'Nothing fashionable about me. I'll be there. And then we can talk. Should I wear twinset and pearls?'

'Just the pearls. Preferably nothing else. Bye, The Emma.'

'Bye, The Barney.'

Abi saw William's car the moment she turned into her street. Her first instinct was to drive away again; indeed, she'd slowed down and was looking for somewhere to turn round when he waved out of the window, and then as she sat there, transfixed with horror, he opened the door and got out, stood waiting for her. This was unbearable, this was unendurable; telling him she didn't want to see him any more over the phone was one thing, being confronted by him, in all his great and terrible niceness, that was something else altogether. But – short of giving chase, for he was sure to follow her – it had to be done. She pulled in behind him, got out of her car, walked up to him, tried to smile.

'Hello, William.'

'Hello, Abi.'

'William, I did say—'

'I know. But I wanted to be sure you were sure. That's all.'

'I am sure.'

'But – why? I don't understand, I really don't. Is it my mother?'

'Of course not. I could perfectly well deal with your mother.'

'I wish you would,' he said, and couldn't help smiling. She smiled back.

'Please, Abi. It would make it – easier for me. Just – explain. Please.' He opened the car door. 'Sorry. It's the old car, I'm afraid.'

She smiled feebly. 'I don't think that's going to make it any worse. Or better.'

'Good. Well, get in.'

She had been in the old car before: an X reg pick-up as opposed to the equally filthy, but comparatively new Land Rover. The well in front of the passenger seat was ankle-deep in old electrical leads, a car battery, several pairs of rusty shears, a shovel, a head collar, what looked like a string shopping bag but William explained was a nosebag, a ball of twine, some lengths of rope and a searchlight.

'You all right there?' he asked as she settled her feet in their high heels gingerly into it. 'Sorry, I didn't think about you getting in. Dad's car was out of juice and he wanted the Land Rover—'

'William, it's all right. It's fine.'

'OK. Well, like I said, I just needed to – to talk a bit more. I'm not much good at all this sort of thing, but I need to know why you – well, why you didn't want to see me any more. I meant it, what I said in my text,' he added, and it was so awful, seeing the honesty and the hurt and the hope mingled in equal parts in his brown eyes, that she had to look away.

'I – I know. And it was great to – to know that. Really great.'

'Don't you believe me?'

'Of course I do.'

'But – you don't – love me? Is that it?'

'William, I don't think I'm capable of loving anyone. I'm awful. Totally awful.'

'Abi, you're not, of course you're not!'

'No, it's true. If you knew what I did on Saturday alone – well, you wouldn't be here. You certainly wouldn't be allowing me to sit in your car. Even the old one,' she added with the ghost of a grin.

'What was that then? What did you do that was so bad?'

'Oh, just killed off a little family. A happy little family.'

'Killed it?'

'Oh, not literally, obviously. I just – just totally destroyed it.' She wasn't sure how much she'd been going to tell him. Suddenly she knew. Everything.

'Whose family? I'm not getting this.'

'Jonathan Gilliatt's family. You know – the doctor at the crash. The doctor I was there with, who was a business colleague?'

'Yes, of course I remember.'

'He – wasn't a business colleague, William. Not at all. He was – well, I was having an affair with him. And it gets worse.'

And it needed to get worse – much worse. He had to know how absolutely rotten she was – in every way; otherwise he'd never accept it. She turned to look at him, heard her voice, astonishingly steady, and it was the most difficult thing, she thought, that she had ever had to do.

'I need to tell you some things about myself, William. I'm so so sorry, but you won't understand until I do.' And she sat there beside him, her feet resting on the car battery, and told him in all its ugly detail why he could not possibly continue to love her.

Chapter 36

'So – where would you like to get married then? Where shall we have our wedding?'

'Our wedding? I hadn't really thought about a wedding.'

'My dearest, you can't be married without a wedding. So maybe you should start thinking. I imagine you'll want it somewhere in England. The bride's prerogative, choosing the venue.'

'Well, yes. I suppose so. I mean, yes of course.'

'In a church?'

'Yes, please.'

'And then perhaps the reception could be at the house.'

'Oh Russell, that's a lovely idea.'

The house – the beautiful house that Russell was buying for them both – it was all too good to be true; the owner was moving abroad and leaving any furniture they wanted; even Mrs Salter was staying. The house was actually called Tadwick House; Mary said that sounded much too grand for her and he had promptly rechristened it Sparrow's Nest.

'But only for our private use; local people don't like the names of houses being changed.'

'Nor do the post office,' said Mary, smiling. Thinking of how Donald had insisted on renaming their last house, the one where she lived now, and what a lot of trouble it had caused with the post office. And the council. But he had battled on. 'Hedges' it had been called, rather pretentiously they had both thought, given that it had one small hedge in front and none at all at the back; but it was in a cul de sac, called Horseshoe Bend, and right in the middle of the curve. 'I want to call it The End House,' he had said, 'for two reasons. It is – in one way, the end, the furthest point of the street. And this is our last house, where we shall live to the end of our days. So what could be better?'

Mary had thought that rather gloomy and said so; and Donald had said why, had she never heard of happy endings? 'Which is what the story of Mary and Donald certainly has.'

She recounted this to Russell now; he smiled.

'I like that. You know, I can see Donald was a remarkable person. I know I would have liked him very much.'

'You would,' said Mary, and it was true. It was one of the things that made her happiest about marrying Russell; that he would have liked Donald and that Donald in his turn would have liked him. She didn't think he would have liked everything about Russell: he might have considered him rather spoiled, and perhaps in need of being brought down a peg or two (one of his favourite expressions), but he would have recognised him as a good man, into whose care he could entrust his beloved Mary.

Which made it all the more sad that Christine had set herself so firmly against him. Mary had continued to try; every Sunday she and Russell suggested Christine joined them for lunch, and at least once during the week they invited her for supper – always at Russell's hotel so that Christine wouldn't feel Russell was taking over her father's house – and she had begged her to come and see the house.

'Please, dear. We could go on our own, without Russell, if you'd prefer. I'd so love to show it to you.'

But Christine, wearing the expression of faint distaste mingled with stubbornness that Mary had come to dread, said she was sorry but she simply couldn't.

'I'm glad you're happy, Mum, very glad, but I don't understand it and you can't ask me to share it with you.'

'Then you can't be very glad,' Mary said on the one occason they had actually had a row about it. 'You clearly preferred it when I was alone and quite often lonely.'

Whereupon Christine had told her not to resort to emotional blackmail and slammed out of the house, leaving Mary in tears; later she had phoned to apologise.

'The last thing I want is to upset you, Mum, but you have to try to understand how I feel.'

Mary said she did understand, and she was very sorry, and she would live in hope that Christine would come round; but so far, it seemed very unlikely.

The rest of the family were much easier. Timothy, Mary's grandson, said it was really cool and he'd be dancing at her wedding all night; when could he meet Russell and would Russell like to be an investor in the IT company he was planning to set up.

'Only joking, Gran. But I would like to meet him, I really would. He sounds great.'

Mary hadn't arranged a meeting because she knew how hard Christine would find it; Gerry too had expressed – rather awkwardly – a desire to meet Russell and had said again how sorry he was that Christine was being what he called 'so difficult' about it.

And Douglas, Donald's pride and joy, the son he had longed for, born eight long years – and several miscarriages – after Christine, had written from Toronto to say how very, very happy he was to hear about Russell and that he couldn't wait to meet him then.

The kids think it's really great, too, he had written. *Don't worry about Chris* – for Mary had felt bound to warn him about Christine's reaction – *she'll come round.*

❊　❊　❊

They agreed on a December wedding, 'So we can spend Christmas together legally,' Russell said. The modest improvements to the house that Mary had requested apart from aquiring some of their own furniture – a lick of paint here and there, and a new bathroom adjacent to the main bedrom – would be completed by then.

'So, very soon now,' Russell had said, 'we must go over to the States, and you must meet my children. Who are extremely excited about you.'

Mary hoped they really were – Russell tended to exaggerate; but in fact, she had received two very sweet letters from his daughters, Coral and Pearl, saying how delighted they were that their father had found her again, what a romantic story it was, and how they longed to meet her. Of course, Mary thought, it must be easier for them, since they had learned to accept and live with Russell's second wife from comparatively early ages. His son had written a slightly stiffer note, but there was no doubt of its friendliness.

'Also,' Russell said, 'I want to show you Connecticut at least, where I think we should have our American house. I know you'll love it, it will suit you very well; I don't think we should buy anywhere there yet, not until the spring, but we can get a feel for what's around.'

When Mary asked him if he was going to sell the apartment, he had looked at her in astonishment.

'No, no, of course not, we'll need a New York base, and I think you'll be happy with it. If you're not, then we'll find another.' He kissed her, then went on, 'So I'll book a flight around the beginning of November. That way you can experience Thanksgiving, very important if you're going to be married to an American, and both girls have expressed a wish to have you there.'

Mary said she wouldn't have much time to organise a wedding if they were going to be in America until the beginning of December; Russell said nonsense, they could do most of it before they went.

'Best draw up a guest-list fairly soon; I guess it will be mainly family, but you can have thousands if you wish.'

Mary said she didn't know thousands and of course it would be mainly family.

'Pity,' said Russell, kissing her again, 'in some ways. I so look forward to showing you off. I hope you're going to wear white.'

'Don't be so ridiculous,' said Mary.

Three homes. A new family. A wedding. It was all rather hard to take in.

William didn't know what to do with himself. Literally. He had been desperately hurt and shocked by Abi's confession; almost unendurably. At first, he had been slightly numbed; then as the days passed and the truth clarified, the pain worsened exponentially.

It hurt so much he could hardly stand it. He kept trying to tell himself it was ridiculous for him to feel this bad, but it didn't help. And it wasn't ridiculous, not really. It wasn't just that she was so sexy and she'd been fantastic company, and he missed her so much. It wasn't even just that she'd lied to him so relentlessly about Jonathan, and that she'd been sleeping with Jonathan, and God only knew how many other men before him. It was that he'd allowed himself to think she'd enjoyed being with him, as much as he'd enjoyed being with her: and she hadn't. Of course she hadn't. She'd just been using him until someone more suitable came along. To think that *he* was suitable, in any way, was moonshine. That he'd allowed himself to believe in the moonshine made him feel worse. Abi clearly wanted excitement, she wanted some flash bloke with plenty of money, who could show her a good time, take her to expensive hotels and restaurants and probably on expensive holidays as well, not some dull, dutiful farmer, who smelled of cowshit a lot of the time and couldn't ever get away from the farm.

And he didn't want someone like her, either: did he? He wanted someone he could trust, who would treat him and his life carefully, someone straightforward and who he understood, not a baffling enigma straight out of a bad TV series, who slept around, and took her sexual pleasures like a cat.

He went about the farm in something of a daze, was silent at mealtimes, spent the evenings at the pub, drinking. He heard himself agreeing to his brother having free shoot days, and to his father spending £20,000 on patching up the roof of the cowshed when he knew they should be investing ten times that in an entirely new building. He didn't care about anything any more. He felt sick, listless and – perhaps worst of all – foolish. How Abi must have seen him coming; probably imagined he was rich, that he would make a good meal-ticket for a while. He couldn't see that he would ever feel any better . . .

'Hi, babe. You all right for Saturday?'

She'd been so far away, in what felt like a parallel universe, that she couldn't think for a moment who it was.

'Sorry?'

'Emma! It's me – your about-to-be absent boyfriend. *Ciao*, baby.'

'Oh – Luke!'

'That's the one. You OK?' He sounded quite concerned.

She made a huge effort. 'Of course. I'm sorry. Difficult day.'

'Yeah? Mine was good. Guy from Birelli came over, took me to lunch. Said he knew I was going to make a real contribution. Looking forward to showing me Milan.'

'Well, that's fantastic, Luke.'

'Yeah. I can't wait. Only ten more days. Then – a totally new life. *Fantastico!*'

'Yes. Lucky you.'

'So – just checking on the weekend. Our last. Well, for a week or two.'

'Mmm.'

'You are all right for it, aren't you?'

'What?' Emma, for God's sake. Get a grip.

'OK. Rewind. Have you still got Saturday and Sunday off? It's my last weekend. Before I go to Italy.'

'Yes. Yes, of course.' She would have to be. Unless by then Barney had . . . but no, he wouldn't. They had agreed. They had to give it a little more time. It was a huge decision he was taking. Huge. She didn't seem to be taking one at all.

'Cool. Now I've got us on the guest-list at Bungalow 8.'

'Fantastic.'

'So we should have a really good night.'

Oh, God. Oh, God oh God. If anything was needed to persuade her that she was doing the right thing, leaving him, this was it. The fact that she was practically dreading Saturday.

'Love you, babe.'

'Love you too,' she said automatically.

Jack Bryant was exactly the sort of person Sergeant Freeman most disliked. Loud, over the top posh accent, old school tie – not that he recognised that one, and he knew most of them, it was a little hobby of his – signet ring, slicked-back hair, highly polished brogues – he was a caricature.

It had not actually been very hard to find him. The motoring division confirmed that the wheel nut came from an E-type; there were several reports of a red E-type on the road that afternoon – immediately in front of the lorry, according to Georgia; and she was quite sure that it had had a personalised numberplate. They had checked with various E-type associations and clubs, and after that it was a simple matter of trawling through the personalised registrations – the DVLA were always very helpful – and making phone calls. The whole thing had been one day's work.

However, Freeman was disappointed to discover he couldn't fault him. Bryant was very articulate, had excellent recall and was eager to help: yes, he had indeed lost a wheel nut, hadn't actually discovered it until a week later, when he was checking his car prior to leaving his friends in Scotland. He'd had no idea when it had come off.

'But I did check the whole car over very, very carefully, Sergeant, two days before I set off for Scotland; my mechanic will confirm that. And I also gave it a personal check that morning – tyres, oil, all that sort of thing – and I also checked the wheel nuts myself. Gave them a final go with the old spanner, just to be on the safe side.'

'The irony of it is,' said Paul Johns from Forensics, 'you can over-tighten those things and the thread goes. What a bloody tragedy. But if it's true what he says, it was definitely not his fault.'

Barney and Emma had had a lovely evening at the Stafford Hotel. They always did. There was guilt and anxiety folded into it, into all of it, but their time together was still astonishingly sweet.

'This can't go on too long,' Barney said.

'I'm in no rush to get back,' she said, deliberately misunderstanding.

'Oh, my Emma, that's not what I mean. I could sit here all night with you and all day tomorrow, and all tomorrow night . . .'

'Oh, really?'

'Yes, really. Couldn't you?'

'Of course I could.'

'What I meant was, we have to – well, to tell them. Don't we?'

He hadn't said that before; confronted their situation,

what it actually meant. She'd been waiting – not too impatiently, for it was he who must act, his life that must so totally change, he who must be surer than sure about the two of them. Luke would be upset, of course, but Amanda would be heartbroken, her world, her present, her future, all in fragments. It was not something Barney could do without terrible difficulty, and without awful remorse; and she knew he dreaded it beyond anything.

'I – suppose we do. But Barney, it's your decision.'

'And I've made it. I love you, Emma. I . . .' He hesitated, his voice shook slightly. 'I don't love Amanda. I never did. I thought I did, but it was an illusion. I am fond of her beyond anything. I hate to make her so unhappy, but I can't marry her. And when she knows, she won't want it either.'

'No,' Emma said, thinking of the truly awful pain that Amanda would have to endure, in order not to want it any longer, not to want Barney, not to want to share her life with him. 'No, I suppose not.'

'She wouldn't. We both have to remember that. So – I will tell her, very soon. I hate these lies, hate living them, day after day. It's awful.'

'Do you think she knows? Suspects anything?'

'I don't know. Would you?'

'I would, I think. Yes.'

'Ah.' He was silent, taking this in, then: 'Well, very soon then. Within the next few days.'

'Oh, Barney.'

'Oh Emma. What about you and Luke?'

'He won't mind that much. He'll think he does, but he won't. He's quite – quite thick-skinned.'

'Really?'

'Yes,' she said, and then added, quickly anxious not to blacken Luke, who had seemed so recently everything she wanted, 'but so lovely in so many ways.'

Barney nodded, looking at her rather solemnly. 'Like you.'

'What, thick?'

'No. Lovely in so many ways. I love you, The Emma. So much.'

'I love you, The Barney. So much.'

They left the Stafford soon after ten: Emma to go back to Swindon, Barney to go home to Amanda.

They walked out of the restaurant hand in hand; they had kissed hello, and during the course of the evening had kissed again from time to time, albeit in a very seemly manner, usually because one of them had said something that particularly delighted the other. There had also been a fair amount of smiling into one another's eyes.

No one could have possibly complained about their behaviour; it had been modest, well-mannered and really rather charming.

No one, that is, who was unaware of a relationship either of them might have been conducting with another party altogether.

But Barney had been wrong when he had judged the Stafford a safe venue; for as they walked out through the foyer, smiling at one another, he failed to recognise that among a rather noisy party of eight, arriving for a post-theatre supper, were Gerald and Jess Richmond, Tamara's parents. And following them, out of a second taxi, together with a couple of other friends, Tamara herself.

Chapter 37

'Barney, hi. This is Tamara. I thought we might have a little drink this evening. My treat. No, just the two of us. What? Oh no, Barney, I think you could spare half an hour. It really is quite important. Great. How about Number One Aldwych? Yes. Well, I know it's a bit of a trek, but maybe better than right on our own doorstep. You know what they say? Only joking . . .'

Patrick woke early on Thursday morning. Early for him, that was, which meant before six. Five-forty, to be precise.

He had slept badly, which he usually did now, since they were weaning him off the sleeping pills. He would take hours to get to sleep and then surface after maybe three or four hours. They were the worst hours, those early ones, when the depression that he could hold off – just – during the day, hung around him like a shroud, when the fears that he would never progress beyond the stage he was at now, bedridden and helpless, never going home, never being together with Maeve and the boys again, never making love to Maeve again – that was one of the worst – those fears were at their strongest, their most dangerous. He had moved himself away – with his own willpower, and the help of the hospital priest – from thoughts of suicide; but the alternative, this death-in-life, seemed little better.

He struggled to distract himself with things, with books, with music, but it was a feeble self-conscious escape; it was as if he was watching himself reading and listening, thinking, 'Ah, there is a man who has escaped from his wretched life, into the stories and the sounds', but he found no real pleasure in it. He was only happy when he was with Maeve, and he knew she would not have believed it, for he was irritable, awkward with her, often unkind, resenting her freedom to come and go from the hospital when he was captive there, unable even to move from his bed to his chair without help.

He looked out of the window at the blackness, thinking about himself and what an absolute disaster his life had become: all as a result of a few seconds' misjudgement. And it hadn't even been his misjudgement: life didn't get much crueller than that. Where had God been when he'd needed Him so badly? Looking the other way, it seemed. Well, that would have been Maeve's explanation . . .

Patrick was an intelligent man; his faith was not entirely simplistic, but until the accident it had been rock solid. Tragedy was not for God to steer away, it was sent to test and to try you – with His help. Over the last few weeks, Patrick had found even this tenet unsatisfactory.

He sighed; he was thirsty and hot. Maybe he could get the dear little night nurse, the one who had found him that night and of whom he had grown rather fond, to make him a cup of tea. He rang the bell.

Sue Brown made him a cup of tea and promised to be back soon, but she had to sort out a couple more patients; it was after seven when she got back to Patrick.

'Right, Patrick, let's get this job done, shall we? Then you can have your breakfast. I'll start with your catheter and then give you a nice wash. Let's see . . . right.'

Sue Brown was intent on her task; she didn't hear the slight intake of breath from the patient as she pulled on the catheter, but as she started to insert the fresh one, there was another. Slightly louder it was, followed by, 'What are you doing down there, Sue, putting a bit of barbed wire in?'

She looked at him, unaware in those first few seconds of the significance of this. Then, afraid even to ask the question, she said, 'Am I hurting you?'

'Not hurting, no. But it's not exactly comfortable.'

Sue Brown closed her eyes briefly. She dared not think how important this might be; or trust her own comparatively inexperienced judgement.

She withdrew the catheter again, laid it gently on the tray and said, 'Sorry, I seem to have forgotten something. I'll be back in one minute – all right?'

Jo Wales was eating an extremely soggy croissant and drinking a very bitter cup of coffee, while thinking that a hospital that had cost over a billion pounds to build might have spent an extra five hundred on a decent coffee machine, when Sue Brown walked in. Or, to be more accurate, as she said afterwards, seemed to explode into the space in front of her.

'Jo – Jo, I don't know what to do! Could you come with me, please?'

'What to do about what, Sue? The patient who came in last night, do you mean? What is it, blood pressure not down? I'd hoped so, it was extremely high.'

'No, no, it's not him. It's Patrick Connell!'

'Patrick? Has he had another bad night? I did think it was too soon to stop the—'

'No, no, it's nothing like that. He – well, I was just changing his catheter . . .'

'Yes? Not blood in the urine, I hope?'

'No, no, Jo. Please listen to me!'

Jo looked at Sue, her face was very flushed and her eyes huge. Something serious had obviously just happened.

'Sorry. Go on.'

'It's – well, he said it was uncomfortable. The catheter.

When I tried to insert it. Or to be precise, he asked was it a piece of barbed wire.'

Jo stared at her; her heart thumped uncomfortably.

'Oh, my God,' she said. 'God, Sue, that is exactly, *exactly* what we've all been waiting for. Let me come in to him straight away. But – nothing must be said to him yet. All right?'

'Of course not!' said Sue Brown, half-indignantly. 'That's exactly why I'm here, not saying anything to him. I wanted your opinion.'

And thus it was that five minutes later, Jo Wales smiled radiantly at Sue Brown across Patrick's bed, having received the same rather plaintive response as she too tried to insert the catheter, and then at Patrick himself and said, very gently, 'Patrick, I think we might have some rather good news here. I'm going to call Mr Osborne straight away.'

Never, as Patrick said to her later, after James Osborne had come up to see him personally and first peered at and then prodded it, had his modestly-sized willy caused so much excitement.

Laura felt rather ashamed of herself. It was almost a week since the party and she still hadn't done anything about her situation. She was still living in Chiswick, still living with Jonathan, hadn't even seen a solicitor. What had happened to the strong steely woman who had behaved so magnificently that night? She seemed to be disappearing, day by day, replaced by someone more like herself, much more fragile and anxious.

Her absolute certainty that she shouldn't stay married to Jonathan hadn't changed; the thought of him even touching her, now that she had seen Abi, knew what she was like, was repulsive; she kept thinking of that swaying sexy walk, those full high breasts on that skinny body, those dark, mocking eyes, and imagining him with her.

She would torture herself with horrible visions of him lying with her, caressing her, entering her – just as he did with her, only it would be different, exciting, and Abi would be knowing, skilful in what she did. Laura knew she was not particularly sexy, she liked sex with Jonathan – indeed, she enjoyed it – but leaving the boundaries not just of what was familiar but what she liked actually distressed her. She got uneasy when, in the early days – it was a long time since he had suggested anything – he'd wanted to make love in the shower, or on the floor, and more so when he kissed and licked and teased her clitoris, or – worst of all – wanted her to take his penis in her mouth. She tried, dutifully, but he could see how much she hated it and he never forced her, just laughed at her tenderly and called her his Little Miss Missionary.

She wondered miserably now whether, if she had done those things, maybe he would not have needed the likes of Abi; and wondered too how many Abis there had been, forcing her into sharing him, without ever knowing it, hearing about her, laughing at her, despising her.

But if she left him how would the little girls who adored him so, how would they manage without their beloved daddy? And Charlie, to whom he was a hero – although Charlie was clearly uncertain at the moment, watchful on the rare occasions they were together.

The three of them would have their lives suddenly disrupted; they'd be robbed of their birthright of absolute security; their times with their father doled out, however generously, their loyalties strained, a life where things like Christmas, birthdays, holidays would become painful and awkward, where the empty seat at the table, in the car, on the plane, would be so horribly poignant, and which – in time – might even be occupied by new people they wouldn't want there, wouldn't welcome, who they would know they should accept.

For them at least, it would be better to do what Jonathan

so plainly wanted, for her to forgive if not forget, to cover the cracks, to fake happiness. But – that was impossible, beyond her. And so she went on, day by miserable day. Watched with considerable scorn by the other Laura, the steely tough Laura who had been so absolutely sure of herself and what she should do.

'So, Barney – what would you like? Cocktail? Beer? Or should we push the boat out and have a glass of champagne? Drink to both our forthcoming nuptials?'

'I'll have a beer, please,' said Barney.

'OK. And I think I'll have something non-alcoholic, now I come to think about it. I want to keep a clear head.'

'Fine.'

'Right. So . . .' She paused while she gave the order, settled back in her chair. She smiled at him, crossed her long legs rather deliberately.

The bar was very crowded; even so, everyone had noticed Tamara. Barney saw them staring at her. Well, she was impossible to ignore. It wasn't just her looks, she carried with her an aura of power and purpose wherever she went. This evening, she was wearing a red dress and black, very high-heeled shoes; she looked – what? Slightly dangerous.

'So, what do you want to talk about?' he asked.

'Oh, this and that. You know.'

'No. I don't.'

'OK. Well, I don't know if Toby's told you, but we've got a new date. Bit tentative, but we're working towards it. Next May.'

'He hasn't, no. I haven't seen him for a bit. Now he's home . . .'

'Ah yes. So you're not hotfooting it down to the hospital every few days. What a good friend you were, Barney. How very unselfish of you that was.'

He shrugged. 'I didn't mind. He's my best friend. He needed me.'

'Of course. Well, I hope you're not implying I didn't do my bit.'

'No, of course not, Tamara. Anyway, May sounds fine. Bit of a way ahead, but—'

'I know. But I really don't want a winter wedding. Apart from anything else, it's a summer wedding dress. Well, you have to think of these things. And the bridesmaids' dresses, of course. Freeze to death they would, poor little things. April might be all right, but still pretty cold in the marquee. So, we're waiting. What about you, Barney? When are you and Amanda going to do it?'

'Oh, next year maybe. You'd better ask her, we haven't really finalised it yet.'

'Just as well perhaps.' She smiled at him over-sweetly. The drinks arrived. 'Oh, thanks,' she said to the waiter. 'Got any olives? Great.'

'Tamara,' said Barney, trying to ignore a rather leaden sensation, somewhere in the bottom of his stomach. 'What did you mean by that?'

'By what?'

'By "just as well".'

'Ah. Yes. Well, you know . . .'

'No. You'll have to explain. I'm a simple sort of chap.'

'Oh Barney, come on. I wouldn't have called you that. I've decided you're rather complex. Actually.'

'Because?'

'Because you seem to be able to conduct two relationships at once. Not the act of a simple chap, surely?'

The leaden feeling took over and sank somewhere deep into him. Taking his stomach with it. The noise around them seemed to intensify; and yet they seemed oddly isolated, set apart from the rest, just the two of them, staring at one another over this dangerous, deadly conversation.

'I saw you, Barney, that's the thing. Leaving the Stafford the other night. With someone who wasn't Amanda. It was the pretty little doctor person, I think. Of course, I didn't see very much of her. You obviously managed to see a great deal. It does rather explain your devoted presence at the hospital, day after day.'

'This is a disgusting conversation,' said Barney. He could feel himself beginning to sweat now. He put down his beer, asked for some water.

'I don't think so. If anything's disgusting, it's you. Playing around, cheating on just about the sweetest girl you could find anywhere.'

'Have you discussed this with Toby?'

'No, I haven't discussed it with anyone. Yet. I wanted to get your version of it.'

'You're not going to get any version of anything out of me, Tamara. I have no intention of discussing my personal life with you.'

'Well, I think you might have to. Unless we start with discussing something else.'

'And what's that?' Jesus, she was clever.

'Starting with the reason you and Toby left so late for the wedding that day. I still haven't had a satisfactory explanation out of either of you. I really want to know that, Barney. And if you don't tell me, I'm going straight to Amanda. Before you have a chance to work up any kind of an explanation.'

'I've told you. A dozen times. Toby was ill. He kept being sick.'

'And why was he being sick?'

'I suppose he had some bug. I don't know.'

'His parents didn't mention it.'

'They didn't know. We – specially Toby – didn't want to worry them.'

'Really? But why not? They could have called their doctor.'

'Which I did. When they'd gone. And then he began to feel better.'

She crossed and uncrossed her legs, began to fiddle with her necklace. It was a complex affair, a mass of small charms on a long silver chain.

'This just so doesn't ring true, you know, Barney.'

'Look, why don't you ask Toby?'

'I have. He says much the same. That he must have eaten something.'

'Well then—'

'But you and his parents were fine.'

'Oh, Christ. You're talking total shit, Tamara.'

'No, Barney, I'm not. Now I know you were stopped by the police and that must have held you up a good twenty–thirty minutes. But then you went to a service station, for Christ's sake. What the fuck for? Making you even later.'

'Toby needed the toilet. Again.'

'No, Barney, he could have thrown up out of the car window if you were that late. I'm sorry. None of this works. I'm going to have to talk to Amanda. This evening, I should think.'

She was looking very complacent now, half-smiling at him; she was clearly enjoying the conversation. Barney suddenly remembered Toby telling him she was a brilliant chess player; he could see why. Her tactics were flawless.

'No!' he said, knowing she must recognise his panic, trying to disguise it. 'No, Tamara, not this evening.'

'Oh, what? So you can think up a pack of lies to tell her first?'

'No. I wouldn't lie to Amanda.'

'That is just so pathetic. Where did she think you were the other night then?'

Barney was silent. Then he said, 'Look, I don't want anyone – *anyone* – talking to Amanda except me. Which is not to say there's anything to talk about. But please, if you don't believe me about the wedding day, ask Toby yourself. Ask him to confirm the story.'

She looked at him, her eyes gimlet-hard, her mouth set.

Then she said, 'All right. I'll give you twenty-four hours.'

'And will you talk to Toby?'

'Yes, I most certainly will. Right. Well, it's been a fun evening, hasn't it? I do like a drink after work, so relaxing. I'm going home now. Bye, Barney.'

And she stalked out of the bar on her impossibly perfect legs, pulling her cloud of hair up into a tight ponytail as she went. It was an oddly pugilistic gesture.

Chapter 38

'Linda? Alex.'

'Oh – Alex. Hello.'

She did have a great voice; husky and sexy and expressive. He supposed it was her theatrical training, the expressiveness at any rate, otherwise how could three words reassure him that she was extremely pleased to hear from him, that she'd enjoyed Saturday night, that she wanted to see him again.

'Busy day?' he asked.

'Mm, it was good. Got a lot done.'

That would constitute a good day. He didn't know her very well yet, but enough to recognise she was terminally restless, filled with energy.

'Saturday was great, Alex.'

'I thought so too.' He was in the car, about to drive home; he smiled into the darkness, feeling a rush of pleasure, partly from hearing her voice, partly from remembering Saturday himself.

They'd gone to the theatre, to see *Chicago*: it had been at his suggestion, since he had a sneaking liking for musicals. She'd said she couldn't believe he hadn't seen it, which he'd found mildly irritating; not everyone could spend every other evening in the theatre; but then said she'd be more than happy to sit through it for the third time. They then went out to dinner, and talked so much and for so long that he really had missed his last train home.

'Damn,' he said, 'I'll have to get a cab. If I can. Or stay in a hotel. If I can find one.'

'Or – stay with me,' she said, and then added, a gleam in her dark brown eyes, 'if you dare.'

And then when he'd got flustered and even, he feared, blushed – not a pretty sight for a man in his mid-forties – she'd laughed and said, 'Alex, I'm not compromising you. I have a very nice spare room, and you're very welcome to it. Don't start talking about taxis and hotels, it's ridiculous.'

And so he'd gone back to her incredibly smart flat, the sort of place he hated, full of aggressively stylish, uncomfortable-looking modern furniture – although she did have two wonderfully large and lush white sofas – and a lot of ridiculous and incomprehensible paintings and rather absurd ornaments – in the corner of the sitting room, for instance, was a two-foot-high red velvet shoe that was a lamp, and painted on the wall of the bathroom, where he had stood rather nervously peeing, a shadowy figure peering in through the non-existent window.

'It's very – nice, your flat,' he'd said politely when he rejoined her in the sitting room.

'I like it. Thank you.'

'I think that man you keep in the bathroom would give me the creeps though.'

'Who? Oh, the *trompe l'œil*. I like him – he keeps me company. What would you like to drink? Brandy?'

'Sounds good to me.'

She returned with a tray, poured him a very large brandy.

'Thanks.' He suddenly felt awkward; a silence formed. He looked round the perfect room, seeking something to say. 'It's all extremely tidy,' he said finally.

'I am extremely tidy. I can't help it. Too tidy, people tell me. It means I'm anally retentive, a control freak, all that sort of stuff. What about you?'

'I'm very untidy. So does that make me not a control freak?'

'Possibly. What do you think?'

'I don't know, Linda. I don't feel I know what I am any more.'

'That's a very sad remark,' she said, and her eyes were thoughtful as she looked at him.

'I'm afraid I've become a bit of a sad person. In the modern sense as well. My daughter constantly upbraids me for being sad.'

'What, as in the get-a-life sense?'

'That's the one.'

'I don't think that matters. Much more important if you're actually not – not happy.'

'I'm not,' he said abruptly. 'I would say I'm quite unhappy. Have been for years.'

Her brown eyes met his; she looked almost shocked. 'Alex, that's dreadful.'

'Oh, I'm exaggerating. I love my work. I love my kids. But – it isn't very nice, living with someone who finds you totally wanting. Knowing they wish you weren't there.'

'This is your wife, I presume.'

'It is. My about-to-be ex-wife. We're trying to sort out accommodation. It's very difficult. I think I told you, we've sold the house, so it's only a matter of time.'

'Do you think you'll feel better then?'

'I hope so. I'll miss the kids horribly.'

'Of course. But you'll still see them, I imagine.'

'Obviously. But that's not quite the same thing as living with them, to put it mildly. And I worry about them, how they'll cope. They seem OK about it at the moment, very cool, but I think a lot of it's an act.'

'Well, I don't know them or anything about them. But living in a miserable household can't be doing them any good either.' Her tone was brisk, almost abrasive; it annoyed him.

'I didn't say the household was miserable, I said *I* was.'

'But Alex, if they have an ounce of sensitivity, which I

560

presume they do, they must know that. And it should worry them.'

'Well, maybe. The fact remains it's all wretched for them and none of it's their fault.'

'No, of course not. I just think if they care about you, and their mother, they'll see it's for the best. And deal with it.'

'I don't think you can know many teenagers,' he said.

'Maybe not teenagers. Thankfully.'

'And I don't think you really know what you're talking about. That's a very simplistic view.'

She stared at him, and flushed suddenly; it was endearing, the first sign he had seen of any crack in her self-confidence.

'Sorry,' she said.

He was silent; he felt depressed and defensive, a shadow over the evening. The silence grew.

Then, 'I'm sorry, Alex,' she said suddenly, surprising him, 'if I upset you. And of course I don't know what I'm talking about.' She smiled at him, rather awkwardly. 'I'm just terribly bossy. I can't help it. Well, I suppose I could, if I really tried, but by the time I realise I'm doing it, it's too late. I'll stop now. I just – well, I just didn't like the idea of you being unhappy all the time.'

'That's very kind of you,' he said, 'but I think I know how to look after myself.' He could hear himself, pompous, a bit stiff.

'Right,' she said, clearly edgy herself, 'how about some coffee?'

'That'd be very nice,' he said. He didn't really want it, but to have turned that away as well as her apology would have seemed very aggressive.

She disappeared, and he leafed rather nervously through a coffee-table book on art deco. This might have been a mistake. The whole thing might have been a mistake.

❋ ❋ ❋

'Well,' she said, on her return, 'let's start again. What shall we talk about – what would be safe? You choose a subject.'

'I'd rather not.'

'Why?'

'Well, to be honest,' he said, 'I'm still a bit nervous of boring you.'

'Boring me! Why? I find you not remotely boring, I promise you that.'

'I'll try to believe you. I mean, you do lead this rather glamorous life. In theatres and so on. And I spend mine . . .'

'Yes, how *do* you spend yours? What do you do? Day by day, I mean. Tell me.'

'Oh, staring into people's orifices. Patching them up. Not the orifices, the people. Dealing with overdoses, cardiac arrests, stab wounds, even the occasional death on site, so to speak. I mean, I love it and it's fascinating, but it can hardly compete with first nights and talent-spotting, can it?'

'Alex, I spend about ten per cent of my time at first nights. The rest is hard graft, talking to a load of rather pretentious people, trying to persuade them that mediocre actors are wonderful, and that wonderful ones are worth hiring. And nannying actors, nursing their egos, making sure they get to auditions, listening to them whining, sorting out their money.'

'Bit like being a parent?'

'Possibly. But . . . I think I might prefer the orifices.'

'You wouldn't,' he said, and laughed. 'Believe me. Not very nice things, orifices. Well, not the ones which land up in Casualty.'

'Tell me,' she said, 'do you really get people coming in with – well, you know – golf balls up their bums, things like that?'

''Fraid so. And people get up to the most extraordinary things with vacuum cleaner hoses.'

'You're kidding! Now that really *is* sad.'

She leaned forward to top up his brandy; he found himself studying her cleavage. She noticed and grinned at him.

'Sorry,' he said.

'Don't be. I don't mind. I'd wear polo necks if I did.'

'Promise me,' he said, laughing, 'you'll never come out with me wearing a polo neck. That would make me very sad indeed.'

'It's a promise.'

'Well, that is – if you *do* come out with me again. I hope I'm not being presumptuous.'

'Oh Alex,' she said, and her voice was impatient, 'of course you're not being presumptuous. You shouldn't put yourself down so much. You're a very attractive, sexy man. Get used to the idea. If you ask me out, I'll come. There you are, that's another promise. Oh God, I'm being bossy again, aren't I? What about your wife? Is she bossy?'

He wasn't sure he wanted to talk about Sam in this sort of way; the complex loyalty of marriage, even a broken marriage, forbade it.

'Not exactly,' he said finally. 'She just does what she wants. But lots of wives do that.'

'Do they? I wouldn't know. Most of my friends aren't wives, you see.'

No, he thought, they wouldn't be. You don't move in a married world, you don't know about marriage. Not really.

She pushed on. 'So, lots of fights?'

'Used to be,' he said. 'I've given up lately.'

'Really,' she said, sipping her brandy, looking at him thoughtfully. 'I'm surprised. I'd have thought you'd be rather good in a fight.'

'What on earth makes you say that?'

'Well, you're quite powerful, aren't you? Emotionally.'

'Linda, you hardly know me.'

'I realise that. But I can rather see you roaring and raging away.'

'I think you're letting your imagination run away with you,' he said, edgy again. 'I told you I don't do much roaring and raging these days. Not at home, anyway.'

'Ah. How about work? From what I could see that day in the hospital, you were quite fierce. I bet you're one of those terrible men who take everything out on their colleagues.' She smiled at him, lay back on the cushions. 'Am I right?'

'That's a dreadful thing to say,' he said. He didn't smile back.

'Oh Alex, I was only joking.' She looked at him, and the dark eyes were defensive now. 'Look, this conversation's going nowhere. Let's go to bed, shall we?'

'Fine.' He stood up. And then added, 'Maybe I should try and get a cab, after all.'

'That really is ridiculous,' she said. 'Why, for God's sake?'

'Because suddenly I don't feel very comfortable here.'

'Oh, please,' she said. 'You should stop being so sorry for yourself, Alex. You know that? You're not the only person who's had a bad marriage; other people go through it and out the other side. Even other people with kids.'

He stared at her, suddenly angry. 'I don't think you're exactly an expert on the subject,' he said. 'By your own admission, you haven't done too well yourself.'

'Oh, do shut up,' she said wearily. 'Good night, Alex. There's a towel on your bed. And a spare toothbrush on the chest of drawers. The bathroom's down the corridor. Just let yourself out quietly in the morning, will you?'

It was the reference to the toothbrush that did it. He suddenly felt rather stricken at his rudeness, and thought that whatever else, she had been very generous, not to mention thoughtful. Not many people kept spare toothbrushes for unexpected guests. He'd been on his way out of the room; he stopped and turned.

'I'm sorry,' he said stiffly, 'if I was rude. You've been very – very hospitable. I shall be glad of the toothbrush. Thank you. Good night.'

He turned away again; and heard the unmistakable sound of a giggle.

'That was the most ridiculous little speech,' she said, 'but thank you for it. I'm glad you think I'm hospitable at least. I seem to have one virtue.'

Alex turned; she was shaking with silent laughter, biting her lip, her lovely face alive as she looked at him.

'I'm sorry,' she said, 'really sorry if I've hurt your feelings. I truly didn't mean to. It was – well, it was seeing you doing your Heathcliff number. All brooding and wounded.'

'I was not doing a number,' he said. And then he grinned back, albeit reluctantly.

'Yes, you were. You are Heathcliff. To the life. Pity you're not an actor, I could get you cast in no time. Don't look so cross. Heathcliff was very sexy as well as brooding. Come on, let's go to bed friends, shall we?' She walked over to him, lifted her face to his, reached up and kissed him. Very lightly on the mouth. But it was enough.

Five minutes later they were in her bed.

'Yes, Saturday was lovely,' she said now, the memory making her, too, smile down the phone. 'Very lovely. Thank you.'

'I thought so too. When—'

'Oh, as soon as possible, I'd think,' she said, 'if that doesn't sound too bossy.'

'Well, it does quite. But I'll try to ignore that. How about the weekend?'

'Weekend'd be good. Friday running over into Saturday, maybe? Or does that sound bossy, too?'

'Very bossy. But I think I can handle it.'

'I'll book somewhere, shall I?'

'No,' he said, 'I'll bloody book. I do know how to. Bye, Linda.'

'Bye, Alex.'

He started the car and drove home quite fast, smiling at the prospect of the weekend and of her. She might be – well, she *was* difficult. But she made him feel as if he mattered. It was a very good sensation.

The note lay on the hall table when Barney got in.

Sorry, darling, tried to ring you, but your phone was switched off. Left a message, but in case you didn't get it, I've gone to see that Keira Knightley film with Nicola. Hope that's OK, knew you'd hate it. Lots of salady stuff in fridge, back about 10. Love you.

Oh God, Barney thought. Oh shit. Well, it bought him some time. He sat down at the kitchen table, pulled out his phone, rang Toby.

'Tobes. It's me, Barney.'

'Hi, Barney. What's up?'

'I'm really sorry, Toby, but Tamara's been on to me. About why we left for the wedding so late. Again.'

'Oh – OK.' Toby sounded remarkably calm, under the circumstances.

'Yeah. So she's going to ask you – again. And I presume you're not going to tell her the truth. So you may have to think of something a bit better than I could manage.'

'Which was?'

'Well, that you were ill. Kept throwing up. I mean, it is sort of true.'

'Only sort of?'

'For Christ's sake, Toby, this isn't a game, it's extremely serious. Tamara's really upset about it. She doesn't believe that story. She's been on about it ever since – well, since it happened.'

There was a silence, then Toby said, 'Right. Well, it looks like I'll have to think of something else, then.'

Maybe he should do it tonight. He wasn't going to be held to ransom by that cow. Wasn't going to hide and be scared and carry on lying. And it wasn't fair on Amanda, the lying. The cheating wasn't fair either, but it was the lying that was so awful. Pretending all the time, smiling at her when he didn't feel like smiling, saying he loved her when she'd said she loved him, because that was the only thing to say.

Returning her kisses, pretending he was too tired for sex; it was all horrible. When she knew, she'd hate that, hate thinking that was what he'd been doing.

But – it was very soon. Being sure enough about Emma after a few weeks: when it had been a few years with Amanda. Well, three years. How much of it was novelty, excitement, the fact it was illicit? How could he know?

He did know though; he had never felt for Amanda what he felt for Emma. Barney was not a poetic soul, he wasn't given to introspection, but – well, meeting Emma had been like a light going on, a brilliant white light. Simple as that.

Yes, he would, he'd tell Amanda tonight. Get it over.

It would be hideous, but if she knew, it was what she'd want.

He poured himself a beer, sat there thinking about her, about Amanda, his Amanda, whom he had once thought he loved. Amanda who was happy, trustful, sure of herself and her future, and was about to be rendered, at his hands, wretched, frightened, lost. How she would hate him, how everyone would hate him . . .

But – it had to be done. The sooner the—

The landline rang sharply, cutting into his thoughts. Who could that be? Who used the landline any more? Except grown-ups, except parents of course . . .

He picked it up.

* * *

Amanda arrived home two hours later. He heard the taxi door slam, heard her pretty light voice saying, 'Thank you so much, goodnight, enjoy the birthday party.'

She was like that with everyone, friendly and chatty and interested. It was a joke among their friends that Amanda would have had a lovely chat with Osama Bin Laden, would have said, 'Oh, he's so sweet, so charming, and he's got this dear little boy . . .'

He sat there thinking of what he must tell her, feeling like an executioner, waiting to do his dreadful deed.

She came in smiling, kissed him, said, 'Hello, darling, it was such a lovely film, I really think you might have liked it . . . Barney, what is it? What's the matter?'

And, 'I'm sorry, Amanda,' he said, 'so, so sorry. I've been trying to get hold of you for the past hour. Look, come on, sit down . . .'

'I'm all right, I don't need to sit down. What is it, please tell me.'

'It's – it's bad news, I'm afraid,' he said, staring at her, hating that he had to tell her.

'Barney, what? Please tell me, quickly.'

'Your mother called,' he said. 'It's your father, Amanda, he's . . . Oh God, I'm so sorry. He's had a heart attack, he's – well, he's dead.'

And then he stood there, holding her as she sobbed and shook with grief, and thought how cruel, how doubly cruel was fate, mostly to her, of course, robbing her of her beloved father, but also in a small part to him, robbing him for the foreseeable future of the chance to set his life straight and to do the right thing and be with the person he really loved.

And hating himself for finding room even to think it.

Chapter 39

'How about *Woodentops*?' Rowe's round face was flushed with excitement.

'I'm sorry?'

'*Woodentops*. For the name on the van?'

'I thought that was some children's programme.'

'It is. But it's also the name of a small builders outfit: just like I said, fences, cupboards. That's the whole point of trademarks, play on words. I think it's worth a try.'

'Where are they based?'

'Reading area. So it would be feasible he was on the road that afternoon. Very feasible.'

'Hmm,' said Freeman. 'Well, it might be worth checking him out, I suppose. Long shot, though. Very long shot.'

'Toby.'

'Yes, Tamara?'

'I want to talk to you about something.'

She was sitting in one of the deep armchairs by the fire in his parents' drawing room; she'd been in a funny mood ever since she'd arrived, extremely late – too late to join the family for supper. His parents had tactfully gone upstairs and he half-wished they hadn't. He'd hoped for an early night; he obviously wasn't going to get one.

'Darling, if it's the date, next May's fine by me.'

'Good. But it's not.'

'Not what?' Toby's leg was still painful and he was tired and easily irritated. He could hear it in his own voice.

'Not the date,' said Tamara impatiently. 'It's about the wedding – the one that didn't happen.'

'Ye-es?'

'Toby, I really want – no, I really need – to know. Why did you leave so late? I'm still no wiser. You've waffled away, all that stuff about you being ill and the police stopping you and then the crash. The fact remains, you should have left literally hours earlier. Why didn't you?'

'Well – Tamara, do we really have to do this?'

'Yes, we really do.'

'I can't see what good it would do. Now.'

'It would do me good, Toby. Because however much I try to believe all that stuff about your being ill, I somehow can't. And if you weren't ill and you didn't leave in time, there was clearly some other very good reason. What was it, Toby? I really have to know.'

Toby looked at her, took a large sip of the wine he was drinking and sat up very straight in his chair.

'Yes, well, I suppose I'd better tell you. I've been keeping it to myself, hoping it wouldn't have to come out.'

'What wouldn't have to come out?'

'It was – well, it was Barney, Tamara. I'm afraid.'

'Barney! How, why?'

'He – well, he got terribly drunk the night before the wedding. I tried to stop him, but he kept saying it was my last night of freedom and we should enjoy it. He must have drunk the best part of two bottles of wine and at least half a bottle of whisky. Honestly, he could hardly walk. I got him to bed somehow. And then in the morning – well, you can imagine the state he was in. Kept throwing up, completely unfit to drive, of course – I just had to sit it out. And, adding insult to injury, if you like, he'd forgotten to fill the car up with petrol. Which was why we came on the motorway – nearest petrol station. I could have killed him, if he hadn't been my best friend. So, there you have it. I'm sorry, darling, really I am. But – non mea culpa.'

'And why the fuck didn't you tell me before? Instead of fobbing me off with this stomach bug nonsense?'

'Oh Tamara, how could I? He's my best buddy. He's been fantastic. Sitting with me all that day when I had my leg done, visiting me endlessly, listening to me moaning. We go back years and years. I couldn't rat on him, could I?'

'Quite easily, I'd have thought, to make me feel better about the whole thing. Who's more important to you, Toby, Barney or me? Seems like it's Barney.'

'Darling, of course it's not. Don't be ridiculous. I mean, what good would it have done, splitting on him? And don't, please I beg of you, don't tell him I told you. He'd be so horrified. He feels quite bad enough as it is. Let's just put it behind us, eh? We've got another one coming up now, let's just look forward to that. And at least I won't be trundling down the aisle in a wheelchair. Or on crutches – surely that's what matters? Next May, you'll be Mrs Toby Weston and this whole thing'll be like a bad dream.'

Tamara sighed. 'I – I suppose so. I still find it pretty hard to cope with. It's not exactly reassuring. I mean, you could have come on your own. Left Barney behind.'

'Darling, he was my best man. Who was going to do that for me, eh?'

'One of the ushers could have stood in. Perfectly well. And he'd have got there somehow. Eventually. Although he might have got hurt in the crash himself. Serve him right if he had. If he'd lost his leg. God . . .'

She was close to tears; Toby reached out, took her hand.

'Try not to be so upset. I'm so, so sorry but it really is all over. Let's look forward, shall we, not back?'

'I don't think it is all over, actually,' said Tamara. 'Not quite.'

'What do you mean by that?'

'Oh, doesn't matter.' She managed to smile at him. 'Could I have a glass of that wine, Tobes? I feel as if I need it.'

'Now, Maeve, please don't laugh but I would be very honoured if you would be my bridesmaid.'

Mary's face was rather pink as she looked at Maeve across the table in the café: the same café that had provided so fateful a meeting-place two months earlier. She had come in to see Patrick, alerted of the wonderful news of his recovery by Maeve.

'It's like a miracle, Mary! Every day there is a little more sensation. He can feel almost the whole of one foot now, and the toes of the other. I can't believe it, and he is so happy – although being a man, of course, we have new complaints now, that the foot itches and the toes cramp up.'

'Yes, well, that's entirely to be expected,' said Mary. 'They're all the same. Donald with a cold, it was pneumonia every time, and his indigestion an ulcer, of course. And Russell is worse. His stiff neck is due to spinal damage, he's convinced, and the fuss over the very little bit of arthritis he has! He is all for rushing me off to see what he calls his heart specialist when we get to New York, convinced we can't possibly know what we're doing here. I've told him I want to enjoy America, not spend the time with doctors. Anyway, it's such wonderful news about Patrick, and I'm simply delighted for you. You deserve it.'

'Well, I don't know about that. I keep popping into the church, lighting another candle, saying Hail Marys for all I'm worth. Anyway, he'll be coming home in a week or so now. And – oh Mary, I'd love to be your bridesmaid, it would be the greatest honour, but what about your daughter? Isn't that her place?'

Mary went even pinker. 'I'm afraid Christine will want to play a very minor role,' she said, 'if she comes at all.'

'What? What are you saying?'

'I'm saying she's still very upset about it, seems to think I'm betraying her father's memory. It's so sad, Maeve, I'm finding it very hard to cope with. I thought she'd be pleased for me, not cast a shadow over the whole thing. There's nothing I can say that will make things better. In fact, everything I do try just makes her worse. My son seems delighted, they're all coming over from Canada for the wedding, and my son-in-law Gerry, he's very happy about it, and my grandson Timothy too. He wants to give me away, in fact. I was very touched by that.'

'Well, most of them are behaving as they should,' said Maeve, 'and that's wonderful. Very well, but if Christine changes her mind, you must tell me at once, and I'll resign the office. Now, what are you going to wear – will it be white?'

'Well – it will. Do you think that's terribly foolish?'

'Of course it's not foolish, it's delightful. You'll look beautiful.'

'I don't know about that,' said Mary, laughing. 'Anyway, I got a dress from a boutique in Bath. It's a two-piece, quite a straight skirt and a beaded jacket. It's a bit hard to describe, but it's very pretty. And then I have some quite high-heeled shoes, I hope I won't fall over, and I'm going to carry just a very small bunch of flowers. I thought white roses, what do you think?'

'I'd say pink would be better,' said Maeve thoughtfully. 'White will hardly show up against your dress. And what in your hair?'

'Oh, a long veil, of course,' said Mary, and they both started to laugh; two women, joyfully engrossed as they went about the centuries-old female business of planning a wedding, and it was of no consequence whatsoever that the bride was three times the age of her bridesmaid, and her bridegroom four times the age of the man who was to give her away.

Emma found herself now in a kind of limbo; suspended not only in time but in emotion. She was afraid to think about Barney, certainly to feel more for him than she could possibly help.

He had called her very late on the Monday evening, with the news of his conversation with Tamara and then of Amanda's father's heart attack.

'I just couldn't tell her, Emma, it was completely impossible. She adores – adored – her dad. I'm taking her down now, to her mother. We're on the M4, we've stopped so she can go to the loo and stuff. We're horribly near you, actually. I just saw a sign to Swindon and the hospital, and it was all I could do not to turn off and come and find you. Take care. I'll speak to you tomorrow probably. Lots of love.'

'Lots of love,' said Emma, and then she had rung off and burst into tears.

Anything might happen now, she thought. Tamara might tell Amanda – although Barney told Emma, in a longer phone call next day, that he didn't think she would.

'I warned her that if she did, I would personally wring her neck. I think she believed me and I think she'll keep her mouth shut. God, she's a cow. God, I dislike her.'

Emma didn't say anything; there seemed no point in slagging off someone she didn't know. Tamara did sound like a cow, but blokes were funny about their best friends' girlfriends. She actually thought that if Toby was really the wonderful person Barney said, then he wouldn't be about to marry someone who was absolutely the reverse. And after all, Amanda was, or was supposed to be, her best friend; Tamara was bound to be angry and upset on her behalf, would feel furious and vindictive towards Barney.

Emma felt very bad about Amanda herself; she had only met her once, but she could still see her standing there in the sunlight, with her perfect peaches and cream skin and her sweet smile; a Sloane she was, and as such a more or less unknown species to Emma. She instinctively mistrusted them – Prince Harry apart – their paths smoothed by money and confidence, over-endowed with life's goodies, with expensive clothes and voices and flats and cars, bought for them by Mummy and Daddy.

Well, if she stayed with Barney— no, Emma, don't go there. All she could do now was wait.

The other thing, the great fear that was consuming her now, was that with Barney being so necessarily close to Amanda, supporting her, comforting her, helping her through the awful days ahead, he might find himself drawn back irrevocably into their relationship. Grief was a powerful force; Amanda would not only be expecting Barney's presence 100 per cent in her life, she had an absolute right to it.

She had taken the coward's way out herself and told Luke she was ill, that she kept throwing up and couldn't come out with him for his last weekend. He had been fairly upset – almost as much, she thought, because of the waste of being on the Bungalow 8 list as not seeing her. She simply couldn't face it. She couldn't face telling him and she couldn't face not telling him; she just wanted to lie down somewhere quiet and dark, for days and days, and not have to speak to anybody. Except Barney, of course. And that wasn't going to happen any time soon.

Chapter 40

'I think I'd be really angry, as well as upset that he just didn't seem to care where she'd gone. That he wasn't more worried . . .'

'Good, Georgia. Much better. So, before we read that scene through again, let's do a bit of improvisation. Maybe you confronted him – your dad – the night before, met him in the kitchen or something – or maybe you'd talk to a friend on the phone about it.'

Georgia felt the awful crawling fear in her stomach that the word 'improvisation' always engendered in her; she looked at all the faces, some of them quite famous, like Davina's, their eyes all fixed on her, and knew she couldn't do it.

Only she had to. You didn't tell Bryn Merrick you couldn't do what he wanted. Maybe it would be easier if she did it as a monologue – on the phone as Bryn had suggested – rather than tried acting something out with Frank Ireland, who had probably the most famous face of them all. Specially as so far she didn't like Frank Ireland; she got the feeling he didn't think she was up to the part. Which she was beginning to think as well . . .

She'd been so excited about this, but it wasn't turning out how she'd imagined it at all. They were sitting in a circle, the whole cast, in a church hall in Acton, just talking endlessly. She knew rehearsals for telly weren't like stage rehearsals, you didn't do read-throughs of whole scenes or even walk-throughs; you spent a lot of time talking about the characters, working scenes out, moving round with other actors, but at least you were following the script. Which she'd been studying so diligently over the past ten days. But Bryn seemed to want to do nothing but talk: talk and initiate improvisations. Davina had already done a brilliant one, where she realised that her mother really was beginning to lose her marbles; you could watch her recognising the terrible years that lay ahead. How could Georgia compete with that? She felt altogether miserable and inadequate.

Arriving there had been horrible. She'd planned to get there really early, so she didn't have to confront everyone at once, but there'd been a hold-up on the Tube from Baker Street and she was actually late. She sat there in the tunnel, trying to stay calm, telling herself that it wasn't her fault, and that there might even be other cast members on the same train, so they'd be late too, but by the time she finally burst into the hall, having run the last half-mile from the Tube station, the rehearsal had actually begun. Everyone was very nice – or nearly everyone – and said the Tube had been hellish that morning, but the fact remained that everyone else had managed to make it on time. Only she, the newcomer, the person so lucky to be with them, had been late.

She felt conspicuous and ill-at-ease as she hadn't for years; it was a bit like getting to a new school, where she was the only new girl and everyone else had a best friend. Or being the only black child at those parties all those years ago. And then, had they been discussing her while they waited, talking about how she'd run away? *Stop it, Georgia, pull yourself together. This isn't doing you any good at all* . . .

'Georgia, dear, come along, we haven't got all day.' Bryn smiled but there was an impatience in his eyes; Georgia felt worse.

'Well . . .'

'Come on, darling.' It was Davina, smiling at her, her huge, almost black eyes soft with sympathy. 'Let's us do one. Sorry about hogging all the limelight, everyone. Now, Rose, it's the night before and I'm asking you how you think your gran is. And you . . .'

'I'm well pissed off – I mean annoyed,' said Georgia, and everyone laughed.

'Sweetie, Rose would have said pissed off,' said Davina. 'That's the whole point of all this. You're her, not Georgia. So – Rose, what's the matter, love? Why are you so cross?'

'It's Gran,' said Georgia slowly. 'She – she – just washed all my socks with her sheets, on a hot wash . . .' Suddenly it was easier, she was flying . . . 'and they're, like, ruined and – Mum, what are we going to do with her? I heard you telling her not to put the machine on, she just ignores you.'

'She can't help it, Rose. I've told you that. Don't get too cross with her. She's so fond of you. More than anyone, probably.'

'I know and I'm well fond of her. Lot more than Ron is.'

'Let's not get into that. Ron does his best for her.'

'No, he doesn't. He's horrible to her. You don't know, you don't see it—'

'Rose—'

'Right, that was fine as far as it went,' said Bryn, interrupting. 'Good. I think we're getting somewhere. Right. Now let's move on to Ron for a bit. Frank, how are you feeling about Ron?'

'I feel I'm getting him,' said Frank, 'but he's a bit two-dimensional. I'm looking to expand him a bit, find some contradictions. The scene with his son and the baby, for instance: I'm wondering if he couldn't be really – really soft with the baby, want to hold it, that sort of thing.'

'Very good,' said Bryn.

* * *

By the end of the day Georgia was exhausted and depressed. She knew she hadn't acquitted herself very well, she could see that Bryn Merrick was getting impatient with her: and that made her nervous and less competent. It was a vicious circle. Maybe Linda would have some ideas; she could talk to her that night. She was staying with her.

'But only for a couple of days, Georgia. I thought you'd have got accommodation sorted out by now.'

She started to put on her coat, listening miserably to the others all laughing loudly in the next room – probably about her. Saying how hopeless she'd been, picking out scenes where she'd done specially badly . . .

Merlin walked in. He'd been out most of the day, thank God. At least he hadn't seen her humiliation, how bad she'd been.

'You look a bit down. Anything wrong?'

'Only a bit of disastrous miscasting,' said Georgia, managing to smile, to show him she wasn't entirely serious.

'Oh really? Who?'

'Me.'

'Don't be ridiculous,' he said, and she could see he was genuinely surprised. 'You're going to be fine. Look, I've just got to have a very quick word with Bryn, be about two minutes, and then do you want to come for a drink?'

Did she want to? Oh, no. Like she wouldn't want to win the lottery? Or get cast opposite George Clooney? Or . . .

'That'd be nice,' she said.

Only the two minutes lengthened to ten and she was still waiting; and then he appeared suddenly, saying, 'Sorry, sweetheart, got to stay and talk sequences. See you tomorrow,' and disappeared again.

'Yeah, cool.' Well, at least he'd called her sweetheart. Not that it meant anything. He probably called the cleaner's cat sweetheart. Time to go home to Linda. 'The lovely Linda' as Merlin called her. Well she was lovely.

Linda wasn't feeling particularly lovely; certainly not towards Georgia. In fact, she was seriously regretting her offer to take her in even for a few days. And she knew Georgia's few days. She really should have got herself sorted, she'd had weeks, for God's sake. The last thing she wanted at the moment was someone else in her flat. Especially not a young person; and even more especially, not a demanding young person.

She needed time and space and privacy to think. She had been feeling great until she'd done it, been so extremely stupid; sleek and relaxed and loved up. She and Alex seemed to be doing rather well. They'd had a fantastic night on Saturday: he'd taken her to the Poule au Pot in Pimlico. She was surprised at his choice; it seemed a bit feminine for him, but he'd always liked it there, he said. He'd been taken there a few times when he was young – she didn't ask who by, in case it had been his wife – and he did like proper French food.

'Most of all I like those set menus you get in small provincial towns – you know, with a paper tablecloth, cassoulets, things like that and quite rough red wine, but there aren't so many of those these days. But this is pretty good. I like the way the menu isn't translated too.'

'I do too. That's so French, isn't it, so charmingly arrogant.'

They talked and talked; he was more relaxed, less defensive, quite funny. They had a couple of arguments, but about abstract things, politics – he was quite fiercely socialist, she was – well, the reverse – architecture – he hated modern stuff, she loved it – but generally they chatted and told each other funny stories about their respective weeks, and then they went back to her flat, quite early and to bed.

The sex was – well, it was stupendous. He enjoyed it so much. He had a way of almost whooping with delight when he came, and then hurling himself off her and saying, 'That was glorious,' or, 'That was superb.' If he was that appreciative of his wife, Linda thought, then she must be a miserable ungrateful cow. He was careful too and considerate with her, especially the first few times, asking her almost anxiously if it had been all right, if she'd had a good time.

'I'm having a wonderful time,' she said, happily snaking herself round him. 'I want it to go on all night and all day tomorrow.'

'I'll do my best,' he said.

They were tired in the morning, happily, wonderfully tired. Linda brought breakfast to bed, and they sat there eating bagels and drinking orange juice and gorgeously strong coffee – 'I like my coffee strong and my men stronger,' she said, misquoting the old joke – and read the papers. She took the *Telegraph* and the *Mail* – 'How can you read that fascist rubbish?' he said, and she said it wasn't fascist or rubbish, it was brilliantly pitched journalism.

He said he'd have to go out and get the *Observer*; she put her hand out and grabbed his.

'You leave this bed now, Alex Pritchard, and you don't come back into it for a long time. I'm enjoying this so, so much, you have no idea. Shall we move on and make the orange juice into Bucks Fizz?'

'Why not?'

She fetched the champagne, handed it to him to open.

'Veuve Clicquot,' he said. 'Bit extravagant for breakfast.'

'Not really. I get sent quite a lot by clients.'

'Lot of perks in your job,' he said.

'A few. D'you get any?'

'Only ones I'm not prepared to accept.'

'What do you mean? Like what?'

'Well, beanos organised by the pharmaceutical companies for the most part. Totally immoral – I wouldn't dream of accepting.'

'Give me a for instance.'

'Well, for instance, this week, something came in, absolutely appalling, trip to South Africa all expenses paid. Four days in Cape Town and then an internal flight to wherever we fancy. Partners invited, all very lush, Club-Class flights, that sort of thing.'

'My God, that does sound absolutely appalling. Alex, what is the matter with you? How on earth can you turn down something like that? Why?'

'Because it's immoral, that's why.'

'In what way?'

'It's obvious, I'd have thought. Thinly disguised bribes.'

'Well, how do they work? What would the conference consist of?'

'Oh – this one, several papers presented by surgeons and physicians on new Intensive and Emergency Care techniques, use of new advances in technology, laser and micro-surgery, that sort of thing. Followed by various leisure activities, five-course dinners—'

'Would there be no value in hearing about the new techniques and treatments? None whatsoever?'

'I could read about them later perfectly well.'

'So why not enjoy the dinners and the leisure activities and get to hear about them sooner? What about meeting the other surgeons? Not remotely useful to you?'

'I wouldn't really want to. Arrogant people, surgeons,' he said, and grinned at her.

She put her coffee down, lay back on the pillows, studied him. He was wonderfully dissolute-looking in the mornings, with his wild black hair and a thick dark shadow of beard.

'You're mad,' she said. 'Completely mad. Why not go, why not enjoy yourself!'

'It's against my principles,' he said.

'Oh please! Do you really think your not going does any good? Do you think they'll cancel it? Someone will go in

582

your place and have a great time, and you'll be stuck in Swindon sulking.'

'I will not be sulking.'

'Sorry! Don't get touchy. I just meant, you don't gain anything for anyone by not going. It's against my principles licking the arses of sleazy directors, but if I didn't, I'd get fewer chances for my actors. They'll still get their arses licked, they're not going to say "Oh please don't" to all the others, just because I've stopped. Besides, South Africa, for instance – poor country, struggling against a difficult economy, tourist trade very important to them. Did you not think of that?'

'That's crap,' he said. 'The tourist trade only exploits the poor anyway.'

'Rubbish. It helps the economy. God, I'd give anything to go on a trip like that. I need a break. When is it?'

'Oh, I don't know. Early spring, I think. I didn't finish reading the letter, I just threw it away.'

'Oh God, Alex . . .'

'Yes?' His voice was irritable. Linda took a deep breath. What, after all, did she have to lose?

'Alex, you go on the trip. Say yes and—'

'No.'

'Don't interrupt. And I'll come with you.'

'What!'

'You heard. It sounds utterly wonderful: we could have just the best time – I've always wanted to go to South Africa. Don't look like that, just think about it. I'll act the perfect spouse. I can, you know; you'd be surprised.'

'I'm sure you could act anything,' he said. He sounded sulky.

'Wouldn't you like to go? With me?'

'I'd love to go to South Africa with you,' he said, 'but not by being beholden to someone I don't approve of.'

'Right. Well, let's go anyway.'

'Linda, I can't possibly afford to take you to South Africa.'

'That's what I thought. So you turn the whole wonderful thing down. You're mad. Go on, Alex, accept. I dare you.'

He hadn't liked that; he'd become withdrawn, had got up, showered, dressed, said he had to get back, that Adam had a football match in the afternoon. She'd lain watching him, feeling slightly panicked. She hadn't expected this. She'd thought the worst thing would be he'd get cross with her, tell her to shut up.

He left, kissing her rather briefly, said he'd ring. So far he hadn't. It was Monday afternoon now, and the phone sat on its hook, silent. Well, not silent, it hadn't bloody stopped all day – mostly directors who wanted their arses licked. No brooding angry surgeons at all. Not one.

You're a complete idiot, Linda Di-Marcello. Complete. Brilliant, brilliant love affair, and you decide to wreck it really efficiently. Well done. Very, very well done . . .

'Woodentops.' The voice was perky. It sounded more suited to the children's TV programme indeed than a firm of carpenters.

'Good morning. This is the Collision Investigation Unit of the Swindon Valley Police.'

'Oh yes.' Slightly less perky.

'We're looking to contact the driver of one of your vans.'

'We have several, I'd need more details, please. Driver's name, number of vehicle . . .'

'Well, I don't have either, I'm afraid. But one of your vans was seen driving up the M4 on the afternoon of the twenty-second of August towards London. Is that any help to you?'

'Let me see . . . it's a while ago now.'

There was a silence; Freeman could hear computer keys clicking in the background. Then: 'That would probably be

Mr Harwood. I'm not sure, you'd need to speak to him. As I said, we do have several vans and—'

'Is Mr Harwood there?'

'No, but I can contact him for you.'

'Perhaps you'd ask him to give me a call. Just a routine enquiry, tell him. The number is . . .'

'Rick, you been speeding again? Naughty boy. Had the police on about you. You'd better not lose your licence – you'll be out of a job if you do. Now it was you, wasn't it, on the M4, afternoon of August the twenty-second? Yeah, I thought so.'

Shit. How had they traced him? Not that it mattered, he hadn't done anything wrong, nothing to worry about. He'd been miles ahead of that accident, anyway. Probably thought he could just provide some information. Bloody police, always harassing the poor bloody motorist.

By the time he phoned them, Rick Harwood had worked himself up into a state of extremely righteous indignation.

'Is that The Emma?'

God. She'd forgotten how lovely it was just to hear his voice.

'Hi, Barney. The Barney. Yes, it is. How – how are things?'

'Bit tough. Yes. How are you?'

'I'm fine. Yes, really fine. Missing you but—'

'Missing you too. So much. It was the funeral today. That was grim.'

'I can imagine.'

'Amanda was incredibly upset.'

'Of course.'

'But being terribly brave, wonderful with her mum.'

She wasn't sure she wanted to hear all this.

'We're staying down here tonight –' she didn't like that

'we'; it conjured up images she could hardly bear – 'and then I'm going back in the morning.'

'Right.'

'Amanda's probably coming up in a day or two. She's had a lot of time off work already.'

'Yes, I'm sure.'

'Emma – I don't – that is, I can't – not until—'

'Barney, it's OK. You don't even have to say it. Just take your time. I understand.'

'I love you, Emma.'

'I—' but she couldn't even finish. She choked on the words. And rang off without saying goodbye.

The second day of rehearsals, things were better. Georgia arrived early – early enough for coffee alone with Merlin – and she began to feel more comfortable with everyone. Davina told her she was doing great, and Anna was there, rehearsing a scene with Georgia and the grandmother. Anna was wonderful to work with, easy, encouraging – and managed to give her character a humour that lifted her scenes beautifully and to which Georgia found herself responding. Best of all, at the end of the day, Merlin said, 'I could have that drink this evening, if you've got time.'

Georgia was able to find the time.

They went to a pub down the street. Even walking into it with him was amazing; she felt everyone must be looking at them and thinking how good looking he was, and what a cool couple they made. As they were in a real old-style Acton pub, mostly filled with old chaps reading their papers, she had to admit this was not terribly likely. Merlin had half a pint of bitter and she had a spritzer, and they settled down in a corner.

'So – things better today?'

'Much better, thank you.'

'Anna is great, isn't she?'

'So cool.'

'She has a fascinating history. Ask her to tell you sometime.'

'Oh, OK. So,' this seemed a good opening, 'so what about you, Merlin? Have you worked on loads of productions?'

'Not that many. Incredibly lucky to be in this one. Bryn is the greatest, you learn such a lot from someone like him.'

'And – did you go to drama school?'

'Yeah, I went to LAMDA, did their two-year stage management course. Haven't been working that long, I'm still only twenty-six, and the money's rubbish, of course, but who cares?'

'Course,' said Georgia, thinking that most twenty-six-year-old people would care a bit about rubbish money. But obviously, Merlin had rich parents.

'Of course, I have to live at home still, but I'm pretty well self-contained, and they don't bother me much.'

'So where is home?' asked Georgia, hoping it wasn't too personal a question, but encouraged that at least he didn't seem to have a live-in girlfriend.

'Oh, Hampstead. Up by the Heath. Know it up there?'
She shook her head.

'Pretty nice. Sometimes, early in the morning, you can believe it's actually the country. Birds carrying on and all that sort of thing. Mummy swims in the Ponds every day.'

'Really?' said Georgia, hoping she sounded as if she knew what the Ponds were.

'Yes. With some of her chums. They're all mad really. She's cool though. We get on pretty well.'

'And your dad? Does he swim too?'

'Oh, not Pa, no. He's a bit of a wimp. Although he does cycle into the college in the summer. If it's not raining, that is.'

'The college?'

'Yeah. He's a lecturer at LSE. In political history.'

587

'Goodness. He must be very clever.'

'He is. God, Georgia, it's been such fun, but I must go. Got to get up to Kensington. I'm going on the Tube, how about you?'

'Oh yes, me too. To Baker Street.'

'Let's go together then.'

He must like her a bit, to want to travel on the Tube with her. Just a bit.

He wasn't in the next day, but she got chatting to Mo and by carefully casual questioning, found out a bit more about Merlin.

'He's a sweetheart,' Mo said, 'and looking like that – God. He ought to be a real brat, but he isn't. Well, not much of one.'

'It sounds as if his parents are quite – rich,' said Georgia.

'Well, quite. But they're incredibly socialist as well. Both fully paid-up members of the Labour Party. Mama runs this second-hand bookshop in Hampstead, and sells loads of political books and does fundraising and stuff. Although they still keep threatening to leave because Tony Blair was such a Tory.'

'Oh, I see.' This was familiar territory for Georgia; both her parents were socialists and had gone on the peace march and then almost resigned from the Party over the Iraq War. 'But Merlin sounds very – well, very posh. I thought he must have gone to Eton or somewhere.'

'God no. Holland Park Comp. Where of course he was bullied terribly, actually beaten up several times; a group of really rough kids decided he was gay, but his parents didn't care. Their principles were much more important. Poor old Merlin. Anyway, he's all right now. Everyone loves him.'

'He's not though, is he?' said Georgia, trying not to sound anxious.

'Not what? Oh, gay, No, of course not. Very red-blooded indeed, our Merlin.'

'He's been so, so nice to me,' Georgia said.

'Yes, well, he is really . . . nice. But—' Mo looked at her and Georgia thought she was about to say something, but then Frank Ireland arrived looking petulant and demanded freshly ground coffee. And then Davina wanted to run through a scene with Georgia and whatever it was was never said.

Wednesday night. Still nothing. This was getting serious, Linda thought. How could she have done that, been so stupid? Thrown up a chance of happiness, of togetherness, possibly – just possibly – love, for the sake of a cheap jibe about principles? Well. She'd got her come-uppance in a big way. Closeness, fun, warmth and great sex: all gone. Just like that. And she deserved it.

The landline rang suddenly – Georgia, no doubt, saying she'd had another terrible day, or she'd had another wonderful day. God, she was tiresome . . . The thought of a whole evening with her seemed unendurable. She must turf her out soon.

She picked it up, reluctantly. 'Georgia?'

But: 'No, it's not Georgia. It's Alex. I hope that's not a disappointment.'

Oh, God. Oh, God. He'd rung to – finish everything. That would be like him. He was inclined to formality, to making sure everything was neatly settled and quite clear. He wouldn't leave things in the air. And anyway, he'd want her to understand exactly why he was finishing it. For some reason she stood up. It seemed appropriate to the occasion.

'No,' she said, grateful that her voice at least sounded steady. 'No, of course it's not a disappointment. Hello, Alex.'

'Hello, Linda. How are you?'

'Oh – fine. Yes. Thank you. How about you?' She couldn't let him know how anxious she was; or how upset. She must go down with her reputation intact. Her cool, self-assured reputation. She couldn't have him feeling sorry for her; on top of everything else . . .

'Not bad. Look . . .' Here it came. He was going to say it now. She closed her eyes, she wasn't sure why. She would have closed her ears, if she could. 'Look, Linda . . .'

'Yes, Alex?'

He was obviously finding it a little bit difficult to say. Maybe she should make it easy for him, say she thought it was best they should part. At least that way she'd retain her dignity.

'Look, this is a bit difficult but—'

'Alex, perhaps I should—'

And then suddenly it happened; his voice lightened, warmed, she could even hear the smile in it. 'I've – well, I've had this invitation, to a medical conference in South Africa. I think I might have mentioned it.'

'Possibly. I'm not quite sure.'

'Well, the thing is, I wondered if you'd like to come with me. As my guest. I might need a bit of support. And I warn you, the "spousal programme" as it's called could be quite tedious. But it would be so – so nice if you were there.'

And then, as she sat down abruptly, unable to speak, he added, 'Go on, Linda. I dare you.'

'Oh Alex,' she said, unable to help herself. 'Oh Alex, I'd absolutely love to. Thank you so, so much.'

And then she heard herself saying – and that really was a bit unbelievable, because she hardly ever did say it to anyone. 'And I'm sorry, Alex. For what I said. Really sorry.'

'You little shit, Barney.'

'What? Who is this?'

'It's Tamara – who do you think it is! The person whose wedding you ruined. I knew it was your fault – I just knew it. Fuck you, Barney, just fuck you.'

Part Five
Afterwards

Chapter 41

William was walking out of a pub in Bristol, quite early in the evening, when he saw Abi. He'd avoided the place as much as he could recently; in fact, he'd found even driving into the city painful, but an old friend from Cirencester days who farmed near Bath had asked him to be best man at his wedding and had invited him and his ushers to discuss the demands and requirements of their roles.

He tried very hard to get into the spirit of the thing, downed a couple of beers and laughed at some pretty unfunny jokes about weddings and the role of the best man, and agreed that the Hunt Ball of the previous week had been terrific, although actually he'd reached a peak of misery there. Gyrating to the pounding rhythms of The Whippersnappers, some outfit that the MFH had discovered, smiling inanely at Fiona Rutherford (with whom he'd had a few entanglements before and whose mother had high hopes of him), he'd looked round at all the other gyrators, some young, some older, but with the identical DNA of the foxhunting classes, cheerful, foolhardy, blinkered folk, clinging to their beleaguered lifestyle: and wondered how he was going to live among them for the rest of his life.

Abi was walking along, laden with bags; Christmas shopping, he supposed. She was wearing black as always; he sometimes wondered if she knew about any other colours. Black leather coat, knee-length black boots, black furry hat. And dark glasses. In the dark. Why did she do that? She saw him, briefly pretended she hadn't, then half-smiled, and said, 'Hello.'

'Hello, Abi.'

'How are you?'

'I'm fine. You?'

'Oh – yes. Fine, thanks.'

He felt awful; wondering if he was going to throw up or pass out. *Get a grip, Grainger. She's history. Just walk on. Say cheers and walk on. It's the only thing to do.*

'Been Christmas shopping?'

'Yeah. God, it's awful out there. Pandemonium.'

OK. That really will do. But –

'Where's your car?'

'Oh – just along there, in the car park. What are you doing here? I'm sure you're not Christmas shopping.'

Just say no and go. Now. Fast.

'No. I've been having a drink with some mates.'

'William! So far from home.' She was smiling now, pulled her glasses off.

'Yeah, well, mate of mine's getting married, he's asked me to be best man. We were just getting together, with the ushers.'

'Really? When's the wedding?'

'In the spring. April time.'

'Lambing time.'

'No, not for us. We do early lambing.'

'Oh, of course you do. In the lambing shed.' She looked at him and smiled. 'See how much I've remembered? Well, I guess I wouldn't have forgotten that.'

Oh God, God, she shouldn't have said that. It had been all right till then, he'd been fine, totally fine, about to move on, say cheers. But the lambing shed . . .

'My car's down there too,' he said. 'Let me help you with your bags.'

'Oh, OK. Thanks.'

There was no tension, no uneasy silence as they walked,

he was amazed; she asked him how he was, what he'd been doing, what was the main activity on the farm in the winter. He'd forgotten how interested she was in everything; and how much he enjoyed the interest. She behaved as if they were old friends, as if nothing of any note, and certainly of any distressing note, had ever happened between them. It was extraordinary; and extraordinarily pleasing.

Her car was on the ground floor; he realised that he'd been hoping it would be a longer trip, that they'd have to go up in the lift, that the encounter might continue as long as possible. Because of course it would be the last – a final tease on the part of fate. It would never happen again, chance would not be working on their behalf a second time; she would be lost to him, he'd be in a future without her. And of course that was a good thing; there could be no other outcome. But it was good that his last memory of her now would be a happier one . . .

She opened the boot. 'Thanks, William. That's really kind of you.'

He put the bags in; she shut the boot, turned to look at him, her dark eyes friendly. He caught the strong heady scent he remembered; he felt a bit dizzy.

'It was so nice to see you,' she said. 'I've often thought how good it would be. Just to – well, to say goodbye more happily. But it didn't seem very likely. I mean, those sorts of things only happen in films, don't they? And books. What are the chances of William Grainger, farmer, and Abi Scott, photographer's assistant, actually bumping into one another by accident? One in millions. Billions, probably.'

'Yes,' he said. 'But we did.'

'I know. Defied the odds. How lucky was that?' She leaned up, gave him a kiss on the cheek. 'Bye, William. Once again, I'm so sorry.'

'What for?' he said, and in that moment he genuinely couldn't think why she should be apologising.

'You know, I'm afraid. Me being me. Right then.' She

turned, walked to the door, opened it. 'Take care. Oh, and Happy Christmas.'

She got in, slammed the door, started the engine. William stood there, mute, helpless, unable to do or say anything. She was there, not in his memory, not in his imagination, but for real. Funny and fun and sexy and interested. Interesting and absolutely on his side. That was the most special thing about her. Only – well, he supposed she hadn't been. Not really. And now she was going – again. Leaving him to his new – or rather old – life, blank, monotone, no sexy texts as he sat on the tractor, nothing to look forward to as he spread slurry in the cold, or fixed one of the interminable broken fences, or even worse, did the hated paperwork.

She put the car into gear, wound down the window, blew him another kiss. 'Bye,' she said again. And still he couldn't speak.

There was a slightly confused expression on her face now; she clearly couldn't make any sense of him, of how he was behaving. Probably thought he just wanted to be rid of her, that he couldn't think of anything to say that wouldn't be offensive. Shit. Shit.

She moved forward; he jumped out of the way, managed to smile. The car accelerated slowly off. She was going, leaving him again, and that had to be right, had to be the only thing. He should just be glad, as she had said, that they could say goodbye more happily. There was absolutely no alternative. None whatsoever.

Barney couldn't believe how much it hurt, losing Toby. Sometimes he thought it was even worse than losing Emma. At least he could have gone and talked about Emma to Toby, the one person in the world – he had thought – he could trust, talk to about anything. God, he'd even told him about that girl he'd met on holiday in Rhodes, the one he'd got incredibly keen on, had told her he was in love with her, practically proposed, and then when they got home she texted him and told him she was married. You couldn't admit to being that foolish to many people. And when Barney got into trouble with his money at Uni, ended up with a massive overdraft and was unable to get any money out of the cashpoint or indeed anywhere at all, he'd lent him five hundred quid – Toby was rather annoyingly good with his money – and hadn't asked him to pay it back until Barney was actually working.

And— Barney shut his mind to any more 'ands': it hurt too much. It was like discovering the Rolex Oyster you'd been given for your twenty-first by your parents was a cheap fake; or the incredibly over-priced flat you'd bought had a dodgy lease. Toby, his best friend all those years, whom he'd have trusted with his life, for whom he'd have done anything, had turned out to be a cheap fake himself. He still couldn't quite believe it. Or, worse, that he'd been so stupid and that Toby had pulled the wool over his eyes for so long. That hurt too: horribly. He also felt incredibly angry quite a lot of the time: angry with Toby, angry with himself, angry with Tamara.

He knew he'd never forget as long as he lived that night she came round and ranted and railed at him; he'd thought she was mad at first, that she'd finally had a nervous breakdown, because of her cancelled wedding.

He'd been quite nice to her, made her sit down, gave her a drink, told her to get a grip and that there must have been some mistake; but then as she calmed down and he managed to get her to tell him just exactly what it was he was supposed to have done, and as the hideous realisation dawned, he felt so terrible he thought he was actually going to be sick.

'Well?' she said, when she had finished. 'What have you got to say, Barney? Did you really think you could get away with it, all that crap?'

There had seemed no point at that moment in telling her

it was Toby who was giving her the crap, Toby who was lying; it was Toby who must be confronted. Barney simply said he was very sorry she was so upset, that there was obviously a terrible misunderstanding and he would do his very best to sort it out. She had left, after hurling a few more insults at him; she was so clearly genuinely upset that Barney had actually felt quite sorry for her.

Toby had lied, of course. Barney had arrived at the house the following evening, had gone straight down from work, told the Westons he was going to take their son out for a drink and then parked a mile down the road and confronted him.

'Mate, she's crazy. She's still so upset, she just won't calm down about it. She must have misunderstood what I said to her.'

'No,' said Barney, 'she didn't misunderstand. She was very, very clear about what you told her. In fact, she repeated it almost word for word. I'd repeat it back to you, if you like, only I don't think I could face hearing any more lies. I don't know why you did it, Toby. I'm baffled.'

'I don't understand myself,' said Toby, and his voice was rather quiet suddenly. It was as if he was putting his hands up. 'I've just had so much to cope with, with the accident and the leg and so on, and it was just easier to tell her that. Calm her down. I'm sorry. I still feel pretty rotten, Barney, in pain a lot of the time, can't sleep . . .'

'Oh, my heart bleeds for you,' said Barney. 'I can cope with you not telling Tamara the truth – obviously. I wouldn't either. But not lying to her about me. It's hideous, Toby. After all we've been to each other – or so I've thought. Seems that was all a bit one-sided. Any other little fibs I need to know about, just so I don't get any more nasty surprises? If not, I'll be off.'

'I—' Toby seemed about to say something, then stopped. 'No, no, Barney, of course not. Nothing else.'

'Good. Don't see what's "of course" about it. Actually.'

'Look, I'm sorry. Very sorry.'

'Yeah, OK. I feel quite sorry too. Anyway, I'll drop you back. You'll have to think of some story to give your mother. Why do I think you'll be able to manage that?'

He had been so upset he'd actually cried after he dropped Toby outside his house, parked his car at the end of the road and sobbed like a small boy. Then he'd driven very slowly and carefully back to London. He still didn't like driving; and he never reached the point on the M4 where the accident had happened without feeling sick and shaky.

He got home at midnight, sat down and got very drunk on whisky, grateful only that Amanda wasn't there; he felt betrayed not just by Toby but by life itself. It just wasn't fucking fair.

When Emma phoned two weeks later to tell him that she'd been doing a lot of thinking and she really couldn't see how they could possibly have a future together, or not one based on making Amanda, whom he obviously still loved so much, deeply unhappy: and moreover not to argue and not to try to see her, he found he was hardly even surprised.

Wretched, wounded, shocked; but not surprised.

'Right,' said Freeman. He tapped the pile of papers on his desk. 'Ready to go, I think. Lot of work there, Rowe. Dozens of interviews, hundreds of hours. But none of it warrants going to the CPS, in my opinion. No real charge against anyone here.'

'Not even our friend Mr Harwood?'

'No chance. Nasty bit of work, and undoubtedly he contributed to the blow-out, but you could never charge him. Motoring offences, maybe, but not with causing death by dangerous driving.'

'Well, maybe he'll be a bit more careful in future.'

'Maybe. For a while. Then it'll be two fingers to us all

and he'll be off again. I'd like to see him fined, at least. But I'd say we simply have an inquest situation here.'

Constable Rowe felt quite sorry for him; he looked as if he was about to burst into tears.

Interviewed at a police station, Rick Harwood had been truculent; yes, he'd had a load of wood on board, that was his job. No, he hadn't been driving dangerously. Or exceeding the speed limit. More than his job was worth, literally.

'And with all these bl— all these cameras everywhere, you wouldn't stand a chance of getting away with it. So – I don't.'

'Well, that's good to hear,' said Freeman. 'And this wood, Mr Harwood: was it properly stowed in your van?'

'Yes, course it was. Expensive stuff, wood. You don't want to risk losing it.'

'And you were taking it where exactly?'

'To the delivery address. In Marlow. I can give you chapter and verse.'

'And it was new wood, was it?'

'Yeah.'

'It had no nails in it, for instance?'

'Course not.'

'Right. Well, perhaps you could explain why several witnesses saw the back doors of your van insecurely fastened, and indeed tied together with some rope?'

'I might have tied some rope round the handles. Nothing wrong with that, is there? Doesn't mean it wasn't properly fastened, rather the reverse.'

'So you're quite sure that some pieces of wood, with nails in them, could not have fallen out of the van onto the road?'

'Yeah, quite sure. I told you, it was new wood.'

'Which you acquired from where, Mr Harwood?'

'Oh – dunno. It was months ago, I can't be expected to remember details like that.'

'Presumably you had some kind of receipt for it, a delivery note, something like that?'

'I might have. I don't keep every bit of paper that comes my way.'

'Surely you have to, sir? In order to complete your VAT return.'

'The office does that.'

'In which case they would need every bit of paper that came your way, I would have thought. Well, we can ask them. Thank you, Mr Harwood, you've been very helpful.'

The man from the woodyard near Stroud had remembered Rick very clearly. Particularly his request that he should dispose of the old timber for him – a request he had refused. And that Harwood had then asked for a length of rope to tie the doors together, which had been insufficient to do the job properly.

Rick was told he would be called as a witness at any trial or inquest on the crash.

'Oh, what! I wasn't anywhere near the bloody crash.'

'People have died, sir,' Freeman said. 'Proper explanations for that have to be found. You could certainly be judged to have played a part in the collision that caused it. You'll be hearing from us in the fullness of time.'

'I think I should move out for a bit,' said Jonathan. 'This isn't getting us anywhere.' He had walked into her studio where she was struggling to work; it was late, the children were all in bed and asleep.

'What isn't getting us anywhere?'

'Well, drifting along like this. With you obviously unable to bear the sight of me.'

'Are you surprised by that?'

'No, Laura, I'm not surprised. But we can't go on like this for the next forty years or whatever.'

'Believe me, I don't want to. I'm just trying to decide what's best. For all of us.'

'I presume by that you mean the children,' he said. 'Rather than me and you.'

'Well, not really. Me as well. But mainly them, yes.'

'Right. Well, I think rather than go on living in this poisonous atmosphere . . .'

'I hope you're not implying I'm creating the poisonous atmosphere.'

'Well – to a degree, you are. Obviously with some justification, but—'

'I can't believe you said that!'

'What?'

'That I was creating the atmosphere. I haven't done anything. I'm not doing anything. Just trying to – to cope with it. With what you've done. You've betrayed me totally, Jonathan, lied and lied to me, broken every promise, all your marriage vows.'

He was silent. Then he said, 'You know, I sometimes wish you'd let me try and explain.'

'Explain! What, why you slept with – with someone else? With her? Why you wanted to? What it did for you? What she did for you? If you even tried, I think I'd throw up.'

'Yes, but Laura, I've said so many times, I'm sorry, desperately sorry. I would give everything I have for it not to have happened.'

'Oh really! Everything? I don't think so. Your precious career, your doting staff, your adoring patients? And if you're that desperate about it, why didn't you realise how wrong it was, what damage you were doing to us and our marriage? No, you must have felt you had some kind of right to it, to her. And in that case, then either you're rotten through and through, which actually I don't think you are, or there's something wanting in our relationship: it doesn't satisfy you. It or me. So don't try and explain because I don't think I could bear it.'

She had kept her feelings so much to herself, ever since the night of the party, she was almost surprised to hear herself expressing them now. It was a relief; but it was also frightening. It was a step along a road from which there was no return, a dangerous, lonely road, and it went against all her usual instincts: the ones that said it was best not to make a fuss, to put up with any hurts or disappointments for the sake of peace, for maintaining family tranquillity. Not that the hurts had been many or the disappointments great, but they had been there – Jonathan's dismissal of what she had struggled to make a career, his frequent failure to be present at things that mattered to her but not to him, like her girlfriends' birthday parties, events sponsored by her clients, private views she had particularly wanted to attend. Of course, there were always reasons: he was tired, he was on call, he had papers to write – but she knew he would have managed to attend, had the people involved been important to him.

He stared at her and she could see she had shocked him; not by what she had said, but that she had said it at all. This was not the Laura he knew berating him, this was not his gentle, softly spoken wife. But then, she thought, he was not the Jonathan she had known, not the loving, loyal husband and father, who had the family at the very centre of his being. They were moving far and fast from their old selves; and there was no knowing where and how far apart they would end up.

'Well, in that case, I'll go,' he said finally. 'There's no point in my staying. I really can't see it's of any benefit to the children, my being here. I mean, I expect they'll miss me, but I'll arrange to see them at weekends and so on. And then we can decide what to do next.'

'Yes. All right.'

She felt sick suddenly, half-wished she'd let him talk to her, but that would have meant being forced to listen to him talking about Abi Scott, and why he'd done what he had, and she didn't think she'd be able to bear it. She couldn't, in fact, bear any of it. It all seemed, at that moment, unendurable.

'I think I'll go to bed,' she said, and picked up her congealing cup of coffee and walked over to the door. There was a scuffle on the stairs; she looked up and saw Charlie staring down at her, his face white, with two brilliant spots of colour forming on his cheeks. He had obviously heard every word.

Georgia was still slightly surprised to find herself in this situation. It all seemed so extremely unlikely, somehow, living with a friend of Merlin's – well, not actually *living* with him, but in a room in his house in the shabby back end of Bayswater. She had imagined herself in a flat with a load of girls, or men and girls, sharing everything, eating together, going around together, not virtually on her own, having to be self-sufficient, having to budget and cook for herself and get herself up and out in the morning. It had all been a bit of a shock at first. But there simply hadn't been an option.

It had all begun with a row with Linda. Linda was being really odd. Far less interested in Georgia than she used to be, demanding, critical, making a fuss about stupid things like a couple of cups left unwashed, or music being played too loudly, and nagging endlessly about her finding a place of her own. It was so unfair, Georgia thought; she was having such a struggle with everything, and she was paying for her keep – well, making a contribution anyway – and how was she supposed to have time to look for a flat when she was working from nine in the morning until quite often seven or eight at night? And she did try very hard to keep out of Linda's hair and the first weekend she'd gone home to see her parents, she'd felt really down and anyway, Linda had practically demanded she was out of the flat until Monday.

She'd had Monday morning free, no shooting, and she'd looked at about a hundred – well, at least ten – rooms and flatshares, and they were all horrible. She'd just never expected it to be so hard. Getting student digs in Manchester had been no problem at all. And then she'd gone in, in the afternoon and Bryn Merrick had actually shouted at her when she kept getting a scene wrong, and everyone was embarrassed, and she could see why, she was making a total hash of it, and she'd half-run out of the hall at six and arrived back at Linda's flat in floods of tears. To find Linda not there. She'd spent a miserable evening on her own until Linda came in at nine o'clock in a foul mood, all because some contract had been cancelled or not signed at the last minute and she'd been with lawyers all evening.

Georgia managed to express sympathy, and to make Linda a cup of tea; but then once Linda had settled on the sofa and reached for the TV remote, she said, 'Linda, I need to talk to you.'

'Georgia, must it be now?'

'Well – yes. If you don't mind.'

'And if I do?'

'I'd still like it.'

'Oh all right.' Linda put the remote down, picked up her cup and looked at her. 'What is it?'

'It's – well, I'm finding it all so hard.'

'Finding what so hard?'

'The series, the rehearsals – all of it. Mostly Bryn Merrick. He just doesn't like me, and that makes me nervous. You know I still feel – bad about the accident and I'm still so aware of what they must think of me. And then Frank, he's so up himself, and today I just totally blew a scene – well, it was my fault, but even so, everyone was so – so like, hostile to me, and I just cried all the way home. I just wondered if you could help, have a word with Bryn or something, or even if I should just resign or something, let them get someone else for Rose . . .'

605

She had seen Linda annoyed with her before; even very cross. She had never seen her totally lose it. Which was what happened then. She put down her cup, stood up and folded her arms and confronted Georgia from across the room.

'Georgia, I'm finding something hard too and I'll tell you what it is. You. You and your self-obsessed, pathetic attitude. You get this part, this amazing opportunity, and ever since the very beginning you've whinged about it. You miss the audition – and don't tell me that was because of the crash, I'm sick of hearing about that bloody crash – you were actually late because you were out the night before; then you couldn't face the auditions, you couldn't face read-throughs, you hated getting your costumes sorted, and now you're no good and nobody likes you. I can tell you I wouldn't like you either if I was on that production. I should think they're all wishing they'd never heard of you. Given that they have and they chose to give you the part, they've now got to live with it and you. God help them. Listen, it is of no interest to them whatsoever that you've had a traumatic time and you're suffering from survivor blame or whatever it's called; although I'm sure initially they were very sympathetic. You've been hired to do a job. Grow up. Life's tough. Get used to it. And find yourself somewhere to live in the process.'

And then she turned and walked out of the room and into her own, and slammed the door shut.

Georgia didn't go to bed at all that night. She sat in the big comfy chair in her room, fully clothed, occasionally dozing, in a state of shock. She longed to make some grand gesture, to pack and just walk out into the night, but she knew she'd have to sleep on a park bench or in a bus shelter, and not even the grandest gesture seemed quite worth that. She kept hearing what Linda had said, replayed it over and over again in her head, trying to make sense of it, trying to believe that Linda could have been so horrible to her; but as the night wore on, a small, sneaky voice began to tell her that there might, actually, be something in what she had said. If only that for the cast, it really wasn't remotely relevant that she had had a horrible time, and that Bryn had taken a big chance on her and she really ought to do her best to justify that and not throw it away. She still felt Linda had been totally out of order and she should have seen that it was support that Georgia needed, not a bollocking, but as long as she could get out of the flat and in somewhere else – someone had suggested the YWCA, which Georgia had been horrified by at the time – it would be better than hanging around crowding Linda's space.

At six o'clock, she woke in acute discomfort, having finally fallen asleep with her head somehow twisted halfway round her shoulders, got up and packed – as noisily as she dared, which was actually quite quietly – wrote a note telling Linda she wouldn't be getting in her way any longer, called a cab and went to the church hall. She knew it would be open, as the cleaners came at six and rehearsing sometimes started at eight, but she hadn't bargained on Merlin being there.

She looked at him in horror and shot into the loo, where she found she looked even worse than she had expected; she stayed there for a few minutes, combing her hair and putting on a bit of make-up, but clearly in the end she was going to have to come out. When she did, he was waiting for her with a huge mug of coffee.

'Heavy night?' he said sympathetically, and, 'No,' she said, 'not in that way,' and started to cry.

Merlin wasn't remotely embarrassed, as most blokes would have been, confronted by a weeping female. He found her a box of Kleenex, sat down beside her, put his arm round her and asked her to tell him what the matter was.

Which, having recovered from the considerable shock of

finding herself where she had dreamed of being for the past four weeks, in close physical contact with Merlin Gerard – which suddenly wasn't particularly exciting, but just cosy and comforting – she did.

All of it.

He really was very sweet: he said he could imagine how terrible she must have felt about the crash, and it being in the papers, and he'd really felt for her – 'so vile, the tabloids' – but he told her no one else had really taken it in at all.

'They all really like you, Georgia. Davina's always saying what a sweetheart you are, and I know Bryn can be terribly awkward, but he's a perfectionist, that's how he's got where he is, and he's not remotely regretting casting you. You're doing really well, and considering it's your first big part—'

'My first part full stop,' said Georgia, sniffing and smiling a watery smile.

'Well, OK, even more remarkable. You're very talented, you know. You should believe in yourself a bit more.'

Georgia sniffed again. 'I don't feel very talented. I don't feel talented at all.'

'Well, you are. Now look, I really have to get on. I came in early to catch up on some stuff, and if Mo finds me sitting here having a goss with you, she'll get very shirty. But – what are you doing this evening?'

'Nothing,' said Georgia, trying very hard to believe this was actually happening. 'Probably trying to find a park bench.'

'Why? Oh yeah, Linda's thrown you out. I'm sure she didn't mean it. But it would be nice to have somewhere of your own. Anyway, I think I can probably help. Hang around if you finish before me and then we'll go for a drink and I'll tell you about it.' He gave her a quick kiss and disappeared into the kitchen; Georgia went through the rest of the day in a trance.

* * *

Merlin's help came in the form of his friend Jaz, who he'd been at school with; Jaz helped his dad with his building business and what he called his property empire, which was the ownership of two large, crumbling houses off the Bayswater Road.

'They're divided into bedsits,' Merlin said, 'and there's usually a couple at least looking for occupants. I'll give him a call.'

Jaz said he did have one and if Merlin would bring Georgia round in an hour or so, he'd show it to her.

Jaz was fun, she liked him. He was tall, taller than Merlin, but heavily built, with close-cropped black hair and almost black eyes; he kept punching Merlin on the arm and calling him his old mate; he also argued with him a lot, mocked his job and told him that he was a bloody great poof. Georgia had been assured more than once by Davina that Merlin's blood was very red indeed, and in tones that implied that Davina knew this for herself, but she still wondered if Jaz knew something she didn't.

He didn't. 'Pardon my French,' he said, grinning, seeing Georgia's embarrassment. 'Just a joke – got stuck with it at school, didn't you, mate? I thought so meself for a bit, used to stand with me back to the wall when he was around, but don't you worry, my love, there's nothing fairy-like about our Merl. OK, let's go and have a look at this accommodation, shall we?'

It was pretty grim, really, right at the top of the house, one of two converted attic rooms, and very cold. It had a gas ring and a sink behind a curtain, and a money-in-the-slot electric meter, and the bathroom was a floor down, not dirty exactly, but grubby, freezing cold, with stains in the bath and a suspicious wetness round the base of the loo which made her think it must be leaking. It was all a bit smelly.

But it had brilliant views, through a rather sweet little dormer window – and she loved the way the ceiling sloped almost to the floor on two sides. And it would be hers. Her very own home. She said she'd take it.

'Right-oh,' said Jaz, 'it's yours. Vacant possession. Next door's some bloke who works for a charity, real do-gooder. Won't cause you no trouble. Anyone does, you just let me know. But we don't take none of your rough types. They're mostly a nice crowd, lotta females, you'll be fine.'

And she was.

She was blissfully happy. She replaced the filthy curtain that shielded the kitchen with a bamboo screen and bought some thick blinds at Ikea, and a gorgeous white furry throw for her bed and another for the lumpy armchair, which she supposed was what made the rooms officially bedsits – and she bought a convector heater which ate money, but even so, she was cold a lot of the time. She had even taken to keeping the two plates on her hob on a lot of the time to help heat the room. That was costing mega bucks.

Nonetheless, she loved it. It was hers, her very own home that she was paying for; she felt independent and pleased with herself, and that kept her going through the very tough times she continued to have on the series.

She had also formed a hugely supportive friendship, not with Davina as she might have expected – she had turned out to be a rather empty vessel, all charm and no substance – but with Anna, who was playing her grandmother's friend.

Anna had had a great life; she had trained as a classical singer, fallen in love with a jazz pianist called Sim Foster and run away with him. Georgia could see how it had happened; she was astonishingly glamorous and sexy out of make-up and looked far younger than her sixty years. She said she loved character roles. 'The less I'm like myself, the better I like it.'

Her parents had lived in Surrey, were terribly conventional, completely horrified that their beloved daughter should be living with what they called a 'coloured' man – in the obligatory hushed tones – and not even married, touring the world with him, singing jazz for fifteen years . . .

'He was fantastic, Georgia – not first division, but definitely top of the second. I adored him, and I adored the life we led, all those wonderful smoky bars – God, how I miss smoky bars. We even played New Orleans.'

They had been in her day quite successful – 'not exactly Cleo Laine and John Dankworth, but we put out the odd album, did quite a bit of TV.'

Sim had died, 'Well, he killed himself really, just one too many cocaine cocktails,' and Anna had come home to make a new life for herself and their daughter Lila.

'She was only four. I couldn't support her on the road, so I started doing modelling, mumsy stuff for the catalogues, and some commercials. I wasn't bad looking and when I met Sim I was actually halfway through a drama course at RADA. One thing led to another, and I got lucky and started acting for real. Twenty years later, here I am.'

Lila was at college, training to be a musician. 'She can play a mean clarinet, I tell you. You remind me of her, Georgia.'

Lila turned up at the set to collect her mother one night; she was very pretty, huge fun, and Georgia was flattered by the comparison.

Anna too had done a lot to help Georgia over her nerves. 'I know what it's like and it was worse for me – was a novice at forty, not twenty. You think it won't be easy, of course, but you got the part, for God's sake, so you must be OK, but everyone else belongs to this club with its own language and customs, and you're on the outside, fighting to get in.'

* * *

They were actually filming now, and she found it much easier in some ways, although there were still serious problems in playing a major part that was also her first. She was the only novice on board; everyone else knew exactly what they were doing, and time and time again she misunderstood an instruction, misjudged timing, failed to interact with the other people in the scene. Even the most brilliant actors – and she knew she was good, possibly even very good, but not brilliant – need experience on their side, to handle complex moves, camera angles, and the misery of reshoots.

Nothing was worse, Georgia had discovered, than knowing you'd done a scene really well, and then having to do it again the next day because the editor and director had looked at the rushes and said it hadn't come off, often through some extraneous factor, like using daylight that they'd thought would have been just strong enough, and wasn't. 'You can get away with a lot through grading,' Merlin had explained to Georgia, 'but there's a limit.'

But she did feel quite differently now. She recognised that her problems were due to inexperience, not everyone being against her; and she felt more self-confident as a result.

And the others were actually very nice to her – with the exception of the appallingly up-himself Frank – and even Bryn Merrick had taken time out to go through certain scenes with her.

She had had a rather emotional reunion with Linda, at which she cried a lot and Linda cried a bit, and Linda told her how proud of her she was and that Bryn Merrick had called her personally to say how well Georgia was working out and how he knew it must be difficult for her. And she was clearly impressed by all that she had done. She had even apologised for her behaviour the night she had lost her temper.

'I'm sorry, darling, it was wrong of me.'

'That's OK,' said Georgia, giving her a hug. 'I'd probably still be here if you hadn't.'

None of it would have happened, of course, without Merlin; Georgia felt she owed him everything. And said so, and even offered to cook him supper to show him her gratitude.

Merlin refused this; she was disappointed, but not really surprised. He moved in such exalted circles, was always mentioning famous writers and artists and even the odd Labour politician who'd been to dinner with his parents. How could he be expected to enjoy a chilli (her only culinary accomplishment) cooked in a bedsit? But he continued to be really friendly, to ask her to go for drinks after work, to pass on any compliments.

He was, she could see, very good at his job. It seemed rather easy to her at first, just a lot of running about and doing what he was told, but she came to see it was much more complex. He had to anticipate moment by moment what might change, who might be needed, where they might have to be, and how to get them there; and if it all went wrong and Bryn Merrick had a hissy fit, which he frequently did, he would shout at Tomo, the first assistant, who would then proceed to shout at Merlin, who had to take it and carry on sorting and rescheduling.

'I have to be really thick-skinned and sensitive all at the same time,' Merlin said to Georgia, 'as well as efficient. That's a tough call.'

He also clearly felt responsible for her personal safety and constantly checked that she wasn't having any problems in the house. Which she wasn't; everyone was friendly and very nice, and the young charity worker who was her neighbour had twice asked her to go to folk evenings at the pub on the corner, and a girl on the floor below who was an art student and her boyfriend who didn't seem to do anything at all had invited her to supper. It had been quite fun, but they had smoked hash throughout the evening and got totally stoned; by the end of it, Georgia, who had no moral objections to hash but simply didn't like it, preferring good, or rather bad red wine, had decided she would duck out of subsequent invitations.

The weather had been a big factor in the shooting; because it was autumn and they had to cope with it, there were many days when they had to move inside and change scenes at a moment's notice. This necessitated wardrobe changes as well as everything else; and was a nightmare for Continuity.

Weather cover meant you built filming alternative scenes into the schedule, but as time went on, they ran out of indoor shots and just had to cope with it.

'You'll quite often see dark clouds in a film and then it gets sunny again, supposedly on the same afternoon,' said Merlin. 'You can do a lot post-production, of course, and anyway, once it's on the screen only a technical boffin will notice.' He seemed to know an awful lot.

One very cold November morning, Georgia had to run down the street, wearing only a vest and shorts, buy an ice cream and stand licking it while she chatted to a woman on a flower stall about her granny; the sun was brilliant, but not exactly warm and it kept going in, and she had to do it five times because in spite of Merlin's best efforts, cars kept coming across shot. It was the sort of day guaranteed to produce one of Bryn's hissy fits – although, as she said to Merlin in the pub, he'd had a thick coat on and a scarf, 'and gloves, for God's sake'. Just the same, she remained puzzled by Merlin's attitude to her. He was so sweet, so attentive, and he didn't seem to have a regular girlfriend, yet he didn't make any kind of a move on her. In spite of telling herself it was ridiculous, she couldn't help being hopeful.

Chapter 42

'Alex, are you going to this wedding on Saturday?' Emma asked.

'I am indeed. I'm told by Maeve that if I don't, she'll never forgive me. I feel a bit of a fraud. I've never done anything for Mrs Bristow, except chatted to her once or twice, but she said the hospital had been so fantastic to her, looked after her so well, and she wanted to have some representatives there. Plus the Connells are going to be there in force, apparently. It's Patrick's first outing, and Mary Bristow said she knew what a lot I'd done for him.'

'I've been asked too.'

'Really? How very nice.'

'Yes. I had a sweet note from Mr Mackenzie – he's the bridegroom, you know, bless him, bless both of them – saying it was a small token of his gratitude for helping him to find Mary that day.'

'I didn't know you did.'

'Bit of a long story. You don't want to hear it.'

'Yes, I do.'

'Well, you're not going to.' She sighed. 'Anyway, maybe we could go together?'

'That would be delightful. I think the whole thing will be delightful. We can feel fraudulent together. You're . . . all right, are you, Emma?'

'Yes, thank you, I'm fine.'

'Good. You look a bit tired, that's all. I wondered if—'

'Alex, I'm fine.'
'Good.'

But she wasn't fine; she felt absolutely terrible. She'd read somewhere that recovery from a love affair worked out at a day for a day; if you'd been with someone for a year, you got better in a year; if it had only been three months, then you only had to get through three months. By that reckoning, she should be feeling quite a bit better by now; and she wasn't. She hurt, all over, physically somehow, as well as emotionally. It was extraordinary. Her skin felt tender and her eyes were permanently sore; and she felt utterly weary, as if her bones were somehow twice their proper weight. When she allowed herself actually to think about Barney, she wanted to cry; and even when she managed not to think about him, the awful sadness was still there, oppressing her. She couldn't imagine ever feeling properly happy again, which she knew was ridiculous, but telling herself so didn't help. She felt as if for the rest of her life she would feel the same, as if a large chunk of herself had gone missing and she had no idea where or how to find it.

She had written to Luke as well, telling him she was very sorry, but she felt it was wrong of her to let him go on thinking she cared about him as she had. She had enclosed the necklace. He had called her, clearly very upset, had asked her to take time to think, to reconsider; he said he couldn't imagine life without her, that he needed her: 'It's not easy, this job, Emma – tougher than I'd thought. I've been really banking on coming home and seeing you at the weekends. Or like I said, getting you out here. It's a really cool city, we could have a great time.'

But she stood firm, told him she was sorry but she couldn't see how it could possibly work out between them; that she liked him and admired him far too much to let him think she loved him when she didn't. He had been quite harsh at that, had told her she'd done a fine job deceiving him in that case; and when she finally put the phone down she had cried bitterly and for quite a long time. She was nonetheless astonished how swiftly her feelings for him had disintegrated; she had felt what she thought was love for him, and it had turned out to be an entirely hollow emotion with no proper heart to it; while all the time, real love, the emotion she now knew was real love, had been waiting for her, quietly watchful, carefully concealed, ready to trip her up, make her stumble, to take her breath quite literally away.

And having stumbled, having been so sweetly ambushed by it, there was no way she could return to the other smoother path; she wasn't just deceiving Luke, she was betraying what she had felt for Barney.

She had been all right in the beginning, when Barney had told her about Amanda's father, and had realised that they must wait a while longer. It had seemed the kind and only right thing to do. She had been sad, very sad; she had missed Barney dreadfully, missed his calls and his smile and his jokes and indeed his presence at the heart of her life. But as time went by, she became increasingly anxious; she was in love with a man who, however much he said he loved her in return, was clearly deeply and tenderly concerned for someone else. Someone he admired, and greatly valued; someone with whom, until he had met Emma, he had wanted to spend the rest of his life. And someone who, for whatever reason, had become his first priority once more; someone who belonged in his life, who had earned her place there. And the more she thought of herself dislodging that person, the more impossible it seemed; how could a brief affair, a flash of desire, replace all that?

It was a daydream, an acutely tempting fantasy; not for her, she had no doubt of the reality of her love for Barney, but for him. She should leave him to be with his Amanda, not be singing her siren song to him, luring him onto the rocks of a cancelled marriage.

For a few days, the very rightness of what she had done buoyed her up; she felt stronger, braver, a better person altogether. And then the misery set in, and she knew she had been right. For Barney had not argued, had not fought for her; he had been quiet, gentle, very sad, while seeming to accept absolutely what she said.

It was over; and it was horrible.

'Barney?'

He was working late; it was quiet on the floor. She was standing by his desk, seemed to have appeared out of nowhere. He hadn't seen her since their last confrontation; surprising in a way, he supposed, since they were in the same building – but then the building contained at least five thousand of them. And he'd certainly done the opposite of seeking her out.

He glanced at her warily. She was looking slightly nervous, her face pale, her lips unglossed, her hair hanging straight onto her shoulders. Tamara undone. This must be serious.

'Hello, Tamara.'

'Barney, this is – well, it's hard for me to say.'

'Try.'

'I'm sorry.'

If she had disappeared into a pall of smoke, leaving only her shoes and bag on the floor, like the wicked witch in *The Wizard of Oz*, he could not have been more astonished. He hadn't thought 'sorry' was a word in Tamara's lexicon.

He sat and waited.

'I – I shouldn't have done that,' she said; she was clearly having difficulty meeting his eyes.

'Done what, Tamara?'

'Shouted at you. Accused you of – well, of what I did.'

'Oh,' he said, 'well I shall probably get over it.'

'Yes. I hope so. The thing is though, I know now Toby was lying to me. It wasn't you who made him late.'

'No. It wasn't.'

'Can I – can I sit here?' She indicated the chair next to his. More diffidence; it was all so unlike her.

'Yes, of course.'

'I – I went to see him last night,' she said, and her expression was suddenly raw with hurt. 'We had a long conversation. Basically, it's over, Barney. We're not – not having a wedding. I don't want to marry him.' A quick, forced little smile. 'Absolutely I don't.'

'I see. But—'

'It's him who's the shit. Not you. I know that now.'

'I see,' said Barney again.

'Yes. I suddenly began to think and I thought – well I realised that you were driving when you were stopped by the police.'

'Ye-es?'

'And they'd have breathalysed you.'

'They did.'

'And actually if you'd been as drunk as Toby made out, you'd still probably have been over the limit.' Her expression was awkward again: embarrassed.

'Possibly.'

'No, definitely. Sorry, Barney. So I said that to Toby and started really asking questions. And he – well he suddenly gave in.'

'Really?' Barney had never thought to feel sorry for Toby again; he did then.

'Yes. He told me everything. About – well all of it, the other girl, everything.'

God, Barney thought, looking at her, this couldn't be easy. This was – well it was brave. Really brave. He smiled at her, said quite gently, 'Tamara, I'm so – so sorry.'

'Not your fault,' she said briskly, 'absolutely not your

fault. God. What a piece of— Well, I delivered a few home truths. You can imagine I expect.'

'Think so.'

'And told him I never wanted to see him again. And left.'

'Right . . .'

'The other thing is, I don't know how things are with you and Amanda now, but she says you've been fantastic over all this, that she'd never have got through it without you . . . So – well, I promise you I'll never say anything to her, ever.'

'Thank you.'

'Right, well I must go now. I just wanted to – well, to set things straight, you know.' She stood up, managed another smile, leaned forward and kissed him briefly on the cheek. 'Night, Barney.'

'Good night, Tamara. And thank you for coming. It was – well it was nice of you.'

'That's OK.' She turned and walked out of the room, her fast, purposeful walk, her task completed, clearly feeling back in control. Barney watched her, not feeling anything much: except extremely tired.

Charlie was being completely impossible. The fact they both knew why didn't help, because he refused to talk about it, or even listen to them. He was cold and insolent to his father and completely uncooperative with Laura, refusing to join the girls for meals, and locking himself away in his room playing with his Game Boy, or painting the Warhammer models that were his new passion, some-times late into the night. If Laura came in and told him to turn the light off and go to bed, he shrugged and didn't even answer. If she turned the light out, he would simply wait until she had gone downstairs and then turn it on again. He did the minimum amount of homework and when his work came back with low marks, once again he simply shrugged. He refused a part in the Christmas play and didn't turn up for soccer practice.

When Jonathan and Laura went in for a parents' evening, his year tutor showed them the reports he had from all his teachers, and they were horrified. The charming, high-achieving Charlie was suddenly being labelled lazy, uncooperative, and even disruptive: they were told there was no chance if he continued in this vein that he'd pass his entrance exam to Westminster.

'Er . . .' David Richards looked awkward. 'I wondered, is there something upsetting him, some problem that we don't know about? The thing is, all boys get a bit like this towards puberty, but this has been so sudden and such a great change, I feel there must be a different explanation.'

'Well—' said Laura; but, 'No,' said Jonathan, 'no problems at all. He's obviously just got a bit out of sorts with it all. I was the same at his age, suddenly didn't want to be one of the good boys any longer. No excuse, of course, but I think that's what it must be. I'll talk to him. Clearly it can't go on.'

'Yes, clearly it can't go on,' Laura said, glaring at him across the table of the restaurant where they had agreed they should talk, safe from Charlie's sharp ears and all-seeing eyes. 'But I don't see how we're going to stop him. He's just so horribly upset and it's his way of telling us so.'

'Fine.'

'What do you mean, fine?'

'I mean, of course he's upset. Unfortunately there's not a lot we can do about that. And yes, I know, I know, it's my fault. But if we can make him see that he's damaging his own chances, then I think he may start behaving a bit better.'

'I hope so,' said Laura. She didn't actually think it was very likely.

'Fuck you!' said Charlie. 'Fuck you, talking to me like that.'

'Charlie, don't you dare swear at me.'

'I'll swear at you if I want to. You're awful. Horrible. Doing that to Mum, sleeping with that girl. How could you, when Mum's so – so good to you!'

'I know she is, Charlie, and I'm deeply ashamed of myself. Terribly, terribly sorry and so sorry too that you had to find out.'

'Yeah, well, if you're so sorry you might have thought a bit harder before you did anything so disgusting.'

'Charlie – if you could just listen to me for a while. I'm not asking you to understand—'

'Yeah? Sounds like it to me.'

'No, I'm not. All I'm saying is, I'm desperately sorry, and I would ask you to—'

'To what? Forgive you, I suppose. For wrecking our family, ruining Mum's life. How am I supposed to forgive that?'

'I wasn't going to say forgive, Charlie. Just to beg you not to ruin your own life, your own chances by behaving as you are. I may have made a mess of mine, but you have everything ahead of you. Don't lose your place at Westminster, don't—'

'I don't care about any stupid place at Westminster. Or anywhere. I don't care if I get expelled, I don't care if I end up in prison. I can't have the only thing I want, which is our family back like it used to be, and you've taken that away from all of us for ever. I wish you weren't my father, I wish you were dead.'

Jonathan walked out of the room, and into his study. When she went in much later, to tell him how distraught Charlie still was, Laura could see that he too had been weeping.

Abi thought she would never forgive herself for what she had done that night, to Jonathan: or rather not to Jonathan, who had deserved every ghastly moment of it, but to his family who had not. She had contemplated every kind of retribution, from writing to Laura to apologise, to seeking out the children and telling them their father was a wonderful man and she was simply a very nasty, angry patient of his and she had been very cross with him. She was afraid none of it would work. The harm had been done; she could not undo it. She could only hope that it had not been too great. Especially to the children. Laura, blameless perfect Laura – God, no wonder he needed a break from her – was an adult, she must surely realise that such things happened, that husbands were unfaithful, that it was an occupational hazard of being a wife, and she would either come to terms with it, sooner or later, and take Jonathan back, or she would decide she could never forgive him and take her revenge. But the children: what she had done to them was savage their innocence and their happiness, tear it apart. All in a spirit of revenge for something that was partly her own fault. She was obviously a bad person to be able to do such a thing; she had to learn to live with that.

Seeing William again had upset Abi badly. She hadn't forgotten – of course – how great he was, how truly nice and good. As well as so sexy and fun and interesting. Being confronted by him again had reminded her horribly, vividly. She felt set back several miles in the recovery process.

But at least she'd ensured he couldn't entertain any foolish fantasies about her. She'd made quite sure of that. It hadn't been easy, but she'd done it. By telling him how rotten she was, what she was capable of.

She had not allowed him to think for one moment that it wasn't really so bad, that it was maybe not her fault, that her early life excused – to an extent – her behaviour. She had actually told him that dreadful night that she didn't really buy all the crap about people being bad because bad things had happened to them; he had looked at her with those great brown eyes and half-laughed and said, 'Abi, how can you possibly say such a thing? Of course people are influenced by how life's treated them.'

She'd said it just felt like a cop-out to her; but she'd been finishing with him then, so it hadn't mattered what she'd said or what he'd believed. She'd been too distraught to care.

She had been beginning to feel better, to rebuild her life. She was looking for a new job, was thinking she might perhaps move into Party Planning, as it was called – well, it would be better than Party Wrecking – she knew she'd be good at it and it looked like fun. She'd told William about that actually, and he'd said that it sounded great: that was the lovely thing about talking to him – he really listened and thought about what you'd said.

Well, she'd advance down the recovery road again, no doubt. If life had taught her anything, it had taught her that. And the fact that she still missed William, really missed him, that it had been an act of great cruelty on the part of fate, bringing them together that day, that she had cried when she had driven away from him, out of that bloody car park, and that she couldn't even contemplate starting a relationship with anyone else . . . well, she should regard all that as some kind of a penance for the wrong she had done, not only to Laura and her children, but to William himself.

William had been equally upset by their meeting. It had been great in a way – they'd almost become friends again; parting had been made somehow less hideous, and in theory a slightly nicer line had been drawn under their relationship. But it had made him miss her horribly all over again; he felt like a reformed alcoholic who had had the fatal, first sip, and he was back in the misery of his addiction.

It was true, of course, what she said; she was not the person he'd thought her to be. In fact, to be brutal about it, she fell extremely short of that person. She was not only happily amoral, which he had more or less realised, she hadn't just slept around and had a good time, she had lied to him, quite thoroughly and extensively – and it would be very hard ever to trust her again.

But then, he thought, as he went about the farm, for he had become unable to think of anything else at all but Abi, Abi and what he might do about her – she had been honest with him in the end; she had not spared herself, she had not taken the liar's way out and continued to deceive him. And that had been brave. She was brave: immensely so. It was a slightly dangerous bravery that she possessed, and it had its dark side, but it was a quality in her that William liked and admired. She wasn't just tough, she was cheerfully so, she didn't whinge about things, she just got on with them. And he missed her – horribly. And so he thought, why not see her again? Without any illusions? The attraction had still been there, what she did for him hadn't changed. Why couldn't he live with the bad, enjoy the good, the sexy, the totally unsuitable, which was – he knew – so much part of the pleasure of her.

He swung from decision to decision, backwards and forwards, as he fed the cows – now in their winter quarters – mended fences and hedges and drilled for winter wheat and delivered calves and checked on the drives and the birds with the gamekeeper, and changed his mind almost hourly. He should forget about her, he would forget about her, it was the only thing to do. It was settled, resolved, they had parted, it was over; she had hurt him, she was the opposite of good for him. But then – where was the sense in that, when she had made him happy, made him laugh, made him feel a different person, when she was still there, a few miles down the road.

What he needed, William thought, as he lay, most unusually sleepless in his extremely uncomfortable bed – he had never noticed before how uncomfortable it was, hard and lumpy at the same time, one of his mother's economies; he might ask her to get him a new one – what he needed was some kind of a sign that would make up his mind for him. Only – what was Abi practically bumping into him, quite clearly fancy free, and clearly pleased to see him, but a sign? Was he really likely to get another one? Almost certainly not.

Chapter 43

Tomorrow she would be a different person. With a new name and a new life ahead of her. She would walk down the aisle of the little church, to be given away, in the age-old tradition; the little church, filled with people who loved her and wished her well. She looked at her dress, hanging in its shroud of muslin, at her veil hanging beside it, at her shoes: and worried that they would be too high and that she would trip over, fall flat on her face. Well, it wouldn't be the end of the world if she did.

Her bouquet would arrive in the morning; the florist was delivering it, together with the bridesmaids' posies. She had had her hair done; it was a bit tight, but it would have dropped a little by tomorrow, so would look more natural. The way he liked it. She must be careful with her make-up too, not to overdo it; she didn't want to make the mistake so many brides did, of looking unlike themselves.

It was all going to be so lovely: they would be so happy. Sharing life, instead of living it separately, learning about one another, each new day a discovery. The only sadness would be the empty place in the church, where one of the people she loved most in the world should have been. But she could remember as she walked down the aisle, conjure him up, his dear face, his proud smile. She would be happy for him, as he would have wished. She . . .

'Mum? You all right up there?'

Mary jumped. She had been lost in the past: in the day before the other wedding, when she had been just as happy, just as sure. And how strange that there had been someone important missing from that wedding too: her father, dear dear Dad, who had died a year earlier, of lung cancer – the legacy, she now knew, but they had not then, of a lifetime of chainsmoking. Dad whose last words to her as he lay fighting for breath in hospital had been of how happy he was that she would marry Donald. 'He's a good man, Mary, the right one for you. You've chosen well.'

And she had; she knew that then and she knew it still, over sixty years later. Donald had indeed been the right one for her and she had chosen well. For that time, for the Mary that she then was. Now she was another Mary in another time: and she had chosen well again. She had no doubts; no misgivings and no sense of disloyalty. Donald would have approved; he would have wished her to be happy.

And he would have minded for her, about that empty place, for it need not be so. Her father would have been there, if he could; her daughter could be there and would not. For Christine still would not yield, refused even to consider sharing her mother's happiness.

'I'm sorry, Mum,' she said, when Mary asked her, 'I can't. It feels wrong, disloyal to Dad. I've tried to accept it, but I can't. Maybe one day, but not now. And please don't ask me again, because I can't change my mind. I'm not being difficult, I just feel very uneasy about it.'

Gerry was coming; indeed, Mary knew he and Christine had had rows about it; and her son Douglas had arrived from Canada with his wife Maureen and their two children. Timothy would take her down the aisle, and that would make up – almost – for Christine's absence. They had always had a very special close relationship, she and Timothy; he had been born six weeks premature and had almost not survived. Mary had sat with Christine night after night as he fought for his life, and when they came home, Christine had been unwell, had developed bronchitis that turned to pneumonia; and Mary had moved in and taken over the household and cared on her own for Tiny Tim as he had come to be called, for nearly three weeks. They had bonded for ever in those weeks, and he had always adored her, asking her to all his birthday parties – except the teenage ones, of course – demanded she was outside the school gates after his first day, invited her to all the interminable football matches he played in and the school plays, and after he had left home, visited her at least once a fortnight, demanding the cottage pie she made, he said, so much better than anyone else.

So there they would all be, and Russell's children too – they had taken her to their hearts, especially his son Morton – they did have the oddest names over there. The girls, Coral and Pearl – not names Mary would have chosen either and indeed, when Russell had written her about them when they were born, she had been bold enough to say so – were very sweet and kind.

She would be surrounded tomorrow – as she had been then – with friends, some old, some new, it would be a wonderful day. But still, it hurt that Christine would not come and more that Christine knew it hurt, and even so was not persuaded.

Mary was still in the house in Bristol. She hadn't wanted to move into Tadwick House until she was married; she had wanted to save that – it felt wrong to move in before. They had been to New York and she had had the most wonderful time; she had met a lot of Russell's friends, of course, and attended so many welcome dinners and cocktail parties that she became exhausted and had to go to bed for two days; but she had also been shown the sights, had gone up the Empire State Building and looked down in awe on the dazzling fairyland that was the city far below, drunk cocktails in the Rainbow Room, done the Circle Line Tour, shopped in Saks and Bloomingdales and taken a horse and carriage ride in Central Park.

But she had gone home at her insistence to her own dear house in Bristol until the wedding in December; she contemplated its sale with deep misery, but then Russell had had the idea of giving it to Timothy. 'It's so tough these days for kids, trying to get a foot on the property ladder, when they can't get a mortgage for love nor money. Try him out, see what he says.'

Timothy had said only one word when she told him, and that four-lettered; he had then gone bright red and said, 'Sorry, Gran, sorry, sorry, but that is just so – so cool. You are the best.'

Christine had been a bit funny about that too, said it wasn't good for young people to have things made too easy for them, but Gerry saw Mary's hurt face and said if anyone had made things a bit easier for him when he'd been young, he might have progressed further than he had.

Douglas and Maureen and their children were staying in the house with her; and Douglas would drive her over to Tadwick Church next day. Russell had moved into Tadwick House, and his three children were staying there. They had said they would go to hotels, but Mary had begged them to use the house. 'I hate to think of it not lived in; it will be wonderful to have you there. And besides, it will be nice for Mrs Salter to have something to do other than wait hand and foot on Russell. So bad for him anyway.'

The girls, as Russell called them, nearing sixty both of them, said they would love to stay. 'But Mary, dear, he's ruined already,' Pearl added, and Coral agreed. 'You have to blame Grandma Mackenzie. She thought he was the nearest thing to an angel on this earth.'

'Heaven help us all,' Mary said, 'if we get up there and find it inhabited by people like your father.' And then she added hastily that actually of course it would be very nice. You couldn't be too careful with stepchildren: even if they were sixty . . .

❋ ❋ ❋

It was a perfect December morning; bright and golden, with frost spangling the hedges and meadows and a sky that was brilliantly clear and blue.

Russell had arrived extremely early at the little church; had admired the red ribbons and holly fixed over the lych-gate, the bundles of white Christmas roses tied to the end of each pew, and the great urns of greenery either side of the aisle. He felt extremely nervous, and after sitting down in the front row with Morton, who was to be his best man, and gazing for a while at the empty space which would hopefully be occupied by Mary in a little under an hour, realised that it had been a mistake to allow so much time and indeed to have a second coffee with breakfast, since the waterworks problem was quite acute.

He agonised over it for a while and then, covered in confusion, whispered as much to Morton who grinned at him and patted his shoulder and said he would see what he could do; he disappeared for a few minutes and then came back with the verger who said that if Mr Mackenzie wished to comb his hair or wash his hands there was a washroom in the vestry – 'a bit primitive, but it serves its purpose'.

The guests started to arrive at eleven-thirty: the first swathe consisting of the remainder of his family, followed by the rest of the American contingent. Russell had been deeply touched by how many people, some of them quite elderly as he remarked to the girls, while clearly and blissfully unaware that this description could be equally applied to him, had accepted and made the long journey to Somerset England, as they all called it. Mary's friends, also quite large in number – there was no doubt they were good healthy stock, their generation – followed them in and the organist began to play, the lovely echoing sound soaring through the little church. Russell felt a dangerous lump in his throat; and gripped Morton's hand suddenly.

❊   ❊   ❊

Alex felt proud to be arriving with not one but two extremely pretty women; he had confessed to Emma that he and Linda had become 'just friends, nothing more, seen each other for a meal once or twice'. Given that he flushed to the roots of his black hair as he said it, and failed to meet Emma's eyes, she guessed that the relationship might be just slightly more meaningful than that, but she nodded politely and said how nice that must be.

Linda had suggested she met them at the hospital; they proceeded in her Mercedes – 'I'm sorry, Alex, but I'm just not prepared to sit in that boneshaker of yours.' The Mercedes was very low-slung and swayed about a lot; and by the time they arrived in Tadwick, Emma, who had obviously been relegated to the back, was feeling extremely sick and had to stand in the lane breathing deeply for five minutes before she trusted herself to go into the church. She was wearing an off-the-shoulder red dress, with a white stole wrapped around her, and high-heeled red shoes, and her long legs were golden and bare. What was it about the young, Alex wondered. What extra, if short-lived, gene did they possess that they didn't feel the cold? His daughter was the same, went out to endless Christmas parties in minute tops that left her midriff bare; occasionally he or Sam would suggest she wore a coat, at which she would look at them in open astonishment, rather as if they had suggested she walked down the street on her hands, or went out blindfold.

Linda was looking staggeringly beautiful in a pale grey silk suit with an ankle-length skirt; she had extraordinarily good ankles, Alex thought, studying them as she walked ahead of him down the aisle, and then as he settled into the pew, found himself thinking rather unsuitably carnal thoughts about the rest of her legs, and rebuked himself and tried to concentrate on the organ music instead.

Dear old chap, the bridegroom looked; Alex had not met him before. He was tall, as far as Alex could make out, and he sat ramrod straight in the pew, occasionally running a hand through his thick white hair and staring fixedly ahead of him; presumably the chap beside him – also quite old, well into his sixties – was his son. And how wonderful it was, Alex thought, that love could flower so sweetly and so late, that two really very old people could be celebrating their marriage in a spirit of such determination.

And these people coming in now, walking to the front of the church, they must be Mary's family: a grey-haired, rather portly man and a very pretty young girl – surely not his wife? And another man, slimmer and fitter-looking, together with a woman in a rather chic yellow coat and brown fur hat, and two girls in trouser suits with very high heels and a lot of make-up.

There was a flurry at the back of the church and three little boys appeared, all dressed identically in tuxedos; fine-looking little chaps, with dark curly hair and brilliant blue eyes, flanking a wheelchair in which sat Patrick Connell – also with the dark hair and the blue eyes and also dressed in a very smart suit, although plain and dark grey, rather than a tuxedo, smiling broadly and pushed by Georgia. Patrick had made such progress, Alex thought, it really was little less than a miracle; he could sit up properly now, no longer belted tightly into the chair, and his legs in their perfectly pressed trousers beginning to look larger somehow, and as if they knew how to work and walk, and less at variance with his heavy shoulders and broad chest.

Georgia looked amazing in a brilliant green dress – also bare-shouldered – with a green feather arrangement in her wild hair. Linda was sporting similar headwear; they were known as fascinators, she had informed Alex on the way down. Emma had enquired rather anxiously if Linda thought she should have something on her head and Linda said absolutely not if she didn't want to, and that anything went at weddings these days, especially if you had long hair, and they had embarked on a rather long and complex discussion about the hats and fascinators worn at various weddings, both of a societal and showbiz nature as clearly studied quite closely by both of them in the pages of *Hello!*.

Georgia urged the three little boys into a pew at the back, and after a whispered conversation with Patrick, inserted herself between them, clearly with a view to minimising talking and giggling, and Patrick beside them in the aisle; every so often she leaned over and patted his legs and asked him if he was all right, and he told her he was wonderfully all right and to stop fussing; anyone would think he was an invalid, the way everyone was going on.

This was a great day, Patrick thought, for all of them: and considered how far he had travelled from that darkest of the dark days four months ago, and how impossible it would have seemed then that he could have been attending a wedding, dressed up to the nines, his conscience clear and his physical outlook so good. He looked at Dr Pritchard and Emma – pretty little thing she was, looked much too young to be a doctor – and knew how much he owed them, and their hospital, for its skill and determination on his behalf and— He was interrupted in this reverie by a change of pace and tune from the organ and a rustle of excitement from the opening door; and saw that the bride was standing in the porch, on the arm of a really most handsome young chap, positively beaming with pride, and behind them, his beloved, beautiful Maeve.

She should be here, Gerry thought, Christine, his wife and Mary's firstborn, her beloved daughter. What demon had possessed her that she had been able to resent her mother's new happiness so deeply; and worse, been unable to suppress it or at the least conceal it? Mary had done so much for Christine: always helping her with Tim in the early days, never refusing any call on her time, never interfering. Unfailingly generous, extremely brave, not even hinting at the raw loneliness of new widowhood, always waiting for invitations, never imposing herself. It was wrong, deeply wrong; and what it displayed, Gerry thought, was a meanness of spirit that he would not have thought Christine capable of. He wondered where it had come from, that meanness – not her mother, for sure – or her father either; Donald had been the sweetest, most unselfish of men. Whatever the reason, he didn't like it in her. He was ashamed of her, and he wasn't sure how he was going to cope with those emotions in the days ahead.

'Stand up, Gerry,' hissed Lorraine, Tim's girlfriend – very nice to have on his arm that day. What did they call girls like her? Oh yes, arm-candy. 'They're here!'

Russell was afraid for a moment that he was going to pass out, so strong was the wave of emotion that passed through him then. The sound of the organ, the opening of the door, the knowledge that she was walking towards him down the aisle at last, after a wait of sixty-three years – it was an experience of such intensity that the light in the church seemed to fade a little, the sound of the organ to diminish and all that existed for him was her, walking slowly towards him, then standing beside him, smiling up at him, his Mary, his adored and adorable Sparrow, dressed all in white, a whiteness that literally shone where the light caught it, her eyes as brilliant and blue as they had been then, her mouth as soft and sweetly smiling, and her hands, shaking a little as she handed over her bouquet to Maeve, as pretty and perfect still as the ones that had clasped his, her tears falling on them, as she said goodbye to him just before he left to go home, a lifetime ago.

And Mary, looking up at him, saw the young Russell again, who she had loved so very much, who she had never forgotten, and never failed. She had feared she might cry, make a fool of herself at this moment, as she put it; but she felt steadfast and strong, purely and intently happy, hardly able to believe in what was taking place for her, and in the faith and courage that had brought them here, uncaring of whether they appeared to be foolish, unafraid of what the future might have in store. Today and for now, they were to be together, two people in love and their age immaterial; and it was a moment of the purest joy.

This was how it should be, Linda thought. This was love she was looking at, true love, not the counterfeit version she had known twice now, and wondered if it was what she felt for the man beside her, who had suddenly and unaccountably gripped her hand; and, This was how I thought it was, Alex thought, and do I dare even to think I've found it now? and, This is what I thought we had, Emma thought, and what I've lost, and will I ever find it again? And first one large tear and then another fell onto her prayer book and for a while she saw everything spangled with tears.

Mary reached up suddenly and kissed Russell, and the gesture was so sweet, so spontaneous that a small fragment of applause started from somewhere near the back of the church and spread round it, and she turned to acknowledge it, smiling, and thought as she did so that she saw the door begin to open; and then she turned back to the vicar as he bade them all welcome and prepared to embark on the lovely, familiar words (while omitting, as they had agreed, those that might appear somewhat ludicrous, about the procreation of children, and carnal lusts and appetites).

But then something truly wonderful happened: as the vicar began to speak, the door at the back did indeed open, everyone heard it, and turned to look; and through it, with no expression on her face whatsoever, except one of absolute determination, came Christine, bare-headed, wearing the old mackintosh in which she walked the dogs and some really quite sturdy boots, and Mary, catching sight of her, provided one of the most beautiful moments of the day, for her small, solemn face fragmented into joy and she left Russell and walked back up the aisle and put her arms round her daughter, her beloved, brave, difficult daughter, and kissed her, and then led her by the hand to her place in the front pew, next to Gerry. Who, in turn, put his own arm round her and gave her a kiss.

The service proceeded without any further departure from convention. Tim gave her away with his eyes suspiciously bright; Russell beamed throughout, until it was his turn to make his vows, and then as he said. 'Thereto I give thee my troth,' his strong voice cracked and two great tears rolled down his handsome old face; and as Mary promised to love, cherish and obey, a giggle rose unbidden in her voice and it was a moment before she could compose herself once more.

And then, having uttered his final solemn exhortation that no man must put them asunder, the vicar pronounced them man and wife and told Russell he might kiss the bride; and Mary was not only kissed but held so tightly and so fervently that it seemed Russell was afraid, even now that she had been pronounced his, of losing her again.

The bells began to peal; Mary turned, took Russell's arm, and walked slowly down the aisle, smiling into the dozens of flashing cameras that had most assuredly not been a feature at her first wedding, waving at people, blowing kisses, and hugging the small boys who scrambled over their father and rushed from their pew to greet her.

'I've been to a great many weddings,' Maeve confided to Tim, who was walking her down the aisle, 'but never in my entire life one more beautiful than this.'

Chapter 44

'I've found a flat.'

'Oh, really? Good.' That was more like it: more like she'd planned to be. Cool. Not clinging.

'Yes. I can be in it in ten days. Well, before Christmas anyway.'

Christmas. How would they deal with that? That most awful of times for Fractured Families. A fractured family. Them.

'Fine. Where is it?'

'In Little Venice. Convenient for the clinic, not bad for the hospital.'

'Excellent. Well, I think that's a very good idea.' She wasn't panicking, it was fine. It would be much better. Just a few small problems, of course. What exactly would she say to their friends? How would she tell the girls? What would she say to Charlie? Charlie, who had actually refused to go to school one day last week . . .

'Yes. So I'll start clearing out of here this weekend.'

Clearing out. Leaving her and the children. Her husband. Her adulterous husband. Would he start seeing Her again? Maybe he would. He certainly could. He'd said it was over, but he'd said so many things.

'All right.'

'I thought we should talk to the girls together. But only if you think that's a good idea. So we can present a – a fairly decent front.'

'Well, yes. Possibly.' How decent? What could they possibly say?

'I thought we could say you and I had not been getting on very well lately, and that we were going to live apart for a while so we could see if we were happier that way.'

'I see. Yes.' And how would they take it, those dear, trusting little girls? 'Your daddy's not going to live here any more, not be with you any more?'

'Unless you've got a better idea?'

'Oh – no.'

'I mean, that's the usual line with children, I believe.'

With other children, not her perfect, golden, happy family. It would be like waking the girls out of their sleep and slapping them repeatedly round the face. That cruel. That brutal. Was this really the right thing to do? Was it genuinely her choice?

'Yes. Well, I suppose we don't have much option.'

'Not really. You can tell Charlie. I can't get through to him at all any more.'

'What do you want me to tell him? The same?'

'Whatever you like, Laura. Whatever you think would be best.'

Nothing would be best. Nothing could be best. It was a choice between bad and very bad. For all of them, all the children.

'Anyway, I must go now. Big clinic today. All those Christmas babies, their mothers wanting to have them induced. Bye, then.'

'Bye, Jonathan.'

Goodbye, Jonathan: not just for today, it had been goodbye for weeks now, and for tomorrow and tomorrow and tomorrow; goodbye not just to Jonathan, but to the marriage, the family, to happiness.

'I'll be out tonight. Got a dinner, actually.'

A dinner. What did that mean?

'You could come, if you wanted to,' he said suddenly. 'I'd love it if you did. But . . .'

She knew what that meant. He'd read her eyes, her flush, her sudden anxiety. And wanted to let her know she was wrong.

'Jonathan, no. Thanks.'

'Fine. Well, see you tomorrow then. I'll be late.'

And he was gone; leaving her looking at the empty place at the breakfast table and thinking that it would always now be thus.

The concert had been Anna's idea. Georgia had been sitting and talking to her in the pub one night, trying to explain how bad she still sometimes felt about the crash: 'And not just about Patrick, the lorry driver, although there he is, three little kids to keep and no job really, although his wife keeps talking as if he'll be back next week; there are other people who are still really hurting. That man whose wife was killed, he's had to give up his job to look after his little boy, and also he's had terrible psychological problems; and several other people have lost their livelihoods through no fault of their own, like one girl who can't walk, and she was a dance teacher; others have had breakdowns, and I just feel so guilty about them. Here I am, having a great time now, and it's not fair, is it?'

Anna had agreed it wasn't fair. 'But it wasn't your fault, Georgia. You have to see that, and come to terms with it somehow.'

'I know it wasn't my fault – well, except for deserting Patrick – but that doesn't stop me feeling terrible. I just wish there was something I could do.'

'Like what?'

'I don't know. Help. In a practical way.'

'What, like raise some money, maybe? Help them at least financially? Quite small things can help a lot. I mean, I raise money for one charity that pays for under-privileged kids to go to the country for a week once a year. Makes all the difference in their lives. You should see the letters – from the parents as well as the kids. And there's another. I did a gig for a concert, just a small one, for a charity that provides special bikes that physically disabled children can control. It means they can hare about like other kids. Don't look at me like that. It's only an idea.'

'Wow. I'm not looking at you like anything. Except in admiration. That could be a really great thing to do. D'you think I could manage it?'

'With a lot of help, yes, I'm sure you could. Mind you, setting up a fund's a big endeavour. You need trustees, and a huge amount just to start it, and God knows what else. But you could maybe organise an event that raised money.'

'What, a sponsored something or other?'

'Possibly. Why not a performance of some kind?'

'My own personal Royal Variety Show?' she said laughing.

'Something like that, yes. Or your own personal Band Aid concert. That'd be good. Look, why don't you put some feelers out, see if it's feasible. And then if it is, you can maybe take it a stage further. I'll help. Or – and here's an idea – why not do it as a fund-raiser for the hospital that helped them all so much? That might be even better, it would give the project a sort of respectability. I'm sure they'd be delighted. Think about it.'

Georgia felt as if a light had gone on in her head, shining onto the dark, ugly memories, and the rotting guilt, and slowly but steadily shrinking them away. She could do something: actually do something to show all those people they hadn't been forgotten, had not been dumped by fate into a hopeless dead-end street. It wouldn't bring much-loved relatives back, or restore damaged muscles or bones or nervous systems; but it would be so, so much better than nothing.

She decided to talk to Linda about it.

Linda was cautiously enthusiastic; she thought it was a great idea – 'But you really have to do it properly, Georgia. You can't just play at something like this. Think long and hard before you get into it, because it could turn into a monster. If you're going to set up a charity, then you have to get it registered, appoint some trustees – I know that sounds like a lot of work and rather daunting, but people will be much more willing to help if it sounds official and not like a lot of kids raising a bit of money for fun. And it's got to be done well: if it goes off at half-cock, it'll be worse than nothing. The venue alone will be a nightmare to find and fund, and you'll have to scale everything to it. No use getting the Stones to agree to play and then offering them a rehearsal hall in Staines. Sorry, I don't mean to discourage you. I just don't want you getting into something you can't cope with.'

Georgia said she was sure she could cope with it, and that she didn't actually envisage getting the Stones; but a few enquiries revealed the extent of the venue problem. Hiring anywhere at all was hugely expensive and would wipe out any profit at a stroke; something radical was clearly required.

Linda inclined to the view that the money should go to the hospital: 'Then if you don't raise as much as you hope, it'll still be extremely welcome. Hospitals always need money, to buy specific things, like scanners or whatever. I'm told.' She blushed as she said this; Georgia hadn't been able to think why at the time, knowing about hospitals and their needs didn't seem quite Linda's thing. Later, it all made more sense . . .

Linda said she'd sound a few people out, that she knew quite a lot of musicians and maybe Georgia might even consider having a couple of dramatic items in the programme. The few people she'd approached were cautiously interested; Georgia didn't want to ask anyone yet on *Moving Away*, she had enough to cope with there, but it would be worth a try when it was over. Merlin, she was sure, knew a lot of people in the music business. He knew a lot of people in every business.

She could see it was all going to take a long time, it was no use thinking about a Christmas concert, as she'd originally imagined; it needed intensive long-term planning. But an optimism had gripped her from the very beginning; she felt absolutely certain something would turn up. In fact, she said this so often that Anna had nicknamed her Miss Micawber.

The other person she talked to about it was Emma; she and Emma had seriously bonded at Mary's wedding, got quite drunk and danced together. Emma said she thought it was a great idea. She agreed with Linda that it might be better to raise the money specifically for the hospital. 'You could ask Alex, see what he says.' She said she didn't think she'd be much use herself, but when Georgia said she was forming a committee and that she was hoping Alex would come on it, she told Georgia to count her in. 'Only if you think I could help, of course. I've – well, I've got a bit of spare time at the moment, so I could write letters for you, stuff like that if you like. My mum works for a school, and she's always being asked to go on fundraising committees. Only small local ones, of course, but the principle's pretty much the same. She might have some ideas.'

Georgia said she was beginning to think quite small and local herself. 'It's hopeless thinking we can do something big in London. It'll cost squillions, and we'd never get the sort of people we'd need. I mean, the crash was local, and the hospital's local and people are bound to remember it. And there must be places in Swindon, for instance, it's not that small – or Reading, maybe. We'd obviously take less cash, but we'd make more profit. Anyway, it's early days.

The great thing is to keep on trucking, as Dr Pritchard calls it. I'm going to start writing letters.'

She and Emma were both very intrigued by the relationship between Linda and Alex, which had become so extremely obvious after Mary's wedding.

'It's a match made in heaven really,' said Georgia. 'I mean, Linda's so lonely and needy . . .'

'Is she? She doesn't come across lonely and needy.'

'No, but that's her whole problem. Ballsy women, especially good-looking ones, just scare men off. I mean, it's obvious really. Anyway, then there's Dr Pritchard, also lonely, you say . . .'

'Well, pretty miserable a lot of the time. His wife is an ace cow. She's literally turfed him out of the house, sold it more or less over his head as far as I can make out. He's had to move into some cruddy flat in Swindon – it's so not fair – while she swans around with her new boyfriend; she actually arrived with him at the hospital the other day, in his Jaguar.'

'Jaguar! Gross!'

'Well, I know. They've got some nice kids though. Like fourteen, fifteen, that sort of age. How'd Linda be with kids, do you think?'

'Mmm . . .' Georgia considered this for a moment. 'Bit impatient. Tough. But – she's been pretty cool to me. We've had a few fights, but we've always worked it out.'

'Yes, but you're twenty-four. And she's not having a relationship with your dad.'

'Fat chance,' said Georgia, laughing. 'My dad is absolutely terrified of her, goes a funny colour every time she speaks to him. I don't know quite what he thinks she might do, but—'

'Well, we'll have to hope for the best,' said Emma. 'I love Alex, I really do – he's such a sweetheart; all bark and really no bite at all. And he does seem much happier recently, although he still has his dark days, when he moods around and shouts a lot. He's been so kind to me. I shall be very sad to leave him.'

'Which is when?'

'Oh, Jan, Feb time. Depends what job I can get.'

'You'd better not go to some hospital in Scotland or something,' said Georgia. 'Not until after the concert anyway.'

'Right now Scotland looks quite appealing,' said Emma with a sigh. 'As far away from London as possible, that's what I want.'

She didn't tell Georgia why and Georgia didn't ask. She could see something was hurting Emma a lot and equally that she didn't want to talk about it. Which usually meant in Georgia's experience that she'd been dumped. Men were such idiots. Who'd dump someone as lovely as Emma?

The days when Alex 'mooded around' as Emma put it and shouted were the days when he was undergoing severe anxieties over his relationship with Linda. She was gorgeous, she was sexy, she seemed to really care about him; on the other hand he had vowed he would not enter another relationship with anyone who didn't totally understand the demands of his career and profession. Linda might understand them, but she was hardly going to give them priority. If it came to a conflict between a First Night or a major audition, and a dinner with other doctors and their wives, the dinner would not win. They had already had a couple of run-ins over the South African trip; having promised to be totally accommodating with the spousal programme – 'I cannot believe there are things called that' – she had said there was no way she was going to go on a boat trip to Robben Island, where Mandela had been imprisoned, without him, or go on what she called an obscene trip to one of the townships. 'Patronising, utterly ghastly. I wouldn't even contemplate it.'

'I seem to remember your saying that the tourist trade benefited the country?'

'I'm sure it does. I just don't think sitting in an air-conditioned car and looking graciously around a series of shanty towns benefits the inhabitants very much. I'm not going to go, Alex, and that's all there is to it.'

'And at the dinner table that night, if you're asked by our hosts whether you enjoyed it or not, what will you say?'

'I'll say I thought it was totally inappropriate and I didn't want to go.'

'Linda, you seem to be embarking on this trip in a rather different spirit from what you'd promised. I really don't think it's viable on this basis, and I don't see how we can go.'

'Alex, that's crap.'

'It is not crap. I said I didn't like any of it, on principle, that I never had, and you talked me round.'

'I did not talk you round!'

'Oh really? I seem to remember a lot of talk about how it wouldn't help anyone, my sulking in Swindon, while someone else went in my place . . .'

'I do dislike the way you play back everything I say to you. All right, then let's not go. Let's not do anything nice. You just sit in your bedsit and contemplate your navel.'

'I think I'd prefer to do that than see you alienating everyone on the trip. Not just your hosts, but the other wives.'

'I'll be delighted to alienate the other wives, if they're the sort of people who enjoy a lot of patronising garbage by way of a meal-ticket.'

He'd left at that, without another word; too angry for twenty-four hours even to return her dozen or so missed calls. Finally she'd texted him: *VV sorry, totally wrong on this, need bottom smacked, xxx*

Alex had replied that he would perform the smacking in person that Saturday; it had all blown over, she had meekly agreed to do everything on the spousal programme – 'even the shopping trip' – but it had left him worried. Not just about the trip, but Linda's whole attitude. He was beginning to be afraid that she wasn't what he needed; she wasn't going to be a supportive consort, the whole incident had illustrated that.

And what about the children, how was she going to cope with them? Now that he was removed from physical day-to-day contact with them, he could feel the rift between them growing almost daily. It was no fault of theirs, they were very sweet whenever he did see them, especially Amy, but what had afternoons in a flat in Swindon to offer them, or even organised trips to London? He needed a proper base, a real home, and a decent set-up, in order to be able to claim their time and attention to any degree. Not to be haring up to Marylebone at every available opportunity to see a mistress who was hardly likely to welcome him with two inevitably awkward children in tow. A mistress moreover who would not in two dozen years consider moving to Swindon. It couldn't work, it was impossible; and the fact that he enjoyed her so much and for so much of the time was depressing in itself. Here she was, lovely and sexy and interesting and looking for someone too, and it seemed he would have to walk away from her, consign himself to miserable singledom again.

Dear Mr Grainger,

I hope you don't mind my writing to you out of the blue, but a friend suggested that you might be able to help in some way, however small.

I'm hoping you will get this safely and that I've got the right address; I looked up Grainger in the directory and your farm was definitely in the right place, if you see what I mean!

My name is Georgia Linley, and I'm the girl you

met wandering round your property on the day of the M4 crash last August. You were very kind to me, and I hope I wasn't rude! I know you were incredibly helpful to everybody that day, allowed the air ambulance to land on your field, and brought water for people to drink and did all sorts of other kind things, so I'm hoping you'll feel sufficiently interested to read on!

I am trying to organise a fundraising concert in aid of St Mark's Hospital in Swindon, where the crash victims were all taken.

Patrick Connell and his family have all become good friends of mine. He was the lorry driver who was at the forefront of the crash, and who had given me a lift that day. He was very badly injured, although he's recovering now. He has three young children and can't work at the moment: he's just an example of one of the many people who were helped by the staff of St Mark's who will, we all hope, soon get him back on his feet.

We are setting up a charity, in order to make sure that everything is done properly, and in a businesslike way. If you log on to *www.crashconcert.linley.com* you can check that as well.

Several musicians have already expressed an interest in performing – nobody very grand yet, I'm afraid – but until we have a venue, we can't get a great deal further and that is proving the biggest obstacle so far.

I wondered if you would be willing to contribute anything, however small, to our setting-up fund; and in due course, obviously, to bring as many people to the concert as possible.

We're also looking for a sponsor: any suggestions in that area would be hugely helpful.

Yours sincerely,

Georgia Linley (Ms)

William sat staring at the letter, concerned not so much with helping Ms Linley who did sound rather engaging, and who he remembered as being extremely pretty, or even with the hospital which had taken in the unfortunate crash victims, undoubtedly a very good cause, but wondering if this was a second enormous nudge on the part of the Almighty in the direction of his re-establishing a relationship with Abi. For hadn't she talked about setting up her own events company? If so, then he should surely respond; before the Almighty gave up on him altogether.

Abi had been at work when he rang; she sat looking at his name on her phone, willing it to go to Missed Call. She could easily send a text saying no, she didn't want to see him, but actually hearing his voice, that would be a bit more difficult. Not impossible, of course, but difficult. *Just hang on for a couple more rings, Abi* – she really must reset this so it cut to message more quickly – then see what he wants and then you can sort it out. Just don't anwer it, there's no point, absolutely no point, and this will clinch it. He won't ring again . . .

'Hi, William.'

'Hello, Abi. You all right?'

'Yes. Yes, I'm fine, thanks. You?'

'Absolutely fine.'

'Good. Look, William, I—'

'Abi, I've had an idea. Well, I've had a letter, actually.'

'Well – which? Or is it a letter with an idea?'

'Um – bit of both.'

'Hmm. Hard to guess this one, William. Film, book, play—'

'What?'

'Charades. Didn't you ever play Charades?'

'Few times. At Christmas. Yes, I see what you mean. Well, what's the sign for concert?'

'There isn't one. William, do spit it out. Please.'

William spat it out.

* * *

Three days later, Georgia arrived in the location house, breathless and flushed. 'Is Merlin here? Or Anna?'

'Anna's in Make-up,' said Mo. 'Don't know where Merlin is.'

Georgia hared up the stairs to the bedroom that doubled as Make-up.

'Anna, Anna, listen to this, it's amazing, totally amazing! I think we've got our venue!'

Chapter 45

The letters arrived just after Christmas. Very courteous, very formal, with little or no information beyond that their presence would be required as witnesses at an inquest on 19 February into the deaths of Sarah Tomkins, Jennifer Marks and Edward Barnes on 22 August on the M4 motorway. Details of the time and place of the inquest were also given; and the letter was signed by the Coroner's Officer.

'Well, thank God it didn't come before Christmas,' said Maeve. 'It would have cast a bit of a blight, not that you've got anything to worry about. But still – good to have it over. A line drawn.'

Patrick nodded; he actually felt he had quite a lot to worry about, however much he'd been reassured that the accident had in no way been his fault, and the police informing him that there were to be no criminal proceedings. The fact remained that his lorry had gone sprawling across the motorway, bursting through the crash barrier, and the result had been three deaths and dozens of injuries, some of them major. It still haunted him, however many times Georgia told him he most certainly had not been asleep, or even sleepy. Every time he thought about the inquest, he felt the old, panicky fear.

Still, at least he had legs and they were beginning to work, and he had the loveliest family and the best wife a man could wish for, and when he managed to walk into Mass on Christmas morning, albeit slowly and awkwardly on his two sticks, he felt that somehow, although he would not wish to relive the past year – or rather the past six months – getting through it had been a wonderful thing.

Abi found the thought of the inquest pretty scary also; she had, after all, lied to the police, albeit about nothing to do with the crash, and she still had nightmares about them charging her in connection with drug offences. She had actually taken legal advice on this; the solicitor had told her that since she had not been in possession of any drugs, either at the time the police talked to her or later, they were extremely unlikely to press charges.

Nevertheless, she was a major witness; she would have to stand in the dock or whatever they had at inquests and swear to tell the truth, the whole truth and nothing but the bloody truth and it could well transpire that she had lied the first time around, and in front of all those people. Plus Jonathan would be there; bloody, bloody Jonathan. And – what if Laura came? How would she feel then? And what might Laura do to her? Physically attack her probably; and quite right too. It was all a complete nightmare.

Abi hated Christmas usually; she had a few misfit friends, equally at odds with their families, and they would spend the day together, drinking mostly, although they'd make some sort of festive meal consisting of Christmas odds and sods from M&S and Tesco, and pull some crackers and even, occasionally, play Charades before the evening really disintegrated, but she was always hugely relieved when it, and its insistence that everyone was part of one great big happy family, was over.

Sylvie, who for all her faults was probably the person Abi was most fond of in the world, with the exception of William, of course, was never there; she had a proper family, dozens of brothers and sisters and cousins, and they had a real Christmas knees-up at one of her aunts' houses. She'd invited Abi once or twice and though it had been great, Abi hadn't really enjoyed it; she felt she was there on sufferance, although everybody was extremely generous to her, and Sylvie always said what a laugh she'd been; but you wanted to belong to the people you were with at Christmas, not have half of them wondering who you were.

The best thing that had happened all Christmas was a text from William which she'd got on Christmas night: *Happy Xmas, hope it's a good one, mine isn't. William x* She struggled not to read too much into it, not to presume his wasn't good because he wasn't with her, and that the kiss wasn't simply what anyone would put at the end of a text on Christmas Day: but the fact remained that he'd been thinking of her enough to send it. She wondered what their Christmas would be like – Mrs Grainger wearing a paper hat perhaps and a determinedly cheerful expression, and the food would be wonderful and apparently William's brother and his wife were coming for the day, but no children and no friends. Abi shuddered and texted back: *Happy one to u2, not bad, thanx, gd 2 hear from you. Abi* and after that a kiss also. She'd put gt at first instead of gd, but that looked a bit keen.

And now astonishingly she was seeing him again; albeit on a completely platonic basis . . .

She was extremely excited about Georgia's concert. It had been her idea that it should be held at the farm, festival style; she had actually once suggested something similar to William before, when he had been talking about diversification and money-making schemes, and he had been surprisingly receptive to the idea then. It really hadn't been too difficult – amazingly easy in fact – to re-persuade him.

It was very scary – on a professional basis – and she wasn't even sure they would be able to pull it off; but if they did . . . she could launch her party planning career on the back of it. And see lots of William into the bargain.

The first meeting about the concert had been – well, it had been extraordinary. An absolutely violent tangle of emotions. She'd expected the tangle, of course, had expected it to be awkward, and painful, seeing William; in fact, she'd been so scared the few days before that she'd almost pulled out of the whole thing, and put Georgia – and him – in touch with a friend who was a party-planner. But she didn't.

Which in any case would have been crazy; her head, so much harder than her heart, told her this was a big chance, professionally if not emotionally. She kept her mind as firmly on that as she possibly could.

They'd agreed to meet in a pub in Bristol, on a Saturday afternoon; nobody could manage a weekday and it had seemed a good compromise, location-wise. Abi had arrived far too early and had spent at least fifteen minutes in the loo, to avoid sitting waiting for them and looking like a complete loser; when she came out, William was sitting at a table with a very pretty black girl, which rattled her considerably at first, until she realised she must be Georgia. And she stood there, just staring at him, drinking him in; watching him smile at Georgia rather awkwardly, look at his watch, look at the door, look round the bar – and she felt a wave of emotion so violent, so charged with regret and love and intense physical memory, it quite literally took her breath away, and it was as much as she could do not to run over to him and put her arms round him. Yes, she had seen him in the street that day – yes, she had talked to him briefly, and it had been a shock, but it had also been purest chance. Fate had brought them together – as indeed it had in the first place – and had seemed to provide a happier, more easeful end to their relationship. It had been upsetting; but it had also been healing.

This was different; this was a new and dangerous journey down a new and dangerous road, and God alone, she thought, could know where it might lead or indeed exactly why she had agreed to travel along it. It was in many ways madness; she had managed to break with William once, she had told him in every ugly detail why they could never be together; she had started to recover . . . and now here she was, risking more unhappiness, more confusion.

She must just stay really cool, she thought, refuse to see it as anything but a business arrangement, as William being kind and good and wanting to help both her and Georgia in a venture that would clearly seem relevant to him as well as to them.

And then, as she stood there, still waiting, still watching, he saw her; and he stood up, as he would have done for anyone, with those bloody old-fashioned manners of his, pulled out a chair, and beckoned to her to join them.

'Hi,' she said, walking over, hearing her own voice, calm and steady, not weak and breathless as she was afraid it might be, smiling at him as you would at any friend who had put a business proposition her way, kissing him briefly, coolly on the cheek – how could she do that when she wanted to kiss him endlessly, desperately – and then turned swiftly to Georgia.

'You must be Georgia. Hi, I'm Abi.'

'Hi, Abi. It's so good of you to come. William – Mr Grainger – has been telling me all about you.'

'Really?' Not *all* about her, surely. Not of endless, giggly conversations, nor of more earnest ones, not of long nights of searing, soaring sex, nor of closeness, warmth, tenderness; not of discovery, of delight, of sheer happiness, however shortlived . . .

'Yes. How you've done this sort of thing before and can tell me how to go about it.'

'Well, he might be taking a slightly optimistic view. But yes, I did get involved with a musician' – damn, that would hurt William, in fact she saw it hurting him – and it would remind him of why he should have nothing more to do with her. But that was good. No point suddenly presenting herself as a nun. She went on, 'A musician who played at a rock festival a couple of years ago. I got sucked into helping with ticket sales and programming and absorbed a lot about the organisation entailed. It's a huge project, Georgia, I hope you realise just how huge.'

'I probably don't. But I'm ready for anything. I'm so, so determined to do it.'

She smiled; she was sweet, pretty, rather serious. It would be fun working with her.

'Good,' was all Abi said.

Gradually, the emotional situation eased as they discussed the form of the thing – 'I did once suggest a rock festival to William, didn't I? But I think maybe you've got more of a single concert in mind' – possible lead times, possible dates, the vast amount of time and planning it would absorb, how with the best will in the world, they would need many more people on board. 'Don't look so frightened,' Abi said to Georgia. 'It's for charity – we can get mostly volunteers. It's a wonderful project, Georgia. I'm really excited about it.'

Not about working with William, not about having endless access to William; that was out of the equation. Entirely.

Georgia said she was just as excited and that they could at least look at a festival. 'Tell us more about what it might entail.'

Abi told them more: much more. Probably too much, she thought afterwards. When she started outlining the need for security guards, parking facilities, police involvement and the infrastructure required, William became visibly worried.

'A road! Abi, I can't start building roads.'

'Well, you might have to. The contractors—'

'What contractors?' asked Georgia.

'The ones building the stage, setting up the sound systems – all that sort of thing. You can't do this using a few old planks of wood and an iPod, you know. Even if it is just a concert. You've got to think big, or it won't work. Anyway, the contractors – and the punters, come to that – need to know they're not going to get stuck in the mud. You do realise it will rain, don't you?'

'No, why?' said William.

'It just always does. Part of the package.'

'Oh,' said William.

Georgia looked at him and then said rather nervously that maybe they should just stick to the idea of a concert. 'An open-air one in the evening, next summer; it could be lovely.'

Abi said a concert would be all right, but it would be hard to make nearly so much of it, 'And certainly not much money. I think a festival would be much more exciting, you'd get far more publicity for a start and a much bigger crowd. Not one of those huge ones like Glastonbury or Reading, obviously, but something where families could come, bring their kids, camp just for one night, have a few bands playing, dance, people really love that sort of thing; it's like a mini-holiday and it's so cool at the moment. That way, you'd probably end up with a couple of thousand people – and you will make a bit of money. And you know, even quite big bands bring their fee down if they know it's for charity. Anyway, whatever the size of the thing, you have to have a stage and audio equipment, and loos of course, and a licence from the council . . .'

'A licence!'

'Yes, of course. They can't actually refuse unless there's a very specific reason, which has to be a real one, not just that your neighbours won't like it, but that it might be dangerous in some way, a fire risk or something.'

'A fire risk?'

'Well, yes,' said Abi patiently, 'from all the electrics and so on, and then people might light barbecues – in fact, they will, it's all part of the fun. William,' she added, seeing his shell-shocked expression, 'are you really up for all this? And are your parents all right about it?'

William said rather airily that they'd been persuaded to do it: he didn't add that he'd been pretty evasive about the implications, had sold it to them as a charity concert which sounded rather charming; he knew they'd be totally opposed to the idea of a festival, with all its unfortunate implications of deafening noise, drugs and general squalor.

'Come on, Dad,' he'd said, seeing his father wavering slightly after a long evening of his mother saying she wouldn't even countenance such a thing. 'You only live once. And we are only talking about once, after all.'

Whereupon his mother had made the sound somewhere between a tut and a sigh so familiar to both of them and left the room saying she hoped they both knew what madness they were considering; and his father had looked at William and half-smiled and said he hoped William did realise that, and that he would hold him personally responsible for any damage to livestock and farm buildings. 'And you know what I mean by that, William – financially responsible.'

William said that was fine, and that he was confident there would be no damage; and, 'Very well,' his father had said and poured them both a large whisky. 'To the concert,' he said, raising his glass. 'What are you going to call it?'

'Golly, Dad, I don't know. That's more the girls' bag.'

'Right. Well, let me know. Could be fun.'

William was still very surprised; it seemed so out of character. A man who resisted change to an almost obsessive degree, giving in to a suggestion that was radical, to put it mildly – it was – well – unexpected. But, 'Thanks, Dad,' he said again.

'That's OK. Just don't let me down.'

'I won't.'

'I went to a music festival once,' his father said, looking half-embarrassed.

'Dad! You didn't!'

'Yes, I did. On the Isle of Wight. Back in the sixties. Marvellous fun it was. Never forgotten it.'

No wonder William thought that wasn't surprising. The number of times his father had left the farm overnight for anything at all could be counted in single figures.

'Did you go with Mother?' he asked.

'Oh no, no, not her sort of thing at all. Even then. No, I went with several friends from Agricultural College. God, we let our hair down. If you know what I mean.'

William said he thought he did: and smiled at his father and sat looking at him as he poured out two more whiskies, dressed in the flannels and sports jacket that his mother insisted he changed into every night for dinner, even if they were eating in the kitchen, and tried to imagine his father letting his hair down, as he put it, and absolutely failed.

'No, they're fine about it,' he said now. 'Specially Dad.'

'Well, that's great,' Abi said. 'Let's just hope they stay on side, because they won't be able to switch very easily. Now, really and truly you need a sponsor, to make it financially viable. They would put up something like – I don't know – a couple of grand say, in return for publicity.'

'That sounds like an awful lot of money,' said Georgia.

'Sweetie, it's a piss in a pot set against the real cost, but a big help nevertheless. You might start thinking who to approach.'

'What, like one of the TV companies or something?'

'Well possibly, although it's unlikely they'll have that sort of money to throw around at the moment. More of a commercial concern, some local manufacturing company or other. I'll think too. Anyway – what do you reckon? Now's the time to say no.'

Georgia emitted a sort of squeak. Abi looked at her. Her

great dark eyes were shining and her hands clasped together, making a sort of fist. Abi was to get to know that gesture well in the months to come.

'I think it sounds wonderful,' she said. 'We've absolutely got to do it – if William – Mr Grainger – is really up for it. It's obviously a very big undertaking.'

'Please call me William,' said William. 'Mr Grainger makes me feel like I'm my dad.'

He looked at the pair of them, two sassy sexy girls, girls he would never have known a year ago, and thought of spending a lot of time with them over the next six months or so. It made him feel dizzy.

'I'm up for it,' he said. 'Yeah, course.'

It was just as well, Georgia thought, that she had the concert to distract her. She viewed the inquest with absolute terror. Her mother, who had attended countless inquests over the years in the course of her job as a senior social worker, had tried to reassure her, to tell her that the whole point about them was that they were about setting records straight, not about casting blame or making judgements, and that coroners in her experience were the most charming and considerate of people. None of it helped. The thought of having to stand up in a courtroom, in front of a crowd of people, several of whom were still grieving, and describe under oath how she had abandoned Patrick Connell in his cab and disappeared, failing to provide the evidence that had been so crucial to him, made her feel violently sick.

She knew there was no way out of it; it had to be got through, but it was still there, driving her back into her guilt and remorse, telling her parents she couldn't face Christmas at home and that she thought she might spend it in London on her own in her room. It was only when Anna, who had become her latest confidante, told her with unusual firmness that she was being selfish, taking it out on her parents by spoiling their Christmas, that Georgia managed to call her mother and apologise and say that of course she would be there.

Moving Away was in the final stages of filming; Georgia had very mixed feelings about it. She'd got really fond of everyone, and it had been a wonderful experience, but she'd been so scared such a lot of the time, and although everyone had been very nice to her, even Bryn, who'd said he couldn't wait to work with her again, she still felt she'd been a disappointment to them all, hadn't quite fulfilled her promise, and it had been hard to keep going, day after day.

Release was planned for the spring; it was now in post-production, was being edited, music added, colour graded; once they got to the final cut, the producer would see it.

'And agree it – we hope,' Merlin said.

It was awful to think she wouldn't be seeing him more or less every day; it had been such an incredibly exciting element in the whole thing, just getting ready in the morning, wondering what to wear, whether he'd be there, what he'd say to her. She was still slightly baffled as to what his feelings about her were; non-existent, she thought on her bad days, but then on the good ones: why ask her to go for a drink so often after they'd finished for the day, why spend so much time with her, why make sure she was all right in Jaz's house.

He'd even, once or twice, asked her to the cinema, to see some incredibly intellectual foreign films at what he called his local, the Hampstead Everyman, which she hadn't understood at all, let alone enjoyed – although she'd pretended to, of course – and one wonderful Saturday he'd called her and said he was going to do some Christmas shopping in the Portobello Market and if she was around, would she like to join him? She'd loved that, wandering along the stalls, not that she bought anything, as it all seemed hideously expensive to her, not a bit like a real market; in fact, Merlin told her that some of the silver was brought along by the really big dealers because they got a better price there than at the other antique markets, or even in Bond Street. 'The tourists, you see, they can rip them off terribly.' When they'd finished, he asked her if she'd like to have lunch at Camden Lock – 'I can't believe you haven't been there yet, all this time in London' – and she'd said, trying to sound totally cool, that she'd like that, and had sat in one of the bars alongside the canal, convinced this was it, that he was going to say he really liked her. But he didn't, he simply said he had to get back quite soon after lunch. 'The parents are having a party tonight, so I have to go back and help.'

'Will it be a big party?' she asked, trying to sound casual, half-wondering if he might be going to invite her.

'Quite big,' he said. 'About a hundred. Anyone else would have proper help, but Mummy won't. It's against her principles, like not having a cleaner, so she's run herself ragged cooking for weeks and Pa just hides in his study and pretends he hasn't noticed.'

'And lots of famous people there?' she said.

'Yeah, I suppose so, lot of Beeb types, Humphrys, Paxman. Benn, I imagine, the Milliband seniors, possibly Charlie Falconer, but not the Blairs, Browns or anyone in that league.'

'God,' she said. 'I call that pretty impressive.'

'Not really. You're so sweet, Georgia,' he added, smiling at her, 'so totally unspoiled still, aren't you? Stay like it, for goodness' sake. Right – I must dash. Can you find your own way back?'

'Yes, of course. I want to look in some of those shops anyway,' she said quickly, and then added, emboldened by the two glasses of white wine she had consumed, 'But look – if you want any help passing round the crisps this evening . . .'

Whereupon he went very pink and said how kind of her, but no, no, it was quite unnecessary, and asked her what she was doing that evening. Georgia was extremely grateful to be able to tell him she was going to the Comedy Store, and didn't add that it was with Anna's daughter, Lila.

And that was how their relationship – or rather their non-relationship – proceeded, two steps forward, two steps back. Exasperating, frustrating – baffling. Most of the time she managed to think it was just luvvie stuff, no more than that, along with the hugs and the brotherly kisses; but she still found grounds for thinking it was more. Although it had never got any further; and yet he wasn't exactly shy. But then maybe he didn't want to get involved with her emotionally until after shooting was finished. Or was that wishful thinking too?

She had never talked about him to anyone involved in the production: deliberately. There was no way she was going to risk being laughed at for having an unrequited crush on him; she preferred they would all think she was as cool about him as he appeared to be about her. And in any case, she wasn't on those sorts of terms with any of them, except for Anna, and she was careful to keep her feelings about Merlin a secret even from her.

She tried to find out about him from Linda, who always knew all the gossip about everybody, but she just said vaguely that she didn't really know much about him, except that he was incredibly talented and would soon be a first assistant, probably in the next production he worked on. 'You don't fancy him, darling, do you?'

'God no,' said Georgia. 'Not my type at all.'

'Good. Because the words little and shit do come rather to mind.'

Georgia ignored this; it was such a typical Linda comment.

❖ ❖ ❖

And then the mystery was solved – painfully.

The wrap party was taking place just a week before Christmas. Georgia was really looking forward to that, had bought a sequinned dress that was virtually non-existent, so short and low-cut it was, and some incredibly long, sequinned fake eyelashes to go with it; she'd been feeling really confident until she saw Sasha. Sasha had gone Goth for the evening; Georgia thought she looked awful, but told herself if anyone knew about style, it had to be Sasha. She had looked Georgia up and down rather pointedly when she arrived and said, 'Sweet dress,' in tones that implied wearing it had been a very serious mistake. Luckily Merlin had come up and told her she looked wonderful or she might have gone home to change.

The party was at Bryn's house in Putney, a wonderful glass-fronted place on the river. She'd never been to a wrap party before, but she'd heard they were really emotional, everyone bonding like crazy and reminiscing about the production and how it had been the best ever; and it certainly lived up to her expectations. At first . . .

Bryn had been incredibly generous, provided champagne by the crateful, and Mrs Bryn, who was a glamorous actress called Jan Lloyd, fantastic food. Particularly kind of her, as she then went out for the evening. 'She says no one should be at the wrap parties of other people's productions,' Bryn said, laughing when he made his little speech, and actually, as Anna said to Georgia, it really wasn't very pleasant: you felt like a complete outsider, understood none of the in-jokes, and were deeply wary of discovering any illicit relationships. 'I should know, I used to hate meeting people Sim had been on the road with when I hadn't. It wasn't even that I thought he'd been sleeping with anyone, although he probably had; there's just this closeness that working with people day after day creates. It's a hell of a bond – and quite an excluding one.'

Georgia could feel herself going over the top, flirting with everyone, including Bryn – and Merlin, of course – making people dance with her, but it was the last time she'd see most of them, for God's sake, and she was enjoying herself so much.

Merlin was a fantastic dancer, and he was looking absolutely amazing, all in black – black skinny jeans, black T-shirt, black leather jacket. She thought he must be rather hot in the jacket, and suggested he took it off more than once, but he said he liked it, and he liked being hot. She hoped he meant what she thought by that.

And then suddenly and without warning, the front doorbell went and Georgia, who was in the hall, opened it. A girl stood there, a really beautiful girl, tall, with long blond hair and astonishingly green eyes; she was wearing a short black dress and black knee boots with very high heels; she smiled at Georgia just slightly dismissively and looked her up and down rather as Sasha had, and then said, 'Hi. Is Merlin here?'

Georgia said he was and that she'd go and find him – the girl was the sort who inspired such behaviour – and had just turned to go into the party when Bryn appeared and said, 'Ticky! Darling! What a surprise. Merlin didn't warn us.'

The girl kissed Bryn and said, 'He didn't know I was flying in today. I promise, Bryn darling, I haven't come to crash your wrap party. I just thought I might steal him away, in a little while.'

'You can crash anything of mine, sweetie. Let me go and find the boy.'

'I will,' said Georgia. She was feeling very sick.

Merlin, it seemed, and Ticky – whoever was called Ticky, and what was it short for, Georgia wondered – were an item. Had been since drama school. Only Ticky, who had a very rich daddy, was now attending the New York film school. And only came back to London for the vacations.

Merlin clearly adored her; so did most of the cast. Davina called her 'darling lamb', Frank kissed her hand and told her she was beauty personified; even Sasha threw her arms round her and told her she looked divine. Which she did, Georgia thought miserably; she was the sort of girl who was on the cover of *Tatler*, or even *Vogue*. Understated, super-confident, totally classy, she had become, briefly, the centre of the party.

And when she and Merlin left after half an hour, looking like a Prada ad, as Sasha said, Georgia sat down next to Anna and trying to sound cool, said, 'What happened to not being at other people's wrap parties?'

'I guess if you look like that, you can be anywhere you damn well like,' Anna said, and then, looking rather hard at Georgia, 'I bet she's pure poison. Trust-fund babe, apparently.'

'No one acted like she was poison,' Georgia said, struggling to sound light-hearted and failing, she knew.

'No, that's true. Maybe she's nice as well. That really would be unfair. Listen, sweetie, you know something? I've had enough. Want to come home with me? Lila's on her own and she'd love to see you – and catch up on the concert. If there's anything to catch up on . . .'

'That'd be great,' said Georgia. 'Thank you.' All she felt now was a consuming terror that the whole production had been laughing at her behind her back.

Anna, who had clearly put two and two together, confronted the issue in the cab home; told her they hadn't.

'I swear to you, nobody ever mentioned it. Listen, even I never guessed. You played it really cool, Georgia. Well done. And good riddance, I'd say. Leading you on like that, never mentioning her. Ticky! What a name.'

'No, no, not really,' said poor Georgia, the tears beginning to flow now. 'And he didn't lead me on, he was just – really kind. Helped me get my room, took me for drinks, cheered me up . . . Oh, I'm sorry, Anna. I think I might change my mind, go home after all.'

'All right,' said Anna, 'of course I understand. But please, please sweetie, believe me. I never heard a whisper about you and Merlin. Honestly.'

It was comfort of a sort.

She had expected to feel terrible; and she did. Stupid, as well as hurt, naïve as well as abandoned. The days were suddenly emptied of excitement, of emotional interest, indeed of any interest at all; she decided to go home early for Christmas. She wasn't needed on the film any more, and had only been hanging around for the pleasure of seeing Merlin.

It was quite nice to get home; her mother was in a whirlwind of preparation and touchingly pleased to have Georgia with her, particularly as Michael wasn't joining them – he'd been invited to join Marissa and her family. Marissa was his rather glamorous barrister girlfriend. Her parents were very rich and had a villa in Barbados where they Christmassed, as Marissa put it. 'I don't think Cardiff can quite compete, do you?' said Bea, laughing.

She was so amazingly well-adjusted and nice, Georgia thought; she knew that she herself would have been totally jealous if her only son had ditched a family Christmas in Wales for one on the beach in Barbados. But Bea just wanted Michael to have a good time.

And as the days went by, in a seasonal haze of shopping and wrapping and mince-pie making and tree decorating, something rather surprising and extremely welcome happened, and Georgia discovered that she was becoming cross where she had been miserable, indignant instead of heartbroken.

How dare he! How dare he treat her like that, present himself as her mentor and guide, deceive her so skilfully. For he *had* deceived her, she could see that now; he must

667

have realised she liked him, that she depended on him even. The very fact that he had never so much as mentioned Ticky was proof of the depth of the deception. Had he really seen Georgia just as a friend, of course he would have talked about a girlfriend, about what Ticky was doing, where she was, her very existence. He had just made sure she remained completely ignorant and then had the fun of flirting with her, enjoying her hero worship, dispensing largesse, making himself seem like Mr Important. She kept hearing Linda saying the words 'little' and 'shit'; she should have listened to her more carefully, asked her what she meant. It was so true; he was indeed a sneaky, sly, self-important little shit. He deserved some kind of come-uppance. She began to have fantasies about Ticky finding some billionaire in New York and dumping Merlin publicly and mercilessly; that would be good. She did some research about Ticky, Googled her; she was indeed a trust-fund babe, an It-girl, always at high-profile parties, featured endlessly in magazines. The quote that gave Georgia most pleasure was 'Ticky Davenport, wannabe actress . . .' in one of the newspapers. Wannabe – that was good. At least no one could say that of her, Georgia thought. She was a real actress, with a real part under her belt. And then was surprised that she had the confidence to think of herself in such terms and knew she must be feeling better.

In the end she actually managed to enjoy Christmas.

Linda had an incredible Christmas. She always enjoyed it, she loved the theatricality of it, spent many hours decorating her flat, went to endless parties, bought a mountain of presents for everyone and went for the day to Francis and his partner who was an incredible cook. None of that was altered this year; except that Alex, who had spent the day with Sam and the children and Sam's sister and her family, came up for the evening and, as Linda put it, they fucked their way into Boxing Day.

Linda didn't know quite what she felt about her relationship with Alex. In many ways it was extremely difficult; he was moody and bad-tempered and introspective to an absurd degree, they fought a great deal, and indeed what felt like at least half their dates ended in rows – the less serious resolved in bed, the more serious unresolved for days. They fought furiously, and passionately; as they got to know one another better, knew where and how to hurt, the rows got nastier. Several times, after he had slammed out of her flat late at night or very early in the morning, or even on one particularly nasty occasion, out of a restaurant, first throwing some money down on the table, she decided that she must finish things. There was no future in any of it, they just made one another unhappy, and indeed would call him to tell him so – and more than once he had agreed. But then somehow, they would resolve things, one or other of them would make some approach, without actually apologising, and they would agree to meet and then having met, found themselves, almost against their respective wills, quite unable to continue with the hostilities. And then they would start again, amusing, charming, pleasing one another, agreeing that they made one another happier than anyone else had ever done – until the next time.

It seemed to Linda quite impossible that it could be a long-term relationship – it was just too uncomfortable and disturbing; on the other hand, she looked into a future without Alex, without the intense colour and interest and drama, and that seemed impossible to contemplate too.

She was perfectly aware what caused the rows; they were both arrogant, opinionated people and for too long had been able to hold on to their opinions and behaviour and not consider anyone else, Linda because she lived alone, with all the self-indulgence that offered, and Alex because he and Sam had long ceased to communicate in any way, and his status at the hospital meant that very few people ever confronted him there either.

On her up days – and Linda was on the whole an extremely up person, she had to be, in order to survive her chosen profession – she would think it was fine, that the drama and passion and difficulty of it all were actually part of the pleasure; but when she was down, contemplating her middle age and beyond, she could see that it was not at all what she needed, not the warm reassurance and companionship she had been dreaming of. Alex was about as reassuring as a roll of thunder. He also brought with him exactly what she had vowed she would never even consider, the burden of teenage children – whom he had not even allowed her to meet, and that in itself had to be significant, and indeed she found it fairly hurtful – and a demanding career entirely out of her orbit.

The only thing she could do, or try to do and it went against her nature, was enjoy the relationship for as long as she could, and to continue to look for someone more suitable. The trouble was that Alex, for all his appalling drawbacks, had set the bar rather high . . .

Laura had hated every moment of Christmas. She had always loved it so much, looked forward to it for months, the planning, the shopping, the decorating, the cooking, creating the perfect performance for everyone; had always thought how lucky she was to be able to do it all on such an extravagant scale; and now she discovered that actually it wasn't the present-giving, or the family feasts, or the delight of doing the tree with the children, or even the carol concerts and the children's party that she and Jonathan had always given – 'everyone gives grown-up parties, too many really; we think it's more fun to have a children's one' – it was the sense of being at the heart of her perfect, happy family. Her family this Christmas was not only not perfect, it was not even happy; and she was not at the heart of it.

At the heart of it this year was a bitter unhappiness, two little girls crying most nights for their daddy and begging her to make sure he came for Christmas, a boy who said he hated his father, and that he would walk out if he came for Christmas, and a house that was a cold showcase for the lights and the tinsel and the tree and the presents underneath it. She had invited her parents to join them as usual, thinking that they would ease not only the atmosphere, but the sense of emptiness, but it didn't really help much. They had all tried; she had lavished enormous sums of money on PlayStations and Nintendo games for Charlie, and dolls and clothes for the girls, and iPods for all of them, they had had the tallest tree and the biggest crackers ever, the most perfect Christmas dinner, and even though the girls had expressed delight and told her they loved their presents and loved her, and had sung Christmas carols determinedly as they helped to lay and decorate the dinner table, and even Charlie had tried to be cheerful and said how cool his PlayStation was, and submitted to his grandfather's endless terrible jokes with a good grace and they had all managed to play a round of Charades and a game of Trivial Pursuit after dinner, there had been a greyness over everything.

And when they hugged and kissed her goodnight and settled into bed with their new books, their iPods clamped to their heads, she knew that above anything else, they were relieved it was over and they could stop trying to seem happy. The compromise reached over Jonathan's visit had been that he would come on Christmas morning and give them presents (during which Charlie glowered from a corner) and then go away 'because I've got to deliver some babies' and then have them on Boxing Day in his flat, and take them to the pantomime at Richmond in the evening. But Charlie had refused to go at the last minute, which had upset the little girls, and there had been the hideous empty seat beside them in the theatre which they could almost hear shouting, 'Charlie should be here!' and they had cried all the way home after Laura collected them.

And left alone in his flat without them, contemplating the ugly, empty day that had passed, Jonathan had cried too.

Barney, like Georgia, was literally having nightmares about the inquest. Indeed, he felt so wretched and so panicky sometimes that he began to wonder if he was having a nervous breakdown. Every time he thought about being asked about the tyres and how he would have to say that Toby hadn't let him check them, he thought he would throw up. The fact that there had been a nail in one of them, initially an immense relief, now seemed of less importance. He should have insisted on doing all he could to ensure the car's safety; that was the whole point.

His memories of the crash now were somehow more intense than they had been for months, as he relived the horror not only of the blow-out, and seeing Toby's white face and staring eyes as he struggled to right the car and regain control of it, but the endless time afterwards while he sat with Toby, spattered with his blood, wondering if he was still alive; and even the awful day of the operation. And that would lead him on to thinking about Emma that day and how happily and quickly they had tumbled into love; and then how much he missed her still. And he would even, in spite of everything, realise how much he missed Toby too, missed having him there to have a laugh with, to send stupid emails to, to get drunk with. He had other friends, of course, but Toby had been there for so long, it was like losing a bit of himself: quite a large bit. Toby would be back at work after Christmas; he was bound to run into him in bars and so on, they'd always had jokes about it: 'We mustn't keep meeting like this,' one or other of them would say, and Amanda was bound to ask why they weren't seeing each other. She knew about Tamara, of course, and the broken engagement, and she'd been very upset, her great blue eyes filled with tears. 'But I suppose it's for the best. Tamara said they'd just fallen out of love – how awful is that?'

How awful indeed.

It had been agreed that he and Amanda and Amanda's mother should spend Christmas Day with Barney's parents. Barney had always rather looked down on people who said they dreaded Christmas, thought they were killjoys; this year he knew how they felt.

Amanda had been at her very best, charming, sweet, thoughtful, incredibly gracious; had bought wonderful presents – and a hamper from Fortnum's – for the Frasers, had helped Barney's mother with the cooking, teased and flirted with Barney's father, and watched over her own mother as tenderly and carefully as if she was the child. She had also, when she and Barney went to bed on Christmas night, thanked him for everything he had done for her and her mother, 'Not just today, but every day since Daddy died. I couldn't have got through it without you, neither of us could.' She gave him a pair of gold Art Deco cufflinks, 'Just to show you how much I love you,' and then urged him to make love to her, 'Because I know I haven't been very – very welcoming lately, but it's not because of you, it's because . . . well, you know, because of Daddy.'

And Barney, lying awake later as she slept, thought how dreadful it would be if she were to know how grateful he had been for the lack of welcome, and how impossible it was to make love to her now without thinking of another body, more passionately loved, and wondered if he would ever manage to forget its owner, or at least to set her safely in the past and concentrate on his great and present good fortune in being loved by someone who was almost literally too good to be true.

* * *

Emma was also dreading Christmas and had been half-hoping she'd be on duty, so as not to have to spend three long days with her family, who she loved very much but who were incorrigibly curious about her life. She would, she knew, be endlessly questioned, not only about her job at St Mark's, now drawing to a close, her future career and where she might go next, but also about her dashing boyfriend. She deeply regretted telling them as much as she had about Luke, but she had been so overcome with excitement about him at the time and had even told her sister about the Tiffany locket; she had managed to avoid much recent questioning by virtue of the simple fact that Luke was in Milan and she hadn't seen him since October, but she could see that wasn't going to work much longer. They'd expect him to appear over Christmas; either she would have to tell them it was over, which would lead to more questioning, or invent some compelling reason for him to stay in Milan. In the end she told them he'd dumped her and she didn't want to talk about it; they respected this, assuming that the almost palpable sadness that hung about her at times must be due to this. She spent much of Christmas trying not to wonder what Barney was doing, which large country house he and Amanda would be staying in, and whether there would be discussion with their families – Christmas being the sort of time such conversations did take place – about their wedding plans.

It was a relief to get back to work.

Mary and Russell had a perfect Christmas. Tadwick House was absurdly over-decorated, with fairylights not only in every room, round every fireplace, and entwined round every stair-rail, but strung along every hedge outside as well. A vast Christmas tree stood in the hall, a second in the drawing room, complete with a mountainous pile of presents; mistletoe hung in every doorway, huge log fires burned in every grate, and the house was filled with the irresistible mingling of woodsmoke and baking. And it was wonderfully, noisily full.

Not only were Christine and Gerry, Douglas and Maureen and their children, Timothy and the lovely Lorraine there for Christmas Day, together with Lorraine's parents, but to Mary's absolute surprise and delight, Coral and Pearl and their respective spouses asked if they might join them as well, an English Christmas having long been a dream of theirs.

'I'm so pleased they want to come,' Mary said, passing the note to Russell. 'It means they like me, you see; they've accepted me as part of your family.'

Russell said no one in their right mind would fail to accept Mary as part of anything, but he was actually delighted as well. Christine's initial rejection of him had hurt him badly, and he felt rather proud that his own daughters were more generous-hearted than Mary's. He still found Christine quite hard to embrace – both physically and emotionally. In spite of her dramatic appearance at the wedding in her mackintosh, she had failed to say anything to him by way of an apology, and every time he looked at her rather self-satisfied, plump face he wondered at her dissimilarity from her mother.

Mrs Salter had worked with Mary for several days, baking and glazing and roasting and icing. She had found it hard at first, as she told her sister, not having her kitchen to herself, and she could see that Mrs Mackenzie, while being very nice, was not the sort used to staff. But she liked her so much that she was prepared to humour her and let her be involved. 'And actually, she's a very interesting lady. The stories she has to tell about the war and that – well, you should just hear them. That was when she met Mr Mackenzie, of course. Now he *is* a gentleman, used to being looked after, but it takes all sorts.'

The weather was most obligingly Christmassy, crisp and sunny; the entire party went to morning service on

Christmas Day, came back for a vast lunch (with a break for the Queen's speech), and then went for a short walk, before having presents in the drawing room. After that, everyone withdrew for a short rest and then reassembled for games and to sing carols round the piano. The piano had been Russell's Christmas present to Mary, who had always longed for one ever since learning to play on her own grandmother's when she was a small girl, and never been allowed one since; it was delivered on Christmas Eve and she wasn't allowed into the drawing room for at least an hour while Russell, with Mrs Salter's help, managed to wrap it entirely in silver paper and tie a huge red bow round it; Mary was then led in and allowed to open it. She was so overwhelmed she cried, and then spent the next hour playing it, a little rustily at first, but by sherry time she was sufficiently adept to play 'Jingle Bells' and 'Away in a Manger'. Russell was a superb pianist and took over for the evening performance, finishing with a flamboyant, concert-style rendition of 'Rhapsody in Blue' which reduced Lorraine's mother and both Coral and Pearl to tears.

The party broke up at about ten, apart from Timothy and Lorraine and the Canadian cousins who were watching an old Bond movie. Christine walked to the bottom of the stairs, then turned and went back to Russell and kissed him.

'It's been wonderful,' she said. 'Thank you very much for having us here today.' She then went very pink and said, 'And I'm very sorry about my – about – well, I can't tell you how pleased I am that you're here. You've made my mother happier than I can ever remember. Since Dad died, that is, of course.'

At which Russell assumed a very respectful expression and kissed her back and said, 'Of course,' and added that he was proud to have succeeded someone who had clearly been so remarkable a gentleman as Donald.

Later, as they sat in bed reading the new books most

thoughtfully provided by Santa – a new Dick Francis for Russell and a Maeve Binchy for Mary – 'they're my favourite books, nothing or no one really horrible ever appears in them' – he leaned over and kissed Mary and said, 'I meant it about Donald. He clearly was most remarkable, to have made you so happy. I'm going to have a tough job living up to him.'

Mary kissed him back and told him he wasn't doing too badly so far.

Chapter 46

She supposed she should have realised; if they squabbled as much as they did when they were living in different houses – and different cities, come to that – what hope was there for them when they were sharing the same room with no escape in any form, even into work?

It wasn't her, of course; it was Alex. He was so terminally untidy. He seemed unable to so much as change his socks without messing up the entire room. At first, she simply went round after him, picking things up and putting them away, but that made him very irritable and he told her to stop. 'You'll be regulating my breathing next.'

'Which wouldn't be a bad thing,' said Linda tartly. 'You might snore a bit more quietly.'

'You knew I snored, Linda.'

'I know I did, Alex. It's one thing knowing it and another thing enduring it night after night.'

'Well, maybe we should get you a separate room.'

'Absolutely not,' said Linda. 'Don't be ridiculous!'

Actually it seemed like a very nice idea, but it would be round the Conference in minutes, she thought, that they didn't want to sleep together, and they were already quite enough of a discussion point, first for not being married and secondly for her having nothing to do with the medical profession whatsoever.

Perversely, she had enjoyed the first part of the trip – the conference in Cape Town – a great deal more than she had expected. She had thought it would be tedious in the extreme, and it had actually turned out to be rather fun. Not least because she was quickly established as something of a star, certainly among the men, not just because of what she looked like and how she dressed, but because of what she did: a glossy, entertaining creature from another world altogether.

She had made two friends in particular, one a rather dashing neurosurgeon, who had first trained as a barrister; he told her life was too short to spend it in one discipline, as he put it, and asked her, his blue eyes dancing with appreciation at her very low-cut black velvet top, what she was going to do when she grew up. Linda told him she was going to be a lapdancer and he laughed so much and so loudly that the entire dining room turned round to look.

The other friend was rather different; he was a part-time primary school teacher called Martin, rather plain but very funny, accompanying his wife; he said he was quite used to coming on the spousal programmes.

'I don't mind a bit. I enjoy it all except the shopping. And the other wives are very nice to me.'

He said he had always looked after the children, ever since his wife, an orthopaedic surgeon, had got her first consultancy. 'I mean, why not? She earns squillions more than I ever could. It works pretty well, we don't have to pay a nanny, and she gives me a very generous dress – I mean golf – allowance. She gets a bit tetchy if dinner isn't ready when she gets home, but I can handle that.'

Linda laughed. Maybe that was what she needed – a house husband. It would be great to get home every night to find dinner cooked, and the fridge stocked. Not to mention all her dry cleaning and laundry sorted, and the cleaners organised. Wonderful. But then, house husbands just weren't very sexy.

They were staying at the Vineyard: a five-star wonder nestled just below Table Mountain, with rambling show-piece gardens, complete with giant tortoises and incredible flowers, and a superb spa. The sun shone relentlessly from an incredibly blue sky, the air was clear and somehow crisp even in the heat of the day, and the food and wine were beyond criticism. It would have taken a churlish spirit not to enjoy this, Linda thought, settling by the pool, a large white-wine spritzer at her side, happily aware that she looked as good in her bikini as all but the youngest of the other guests. Sometimes, just sometimes, all those hours at the gym seemed worthwhile.

On the second day the spousal programme took them up Table Mountain via the cable car. Linda walked round the top with Martin, the teacher; they admired the views, the almost literally intoxicating air, and agreed that they might both duck out of the visit to the township the following day.

'But my— Alex tells me they don't like that,' she said.

'Oh, they don't mind once or twice. I usually say I've got my period.'

Linda giggled. She really hadn't expected someone as fun as this.

'Your husband comes on these things a lot?'

'My partner. We're not married. Well, actually, and if you can keep a secret, he's just my boyfriend. I dared him to bring me on this and he did.'

'I won't tell a soul. Why should you need to dare him? Any normal red-blooded man would be dying to take you anywhere. Or is his blood a bit pink?'

'No, of course not,' said Linda, laughing. 'And it's a bit of an in-joke, the dares. Anyway, he doesn't approve of these trips really. Says they're thinly disguised bribes.'

'Quite right. Fortunately my wife doesn't have such principles.'

And all might have been well, had he not brought his wife – a pretty girl with freckles and a Scottish accent called Fiona – to meet Alex and Linda at pre-dinner drinks and told Alex what Linda had said about the bribery, and how much he agreed with him.

'Frightful racket. Still, who are we to complain?'

'Well, you certainly don't,' said Fiona. 'I have to work very hard for it. Anyway, it's not exactly true.'

'Of course it's not,' said Alex. He glared at Linda.

'I call the spousal programme pretty hard work,' said Martin. 'Linda and I are ducking out tomorrow, aren't we?'

'Yes. Doing a heavy day at the spa,' said Linda, and then rather hurriedly, 'And how was today's conference session?'

'Very good,' said Fiona. 'Some really interesting ideas, didn't you think, Alex?'

'Yes, not bad.'

'Well, if it isn't the lapdancer. Not working tonight?'

It was the neurosurgeon. Linda, who had already had two glassses of champagne, reached up to kiss him.

'Hi. Not yet. I don't usually start until after dinner.'

'I'll look forward to it. Come and rescue my wife, will you? I've told her about you, she's longing to meet you and she's stuck with some gnome from R and D. Can you spare her, Alex, old chap?'

'Yes, of course,' said Alex. He smiled at the neurosurgeon. Linda knew that smile. It came with great difficulty. She winked at him, said she'd soon be back, and followed the neurosurgeon across the room.

Mrs N-S was rather fun: a doctor herself, a GP from Ireland. She was extremely grateful for the rescue – 'I really thought I'd pass out with boredom in a minute' – and asked Linda who her husband was.

'Ah yes,' she said, squinting across the room. 'Very sexy, I thought. Touch of the Heathcliffs.'

'That's exactly what I thought, the first time I saw him,' said Linda. 'And the resemblance doesn't end there. Very dark and brooding he can be. Not that full of sunshine right this minute actually. I think he's cross because I'm ducking out of the programme tomorrow.'

'I might join you in that. Hate the idea of it. What are you doing instead?'

'Beautifying myself in the spa.'

'Sounds good. Well, see you there maybe. We've got to go into dinner.'

Alex scowled at Linda as she sat down beside him.

'Lovely to see you too,' she said, kissing him.

'Linda, how dare you go round telling people I regard these things as bribery. It's outrageous!'

'But you do. You said so.'

'That was a private remark. Passing it on here is rather like telling your hostess you don't like her cooking. I can't believe you can be so socially inept. Not to mention rude.'

'Sorry,' she said, slightly alarmed at his anger. 'I really am.'

'And please, Linda, don't duck out of any more of the programme. You know what we agreed.'

'All right. Sorry. I'll be as good as gold tomorrow. You know, I'm really enjoying it all. It's a bit like being back at school.'

'Well, try not to behave as if you actually were.'

'Oh, do stop scowling at me, Alex, I've said I'm sorry. And you should be glad I'm enjoying myself.'

'I'm afraid not. Or rather not the way you've chosen.'

'Oh God,' she said, putting down her fork, 'you really are a miserable bastard, aren't you? First sign of a bit of a laugh, and you're down on everyone like a load of shit. I'm glad I don't work at that hospital of yours.'

'Linda, you know perfectly well what I mean. It's very discourteous, setting yourself up in some rebel group like this. You wanted to come and—'

'Oh fuck off,' she said, and turned her attention to the man the other side of her. He wasn't as charming or attractive as the neurosurgeon; by the end of the meal her face ached from smiling at him and looking interested.

'Shall we go to the bar?' she said, finally turning back to Alex.

'I'd rather not. I'm tired. I'm going upstairs. You can join me if you like.'

'I've had more promising invitations,' she said. 'I'll see you later.'

She had one drink with Martin and his wife, and then said goodnight to everyone and went up to their room. Alex was in bed, reading.

'Hi,' she said.

'Hello.'

'Good book?'

'Very.'

She pulled off her clothes, slid into bed beside him. 'Let me distract you from it.'

He turned away slightly; she snatched the book from him. 'Oh, Alex. You're so sexy when you're cross.'

Against all the odds he laughed. 'I must be sexy a lot of the time, in that case.'

'You are. And I'm not the only one who thinks so. Mrs Neurosurgeon was saying how sexy you were.'

'Really?'

'Really. And don't try to look as if you aren't pleased.'

'Oh Linda,' he said, switching the light off, taking her in his arms. 'I'm sorry. You're a very – generous woman.'

'I am?'

'Yes. Sam would never have told me some other woman thought I was attractive. Are we friends again?'

'I never wasn't,' she said.

She managed to behave after that more as Alex would have wished. She went on the obligatory shopping trip – not exactly a hardship in the delicious bounty of Cape Town stores – bought an enormous number of clothes, and went on the other major outing, down the winding coast road to Chapman's Peak, an incredibly beautiful promontory carved out of the cliffs, and then on to Cape Point.

'It was truly amazing,' she said to Alex as they dressed for dinner. 'This road just going on and on into infinity, getting narrower and narrower; there were ostriches grazing by the road like ponies, and baboons just running along, looking like they'd missed the bus or something, and then we got there, right at the very edge of the world it felt like, on this long narrow tip of peninsula, the sea below us and behind us and all round us, shining in the sun, and mountains lining the sea in either direction and the water was green, not blue. I couldn't believe it, it was so lovely. I just wanted you there. I hate doing things – nice things, that is – without you now,' she added suddenly. The thought had struck her rather forcibly; she was surprised. 'It feels as if there's something missing.'

'Well, there is. There's me. Or rather not me.'

'Oh, don't be so prosaic. Here I am, getting all romantic and – well, anyway, it's been really fun, the whole thing. I almost don't want to leave them. Some of them anyway, like Martin and the neurosurgeons. We must see them again. I've got their emails.'

'Their emails! Why, for God's sake?'

'I told you, so we could see them again.'

'But why ever should we?'

'I don't know, Alex, we might.'

'But—'

'Oh stop it. I'm not asking them to move in with me. Look, it's what I do, it's called networking. Get used to it.'

They were heading north after that, to do a few days' safari; travelling on the Blue Train for the first leg to Pretoria, where they were picking up a small private plane to the Kruger Park.

The Blue Train was her idea, and her contribution to the trip. 'If you think I'm going on an ordinary old plane for two hours when we can do the same thing in total luxury in twenty-four, then you've brought the wrong woman.'

The Blue Train was sheer indulgence, an excessive treat which made her feel, she said, like Lauren Bacall in *Murder on the Orient Express*. She and Alex had their own private suite, a drawing room which converted into a bedroom, complete with immense double bed, and an elaborate bathroom in which you could take a deep, hot bath and enjoy the landscape at the same time – a peculiarly heady, sexy pleasure. They also had their own butler; all the suites did. Alex didn't approve, was hating most of it: Linda didn't care.

They arrived at the Blue Train arrival lounge at midday; it was indeed straight out of an Agatha Christie movie, with large chintz sofas, an attentive staff and a bar serving champagne and delicious nibbles.

They watched people arrive, or rather Linda did, constantly nudging Alex. 'Look, I bet he's the murderer – oh, now here we go, mother and daughter . . . wow, Mum's so much more glamorous, bet she's a bully. Oh Alex, just look at those two gay men, so sweet, so in love . . .'

He became increasingly irritable, refusing to join in the game. Linda sighed and finally gave up. Maybe she could find someone else to talk to . . .

They had the first squabble before lunch, as she tidied up the suite for the third time.

'Linda, do for God's sake stop that. I can't stand it.'

'Well, I can't stand the mess.'

'Go and sit in the lounge then.'

'I will.' She sat there, watching the incredible mountain ranges go past, sipping a glass of very nice Sancerre and felt better-tempered; by the time lunch was served she was feeling very sleek and told Alex so.

'I know what that means,' he said, grinning at her.

'You do?'

'Yes. Some considerable activity a little later.'

'You're being very presumptuous.'

'Sorry. Am I wrong?'

'No, Alex,' she said, closing her eyes briefly and smiling at the intense sensation that quite literally swept through her, leaving her almost dizzy. 'No, you're not wrong.'

'Thank Christ for that. I was beginning to think I'd never say the right thing again.'

'I'm not terribly interested in what you say,' she said, reaching under the table, gently massaging his thigh, 'not just now. More what you do.'

'Oh, OK. Linda, do stop that. I can't enjoy my food while I'm having an erection.'

'Try,' she said. 'It's my challenge for the afternoon.'

Much, much later she sat in the bath, with yet another glass of champagne; he sat on the edge and smiled down at her.

'That was very lovely.'

'Yes, it was. Oh look, Alex, there's some wildebeest! See – there. God, how amazing, to sit in a bath drinking champagne and watching wildebeest. I told you it would be wonderful.'

'You were right,' he said, reaching out, tracing the outline of one of her nipples with his thumb. 'It is very wonderful. All of it.'

'Please, please don't do that,' she said, reaching down for his hand, kissing it, then replacing it. 'You know I can't bear it.'

'I thought you liked it.'

'I do. I love it. But it makes me feel I'll have to – oh God, Alex, I'll have to – we'll have to . . .'

'Have to what?'

'You know.' She stood up, she was very wet, her red hair slicked back. He stood up too, lifted her out, bent his head and kissed her; very slowly, she eased off his bathrobe, and then reached out to pull down the bathroom blind.

'Who do you think's going to see us?' he said, laughing. 'The wildebeest?'

❊   ❊   ❊

When they came back after dinner, their sofa had been transformed into a vast pillowy double bed.

'I'm not sure I can do that justice,' Alex said. 'I'm an old man.'

'Never mind. I probably can't either. Let's just watch the stars.'

They fell asleep gazing out of the window, up at the star-littered black sky. And as the incredible orange dawn streaked out over the veldt, they managed to do the bed justice after all.

It was their first night at the lodge that the trouble really began; set unfenced in the middle of the park, their hotel consisted of a main building and then a series of bungalows. Beautifully furnished, colonial style, with its own Jacuzzi in its own small garden, and a huge deck, lit only by candles and oil lamps, it was, as Linda happily said, like something out of one of the really posh travel magazines.

She sat in the hot bubbling Jacuzzi as the dusk fell and the chill came in; it was a wonderfully surreal sensation.

Dinner was outside, under the stars, the tables set in a horseshoe round a vast fire; afterwards they were escorted back to their room by a guide, complete with rifle.

'Never, ever do this walk alone at night,' he said. 'It's very dangerous. Remember, we're not fenced. The animals can get in and they're not pets. They're wild and they kill. And there are snakes, really nasty pieces of work. Breakfast's at six,' he added cheerfully. 'I'll knock on the door at five-thirty, for morning safari.'

'Oh wow,' said Linda, wandering into the candle-lit room, 'this is my idea of true heaven. Such a wonderful idea, Alex. Thank you so, so much. I might not get up at five-thirty though. Give that bit a miss.'

'Linda, you have to. It's the reason we're here, to go on safari, see the animals.'

'Yeah, OK, but there's another in the afternoon. I can see them then.'

'You're expected to go on both each day. They're all different.'

'Yeah, bit like the spousal programme. Alex, I don't want to. Not tomorrow. I'm tired.'

'Well, I think that's a little pathetic,' he said.

'Oh, don't be so stuffy. This is a holiday, not an Army workout.'

'Yes, and a very expensive holiday. I was expecting you'd participate rather more fully. I'm disappointed.'

'Alex, you are joking, aren't you? No, you're not. Expensive indeed! Is that supposed to make me change my mind?'

'I'd have thought it was a factor.'

'Well, I'm sorry if I'm a disappointment to you, but I hadn't expected to have to earn my stay here.'

'That's a filthy thing to say.'

'It's pretty filthy talking about how much it cost. Remind me to write you a cheque when we get back.'

'Oh, for fuck's sake. I'm going to bed.'

'Good. Because I'm going back to the bar. And don't worry, I'll pay for my own drinks.'

She phoned for the escort; and slammed the door after her.

In the morning when she woke, he was gone; she turned over, went back to sleep and was sitting in the Jacuzzi when he returned.

'Good safari?'

'Very good.'

'What did you see?'

'Animals. Wild animals,' he said stiffly. 'I'm going to have breakfast. I'll see you later.'

Linda stuck out her tongue at his back. It spoke of huge hostility, that back. In fact, it was the most expressive back she knew.

Later they made up, lunched by the pool, and went out on the evening safari together. It was very wonderful. Nothing could have prepared Linda for the moment when a pride of lions walked by in a long, sinuous line, so close to the Land Rover they could have touched them. Or when two giraffes stalked languidly past them supermodel-style, heads held high, eyes on some far horizon, totally ignoring them. She'd somehow expected the animals to be about 200 yards away, not within blinking distance. It was astonishing enough to get her up at five-thirty the following day for more.

The highlight of that morning's safari was an elephant and her baby; just a few days old, it was being caressed and urged along by its mother's swishing trunk.

'So sweet,' Linda said to the ranger, 'and so gentle. But elephants always are, aren't they?'

'Until they're threatened. Let her think you might hurt that little chap and you'd have three tons of aggression heaped onto you.'

Probably because Linda was tired, they quarrelled dramatically that afternoon, so dramatically indeed that when they emerged from their bungalow for dinner, having missed the safari, they realised from their slightly embarrassed, distant expressions that their fellow guests must have heard them. The initial cause was Linda's getting sunburned; Alex told her she was a fool to lie out in the midday sun, she told him he was a stuffy old fart, he said he had seen enough skin cancer cases to make him cautious, she accused him of being over-dramatic and depressing. Somehow after that they got on to the children, with him informing her it was as well she'd never become a mother, given her total irresponsibility of attitude: which was, she informed him, so far below the belt as to be totally obscene.

He did apologise for that; they had a making up of sorts

and braved dinner, but afterwards, alone in the bungalow, she said, 'Just as a matter of interest, Alex, why have you never allowed me to meet your children?'

'What do you mean, never?' he said. 'We've only known one another a few weeks.'

'Months. Actually.'

'All right. But we don't meet very frequently. It just hasn't been practicable.'

'I hope that is the reason. I'd have thought if you were in the least serious about me, you'd have thought I'd like to meet them. And them me.'

'Linda, you know I'm serious about you. Neither of us would be here if I wasn't.'

'OK then. Maybe it's even worse than that, maybe you think they won't like me.'

'They probably won't.'

'Oh, what? Alex, how can you talk to me like that! You really are—'

'You misunderstood deliberately. I mean, of course, they won't like you, because you're not their mother.'

'I'm sorry?'

'They're very attached to their mother. They're bound to be hostile to any new girlfriend.'

'What about her boyfriend?'

'Yes, well, they certainly don't like him.'

'I thought they lived with him?'

'No, they don't. His house is in Marlow, Sam has her own near Cirencester.'

'I thought they all spent lots of lovely cosy weekends together.'

'They do spend the weekends together, some of the time. I don't think they're particularly cosy.'

'But they do see him?'

'They have to.'

'Well, why don't they have to see me?'

'Linda, can we stop this? It's absurd. Of course they

690

don't have to see you – I'm not in a permanent relationship with you.'

'Well, thanks for that.'

'You know very well what I mean.'

'Yes, Alex, I do. I'm glad to have it spelled out.' Whereupon she pulled on a jacket, opened the door and walked out into the darkness.

Alex waited for a few minutes; he was sure she'd be back. The bar was closed, there was nowhere for her to go. And she'd never dare walk far, without an escort. An escort with a gun. And he felt in those first few minutes so angry with her he really didn't care. If a pride of lions came for her, she deserved it.

Five minutes later, he was growing anxious. The rules were clear and it wasn't some idle threat, there was a host of dangerous animals out there, beyond the compound; only a few months ago a tourist had been savaged by a lion, when he had got out of the Land Rover (totally against instruction) and crept up on a lioness and her cub to take photographs. Both lioness and lion had been shot.

They had all sat soberly in the Land Rover while the scout told them this story, shocked into submission; no one had even moved for a while. And now here was Linda, doing something even more insane, out in the darkness, endangering not only her own life but that of the people who must find her. Stupid, bloody-minded stubborn woman. Arrogant beyond belief. Self-centred, over-dramatic; she deserved all she got.

Alex rang for help.

There was a track leading away from the lodge; one way it broadened into a wide, dirt road, the other into the track the Land Rovers drove along on safari. Linda could see that might be a little dangerous; she simply could not imagine the road could be in any way so. They would exaggerate the dangers, to make everything more exciting, and so that people didn't take silly risks. There certainly hadn't been anything more aggressive than an impala as they drove along it on their way.

Fucking Alex; God, she hated him. How dare he talk to her like that, like some patronising father figure – and then tell her his children wouldn't like her! That had been hugely hurtful. In fact, it had been endless, one long attack after another, all holiday. Thank God tomorrow it would be over and they would be going home. She realised she was crying: as much at the disappointment of the trip, which she had so hoped would be happy and fun, as at the hurt he had just slung at her. Thank God they weren't in much of a relationship; they could part at the airport and never meet again. Apart from the toothbrush and razor he kept at her flat, there would be no trace of him left in her life. Bastard! Bloody arrogant, bad-tempered bastard! She hated him. She—

Linda turned; better not go too far, it was very black, and it was the middle of the night. The park was noisy, sound cutting through the thick darkness, the raw cries of the birds and the chattering of the monkeys mixed with the occasional bellow or roar. Something moved on the ground horribly close to her; she jumped. Couldn't have been a snake, could it? No, of course not. She heard, from about fifty yards away, a rustling in the undergrowth; nothing dangerous, she was sure, a bird probably. But still – best get back.

She turned; and realised that she had actually wandered off the main track, had taken in the darkness a minor one; grass brushed at her ankles. Damn. Bloody silly. Well, she couldn't be far from the compound; she'd only been walking a few minutes. Actually, looking at her watch, nearly ten. You could walk quite a way in ten minutes. Still, she was fine; it was fine. The hotel lights were – shit, where were they? The track sloped slightly; she must just walk back down it, rather than up, and she'd hit the main track. Then she could easily . . .

Fuck. She couldn't easily anything. It was pitch black, there was no moon, she hadn't even had the sense to bring the torch. Well, that was Alex's fault, she'd been too upset to think. She walked a few steps tentatively; was that up or downhill? Hard to tell, the slope was very slight. She could be walking further into the bush, or out of it. It was impossible to tell. Maybe she should shout for help. But if she did, an animal could hear her. A hungry animal. Like the lion that had caught the tourist. Or the mother elephant, startled into defending her baby. What had the ranger said? Three tons of aggression. So – no shouting then. *Just keep calm, Linda, walk steadily back*. But she didn't know which way was back.

She stood there, willing herself not to panic, her mouth dry, her heart thudding. What should she do? What on God's earth should she do?

'Several of us will go,' the ranger told Alex, 'since you have no idea where she went.' His voice was calm, but cold. He was obviously very angry: with good reason.

'Yes. Thank you. I'm so – so sorry. Should I come with you?'

'Absolutely not. No, stay here. If she turns up, if you find she's just sitting by the pool or something, tell them at the hotel. And they can radio us.'

'Of course,' said Alex. He was absolutely confident Linda was not sitting by the pool. Or the bar. Or anywhere. She was out there, in all that danger, possibly even now being savaged by something, her lovely body being ripped quite literally apart – and it was his fault for being so harsh with her, so critical, so cruel. Sam had been right, he really wasn't worth having a relationship with.

He stood at the doorway, the light of the room behind him, that gentle, sweet candlelight, so at odds with what he was feeling, with what was happening. He strained his eyes into the darkness. He couldn't see or hear anything, except the Land Rovers which the rangers had taken. Jesus, those lions the other day had only been a mile or so away. Several of the other bungalows were lit up, he could see faces at the windows. What stories these people would have to tell when they got home: about this misfit couple, who fought endlessly, put the safety of the whole camp and all the rangers at risk . . .

He tensed; he could hear a Land Rover now, drawing nearer. It pulled into the courtyard, its engine silenced; Alex stood, unable to move, more fearful than he could ever remember. They had called off the search; she had been found dead, or horribly mutilated. No one could find her, she . . .

'Right, Alex. Here she is. Safe and sound, although she might not have been much longer. Something quite big out there, could have been anything – leopard, lion. Please don't do that again, Linda. You're putting us at risk as well as yourself. Good night.'

'Good night.' Linda's face was drawn and tear-stained, distorted by fear and remorse. 'I'm so, so sorry.'

'That's OK. Night.' He looked pretty cheesed off, Alex thought. He would have been too. Some silly cow endangering his life, all for a bit of drama. He took Linda's arm, pulled her in, shut the door. He shook her: hard. Again and again. Her eyes were shocked and afraid in her white face.

'I'm sorry, Alex. I'm so sorry.'

'You stupid, fucking, thoughtless bitch. How could you be so selfish, so insanely stupid!'

'I don't know. I'm sorry. I – well, I'm sorry.'

'You'd better be.' He stopped shaking her suddenly, set her away from him. 'You know, I could—'

'What?'

Suddenly, he couldn't stand it any longer. Her fear, her

694

misery, his relief. He sat down abruptly on the bed, his legs weak, sat looking up at her. She didn't move, just stood there, staring back at him.

'What?' she said again.

'Oh Linda,' he said, after a long silence. 'I'm afraid I love you. That's what.'

Chapter 47

It was very odd, to be seeing him again. Being with him, talking to him, having a laugh with him, doing everything with him really – except touching him. That seemed to be totally off-limits. And it was all, really, she wanted to do. Well, more or less. The talking and drinking and having a laugh were fine – great, in fact; but every time they met, which was fairly often, on account of planning the concert, she just fancied him more, wanted him more, fantasised about him more. She quite often dreamed she was in bed with him, and would wake restless, fretful, wondering if it was ever going to happen again. She feared very much it was not. He had clearly forgiven her, accepted her even, sufficiently to be friends; but no further. She was tarnished, labelled A Bad Girl: fun, good company, exciting even, but not to be trusted with his heart.

Still – it was something, even to be working with him.

And Georgia was great. Really cool; bit immature, bit spoiled, but funny and clever, and really good to work with, full of ideas, willing to do anything, put in endless hours. A real trouper.

They had formed a committee, which met regularly and then issued properly reported minutes at Abi's instigation. 'Formalising it all is the only way to push it forward, otherwise it just turns into a wank, everyone discussing their wonderful ideas and never doing anything.'

The committee members were Abi, who was Chair – 'only because I've been involved in all this stuff a bit before', Georgia and William. 'Well, I think you should be on the committee,' Abi had said, 'since every possible aspect of it's going to affect you. If you're up for coming to all the meetings, that is.' William said he was up for it.

Then there was Emma, representing the hospital, and a friend of Abi's called Fred, who worked for a charity and knew a great deal about the ins and outs of that industry, about fundraising, about sponsorship, and running events in general. He said he might even be able to find a sponsor for them. He was doing it for nothing, out of the goodness of his heart, he said, adding with a grin that it was the only bit of his heart that was good, but they were welcome to it.

Abi and Fred went back a long way. They'd been at school together, and were the only two people from their year who'd made anything of their lives. Fred wasn't too much like anyone would expect a charity worker to be – he looked like a secondhand car salesman, as Abi said when she introduced him to the group. Fred had taken the implied criticism of this with great good nature and said that selling charities and selling cars were much more similar than anyone would think. 'You're still getting people to part with more than they want for something. Charities are easier really, in a way, because you can work on their consciences.'

Abi knew that William had thought initially that Fred was doing it because he fancied her, but in fact he wasn't; he was a happily unmarried man as he put it, with a sweet-faced girlfriend called Milly, and a baby on the way. Abi spent a lot of time asking Fred about Milly and the baby and when it might be due, at the first meeting she brought him to.

They had a notional date now, of 8 and 9 July, but as Abi said, it was no use setting anything in stone until they knew they could get some bands.

'There are literally thousands of them,' she said, 'and they'll all be on MySpace. You'll only get unsigned ones to

697

come, obviously, although it would be great to have one slightly bigger name.'

'Would a slightly bigger name come?' Georgia asked, and Fred said they might, if the idea appealed, and there was going to be some good publicity.

'Which there will be, won't there?'

'There certainly will,' said Abi coolly. 'And quite big bands will bring their fee right down if it's for charity. The smaller ones will probably do it for cost, just to get the chance to play and be heard. We're going to have to hit the keyboard, Georgia, email all their agents – those who have them. We also want quite a good spread of music styles. Like rock, obviously, but also jazz, bit of folk even, for the families.'

It was William who came in with the really clever idea: 'I was talking to a bloke the other night in the pub, telling him what we were going to do, and he was awfully impressed. Anyway, he'd been to a small festival the other side of Bath and what they did was have a whole load of sort of auditions – play-offs, he called them, or Battle of the Bands – in pubs. Each area fielded a few bands and they played in the pub and the punters voted and the winner was put forward to play. He said it was great because everyone who'd voted wanted to go to the festival and hear their band. So they got loads more people than they would have done.'

'That is such a good idea,' said Georgia. 'Wonderful local publicity too. You are clever, William. Isn't that clever, Fred?'

Fred said it was a good idea. 'Only thing is, what sort of standard would the bands be? Bit of a gamble.'

'No worse a gamble than if we chose them from MySpace,' said Abi briskly. 'And obviously we'd hear them too and if they were dreadful we wouldn't book them. We should get cracking on this straight away. William, you give us a list of villages, or small towns, I suppose might be better, not too close together, with really good pubs who you think'd cooperate, and we'll get some flyers done – I can run them off at work. Oh God, if only we had some money. And a name. We've got to have a name. Georgia, you're the creative one, get us a name.'

William felt rather pleased with himself at having made such a large contribution on what he thought of as the theatrical side. Everyone, including him, had seen his role as strictly functional; providing the site, finding the contractors, organising the infrastructure. The cost of providing power lines and building the arena was eye-watering: he hoped his father would never find out. They had settled on a ticket fee of thirty pounds, children half-price; it sounded a lot, but not set against the thousands they were going to have to fork out. In his darker moments, he worried that they wouldn't make any money at all, just a whacking loss; and half-wished he had said no in the first place. But then he thought of the heady pleasure of the thing, the sense of purpose it had given them all, and of creating something so original and exciting – and he would know it was worth it.

And besides, it meant he could spend time with Abi.

It was very odd to be seeing so much of her. Being with her, talking to her, having a laugh with her . . . everything really, except touching her. That really did seem to be off-limits. And it was increasingly all he wanted to do . . .

The hurt had gone; he just longed now to go back to where they had been. She clearly felt quite differently; and working with her on the festival, seeing her more on her home turf, so to speak, he imagined himself through her eyes – very sound, nice, bit dull, someone she had once undoubtedly been fond of, and had fun with, a good friend, but who really was not in her orbit of consideration for anything more.

*   *   *

Laura was sitting in her mother's kitchen, crying. She was in complete despair over Charlie, and her mother had always been very close to him; she thought she might be able to help. Jonathan moving out had made him slightly less tense, but his behaviour was no better. Indeed, his year tutor had said that there was little point his sitting the Common Entrance exam, as his work was increasingly erratic, 'And quite honestly, Mrs Gilliatt, he seems to have lost most of his social skills as well. I can't see him doing very well at interviews.'

She had tried everything: persuasion, threats, bribes, even emotional blackmail: 'You could do it for me, Charlie, even if you won't for Dad. It upsets me so much, your behaving like this, and life is already quite difficult enough just at the moment.'

She got little response beyond the now horribly predictable shrug; he clearly felt she must bear some of the blame for his father's behaviour.

Occasionally she thought she had made a breakthrough; one night he had found her crying, after the girls had gone to bed. He had sat down beside her on the sofa, put his arms round her and asked her if there was anything he could do.

'I'm so sorry, Mum, it must be horrible for you.'

Laura told him it would make her feel better if he started working at school again, what his year tutor had said: that had been a mistake.

'Mum, I don't mind helping at home, or trying to cheer the girls up, but I can't go back to being good little Charlie again. He's gone. Dad's sent him packing.'

'But Charlie, that's not fair. To me or to you. You could perfectly well start working again if you wanted to.'

'Yeah, but I don't want to. Don't ask me why, I just don't. Maybe in time, but not right now. I don't see the point.'

'The point is your future, darling. Doesn't that matter to you?'

He shrugged. 'Not much, no. I couldn't care less about it.'

'I don't know what to do, Mummy,' Laura said now, blowing her nose. 'He's just wrecking his own life. I can't get that through to him.'

'I'm no psychologist, darling, but I'd say he was feeling completely disillusioned.'

'Disillusioned!'

* 'Yes. With everything. He idolised his father and he feels utterly let down. And not just with Jonathan, but Jonathan's way of life. Why should he try to be like him, to emulate him in any way, when he despises him so much?'

'But that doesn't make sense!'

'I think you'd find it did to Charlie. He's rejected the way Jonathan brought him up, and that includes working hard and doing well.'

'Oh, God,' said Laura, 'it's all so hideous. Tell me what to do, Mummy. I can't think straight any more.'

'Nothing for now, darling. Give it time. You have no idea how things might turn out.'

'Yes, I do. Jonathan's not coming back, because I couldn't bear it if he did. Charlie won't forgive Jonathan, or change his attitude in any way. I can't see how anything could change.'

'Laura, just now, neither can I. I only know after living for quite a long time, that things do. Stuff happens, as the horrible expression goes. Try to be patient. Charlie's young for his year, he can take the exam next January instead. It's all so hard, I know, but . . .'

'Oh Mummy, you know what I often think?'

'No, what do you often think?'

'That if it hadn't been for that bloody car crash, everything would have been all right. I'd never have known about Abi Scott, it would have played itself out, Jonathan would have got sick of her—'

'He might not have.'

'Well, thanks for that!'

'Darling, don't get me wrong. I think what Jonathan's done is unforgivable, when you've been such a perfect wife to him. I can hardly bear to see you so unhappy. And if he wanted to come back, if you did forgive him, I'd find it very hard to accept. All I'm saying is that men do seem to need these – relationships – sometimes. Well, saying they need them rather over-dignifies it. They decide they're going to have them. Especially at Jonathan's age – it's a grab at their lost youth. If it hadn't been Abi Scott, it might have been someone else.'

'Daddy didn't do that, did he?' She stared at her mother, suddenly understanding for a brief moment how Charlie felt, the shock of betrayal.

'No, he didn't, he never cheated on me, thank God, but several of my friends had to endure it. Some of the marriages survived. Well, most of them, actually. They did in those days. And there was a lot of turning a blind eye, pretending you didn't know.'

'So – are you saying I should take him back?'

'No, of course not. Unless you really want to. And as I say, I wouldn't find it easy if you did. I'm simply saying that you're not the first woman to have to endure this.'

'No, I know.' Laura hesitated. 'He – well, he did say he was about to finish the relationship. That it was over.'

'Well, that's something in his favour.'

'You don't believe that, do you?'

'Laura, you know Jonathan a great deal better than I do. If you believe him, then I'd trust your judgement. And maybe you've been too perfect, too good to him. You do – well, you did – spoil him dreadfully.'

'That's what Serena says,' said Laura. 'She says I should have kicked him around more, like she does Mark, given him a harder time, so he was more – more scared of me. Bit of grit in the mixture, as she put it. But it's too late

702

now, I'm afraid. It's happened and I could never trust him again.'

'Would you like to go for a walk, Russell, dear?' asked Mary, coming into the morning room where Russell was reading the *Financial Times*. He had been persuaded to take it instead of the *Wall Street Journal*; he complained every day how unsatisfactory it was, and made a great thing of reading the *Journal* online, but Mary had observed he still became totally absorbed in the *FT* for at least an hour and a half each morning. Which was a relief, actually; now that all the excitement of the wedding and Christmas was over, Russell was often restless. He spent a lot of time on the internet studying the markets and then instructing his broker to buy this or sell that. And he was on the phone for at least an hour a day to Morton, discussing the business. Mary had a pretty shrewd idea that Morton didn't welcome these calls, and indeed, he had told her over Christmas that it was wonderful to see his father so relaxed and happy.

'He really seems to be letting go of the reins at last.'

'The reins?'

'Yeah, of the business. He was supposed to have retired ten years ago – we gave him a dinner, everyone made speeches, we presented him with a wonderful vintage gold watch – that was a kind of a joke, of course – and he even wept a bit, and said goodbye to everyone. Monday morning, nine a.m. he was back at his desk. He's cut down a bit since then, of course, but I'd like to see him taking it really easy.'

Mary could see very clearly that what Morton meant was that he'd thank God on bended knees for his father to be taking it really easy and assured him that she absolutely agreed and that she had all sorts of plans for the coming year. 'A bit of travelling for a start. We haven't had our honeymoon yet, and I'm not letting him get away with that,' she said. 'And he seems to have plans for making over some of the land here to what he calls a vegetable farm. So that we can be self-sufficient, he said.'

Morton grinned at her. 'Sounds good to me. He needs new projects. May I warn you though, he could get tired of the vegetable farm . . .'

Mary said she didn't need the warning. 'It's a problem with retirement, Morton. Donald – my first husband – had his birdwatching, it had been a passion all his life, he'd longed for more time to spend on it, and after a few months, he even got bored with that. We started learning bridge just so he could focus on something else.'

'Don't play bridge with my father, Mary,' said Morton. 'He becomes extremely aggressive.'

'Morton, I wouldn't play so much as a game of Tiddlywinks with your father.'

'Pardon me? What's Tiddlywinks?'

'Oh, a game children play, or used to play, flicking small plastic discs into an egg cup. The aim clearly is to get more in than your opponent.'

'How right you are. My father would be taking special tuition and practising far into the night.'

'How do you think he'd be on archaeology? That's always interested me.'

Morton considered this for a bit. 'I can only say the world would hear of some amazing new buried city within months. As for the archaeological outfitters, how are they on bespoke shorts?'

'Russell dear, do listen to me. I said would you like to go for a walk?'

'Not just now, Sparrow. I'm worried about some of my stocks. Thinking of selling them. I'm going to draft a letter to my accountant just as soon as I've finished reading this.'

'Well, all right, dear. I'll go on my own.'

'Mary, you know I don't like you going out on your own.'

'Oh, for goodness' sake,' said Mary impatiently, 'what on earth do you think might happen to me? Might I meet a marauding gang of skinheads from Bath? Or come across a herd of wild boar in the lane?'

'Don't mock me, Sparrow,' he said, and his eyes were quite hurt. 'I want to look after you.'

'I know you do. But I need to get out. Can't the stocks wait another day?'

'Possibly. Yes, all right.'

'Now, Russell dear,' she said, tucking her arm into his as they walked through the gate at the bottom of the garden and into the wood, 'I really would like to start planning our honeymoon. I don't want to be cheated of it. Where would you like to go?'

'Anywhere you like, Sparrow. Italy maybe? I've always longed to go there again and with you – I find those works of art so wonderful. Or maybe the Seychelles, or even Vietnam . . .'

'Russell, I don't think I want to do anything quite as adventurous as that,' said Mary.

'Well, why on earth not?' he said, looking genuinely puzzled. 'We should do these things while we can, Mary, before we get old and stuck in our ways.'

'Oh Russell,' she said, reaching up to kiss him, 'I love you for so many reasons, but perhaps most because you don't see us as old.'

'Well, of course I don't. We're not old. We're certainly quite young enough to enjoy ourselves.'

'Yes, of course. But – well, I would still rather have a quiet honeymoon. I've never been to the Lake District. Wonderful scenery, good driving – and walking. Would you consider that? Just for now?'

'If that's what you want, Sparrow. As long as we can go to Egypt in the spring.'

'I promise you,' she said, 'we'll go to Egypt in the spring.'

It had gone – not badly, but not very well either, Linda thought. They had been polite, but wary, undemonstrative. And Alex had been pretty similar; obviously nervous of appearing in any way foolish, romantically inclined, uncool. He hadn't even touched her, except to kiss her hello and goodbye. And she felt under inspection by him, all over again, seeing her through their eyes.

It had been her idea to take them to a preview. A restaurant meal would be a minefield: where would they go? Somewhere easy and informal, obviously, but high profile like Joe Allen's or the Bluebird, or really local and undemanding? And then the former might seem like trying too hard, the latter like selling them short and not bothering much. And then it would be a minefield as well of silences and studied manners. If it had just been Amy, then maybe they could have gone shopping; although what self-respecting fifteen year old would want to go shopping with someone knocking on forty – and where on earth could she take her? And would she buy her lots of stuff, which would look like trying too hard, or not anything at all, which would look mean.

Not shopping then. Anyway, they were all coming together, the three of them, Alex, Amy and Adam. And then the tickets arrived, for the new comedy smash hit, and that seemed too good to be true. She was sent two, asked for two more. The show was for early Friday evening, which was ideal really; they could just go for a pizza afterwards, the ice broken by laughing – hopefully – and if it was going really badly, just a coffee at Starbucks and then Alex could take them home.

She chose what to wear with as much anguish as if she was going to meet the Queen or Brad Pitt. Both of whom would actually have been easier, she thought. In the end she settled on a short black skirt and sweater, and a leather jacket. Any hint of cleavage seemed a bad idea; the skirt was short-ish, but seemed all right. She initially put on pumps but they looked wrong and frumpy, so slightly anxiously changed into some Christian Louboutin high heels. She removed her red nail varnish, and wore much less eye make-up than usual.

Alex brought them to her office, because that seemed safer territory than her flat and a bit more welcoming than the cinema lobby; an acknowledgement that she was a bit more than a casual acquaintance, a bit less than a permanent fixture.

They walked in, smiled, shook her hand, said how do you do; she was pleasantly surprised by that, and by their slightly formal clothes. She had half-expected grunting hoodies. They were good-looking children, both of them, Amy an incipient beauty, with Alex's dark colouring, all pushed-back hair and posh languid voice; Adam blond, over-tall and thin and horribly self-conscious, with spots, braces on his teeth, and a voice perilously close to breaking. Amy wandered round the office, looking at photographs, expressing polite interest when she recognised someone. Adam sat on the sofa, trying not to look at anyone as he sipped his Coke.

The taxi ride was silent; they arrived at the preview cinema in Wardour Street half an hour early. Not good. Linda met a couple of people, introduced them and then withdrew into the safety of showbiz gossip. Amy looked bored, Adam embarrassed, Alex glowering and Heathcliff-like.

The film was a success; very funny, very glossy, quite cool. Linda sat between Amy and Alex. They both laughed a lot and afterwards Amy turned to her and said, 'That was really cool, thank you so much.' Adam shuffled out, muttering, 'Great, cool, yeah.'

'So – pizza, anyone? Or shall we just go to Starbucks or somewhere for a coffee? You guys choose.' Guys? Should she have said that? More pathetic groping for street-cred.

'Pizza?' said Amy.

'Don't mind,' said Adam. They went to Cafe Boheme, the kids talking and giggling between themselves. What were they saying? Linda wondered. Were they agreeing that she was gross, or pathetic or even – just possibly – nice? There was no clue from the subsequent exchanges.

They ordered pizzas, preceded by garlic bread; conversation was strained and mostly about the film and other films they had seen. She longed to ask them what they wanted to do when they grew up, but knew that this above all was what people their age hated. She asked them their plans for the weekend and they both said they didn't know.

She then asked them if their father had told them much about South Africa and Amy said yes, and it had sounded really cool. Adam said yes, it had sounded great.

She had ordered one small glass of wine, but it was gone in her nervousness before they had even finished the garlic bread; she ordered another – 'a large one this time, please' – and then worried they might put her down as an alcoholic.

A very large silence now settled; she almost let it go on, and then thinking things could hardly be worse, asked them if they had heard about the music festival that Georgia, one of her clients, was putting on, 'For your dad's hospital. The victims of the M4 crash last summer were taken there. I'm sure your father will have told you about it.'

'He tells us about so many awful things,' said Amy, smiling suddenly at her father, then at her, 'we wouldn't remember.'

'Oh, right. Well, Georgia, Georgia Linley she's called, going to be in a big new thriller series in March; she was involved in the crash and wanted to raise some money for the hospital.'

'Cool,' said Amy. 'Was that her, the black girl in the photograph with you?'

'Yes, that's right.'

'So, when's the festival?'

'Oh, July.'

'Where?'

'On someone's farm. Nice young guy called William Grainger – his farm borders the M4, and the air ambulance landed on his field.'

'Oh, OK.'

'Would you like to go?' said Alex. It was virtually the first time he'd spoken since they got to the restaurant.

'Yeah, maybe. What's it called?'

'I don't think it's got a name yet,' said Linda. 'They can't seem to get it quite right, the last thing I heard. Got any ideas? All suggestions welcomed.'

'God, no,' said Amy.

Adam shrugged.

Shortly after that, they left; Alex was driving them home to their mother. He still hadn't found anywhere decent to live.

'You've been a great help,' hissed Linda, as they stood at the edge of the pavement, hailing taxis for her rather fruitlessly.

'Sorry. I thought it was better to let you make the running.'

'Hmm. Oh shit – look, there's one miles down the road, hasn't seen us. I really do want to get home. Oh hell . . .' She put two fingers in her mouth and whistled loudly. Amy and Adam looked startled, then grinned at her. Or were they laughing at her? How loud, how brash, not the sort of thing a nice, seemly stepmother should be doing.

'Bye then,' she said, holding out her hand, taking theirs one by one. 'It's been really fun. I'm glad you liked the film.'

'Bye,' said Amy. 'And thanks.'

'Bye,' said Adam. 'Yeah, thanks.'

'Bye, Linda,' said Alex.

The last she saw of them were the two children, heads together, laughing – at her again, no doubt, pathetic, would-be cool woman, and Alex, looking ferocious.

What a disaster. What a bloody disaster. He'd never want to marry her now.

She went home, drank almost a bottle of wine, watched a re-run of *Sex and the City*, telling herself that no love, however passionate, could survive a relationship with hostile teenagers, had a hot bath and went to bed. She was half-asleep when the phone rang.

'Hi.' It was Alex.

'Oh, hi. You OK?'

'Yes, thanks. I'm fine.'

'Sorry, Alex.'

'What on earth for? Right – now, as the kids would say, were you a hit, or were you a hit?'

'What?'

'You, my darling beloved, are just *soooo* cool. That's Amy's verdict. You are pretty nice. That's Adam's. You have great legs. That was also Adam. You are *so* not embarrassing. Amy again. She wants to come and see you on her own, maybe; go shopping, your shoes were just uh-may-zing. And ohmigod, the way you whistled for the cab. Oh, Linda. I love you.'

'I love you too,' she said.

It felt like any other evening. Not good, not bad, Barney thought, just an evening. For going home, eating dinner – dutifully, smiling a lot – talking carefully and listening even more carefully. Trying not to think too much, not to remember – and most of all, not to look forward. Forward into God knew what. More of this? This odd calm sadness, this lie of a life. Lived with someone who loved him so much. Whom he still loved too. In a concerned, tender, guilty way.

It was a horrible night, wet, cold, windy. He was carrying a brown paper bag with a couple of bottles of wine in it, and it was getting dangerously soggy. He'd also got Amanda some flowers. Those Kenyan, two-tone roses that she liked so much. It was Wednesday and he always bought her flowers on Wednesday, it was half-joke, half-tradition. She said if he ever forgot, she'd know there was something terribly wrong. Well, he hadn't forgotten yet.

When he got home, she wasn't there. Which wasn't particularly unusual; Amanda was terminally sociable, always having quick drinks or even supper with girlfriends after work. Although he couldn't remember her saying anything about this evening.

He went in, put the wine in the fridge, the roses in water – without cutting the stems, which would have induced a ticking-off if she'd known, she was very strict about such things: 'Barney, darling, it doesn't take a minute, and they live so much longer. You're just lazy.'

He wondered if Emma fussed over rose-stems and decided it was very unlikely. *Don't start thinking about Emma, Fraser, just don't. Doesn't help.*

He wondered if he should do something about supper. He looked in the fridge – there didn't seem to be much in there. Well, if she was much later, they could go out. Only if she'd eaten . . . He'd call her. See what she was doing. She'd be amused, not cross, if he'd forgotten some arrangement; would tell him he was hopeless, that she'd be home soon.

Her mobile was switched off.

He sat down, turned on the TV, was watching the end of the seven o'clock news when he heard her footsteps in the street, heard her key in the lock. She'd be soaked, miserable; he should make her a cup of tea.

He went into the kitchen and was filling the kettle when she came in. He turned to smile at her, and then saw her

711

face. It wasn't quite right somehow. It wasn't wearing its usual smile; her eyes weren't warm, in fact they were staring at him as if she had never seen him before. Barney put the kettle down.

She was taking her coat off, her wet coat; he reached for it to hang it up.

'It's all right,' she said. 'I can do it.'

He followed her as she walked out of the kitchen, throwing the coat down on a chair – unthinkable, that – went into the sitting room and sat down. Barney sat opposite her. It seemed the only thing to do.

A silence, then: 'Barney, why didn't you tell me?'

His stomach lurched hideously. 'Tell you what?'

'You know perfectly well what. I saw Tamara today, and she told me all about it.'

The cow. The bitch. How dare she? How *dare* she? She'd promised, as he had; that was what came of making a pact with the devil.

'Yes,' he said. 'Yes, I see. Well, she had no right to do that. To tell you. It's nothing to do with her.'

'Well, it is a bit. I think. She is my best friend.'

'Yes, I know, but—' How had they ever got to be best friends, these two? One so good, so transparently sweet and kind, the other so bad, so devious and cruel.

'Well anyway, she has. Do you want to talk about it?'

'If you do.'

'Well, of course I do. It affects us both, doesn't it?'

'Yes, Amanda, it does.'

'Well – go on.'

'I think I might,' he pushed his hair back, 'think I might have a beer. You?'

'Not a beer. Maybe a glass of wine.'

He poured her her favourite, Chardonnay, not very smart as she often said, but it was so lovely who cared about smart? And poured himself a Becks.

He had been half-expecting, half-rehearsing indeed, this

conversation for two months now. Sometimes in his imagination he had instigated it, sometimes Amanda, but it finally seemed to be happening for real. And he felt so scared his hand was shaking as he picked up his glass.

'Come on, Barney, please. I do need to know.'

Oh God. God, how do I get through this? He looked at her. Her pretty, peaches and cream face was very calm, her blue eyes fixed on him intently.

'Well,' he said, 'well, it – it all happened because of the crash. And while Toby was in hospital.'

'Yes, that's what Tamara said. Well, sort of.'

'Let's forget about what Tamara might have said. I want you to have the story as it really happened. I – never meant it to happen, Amanda. I loved you so much. I *do* love you so much. It just – well, it sort of took me over.'

She was silent; he didn't dare look at her. Then she said, 'I don't quite see what that's got to do with it.'

'Amanda, of course it has!'

'Well – go on.'

'Yes, well, I think it was partly the emotion about Toby, you know. And I was full of guilt about the crash. She – well, she helped me over that.'

'Who, Tamara?'

'No, of course not Tamara. Her. Emma.'

'Emma? Just a minute, Barney, I'm losing it a bit here.'

Afterwards, he thought, if he'd looked at her then . . . but he didn't.

'Yes, she's a doctor there. Well, you met her actually, the day after the accident. Outside. I don't suppose you remember.'

'I – don't think so . . .'

'I'm not surprised. Oh Amanda, I'm so, so sorry. Anyway, she was just fantastic the day Toby had his operation. I couldn't have got through it without her. Of course, if you'd been there . . . but you weren't.'

'No. No, I wasn't.'

He did look at her now; she was very pale suddenly, and very still, her eyes darker.

'Go on,' she said. Her voice was strange, rather breathless.

'And – well, it just went on from there. Our relationship. It developed so quickly. It sounds kind of – well, cheesy, I know, but I couldn't seem to help it. Neither of us could. We saw each other a few times, not many at all, but we did decide . . . Well, I – I was going to tell you, that night.'

'What night?' she said. Very slowly.

'The night your father died. I was waiting for you, and then while I was waiting your mother phoned and of course I couldn't – then.'

'No. Well, that was – very good of you.' Her voice wasn't breathless now, it was low and very level.

'I know I'm a shit, Amanda. I know I behaved badly. Terribly badly. But – well, I did want to take care of you, while you were so unhappy.'

'Yes, I see. And what about her? Emma? While I was so unhappy?'

'I didn't see her. Of course. We agreed it would be very wrong.'

'Nice of you both.'

He was silent, then he said, 'Anyway, it is over. For what it's worth. Finally, I mean. She – finished it. She said it mustn't go on.'

'Right. Well, that was very noble of her.' There was a silence, while she looked round the room rather wildly, as if she was seeking an escape, her eyes brilliant with tears. Her voice wasn't tearful though, it was still very level. 'Yes, Barney. Very noble. I don't suppose it occurred to her that it shouldn't have gone on while you were engaged to someone else. Or to you.'

'Of course it shouldn't have gone on! I can't justify

714

it or even explain it. I just didn't seem to be able to help it.'

'No. So you keep saying. Anyway, it's – it's over is it? Have you seen her since?'

'No, I haven't. And yes, it is over. But – well, that doesn't quite alter what I feel for you. Now.'

Another silence; he could feel her gathering her courage to go on. 'And what's that?' she said finally.

'It's not the same, Amanda. It just isn't. It doesn't feel right any more. It used to be so perfect and now it isn't. I still love you very much but—'

'Oh, please. So all that time while I was so wretched over Daddy and his funeral and even Christmas, you were thinking about her?'

'Well, in a way, yes. I was.'

She was crying now. 'But it was her that finished it?'

'Yes, it was.'

'Well, good for her. At least she has some sense of right and wrong. I suppose you thought you'd just let it go on and on, enjoying both of us – or maybe you weren't enjoying me. Just staying with me because you were sorry for me. God, Barney, that's so horrible.'

'Amanda, I'm sorry. I can't say it enough. I do still love you. Very much.'

'Yes, you keep saying. But – you – you don't want to marry me, is that it?'

There was a long silence; it was the most difficult thing he had ever done, but he managed it.

'Yes, Amanda,' he said. 'I'm so sorry, but that is it.'

She was very good, very calm. She called her mother, who was in the family mews house in London, and said she'd like to go round there. She packed a few things, and took her car keys from the hook in the hall where they both always kept such things.

'Bye then, Barney.'

'Will you be all right driving? I could call you a cab.'

'No, I'll drive. It's only a little way. And I've always found driving very therapeutic.'

This was true; she'd even gone for a drive the morning of her father's funeral.

'You know I'd leave if you like,' he said.

'No, no, I'd like to be with Mummy. We can decide what to do about the house and everything in a day or so, I can't bear to think about it now. Bye, Barney.'

'Bye, Amanda.'

When he heard the car finally pulling away from the house he picked up the phone and called Tamara.

'You cow,' he said. 'How dare you! How dare you do that!'

'Do what?'

'You know perfectly fucking well what. Tell Amanda about me and Emma.'

There was a long silence; then she said, 'Barney, I didn't. I really, really didn't.'

'But –' now he really was going to throw up – 'but she knew. She said you told her.'

'I didn't tell her about you and Emma, Barney. I told her about Toby and what he'd done to you. And me. That's all. I swear to you, that's absolutely all.'

Chapter 48

'Mummy, I want to go and get some sweets and my magazines.'

'Daisy, darling, I'm awfully busy. I've got these plans to finish for someone.'

'You're always busy now.'

This was true; it was the only way she could distract herself.

'I'm sorry, sweetie. Maybe when I've finished – oh no, Granny's coming to take you all to the Science Museum.'

'Again? Bor-ing.' This was Charlie.

'Charlie, don't be rude. If you can't find anything to interest you there, then I'm sorry for you.'

He shrugged. 'So? It's still bor-ing.'

'But Mummy,' Daisy wailed, 'I so want my magazines. Especially *Animals and You*, it's got a free necklace. I could wear it to the Museum, and show Granny.'

'Daisy, I just haven't got time.'

'It's not fair. You never have time any more.'

'Yes, darling, and I'm sorry. After this job, I won't be so busy. Promise.'

'You said that last time,' said Charlie.

'Charlie, will you please stop being so difficult.'

'I'm not. I'm just telling the truth. And why shouldn't Daisy get her stuff if she wants to.'

'Could Charlie take me?' said Daisy.

This had happened before, several times. The shop was

only at the end of the terrace, there were no roads to cross, and Charlie had always been a very reliable chaperon.

'I'm not taking her,' he said.

'That's not very helpful.'

'So? I don't want to, I'm going to go on the computer, look at my Warhammer stuff.'

'Charlie, you are not going on the computer.'

'Why not?'

'Because I'm about to need it, that's why.'

'That is just so mean. Anyway, I'm not taking her to get her stupid comic.'

'It's not a comic.'

'Daisy, it's so a comic.'

Laura suddenly lost her temper. 'Charlie, stop being so difficult! Now, get your coat and Daisy's and take her to the shop.'

'No.'

'I hate you!' shouted Daisy. 'You're so mean!'

'Charlie, I'm not telling you again. If you don't take her, you don't get your pocket money and then you won't be able to buy any more Warhammer stuff.'

'That's blackmail.'

'I don't care. Go and get the coats. And look after her properly. Don't walk miles ahead.'

She'd at least get ten minutes' peace. And maybe if she finished sooner, she could go and meet them all at the Science Musem for tea.

It was a difficult job this one, a very dull modern flat, purpose-built, which the owner had requested be given 'some character. Only not too modern. Maybe a bit pretty even. Curtains, not blinds, that sort of thing. But still contemporary. I don't want it to look like something out of the seventies.'

Such instructions were fairly common.

* * *

Charlie and Daisy walked along the terrace, Daisy chattering, Charlie kicking a stone, ignoring her.

'Charlie, if I got a kitten, which I think I might, Mummy said just possibly, what shall I call it?'

He shrugged.

'I thought Paddypaws would be a nice name.'

'It's a stupid name.'

'It's not. It's sweet. Well, what would you call it?'

'I don't want a stupid kitten.'

'Kittens aren't stupid.'

'Course they are.'

'Well, what pet would you like?'

'I don't want a pet.'

'Everyone wants pets.'

'I don't. Well, maybe a boa constrictor.'

'What's that?'

'A snake.'

'A snake! You couldn't have a snake, where would you keep it?'

'In my room.'

'Charlie, you're so stupid.'

'Oh, and you're not, I suppose. Look, here we are, I'll wait outside. Be quick, don't start looking at all the other comics.'

'They're *not* comics.'

He shrugged.

She came out, clutching several magazines and a bag of sweets.

'OK. All done.'

He began to walk faster; Daisy had to half-run to keep up with him, and dropped one of her magazines.

'Charlie! Wait for me!'

'Well, buck up then.'

'I can't buck up, I've dropped one of my magazines.'

He stood, arms folded, elaborately patient, while she picked everything up, then set off again.

'Look, here's a picture of a kitten – isn't it sweet?'

'No.'

'It is. And— Charlie, please wait, you're doing it again, I can't keep up . . .'

'Well, walk faster then.'

'I *am* walking faster. Oh no, now the cover's ripped off, it's got the necklace on it. Charlie, wait, wait . . .'

But he didn't wait; and he didn't see the crumpled cover of the magazine caught by the wind and blown across the road; nor did he see Daisy dashing into the street after it. He only heard things: a car, driving fast, faster than usual down the terrace, a scream, a screech of brakes, a hideous silence. And then he turned and he did see; the car halted, slewed across the street; a man, not much more than a boy, his face distorted with fear, getting out of it; and Daisy, lying horribly, horribly still where it had flung her, face down, her long fair hair splayed out, one small hand still clutching her bag of sweets, and her pastel-coloured magazines, filled with pictures of smiling little girls, fluttering away down the street.

Jonathan was in the shower when his phone rang; he'd been to the gym, there was a queue for the showers – bad that, they really should have enough, even for a Saturday morning – and he'd decided to drive home and shower there. He didn't even hear his phone; it was only when he picked it up and checked it minutes later that he saw a message.

It was from Laura.

Could he come to A&E at St Peter's Hospital, Brentford, immediately; Daisy had been knocked down by a car.

She's alive, but she's badly hurt. Please hurry.

They were sitting there together, when he arrived. Lily and Charlie. Lily hurled herself at him, crying: 'Daddy, Daddy, do something, please, please, make her better, make her better.'

Charlie was sitting, arms folded, shoulders hunched, his head somehow sunk down into his body. He didn't look up.

A young man with a shaven head was sitting two chairs away from them; he was a greenish colour.

'Where's Mummy?'

'In there,' said Lily. She nodded towards a set of double doors. 'With Daisy.' Her blue eyes were enormous with fear; she was shuddering with sobs, tears streaming down her face.

'Charlie, what happened?'

'She – she ran in the road.'

'In the road? But how? Why?'

The young man stood up, came over. 'You the dad?'

'Yes.'

'I hit her,' he said.

'You hit her. With your car?'

'Yeah. I'm – well, I'm sorry. She just – ran out. I couldn't help it. I really couldn't. I'm sorry. Really sorry. I . . .' He started to sob himself, like a child.

'Yes, all right, all right.' Jonathan could feel a steely professional calm taking over; just as well, they couldn't all be hysterical. 'Try to pull yourself together. How bad is she? What sort of injuries?'

'I don't know. I didn't – well, I didn't go over her, if that's what you mean. Just hit her.'

'The ambulance man said internal injuries,' said Charlie. His voice was hoarse, odd. Then he suddenly leaned forward and threw up.

'Poor old chap. Don't worry . . .'

A weary-looking woman came over, looked at the pile of vomit and sighed. 'That'll need clearing up.'

'Yes, indeed it will. Maybe you could find someone to do it,' said Jonathan. 'Look, Charlie, go into the toilet, have a wash – I must go and find Mummy. And Daisy. Lily, you stay here. I – oh, look, here's Granny. She'll stay with you.

721

Hello, Stella. Could you get Charlie some water, he's just been sick.'

'Yes, of course. How is she? What's happened?'

'I don't know. I only just got here. I'm going to try and find out.'

'You can't go in there,' the woman on reception called to him as he pushed open the double doors Lily had indicated. 'That's for medical staff only.'

'I am medical staff,' said Jonathan, and disappeared.

Laura was standing outside a curtained cubicle, very pale, very calm. She looked at him and almost smiled.

'Hello.'

'Hello. How is she?'

'We don't know. Internal injuries, that's all they'll say. A doctor's with her now.'

'Is she conscious?'

'No.'

'Has she come round? Since it happened?'

'Not, not really. Well – a bit, in and out. Mostly out.'

'Oh God. Jesus. Laura, how—'

'It was my fault.'

'Yours?'

'Yes. She wanted to go to the shop, get some sweets, I didn't have time.'

'She didn't go alone?'

'No, no.'

'Helga?'

'No, she went with – with Charlie.'

'Charlie!'

'Yes. Don't look like that, he's taken her before. And Lily. Several times before – well, you know he has. It was you said he could in the first place.'

It was true. He had. It had been a huge adventure – for Charlie. They had watched him from the gateway as he had walked carefully and proudly down the road, never taking his eyes off Lily, calling her back if she went so much as five yards ahead of him. They had had to keep ducking out of sight, in case he saw them; when the children were nearly back they both fled into the house, laughing, Laura to the kitchen, Jonathan to his study, had pretended they hadn't even heard them come in, expressing huge surprise when Charlie called out, 'We're back.'

Different times. Happy, safe times.

'Anyway, she ran into the road, she'd dropped her comic. Some lad was driving up – much too fast, I imagine.'

'Yes, he's out there.'

'To give him his due, he stayed with her while Charlie came for me, insisted on coming to the hospital. He's all right really, nice boy, just desperately frightened. Has Mummy come?'

'Yes, she's there. Charlie's just thrown up.'

'I'm not surprised. He's beside himself. He was hysterical, I couldn't stop him crying, screaming almost at first. Then he went terribly quiet, sort of disappeared into himself.'

'So what actually happened? I mean, why did she run in the road?'

'I told you, to get her comic, it was blowing away.'

'She knows better than that.'

'I know she does. But Charlie said she was all stressed, as he put it; she kept dropping things.'

'Chap must have been going at a hell of a lick. Or he'd have seen her.'

'I know, I know.'

They stood there, staring at one another; she wild-eyed, ashen, shaking, he frozen-faced, shock-still. Unable to reach each other, comfort each other; each filled with the torment of guilt.

'I'm so, so sorry, Jonathan.'

'Laura, it wasn't your fault.'

'It was, it was. I wasn't there . . .'

'Neither was I,' he said, his voice hardly audible. 'Was I?' He took a deep breath, stood silent for a moment, then, 'What does the lad say? The driver?'

'He says he doesn't know what happened. But he said – well . . .'

'Yes?'

'He said Charlie came running back to the car. So it sounds like he'd gone ahead. He wasn't with Daisy. Not looking after her.'

'Oh, Christ.'

'Yes. He didn't want to go, Jonathan, he was arguing with me, saying he wanted to go on the computer, do his wretched Warhammer stuff. I – well, I made him. I shouldn't have, I should have seen what might happen. Oh God.' She dropped her face into her hands, began to cry.

'Don't,' he said, and his voice was odd, cracked. 'Don't cry. It's all right. It was an accident. These things happpen.'

'They don't have to. They—'

The curtains opened abruptly; a doctor came out. Behind him they could see Daisy, very white and still, a nurse standing by her, checking her pulse.

'I'm her father,' said Jonathan quickly, 'and a doctor. What's the verdict?'

'Well, it's hard to say with any confidence. We need to do a brain scan, see if there's any real damage to the skull. It could be just the violence of the contact, rather than a direct blow: it's the equivalent of a very hard shaking. She's certainly in shock – medical shock, that is. Only half-conscious, very distressed. Her blood pressure's very low, which is worrying, it would indicate some internal bleeding. She may need surgery on her chest or abdomen, or at the very least we'll need to put in a chest drain. She has some broken ribs, which could cause liver damage. Or indeed lung damage. One of her legs is broken and one arm as well. And I think possibly her pelvis.'

'Oh God,' said Laura. 'Poor little girl.'

'We're setting a drip up, make sure she's stable, and then we'll send her down for a full scan. And we're probably going to intubate her – she's having a bit of trouble breathing. I'm getting my colleague, Mr Armstrong, down to have a look at her – he's the main chest and lung consultant here. You're lucky, he's often in the country on Saturdays, but he's on call today.'

'I know him,' said Jonathan. 'Tony Armstrong. Good bloke,' he added to Laura. 'Really excellent.'

The young doctor looked at him and he seemed to be having trouble speaking. Finally: 'I'm afraid this child is very sick,' he said. 'Very sick indeed.'

Chapter 49

It was very quiet on the ward; they called it a ward, ICU, standing for Intensive Care Unit, but actually it was a long corridor, outside some doors. Behind each door was someone very ill indeed, in need of the Intensive Care. Like Daisy. He hadn't been allowed into the room where she was, but he had got a glimpse once when his father came out: it was a mass of machines and screens. She lay on a high bed, her eyes closed; there was a tube in her nose, which his father said was helping her to breathe. Her hair was spread out over the pillow.

Charlie felt so afraid and so sick that he didn't know what to do with himself. Keeping still was awful, because his head just filled up with what he had done. He saw pictures over and over again, and they seemed to go backwards in time, first of Daisy lying in the road, near the car, then Daisy running along behind him, asking him to wait, then Daisy trying to show him pictures in her magazine, then Daisy skipping out of the gate ahead of him, calling, 'Bye, Mummy.'

She'd been fine then: he hadn't done it then, hadn't killed her. He hadn't argued with her, told her she was stupid, hadn't got crosser and crosser with her, hadn't not seen the car, hadn't not seen her running after the cover of her magazine; she'd been safe, held in the past, happy, laughing, alive, alive, alive . . .

At this point he felt so terrible he had to get up and walk down the corridor away from the pictures; he kept going into the lavatory, thinking he was going to be sick, standing there, bending over the bowl, staring down into it, wondering how he was going to get through the next five minutes even, let alone the rest of his life. He hoped he could find some way of dying too, maybe run under a car himself, that would be right really, that would make it fair, his death traded for hers; he certainly couldn't contemplate years of this, or even many more hours . . .

His grandmother had gone, taking Lily with her; his parents sat on the chairs in the corridor outside the room. They had been told they could have a parents' room for the night, but they'd both refused, said they wanted to be near Daisy.

It was when they'd said that, he'd known: known it was so bad that she really was likely to die. Until then, he'd known it had been terribly serious, that she was very, very badly hurt, in danger of dying; but now he could see from their faces, hear from their voices that it was actually more likely that she would.

They'd told him to go with Lily, but he refused; he didn't actually argue, he didn't seem to be able to say anything anyway, he couldn't remember speaking since it had happened; he just shook his head and then folded his arms, and stood there, daring them to make him go against his will.

'Darling,' his mother said, 'you'll be better with Granny, and the minute we know anything we'll call you, promise, even if it's the middle of the night.'

But he'd shaken his head again, furiously, and his father had said, quite gently, 'Laura, let him be. He's better here.'

His father had been terribly nice to him, they both had; he wished they hadn't, he wished they'd both attack him, shout at him, beat him up, injure him really badly so he'd be hurt too, so he might need Intensive Care too, and then when he was all wired up, he could pull the wires all out so he couldn't breathe or live any longer.

He walked back to them now, after another visit to the lavatory; his mother was holding his father's hand, her head on his shoulder. For a minute he thought she was asleep, but then he saw her eyes were staring down at the floor.

'Hello,' his father said. 'You OK?'

But still he couldn't speak; just nodded and sat down next to his mother.

His father had explained as much as he could to him; Daisy had had a brain scan, and her skull had what was called a hairline crack in it. She also had some damage to her spleen, which had caused it to bleed inside her, and that meant giving her some blood. The most worrying thing, it seemed, was that she had some broken ribs and one of them had punctured her lung, which could lead to an infection. 'That's why she's got a drain in her chest. And you see, as she's very poorly, she'll have trouble fighting infection. So they're giving her some antibiotics as well.' The other things, the broken leg and arm, sounded like nothing in comparison.

He wanted, more than anything, to say how sorry he was, but somehow he couldn't. It was such a useless thing to say, because it wouldn't do any good, it wouldn't bring Daisy back or make her better, and anyway, it was too easy: saying sorry was what you did when you'd spilled or broken something or not done your homework. Not when what you'd broken was your sister, broken her into what seemed like fragments, so that she could never be mended again.

The man who'd been driving the car was still downstairs; Charlie felt almost sorry for him. He had been driving a bit fast, but it hadn't been all his fault – Daisy had run into the road in front of him – it had been Charlie's fault, for not looking after her, not seeing what she was doing, what she might do; she'd been crying in the end, no one knew that except him: he'd heard the tears in her high little voice, as she called, 'Charlie, please, please, wait,' and thought how stupid and annoying she was, and how he wasn't going to give in to her, make her more of a spoiled baby than she was already. It was completely his fault.

Suddenly he really couldn't bear it any longer; he managed to speak, to say, 'I'm going for a walk, OK?'

His mother said, 'Darling, don't go away, or at least let one of us go with you,' but he'd shaken his head, said he'd be OK, and his father had said, 'Let him go, Laura, he'll be fine. Charlie, don't go into any of the wards, just go down to the front hall, I would, and if you get lost, just ask anyone where ICU is and they'll show you.'

He nodded and stood up, walked rather quickly down the corridor and into the lift; it felt better, walking away from it. It felt like he could escape.

He went into the main reception area, and then walked down towards A&E. As he went in through the door, he saw the man, Mick, lying down on three chairs which he'd pushed together. He was all right, Mick was, staying all this time.

He thought he was asleep, but he was awake, like his mother, staring at the ceiling; he saw Charlie and jumped, sat up with a rush, said, 'What's happened, has she—'

'Nothing's happened,' Charlie said. 'She's the same. Just the same.'

'Oh shit,' Mick said and lay down again; and then, 'I'm going out for a fag. I'll be just outside the main door if there's any news, OK?'

Charlie nodded.

He sat down on a chair in A&E for a bit, but then the pictures began to come back and he started pacing up and down, between the front door and the lift, and then when they stayed with him there as well, he went to the front door and looked out into the area where the ambulances came in, and beyond that to the high lights of the car park and thought maybe it would be better if he ran, maybe he could get away from them that way; and he ran round the car park, round and round, weaving his way in between the few cars, until he was breathless and sat down on the wall by the road, staring out at it and wondering if he had the courage to run into a car himself now, get it over. He looked back at the hospital, up at the third floor, at the lighted window where Daisy lay, probably dying, was maybe even dead; and then back across the car park, and saw his father walking towards him, waving at him, calling his name. This was it then, he'd come to tell him it was over; he'd not just nearly killed her now, he'd actually killed her, and he closed his eyes and waited, waited for the words.

But, 'You all right, Charlie?' his father said, and he shook his head, and finally managed, 'What – what's happened?'

'Nothing. She's just the same. I came to find you, make sure you were OK.'

He didn't deserve this, this kindness; it was wrong, all wrong! Why couldn't they be cruel, as cruel as he'd been? And then his father put his hand on his shoulder and something happened, inside his head, and he started to cry, quite quietly, but desperately, and his father said, 'Come on, old chap. Let's go inside, see if we can find somewhere a bit nice to sit, shall we?'

They couldn't find anywhere exactly nice, but they did find a corner near a radiator, and his father fetched two chairs from down the corridor, and they sat down. Charlie felt a bit dizzy and leaned forward, put his head on his knees.

'Poor old boy,' his father said, and Charlie felt his hand gently rubbing his back; and he sat up and pushed him away, saying through his tears, 'Don't, don't do that, don't be so nice to me! Why don't you hit me – go on, hit me hard, please, please . . .'

But then somehow, he was in his father's arms, where he had never thought he would be again, and his face was buried in Jonathan's chest, and he was sobbing and clutching at him desperately, as if he might go away, and then he stopped suddenly and looked up and said, 'Dad, it was my fault.'

And instead of saying something stupid and trying to comfort him, as if he was some kind of a retard, his father looked back at him very steadily and said, 'Yes, I know it was.'

The words hit him like a lash; they were shocking, but they helped, made him calmer, stopped his tears.

'Did – did Mum tell you?'

'Sort of. Of course she didn't see, she wasn't there, but Mick told me as well what happened and I can put two and two together. Not all your fault, Charlie, these things never are. Mummy and I both played our part, but – well, in a way of course it was, yes. I can see why you feel so bad.'

'Not even in a way,' Charlie said, and the relief of being able to talk about it, to let the pictures out, made him feel better, in a strange way. 'I – I wasn't looking after her. That was why it happened. No other reason.'

'Go on. Just hang on a minute.' Jonathan pulled his mobile out of his pocket and looked at it. 'No, it's OK. Just wanted to check Mummy hadn't called me. Sorry.' He pressed a key, said, 'Hi. I've got him, he's fine, we're downstairs together having a chat. Any news? No, OK. Ring me if you want me.'

'I thought you weren't allowed to use mobiles in hospitals,' said Charlie.

'You're not.' His father smiled at him suddenly – a warm, almost cheerful smile. 'They'd better not tell me not to, that's all.'

'I'm sure they won't.'

'I'm sure too. Now – want to go on?'

He nodded, settled back on his chair. The words came slowly, had to be forced out. 'She was annoying me. Making me cross. I couldn't help it. I know I shouldn't have felt like that, but anyway, Mum made me take her to the shop, and

I wanted to go on the computer, and I was horrible to her, really horrible, telling her she was stupid, when she went on about some kitten she wanted—' He stopped, remembering Daisy's face as she talked about the kitten, so serious, so anxious to discuss the kitten's possible name; she'd been all right then, fine. He gulped, swallowed some tears. 'It was on the way back. I just walked ahead, faster and faster; she was dropping things, Dad, and I wouldn't help, wouldn't wait. I knew she was getting upset, you know how she does.'

'Yes, I do. Go on.'

'Well, that was it. I was walking further and further ahead, and she called to me to wait, to help her, said the cover had come off her comic, and I still walked on and then – then I heard it. Heard the car.'

'You didn't see it?'

'No, and I don't know why, because it all happened really slowly . . .'

'Accidents do. Or seem to.'

'I just heard the brakes and I heard her scream and I turned round then and – there she was. On the road. Like a . . .' *a dead person*, he had been going to say and he couldn't, and then he started crying harder again, and hurled himself at his father, clutching at him, and saying, 'I'm sorry, Dad. I'm so, so sorry,' over and over again.

Finally he stopped, looked up at him and waited. Waited for the words, the shocked and shocking, angry words. Or worse, the stupid, rubbish words, saying he couldn't have helped it. They didn't come. Nothing came. Just a silence. His father was just staring in front of him, and his eyes were sadder than Charlie had ever seen them; and then finally he looked at him and said, 'Charlie, we all make mistakes. Some don't matter very much, some are terrible. Terrible mistakes, that make other people very unhappy. Mistakes we'd give anything, anything at all, to change. To take back. But – we can't. I made one, as you know. You've made one. Both serious mistakes that can't be unmade. And that's the thing. They are unchangeable. They won't go away, whatever you do. So – the only thing to do is to live with them. Do the best you can. You can't put them right. But you can put them behind you. Which isn't easy, but – well, it isn't easy.'

He was silent again; Charlie sat looking at him, his sobs quietened, his feelings oddly quieter too. After a while, Jonathan put his arm round him, pulled him closer; Charlie relaxed against him, rested his head on his chest.

And then Jonathan said, 'I love you, Charlie. Very much,' and after quite a long time, Charlie heard his own voice, very quiet, almost as if it didn't belong to him, 'I love you too, Dad.'

'Oh, God. That's so awful.'

'What?' Sylvie looked up from the TV; Abi was sitting at the table, staring at the newspaper, her face very white.

'I – Sylvie, look at this.'

Sylvie looked: a small paragraph, next to an item about yet another politician caught taking bribes. *Hero Doctor's Child in Coma*, it was headed. *Daisy Gilliatt, eight-year-old daughter of top gynaecologist Jonathan Gilliatt, dubbed the hero of the M4 crash last August, has been knocked down by a car and is in Intensive Care. Her parents and her elder brother were at her bedside last night. No one from the hospital was available for comment. Our medical correspondent writes . . .*

'God,' said Sylvie. 'How sad.'

'I don't know what to do, Sylvie.'

'What do you mean? What could you do?'

'Like I said, I don't know. But I ought to do something, don't you think? Call him maybe, send some flowers to the mother?'

'Abi, are you out of your head! Do you really think that

733

poor woman would feel any better if she got some flowers from *you*? I don't want to be offensive, but it'd probably make her feel much worse.'

'Yeah, yeah, I suppose so. You're right. I just feel – well, I don't know. I met those kids, you know.'

'Yes, I know. And I can see why you're upset. But I really don't think you can do anything because he really is not going to feel better if he hears from you.'

'No. No, you're right. Oh shit, Sylvie, where is this thing going to end?'

'What do you mean?'

'I mean, it just won't let me go. The crash.'

'I can't see what the poor kid getting run over has got to do with the crash. Or you, if that's what you're thinking.'

'Well, maybe it has. Maybe finding out about me stopped the mother from looking after them properly. Don't look at me like that, Sylvie, it's possible.'

'Of course it's not possible. Mothers aren't like that. They function whatever. My Auntie Cath didn't start letting her kids run around doing what they liked when my uncle ran off with that totty from his firm. She got harder on them, if anything. Stop beating yourself up, Abi.'

'Yeah, OK, I'll try. But—'

'Abi!'

'Sorry. Look, we've got a committee meeting here this afternoon – you want to go out, or what?'

'No, I'll stay, if you don't mind. I won't get in the way. And I always enjoy the sexy farmer.'

'Yeah, well. Anyway, get in the way as much as you like. You might have some ideas. We need them. Oh shit, and it's the inquest in a fortnight. Suppose the kid doesn't get any better – how will Jonathan cope with that?'

Sylvie sighed. 'I don't know, Abi. But it's not your problem, honestly. Want a croissant?'

⁂ ⁂ ⁂

'It's the first forty-eight hours that are crucial.' The paediatrician looked at Jonathan. 'She gets through that, then we have reason for optimism.'

'And now? It's twenty-four. How's she doing?'

'Well, she's holding her own. The bp's gone up, which is good. She's definitely coming out of it a bit. She's woken up several times this morning, Sister tells me. Which is excellent. Those fractures are nothing – apart from the fact her lung's been punctured. The biggest worry now, to be honest, is infection. She's running a bit of a fever.'

'What is it?'

'Oh, only thirty-nine.'

He spoke over-casually; Jonathan winced.

'Thirty-nine is high.'

'Ish.'

'No, it's high. She's still on the antibiotics, isn't she?'

'Of course. You know she is. Intravenously. Look, have you been in to see her this morning?'

'Yes, of course.'

'Well, how does she look to you?'

'Pretty bad,' said Jonathan. 'To be honest.'

Laura stood, watching her daughter. Her pretty, sweet, merry-hearted little daughter. Reduced to something devoid of personality, a still, white ghost, most of her bodily functions taken over by machines. It was all very well for the doctors to keep saying her vital signs were good, that the concussion was serious but far from fatal, that a few broken limbs were of no great importance. The fact remained she was extremely badly hurt, her small slender body knocked about by half a ton of moving metal, her small skull cracked, one of her lungs ruptured, a mounting fever invading her. They were talking now of packing her in ice; Laura knew what that meant. It meant the fever was very serious, very high. She was in pain, too, restless, turning her head constantly; her hair had been getting tangled, and Laura had asked if she might tie it back somehow, but it was difficult. Daisy seemed aware that something was bothering her, tried to push her away with her good arm.

More than anything, Laura wanted to hold her, hold her safe, as she had through all her small troubles, her minor childish illnesses and the more major recent hurts, to be able to say, 'It's all right, Mummy's here, Mummy will look after you, Mummy loves you.' But she couldn't look after her, however much she loved her; her efforts were of absolutely no value. Indeed, if she held her now, she would die. The only things that could help her were the machines – cold, unfeeling, efficient machines – helping her breathe, hydrating her, dulling her pain, telling them when her pulse rose, her blood pressure dropped.

She hated the machines, even while she knew she must be grateful to them. She wanted Daisy to be able to tell her that she hurt, that she was hot, that she felt sick; she didn't want her function as a mother negated, didn't want to be told that all she must do was stand back, be quiet, wait, not interfere. It was wrong, against the natural order of things: and yet she knew that without the machines, and without the skills of the doctors and the awesome power of the drugs, Daisy would most certainly have died by now.

Jonathan came in, stood watching Daisy with her, put his arm round her.

'All right?'

'Yes. I'm all right. Where's Charlie?'

'He's asleep in the parents' room. I mustn't be long – I promised I'd be there when he woke up.'

'How is he?'

'Oh, you know. Poor little boy.'

Jonathan was being amazing; not just sympathetic, not just supportive, but calm, positive, absolutely unreproach-ful. She had said she was sorry, that she knew she shouldn't

736

have sent Daisy out with Charlie, and he'd said nonsense, that she was right, they'd done it countless times, that children couldn't be wrapped in cotton wool. 'But they should be!' she'd cried, tears coming suddenly. 'We should wrap them in cotton wool, that's exactly what we ought to do, then they'd be safe, stay safe . . .'

'And grow up helpless, unable to look after themselves.'

'They'd grow up at least,' she'd said, and he was powerless to answer that.

'How's Lily?' she said then.

'She's all right. Your mother's being so good. She said should she bring her over, did I want her to fetch Charlie, should she bring some food in – all sorts of helpful things.'

'Should she bring Lily? Do you think?'

'No,' he said, 'not unless she really wants to come. And your mother said she was better at home with her. They're watching movies. Of course, if—'

'Don't. Don't say it.' She knew what he meant. If Daisy got worse, if they had to say goodbye, then Lily must be there too.

'Right. Well, I think that's about it. Well done, everybody.' God, this was an effort. It was hard to think the wretched festival mattered. While that poor little girl . . .

'We'll go firm on the date then?'

'Ye-es. Still no headliner but the dates for the play-offs are fine. No news on a sponsor, I suppose, Fred?'

'Nope, sorry. They like higher-profile causes, most of them.'

'Surely not local ones?'

'Well, maybe.'

'Fred, haven't you tried locally at all? Georgia?'

'Not, not really.'

'Well, why not, for fuck's sake! Jesus, I thought you were going to take all that off us. I suppose I'll have to do it, like I do everything else.'

'Abi,' said Georgia, 'I'm sure Fred's doing his best, we all are. But everyone's busy.'

'You're not.'

'Well, thanks for that. I am actually, got three auditions this week. Look, I know this was all my idea, but it seems to be getting everyone down, and it's running away with us. Maybe we should rethink.'

'No,' said Abi. 'Sorry, I shouldn't have lost it. Sorry, Fred.'

'That's OK. I should have done more, you're right.'

'No, you've got a lot on. And you're not even personally involved like the rest of us. I'll take that over.'

'Well, if you can pull a few things out of the bag . . .'

'Sure.'

'I might go then, if that's all right. Stuff happening at home this weekend.'

'Fine. Sorry again, I'm – well, I'm a bit worried about something.'

'I'll see you out,' said Sylvie, standing up. 'Georgia, William, want a coffee or anything?'

'I should go too,' said Georgia. 'Promised my mum I'd be back for this evening. Thanks, everyone, so much. Fred, wait for me.'

She was going to apologise to him again, on her own behalf, Abi thought. Perversely, it annoyed her.

'I'll have a coffee, please, Sylvie,' said William, smiling at her. He quite clearly fancied her, Abi thought. And she played up to it. Bit annoying.

'I'll have some wine, Sylvie, please,' she said tartly. Then: 'Oh dear,' she looked at William. 'I'm a prize cow, aren't I?'

'I don't think you'd get many prizes,' he said, 'not at the shows I go to.'

'Don't joke. I am. I shouldn't have said that to Fred.'

'Maybe not. What are you worried about?'

'Oh, doesn't matter.' Of all the things William wouldn't want to hear about, or be reminded of, it was the Gilliatt family.

738

'It obviously does. Come on, Abi, tell me.'

'I – that is – oh God, William, Jonathan Gilliatt's little girl's been run over. She's in hospital. In Intensive Care.'

'That's very sad.'

'I know. It's worse than sad. It's terrible. They don't deserve that, do they?'

'Well – no. Life isn't about what you deserve though, is it? Not always.' There was a pause, then he said, obviously with difficulty, 'How – how do you know?'

Jesus, she thought, fuck, he thinks I'm still in touch with Jonathan. How awful was that.

'I read it in the paper,' she said, 'this morning.' She looked at him; his large brown eyes were thoughtful, doubtful even. 'William, I swear to you, I have not spoken to Jonathan since that night. You really can't think that.'

'No. No, of course not.' But he didn't sound completely sure.

'Look,' she said, reaching for the paper, 'it's here – see? William, please believe me.'

'I – do,' he said. 'Yes, of course I do. Well, this was yesterday's news. How is she today?'

'I don't know,' she said. 'How could I?'

'You could ring the hospital.'

'William, it doesn't say what hospital she's in, even. And anyway, they wouldn't tell me. They never do unless you're family.'

'No, no, I suppose not.'

Shock at his clearly still not quite trusting her, combined with anxiety and guilt, suddenly got the better of her and she started to cry.

'I feel so bad about it,' she said, 'so bad.'

'But why?'

'Because maybe what I did, having the affair with Jonathan, going to the house that night, maybe that contributed in some way. I don't know. Maybe the little girl was upset, maybe her mother was upset, maybe she wasn't looking after her properly . . .'

'Abi, Abi,' he said, and he came round the table to where she was sitting, put his arm rather clumsily round her shoulders. 'You can't go on blaming yourself for what you might or might not have done to that family. It's a while ago now . . .'

'Yes, I know, I know,' she said, looking up, trying to smile, wiping her nose on the back of her hand. Sylvie had come in with the drinks, stood looking awkward.

'Thanks,' he said, withdrawing his arm. 'Here, Abi, have a hanky.'

'No, it's OK,' she said. 'I've got some tissues in the kitchen. Excuse me . . .'

'It's all right,' he said, grinning suddenly, 'it hasn't been up some cow's bottom or anything, if that's what you think. Clean out of my drawer, when I left. Where my mother'd put it.'

'Your mother spoils you, obviously,' said Sylvie. 'Abs, I'm off now. See you later.'

'OK. Cheers. William,' she said, when the door had shut, 'you don't really think I'm still in touch with Jonathan, do you?'

'No,' he said, and this time he managed to smile back. 'No, I suppose not. But I can't help wondering sometimes . . .'

'I swear to you, I still hate him. I just – well, I feel bad for the little girl. And Laura.'

'Of course. Right – well, I'd better go. Milking to do. And the ewes' feeding to sort out.'

'The ewes?'

'Yes. About this time of year, we scan them. See how many lambs they're having.'

'You scan them?'

'Yup.'

'What, like you scan pregnant women?'

'Pretty much. Of course they don't lie on their backs, but—'

'And then what?'

'And then we separate out the ones who are having triplets and twins from the singletons.'

'Why?'

'Well, to adjust their feeds. So that the ones having more lambs get more food. Makes sense, if you think about it.'

'Yes. Of course it does. How clever.'

'Not really. Just common sense.'

'I suppose so. Well, thanks, William. Thanks for coming. It's such a long way.'

A long way, William thought, starting up the truck. If only she knew.

'Oh, my God. Abi, are you mental or what?'

'What do you mean?'

'William. God, he's well fit, isn't he?'

'Yeah, OK. What about him?'

'He's still nuts about you. Obviously.'

'Sylvie, don't be stupid. He never says or does anything.'

'I don't know what's happened to you, Abi. You've got so thick. He might not *do* anything, but he wants to. Blimey. It shows all right.'

'D'you think so?'

'Yeah, course. I mean, he had his arm round you last night, for God's sake.'

'Because I was crying. That's all.'

'Why were you crying?'

'Oh – about that little girl.'

'Must have been nice for William, to have you crying over that lot.'

'What do you mean?'

'Well, I don't suppose he likes thinking about *him* too much. About you and him, that is.'

'No,' said Abi slowly, remembering William's hurt face.

'No, I don't think he does. But that doesn't mean he still fancies me.'

'Well, it would make it worse,' said Sylvie, 'make him mind more. Don't you think?'

'Suppose so. Yeah. Oh shit. It's all such a mess. Still . . .'

'Mr Gilliatt! Could you come in, please. Quickly.'

This was it. She was dying. Or she'd died.

He went in, very quietly, shut the door behind him. She was lying, very still, apparently sleeping. Her face was pale, her expression very peaceful. Surely, surely she hadn't – not without him saying goodbye, sending her on her way, with his love. His special love. It was special. She was his baby – he still thought of her as three or four; it made her – used to make her – cross. 'I'm not a baby,' she used to say indignantly. 'Don't treat me like one, Daddy. I'm eight.' She used to say, she used to say . . . And now she'd never be nine; never grow up, never change, always stay thus in his memory, Daisy, who he'd loved so much, who loved him so much. 'My daddy,' she used to say, putting the emphasis on the my. 'My special daddy.'

Who'd also, just by the way, betrayed her; her and her sister and her brother and her mother. How could he have done that, failed them all, shattered their security, broken the faith.

'Oh God,' he said, and for the first time since it had happened, his calm broke; he felt the tears, hot fierce tears, filling his eyes, a sob rising in his throat. He stepped forward, took her hand – no longer hot, cool even – smoothed back her hair . . .

'Mr Gilliatt, she's—'

'Yes, yes, I know,' he said, and felt a tear drop onto their hands, their two joined hands. It would never be in his again, that hand, that small trusting hand, letting him lead her, running with her, skipping with her; she loved him to skip, it made her giggle, he would haul her off the ground

742

as he took great bounds, laughing too. 'I know. I understand.'

'No, you don't know. She's better. Really she is. Her temperature's down, she's peaceful, I'm just going to call Mr Armstrong to discuss removing the tube.'

'Oh God. Dear God. I—' And then he really started to weep, bent over Daisy, kissed her cheek, and then her hand, over and over again; and then said, 'Stay there, my darling,' as if she could do anything else, and went out to find Laura and Charlie, who were together, in the parents' room.

Laura looked up as he went in, saw the tears streaming down his face, and just for a moment thought, as he had, what he had; and then she saw that he was smiling, laughing even, as he cried, and she said only, 'Is she?' and he said, 'Yes, yes, she's better, she's going to be all right, her temperature's right down. Charlie, come here, give me a hug, your sister's better, she's going to be fine.' And they stood there, their arms around one another, the three of them, laughing and crying, bound together by their relief and joy and their love of the small precious being they had thought was lost to them for ever and who, by some miracle, worked by either God or science, or even her small determined self, and quite possibly all three, had been given back safely to them once more.

Chapter 50

Barney was horribly depressed. He might have fallen out of love with Amanda, but he missed her, missed her sweetness and her thoughtfulness, the way she cared for him, the sense of order she had created in their lives. She was so efficient, she ran the house and their life so well, and she was so happy always, so optimistic, distracting him when he was stressed about work, always ready with some new plan or idea for a holiday or a weekend or a dinner party.

He had moved out of the house and into a flat. His life seemed to be disintegrating into a dismal chaos. He didn't want to see anyone, he couldn't be bothered to cook for himself or even get his laundry organised; he spent a fortune on new shirts, as the dirty ones piled up in the bathroom and washing them seemed more difficult than simply buying a whole lot more. It wasn't just Amanda, of course, it was Toby; he had lost both of them, both his best friends. Nobody else seemed worth spending time on. It involved too many explanations, too much effort. He just drifted along aimlessly, working absurdly long hours, and dreading the inquest. He'd be under oath and therefore required to recount what had happened over the tyre, and worse, he would have to face Toby across the court. However disillusioned he was about Toby, he had no wish to see his reputation blackened, and possibly for him to face legal redress.

He spent a lot of time now wondering what Emma was

doing. Back with the boyfriend, maybe; which quite hurt. Or with someone new, which hurt more; or with no one at all, which hurt more than anything. Of course, she didn't know that it was over with Amanda, but some odd sense of pride kept him from telling her. She had finished it; she had decided it wasn't to be, that she didn't want to wait until Amanda could cope with her engagement being broken off – and he could hardly blame her. It did slightly cast her in the role of understudy – and she had obviously decided she couldn't cope with any of it. What price love then, Barney thought, remembering those fierce few weeks, when the world had changed and him with it: when he had looked at a relationship he had thought was for ever and found it wanting, and found another that had seemed not to want for anything at all.

It wasn't the best of times.

Alex had been called as a witness at the inquest; he had asked Emma if she would like to go – 'might be interesting for you' – and she had looked at him in horror and said no way, and she was surely going to be more useful at the hospital.

'Someone has to care for Swindon's sick and wounded,' she said.

What she meant, of course, was that she knew Barney would be there, possibly with Amanda, and that would be more than she would be able to bear.

In the event, Mark Collins said he would like to go with Alex, 'If that's OK. Having operated on so many of the victims, I'd like to hear the official verdict. Still all sounds a bit messy to me.'

Alex and Linda had settled into an uneasy peace: or as Alex called it 'an easy war'. Their relationship was never going to be comfortable; they continued to argue, to compete, to fight and reunite, and to enjoy one another physically and emotionally with a passion which still half-surprised them. Their latest battleground was where they would live: they had agreed that they wanted to live together, that had been the easy part. Where was proving impossible. Clearly Linda was not going to settle down in Swindon, nor Alex move to NW1; various compromises like Windsor, Beaconsfield and even Ealing had been scrutinised and dismissed as too surburban, too far out and just too horrible. Currently Alex was looking at Gloucestershire and Wiltshire cottages where they could weekend together at least; it was a compromise, and like all compromises provided the worst as well as the best of both worlds.

Linda was going to the inquest too, partly as support for Alex, which he said was very nice but hardly essential, since he'd attended thousands of the bloody things, but mainly as support for Georgia. The girl was absolutely terrified: at having the whole thing relived, and her own behaviour and what she saw as her cowardice publicly recorded. She dreamed about it, night after night, couldn't eat, was irritable and tearful. None of which, as Linda remarked to Alex, was unusual.

The only good thing was that she had got a part in another production. It wasn't quite such a good one as *Moving Away*, in fact, nothing probably ever would be so perfect for her again she thought, but it was pretty nice, a comedy series about a threesome, two girls and a boy, living together supposedly platonically; both the girls were secretly in love with the boy and he was meanwhile hopelessly – and also secretly – in love with someone else entirely.

'It's a marvellous script,' Linda said to Georgia. 'Shades of Noël Coward. You're a lucky girl.'

It wasn't until she turned up for a pre-production meeting that she discovered the first assistant director was Merlin Gerard . . .

'Georgia, hi,' he had said, smiling at her. 'Lovely to see you. And wonderful to be working with you again.'

'Yes. Yes, it's great.' Thinking thank God, thank God she had never let him know how hurt she'd been, how deceived she'd felt. 'Er – how's Ticky?'

'She's great, thanks. Yeah. Gone back to New York, of course.'

'Of course.'

'Want to come for a drink tonight?'

'I'm sorry, Merlin, I can't. Not tonight. Another time, maybe.' She'd even managed to smile at him.

She'd never felt more proud of herself than she had at that moment.

'You total star,' Lila said, when she told her, later that day. Lila had become just about her best friend. They spent a lot of time together, shopping, going to the cinema and to clubs when they could afford it, sometimes jazz clubs – Lila and Anna had introduced Georgia to jazz, and she was slightly surprised by how much she loved it – but mostly just talking, often late into the night.

'Yeah, I was rather pleased with myself. He looked pretty surprised when I said no.'

'Good. He needs to be. And – did you still fancy him?'

'Oh, yes. Completely,' said Georgia rather sadly.

Anna had agreed – rather nervously, but with great delight – that she and Lila would play a set at the festival. Abi had said she thought they should have some jazz, and Georgia, who was still a little in awe of Abi, said rather tentatively that she knew someone who had played jazz in quite a big way. Abi had never heard of Sim Foster, but she mentioned his name to a jazz enthusiast at work and had been astonished at his reaction.

'My God, Abi, you've never heard of Sim Foster? I can't believe it. He was one of the greats, you know. Some of his early stuff, absolute classics. And Anna was fantastic too, great voice. Anyone who knows anything about jazz'd give a lot to hear her, even without him. They were an absolute legend.'

Abi went back rather humbly to Georgia and told her to ask the legend if she'd be kind enough to consider playing at the festival.

She was totally dreading the inquest; she shrank from having her relationship with Jonathan brought out in court, together with the fact that she had lied when she had first given evidence. She couldn't imagine what the outcome might be; in her darkest hours, she saw herself in jail, or at best with a criminal record. William had tried rather cursorily to reassure her once, but after that refused to discuss the whole thing. William just wanted it over: for more reasons than one. The thought of being in the same courtroom as Jonathan Gilliatt was not appealing.

Daisy was home now, frail, and very thin, moving around with great difficulty but equal determination; fortunately it was her left leg but her right arm that were broken, so she could use a crutch to hobble from room to room. The family room had been turned into a bedroom for her, and her toys installed, so that she didn't have to cope with the stairs.

With the resilience of children, she seemed fairly unaffected by her trauma emotionally; no nightmares, no display of anxiety. The thing that most worried her was that she had broken the rules, done what was expressly forbidden, and she said over and over again that she was very sorry she had run into the road, and that she would never do such a thing again; Laura had privately resolved that Daisy would never run or indeed walk anywhere unaccompanied again, or not for a very long time.

The person perhaps most adversely affected by the whole thing was Lily, whose pretty little nose had been put distinctly out of joint by all the attention lavished on her sister. Initially delighted when Daisy was pronounced out of danger, and especially when she was allowed home, she now spent a large part of every day quarrelling with her, and demanding that the bounty of new toys pouring into Daisy's possession, supplied not only by her parents and grandparents, but schoolfriends and neighbours, be replicated in her own, and bursting into hysterical tears when she was told they would not.

Charlie, who appeared in some ways to have become at least five years older than he had been before the accident, was alternately to be found telling her to shut up and to be glad she still had a sister to fight with, and patiently playing games with one or the other of them. He had pleaded not to have to go back to school until Daisy was completely well; after two weeks of acting the perfect brother he suddenly announced that even sitting his Common Entrance was preferable. Laura and Jonathan, who had been a little worried by his newly saintly persona, were secretly relieved.

Jonathan had moved back home. Charlie had begged him to, and so had the girls; Laura could hardly refuse. She didn't exactly want to refuse. But even given the surge of positive emotion towards him that she had experienced in the hospital, she wasn't sure that she was remotely ready to start living with him again. Or indeed if she ever would be. A slow, but savage surge of anger and resentment was filling her once more; in the adrenaline crash after Daisy's initial recovery, it shocked her. She had thought, felt indeed, that if Daisy was given back to her, she would never mind anything again and was horrified to discover that she still minded about Jonathan and Abi Scott, very much indeed.

Once the desperate, clawing fear had subsided, once they had gone home, properly home, faced with the long, long days of sitting at Daisy's bedside, the exhaustion of coping with her querulous demands, her boredom, and her pain, then it began. She would look at him over the table as he laughed and joked with Charlie, teased Lily, as he sat by Daisy reading to her, as he helped her with things like shopping and the school-run, for he had taken compassionate leave, watched him being the perfect husband and the perfect father once more and at times she still hated him. And was shocked at herself for it.

She struggled to fight it, she reminded herself constantly of his courage and his tenderness in the dreadful days at the hospital, when Daisy had swung so close to death, she told herself that more than ever now he had earned her generosity and her forgiveness – but she was still haunted by the betrayal, the easy lies that he had shown himself to be capable of, and the way he had allowed Abi Scott to cut into the heart of their marriage.

And the thought of sleeping with him remained abhorrent; she could not imagine it ever again. There would be a third person in their bed for evermore now, and no longer a shadowy presence, a vague threat, but one she had seen, heard, smelled – she would never forget that rich, cloying perfume – and watched as she sashayed across the room and kissed her husband's mouth.

Jonathan had not suggested that he join her in their bed; he continued to sleep in the spare room without comment, and indeed as if he assumed it was the proper place for him; but one night, quite late, after they had been reading in the drawing room and she said she was tired and thought she would go to bed, he had looked at her and said, 'Do, darling. You look tired. Shall I make you a nightcap?'

He had always done that in the old days, when she was particularly exhausted, brought her a hot toddy; she hardly ever drank spirits, but she loved that – the effect of the whisky in the hot milk never failed to make her sleep. But for some reason tonight, she found the thought of it unbearable, that he was trying to deny the present, to work back into the past, when it had been a source of comfort, not pain, and she stood up and said, 'No, thank you, I can do that for myself,' and she could hear the coldness, the rejection in her own voice. His eyes as he looked at her then were surprised, hurt even.

'All right, darling,' he said, 'but the offer's there.'

And suddenly, it happened; she could hold it back no longer, the force of her rage.

'Jonathan, don't call me darling, please,' was all she said, but her tone was ugly, almost savage and he could only react.

'I'm sorry,' he said, and his voice in its turn was ice-cold, heavy with anger. 'I didn't realise you still felt so strongly against me.'

'Is that so?' she said. 'You didn't realise? What did you think then? That I had forgotten about what you did, your lies, how you betrayed me, betrayed us all?'

'No,' he said, 'of course not. But I thought – perhaps – we had moved on. That you could at least begin to – to accept it, if not forgive.'

'Jonathan, how could you even begin to think that? Accept it, you say! Accept the fact that you preferred her to me.'

'I did not prefer her,' he said wearily. 'No comparison came into it. She was – well, she was what she was. Nothing to do with you. I love you—'

'Oh, please! You love me! So much that you fucked someone else. Not just once, I could endure that, but many times. And not just fucked her, you slept with her, really slept with her, lay with her all night, woke up with her beside you. Lied and lied to me, so that you could. How could you do that, Jonathan? How could you want to do that?'

'I – don't know,' he said, 'I really don't know. It was some kind of – madness. I know, all erring husbands say that, but it's true. It was as if I became someone else. I didn't stop loving you, Laura, I didn't love you any less; it was greed, a grab at something else that I knew I shouldn't have. I can't expect you to understand, but—'

'No,' she said, 'I don't understand. Of course I don't. Well, I can see that you would want her, but the fact is you couldn't want her without rejecting me. That's how I see it, a rejection of me, of what I could do for you, what I could offer. It makes me feel so – so lacking.'

'Lacking in what?' he asked, and he looked so bewildered she almost smiled.

'In myself, Jonathan. I know . . .' She faltered, took a breath, started again. 'I know I'm not particularly sexy. I know that very well. I mean, I like sex, of course.'

'And why do you say of course?' he said. 'It's not compulsory, you know, liking it.'

'What do you mean?' she said, staring at him in astonishment. 'Of course it is. It's part of a marriage, part of loving someone.'

'And did you really see it as part of loving me?'

'Of course I did!' and she was shouting now. 'Of course I saw it as that. It was so precious to me – it was ours, and no one else's, what we shared, only between us. Now it's not any more, it's hers, she's taken it, or rather you've given it. It's gone, it's gone for ever and no one can bring it back.'

He was absolutely silent, looking at her with a dreadful sadness in his eyes; then he said, 'Well, it seems we are done for then. We can't be as we were again, can we?'

'No,' she said. 'No, we can't. Never.'

'In that case, maybe I should go again. But I want to say a few things first. Things that really need saying. I did love you. So very, very much. I *do* love you so very, very much. You are the centre of my life and the centre of our family. I can't contemplate life without you, Laura. Oh, that's not some idle suicidal threat, it's true. Of course I'd go on living, but I'd be changed. I'd be lost. I'd be pathetic, useless, dysfunctional.'

'Don't be ridiculous. You'd be just fine. Still the successful, attractive, wonderful Jonathan Gilliatt.'

'Laura, I wouldn't. I'm only those things because I have

you. I'd be anxious, I'd lose confidence, judgement. God in heaven, that happened even when I was living away for those few weeks. I dithered, I took second opinions, I did what others said instead of what I knew was right – I didn't even know what was right any more. I made one appalling mistake, I didn't tell you about it and you wouldn't have cared, I should think, given the circumstances, but I missed a cord presentation – you know what that is?'

'The baby's head pressing on the cord?'

'Exactly. Anyway, the baby nearly died; could so well have been brain damaged. And I missed it, because I was so wretched, so – so lost. And deservedly so, no doubt you would say. But – well, that is how dependent on you I am. I'm nothing without you, Laura, nothing at all.'

She was silent.

'I'm talking professionally, of course, but it extends to everything. The charming, attractive Jonathan Gilliatt as you call him is a pathetically different chap on his own.'

'Jonathan, this is all very touching, but if I'm so important to you, why risk losing me? Why start an affair with someone else? It doesn't quite add up. Sorry.'

'I know that. Of course I do. It was insanity. It was dangerous insanity. And I had never done anything like it before, and I never would again. And I know you don't believe me when I tell you it was over, that I'd finished with her that day, but it's true. But haven't you ever, in your perfectly controlled, beautifully behaved life, Laura, done anything remotely wrong? Or dangerous? Haven't you ever been tempted to kick over the traces – oh, not to have an affair, but – I don't know, spend too much and lie to me about it, or take a day off from cooking and buy McDonald's for the children, or go back to bed or spend the day with your girlfriends, and not do any work, or not help with the homework, or . . .'

'No,' she said, after a few moments' thought. 'No, I haven't.'

'Well then,' he said, and he almost smiled. 'There you have it, perhaps.'

'What do you mean?'

'I mean, it's quite tough being married to you.'

'Jonathan, I devote my entire life to you. To doing what you want, going where you want me to be. It's me it's tough for, I'd say. Not you.'

'No,' he said, 'well, it may be. But that's why – I think – I had this affair with Abi Scott. I'm trying to be honest now. Because she was bad, quite a lot of the time. She's greedy, and amoral and she tells lies all the time. I didn't have to live up to her. And I have to say, I treated her very badly.'

'Oh, my heart bleeds for her. I'm so sorry.'

'I am sorry – actually. I should have shown her some consideration, after the crash. It was a trauma for her as well, a dreadful one. And what did I do? I was so shit scared of you finding out about her that I threatened her.'

'You did what?' She was shocked by that.

'I told her that if she didn't go along with my story, that she was a work colleague, I'd tell the police about her drug habit. Not nice behaviour.'

'No. Not really. But—'

'But it was for you. I was so terrified of you finding out, not because you'd be angry, which you'd have every right to be, but because you'd be desperately hurt, that I bullied her. Harassed her ruthlessly. The irony is that if I'd been a bit nicer to her, she probably wouldn't have turned up here that night. At my party. I was a complete shit. I am a complete shit. Oh God . . .'

He looked at her and she could see tears in his eyes. He brushed them away.

'But Jonathan,' she said, 'I can't be what I'm not. I'm me. I can't start being lazy or extravagant, or neglecting the children, just so that you don't have to live up to me, as you put it. It's crazy, you're talking rubbish. Self-indulgent rubbish.'

754

'It may be self-indulgent,' he said, 'but it isn't rubbish. Everyone's so fucking envious of me. Or was. Lucky chap, they used to say, being married to Laura; wish my wife was more like her. God, Mark never stopped going on about it and how Serena never let him get away with anything, how wonderful you were. You remember that song, that music-hall song, "she's only a bird in a gilded cage". I felt like a bird in a gilded cage, and I flew out of it – just once, once for the hell of it. Or so I thought. Fate trapped me, shut the door behind me, and I'll never be back in it now and it serves me right.'

She said nothing: trying to make sense of what he was saying.

He stood up now, in front of her, staring down into her eyes. 'I guess that's it, by way of explanation. I have never regretted anything more. I would give everything I have – everything except you and the children – to alter it. But I can't. As I said to Charlie in the hospital, you have to live with what you've done. There's no alternative. It's hardly a justification, I know, but—'

'No,' she said, 'it isn't.'

'Well, that's my swansong. I'll go, Laura. Don't worry. Or if you'd prefer it, I'll stay here, for the sake of the children, carry on pretending. I'm not sure they could face losing me again. That's not meant to be emotional blackmail, it's a fact. But I won't ask anything of you, anything at all. And when they're older, maybe we can get divorced. It's up to you. Whatever you want. It's the least I can do for you. To make amends. I only ask one thing, that you try to believe how much I love you.'

'I'll try,' she said after a very long time. 'I really will try. And – don't go, Jonathan. You're right. The children couldn't bear it.'

She wasn't sure she would be able to bear it herself. But she wasn't quite ready to say that.

Chapter 51

Michael Andrews always said the most important quality a coroner should possess was courtesy. And indeed, he had never come across one who didn't. It was important for all concerned: for the relatives of the deceased, of course, still grieving, often disappointed that there was to be no criminal trial, so that they might find retribution for the death of their loved ones, and at least anxious to establish the truth; for the police who had worked so hard to establish that truth and whose evidence, often rather ponderous, must be heard in full, that the hard work might be justified; for the witnesses, often distressed themselves, always nervous; and of course for the Coroner's Office staff, so at pains to be courteous themselves, to put people at ease, to ensure that proceedings ran smoothly and as swiftly as possible.

The inquest he was to conduct the following week, on the people who had died in the M4 crash the previous August, would be long, but he hoped very much to get it over with in one day. There were three deceased, and many witnesses; the crash had been complex and high-profile. It would test his skills considerably, and he would need to prepare for it with great care.

Since it was to be so large, and with so many attendees, it was to be held in the Council Chamber at the County Court, rather than in one of the committee rooms; in a way people preferred that, they felt the death of their loved ones was being considered a matter of some importance, accorded proper dignity. The other important thing about inquests, of course, was that they differed from criminal inquiries in that all the witnesses heard all the evidence. It gave a sense of greater openness and fairness, and it meant those involved could more easily see any concerns laid properly to rest. There would be lawyers present, of course, because of insurance issues; and several doctors. One of the doctors, Mr Jonathan Gilliatt, would be giving evidence on two counts: his own involvement in the crash, and his professional observations of the injured and deceased.

It would be wrong, Michael Andrews supposed, to say he was looking forward to the inquest, since it would be both gruelling and sad, but it did promise to be what he privately called a yardstick, one by which he would judge and compare others.

His wife, Susan, was prepared for a somewhat solitary weekend.

'All rise.'

Michael Andrews liked this moment, as he walked into the court: not from any delusions of grandeur, but because it was an acknowledgement of his authority and, through him, the court's.

He sat, in the Council Chamber, on a high dais: flanked by his clerk and Coroner's Officer. The public sat before him, the seats ranged amphitheatre-style and banking up towards the back of the chamber. The witness table, also slightly raised and complete with microphone and Bible, was to his left.

He began as he always did by welcoming everyone; by explaining the purpose of the inquest: 'We are here to answer four questions. Who the deceased were, and when, where and how they came to their deaths. It is not to establish any blame and no charges will be brought as a result.' He paused. 'Three of the four answers are straightforward. The fourth, establishing by what means death arose, is the main purpose of this inquest. The families, if they wish, may ask relevant questions.'

The families, sitting together in their prescribed area, all looked at one another and then nervously about them. He knew from experience that at least one of them would ask questions, probably of the pathologist. He also knew what the first question was likely to be: would the victim have suffered at all?

He named the deceased and described them briefly, their ages, their status, where they lived: the young girl, Sarah Tomkins, the mini-bus driver, Edward Barnes, the young mother, Jennifer Marks.

He called the pathologist, Dr Paul Jackson from St Mark's Hospital, who had carried out the post mortems on the deceased and asked him to take the oath. People were very respectful of the oath; they spoke it clearly and audibly, even if they became less so as they gave their evidence. And it reassured the relatives further, he knew: that no one was going to lie, to prevaricate; they were going to hear, finally, exactly what had happened to those they loved.

Dr Jackson gave his evidence; the awful bald facts, the exact cause in each case of the deaths. The mother of the young girl began to cry; the husband blew his nose hard and repeatedly. When Andrews asked if there were any questions, the wife of the mini-bus driver, a middle-aged woman, her face pale and etched with strain, said, 'I would like to ask a question. In your opinion, Doctor,' she said, speaking to the pathologist, 'would my husband have suffered at all?'

'I think I can state quite categorically,' Dr Jackson said, 'that he would not. It is my professional opinion that all three would have died instantly.'

'Thank you,' said the woman. The others looked at her and half-smiled; Sarah's mother said, her voice shaky with nerves and emotion, 'I was going to ask the same thing. But I wondered if whoever found my daughter – I believe it was another doctor – would have agreed.'

'We shall come to that evidence a little later,' said Andrews, 'and you will be free to speak to the gentleman in question, who was indeed a doctor, then.'

The police evidence followed, describing the background of the victims and how they had come to be on the road that afternoon: the always-tragic accounts of lives ended too soon. They were rich in clichés: 'a devoted and selfless mother', 'a lively, popular and clever daughter', 'a loving and generous grandfather'. Michael Andrews hated the clichés, but they seemed de rigueur; they were what people told the police, and in any case, they undoubtedly comforted the families.

He called Dr Alexander Pritchard, the A&E consultant at St Mark's, to describe what medical procedures, if any, were carried out on the victims. Pritchard who, like the pathologist, had clearly given evidence at many inquests before this one, spoke straightforwardly and with equal and careful tact: no procedures were carried out, the victims were all dead on arrival, and neither basic nor intensive life support techniques were indicated. He added that in his opinion also, the deaths would all have been instantaneous.

Nice man, Andrews thought: an old-fashioned doctor of the best kind.

The inquest machinery ground on.

A large sheaf of photographs of the crash, taken from every angle, with relevant vehicles and trajectories painstakingly marked, were handed out to everyone. A description of the crash was given by Constable Greg Dixon; he said people were for the most part very calm and helpful and that he would like to pay tribute to the courage of a doctor on the scene: 'Mr Jonathan Gilliatt, who worked tirelessly among the injured for many hours, and cared for a woman who had gone into premature labour, reassuring her and monitoring her condition until the ambulance arrived. He also most courageously climbed up into the lorry to turn the ignition off.'

Andrews asked for the forensic evidence; it was complex and highly technical. Clearly the cause of the accident had been the wheel nut shattering the lorry's windscreen. There was also considerable detail about a car two places behind the lorry, which had apparently had a blow-out, and caused considerable further damage. It had had a large rusty nail in one of its tyres which would certainly have contributed to, if not caused, the burst tyre.

Michael Andrews called Sergeant Freeman, to present the police evidence. He liked and respected Freeman, from whom he had heard evidence many times. Freeman had a certain lack of humour, and he tended to be rather self-important, but was inordinately thorough, incredibly hard working, and he presented his evidence with great clarity. It took almost half an hour; at the end of it, Andrews was already tired, and it was only eleven. The concentration required by these big cases was exhausting; it never ceased to surprise him. He called a break for fifteen minutes, and sank gratefully into the peace of his own room, savoured a huge mug of strong sweet coffee supplied by his staff. He worried sometimes that at the age of fifty he was getting a bit old for this game; and then reminded himself that he had found it tough at thirty.

Patrick Connell had obviously once been a big man, Andrews thought, watching him as he came to the witness stand; he was tall, but frail, and walked leaning on two sticks and with a heavy limp. He asked him if he would like to sit down to give his evidence; Connell said he would rather stand, but halfway through what was obviously a gruelling experience, he was forced to give in and sit.

'Now, Mr Connell, tell us about your experience, as much as you can remember. We have heard you suffered memory loss, but anything you can tell us will be important.'

The evidence was faltering, faulty indeed; Connell had no real memory of the crash and indeed very little of the next few days; his memory had begun to return, but only in fragments. 'It was a very disturbing time, sir, as you can imagine, I'm sure.'

'Indeed. Now – you weren't feeling sleepy beforehand? It says in your statement, if I might remind you again, that you had been to see your doctor about this tendency of yours to feel sleepy on the road. Remember you are under oath.'

A hesitation; he could feel the lawyers stiffen.

'I had been, sir, yes. About half an hour earlier. But I'd stopped for a coffee, and I was eating sweets – jelly babies – they're my life savers, odd though it may sound to you, sir, and I was talking to my passenger, immediately before the crash. I do remember that very clearly . . .'

He had gained confidence now; he gave a clearly honest description of blame-free driving, within the speed limit, of the other vehicles, of the E-type ahead of him, 'Just pulling ahead – he was driving very nicely, as a matter of fact.'

'I'm pleased to hear it . . . and may I also say how pleased I am that you have made such a good recovery from your injuries, Mr Connell. You may step down.'

'Thank you, sir.'

Andrews asked for Connell's passenger next. He looked at her as she took the stand – a young, so young, pretty little thing, clearly absolutely terrified – and asked her very gently to take the oath. Her hand shook as she held the card; he wondered how good a witness she would be.

Unexpectedly, she was very good, calm and clear, describing how one moment everything had seemed perfectly fine, nobody speeding, nobody cutting across anybody, when their windscreen had so suddenly shattered. 'It was terrifying. Like being in a thick fog. And then somehow, we stopped and we were in the middle of all this – this chaos.'

'How long would you say it was before you felt the lorry veer over across the lanes of the motorway?'

'Oh – it all happened so slowly. It seemed like hours, although I suppose it couldn't have been more than what – twenty seconds. And then quite quickly there was this terrible, awful noise and horns going and brakes screaming, and then we stopped.'

'Yes. I don't think we need to go over the next few minutes. Your statement was very clear and it must have been very traumatic for you.'

He felt bound, driven by personal as much as professional curiosity, to ask her why she left the scene of the crash.

'I don't know,' she said simply. 'I wish I did, and I'm terribly ashamed of it. But I can't explain it, I really can't. I suppose I panicked. I remember thinking that if I got away, left the accident, it would be all right. No one would know I'd been there, and I could just – just forget about it. It was so horrible, all the injured people, especially Patrick – Mr Connell – and the wrecked cars, and people shouting and screaming. I felt I – well, I had to get away.'

'So you walked quite a long way, you say, and then hitched another lift, and went home to Cardiff?'

'Yes, that's right. And then I sort of managed to persuade myself that it hadn't happened. Or rather that I hadn't been there. That it was nothing to do with me. And the more time passed, the more impossible it got to admit I'd been there. Until there were stories in the press, implying that Patrick – Mr Connell – had gone to sleep.' She started to cry.

Michael Andrews waited patiently, then said, 'Try not to

feel too distressed, Miss Linley. We all make mistakes and do things we can't explain. I'm sure Mr and Mrs Connell are most grateful that you told your story when you did.'

'Yes. Thank you. And we have become good friends now. But only because they're so good, they've been so forgiving.'

Andrews found himself rather taken by her; he thanked her for all her evidence, and then asked if she had managed to get the part she'd been auditioning for. He did that sometimes, ventured into the personal or light-hearted where he felt it would help the atmosphere; Georgia said she had, and added that the series would be shown on Channel 4 in the spring.

'I have to tell you, Miss Linley,' he said, 'commercial advertising is not normally allowed in the courtroom. However, I will make an exception in this case.'

He heard the evidence of Jack Bryant, the owner of the E-type Jaguar. He couldn't think who he reminded him of and then realised he was a dead ringer for that Nigel Havers character, the Charmer. He had the same smooth dress-style, the same confident public-school manner. Andrews was about to dislike him, when he said right at the beginning of his evidence, after taking the oath, 'I feel absolutely ghastly about this. Terrible. The whole thing could be said to be my fault.'

'Mr Bryant,' said Andrews, 'as I said at the beginning, we are not here to establish blame. Merely to find out what happened. Now, we have heard it was one of your wheel nuts that flew off and shattered the windscreen of Mr Connell's lorry; can you tell us how you think this could have happened?'

'No,' said Bryant, 'I really can't. I checked them all really carefully, my mechanic will confirm that, before I set out. I was going to Scotland, long way, for a bit of shooting, and I wanted everything to be as safe as possible.'

'Indeed. And you weren't speeding at all?'

'No, I most definitely was not. Chance'd be a fine thing, in that car. Very beautiful, but not much of a goer these days. She's an old lady, bit past her prime.'

Every inquest has its turning point; this one was provided by one of the experts at the police Forensics department.

'Thing is, you can over-tighten those old nuts. One turn too far and it can break the thread. In our opinion and on examining the car when it came into our possession, that's what happened.'

Andrews looked at Bryant: he was visibly limp with relief. And then at the families: it was the kind of thing that was in a way most painful, the fatal event that was still an accident, an act that had killed, but committed in good faith. He was not surprised to see them all sitting up very straight suddenly, their faces taut, and in the case of the young girl's mother, already in tears . . .

The morning moved on. He heard some excellent evidence given by a young man, William Grainger, a farmer whose land bordered the M4; clear, concise, very helpful. Some more, very painful to hear, from the husband of the young mother who had been killed; they broke for lunch after this.

In the afternoon Jonathan Gilliatt took the stand. Now here was a smoothie, Andrews thought, even if he was a hero. Very self-confident he'd be, his evidence very well presented.

He was wrong; and it was not.

Gilliatt was uncomfortable, nervous, unclear as to exactly what he had seen of the crash, admitted – wiping his forehead repeatedly – that he and his passenger had been having what he called 'a rather heated exchange' just beforehand.

'Sufficiently heated to distract you?' Andrews asked, and yes, he said, and he was very ashamed that he had allowed it to do so.

'Not a good thing to be distracted on a crowded motorway, I'm afraid. Fortunate you were on the inside lane. You had met your passenger at a business function, I believe?'

'We had met through business, yes.'

Cagey answer. Should he press this? Andrews asked himself. No. It was hardly relevant. 'Now I believe also that you were on the phone, which must have added to your distraction.'

'I was, yes. Very, very briefly.'

'You don't have a handsfree?'

'Not in the car I was driving, no. Well – that is to say, I do, but it wasn't working properly. The car was brand new, and there were teething troubles generally with the communication systems. The Satnav wasn't working properly either. I knew I shouldn't have answered the phone, but I was pretty sure it was my wife – she'd been trying to get through, and she'd have been worried. And I had to get to my clinic in Harley Street.'

'I see. But you were obviously driving slowly, given that you were under pressure. Why was that?'

'Well, as I said, there'd been the storm, conditions were nasty. I was tired, I think I must have been feeling generally nervous.'

'And then?'

'Then, as it says in my statement, I realised the lorry was all over the place, that it could be very dangerous. I literally flung the phone into the back and – next thing I knew, I was on the hard shoulder. With all the – the carnage about a hundred metres behind me.'

'And then you walked back to see what you could do?'

'Yes, that's right.'

'Which was very commendable. Well done. Now – I

would like to ask you about the victims, and your undoubtedly splendid work amongst the injured – and I think that when I have finished, some of the relatives may want to question you. I hope that's all right.'

'Of course.'

'I would like to call Abigail Scott. Miss Scott, please take the oath. But first we shall hear your statement, from Sergeant Freeman.'

Bit of a baggage, this one, Andrews thought. Very attractive, and very, very sexy. Unlikely the relationship with Gilliatt had been purely professional. No doubt he'd considered himself perfectly safe – and then found himself skewered by fate.

'Miss Scott. You were in the car with Mr Gilliatt. I wonder if you can add to his evidence in any way, or rather confirm that as far as you could see, there was no question of anything cutting in front of Mr Connell's lorry, from any direction, that might have caused him to swerve.'

'No, nothing. I saw the whole thing, obviously, and everyone seemed to be driving very carefully and well.'

'Including Mr Gilliatt?'

'Yes, he was driving very carefully.'

'But he admits himself he was distracted, that you and he were having a – a heated discussion?'

'Yes, we were. But it wasn't making him drive badly. He – he's a very good and careful driver always.'

'You've been driven by Mr Gilliatt before, I assume from that?'

'Yes. Yes, I had.'

'In the course of your mutual professional duties, I presume?'

There was a long silence; the legendary pin dropping would have sounded like thunder.

Then: 'Not always, no.'

Andrews could feel the entire courtroom tautening.

'Your relationship wasn't entirely professional. Is that what you're telling us? Remember, you are under oath.'

'Yes. I mean, it wasn't. I – liked him a lot. For a while.'

'I see. So – I want to keep this conversation relevant to the proceedings, Miss Scott.'

'Of course.'

'So – this heated exchange – was it of a personal nature? I ask only because it seems to me that it could have been more distracting for him.'

'Well, it was personal. Yes. He had told me that he didn't think we should continue with our – our friendship.'

'And?'

'And I was disappointed. So I was arguing with him.'

'And did you win this argument?'

'No. No, I didn't. Any ideas I had of continuing with our – relationship were over. He made that very clear.'

'Your relationship? I thought you said it was a friendship. Or do you regard the two as the same?'

'Not really,' she said, and her eyes meeting his were what Andrews could only describe as bold. 'I suppose you could say it was – had been – more than a friendship.'

'Well, we need not concern ourselves with the precise nature of it,' said Andrews, aware that the entire court longed to concern itself exactly thus. 'But you are still quite sure that this conversation didn't distract him in any way from his driving?'

'I'm quite sure.'

'Or that you might have failed to notice something untoward or dangerous yourself?'

'I'm sure about that too.'

Then: 'How did you get home from the crash? Did Mr Gilliatt drive you?'

'No, of course not. I told you. Our relationship was over. Anyway, I was helping to look after some boys, the Cubs from the mini-bus. I went back to the hospital in the ambulance with one of them, who was having an asthma attack. Shaun, he was called, he was a great little boy. I'd had asthma as a child, so I knew how to help.'

'Well – thank you for your frankness, Miss Scott. It's been most helpful and much appreciated. You may step down.'

Andrews looked round the court; if this was a play, he thought – and inquests so frequently provided wonderful theatre – it would be the obvious point for an interval. He called another short break. He desperately wanted to get this over in one day.

He heard evidence then from the young couple whose baby had been induced prematurely by the accident. And then said he would like to hear from Toby Weston, the bridegroom who had crashed into the back of them following a blow-out.

'But first we should hear your statement, Mr Weston. Sergeant Freeman . . .'

Weston stood up: good-looking young chap, Andrews thought, seemed pleasant, very conventionally dressed. He'd had a tough time, almost lost his leg. And missed his wedding. Fate again: relentless unpredictable fate.

'Er, could I say something please?' Weston said.

'You may, Mr Weston, as much as you like. Once you have taken the oath. First we should hear your statement.'

'Yes, but—'

'Sergeant Freeman, please go on.'

Freeman cleared his throat and began to read the statement; told of the desperate rush to get to the church, the build-up of delays – and how Weston had wanted to check the tyre pressures, had been concerned that one of them was soft. 'However, Mr Fraser, my best man, persuaded me not to, said it was unnecessary and that we should get on our way again.'

At which point another young man, presumably Fraser,

stood up very suddenly in his seat and said, 'But I – that's not—' His face was scarlet and distorted with some kind of emotion.

Andrews held up his hand.

'Your turn will come,' he said. 'And I will decide when. Please sit down and be good enough not to interrupt proceedings again. I would remind you this is a court of law and you are required to show it a proper respect. Sergeant Freeman, continue, please.'

Freeman continued, and then Weston took the stand and the oath. Andrews watched him with interest. Another emotional revelation, perhaps?

'Now, Mr Weston. Perhaps you would like to start by telling us what you wanted to say.'

'Ah, yes. Well, you see . . . well, that is, my statement wasn't entirely correct.'

'Really?' Andrews' voice was full of innocent disbelief.

'No. No, the thing is – that bit about the tyres, that's not right. I – when I gave my statement to the sergeant, I wasn't at all well. I was in a lot of pain, I'd been running a temperature, I had an infection in my leg, they – well, they thought they might have to amputate. It had all been very traumatic. I was still very upset. And confused.'

'I'm sure. Very understandable. I believe your leg is to a large extent recovered now?'

'Yes. Yes, it is, thank you. Anyway, it was not correct to say that Barney – Mr Fraser – had persuaded me not to check the tyre pressures. It was at *my* insistence that we left immediately and drove on. I'd had a rather pressing call from my father-in-law. My father-in-law to be, that is. I just felt that we had to get to the wedding no matter what. Mr Fraser was very anxious to check the tyres, very unhappy at leaving them. I'm extremely sorry about the – the confusion. Really very sorry indeed.'

'Well, well,' said Andrews. 'Thank you for that, Mr Weston. Of course we have heard from Forensics that in their opinion, the blow-out was caused by the presence of the nail in the tyre, so I don't think you need to worry on that score. But accuracy in statements is, of course, very important, as I'm sure you realise, and it can waste time and even change the outcome of an inquiry in certain instances. It's always a pity when it is lacking and indeed deliberate inaccuracies can be regarded as an offence. Do you have any other corrections?'

'No, no others.'

'Good. Then let's go on.'

Weston's evidence was without further dramatic input.

Fraser, his best man, he who had clearly been so distressed earlier, was called; he appeared strained, his answers often faltering; then suddenly he spoke of his remorse that he had escaped, 'Literally without a scratch while everyone around us, it seemed, was horribly hurt. To this day, I feel bad. One of the doctors at the hospital was great; she told me how common it was, helped me to come to terms with it, this survivor guilt thing. She helped me so much.'

'I'm glad to hear it, Mr Fraser. May I say, this kind of remorse is very common. It doesn't mean you should feel you bear any of the blame. And as we now know . . .' he added, looking directly at Toby, 'that you were keen to do the right thing and check your tyres, I think you will find that gradually you will lose your sense of guilt. I hope so.'

More evidence followed, from a rather sleazy-looking chap, the white van driver, whose nail-studded planks had slithered out onto the road. Andrews rather enjoyed questioning him very closely as to how this had happened. It was not for him to apportion blame; however, it was still possible to make plain where blame lay.

And finally, an old lady gave evidence, a very anxious old lady, who said that she felt responsible in a small way, because she'd made Mr Weston wait while she paid for her own things.

'I feel absolutely terrible,' she said. 'I kept thinking how wrong of me it had been. He asked to go first, he said he was in a terrible hurry, and for some reason, I told him he had to take his turn. Who knows, had I not done that, those young men might have not been caught in the accident, but arrived at the church in time, and – well, I'd like to apologise to them.' She looked across at them both rather nervously.

'I really don't think, Mrs Mackenzie, you should feel too bad,' said Michael Andrews gently. 'It would have made so little difference to the time, and—'

'Yes, yes, but that little difference might have been crucial, don't you think? I'm sure you know the old parable about the horse-shoe nail?'

'I'm not sure,' said Andrews.

And as he waited, clearly expectant, she went on, 'Well, it goes like this:

'For want of a nail the shoe was lost, for want of a shoe the horse was lost, for want of a horse the rider was lost, for want of a rider the battle was lost, for want of a battle the kingdom was lost. And all for the want of a horseshoe nail. Who knows, I might have been that nail. If you follow me.'

'I – think so, yes. But I also think that nail alone would not have kept them from the wedding, you know. Still, it's a very interesting thought. Thank you, Mrs Mackenzie. You may step down now.'

It was five o'clock when Andrews rose to do his summing up. He was surprised by how positive an experience this inquest had been. Long, gruelling, and very sad at times, but uplifting in its own way, due to the courage displayed by the victims' families, and indeed by some of the witnesses, and the general clarity of the evidence. It had also been very satisfying to conduct; there had been no serious confusion, no conflicting evidence, no self-justification – except for that ghastly van-driver chap.

It had been one of those rare things this, an accident pure and simple. Nevertheless, for the families of the victims, this was little comfort.

He began by speaking to them, saying how sad it was when lives were cut short. 'Any lives, not only young lives; one cannot compare or quantify losses or tragedies. Mr Barnes had much to look forward to in his retirement, Sarah Tomkins had her whole life ahead of her, and for the Marks family a wife and a mother have both been lost. I am sure I speak for the whole court today when I say our hearts go out to you. Accidents are terrible things: one moment everything is under our control, the next we lose that control, fate takes over and the world changes. No one can anticipate accidents and they are in many cases virtually unavoidable. We have heard how the road on the afternoon in question was dangerous, because of the recent spell of hot dry weather and the heavy hailstorm; we have also heard that no one was driving in any way dangerously, that the nut came off the wheel of Mr Bryant's E-type Jaguar not through lack of care but if anything, too much care. We know that Mr Connell was driving meticulously and that nothing could have prevented his lorry from jack-knifing and his load spilling on the road. We have heard of much courageous and unselfish behaviour, and I would like to pay tribute in particular to Mr Gilliatt, and of course to the emergency services and the staff at St Mark's Hospital Swindon. And I would like to thank certain witnesses for their courage in coming forward when they were clearly nervous as to the outcome.

'There is much talk these days of the perfect storm – a congruence of weather patterns that separately would not be fatal or even dangerous, but which combine to be both; I would make an analogy between those perfect storms and this accident – everything conspiring to make it happen as and when it did. Rather as in the rhyme that Mrs Mackenzie quoted to us. It is so easy to say *if*: and yes, *if*

Mr Weston had left the petrol station a few minutes earlier, *if* there had not been the queue for petrol, *if* the hailstorm had not taken place . . . one can go on ad infinitum: the fact remains that it was not because these things happened in isolation, it was because they happened in a sequence, that it was tragically fatal.

'I therefore return the only verdict I can, that of misadventure.'

Chapter 52

Abi walked out of the building, feeling near to tears. She looked behind her; there was no sign of William. Shit. She'd really upset him; he must have felt utterly betrayed. Dragging it all up again, more or less spelling out that she'd been chasing Gilliatt, when she'd always sworn he'd done the chasing.

But – she knew that she had done the right thing. Her evidence had been, in a strange, subliminal way, a public apology to Laura. Not for having the affair with Jonathan, although she was pretty fucking sorry about that on her own account, but for what she'd done that night, at the party. It had been hard, and it had certainly taken her by surprise; she'd never meant to say any of it, but she'd done it. Without telling a word of a lie either. Not technically anyway, and certainly not in a way that would pervert the course of justice. She could see dear old Sergeant Freeman looking at her a bit puzzled; but there was nothing he could say or do.

As she had returned to her seat, she'd been aware of two things. One was that William had turned his back on her, as far as he was able. And then Laura turned towards her, and her green eyes, meeting Abi's dark ones, were very steady, no longer hostile. She didn't smile at her, but there was gratitude in that look. She'd got the message: an affirmation that what Jonathan had told her – that he had finished the affair that day, the day of the crash – was true. She need feel humiliated no longer.

774

Abi had made her amends to Laura at last. She could close the book.

'Abi!' It was William. His face was dark with anger. She hadn't seen him look like that before. He was always so even tempered, so level altogether.

'Yes, William?'

'What the fuck was that about?' He never usually swore either. Not real swearing.

'I can't talk about it here.'

'You're going to bloody well have to talk about it somewhere.'

'Why?'

'Why? Because I want some answers.'

'To what?'

'Oh, for heaven's sake!'

'William, please leave me alone. You must have something to milk, or scan or something.'

He turned then, walked away over to his mother; she watched them getting into the Land Rover, saw it drive off, saw his bleak, set face. She struggled not to cry.

Sending the message to Laura might have been the right thing to do, she thought, but it had cost her dear: it had lost her William, once again and this time for ever. She stared after the Land Rover, her eyes filled with tears; and then walked over to her own car and got into it, sat staring out at the darkening day. Someone tapped on the window; it was Georgia.

'Hi, Abi. You OK?'

'Oh – yes. Yes thanks. Glad it's over . . .'

'Me too. Listen, my mum and dad are here, do you want to come and have a coffee or something with us? They've heard such a lot about you, and how wonderful you are, they'd love to meet you—'

'Wonderful! Me? I don't think so.'

'Of course you are. I think so, William thinks so, we all do . . .'

'William!'

'Yes, course. He's, like totally in awe of you. And, actually, I reckon he fancies you rotten.'

'Now you are talking rubbish.'

'Abi, I'm not. You've only got to watch him in those meetings. Anyway, want to come and meet my mum and dad?'

'Darling, I can't. Sorry. I really have to get back. Sorry. Maybe at the festival, tell them.' She watched Georgia running off and suddenly felt better. Maybe she wasn't quite a lost cause. Maybe she could still put things right. And suddenly she knew, with a certainty that took her by surprise, that she had to talk to William, to try to explain and tell him that even while it was clearly hopeless, she did love him. She had to tell him that, in order to be able to wipe the slate clean. She couldn't leave it unsaid. She'd humiliated herself over one man today, in front of a crowded courtroom; she could certainly do it over another in private.

His head ached, and he felt deadly weary – and about a hundred years old. Well – at least it was over. Sort of. His own life was still in a mess. A hell of a mess. He decided before he started on the drive home he needed a pee, and walked into the Gents. And found himself confronted by Toby who was just walking out. He went white, clearly as shocked by the encounter as Barney; he stood there, they both did, frozen in time and then finally Toby said, 'Hi.' Barney said nothing.

'Er – you OK?' Toby asked.

'Yeah, sure. Of course. Never better.'

A strange expression crossed Toby's face: almost disbelief, almost relief, almost a smile.

'Er – great. Good. Yeah. No – no hard feelings then?'

A long silence while Barney fought with an extraordinarily strong temptation to hit him: hard. But he didn't. He just said and was amazed at how mild his voice sounded, 'Fuck off, Weston. Just fuck off. Get out of my way. Out of my life. You total, total arsehole.'

'But Barney—'

He'd be suggesting they had a drink next.

'I said fuck off.'

'Yeah. Sure. Yeah.'

And he was gone.

Barney had his pee, went out of the building; across the car park he saw Toby getting into a car with someone who looked like a driver. How did people get to be shits on that kind of scale? And how could people like him be mug enough to trust them? He felt sick, just thinking about the whole thing, the betrayal, Toby's willingness to send him to the wall, not just once but over and over again, to save his own skin. His best friend. His lifelong best friend. OK, he might have done the decent thing in the end – but only because he was so shit scared of lying under oath. That had been almost laughably clear. Bastard. Complete bastard. Barney felt he would never trust anyone again.

He saw the Abi girl, sitting in her car. Some girl, that. It had all been rather – coded, but no one could fail to get the drift. How extraordinary, saying all that in court. Humiliating herself, in a way. Very brave. Dead sexy she looked. Gilliatt must be a cool customer, to turn his back on her. The pretty blonde wife – bit of a Sloane, bit of an Amanda – must be very good at her job as well. Her job as a wife, that was. As Amanda would have been too. She—

'Hi. Nice to see you. Barney, isn't it? How's it going?' It was Mark Collins, the surgeon who'd operated on Toby that day. In another time, another life altogether. When Barney had had a lot. Instead of nothing.

'Yes. Hello.' He didn't really want to talk to him. He

didn't want to talk to anybody. Ever again. But he managed to smile, shook Collins' outstretched hand.

'And your friend, Toby. I see he's walking pretty well.'

'Pretty well, yes,' said Barney shortly.

'Has the wedding taken place yet? I was thinking about it the other day, wondering if you'd be here.'

'No,' said Barney, 'no, it hasn't.' He heard his own voice, suddenly rather harsh. 'The wedding's off. Cancelled. Actually.'

'I see.' Mark was clearly taken aback. 'Oh – I'm sorry. What about yours? Weren't you getting married too?'

'I was, yes. That's off as well.'

'I see.' Now he was really embarrassed, poor sod. Thought he was going to have a quick cheerful chat, and he'd got lumbered with an episode from some kind of a soap opera. Well, it couldn't be helped.

'Er, how's Emma?' He was astonished to hear himself asking; so terrified was he of the answer.

'Oh, she's fine, yes. Off to pastures new when she can organise it.'

'Really? What, you mean to – to Milan?'

'What? Oh no, that's history, I think. No, she's applying for new jobs. She's very excited about something up in Scotland, not sure how that's going.'

'Great. I mean, well, I hope she gets it. Give her – that is, remember me to her, please.'

'I will, Barney. Look – I'd better go. Dr Pritchard's waiting. Nice to see you anyway.'

'Yes, sure. And – do give my regards to Emma.'

'I will. Cheers.'

And he was gone.

So – what had that meant? About Milan being history? That the boyfriend was history? Or just that he was no longer in Milan? Maybe he should call her. But supposing she was with Luke again, it would be painful for her. Well, he'd made it pretty clear he hadn't forgotten her. Forgotten her. If only. If only you could do that to order, just neatly get rid of something, remove it, throw it away.

Throw away something that had become an intrinsic part of you, grown into you; entwined itself into your memories, tangled itself into your feelings, changed for ever the way you were.

If only.

He got into his car and headed for the M4. The M4, where so much of his life had been changed for ever. He would never hear the words again without a sense of absolute despair.

'Good day, dear?' Susan Andrews had been making marmalade; the house was warm and tangy and welcoming. Michael Andrews felt as he so often did after a day spent hearing sad stories of cut-off lives, that he was inordinately blessed.

'Yes. Pretty good, I think.'

'Difficult?'

'No, not really. It's perfectly clear what happened. But – surprising in some ways. Extraordinary things, human beings. I'm always saying that, aren't I?'

'Yes, dear, you are.'

'Brave and cowardly, foolish and wise, reckless and careful. All at one and the same time. Unbelievable, really.'

Susan Andrews looked at her husband. He was looking very drawn, in spite of his positive words.

'Come into the kitchen and have a cup of tea,' she said, 'and tell me about it.'

Emma had been trying not to think about the inquest all day; but first Alex and then Mark had come in to tell her about it. About the various people they'd been involved with who were there, most notably Patrick Connell and of course Toby. 'Funny chap that,' Mark had said. 'Some confusion over his evidence, he got very aerated. Oh,

779

and your boyfriend was there, of course.'

'My boyfriend? What do you mean?' she asked, assuming they must mean Luke – not that they knew Luke.

'You know, the good-looking one, best man, you brought him up to theatre that day when I operated on Weston's leg.'

'Oh,' she'd said. 'Him. Yes, well, I suppose he would have been there.'

'Nice chap,' said Mark, and then proceeded to tell her that not only was Toby's wedding off, but so was Barney's engagement. Adding that Barney had asked to be remembered to her. That had hurt her so much she could hardly bear it; she'd had to say she was in the middle of something and run to the loo, where she cried for a long time.

Barney had finished with Amanda, but he hadn't got in touch with her. As rejections went, that was pretty final. How could it have happened? Where had it gone, that lovely singing happiness they had found together, that instant closeness, that absolute certainty that they were right for each other? OK, their relationship hadn't lasted long; it hadn't needed to. It had been like a firework show: starting from nowhere and suddenly everywhere, explosive, amazing, impossible to ignore. And now – what? A poor, damp squib had landed, leaving nothing behind it, a sorry memento of the blazing display.

She knew now, absolutely certainly, that he didn't want her. If he had, he would have called her; there was no reason on earth left not to. It had just been a fling for him after all; fun, but no more. The commitment had been fake, the love phoney; he was probably even now pursuing some other well-bred, Sloaney creature, more suited to his background.

She would have been outraged, had she not been so totally miserable; and maybe that would come. She hoped so. Meanwhile she felt like one of the girls she most despised: feebly clinging to what-might-have-been, unable to break totally away.

He's gone, Emma, get over it.

But she hadn't; and she couldn't . . .

Abi drove into the farmyard just after six. The lights were on, and she could see Mrs Grainger in the kitchen, bending over the table, making some no doubt wonderful dish or other. William often described what they'd had for lunch or supper – he was very keen on his food – his mother was clearly the most wonderful cook. Well, fine. William was never going to have to live with her cooking, her spag bol (usually burned), her lamb chops (always burned), her pasta salad (not burned, but pretty tasteless really). After today, he wasn't going to have to have anything to do with her; he'd probably pull out of the festival even. They'd have to find a new venue, Georgia would go mental, they'd—

'Yes?'

'Oh. Hello, Mrs Grainger.' She'd been so absorbed in her thoughts of William, she'd hardly realised she'd got out of the car and banged on the farmhouse door.

'Miss Scott!'

'Yes. It's me. Sorry.'

'That's perfectly all right. But if you want to see William, I'm afraid you're out of luck. He's out.'

'Out? Where? I thought I saw his car.'

'No, out on the farm.'

'Oh, right. What, in the dark?'

'Well, he's in one of the buildings. He went off with his father.'

'Yes, I see. What, the milking parlour? Or the grain store, somewhere like that?'

'I imagine so.'

'But you don't know which.'

'No, I couldn't possibly say.'

'How long might they be?'

781

'I have no idea. As even you must realise,' God, she was an offensive woman, 'farming is not a nine to five occupation. I think the best thing you can do is go home, and I'll tell William you called. Then he can contact you in his own good time.'

'Mrs Grainger, I really want to see him.'

'Well, no doubt you will.'

She began to close the door; Abi put her foot into it.

'Please tell me where he is. I really won't keep him long.'

'Miss Scott, I don't know where he is—'

At this point, the old farm truck swung onto the yard; Mr Grainger got out of it. Abi knew it was Mr Grainger, not because she had ever been introduced to him, but because he looked exactly like William, or rather exactly as William might look in thirty-odd years. He stared at her rather uncertainly as she walked towards him.

'Hi. Mr Grainger?'

'Good evening.'

'I'm looking for William. I'm a friend of his – Abi Scott. William might have mentioned me.'

'Ah yes. The young lady involved in the concert.' Totally unexpectedly, he winked at her; Abi would have giggled under other circumstances. 'How's it coming along?'

'Oh, pretty well. We're so, so pleased to be able to have it here. Um – I wonder if you could tell me where William is?'

'Well, he was in the lambing shed. I left him there, working on the accounts. Would you like me to call him, to find out if he's still there?'

'No, it's OK, thank you. I know where it is. I'll just go and find him, if that's all right.'

'Well – I suppose so, yes. You'll drive down there, will you? Won't do that smart car of yours much good.' He smiled at her. He seemed rather nice. What on earth was he doing with the old bat?

'Oh, it's fine. Really. Yes. Thank you. Thank you, Mr

Grainger. And you, Mrs Grainger, for your help,' she called towards the lighted doorway. Mrs Grainger turned and went inside, followed by her husband.

'She seemed very nice,' he said. 'Attractive girl, isn't she? Not William's usual type. Is there anything still going on, do you think?'

'I really couldn't say,' said Mrs Grainger. She had been making bread; she was kneading it now, almost viciously, her husband thought.

Abi drove down the track to the lambing shed. During the time spent in Cottage Number One, she'd got to know her way round the farm quite well.

It was very dark; she put her lights on full beam. Rabbits ran constantly out onto the track, and she kept stopping, fearful of running over them. William would have found that hugely amusing, she thought; he'd told her how he and his brother had parked the jeep in the fields at night, turned the lights full on and then shot the unsuspecting rabbits that were caught petrified in the beam.

'It's so cruel, how could you, they're so sweet,' she'd said, and he'd grinned at her. 'Abi, rabbits are total pests, they consume vast qantities of cereal if they're not kept under control. And they make wonderful stew.'

Other smaller animals ran across her path as well. God knew what they were – weasels, she seemed to remember hearing about – and stoats, and there indeed was a rabbit, frozen with terror, until she turned the lights off and waited patiently while it hopped away. A large bird suddenly swooped past her windscreen. An owl, she supposed; the first time William had pointed one out, she'd been amazed by how big its wingspan was. She'd learned a lot, in her time with him.

She reached the shed; the office was at the far end of it, so he wouldn't have seen her, although he might have heard the car. And probably thought it was his father. She switched the lights off, got out; the quiet was stifling. An owl – maybe the same one – hooted; something scuffled in the hedgerow near her. She reached for her bag – how absurd was that, to take a handbag with her. William was always teasing her about it, but it held her phone and her car keys, easier than carrying them separately.

She stepped forward; it was very muddy, and that was – oh, what! gross – she'd stepped in a cow-pat. She could see it, in the light from the shed. A great round, liquid pile of shit, and her boot, one of her precious new boots from Office, had sunk deep into it. She stood there, staring down at it, and thought it was rather symbolic; of her, also sunk deep into shit.

She eased her foot out, stepped gingerly forward, wary of finding another. The cows didn't usually come this way, it wasn't their territory; maybe they'd got out of whatever field they were meant to be in. They did that, William had told her. They leaned on the fences endlessly, unless they were electric, all together, usually because they could see some better, lusher grass, with their great solid bulk, and every so often they managed to push them over and wander out. Only – actually, she'd thought they were usually kept inside this time of year, in the cowshed. More yokel knowledge, as she'd called it, teasing William one night.

She made the door of the shed without further mishap, opened it, looked inside. It was still empty, no lambing going on yet, and very quiet. She closed the door after her, and walked, as quietly as she could, down to the other end of the building, towards the outline of light round the door that had William behind it.

When she got there, she was suddenly rather frightened. Suppose he was abusive, started shouting at her. Suppose he actually hit her. She wouldn't be able to blame him, if he did. Then she thought it would be totally out of his gentle character if he did; and anyway, whatever happened, she

784

couldn't feel worse. Her sense of nobility from her actions in the court had left her; she just felt miserable and rather foolish. She opened the door carefully; he was sitting at the desk with his back to her, didn't even hear her at first. He was engrossed in a pile of forms; then he suddenly thrust them aside and sighed, very heavily, and pushed his hands through his hair.

'Hello,' she said. 'Hello, William.'

He swung round; he looked extremely shocked. Not just surprised, but shocked. Well, more like horrified, if she was truthful.

'Hello,' she said again.

'Hi.' His voice was dull, flat.

'I – came to find you.'

'As I see.'

'I – wanted to talk to you.'

'I really don't think there's anything to talk about.'

'There is, William.'

'Abi, there is not. I'm so tired of hearing your lies and your excuses and your phoney concerns. Just go away would you? I'm very busy.'

'No. Not till I've said what I've come to say.'

'I don't see any point in your saying it. I won't be able to believe it.'

'You could try.' She looked down at her boot; it was a hideous sight, the greenish-brown cowshit beginning to dry a little, cake round the edges.

'Um – do you have any newspaper or anything? Or maybe I could go into the toilet?'

'What for?'

'I stepped in some cowshit. Outside.'

'Oh yes?'

He sounded absolutely disinterested. She felt a pang of panic.

'Yes. Actually, I was surprised, as I thought you said you were keeping the cows in this time of year?'

'We're keeping a few out this winter, as an experiment. To see if we can . . .' He stopped.

'If you can what?'

'Abi, you're not really interested in cows. Or farming. Or me, come to that. Certainly not me. It's all a bloody act and I can't cope with it. Now go and clean up your fucking boot in the lavatory and then leave. Please.'

Well, that was pretty final. She really had blown it this time. She couldn't imagine getting past this wall of indifference. And dislike. And mistrust. Better leave. She'd tried at least. Given it a go.

She walked through to the loo, pulled off her boot, sat wiping it with the toilet paper, rather feebly and helplessly. She didn't seem to be able to see properly, and realised that her eyes were filled with tears. God, she was an idiot. Such a stupid, pathetic, hopeless idiot. He must hate her. Really hate her. Well, all she could hope for now was to escape with a bit of dignity. Dignity! Precious little she'd left for herself in the court that day. Saying to them all, 'I fancied this man, this married man. I was running after him, actually, and he didn't want me.' They must have all found it highly amusing.

She stood up again, and walked back into the office. William was apparently absorbed in the forms again. He didn't look round.

'Right,' she said. 'Well, bye, William, then. I'm – sorry.'

'I'm sure you are,' he said, and then suddenly: 'Why did you do that today, for Christ's sake? Why? In front of all those people, in front of me, rubbing my nose in it, telling everyone you – you'd wanted to go on with it, with that – that pile of shit, after what he'd done to you. Are you still in love with him or something? I don't understand.'

'Oh God,' she said, 'no, of course I'm not in love with him. I loathe him! I'd like to see him strung up by his balls—'

786

'Well then . . .'

'William, it's so complicated. But I've always felt so bad, you know I have, about what I did that night. It's not her fault, not Laura's fault. You say I rubbed your nose in it – what did I do to her? And her kids? It was such a ghastly thing to do. And suddenly today, I thought – well, I didn't exactly think, I just could see how I could put it a bit right. Let her know that her vile, slimy husband – how she can still be with him I don't know – but anyway, that he had wanted to finish it that day. To get rid of me. That it hadn't still been going on. I felt I owed it to her. It wasn't easy,' she added.

'And how do I know that's true?' he said, and his face was harsh and distorted, a stranger's face, not kind, gentle William's at all. 'How do I know it wasn't some kind of a – a bid to get him back? To have him thinking well of you again? You've told me so many lies, Abi – about him, about your relationship – how can I be expected to believe anything? And then there was all that shit about how terrible you felt about the child being run over. I had to listen to that, and did I think you should ring him – *ring him*, for Christ's sake, you ask me that! – and then how scared you were of the inquest today. It was fucking endless. Endless. And you seemed to have no idea at all how much it hurt, how horrible it was for me. It was all about you, you, you. You didn't seem very scared incidentally; you seemed very cool and collected. Almost enjoying it, I'd say. Star of the show.'

'That's a horrible thing to say.'

'Well, it was a horrible thing to do. Now please, just go away. Leave me alone.'

She walked the length of the shed, her heels clacking on the stone floor. And then stopped. She'd left her bag behind. How stupid was that. She'd have to return, go back into that office, confront him again, confront all that dislike, that sullen, heavy hostility. Horrible. She might have left her bag there, if it hadn't had her car keys in it. But she couldn't get home without them. She turned, walked back, opened the door.

'Sorry,' she said. 'Sorry, William, I—' And then stopped. Because he wasn't looking at the forms any more, he was sitting with his head in his arms on the desk; and when he looked round at her, she saw that he was weeping.

'Oh William,' she said, her own tears blurring her eyes again, stepping forward, bending over him, putting her arm on his shoulders. 'William, I—'

'Don't touch me,' he said, turning away, so that she couldn't see his face.

'But—'

'*Don't*,' he said. 'I'll go mad if you do.'

'All right.' And very slowly, reluctantly almost, she drew back and would have left then; only he suddenly put out his hand and caught hers in it, and held it, and sat looking at it, as if he wasn't sure how it had come to be there at all; and then he turned it, palm upwards, and bent his head and kissed it, kissed the palm, very sweetly and tenderly and then— 'Christ,' he said, 'dear God, Abi, what are you?' And then she pushed his head up, and began to kiss him, desperate, hungry for him, her mouth working frantically at his, moaning, almost crying with wanting him, and then suddenly she was astride him on the chair and he had pushed up her sweater and his mouth was on her breasts, licking, teasing, pleasing them, and then she stood up and wrenched off her skirt and her pants and then she was astride him again, and he was sinking into her, up her, creating great searing waves in her of a raw sweet violence and pleasure that was so close to pain she could hardly bear it and she came so fast it was shocking, and felt him come too; and they both stayed there for what seemed like a long time, his head on her breast, and she felt him sigh, and then sigh again, then he said, his voice still heavy, 'I shouldn't have done that, I'm sorry.'

'William, you should, you should, it was wonderful, so, so lovely, I've wanted it for so long.'

'For so long?' he said. 'You can't have, you . . .' and, 'I did, I did,' she said, 'so much I could hardly bear it. Every time I saw you I wanted it and—'

'You too,' he said, and suddenly it came, his wonderful giggle. 'That is just so – so ridiculous.'

'What do you mean, "you too"? You're not saying you wanted it too?' she said.

'Yes,' he said. 'Of course I did, you silly cow.'

'Don't call me a silly cow.'

'Why not, it's a compliment. You know how much I love my girls.'

'Oh, all right. Go on.'

'Abi, it was driving me insane. I wanted you so much, and I thought you didn't want me, that you just saw me as a, a – well, I didn't know how you saw me. Some kind of loser, I suppose . . .'

'Loser! You can't have thought that!'

'Well I did, of course I did, and then today—'

'Oh God,' she said. 'Oh William, I'm so, so sorry about today. I really am.'

'Don't keep saying that,' he said, 'please. Let today go. It upsets me, even now. I don't want to think about it.'

'All right. But I have something to tell you – something rather awful in a way. I don't know what to do about it, but I have to tell you.'

'Jesus,' he said, and his expression had changed, was wary suddenly, almost scared. 'Jesus, Abi, there's someone else – is that what you—'

'Someone else! William, how can you even think such a thing? There's never going to be someone else, not now, not ever. I love you, William. That's what I have to tell you. I – well I love you.'

'You what?' he said, and his tone was so odd, filled with disbelief, and his face too, with something close to shock, and she felt quite scared herself, but she had to go on, had to know he knew, just so they could go forward, in whatever direction that might be.

'I said I love you, and I don't care what you think, I don't care if you don't want to hear it, I love you, William. So, so much, I can't begin to tell you. But if you don't want me, and I wouldn't blame you, I swear I'll never come near you again. I absolutely swear it.'

'You'd better bloody not,' he said, and her heart literally sank. She felt it, heavy and sad and infinitely disappointed.

'I won't,' she said.

'No,' he said, 'I meant you'd better bloody *not* swear it. Do you think I want to lose you, you stupid, stupid girl? Do you think I don't want you?'

'Well, I . . .'

'Abi. Say it again. Keep saying it. I can't hear it enough.'

'All right,' she said. 'OK, I love you, William. I really love you. I've never said that before, except to my dad – or maybe to that boy I told you about, the one who—'

'Do shut up,' he said. 'I don't want to hear about any boys.'

'No, sorry, I'm just trying to be truthful. Completely truthful. I love you, William. I always have, from that first day, I think, only I . . .'

'You can't have,' he said, staring at her.

'But I can. If you mean because of how I've behaved – well, I'm pretty bloody stupid, as you know. But ignoring that, I do love you. I love everything about you. I love the way you look and the way you talk, and the way you giggle, and I love having sex with you so, so much, it's just – oh, don't laugh, William, don't laugh at me. It's not funny, it's pathetic really, sitting here without any clothes on, telling you all this when you made it pretty clear about half an hour ago that you thoroughly dislike me.'

'Of course I don't dislike you!' he said, his tone impatient. 'I love you too, Abi. I've told you before, for

God's sake. I really, really do love you. I can't imagine life without you now, that was why I was so miserable and – and hostile to you. I – oh, hell. Look, do you think we could move? I'm getting cramp in one of my legs.'

'You – love me?'

'Yes, I love you too. I just said so, didn't I? I'm a simple sort of chap, you know, I don't go in for anything very complex.'

Abi stood up. She felt very odd. Odd and physically feeble.

'OK. Sorry about the cramp. Shall we move over to the couch? And maybe we could . . . why are you laughing, William? I don't see what's so funny.'

'You are,' he said. 'If you could see yourself, you'd realise. Stark naked from the waist down, except for a pair of boots – one covered in cowshit. Quite appropriate really.'

She looked down at herself and grinned. 'No wonder I was getting cold.'

'Here.' He went and pulled a large green sheet off a hook on the door. 'Let's put this over us.'

'What is it? It looks sort of waterproof.'

'It is. We use it for – well, never mind. It might put you off.'

'It stinks,' she said.

'Yes, well so do I, quite a lot of the time. I'm not always freshly washed and brushed up, you know. You're going to have to get used to smells. If you're going to be a farmer's wife.'

'A what?'

'A farmer's wife. Well, I'm not going to change careers. Even for you.'

'Did you say wife?'

'Yes, I did. It seems the best thing to me. Don't you want that?'

'William, William, but I can't cook.'

'You'll learn.'

'And I feel sorry for rabbits.'

'You'll get over it.'

'And foxes.'

'You'll certainly have to get over that.'

'And I'm not posh.'

'Good.'

'Oh William, I'd love to marry you. God knows how it would work out, but I would love love love it.'

'Me too.' He looked at her and grinned suddenly. 'Really love it. Now, if we could just . . . ah, I think . . . yes, someone's coming through the shed. Um – ah, hello, Mother.'

Mrs Grainger, clad in Barbour and headscarf and heavy green wellies, looked at Abi; at her naked lower half, her tousled hair, her smudged eye make-up, her high-heeled, shitty boots.

'Yes, hello, William,' she said.

'Mother, I have some really exciting news. Abi has agreed to marry me.'

Chapter 53

Laura sat staring into the darkness as Jonathan drove them back to London. Neither of them spoke. There was too much to think about, to be absorbed into their lives: their new lives, as Laura saw them.

Everything had changed again, that day; Abi had done that for them. She would haunt them no longer; she had written herself neatly and gracefully out of the plot. It was hard for Laura to think of her in such a way, but it had been a truly generous act. She had told of Jonathan's rejection of her; and thus told Laura she had him back once more.

He had always said that, Laura thought; he had always said it was over that day. She had not believed him – why should she? – but there was a sweet, odd relief in having it confirmed. It wasn't everything, it wasn't even almost everything; but it was an important something and of huge comfort.

He had sat, while Abi was giving her evidence, rigidly still, his eyes fixed on the floor; and when Abi had spoken of their relationship, he had closed his eyes and shaken his head. Laura could not have said she loved him in that moment, but she felt the beginning at least of forgiveness. And she had been able to feel proud of him that day; genuinely proud. Her bitterness had not worked some ugly alchemy, had not distorted the tributes paid to him by everyone, not just by the coroner and even the police, but by the people he had helped. He had clearly behaved superbly; whatever might have gone before.

He glanced over to her and his face was wary. 'Tired?'

'No, not really.'

'It must have been so hard,' he said, 'being there, looking at her, listening to her.'

'Not so much. Not today. In fact, not at all, today.'

'Really?'

'Really. Yes. She – it – helped.'

'I'm glad.'

Suddenly, she wanted to touch him; she put out her hand, tentatively reached for his. He looked at her, startled; the car swerved.

'Jonathan, look out. You'll cause a crash.'

'I think we've had enough of those,' he said, 'for a lifetime.'

'Yes. But we've survived it.'

'Have we?' and his voice was very tentative. 'Have we really survived it?'

'Yes, Jonathan,' she said. 'I think we have.'

He took the hand she had offered him, raised it to his lips. 'Thank God,' was all he said.

Of course it wasn't properly over, she thought; she would still – sometimes, and probably quite frequently – feel angry, hurt, diminished. But the worst was over, and indeed had receded a long way. He had done all he could; now it was her turn. She was able to feel she could begin.

This is what happiness looks and sounds like, Mary thought, smiling at Russell; a warm room, thick curtains closed against the cold February night, a big jug of winter jasmine on the mantelpiece, a log fire, a concert (Haydn) on the wireless – now, Mary, not a wireless but Russell's state-of-the-art sound system, not that it mattered, the music was lovely anyway – new silks for a new tapestry spread out on her sewing-table, Russell contentedly sipping at his bourbon and leafing through travel brochures, planning a trip to Italy for them in the spring, and by the hearth, slumbering sweetly, curled up with one another, the latest additions to their household, two Persian blue kittens.

How lucky she was, how lucky they both were: to have found so much so late, and not to have been disappointed by it in any respect.

'You obviously did so well today, Sparrow. I wish I'd come now, I'd have been so proud of you.'

'Don't be so ridiculous, there was nothing to be proud of.'

'Oh, now you say that, but Georgia told me how you recited that rhyme to the judge—'

'The coroner.'

'Pardon me, the coroner.'

'And what on earth was Georgia telling you that for?'

'She said you'd told her I was tired, and she was worried about me. Really Sparrow, people will think I'm an invalid or an old man if you keep talking like that.'

'How could anyone think you were an old man?' said Mary, walking over to him and kissing the top of his head. 'When you look so extremely youthful and handsome. Anyway, I didn't recite it exactly . . .'

'She said you did.'

'Well, maybe I did. Anyway, it caught his fancy and he quoted it in his summing-up at the end. Which was very nice. And I said how anxious I had been about holding up the young man – the bridegroom, you know – and the coroner said – such a courteous, kind man – that I should have no concerns about it, that it would have made no difference. I still think perhaps it might, but – he was so very good at his job, Russell. Everyone left looking happier, even the poor families of those who died.'

'Good. And Georgia was happier at the end of it?'

'So much happier. He was very gentle with her.'

'Good. Well, he sounds like a fine chap.'

'He is a fine chap.'

'Well done anyway. Oh, my Sparrow. You don't have any regrets, do you?'

'Regrets?' she said, surprised at the question. 'Of course not. Unless it is that we weren't together sooner. But then, we couldn't have been, could we?'

'Not playing it your way, no. If it had been down to me, we'd have had sixty years together now, instead of six months.'

'I know, I know. But we did the right thing.' She sat smiling into the fire, remembering. She had been seventeen at the beginning of the war, Donald nineteen; she had loved him so much and if anyone had told her she would fall in love with someone else, she would not have believed them. She would have said her heart was far too occupied, her future too settled. But Russell had been irresistible. She told him so now.

'I wasn't though, Sparrow, was I? You resisted me very well.'

'I know. But it was more, as you know, keeping faith with Donald. You remember Marilyn?'

'Marilyn? Oh, Marilyn with the dyed hair. You were so cross with me about her hair.'

'Quite rightly so. You were very rude.'

'I'm sorry,' he said meekly.

'So you should be. Anyway, you know Marilyn thought I should marry you.'

'She did! Now you tell me.'

'Yes. She thought it was terribly exciting.' She remembered Marilyn's actual words. 'He's rich and handsome, Mary, for heaven's sake, and so romantic. You could marry him after the war, go and live in America in a big house, have one of those Cadillacs, why not?'

'And yet still you refused me.'

'I know. I suppose I might have changed my mind, at one stage. But then you know . . .'

'I know. The letters.'

The many letters from Donald, in a prisoner-of-war camp in Italy, all telling her that it was only knowing she was there, waiting for him, that was keeping him going at all.

'Yes. I couldn't have failed him, Russell, could I?'

'I don't believe you could. Being you.'

'And I was happy, and so indeed were you. And we have each other now. It's been so perfectly lovely, these past months. At long, long last. Worth waiting for.'

'Worth it indeed. Now, Mary, do you think Rome and then Florence or the other way round for our trip? Remember we'll have just spent a month in New York. I'll have been working, so we'll need a proper break. Maybe we should take a villa in the Tuscan hills and base ourselves there, and then we can journey at our leisure. We could hire a driver, or we could take the train between the two – that sounds a lovely journey.'

'I think either would be very nice. You do have to do that month in New York, do you, working so hard? I'm sure Morton could manage with you being there for a shorter time.'

'Mary, we have a very big shareholders' meeting at the beginning of April. It's essential I'm there, and we have to prepare for that.'

'Yes, but Russell dear, perhaps you don't. You've been tired lately, even living down here, and—'

'That's purely because I had a touch of flu. I'm never tired normally, as you very well know.'

'Of course not, dear. Well, I think the villa sounds a wonderful idea. Although . . .'

'Yes?' Russell smiled at her. 'I'm getting to know your "althoughs".'

'Well, you know, we could just stay here. Spring in England is so very lovely, and I can't imagine anything nicer than sitting in the garden and going for walks and just – well – just sharing all of it with you. The birds sing so beautifully in the spring – oh, and I've been meaning to tell you, I think there's a thrush nesting in the apple tree. I've been watching either Mr or Mrs Thrush, I'm never sure which, flying in and out with twigs – we'll have to keep an eye on our wicked kittens, we don't want any tragedies. And then we can see the bulbs come up – we don't know what will grow where, it will be so exciting – and then there'll be the blossom on the trees in the orchard, and— But of course if you've set your heart on Italy . . .'

'I think I have, dearest Sparrow. We have plenty of years to enjoy the English spring, and I do so want to see Italy with you—'

Mary was bending over her silks now, sorting out the blues and the greens; she was not looking at Russell, so she did not see his face suddenly change, did not see him momentarily thump at his chest, nor the fright in his eyes, nor did she notice that he was slowly slumping down in his chair; all she was aware of was an odd sound, halfway between a whimper and a gasp, and by the time she did look up, he was losing consciousness fast and she was never to know whether he heard her as she cradled his head in her arms and whispered again and again how much she loved him.

Chapter 54

It had been a stroke, they said; a massive haemorrhage in his brain. If he had recovered, he would not have been himself, he would have been paralysed, probably unable to speak. Or to smile, Mary thought. There would have been no more of that wonderful quick, loving smile; or indeed of anything else that made him Russell. Not just the brilliant blue eyes, the thick white hair, the beautifully kept hands, the proudly erect back; but the fast, almost urgent walk, the swift turn of his head, the way he sat lost to the world, visibly devouring books, the absurdly careful way he folded things: his table napkin, his scarf, the *Financial Times* – how often had she teased him about that – the way he laughed, slowly at first, almost reluctantly, then throwing his head back and giving himself up to jokes, to amusement, to fun.

And his voice, not deep, quite light really, but very clear, calling her as he did a hundred times a day, for he liked to know where she was in the house, not so much to be constantly with her as to be able to find her if he needed to. 'Where are you, Sparrow?' he would shout from the hall, the kitchen, his study, and she would answer him, quite impatiently sometimes, for she liked to do as she pleased, be where she wished – and what would she have given now, she thought, arriving home that first day from the hospital, arriving home to that quiet, dead house, to be summoned, called to account. Now she could wander where she would, from room to room, to the garden and beyond, and no one would care or need to know.

He had died peacefully and apparently happily, twenty-four hours after the stroke, with Mary holding his hand; she hoped above all things that he knew she was there. The nurses assured her he would.

She had sat by him almost all that time. 'They don't make them like that any more,' one of the nurses said, looking at her small upright figure, her eyes fixed on Russell's face, and indeed they did not, the doctor had agreed; they were a special breed, her generation, with the courage to face down for six long years the worst that a savage enemy could do to them and still remain strong, generous, merry-hearted.

When she finally became exhausted, they urged her to sleep, but she refused to leave the room and they brought her a bed so that she could stay with him. She slept fitfully, woke every hour or so to make sure that he had not gone, and was afraid even to go to the bathroom they had made available to her.

'He won't go without you, Mary,' the ward sister had said. 'He'll wait until you are back with him again – they do, I promise you,' but she didn't believe her and each time came scuttling back into the room fearful of not having properly been with him at this, their darkest hour together.

She had been told that hearing was the last sense to go and she talked to him from time to time, told him how much she loved him, how happy she had been with him, how wonderful their few months together.

'I shall go to Italy, dearest Russell,' she said, 'even without you. I will see it for you, all those wonders, as I know you would have wished. And I shall watch the spring garden grow and the apple trees blossom in the orchard, and when the baby thrushes fly, I will know you are part of it all.'

Every so often, his hold on her hand tightened and she would tense, thinking he was coming back to her; once he seemed to try to speak; once he half-smiled. But in the end he left her, slipped away with a sigh and a long, long breath, and she knew it was over without having to be told, knew that she was alone now, alone in the room, alone in the world.

They all came, of course, his children; with their husbands and wives. Shocked, grieving, but saying that it had after all been a blessing, given how much he would have been changed, how poor the quality of his life would have been, and that he could not have suffered, it had been so swift, so mercifully swift. Mary listened, politely patient, nodding, smiling, sometimes weeping; but thinking that he was their father, not their husband; he was not the centre of their worlds any more. So much easier to see it as a blessing, given all that; so very much harder for her.

Her children came too, Christine remorseful, as well as visibly grieving, Douglas shocked, and Tim and Lorraine, both genuinely and horribly upset. All rallying round, loving her, but quite unable to comfort her, to ease the jagged place in her heart. She kept telling herself that a year ago, Russell had been no more to her than a writer of letters, a happy memory; she had been content then, she would be content again. But it was not quite true; for she had changed, Russell's love and vigour and generosity had brought her back to life, had given her indeed more life, a new, broader, richer one. She had grown accustomed to a voice in the darkness, a presence in the bed, a smile first thing in the morning, a kiss last thing at night; to a face opposite her at table, an arm to take as she walked. She had come to enjoy ideas, suggestions, being argued and reasoned with, being appreciated, being loved.

The funeral was small, family only, apart from the Connells, who had become like family. It took place in the same little church where the wedding had been. Maeve found it almost unbearable, looking at Mary standing beside the flower-covered coffin, all alone, when just under three months earlier she had stood beside Russell, becoming so happily his wife. She was brave, so brave; cried only once, when the coffin was carried in, and after that, held her small, strong self together.

Morton spoke of a wise and wonderful father, who had been all the world to him; and then Tim, briefly, of a new grandfather in his life who he had come to love and revere, 'And who made my grandmother completely happy. They never seemed old to us, just a wonderful couple who had found one another, and relaunched their lives. We shall remember him always. And we will take care of Grandma for him.'

And then Russell left the church again, and was buried in the small churchyard. Mary stood looking down into the grave, quite composed, even when she threw the handful of earth onto the coffin; then she walked quickly away, on Tim's arm. Her flowers went into the coffin, with her simple message: *Russell, thank you, with all my love.*

Morton stayed only a few days, Coral and Pearl for over a week. Mary was glad of their company but more glad when they left. She wanted the house to herself, to grieve and to explore her feelings. It seemed very large, very empty, very silent. But Russell lingered in every room.

One of the hardest things to deal with was his clothes. The vast dressing room contained literally dozens of suits – more than Donald had had in his whole life, she thought, along with jackets, trousers, shirts, drawers full of ties and sweaters and belts and the silk pyjamas without which he said he would not be able to sleep. She stood there one afternoon, looking at them all, remembering him buying them – or some of them – seeing him wearing them, wondering where to begin sorting them out and getting rid of them . . . and then realised she did not have to begin at all. They could stay there, for as long as she wished.

She applied the same principle to his study, to all his gadgets, some of them hardly used, most of them quite useless to her; she called Timothy and told him to come and take what he wanted, and then after that she simply kept it all. It was all part of Russell, this super-abundance of things; and therefore now part of her.

She found routine helpful; she walked in the morning, watched TV in the evenings, in the company of the kittens – another source of comfort – making a great effort to watch at least some of the vast number of DVDs Russell had bought and told her she would enjoy – and in the afternoon, she played the piano, his last gift to her. She found this more comforting than anything; she had become extremely rusty and had found a teacher, a sparky sixty year old called Genevieve, who came to the house twice a week, saw exactly what Mary needed and created quite a punishing programme of pieces and practice. Moreover, if Mary hadn't done her practice, she didn't tell her it didn't matter, but that if she hadn't improved by her next lesson, she wouldn't teach her any more. She also entered Mary for her Grade Three piano exam (she had passed One and Two as a child), and booked several concerts for them to attend together in Bath: 'Just so you can hear how it should be done.'

Mary was frequently to be found weeping over the piano in the afternoons; partly through frustration, partly through sorrow, but she knew it was helping her more than she would have believed.

People were very kind. Tim and Lorraine came once a week, sometimes in the evening, sometimes at the weekend, and Christine came twice weekly, once to take her mother to the farmers' market which she enjoyed, and once to have lunch with her at home. She had ventured quite early on into the realms of apology for her hostility to Russell; Mary told her quite briskly to be quiet.

'You came to the wedding, dear, that was wonderful, and you became friends with Russell after that, and I really don't want to discuss it any further.'

Everyone told her she was being wonderful; Mary thought they should see her at night, when she had gone to bed, and wept and sometimes howled with misery.

Other people visited her. Georgia had been terribly upset and wept so long and so copiously after Tim had called her – they had made rather good friends at the wedding, so good indeed that Lorraine had become quite spiky – that her mother thought something dreadful had happened to her.

'It *is* dreadful,' Georgia wailed. 'Russell has died and I was going to visit them the very next week and now I'll never see him again and I can't bear it.'

'You won't see him again, Georgia, no, but neither will Mary. She's the one something dreadful has happened to, and I think she's the one who feels she can't bear it. Go and see her, keep her company, tell her about your life, go for walks with her, that's what you can do for her now.'

'Sometimes,' Bea said to her husband with a sigh, 'I feel Georgia's development was arrested at about the age of six.'

Georgia telephoned Mary to arrange a day and Mary said that if she was coming on the train, then she would send the car to meet her in Bath. Georgia, who felt her visit should be as difficult as possible by way of reparation for her selfish reaction, said that wouldn't be necessary and arrived therefore an hour and a half late on the twice-daily bus to Tadwick. Mary, who had by then decided she couldn't be coming, was trying to comfort herself by playing the piano; which was in fact rather fortuitous, as Georgia found some old sheet music of Russell's and they spent an extremely happy afternoon together, Georgia singing while Mary accompanied her.

'Right,' Georgia said when they were both exhausted and she was hoarse, 'that's *Oklahoma!* and *My Fair Lady* ticked off: next week we'll do *Annie Get your Gun* and *Carousel*. And how do you think you'd be with Scott Joplin? This is fun.'

'It is indeed,' said Mary, 'and next week, dear, please do allow yourself to be collected. We'll have more time together – we can even go for a walk as well.' Georgia's visit had cheered her immensely; she insisted on hearing all about the festival and said she'd be there.

'Really? Goodness, Mary, that would be – well, wonderful . . .' said Georgia, cautiously 'but it'll be very noisy and – well very noisy. And lots of people will be there.'

'That's fine, I like noise and lots of people. Tim and Lorraine can look after me or perhaps the Connells – I presume they'll be there. I may not stay very long, and I certainly won't be camping, but I'd love to see it all.'

'You are so cool,' said Georgia, giving her a kiss.

Two days later, a letter arrived from Mary, enclosing a cheque for a thousand pounds.

You said you were hoping to find a sponsor for your festival. Of course, I am not in that league, and I'm sure this won't make a great deal of difference, but it might pay for some posters or something. I know that Russell would have loved to have helped you, he so enjoyed being with young people – as I do – and got involved himself. In fact, he rather fancied himself as a song and dance man, so you might have got more than you bargained for. Please pass this to your committee as a token of my great interest and pleasure in being involved, in a small way.

'Shit!' said Abi, when Georgia told her. 'A thousand fucking quid! Shit!'

Georgia felt that this was not quite the response Mary might have expected; but thought that she would have recognised its sincerity all the same.

The other person who came to visit, to Mary's great delight, was Emma. She was very upset to hear that Russell had died. *I shall never forget seeing him in the Dorchester that night*, she wrote, *and thinking how handsome he was. And it was such a privilege to come to your wedding. If you'd like a little visit from me, please let me know; if not don't give it a moment's thought.*

Mary wrote back and said that the only thought she had given it was how very nice it would be to see her. *Come and have lunch with me, when you can. I shall look forward to it so much.*

Emma arrived with a large bunch of daffodils, and was then mortified to see the drive down from the gate to the house lined with them.

'I'm so sorry,' she said. 'Talk about coals to Newcastle.'

'Not at all,' said Mary, taking the daffodils, leading her into the kitchen, where Mrs Salter found them a huge white jug. 'I hate picking them. You see, they die so quickly, and it's wonderful to have yours.'

'Well, I'm glad,' said Emma slightly doubtfully. 'Goodness, that is a lovely smell!'

'What, dear, the daffodils? I never can find much of a perfume in them, to be honest.'

'No, no, it's bread. Baking bread. Isn't it?' she asked Mrs Salter.

'It is, my dear, yes.'

'My mum used to make bread when we were all at home,' said Emma. 'I've never done it, although I sort of know how. It's hardly worth it just for me.'

'Time enough when you have a family of your own,' said Mrs Salter.

Emma nodded and smiled politely, thinking that while it was clearly ridiculous to completely write off the family of her own, and the bread she might make for it, its likelihood in the near future was about zero, given that the only person she would wish to have fathered the family clearly cared for her not in the least and she had neither the energy nor the inclination to even begin looking for another. Damn Barney. Damn him! It was as if he'd cast a spell on her, rendered her incapable of normal sexual and emotional thought. She had to get over him; she had to.

Mary suggested a walk round the garden after lunch.

'I was half-thinking you might be at the inquest,' she said, tucking her arm into Emma's.

'Oh – no. I had nothing to do with it. No point really.'

'Dr Pritchard was there. He gave some very good evidence, spoke so well. Such a charming man.'

'Yes, he is a sweetheart. And he's very happy with Linda, you know? The lady he brought to your – your . . .' She stopped, clearly afraid of stirring up unhappy emotions.

Mary smiled at her, patted her arm. 'My wedding. Nothing makes me happier than thinking about that day, Emma. Wonderful things, good memories.'

'Yes, indeed,' said Emma. She sighed without meaning to, then thought how selfish she was. 'Sorry.'

'Is anything the matter, dear? You look sad.'

'No, no, I'm fine. Really. Well, maybe a bit tired. It's hard work, A and E. I was on nights all last week. Takes a time to get over that.'

'I'm sure. Well, if that's all . . . Now I wonder if you heard from Georgia, but those two young men, the bridegroom, Mr Weston, I think his name was, and his best man, Barney someone . . .'

'Fraser.'

'Yes, that's right. They were both there, of course. I was able to apologise to them, rather obliquely. I always felt I'd held them up, you know, wouldn't let Mr Weston go in front of me in the queue. And then Barney paid a tribute to someone I thought might have been you.'

'Me!'

'Yes, dear. He said how a doctor at the hospital had helped him so much to get over his guilt at escaping from the whole thing without a scratch. I believe there's some technical phrase for it.'

'Yes, there is. Survivor guilt.'

'That's it. Yes, and Georgia said you'd been wonderful with her, very kind and patient.'

'Goodness.' Emma felt herself blushing. 'Um, what – what exactly did he say, can you remember?'

'Let me think. Not much more than that really. But I thought it was you because he said "she". "She helped me so much," he said.'

'Oh.' And as the memories swept over her, of those early conversations with Barney, of how she tried to comfort him and to reassure him about Toby, and then the day, the fateful day of Toby's operation, when it had all begun between them, she suddenly felt her eyes fill with tears.

'Oh now, you mustn't cry.' Mary looked at her with great concern. 'Or rather, cry as much as you like, so helpful tears I've always found, but then tell me all about it, what's upsetting you? Shall we go back inside? Mrs Salter has made some scones, I do know that.'

'I'd better not come and see you too often, or I'll be the size of a house,' said Emma, smiling through her tears.

'I hardly think so, dear. And if you mean that, I shall give you a glass of water and a dry biscuit next time. Come along, let's go in. Here, I've got a hanky you can borrow, it's quite clean . . .'

'. . . and it's just so stupid,' said Emma. 'I mean, why can't I get over him, just forget about him and move on?'

'I expect because it has never been properly resolved,' said Mary gently. 'You parted thinking it was only for a few weeks, knowing you loved one another . . .'

'Thinking we loved one another. He clearly doesn't love me.'

'And how do you know that?'

'Mary, if he did, then surely he'd have contacted me. He knows I'm not with Luke – that was my boyfriend before, the one at the Dorchester that night, and I know he's not with Amanda. So, if he wanted to see me, then surely he would have called me. Or something.'

'He might be thinking exactly as you are. Why haven't you contacted him, when you know it's over with Amanda?'

'He doesn't know I know.'

'I thought you said he told your doctor friend.'

'Oh – yes. Yes, that's right.'

'Well?'

'Oh Mary, I'd look such a fool. If there was someone else.'

'Does that matter so much? There are worse things, after all.'

She considered this. 'Maybe not. It would be a terrible risk.'

'Most worthwhile things are a risk, Emma. It was a risk for me, you know, meeting Russell again, after all those years. It could have spoiled everything, spoiled all those wonderful memories; it could have been dreadful. But I decided it was worth it. You ring your Barney. The worst that can happen is that you'll know he doesn't love you any more. Know for certain. And you'll feel a little foolish. And then at least you can move on.'

'Yes, but Mary, it's been so long now. Months and months, since we met. However much he cared for me, if he did, surely he'd have got over it by now. Forgotten me.'

'My darling,' said Mary very gently, 'Russell didn't forget me or get over me, nor I him. We waited sixty years for one another. Love survives, you know. For ever if needs be.'

Chapter 55

It was all very astonishing. She still couldn't quite believe it. That she was actually in a relationship with him, seeing him all the time, sleeping with him even. It just didn't seem possible.

But – it was.

It had all begun the day after the inquest. He'd asked her for a drink – again – and when she'd said she didn't think so, he'd said, 'Please, Georgia. I want to hear about how yesterday went. I was thinking about you all day.'

She was touched by that; that he should care.

'Well, all right. A quick one,' she said. 'Thank you.'

They were rehearsing in downtown Chiswick; he took her to a bar in the High Road, not the pub, insisted on buying her a cocktail. She was surprised, but tried not to read too much into it. Maybe he had more money, now that he was a first assistant. She'd told him about the inquest, in some detail. She thought he might be bored, but she didn't care. It was good to talk about it, and she wasn't into impressing Merlin any more. There was no point.

'It must have been terrifying,' he said, 'reliving it publicly like that. Such a ghastly experience.'

'Yes, it was. Especially having to talk about why I – well, ran away. But you know, it was actually the best thing. I really feel it's over now. I never did before.'

'Well, good for you,' he said, and then added, looking as close to bashful as Merlin ever could, 'I think you're marvellous, Georgia.'

'Oh, for goodness' sake,' she said, mildly irritated by such excess. 'Of course I'm not. I'm a wimp. You of all people know that. Weeping and wailing all over the set of *Moving Away*, thinking everyone hated me, that I couldn't do the part. I'm not marvellous at all.'

'Well, I'm entitled to my opinion,' he said, smiling at her. 'Another one of those?'

'Oh, why not.' They had to work together, after all.

When he came back with the drinks, she took a deep breath and said, 'How's Ticky?'

'Oh, she's fine. Yes. Fine.'

'Good.' She could hear a 'but' somewhere; she didn't even dare think about what it might be.

'Yes. Fine. Doing really well in New York. But,' here it came, 'she – I – well, we're not together any more.'

'You're not together? Oh Merlin, I'm sorry.' He looked so wretched, she really was. She didn't feel remotely glad. Well, not very.

'Yeah, well. You know, it was hard, conducting a relationship across two continents. It just wasn't working any more.'

And if anyone had stopped it working, Georgia thought, it would have been Ticky. Not Merlin. No doubt whatsoever about that.

He sighed. 'I miss her, of course. I miss her like hell. But – we were never together anyway. Or hardly. So what's new?'

'A lot, I guess,' Georgia said. And she then said again, 'I'm sorry, Merlin.'

'You're so sweet,' he said, 'to be so nice about it. But then you would be. You're such a nice person, Georgia.' There was a pause, then he said, 'I hope you didn't feel I was – well, playing around with you a bit. On *Moving Away*. I mean I wasn't, I really enjoyed your company and I hoped I was helping. But after the party, I thought that maybe—'

'Merlin, of course I didn't,' she said, her eyes meeting his in absolute astonishment. 'Of course not! I was just so glad to have you as a friend. A sort of wonderful big brother. But – heavens, no, it never even crossed my mind.'

If I ever get an Oscar, she thought, I won't have acted any better than that.

The next thing that happened was that he became involved in the festival. He thought it was a wonderful idea; he was clearly and genuinely impressed by how much they had achieved. And it turned out that he knew a lot of bands as friends, 'Mostly unsigned, but . . .'

'We're looking for unsigned. Although we're hoping to find quite a lot through these play-offs we're organising. We've had a pretty big response to our flyers.'

'Yeah, that's a very clever idea.'

'It is, isn't it? We still need a headliner though. Do you know anyone remotely famous?'

He thought, then said, 'I might. I'll see what I can do.'

Three days later, she rang Abi and said, 'You're never going to believe this!'

'Try me.'

'We've got BroadBand. And they can do the eighth. So we can get the website up and running.'

'Omigod. Oh. My. God. BroadBand! How, why—'

'Oh, you know what they say,' said Georgia carelessly. 'It's not what you know, it's who you know.'

Merlin came to the next committee meeting. Abi was initially deeply suspicious of him – in fact, she'd told Georgia he sounded like a complete wanker. Georgia defended him rather feebly.

'He really isn't, Abi. He's actually very sweet and kind. Honestly.'

'Doesn't sound too sweet and kind to me, treating you how he did.'

'No, no, you don't understand. He didn't treat me any way, not like that. He really just wanted to help, he told me, and he apologised if I felt he'd – well, you know.'

'Played around with you?'

'Yes. But he didn't. He behaved like a gentleman, honestly, always. He never tried anything—'

'I never did like gentlemen,' said Abi.

'But you're marrying one.'

Abi was silent for a moment; then she grinned.

'Yeah. Suppose I am. Still can't believe it. God, Georgia, he's bought me the most amazing rock, it's being sized right now, but it's just so beautiful. Mind you, I'll make the most terrible farmer's wife. I don't understand any of it, and God knows how I'm going to deal with the in-laws. Specially *her*.'

'Abi, I'd back you against any mother-in-law. Against anything on the planet, really. I'm sure you'll do fine.'

In the event, Abi quite liked Merlin; he made her laugh, and he certainly knew a lot about festivals.

'My parents used to take me to Glasto every year, and I loved it. It's a kid's idea of heaven, all that mud and not having to have a bath. Have you thought about what you should do for the kids?'

'Like what?'

'Well, like face painting and weaving, stuff like that; it'll all add to the atmosphere and anyway, it'll make more money.'

'No, we hadn't thought of that. Good idea.'

'And then you should sell tents, the little ones, and those waterproof cape things and wellies.'

'Yeah, and someone suggested blankets to me,' Abi said.

'Blankets definitely. And I don't know what you're thinking about food, but I went to Reading last year, and they had some massive paella bubbling away, and the punters just came and got bowlfuls, made a change from burgers, really popular. Oh, now here's another thought; you could do a CD of the festival. It needn't cost much, honestly. I know a bloke who knocks them out – well, you know him, Georgia, Jaz.'

'Oh, really? Jaz is great,' she said to Abi, 'you'd love him. He's my landlord.'

'CDs are a brilliant idea,' said Abi, scribbling furiously. 'You're a real find, Merlin. This is all great stuff.'

'What did you think of Merlin?' Abi asked William later.

'He was all right. Wasn't too keen on the bracelets.'

'Yeah. I wouldn't be surprised to hear he swings both ways.'

'What does that mean?' said William, looking genuinely puzzled.

Abi stared at him, then she smiled and leaned forward to kiss him.

'Oh William,' she said, 'I love you so much. You're so – so wonderful.'

William gave up.

Things escalated fairly fast after that. Merlin drove Georgia back to London, took her out for a meal and then to a club. When the cab stopped outside her house, he kissed her good night, rather chastely, and then said, 'Do you really see me as a big brother, Georgia?'

'Course.'

'Right. Good. Well, good night.'

'Night, Merlin. And thank you again. Not just for the evening, but for coming today.'

'It's fine. See you on Monday.'

'Yeah, Monday.'

This wasn't easy. It so wasn't easy.

❖ ❖ ❖

They were rehearsing *Three or Four?* until really late on Monday; Georgia was depressed, felt she'd done badly.

'It's so hard, doing comedy,' she said to Merlin. 'So different. I feel I'm right back to square one.'

'You're not. Come on, let's grab something to eat.'

They went to a Pizza Express; she picked at her lasagne rather half-heartedly.

'Come on,' he said, 'cheer up. You're doing great. Honestly.'

'You really think so?'

'I really think so. I'll tell you who isn't – Molly.'

'Oh really?' Molly Buchanan was playing the other girl.

'Yeah. She's our problem – she's what's making you feel you're crap.'

'Oh. Well, maybe. I do find her quite over the top.'

'Exactly. She's playing it like it's *Romeo and Juliet*. Very, very difficult to deal with. But I think Bryn's on to her. I saw him talking to her rather intently as we left.'

'Mmm. Maybe. Suddenly I feel hungrier.'

'Good. Big Brother at work again.' He raised his glass to her. 'To stardom. You'll get there.'

Georgia looked at him. He was wearing a white T-shirt and blue jeans; his face was tanned still from a family skiing holiday. He looked – well, he looked amazing.

'Yeah,' she said with great difficulty. 'Yeah, you're a really great brother.'

Merlin put down his glass and looked at her in silence for a moment. His eyes moved over her face. She sat there, trying to appear cool.

'I have to tell you something,' he said. 'You can tell me to get lost if you like.'

'Yes?'

'I don't exactly see you the same way,' he said. 'Not really as a sister at all.'

'No?'

'No, not in the least. I think you're utterly gorgeous. Sorry.'

Georgia stared at him; then she stood up, went round the table and put her arms round his neck.

'Oh Merlin,' she said, kissing him repeatedly, first on his cheek, then on his forehead, then finally and rather recklessly on the mouth. 'Oh Merlin, don't say sorry. I—'

'Let's get out of here,' he said.

They went to her room. She said she'd rather, although he did offer her his place in Hampstead.

'I'm self-contained,' he said, 'and anyway, they won't mind, it's part of their religion.'

'No, no, I wouldn't feel happy.'

'I want you to feel happy,' he said. 'Come on.'

She was nervous again; going back to hers. He was probably incredibly experienced, which she wasn't. He'd find her dull, disappointing, and she hadn't made the bed properly that morning, so he'd also think she was a slut. *And* she was wearing some really grotty old pants, when he must be used to the likes of Ticky in Agent Provocateur . . .

None of it mattered. He clearly didn't find her dull; in fact, he was surprisingly straightforward, which was a relief, and there certainly wasn't time to notice the unmade bed, for they were on it in seconds after shutting the door behind them, and as for her knickers, well, he just yanked them off completely unceremoniously, so anything better would have been a complete waste.

In fact, it was all wonderful; it was as if they had been ready and waiting for one another, perfectly matched, perfectly tuned. 'That was totally amazing,' he said afterwards, lying with his face buried in her hair. 'We saw, we conquered, we came.'

She hoped he didn't say that to all the girls.

That was the only thing that worried her; how could he be so suddenly and so totally taken with her, Merlin Gerard, so gorgeous, so sexy, so – so sophisticated. Merlin, who was used to girls like Ticky, as gorgeous and sexy and sophisticated as he was, how could he want to be involved with her?

After a few days, a few nights, when she was beginning to feel more confident, she managed to ask him that; he smiled and kissed her and sat up on the pillows.

'I find you totally gorgeous and sexy, Georgia. I always did. You're so special. Unique. So not like anyone else. The first moment I saw you, I felt a catch in my heart—'

'Merlin!' That really did sound a bit rehearsed.

'No, I did. But—'

'Well, but you had Ticky then.'

'Yes, of course. And now I've got you. My own, beautiful brown bird. Would you like to sing for me once more? Before we go to sleep?'

Crushing the distaste for this, telling herself he was just wonderfully poetic, that was all, she smiled at him ecstatically and climbed onto him, her legs straddling him.

'I love your energy,' he said, 'it's so amazing.' They fell asleep with his head on her breast.

In the morning, they met Jaz on his early rounds, as he put it; checking the terminally leaking taps, the blocked lavatories in the house.

'Ah,' he said, 'very nice. Thought that might be how it was. Merlin, you old bugger, how come you get to pull all the best ones? Georgia, my lovely, any trouble with him, you come straight to me, OK?'

She laughed and said OK; she loved Jaz.

And now, nearly three weeks later, she could hardly imagine life being any different. It was totally, totally wonderful; she was the luckiest, happiest girl in the world.

❋   ❋   ❋

Emma hadn't got the job in Glasgow; she went to see Alex, almost in tears.

'That's the second. I'm beginning to feel victimised.'

'My dear Emma, you wait till you're trying to get a consultancy. That really does feel like victimisation. Nine jobs I went for, before I got this one, it was ghastly. You get there and you see the same old faces each time, with a few variations, and it's always the bloke you least like who gets it, gets called into the boardroom while you all sit waiting like a load of cretins, and then you all shake hands and say you never really wanted it anyway, and crawl back to your hospital with your tail between your legs. I had a special interview shirt, it got quite threadbare towards the end.'

'Yes, well, thanks for all that. I can't wait,' said Emma. 'Meanwhile, it's tail between the legs time for me. Can I stay, Alex?'

'Of course you can. Nothing could please me more. Sorry – not what you want to hear.'

'It sort of is. Thank you. There are lots more jobs I can apply for in the pipeline, but—'

'Emma, the thing about obstetrics is that it's a very popular discipline. There's always going to be lots of jobs, but also lots of people applying for them. You'll get one in the end, promise. Meanwhile, you're a fantastic member of the team here. You can stay as long as you like.'

At least she still had a job – even if she didn't have anything else.

'Barney! Hi, darling! How are you?'

'Fine, Tamara, Yes. Thanks. And you?'

'Oh, pretty good. I called to invite you to my leaving do.'

'Your leaving do! That's a bit sudden, isn't it?'

'Not really. It's just that it's so long since we talked. I've done my time. Start at CKD in a fortnight, at the French desk there. Taking a bit of a break first.'

'Yeah?'

'Yeah. We – Micky and I – are off to Barbados for ten days.'

'Micky?'

'Yes, I can't believe you haven't heard. I'm engaged. Again. To Micky Burne Proctor. Getting married in the summer. Slightly déjà vu, but at least I'll be in a different dress. I thought that really would be unlucky, wearing the same. Or could be. But – otherwise, same venue, same church, same time of day even, I think. Mummy and I are working on that one. Anyway, this Friday evening, six-ish, Terminus. Hope you can come.'

Well. She didn't let the grass grow under her feet. You had to hand it to her, Barney thought, with a sense of grudging admiration; she'd survive an earthquake and hurricane combined, Tamara would. And come up looking immaculate. And sexy. Micky Burne Proctor, eh? In the *Sunday Times* rich list, the previous year. Hedge-fund boy. Better prospect than Toby.

He couldn't think why she'd want him at her leaving do. But – might be fun. He hadn't had much of that lately. He wondered if Toby knew. Or cared.

'Order, order. Georgia, you first.'

'Right. Well, the play-offs are going brilliantly. We've already got three winners from three pubs. One's really fantastic. Called Literate. I don't think they'll be unsigned for much longer. Oh, and a sweet folk band as well. Lots of stalls are coming on board – face painting, weaving, a little roundabout, a Bouncy Castle. Everything we discussed, really. Some guy's got a hat stall – says they went really well at Glastonbury.'

'What sort of hats?' Abi asked.

'Every sort. Baseball hats, trilbies, berets, reggae hats, sun hats for kids. Oh, and some really nice girl has got a beauty stall – does, like, makeovers and massages and all stuff like that. What do you think?'

'Mmm.' Abi considered this. 'No, don't think so. Doesn't go with the family feel. But I quite like the hats idea. And what about a welly stall?'

'Oh yes, got one of those. Merlin says it's essential, don't you, Merlin?'

'Yup.'

'Oh, I do hope it doesn't rain,' said Emma.

'It will,' said Abi. 'Best to accept it. After that, anything's a bonus. We might even get some good gear out of it.'

'What do you mean?'

'Some guy I met, friend of William's, he had a festival on his land. It rained so hard, two-day festival it was, people were just getting into their cars at the end, stepping out of their filthy muddy clothes, and just leaving them. This guy said lots of it was really good stuff, Fat Face, Abercrombie, all that; his wife washed it about three times and then they wore it. And their kids – loads of Boden.'

'Cool. Best pray for rain then.'

'Who's responsible for litter?' asked Merlin.

'Me, I suppose,' said Abi. 'Comes under the heading of site management.'

'Make sure you've got loads and loads of bins and bags. Twice as much as you think.'

'Yes, please do,' said William. He had a sudden vision of endless acres of litter and what his father might say or do.

'OK, OK.'

'You need people specially briefed to pick it up too,' said Merlin. 'It's really important. And loos – Abi, is that you?'

'Yeah, I'm Toilet Queen.'

'Can we not have those awful urinals in rows where you face the other blokes and try not to look at them, and you all pee into a pit in the middle?'

'Sounds fun. I'll do my best. How are the bookings looking, Georgia?'

'Oh, nothing much yet. But the website's only been up and running a couple of weeks. Lots of hits though.'

'Great. Any reactions to the name?'

'Nope. Well, only from my mum. She thinks it's great. She had an LP called *In Good Company* in the seventies.'

'Great. Exactly the image we're after. Mum's favourites. Oh dear. Maybe we should change it.'

'We shouldn't,' said Merlin firmly. 'It's a great name.'

'Yeah, well, you would say that,' said Georgia. 'You thought of it.'

'Shut up. Any other objections?'

There weren't.

'OK. Well, I've got everything booked site-wise,' said Abi. 'Arena, electrics, sound systems, water. What does everyone think about camp fires?'

'We think no camp fires,' said William firmly.

'Barbecues?'

'Not happy.'

'William!' said Abi. 'People love them. Specially families.'

'I'll think about it.'

'Bless. We've got the alcohol licence, the police are on side. Got St John's for the First Aid tent as well.'

'You've done so well,' said Georgia, beaming at Abi. 'Security?'

'I've talked to a couple of firms. Both very expensive.'

'You have to have security,' said Merlin. 'And they have to check for drugs.'

'Yes, all right. I know that. I just said they were expensive. Now, what are we going to do with our thousand pounds from wonderful Mrs Mackenzie? Blow the lot on publicity, say, or split it, put it into the various pots.'

'I think split it,' said William, 'in case we don't get any more.'

'William, you are such a ray of sunshine,' said Georgia irritably.

※　※　※

She was very jumpy now. *Moving Away* was going on air in three weeks, and the publicity machine was cranking up. Davina and Bryn Merrick had been the most in demand – Davina's lovely, laughing face had been everywhere – but Georgia had done two interviews already, one for the *Daily News* Arts round up and one for *You* magazine, both of them talking her up as one of the new faces of the summer. She was surprised about it, hadn't thought anyone would take any notice of her. The one in *You* had been a big profile, very personal, had asked her about being adopted – and by white parents, had that been difficult, how had she coped – and had mentioned, inevitably, the crash. She'd hated it, but Linda told her it was fantastic she was getting so much coverage, she should just be grateful.

'You're getting talked about; most people at your stage would give their eye-teeth for any publicity.'

The DVDs of the show hadn't gone out to the critics yet; she was dreading that, everyone seeing how bad she'd been. Although the girl from *You* magazine, who had managed to wangle one out of the press office, said she'd been 'stunningly good'. Well, what did she know?

The meeting was over; the others left. Abi looked at William and smiled. 'Love you.'

'Love you too. You busy right now?'

'Not terribly. You?'

'I've got an hour or so.'

'Cool.'

'Where's Sylvie?'

'Out for the night. With Mr Perve.'

'Right then. Shall we—'

'Yeah. I want to show you something first though.'

'That'll be nice.'

'No, no, it's what I'm going to wear on Friday.'

'Couldn't it be afterwards?'

'No. You might find it exciting, you never know.

Although actually, I hope not. Give me five minutes.'

'OK. No more though.'

'No, promise.' She was back in ten. 'How do I look?'

'Blimey,' said William.

'Is that it? Don't you like it?'

'Er . . . you don't look quite yourself.'

'That was the idea.'

'Abi, you are yourself. That's why I love you.'

'I know, but . . .'

She walked out into the hall, looked at herself in the long mirror there. It was true, she didn't look quite herself. She looked good though, she thought. She was wearing grey trousers and a pink wrapover sweater. And low-heeled shoes. Her make-up was rather nice, she thought. Grey eyeshadow, grey eyeliner, not much mascara, pink lipgloss. Her hair was tied back.

She went back to William. 'I think I look great.'

'Well – you do. But – not yourself. Like I said. And why?'

'I thought it would be more suitable this way. More the sort of girl they'd like. Approve of.'

'I'm afraid it's a bit late for that.'

'It's never too late. That's my motto.'

'Abi, my mother's already seen you starkers. Twice.'

'Not starkers. I've always worn shoes at least. Oh, you're so disappointing, William. Here I am, trying to be a lady, and you tell me there's no point.'

'I don't want a lady. I want you.'

'This isn't for you. Anyway, this is what I'm wearing on Friday.'

'OK. But get it off now. Please.'

They were going to have dinner with the Graingers on Friday; at the farm. It was not a keenly anticipated evening. Except just possibly by Mr Grainger.

Emma was sitting in her flat with a large glass of wine, holding her mobile. Looking at her mobile. Even, sometimes, scrolling down and looking at Barney's name on her mobile. Even, once, dialling; and then, panic-stricken, hanging up almost simultaneously. And sitting there, heart thudding painfully, dreading that the call might have registered and he'd know. And then, after five minutes, wondering if the call might have registered and if he did know. And then what he might be doing now if he did. And then wondering why he hadn't rung straight back if he did.

Oh, it was useless. Hopeless. She just couldn't do it. Whatever Mary said.

Chapter 56

'So – tonight's the night, is it?'

'Yup. I am shit scared.'

'Oh, don't be so ridiculous. When were you frightened of anything?'

'I'm frightened of Mrs Grainger. Or rather, upsetting Mrs Grainger.'

'I'd have thought you'd done that plenty already.'

'Well – OK. But I do want tonight to go well. She's being very good, he said—'

'That's big of her.'

'Georgia, you're not being very helpful. She's said, apparently, that she's considering letting us have Cottage Number One, to live in.'

'Even bigger!'

'No, well, it is a source of income for them.'

'So is William.'

'I suppose. Anyway, it would be cool. It's really sweet, or could be. Needs tarting up a bit. But it's got three bedrooms . . .'

'One for you, one for the children, one for her.'

'Oh stop it. No, I could use one as an office. When I start my company. I mean, it doesn't matter these days where you work, does it? I can go and see clients, they don't have to come to me. I'm really excited about it.'

'Won't you be living on her doorstep? Literally?'

'Well, sort of. But it's about a quarter of a mile from the farmhouse, right at the bottom of a track thing. I don't think we'd have to see much of her. Anyway, listen, what I've really rung to say is, have you seen the *Mail*?'

'No. Why? I've had two missed calls from Linda, could that be a clue? I was just going to ring her back.'

'Could be. It's got a really nice piece in it about *Moving Away*. Saying how great it is, and Frank Thingy's best work for years.'

'Oh, yeah?'

'Yeah. And then it says something about some promising newcomer, Georgia Linley.'

'What, like she's crap, lets the whole thing down?'

'Well, obviously. But then it says your performance is . . . let's see, oh yes, extraordinary. And that you're . . . yes, here it is: "that rare thing, a completely fresh, individual talent. One minute funny, the next heartbreaking, she looks set to steal the show".'

'Oh. My. God. OH MY GOD.'

'Yeah, I know. So cool. Georgia, you're not crying, are you? How extremely unusual.'

Friday. Her lucky day. Always used to be. She'd met Barney on a Friday – and Luke, come to that. And got her finals results. And passed her Grade Five ballet with distinction.

So – this would be the day to do it. She really would. She'd . . . well, that was a good idea, she'd text him – that would be so much less embarrassing for both of them; why hadn't she thought of that before? He could ignore a text, or send her something non-committal back, like, *Nice to hear from you*. He wouldn't have to struggle to find the right words, or to sound pleased to hear from her. And she wouldn't have to act either, trying to sound all casual and as if she'd just suddenly thought she might phone him, just for old times' sake. Yes, that's what she'd do. When she was on her way out for the evening, not a Billy-no-mates, sitting in her room at the hospital. Mark and some of the others had asked her out for a curry. Or she could even do it when she'd had a couple of drinks. Nothing like a bit of drink dialling . . .

Abi had gone to have her hair blow-dried. It was the only way to get it all silky smooth, like those posh girls had. Then she'd go home, change, and set off in enough time to arrive really cool and collected. She'd even bought a much lighter perfume, not her usual heavy stuff.

She had a manicure as well, no colour on her nails, just left them all natural and shiny. She was going to do William really proud. He'd told her to arrive at about seven-thirty: 'Then we can have a drink. Mother likes to feed everybody at eight sharp.'

She resisted the temptation to say what if everybody didn't want to be fed at eight sharp? Tonight, the world was going to see a new Abi. Or rather the Graingers were. And who knew, she might even stay that way.

She'd read a *Telegraph* that was lying around the office, so she could converse intelligently if required on politics or whatever. Not the foreign stuff, that completely baffled her. And listened to *PM* on Radio Four as she drove back from the hairdresser. God, it was boring: how could people like that stuff?

She left Bristol at six; that would give her so much time.

'Oh – Barney! Hello.'

It was Amanda. He'd been dreading this for some time, this meeting, had been amazed it hadn't happened already, so closely were their worlds, professional and social, intertwined.

'Hello, Amanda,' he said.

She looked exactly the same: pretty, smiling, and – really very well. Glowing in fact. And why shouldn't she? Just because he'd lost weight, and had the dark-eyed look of the terminally sleepless didn't mean she should. For her at least, their separation had clearly been a very good thing. Which was entirely as it should be. If anyone deserved happiness, it was Amanda.

'How are you, Barney?'

'Oh – fine. Yes. Thanks. And you?'

'Oh, very well indeed, thank you. I've just got back from Val d'Isère.'

Ah. A skiing holiday. She was a very good skier. Better than him, actually. They had always gone, every year. Not to Val d'Isère though. Last trip had been to Vail, Colorado.

'Good snow?'

'Oh yes, excellent. Huge fun, great crowd.'

'Good. Yes. Er – you're not going to Tamara's party, are you?' Because if she was, he wasn't.

'What, her leaving party? No. I couldn't quite face it. You?'

'Oh – might look in. Yes. Not sure.'

'No, I'm off to dinner. With Ned. Ned Parfitt, you know?' Of course he knew. Ned Parfitt was a lawyer, big city firm, tipped for stardom. Rich, charming, flat in Sloane Mansions, bit of a time warp. But incredibly nice. And incredibly perfect for Amanda.

'Yes. Course. Give him my regards.'

'Yes, I will. He was in Val d'Isère, of course.' He knew why she'd told him that; so he could be quite sure that she was all right, not alone, rather the opposite, happily headed for a new, safe future. Which was wonderful. He bent down and rather to his own surprise, kissed her on the cheek.

'Lovely to see you, Amanda. You look marvellous.'

'I feel it,' she said, and then with a quick glance at her watch, 'gosh, I must fly. I'm late. Bye, Barney. Take care.'

'Bye, Amanda.'

Well, that was excellent. He was really, really happy for her. So – why did he feel more wretched than ever?

'Barney, hi. Lovely to see you. Come along in. You'll know nearly everyone, I'm sure – Micky darling, have you met Barney Fraser? He's at BKM, on the commodities desk.'

'Not sure. Hi, Barney.' Micky Burne Proctor gave Barney an ice-cold smile.

What a cliché, Barney thought, the Etonian drawl, the slicked-back blond hair, the blue eyes, the striped pink and white shirt, worn tie-less under the excruciatingly well-cut dark suit – and worth how many millions? Well, it was usually billions now, on that list. A good few anyway. He reputedly took home over a million every year in salary and bonuses alone. Well done, Tamara.

'Hi,' said Barney. 'Congratulations.'

'Yeah, great, thanks.'

'Off to Barbados I hear.'

'Yah, well, not quite Barbados – one of the little islands off that coast I've bought. Should be fun. And Tam needs a break – she's had a tough time.'

'Indeed,' said Barney.

'Well, nice to have met you. Hope we'll be seeing you when we're settled.'

Yeah, right. He was about as likely to receive an invitation from the Burne Proctors as the Queen. Probably rather less.

He looked around the bar. It was huge, very long, one of the old-fashioned brass and glass jobs. The usual impossible din was going on. He must be getting old to notice that. Tamara was right, he did know nearly everyone. Well, they did work for the same firm, so it was hardly surprising. Loads of pretty girls, which was nice. They all looked the same, these girls, with their long hair and their long legs and their dark suits and their high heels. One of the things about Emma was that she didn't look like that. Well, she had long hair and long legs, but she was quirkily pretty, not one of your Sloane monotones; her voice was quick and light, she never drawled, and when she smiled – God, she'd light up the city of London unaided with that smile. And he loved her nose, and the way it wrinkled up when she giggled.

Shit, Barney, stop thinking about the girl, and call her. Go on. Just do it. Lay the ghost if nothing else. Go and— Damn. He'd left his phone on his desk. He never did that, ever. Better go and get it.

'Barney! Hi! Lovely to see you. You know Sasha, don't you? Yes, I thought you did. Sasha's got the most incredible new job, out in Dubai. How are you, you old bastard? Come and tell us what you've been up to.'

The phone would have to wait.

She'd written the text; she just hadn't sent it. She'd do that bit later. When she'd got her courage up.

She'd written it on the bus: *Hi Barney. How are you? I was thinking about you and wondering if we could meet some time. Just for a chat. Call me if you have a minute. Emma.*

She'd added two kisses and then taken them off again about six times. At the moment they were there.

Her phone rang sharply; she jumped. Had she sent it already, by mistake? Was he ringing her? *Don't be ridiculous, Emma, you're getting Alzheimer's.*

'Emma? It's Mark. Listen, we're in a different place, not the Indian. It's a Thai, just by the big shopping arcade – that OK? Got a pen?'

Emma scribbled down the address; and went back to looking at her text. And deleting and reinstating the kisses.

This was good. She was in really good time. She'd even had a chance to put her car through the car wash. That would amuse William, who didn't believe in cleaning cars. He treated his cars like shit. Not like his tractors. He tended them as carefully as if they were his animals. One of his cows. One of his girls.

It was a funny thing, their relationship. Everyone was baffled by it, she could see that. Even Sylvie, who was always going on about how fit William was.

'You can't marry him, Abi,' she'd said. 'You don't have anything in common. What are you going to do in the evenings, talk to the sheep or something?'

As long as it was in the lambing shed, Abi thought, that'd be fine. She really couldn't see the problem with having nothing in common with William. It made life more interesting. Anyway, they did. They found the same things funny, they liked the same people – she even liked his farming friends, and they certainly seemed to like her, and he loved people like Georgia – and actually she did find the farming genuinely interesting. The pattern of it intrigued her, the progress through the year, the hatching and dispatching of animals, as William called it, the way it all worked. Stuff was planted and grew and was harvested and then you started all over again, and it was all rather – neat. Neat and satisfying.

She was not particularly fastidious, so she didn't mind the mess and the smells – except perhaps the silage, that was quite gross – and she genuinely liked the animals. Especially the cows. They were so sweet with their big curious faces and kindly eyes, their swinging walk. She had seen a calf born a couple of weeks earlier, and she had found it wonderful; this little thing, slithering out, wet and curly and a bit bewildered, and the mother's great tongue licking it, and the hot sweet strong smell. William said it wasn't always like that, they often didn't slither out, they had to be hauled, brutally; she'd been lucky.

He'd promised her a night in the lambing shed when the lambs were born. 'You'll like that, it's such chaos, and so noisy; they come out, one after the other, it's like a sort of conveyor belt. You've hardly delivered one, or rather a set, when there's another one on the go. And they just come out, stagger up on their little legs, make for the milk and –

don't look at me like that, there'll be no time for us to do anything. Together, that is. You'll have too much to do. You won't be able to just watch.'

She was impressed by the rams' performances: 'One ram to fifty ewes, thereabouts.'

'Not even you could manage that, William, could you?' she said and, 'Oh, I don't know,' he said. 'Over a few days, you'd be surprised.'

They had discussed the matter of children; they both liked children, wanted several.

'But not yet, I want to get my company up and running first,' Abi told him.

'That's fine. I can wait – although not too long. You're marrying an old man, don't forget.'

She did forget how old he was: ten years more than her. It was quite a lot.

He was completely relaxed about her working. He said it was what made her interesting. He didn't want her hanging about, bored.

'You can carry on working when we have kids, if you like. It's fine by me. Just don't expect any help, all right? Farmers are not new men.'

Abi said she wasn't too keen on new men, they always seemed a bit suspect to her. 'All that wanting to breastfeed their own babies. Yuk!'

'Sherry, Abi?'

She was doing it on purpose, Abi thought. She must know that nobody young drank sherry. Mrs Grainger had done a double-take when she walked in; her disguise as nice, well-brought-up girl had certainly worked.

'How nice to see you,' she said. 'William, take Miss Scott's coat.'

'Please call me Abi,' she said, thinking how bizarre it was to be addressed as Miss Scott by a woman who had seen her pubes. Twice. 'Very well – Abi,' Mrs Grainger had said.

Mr Grainger had pumped her hand vigorously and told her it was jolly good to see her; he was a bit of a sweetheart, she'd decided, definitely where William got his charm from.

'Now I do hope you don't mind,' said Mrs Grainger, 'if we eat in the kitchen. It's just scruffy supper, as I'm sure William will have told you.' What was scruffy supper, for God's sake? 'Do forgive me, but I've been so busy this week. But let's go through to the drawing room and have a drink.'

The drawing room was the room where Abi had sat that first day after the crash, waiting for William: it looked rather better as William had lit a fire in the huge fireplace, but struggle as it did, the fire wasn't making much of a job of heating the room. She made for the chair nearest to it, then drew back, fearing that was not what posh people did. They were used to the cold; for some reason central heating seemed to be regarded by the older generation at any rate as a bit common. Well, Cottage Number One was going to be dead common; she'd make sure of that.

'Congratulations to you both,' said Mr Grainger. 'Jolly well done.' He smiled, and winked at her; he did a lot of winking; he was best decribed, she thought, by that old-fashioned adjective 'roguish'. He was fun; she liked him.

'Yes, it's very – nice,' said Mrs Grainger. Nice was clearly the best she could do.

'Any idea when you'll be actually tying the knot?' said Mr Grainger. 'William's been a bit vague about it.'

'Oh, we're both pretty vague, I think,' said Abi. 'Probably when William's not too busy.'

'I'm afraid there's no such time,' said Mrs Grainger stiffly. 'Farming is a non-stop process, as you will discover.'

'Um – yes.' Abi looked at William for help. He smiled at her rather foolishly.

'We don't want to leave it too long actually,' he said. 'I can't wait to have Abi here instead of miles down the road.'

'Ah yes,' said Mrs Grainger. 'Now I don't know if William has told you, Abi, but we are proposing you have one of the cottages to live in.'

'Yes, he did, it sounds wonderful. Thank you.'

'I hope you'll be comfortable there. Of course, we've had to take it out of the brochures. We have families who come back year after year. They'll be very distressed, I imagine, to find that their holiday home is no longer available.'

Very distressed. What an extraordinary thing to say! God, she was a strange woman. Was it really going to be worth it? Living next door to her? Then she looked at William, grinning at her, lounging back in his chair, dressed up for the occasion in clean jeans and a pair of suspiciously new-looking boots, and knew it was.

'You must tell us about your job,' said Mr Grainger. 'I don't really understand it, I'm afraid. I think William said you were involved in photography.'

'Well – sort of. But I'm hoping to set up on my own.'

'Taking photographs?'

'No, no, organising events. You know, like for companies. Conferences and so on.'

'Will it be worth it, starting something now?' said Mrs Grainger. She was looking very determinedly puzzled. 'I mean, surely once you're married, you'll be needed by William up here.'

'Well, I'm not sure . . .' She looked at William helplessly.

'Well, of course you will. You marry a farmer, you marry the farm.'

'She could organise some shoots for us,' said Mr Grainger, winking again.

'I – don't know anything about shooting. Yet. I'm sure William can teach me.'

'You won't be going out with the guns,' said Mrs Grainger. 'Wives don't, for the most part. Unless you do some picking up.'

Picking up? Picking up what? The farmers? Well, there were a few she could fancy.

'It's the lunches, coffees, all that sort of thing. I – well, I . . .' She appeared to be struggling to get some words out; finally she managed it. 'I shall certainly appreciate some help with it all. It's very hard work, and I'm beginning to find it very tiring.' She actually managed a smile. Abi smiled back.

'I'm not much of a cook,' she said carefully, 'but of course I'd like to help. You can guide me, I'm sure.'

'Indeed. Melanie did wonderful lunches, didn't she, William? I remember once I was ill and she produced lunch for twenty-eight without turning a hair. Melanie was one of William's former girlfriends,' she added.

OK, you old witch. So it's to be war. In spite of the low heels. She might as well have saved the money.

But, 'Still, as I say, I'm sure we'll get along very well.'

That was a concession. A big one. She was at least trying.

'More sherry, Abi?' said Mr Grainger.

'That would be lovely. And then I'm so looking forward to my scruffy supper . . .'

She couldn't do it. She just couldn't. She'd look so pathetic, he'd be so embarrassed, it was ridiculous. Totally, totally a bad idea. She deleted the text, switched her phone off, and walked into the restaurant.

God, he needed to get out of here. He'd drunk far too much. And stayed far too long. He'd reckoned on half an hour. It was – God, nearly nine. He'd just retrieve his phone and—

'Barney! Oh Barney, I'm going to miss you!' Tamara's arms were round his neck, her lips on his cheek, her thick scent everywhere.

'Well, I'll miss you too. But CKD isn't exactly in another country. I'm sure we'll see each other around.'

'Yeah, course. Isn't Micky sweet? Aren't I lucky?'

'You are, yes,' said Barney, adding dutifully, 'And he's lucky too.'

He suddenly saw himself as he must seem to her; rather pathetic, a none-too-successful relic of their old life. While she'd got everything perfectly sorted, looked at that life, rejected it and ordered a new one rather more to her satisfaction. Sleek, sassy, winner-takes-all Tamara.

'Sweet of you to say so. It does all seem terribly meant. Just think, if there hadn't been that crash, Toby and I would have been an old married couple by now.'

'Indeed.'

'And so might you and Amanda.'

'Possibly.'

'And – Emma? You with her?'

'Oh – no, no.'

'No! Why not? I thought that was why—'

'You thought wrong,' said Barney briskly.

'Barney! So what happened? Come on, you can tell me.'

'I—' How could he possibly tell her, Tamara of all people, about his broken heart. That most definitely wasn't a cliché, he thought. His heart did indeed feel as if it was snapped in two. Or no, more like dead and crumbling to dust. But then . . .

'It was all a terrible mistake,' he said finally. 'We'd – *I'd* got it wrong.'

'In what way?' She looked round, took his hand. 'Come on, Barney, let's go outside. I can't hear you in this.'

'But—'

'No, I insist. It sounds important.'

Outside, in the cold, she listened as he gave her a brief resumé, her dark eyes fixed on his face. Then she said, 'You absolutely have to call her.'

'Tamara, why? She finished it.'

'Only because she thought you were still with Amanda.'

'Well . . .' He digested this for a moment, then he said,

'Well, she knows I'm not any more. So she could have rung me.'

'Oh, Barney, please! Girls do *not* make those sorts of phone calls. That's a bloke's job. Is she with anyone else?'

'Don't think so. No. No, she's not.'

'Then for God's sake, what are you waiting for? Look, you don't have anything to lose, do you? It's crazy, what you're not doing. Just get out your phone and give her a call. It is so, so obvious. I can't believe it. Anyway, I'd better get back, or Micky will think I've run away with you.'

'I don't think so,' said Barney. 'Loser like me.'

'Barney, you are *so* not a loser. You're just great. Never tell anyone, but I really, really fancied you for ages. If you'd asked me first, I'd have married you, not Toby. Anyway, just as well, I'd have made your life a complete misery. Bye, darling. And just make that call. Otherwise I will.'

'You don't have her number,' said Barney. He was smiling now, thinking how wrong he'd been about her. Or partly wrong anyway.

'I can ring the hospital. I mean it. Promise me.'

'I promise,' said Barney. He leaned forward, gave her a kiss. 'Thanks, Tamara. And thanks for the party. And have a great wedding.'

'I will.'

She would. She got everything she wanted. But – she knew how to get it.

No possible doubt about that.

The food was great, she had to admit that. A wonderful chicken pie, and before that, tiny salmon parcels. Followed by a gooseberry mousse. And thick, thick cream. If this was scruffy supper, what would the full-blown dinner-party be like? And if this was the sort of food William was used to, he was going to be popping home from Cottage Number One pretty often.

The wine was very nice too, and Mr Grainger had

ceremoniously asked her to taste it, to make sure she liked it, but – God! One bottle between the four of them. She finished her two small glasses, made a great thing of lifting it and looking in it, and then at William, but he was studiously ignoring her. In more ways than one; he and his father had started talking about GM crops and whether they might consider a trial. Finally, as she sipped at her empty glass for about the tenth time, Mrs Grainger said, 'Would you like a soft drink, Abi? I thought as you were driving . . .'

'Oh, but . . .' She looked at William. 'I thought – well, I thought I was staying here tonight.'

'Really? I wish you'd said something to me, William,' said Mrs Grainger. 'I would have made up the spare room bed.'

Abi waited for William to say something that would indicate she wouldn't be needing the spare room, but he smiled rather awkwardly at her, passed her the bottle of red he was sharing with his father and returned to the discussion.

Abi poured herself a large glass, smiled at Mrs Grainger and wondered what on earth she could find to say to her; in the end she just sat and ate and learned a lot about GM crops.

It was very quiet on the trading floor. He didn't often see it like this. It looked and sounded dead; the screens blank, the phones silent. He went over to his desk; his phone was still there. Well, it would have been; it was hardly state-of-the-art any more. He was getting one of the new generation of iPhones, but it was taking a time to arrive.

He sat looking at it, hearing Tamara's voice. *It's crazy what you're not doing.*

He scrolled down the numbers, found her name; took a deep breath, as if he was about to do something physically difficult, and pressed the button. And listened. Listened for her voice. Her pretty, slightly breathless voice.

It came. *Hi, this is Emma. Sorry I'm not around, just leave a message and I'll get back to you.*

Shit. He hadn't expected that. And why not? Had he really thought she'd just be sitting there, waiting patiently for him to call? Of course not. She was probably out somewhere; or maybe she was working. Yes, that'd be it, she was at the hospital. He called the number, asked for the doctor's station in A&E. A female, rather bored voice said, 'Accident and Emergency.'

'Oh,' said Barney. 'Ah. Yes. Er – is – that is, is Dr King there? Dr Emma King?'

'No, she's not on duty tonight.'

'Ah. Well, what about tomorrow?'

'Not sure. Do you want me to find out?'

No, thought Barney, of course not, that's why I asked. 'That'd be great.'

'Just hold on.' She was a long time; when she came back, she said, 'Yes, she's on duty from six a.m.'

'Right. Fine. OK. Er – thank you. Thank you very much.' He felt quite differently now. Charged, up and running.

He sat for a moment thinking. If she was on duty from six, she was unlikely to be anywhere but in that flat of hers. That rather dreary flat, where he had spent those few, extremely happy hours. OK, he'd go there. He'd drive down, right now – no, maybe not, he'd had far too much to drink. Well, never mind. He'd take the train. And then get a cab. Easy. And if – well, if she told him to get lost, he could – well, he didn't know quite what he'd do then. Best not to think about it. Live for now. As Tamara would have done. Of all the advice from all the people in the world . . . it was very ironic.

He called Emma again; her mobile was still switched off. He left a message this time. *Emma, it's me. I'm coming down to Swindon.*

That was all.

He left the building, hailed a cab.

'Now you must tell us about this concert, Abigail.' Mr Grainger clearly felt he and William had been talking about GM crops long enough. 'We're looking forward to it, aren't we, Barbara?' he added to his wife. She gave him one of her pained smiles.

'July isn't it? July the eighth.'

'And ninth,' said Abi.

'The ninth as well? There are two?'

'No,' said Abi, looking at William in bewilderment, 'it's running over two days. It's a music festival. People will be staying, camping . . .'

There was a silence, then Mrs Grainger said, quite firmly, 'Oh no, that won't be possible.'

William looked at her startled. 'What do you mean, Mother, it won't be possible?'

'I mean exactly that. I – we can't have strangers camping on the farm. It's ridiculous. I had no idea. We shall have people breaking into the house, frightening the animals, letting them out onto the roads quite possibly. Peter, did you realise this was happening?'

'I – not exactly,' said Mr Grainger. He was looking very uncomfortable.

'Dad!' said William. 'Come on! I did explain.'

'Perhaps you did. I don't remember.'

'Well, whether you remember or not, it's not going to happen,' said Mrs Grainger. 'It must be cancelled.'

'It can't be,' said Abi. 'Not now.'

'I beg your pardon?'

'I said it can't be cancelled. Tickets have been sold, bands have been booked, there's a website, people will come anyway.'

'This is appalling,' said Mrs Grainger. 'Absolutely appalling. Well, you'll just have to return the tickets, and say on the website that it's been cancelled. I've never heard of anything quite so – so high-handed. Or so rude,' she added.

'Mother!'

'Well, it is.'

'Honestly,' said Abi, endeavouring to ease the atmosphere a little, 'there'll be no trouble with break-ins or letting the cattle out. We've got a very good firm handling the security.'

'You've got a very good firm handling the security! With whose permission, may I ask? I'm sorry, but I'm finding this completely incomprehensible. I absolutely refuse to agree to any of it. I was opposed even to what I thought was a small concert in the first place, I was afraid it would get out of hand. But a – a campsite. On our land. With bands!' Her tone implied unspeakable connotations. 'No doubt there'll be drugs, knives probably, all sorts of undesirables . . .'

'They'll be searched for drugs and knives,' said Abi.

'They won't. Because none of it will take place. I'm sorry if you've been under a misapprehension, but I do assure you, so have I. William, I'm astonished at you.'

William, William, thought Abi, stand up to her, fight back; but he didn't. He just sat there, flushed, wretched, raking his hands through his hair.

She stood up, pushed her chair back, enjoying the ugly harsh sound it made on the flagged floor, and left.

'I think I'll go,' said Emma. The evening was turning into hard work, her head ached, and she wanted to be home. Home alone. Again. 'Sorry. Just feeling a bit tired. Hard week. And I'm on duty at six in the morning.'

'You party pooper!' said Mark. 'OK, we understand. Want me to get you a cab?'

'No, it's OK.' She stood up. 'I'll get the bus.'

'Emma, you are not getting the bus. Not the nicest place, Swindon, this time of night. I'll phone for one. Finish your drink.' He looked up at her. 'It'll be about half an hour – all right?'

'Yes, thanks.'

She felt the bus might have been quicker, but she was too tired to argue.

Abi was crying so hard, she could barely see; she stopped at the end of the road, sat there sobbing for what seemed ages, trying to pull herself together. How could he be so pathetic, so cowardly: how could he? Thank God she'd found out. How awful if she'd gone ahead and married him. Sylvie was right. She'd have married the mother as well. It could never, ever have worked.

God, she was a bitch. But she was allowed to be. That was the worst thing. William and his father just allowed her to get away with everything. They were obviously both terrified of her. All those brave words of William's, and they hadn't meant a thing. He was . . . he was . . .

A car had pulled up behind her and was flashing at her. Someone was getting out. It was William. He was running over to her; she wound down the window and put her head out. She realised it was pouring with rain.

'Fuck off. Just fuck off. You're a wimp and a coward and I never, ever want to see you again. Ever.'

'Abi, I—'

'No, just shut the fuck up. I can't believe how you behaved in there. How you let *her* behave. It was pitiful. Pathetic. I'm going home and I never ever want to see you again. Mummy's boy! Thirty-four-year-old Mummy's boy. You make me feel sick.'

'Abi, please. Listen. Just for one second. I'm sorry. I'm really sorry. It's my fault and—'

'It's not your fault she's so rude and vile and snobbish. I know her sort. She thinks I'm common so she can treat me exactly how she likes. Well, I may be common – I am actually, very common – but that's for me to decide, not her. Please get out of my way, William, I want to go home. At least I won't have to sleep in the guest room.'

'No,' he said, 'you won't.'

'Is that all you have to say?'

'No. You'll be sleeping in the cottage. With me. OK?'

'I don't believe you. I'm not sure I want to anyway.'

'Yes, you do. I told her so. And I told her she'd been incredibly rude to you and she was to apologise. And I said there was no question of cancelling the festival, and if she tried to, then I was leaving. Leaving home, leaving the farm.'

'You can't do that!' said Abi. 'You love the farm.'

'I know. But not as much as I love you. I meant it, I wasn't just saying it.'

'But – what would you do?'

'I don't know. Help you with your events company.'

'You'd be terrible at that,' said Abi. 'Really terrible.'

'Thanks. OK, well I'll go and run someone else's farm. Abi, I'm so sorry. I suppose we're so used to her, we just let her behave how she does for the sake of peace. When we notice, that is. She's not such a bad old thing underneath. Her bark's so much worse than her bite. But – well, that was so awful tonight. I was so ashamed. Of her and myself. I have been feeble, I know I have, but I just kept hoping she wouldn't find out about the festival until it was too late.'

'William,' said Abi, 'it would never have been too late. She'd have turfed everyone off when the bands were playing, and I've got to hand it to her, she's very formidable. She should have gone into politics. Mrs Thatcher rides again.'

'Well, maybe. But please, Abi, please come back. I'm so sorry. I love you so much. I can't lose you again. Please.'

She hesitated, then looked at him and grinned. A wide happy glorious grin.

'OK,' she said, 'you win. Fair enough. I don't suppose it'll be the last battle we have with her, but that's OK. Oh shit, William, I love you too. You're getting awfully wet.'

'Lock your car up,' he said. 'I'll drive you to the cottage. I've got the key.'

'OK.'

Inside the door, he looked at her and beamed. 'You know, I told you those clothes weren't a good idea. You'd have done much better if you'd worn your usual stuff. I think you should take them off right now. Starting with those very boring trousers . . .'

And thus it was that when Mrs Grainger arrived at Cottage Number One, wearing a most determined smile, her arms full of clean linen, and bearing a flask of hot coffee, she found Abi sitting on the stairs, naked from the waist down, and William tenderly removing her shoes, kissing her toes as he did so.

In the event, the cab took at least forty minutes to arrive; they always were late, Emma thought. Why did they do that, say they'd be there before it was remotely possible? She had finished her drink long since, and had actually left the table, was waiting in the lobby of the restaurant, amongst the wet coats and umbrellas. She didn't think she'd ever felt so unhappy. Yes, she had. Lots of times lately. God, she was turning into a misery. What had happened to her? Where had the bouncy, smiling, always happy Emma gone? Maybe it was just as well, she'd probably been a bit annoying . . .

The taxi seemed to be going a long way round; the fare would be running up into thousands. Well, tens anyway.

'You know I wanted Rosemary Gardens, don't you?' she said finally. 'By Rosemary Park.'

The driver didn't seem to hear her. He just carried on speaking into his phone, a headset, in Polish. Or Bulgarian. Or Czech. He probably didn't understand English anyway, she thought. He was taking her to some completely different place, that she didn't know, and the fare would be so stupendous, she wouldn't have enough money and—'

'We here. Fifty pounds.'

'Fifty!'

'No. Fifty. One five.'

'Oh – fifteen.'

'That's what I said. Fifty.'

'OK.'

She counted out sixteen pounds, got out. It was absolutely pouring. There was another car parked in the street. It had its interior light on. The person in the back was reading. Must be waiting for someone.

She got out of the cab, ran towards the house, went inside, slammed the door shut. She thought she'd heard footsteps behind her; she didn't want to hang about. She put the chain on the door, turned away.

The bell rang. She ignored it. It rang again. She really didn't want to open it, not at this time of night. But maybe she'd locked one of the other residents out.

'Who is it?' she called finally.

There was a silence, then: 'It's Barney.'

This had happened so many times in her imagination, and her dreams, that she more or less assumed he couldn't be real. She waited, unable even to move the chain, to open the door a crack, too afraid that if she did, she would wake up, or he would simply not be there.

'Emma! Please open the door. Please.'

It did sound like him. It really did. There was a big mirror in the hall; she looked at herself in it. She looked terrible. She was very pale, and her eye make-up had smudged, and her hair was all lank and wet. She couldn't open the door to Barney looking like that. If it was him.

She rummaged in her bag, pulled out a comb, dragged it through her hair. Wiped a tissue under her eyes, which promptly seemed to smudge more, licked it and tried again, tried desperately to find her make-up bag—

'Emma, what on earth are you doing?'

'Sorry. Sorry.' She had to do it, had to open the door. Whatever she looked like. She did, very cautiously, leaving it on the chain. She peered through the crack. And— 'It is you. Isn't it?'

'Of course it's me. Who else would it be, standing here in the pouring rain, begging you to open the door?'

She fumbled at the chain; it seemed to be jammed, it took ages. Finally she pulled it out. Opened the door. And . . .

'Hello, Emma.' There was a pause. Then he added, and then she knew it was him, 'Hello, The Emma. You all right?' He was staring at her, very intently.

'I'm fine. Yes. Hello, Barney. The Barney. Come – come in. Please.'

He came in. She stood looking at him, trying to take in the enormity of it, that he was really here, actually standing in front of her, looking a little dishevelled, not smiling.

'I can't believe I'm really here,' he said. And put out his hand to touch her arm. She put hers out. And absurdly took his hand and shook it. And giggled.

'Oh God,' she said, snatching her hand back. 'I'm sorry. This is so, so stupid. Oh Barney, Barney, but why are you here?'

'I'm here,' he said, 'because Tamara told me to.'

'Tamara! Now I know I'm dreaming.'

'No,' he said. 'You're not.'

'You'll have to explain.'

'All right.'

'Well . . .' She caught sight of herself again in the mirror. 'I'm sorry I look so awful.'

'You don't. You look beautiful to me. Absolutely beautiful.'

It was still all rather surreal.

And then they were standing inside her flat and he was still staring at her and looking very serious, and not touching her, and he said, 'I can't believe this is happening. I really can't.'

'Nor can I.'

'I've tried so hard to get over you. I couldn't.'

'Nor could I. Get over you.'

'I – wanted to call you so much, find out what had happened. But I just couldn't.'

'Nor could I. Even after I knew you'd finished with Amanda.'

'I was so afraid you'd . . . you'd . . .'

'I know,' she said. 'I know what you were afraid of. Same as me. That I was getting over it, had someone else.'

'And,' he said, moving towards her, reaching out, taking one strand of her hair, winding it just a little round his finger, beginning to smile now, 'how stupid was that. How stupid.'

'Of both of us,' she said. 'So, so stupid. As if that would have been possible.'

'As if, indeed.'

'So – what happened?'

'Well, like I said, Tamara told me to ring you. So I did.'

'Since when did you do what Tamara says?'

'Since tonight. She's my new very, very best friend. Yes, she really is.'

'Mary told me I should ring you. Only I wasn't so sensible. I went on being too scared.'

'Who's Mary, for heaven's sake?'

'Oh, Barney. You know. The old lady who was in the crash. I told you, she was meeting her boyfriend from the war; it was so, so sweet.'

'Oh, the one you met in the restaurant. Yes.' He was staring at her, absolutely still, looking dazed. 'I love you, Emma. I can't bear it, I love you so much. What was so sweet? Did you say?'

'I love you too. I can't believe it. So much. What was so sweet was, she told me to call you to get in touch. It's so sad, her Russell's died now. She's been widowed twice.'

'Poor Mary. Poor Russell.'

'I know.'

'Go on telling me what she said.'

'She said I should call you. And I said you'd probably have forgotten about me by now, it was such a long time. And she said you wouldn't have. That Russell hadn't forgotten her, not even after sixty years. How amazing is that?'

'Well, Emma King,' he said, 'I'm not being beaten at love by anyone. I couldn't forget you if I didn't see you for – for seventy years. How's that?'

'We'd have to be quite old,' she said, 'for you to remember me for seventy years.'

'I'd hang on,' he said. 'I'd just hang on, if I thought I was going to see you again. One day. I'd wait.'

'Well – you don't have to.'

'No, I don't, thank God. I'll have you with me. For all of seventy years, I hope. I love you, Emma. I never ever want to spend another hour without you.'

'You might have to spend an hour. Here and there. While you're banking and I'm doctoring. But after that . . .'

'After that, it'd be OK. So OK. And you know something, my darling lovely Emma?'

'No. What?'

'You don't look old enough to be a doctor.'

Epilogue

Abi woke to the sound of rain. Not just a light July shower, but proper, torrential rain. Mud-making, wheel-sticking, tent-soaking, barbecue-quenching, spirit-sapping, off-putting RAIN. Well, she'd said it would. Only she'd kind of thought if she said it enough, allowed for it sufficiently, it wouldn't happen. Wrong. It had happened.

Well, a little rain had never hurt Glastonbury. It was half the point of Glastonbury. Or had become so. But then Glastonbury was famous. People would go if it snowed, just to say they'd been there. In Good Company wasn't famous. This was its first year. Its only year, if Mrs Grainger Senior had anything to do with it. Mrs Grainger Junior had more ambitious plans for it.

There had been a Mrs Grainger Junior for three months now. Three pretty good months. There'd been some ups and downs, of course (mostly to do with Mrs Grainger Senior), but she wouldn't have changed it for the world.

They had got married on a brilliantly dappled April day, when the sun had shone one minute, and the clouds had re-gathered the next; when they had walked into the register office leaving a doomily dark world behind them and come out an hour later into a radiantly blue and gold one. Which, as Georgia said, was an absolutely fitting portent.

They had agreed, William and she, that there was absolutely nothing to wait for. No complex family to worry about – none at all in Abi's case, and while William's was worrying, it wasn't complex – no one's permission to be sought, no need to find somewhere to live. Abi had no desire, she said, for a big wedding. She didn't want to walk down the aisle in a meringue, indeed she didn't want to walk down any aisle in anything, she was a staunch atheist. The only thing she believed in, she said, was William, and how much she loved him, which she repeated in her wedding speech – she had insisted on making a speech – and which reduced almost everyone in the room, with a few notable and predictable exceptions, to misty-eyed and foolish laughter.

She said she'd quite like a good party, but not so big she couldn't dance with everyone in the room; and since she and William had very few friends in common and she didn't want anyone there who didn't understand what they were doing together, the party was just the right size.

There had been about forty altogether; for a late lunch and then dancing in the Royal Crescent Hotel in Bath. Mr Grainger had insisted on paying for it. Abi had wanted to pay for it herself, and not be any further beholden to the Graingers, but 'Let him,' William said, 'it's his way of apologising for my mother's behaviour.'

Abi managed to contact her dad, who was always up for a party, but her mother sent a note in answer to the invitation, saying thanks very much for the invite, and she wished her well, but she wouldn't be coming, as she hadn't seen Abi for over ten years and it would feel like being at a stranger's wedding. This did reduce Abi briefly to tears and quite upset William as well; but it did bring home to him exactly where Abi's toughness and honesty and independence of spirit came from. One day, he thought, he would like to meet the ex-Mrs Scott. It would be interesting.

Sylvie was there, of course, with a new boyfriend called Alan Wallis who worked in the men's department of Marks & Spencer. When Abi first met him, she told Sylvie she must need her hormones examined, he was bound to be gay, but Sylvie assured her he was most definitely not. Abi, in a spirit of pure mischief, made him go and ask Mrs Grainger to dance, but in fact, Alan Wallis had the most beautiful formal manners and had done an advanced ballroom dancing course; he steered Mrs Grainger most expertly round the room and she was later heard to tell William that he was a charming young man and that they had had a very interesting discussion about the rise and fall in the Marks & Spencer share price, and the reasons behind it.

Mr Grainger was in his turn very taken with Sylvie. 'Maybe they could set up a *maison à quatre*,' Abi remarked cheerfully to William. 'That would solve an awful lot of problems.'

William's brother and sister and their respective families came. Abi quite liked Martin, who was not unlike William to look at, but a lot smoother, but she thought his sister Alison was frightful and was almost moved to feel pity for Mrs Grainger when she saw her being snubbed repeatedly by her, and even more frequently by her son-in-law.

Georgia was there, of course, and so was Merlin; Georgia was interestingly and rather overtly impatient with Merlin, Abi noticed. He kept paying everyone very lavish compliments; he told Abi she made his heart stop, she looked so lovely, and William that he was the luckiest man in the universe – that really annoyed Georgia – and Sylvie that she danced like the proverbial angel. In the end, Georgia actually snapped at him and told him to stop behaving as if he was in front of – or behind – the cameras. He looked quite hurt and Sylvie, bored by now with Mr Grainger, took it upon herself to comfort him, which made Georgia crosser still.

Emma was there with Barney; they were officially engaged now and Emma had a rock quite as big as Abi's on her finger. She told Abi privately that she would have given anything to have a quiet wedding too, but her mother had gone into overdrive about the whole thing and her rating on the Bride's Nightmare Mother scale of zero to ten was about eleven and a half.

'It's a bit like you, in a way. Barney and his family are so posh and me and my family aren't, and I can just see it all ending in tears.' Abi had told her to elope with Barney, or run away and get married on a beach somewhere, but Emma said she couldn't possibly do that to her mother. She also, Abi suspected, actually wanted very much to walk down the aisle in a meringue.

William had invited a few of his farming friends and their wives – jolly horsey girls for the most part, who danced energetically long after everyone else had given up – and Abi had invited a small number – three, to be precise – of her better-behaved girlfriends, who would be an adornment to the company and could be more or less relied upon not to get so drunk that they were sick or to bring any drugs onto the premises. And that was that.

'And you know what?' she said to William as they undressed late that night in their suite of the Edwardian Radisson Hotel at Heathrow, prior to a 6 a.m. flight to Barbados, 'it went exactly how I hoped. Everyone seemed happy, most people got on with most people, and even your mother smiled quite a lot.'

William agreed, rather absently; he was goggle-eyed at the excesses of the hotel, with its vast atrium, its marble floors and pillars, its lush palm trees and gilded mirrors, never having seen anything like it in his life, and extremely excited at the prospect of the sort of sun, sea and sex holiday he had never experienced either.

'I've only actually been away three times,' he confided to his new wife. 'Twice with Nanny to Frinton and once with my dad fishing in Scotland.'

Abi told him she thought she could probably improve on that.

* * *

The honeymoon had been wonderful. They had stayed at the hotel, and done all the touristy things – parasailed, surfed, swum with dolphins, and danced to various wonderful bands night after night on various wonderful beaches. And then returned home to the reality of Cottage Number One.

Actually, Abi was very happy there. She was absorbed with starting her company, planning the festival, learning to ride – at which she proved rather adept: 'We'll have you out with the hounds soon – all two of them,' Mr Grainger had said with his usual heavy wink – and struggling to cook. After a few weeks of over-ambitious failures, she gave up and simply served endless enormous roasts which were easy and satisfied William's awesome appetite. Mrs Grainger left her alone for the most part, occasionally arriving at Cottage Number One with pies and puddings and chutneys and jams – 'I know how busy you are, this might help a bit' – which Abi began by resenting and became swiftly grateful for. She knew her mother-in-law's motives were not entirely good, being partly to contrast with her own efforts, but on the other hand it all tasted wonderful.

And here they were on the morning of the festival, with 3,000 tickets sold. 'Three thousand – I can't believe it!' Georgia had said. 'It's amazing.' Abi told her it wasn't amazing enough, they needed twice that to make any real money; they were way over budget on the bands. 'But we should get loads more on the day, as long as it isn't tipping it down.'

'You said it would be tipping it down,' said Georgia. 'You can't get out of it that easily.'

The best thing was that Barney's bank, BKM, had agreed to sponsor it.

'Only a rather modest amount, I'm afraid,' Barney had told Abi. 'Ten grand, a piss in a pot to them, but it should help a bit. And they'll want their pound of flesh or whatever, be credited on all the publicity and so on. They're actually rather tickled by it. My boss said he'd bring a few friends if it's a good day.'

Abi told him she didn't see ten grand as either modest or a piss in a pot, and that she'd thank Barney's boss personally in the best way she knew how.

'Best not,' said Barney, grinning at her. 'He's gay.'

She got up now, and pulled on some jeans, her wellies and her Barbour – 'Who'd ever have thought I'd be seen alive in a Barbour!' she had recently said to Georgia, 'but they really do keep the water out better than anything' – and drove down to the site.

It was still only seven, but the place was already full of people. She looked at it from the top of the hill, at her creation, at the transformation of the small lush valley into something so unrecognisably different, and felt a mixture of pride and terror in more or less equal proportions. The cows had been moved out, mildly protesting, a week ago, ousted by a rival herd of huge lorries, massive power lines, tall arc-lights, neat rows of Portaloos and showers. The brilliant red-and-yellow striped arena stood at the heart of the site, a flag fluttering from the top bearing the words *In Good Company*, a battery of lights above the stage, a rather random array of mikes and other sound equipment standing on it, together with keyboards, drum kits, waiting to be called to order by their musician masters, and even a rather incongruous-looking piano – that would be for Georgia's friend Anna, the jazz singer, and her daughter – and on either side of it, two huge screens. She parked her car at the site entrance; a couple of Portakabins stood just inside the gate. Rosie, the site manager, waved at her and ran over, pulling the hood of her jacket up over her head.

'Hi, Abi. Lovely day.'

'Shit, isn't it?'

'Oh, don't worry. I've seen worse. Good thing we

persuaded William to put down that hard-core. You'll need this.' She wrapped a brilliant green plastic strap round Abi's wrist. 'Being Mrs Farmer won't get you far today. Green is all areas, for people like us and the bands, yellow for all the stall-holders, red for the punters, so don't take it off whatever you do. Security don't take prisoners. They've arrived too, they're in the other hut.'

'OK, thanks. What time did you get here?'

'Four,' said Rosie cheerfully. 'So much to do.'

'Four!' said Abi. 'I hope we're not paying you overtime.'

'Course you are. No, it's fine. My big worry now is Health and Safety. You know they come to do their final inspection an hour before the first band play . . .'

'Yeah.'

'Well, they called late last night to say they might be late, got another to do the other side of the M4. Which is a total bugger; it could hold us up for hours if they find a cable they're not happy with or something.'

'Yeah. William's friend who does one of these every year, said they once held them up till ten-thirty. Oh God. You'd think there'd be enough of them to go round, wouldn't you?'

'No,' said Rosie, 'and oh look, here comes food. I said they could come any time after seven. They won't mind the rain, they sell more.' A small armada of trailer-towing vans was moving down the hill, into the site. 'I'll have to go, tell them where to park. Still happy with what we agreed?'

'Course,' Abi said.

She wondered what on earth Mrs Grainger might be doing, sent up a small but fervent prayer for a brief, violent and non-fatal illness, and walked across to a desperate-looking girl at the entrance who said she was in charge of what she called the kiddy roundabouts; one of her trailers had driven into the farmyard by mistake and been unable to turn round, and a very unhelpful woman had refused to move her Land Rover which would make things much easier. No violent illnesses yet then, Abi thought, and told the girl to follow her back up the track.

Emma and Barney arrived at eleven, just as a very large white van got hopelessly stuck in the mud.

'What are we going to do?' wailed Abi. 'It's going to block the way for everyone else, half the stalls aren't here yet and—'

'Abi, I'm no farmer,' said Barney, 'but a tractor'd sort that out, no time. Where's William?'

'He's trying to fix some problem with the power leads. The supply isn't enough, apparently – now they tell us. Over there, look.'

'I'll go and ask him,' said Barney. He came back grinning. 'He says he can't stop what he's doing, but if I could get his dad or the cowman, they'd bring a tractor down. Where do I find either of those people?'

'No idea where his dad is. Strangling his wife, I hope. But the cowman – Ted, he's called – he'll almost certainly be up in the cowshed. There's a cow calving, apparently she's in real trouble; they're getting the vet, so he won't be able to leave her just to drive the tractor. Oh God!'

'I can drive a tractor,' said Barney unexpectedly. 'If it's OK with William?'

'God, I don't know. He loves those tractors. Far more than he loves me.'

'Do you know where I might find one?'

'Well, yes. There's one parked outside the lambing shed. I saw it as I came down.'

'Take me to it. I'll risk William's wrath.'

'But Barney— oh shit. What a nightmare. Can you really drive a tractor? I mean really.'

'I really can. Chap I was at school with, his dad had a farm, we used to drive the tractors all over the place whenever I went to stay with him.'

'But—'

'I'm sure he wouldn't say he could drive a tractor if he couldn't, Abi,' said Emma. 'He's awfully clever.'

'Emma, you'd think Barney could drive a rocket into space. I've never known love make anyone so blind.'

'Yes, OK. But—'

'Look, we've got to do something,' said Barney. He pointed at the van; the driver had got out and was squaring up to the security guard, calling him an evil nancy boy. The security guard pulled his radio out of his belt and started alternately talking into it, and shouting at the van driver.

'Oh, OK. I'll drive you up there. Emma, you stay here and tell William some lie if he comes over.'

'OK,' said Emma cheerfully. She looked around her. It all looked – stuck van apart – extremely well organised. The food trailers were all in place and putting up their shutters, revealing signs that said things like *Bobby's Burgers* and *The Fry Up*. A couple of girls were standing by a children's roundabout, giving a child a ride; two rainbow-coloured tents side by side announced that they were *Face Painting* and *Willow Weaving*; someone clearly with a sense of humour was hoisting a large hot-air balloon over the loos, that read *In Good Company*. A St John's Ambulance tent was going up, a girl and a man were constructing a large barbecue under a pagoda tent, with a sign that said *Paella: Biggest portions* and a small but determined-looking queue was forming across the valley where the punters' entrance was.

Everyone seemed to know exactly what they were supposed to be doing and getting on with it. The air was thick with the crackle of walkie-talkies, the honky tonk music of the roundabouts, and the occasional burst of rock music as someone checked a sound system. And all the time the picture grew: more vans, more tents, more colour, more stalls. It was astonishing, rather like watching someone doing a giant jigsaw. God, Abi was a wonder. She'd masterminded all of this; without any of the histrionics Georgia had brought to it, she'd just got on and done it. William was a lucky chap; she hoped he knew it.

'Oh, William!' she said, realising he was behind her. 'Hi.'

'Hi, Emma. Everything all right? Abi gone to find Ted?'

'Yes. I – think so.'

'Great. Sorry I can't look after you properly. If you want a coffee, the site manager's cabin's got a kettle and stuff.'

'William, I don't need looking after. Did you get the power problem sorted?'

'No, not yet. And that van's causing chaos. God. If only this bloody rain would stop . . .'

'I think it is stopping,' said Emma. 'Or at least, it's much lighter, more of a sort of drizzle, don't you think?'

'No,' said William, looking up at the lowering sky, 'I don't. Oh good, here comes Ted now. No, it's not, it's Barney. What the hell is he doing, driving my tractor? Barney, you wanker, get out of that, for God's sake! You'll do the most terrible damage!'

'Piss off, William,' Abi shouted above the din. 'Barney's fine, he can drive this perfectly well and you'd better get up to the cowshed: that calf's a breech, and the vet needs help.'

'Where's Ted?'

'Seeing to another calf. Go on, William, for God's sake!'

William roared up the track in the Land Rover, with another agonised yell at Barney of: 'You break my tractor, Fraser, I'll have your goolies off.'

'You know what they say,' Abi said, grinning at Emma. 'You wait ages for a calf and then they all come at once.'

'You'd think they might have waited another day,' said Emma. 'It's so inconsiderate, they must have known what was going on. Abi, would you agree with me that the rain's much lighter? Almost stopped?'

'Mmm, not sure,' said Abi, and then, 'God, good old Barney, he's doing wonders with that thing. I hope that cow's all right. We lost one last week, can't afford to lose another.'

Emma looked at her, her respect growing by the minute.

'Are you Abi? Security sent me over.' It was a girl, dressed totally unsuitably in high-heeled red sandals and white trousers. 'Carol Standish, Wiltshire Radio.'

'Oh – God. Yes. Cool. They said you might be coming. Let's go over to the arena. Have you got any other shoes?'

'No. So stupid, but I wasn't expecting to come this morning.'

'Tell you what,' said Abi, 'we pass the welly stall. You can be our first paying customer. Here, look. Rainbow-coloured, madam? Spotted? Or even a pair of Hunters?'

Georgia was driving down the M4 just before one when she heard Carol Standish: 'Coming to you from *In Good Company*, the two-day music festival based at Paget's Farm, just off the M4 near Bridbourne. And I can tell you, if you're thinking of coming, you're in for a treat. It looks fantastic! There's an incredible array of stalls, wonderful bands on the programme, lots of them local, a great camping area, stuff for the kids to do, and the most amazing setting. It could have been purpose-built for the occasion, a sort of natural amphitheatre – and don't be put off by the weather, because the rain's stopping here now and there's even a bit of sun fighting its way through. Now the headline band is BroadBand, playing at eight tonight, but there are loads of others, starting with a folk band called – what are they called . . . oh yes, Slow-mo. They're on at three. And it's all for charity, in aid of St Mark's Hospital, Swindon, so you'll be doing some majorly good work if you come.'

It was awful to be so late, Georgia thought guiltily. She'd wanted to be down first thing, really make herself useful, but the second assistant director on the new TV series had suddenly called her and said they needed rain to shoot a scene and here it was, most obligingly, so could she get over right away? So she'd had to get over.

Georgia had had a pretty amazing three months since *Moving Away* had gone on to the nation's television screens. She had had rave notices: been proclaimed by various critics as 'an incredible new talent', giving a 'near-perfect performance' and being both 'exquisitely touching' and 'a superbly intuitive actress'.

'I don't understand it,' she'd said to Linda. 'I know I wasn't that good, I just know it. I'm not daft.'

'Maybe, but the thing is, darling, the camera loves you. It isn't just models you hear that of, there are certain actors it's true of too. It found more in your performance than you knew was there, maybe more than actually *was* there. Frankly, Georgia, and I've always been one of your biggest fans, I didn't see you getting rave notices like this. You're a one-in-a-million screen actress and you should thank God fasting for it. And don't come running to me after a bit saying you want to play Juliet at Stratford, that you don't feel fulfilled . . .'

'Of course I won't,' said Georgia.

'Darling, you'd be surprised how many do. Just enjoy this. It's great.'

Her face was everywhere; apart from the Arts pages. *Vogue* had used her for a fashion shoot, she'd appeared in the *Style* section of *The Sunday Times* and in the *Guardian* as their *Close Up* spread in the Monday fashion slot. She'd been interviewed just about everywhere, and wonderfully had been able to plug the festival several times – and most importantly had a part in a new BBC series, filming in the autumn, and after that in a main feature film, a screen adaptation of a new novel set against the background of what the publicity called 'Thatcher's Britain'. Georgia couldn't actually see it was that different from the present Britain, although her mother inevitably could, but it was going to be a great movie, and she had a great part.

She had moved out of her room in Jaz's house and got a mortgage on a minute flat in Finchley; she had also bought a ton of clothes from Topshop and TK Maxx and a couple of dresses from Stella McCartney for special occasions, and one of the new Minis, and she and Merlin were going on holiday to Thailand for a week when the BBC series was finished. Life had changed a bit, as she said to Abi, but she felt exactly the same. 'Just as worried about everything, just as insecure, just as—'

'Nuts?' Abi said with a grin. And yes, Georgia said, she supposed that was right.

'I'd so love to be cool like you, Abi, cool and sorted. I can't see it ever happening. Maybe I need a husband.'

Abi said she thought a husband was the last thing Georgia needed. 'Who could cope with you anyway, all famous like you are? You'd have to find another luvvie, and anyway, how about Merlin – what's wrong with him?'

Whereupon Georgia sighed and said, 'Nothing.' And Abi said, 'Yes, there is, I can tell. What's the matter, trouble in paradise?'

'Paradise?'

'Yes. Merlin told me being with you was total paradise. I thought it was sweet.'

'Well it isn't,' Georgia said. 'I can't bear it when he says things like that.'

'I wouldn't mind. The best William could manage was that life's got a lot better since we married, but he's not so sure about this week.'

'Yes, but he means it. Merlin doesn't.'

'How do you know?'

'Oh, it's all so corny. I swear he practises it in front of a mirror. And he's *sooo* vain. I don't know, Abi, I'd much rather have someone all lovely and steady like William. I'd love to be a farmer's wife.'

'Georgia,' said Abi, 'you couldn't possibly marry a farmer, you'd be crying all the time. Think about the lambs going off to market, or the poor little bull-calves . . .'

'Why – what happens to them?'

'I'm not even going to tell you,' said Abi; but Georgia was intrigued and asked William, and then as Abi had predicted, sat with tears rolling down her face at the plight of the poor things, off to market to be turned into veal.

Anyway, the festival looked like it was going to be great; a cautiously optimistic call from Abi at midday had reported a 'huge queue' at the gates. 'I just drove along the road, saw them from there, a great line of them, straggling between the cornfields – you know, the ones leading across to the end of the farm. Just get here, Linley, you've got work to do. And where's your friend?'

'She should be there,' said Georgia. 'I spoke to them about an hour ago, they were at Swindon or thereabouts. I hope nothing's happened to them.'

'No, not them, they're here and absolutely great. We managed to get them a plug on the radio. And a couple of blokes with beards and prehistoric sandals said they couldn't believe they were going to hear Sim Foster's wife and daughter. They were well pleased. No, I mean the CD guy. No sign of him.'

'Oh, Jaz. He's coming down with Merlin, they're only about twenty minutes behind me.'

Anna and Lila were doing a half-hour set at seven – Lila on saxophone, Anna on piano. They'd turned out to be a big draw with both what Abi called 'the Boden lot' as well as the fanatics.

'It adds a bit of class, such a lovely story for the publicity, tying in with you and the TV series and everything. He was huge in his day, her husband – I Googled him – wonderful for us to talk about. And Lila is just totally gorgeous, isn't she?'

✵ ✵ ✵

Georgia arrived just as the sun came out in earnest; she parked at the top of the hill, looked down, smiling. The sky was a rather uncertain blue, but the clouds had gone, and the tents were going up now, hundreds of them, filling the first field – they'd obviously need the second, Abi had been wrong – all different colours, small igloos for the couples, and bigger frame jobs for the families. She could hear the sound of thousands of pegs being hammered into the ground, of children laughing and shrieking as they ran about, of people calling to each other over the hurdy-gurdy music of the little roundabouts; it was all so lovely, their dream almost unbelievably coming true. A few people had already lit barbecues and she could smell the smoke drifting into the moist air; and across on the other side of the valley, the seemingly endless line of vehicles and people, queuing in the sunshine.

'Hello, sweetheart. How you doing?'

'Jaz! How lovely. Fine, yes.' He was grinning at her appreciatively, pulling off his leather jacket, revealing huge muscles and sunburned arms. He was so – so tough, Georgia thought, and so funny and sexy and un-luvvie-like. And then she berated herself for even thinking so disloyally. Merlin was wonderful. And she – well she loved him, of course.

'Pretty good, isn't it? Your friend's done a great job.'

'Have you seen her? She was worrying about you being late.'

'Yeah, I've left Merl talking to her. And some bird in white trousers. Well, they *were* white. Pretty muddy now. She had a microphone. Well, I mean, show Merlin a microphone and he's off, isn't he? I mean, he's a great guy, but he don't half like the sound of his own voice. You and him a permanent item now, Georgia?'

'No!' said Georgia, and was shocked at the fervour with which her reply came out. 'No, we're just – well, you know.'

'Yeah, think so. Well, you're a big improvement on the last one, I'll give you that.'

'I thought you'd have liked Ticky,' said Georgia.

'No, not for me, love. All fur coat and no knickers, she was. Not my type at all.'

'And what is your type?' asked Georgia, genuinely curious.

'Oh – it varies. I know it when I see it. Look at old Merl, working the field. He do love a fresh audience.'

She looked; it was true. He was moving amongst the tents, talking to people, she could see him occasionally pointing up to the loos, across to the food stalls, good-naturedly helping them, he was holding ropes, mallets, children's hands. He looked amazing, of course – wearing jeans and brown riding boots and a white collarless shirt. He was such a sweetheart; she should appreciate him more, stop complaining about him being irritating.

She parked her car, and went to find Anna and Lila. Anna was down by the arena, checking everything out.

'Great piano,' she said, 'Japanese job. Just what I hoped for. And really well wired up. Lila's just been sick for the fourth time. She can do stage-fright better than anyone.'

'Oh, poor darling.' It was Merlin. 'Nothing worse. She'll be fine. I'll go and talk to her, see what I can do.'

'That won't help,' said Georgia tartly to Anna as he hurried off. 'Enough to make her sick again, I should think,' and then realised she had already broken her resolution to be nicer about him. How could she do this, when six months ago, she would have killed to have Merlin at her side, marked out as her boyfriend. What was the matter with her? And she did still like him so much, she really did. She was just a bit edgy. She'd be better when they'd finished this production; it was killing her.

Lila staggered over from behind the arena, where she'd been throwing up. Merlin had obviously been unable to find her.

'Mum, I can't do this.'

'Course you can,' said Georgia, putting her arm round her. 'You've got to anyway. Come on, let's go and talk to Merlin.'

Merlin was now sitting on the ground, sharing a bottle of water with a little girl wearing a long skirt, wellies and a patchwork hat. Her forehead wore a rainbow.

'Hi, Georgia, Lila. This is Saffron. This is her fourth festival this year.'

'Goodness,' said Georgia. 'That's impressive. Hi, Saffron. You having fun?'

'So fun, yes.'

'I like your hat.'

'My mummy bought it for me. From over there.' She pointed at the hat stall. 'She got one too.'

'Very nice.' Georgia smiled at Saffron's mum, a pretty dark-haired girl, who was wearing an identical hat to her daughter. Then she added: 'I want you to know, that stall was my idea.'

'Well, it was a very good one,' said Saffron's mum, 'it's lovely isn't it? We're great festival people. We always feel they're like mini-holidays. No stress, such freedom for the kids, and this is such a wonderful place. We've never been to one here before.'

'That's because there hasn't been one here before,' said Georgia. 'I know what you mean about festivals though. You're all together, and everyone's the same kind of person – nobody sort of jars, it's really cool.'

'Really cool! You look familiar – have I met you somewhere before?'

'Er, don't think so,' said Georgia. These small, sudden signs of her fame which had initially seemed so exciting had swiftly become burdensome. It was incredibly tedious: everyone asked the same questions, about the production, what various other people in it were like, how she'd got into acting, and – if the questioners were young – how she thought they might get into it. 'I've always loved acting,' they would say, as if that was more than enough. 'I did drama for my GCSEs. How do you get to hear about auditions, that sort of thing?'

She looked over at Merlin for help, but he was standing with Lila, talking to her rather intently. For some reason it annoyed her.

'Where's your tent?' she asked Anna. 'I might set up near you.'

'Oh, darling, do.'

'Georgia!' It was Abi, looking sensational in denim shorts, pink wellies and a pink T-shirt. 'How great is this. Listen, I need you to go and talk to that incredibly annoying girl from the local radio. She wants to interview you.'

'Do I have to? I want to go and talk to my parents. They've just arrived.'

'Yes, you bloody well do. Georgia, you haven't done anything at all yet today. Emma's been here since dawn and so has Barney. I could really have done with you . . .'

'All right, all right. I was actually working, you know.'

'Yes, I do know. You've told me at least six times. Go on, she's over there, in those rainbow-coloured wellies. Quickly, the first band's on in ten minutes – at least I hope they are, if Health and Safety have finished their checks.'

'Oh doesn't that look lovely?' said Linda, taking Alex's hand. 'It's so good that the rain's stopped. Smells so lovely too, the barbecues and . . . what's that other smell? Oh, I know – candy floss. Amy, darling, go and buy us all some yummy candy floss, would you?'

'Sure.'

'Not all of us,' said Alex. 'I can't stand the stuff. E-numbers on a stick. Terribly bad for you, give you a sugar rush.'

'You're such a misery, Dad.'

'My sentiments entirely,' said Linda. 'No, it's all wonderful. Even the music's not too bad.'

'All right if you like folk,' said Amy. 'Still, it's early, isn't it? It'll get better. I still can't believe they've got BroadBand. I think I might go and find my friends. They're all here. And—'

'Hi, Linda.' It was Abi. 'So lovely of you to come. Not really your thing, I'm sure.'

'Now why should you think that?' said Linda. 'I'm a veteran of the Reading festival. I've kept all the wristbands from the very first year.'

'Really? That is so cool. You must be Amy, hi. Having a good time?'

'Not yet she's not,' said Linda, 'but she's about to go and find her friends.'

'Yes, I was just saying I couldn't believe you'd got Broad-Band.'

'Nor can I, Amy. And you know, they're really quite nice.'

'Really?'

'Yes, really friendly. Chatty even. Tell you what, if you come and find me about twenty minutes before they play, if I'm still alive, I'll make sure you can be right at the front. You might be able to meet them. They said they wouldn't be rushing off.'

'Oh. My. God.' Amy's face went bright red. 'That would be just *sooo* cool.'

'Sure. And your friends. I'll be inside the arena – we've got a little base behind the bar.'

'Wow. Well – I'll see you then. God. So cool!'

'I think you've impressed her,' said Linda, laughing. 'Not easy, is it, Alex?'

'Not terribly.'

'It's so great you're here, Alex,' said Abi. 'I'm so glad.'

'Abi, this is partly for my hospital, so of course I'm here. I'm thrilled. Thrilled and grateful. We won't actually be camping but—'

'We would have been,' said Linda, 'if it had been up to me.'

867

'That is a filthy lie,' said Alex. 'This is the woman, Abi, who said she wouldn't so much as go inside a tent.'

'It is not a lie. I love camping. At times like this.'

'Well, there are plenty of tents for sale,' said Abi.

'Oh really?'

'Yeah, course. Over there, look. Only fifteen quid.'

'Well, we might,' said Linda. 'You never know.'

'Go on. Let your hair down. Lord, I must go. Health and Safety are approaching. Pray they're happy. We've had one hiccup already. They let us start, but said they'd be back to check we'd done what they said, and if we hadn't, they'd pull the plug. We have obviously, but – bye for now.'

'Gorgeous girl,' said Alex, looking after her appreciatively.

'Gorgeous. Do you think I'd look good in shorts and wellies?'

'Possibly. Then again, possibly not. You're not really going to buy a tent, are you?'

'Yes. I think I might. Why not?'

'You're such a bloody hypocrite. All that fuss insisting on booking into a hotel—'

'I'm not a hypocrite. I'm a spontaneous person, that's all. I suddenly realise it'd be really pathetic and – and middle-aged – to leave all this, go to a hotel.'

'Well, we are middle-aged.'

'You might be. I'm not. And if I may say so, you're acting more than middle-aged. More like old.'

'Thanks. Well, you'll be sleeping in the tent on your own, let me tell you.'

'Cool, as your daughter would say.'

'Oh, this is lovely!'

'Isn't it? You're not cold, are you, Mary?' asked Maeve.

'Why on earth should I be cold? The sun's perfectly beautiful.'

They were sitting, well wrapped up for it was evening

now, in picnic chairs, halfway up the hill facing the arena. There was a small metal road dividing the area where they were from the campsite, and the arena was beyond that; it was rather like being in the dress circle of a theatre, as Mary had said.

'Donald would have liked this,' Mary added. 'He loved folk music.'

'And Russell?'

'Oh, now Russell would have adored those two women. Really very, very good they were. I remember her husband, you know, he was one of the greats. One night he was on at Ronnie Scott's. I so wanted to go, but Donald hadn't been well. He always was inclined to chest trouble – I think it was being in that prisoner-of-war camp in Italy for so long.'

'I didn't know he was a prisoner of war?'

'Oh yes, he was. For over a year. Terrible conditions. They didn't get nearly enough to eat and in the winter, they were always cold. When he finally got home, he seemed to have shrunk, skin and bone, and was somehow shorter and with this terrible cough. But we fed him up and the doctor told him he should spend as much time as possible in the fresh air. He got an allotment and it did him so much good. It works a kind of magic, gardening does.'

'What a time you all had of it,' said Maeve.

'Yes, it was hard. But you know, it toughened us up.'

'It certainly seems to have done that. And you'd never have met Russell without it.'

'No. And missed out on so much happiness. Oh, now Georgia dear, how lovely to see you.'

'Abi said you were all here.' Georgia bent and kissed her. 'Enjoying yourselves?'

'So much. Aren't we, Maeve?'

'Where are the boys?' Georgia asked, looking around.

'On that carousel for the fourth or is it the fifth time,' said Maeve. 'They've had their faces painted and Liam has made a fine willow basket. It's such a success, Georgia. I do congratulate you.'

'I didn't do much. It's Abi who's made it happen. Is Tim around?'

'He certainly is,' said Mary. 'He and Lorraine brought me over. They think it's wonderful.'

'You've got a grandstand seat up here, haven't you?'

'We have indeed,' said Maeve. 'And we're about to open our Thermos of tea. Would you join us, Georgia?'

'That'd be lovely, but I promised Abi I'd go back down. Some television company have turned up now. We've done so well for publicity, and they want to – well, to . . .'

'To have you on, I'm sure,' said Mary, 'Of course. The festival celebrity.'

'Mary, hardly. There are masses of celebrities here. Some really well-known musicians. Very small beer, I am.'

'Somehow I don't think so,' said Mary. 'There are very few who've been on TV at peak viewing time. I felt so proud of you, dear.'

'Well, that's very nice. Look – I'll be back later. How long do you think you'll stay?'

'Certainly for another hour. And then we'll probably set out for home. They're all coming back to Tadwick for the night.'

'You must miss Russell so much,' said Georgia gently.

'I do, dear. But you know Patrick has his fine new job now.'

'Really? I'm so pleased. I didn't know.'

'Yes, he's office manager of a haulage company,' said Maeve, 'and even better, he's to be based in Reading, so that we can all see one another very much more easily, and Mary comes up nearly every weekend at the moment, to help and to babysit, so that Patrick and I can go out for an hour or two now and again.'

'That sounds really nice. I'm so pleased. Look, I must go, Abi's waving at me. I'll come back later, promise.'

'Don't worry too much, dear. You've got a lot on your plate.'

'I'm going down to find the boys,' said Maeve. 'They'll be sick if they have any more rides on that thing, on top of those burgers and the candy floss. Patrick has no idea how to refuse them anything. I won't be long, Mary.'

'No hurry,' said Mary. 'I'm very happy.'

And she was. She sat, looking down into the golden evening, at the little families wandering about, smiling, holding hands, at the young couples, arms around one another, at the lights of the roundabouts and the small old-fashioned carousel, turning so tirelessly, at the stage with the small figures playing on it, beside their larger selves on the screens, at the hundreds of tents, snuggled down into the grass, barbecues smoking gently, at the lovely evening-blue July sky, a few clouds drifting across it streaked with the sunset, and she felt an immense gratitude all of a sudden and thought how blessed she had been in her life, her long, mostly uneventful life, to have loved and been loved so much and known so much happiness, in spite of the sadness that she had had to bear. One could not ask for more than this, she thought; to be in a beautiful place, on a beautiful evening, surrounded even now by people she loved, and who cared for her, and with a head full of memories, wonderful charmed memories, and not one of them bitter, or angry, or ugly in any way. If her two husbands – both of whom she had loved so much and been so happy with – could be aware of her happiness now, they would be well pleased. And somehow, this evening, looking at the sky and the dusk just beginning to appear above the sunset, she felt it was very possible they were.

Laura was sitting on the sofa with Daisy, watching the evening news, when the announcer suddenly said, 'And now, as some properly seasonal weather seems finally to have arrived, and with more of the same promised for days to come, we take you over to one of those great icons of summer, a music festival. A rather special festival, one created for charity, in aid of the hospital which cared for the victims of the M4 crash in August last year. The brainchild of two of the people involved, although not hurt, in the crash, Abi Grainger and Georgia Linley – you may remember Georgia from *Moving Away*, the haunting Channel Four drama early this spring – they conceived it, nurtured it and brought it to life today. It is being held indeed, on the farm of William Grainger, on whose land the air ambulance landed that day; and who, incidentally, married Abi just three months ago. Isn't that right, Abi?'

And there she was, Laura thought, waiting to feel all the ugly, angry things for this girl, this beautiful sexy girl, in spite of her generosity towards her in the courtroom, smiling at the camera, dressed in shorts and a T-shirt and hugging the arm of her husband and saying, 'Yes, that's right, and none of this could have happened without the generosity of William and his parents, in allowing it to be held on their land.'

'I imagine it could all have been pretty alarming to someone not used to these things,' said the interviewer, a rather uneasy-looking young man, dressed for some reason all in black.

'Oh, it was pretty alarming to all of us, used to them or not. Including William's cows. But it's all turned out brilliantly. We've earned shi— huge loads of money for the charity, and any minute now one of the newest, most exciting bands in the country is going to play. So – go, BroadBand, go! And anyone in the vicinity, it's not too late, come on down and join us. Thanks. Thank you so much.'

And funnily enough, Laura didn't feel anything ugly at all, just a wave of relief that it was all finally over, the sadness and the bitterness, and a certain admiration for the new young Mrs Grainger who could so successfully turn tragedy into at least some kind of triumph.

'That looks fun,' said Daisy, gazing rather wistfully at the camera, weaving now among the crowds, the bizarrely dressed young, fairies, nuns, angels, all dancing in the semi-darkness, the children dancing too in circles, in and out of the tents and the barbecues, holding hands. 'Look, there's a whole family dancing there, and they've got sparklers, see? I wish we could go to a festival, Mummy. I'd really love that.'

'We will go, darling. Together. I'd like it too.'

It was Jonathan; he had come into the room and was standing beside the sofa, one hand on Laura's shoulder. 'If Mummy would like that.'

'Mummy would like it,' said Laura, not looking at him. 'Maybe not that one, but—'

'No,' he said, 'not that one,' and bent and kissed the top of her head. 'All right?'

'Yes, I'm all right,' said Laura. And realised that at last she was.

'You did a grand job with this, Abi.'

She turned; it was Jaz, Merlin's hugely sexy friend. How they could be friends, she wasn't sure, she couldn't imagine two people more different, but then people still kept saying that about her and William.

'Thank you. Yes, I'm pretty pleased. It was Georgia's idea in the first place, you know.'

'I do know. Now there's a little sweetheart. Too good for Merlin, I keep telling her.'

'Really?'

'Well, you know, he's seriously in love with himself. I'm well fond of him, in fact I'd say he's one of my best friends, but a little of him goes a long way, know what I mean?'

'I – think so,' said Abi carefully, 'but he's awfully sweet.'

'Course he is. Just knows it, that's all. But he's all right.'

She longed to continue with the conversation, but the last thing she wanted was to mess things up between Georgia and Merlin.

'Um – is the recording OK?'

'Yeah, it's fine, darling. Sid, me little brother, he's keeping an eye on it. Or rather an ear. Better go and check on him, I suppose. See you later.'

'Shit, look at that.' It was Georgia, her small face near to tears.

'Now what?'

'Merlin and Lila. They've been dancing together for ages.'

'So?'

'What do you mean, so? He's my boyfriend.'

'So?' said Abi again. 'You've been complaining about him for weeks. And he's only dancing with her, for God's sake.'

'Oh, I know. I'm sorry. I guess I'm just . . . confused. We do squabble an awful lot these days. It's so sad.' She sighed. 'Abi, what's wrong with me? I can't get it together properly with anyone. Even someone as lovely as Merlin.'

'I don't know why you want to,' said Abi. 'Half the country's in love with you.'

'Oh, don't be so ridiculous!'

'Yes. They are. You're famous. What you've always wanted. You've got an incredible time ahead of you, you'll probably be in Hollywood next—'

'Oh, right.'

'You will. You know what it is with you, Georgia, you just want so much. Fame, success, all that stuff. And you're beginning to get it. Why don't you just settle for that for a bit? Forget about lurve. You don't have to marry Merlin, for God's sake, you can just enjoy him. And then . . . well, let it take care of itself. I would.'

'I suppose you're right,' said Georgia slowly. 'I do feel I've come rather a long way. Since I first set eyes on Merlin, fell in love with him.'

'You have. You've dealt with so much crap, had all this success – make the most of it. It may not last. And then you'll kick yourself, that you didn't enjoy it more.'

'Yeah. Yeah, you're right. Sorry, Abi. I've been a pain. As usual.'

'Well, that's why we love you,' said Abi, grinning at her. 'We're used to it anyway. Oh hi, Jaz. Everything OK?'

'Everything's fine, yeah. Sid's doing a good job. Wondered if you'd like to come down and have a quick dance, Georgia?'

'I'd love to.'

'Right-oh. Mind you, I'm a terrible dancer.'

'I'm sure you're not.'

'Darlin', I am. Not like our Merl. I know me limitations. Don't mean I don't enjoy it though. Come on then.'

He was all right, Abi thought, smiling, watching them go off. Dead sexy, funny, cool, with none of Merlin's intense self-regard. Much more suitable for Georgia really . . . Now she was doing it, trying to get Georgia settled. She shouldn't be settled, she was a wild card, a loose cannon, she needed to make her own way. And she would. She really would.

'Right,' said Linda. 'I've got a tent.'

'You haven't.'

'Yes, I have. Look, it cost me fifteen quid, just like Abi said. Where shall we put it up?'

'There's no room for it anywhere. You'll be able to hear everybody else breathing, wherever it goes. Linda, do let's leave and go to the hotel.'

'I don't want to. I'm having an adventure. *We're* having an adventure.'

'Oh, for God's sake! The music, if you can call it that, is ghastly, it's getting cold, I'm tired—'

'OK. You go. That's fine.'

'You can't stay here on your own,' said Alex irritably.

'Yes, I can. I'll be fine.'

'Linda, you are not staying here on your own.'

'Well, I'm not leaving.'

'Oh, for fuck's sake! Why do you have to be so bloody dramatic!'

'I'm not being dramatic. I'm just entering into the spirit of the thing – which, considering your hospital is going to benefit so much, I'd have thought you should too. You're such a killjoy, Alex. You really are.'

'Well, thanks for that.' He'd been waiting for her, not far from where Mary had been, on the far side of the small valley. He sat down in the grass, glared gloomily down at the arena. 'You know, sometimes I wonder if this is worth it.'

'What on earth do you mean?'

'Well, we only see each other for two days a week, sometimes less, the occasional evening, and when we do, we fight. Where's the joy in that?'

'I – don't know. What are you trying to say?'

'That this is hardly an ideal existence, simply being together at the weekends. Maybe we should try again to find somewhere we can live together. Or even call it a day.'

'Do you really want to do that? Call it a day?' There was a shake in her voice.

He looked at her, put out his hand and took hers.

'No, of course not. I love you far too much. But this isn't working terribly well, is it?'

There was a long silence, then she said, 'No. Not terribly. Um, Alex . . .'

'Yes?'

'I – well, actually I have been thinking maybe I could, after all, move out a bit. Say to Windsor.'

'I hated Windsor. Maidenhead was OK.'

'I loathed Maidenhead.'

'Well, clearly we'll be settled in no time. But why, suddenly?'

'Because I think I could run my business at least two days a week from further out. I mean, I can always go in for meetings. And keep the office on. What would you think about that?'

'I'd think it would be amazing. Wonderful. But I don't believe it. It's a bit like Cherie Blair or Lady Thatcher suddenly announcing a woman's place is in the home.'

'Don't compare me to those awful women.'

'Sorry.'

'Anyway, I think you might have to. Believe it.'

'What do you mean?'

'I was – well, I was sick this morning.'

'Poor darling. You're obviously run down.'

'And the morning before. And the one before that.'

'Oh, dear.' He was rummaging in the picnic basket, muttering, 'I'm sure there was some wine left.'

'Alex! God, you medics are all the same. So unsympathetic. Didn't you hear what I said?'

'Yes, of course I did. You said you'd been sick this morning.'

'So?'

'Yes, and the two mornings before that.'

'So?'

'For Christ's sake! So – I think I might be pregnant. Well, I'm pretty sure I'm pregnant. Actually.'

'You what?'

'Alex, you're not deaf yet. I said I was pregnant.'

'Oh my God,' he said, staring at her, his face frozen with shock. 'God. Linda. Oh, my Linda.' He sat back on the grass staring at her in total silence, then put out his hand and stroked her cheek. Very gently. 'How did that happen?'

'Usual way, I suppose.'

'Yes, but—'

'I had that stomach upset last month, remember? Not good with the pill.'

'Oh my God.'

877

'So are you pleased?'

'Oh no,' he said, 'I'm not pleased.' Then: 'I'm ecstatic! Totally, gloriously ecstatic! It's wonderful. Amazing. You?'

'I'm – moderately ecstatic. Bit thoughtful. I don't know how I'll do at it.'

'How you do at everything else, that's how. Brilliantly. Oh Linda, I'm so . . .' He stopped. Seemed near to tears. She smiled at him, leaned forward and kissed him.

'I'm glad you're pleased.'

'I'm – well, I'm much more than pleased. How do you feel though?'

'Fine. Except in the morning. As you'll probably find out tomorrow. Oh – and tired. Bit tired.'

'We must get you back to the hotel, straight away.'

'Alex, I don't want to go back to the hotel. I really want to stay here, in this tent, with you.'

'Oh, don't be so ridiculous!'

'Please,' she said, and even in the darkness he could see her eyes shining. 'Please. For a little while anyway. Go on, Alex. I dare you.'

'Well, Abi, what a success, eh?' It was Peter Grainger, smiling at her. 'I take my hat off to you. It was quite something, but you've pulled it off. And so far – no problems.'

'No, not yet,' said Abi. 'Don't speak too soon.'

'Oh, I have total faith in you, you and your arrangements. I must admit I had my doubts, but I was wrong. Where's young William?'

'I don't know. I haven't seen him for ages. Um – where's . . . Barbara?' She still had the utmost difficulty in referring to Mrs Grainger by her Christian name.

'She's in bed, I'm afraid.'

'Oh, no. What's wrong?'

'Obviously eaten something very nasty. Keeps being sick. And – well, never mind. I'm sure she'll be better tomorrow.'

'Oh, that's terrible,' said Abi. 'I'm so sorry.' Thinking of her silent prayer of the morning and wondering if the God she so firmly didn't believe in had actually sent Mrs Grainger's illness as a sign to her of His existence.

'Yes, but you know, I don't think she'd have enjoyed this too much. And she'd have felt bound to come down and have a look. And then she'd have started worrying about everything.'

'Yes. Yes, I suppose so. But she must be bothered by the noise.'

'Funnily enough, you can hardly hear it in the house. Something to do with the sound going over the top of the trees, perhaps. I don't know. Anyway, she'll be fine tomorrow, don't you worry. Now, this isn't really my sort of music, but I wonder if we could have a dance.'

And William, arriving back at the arena, was met by the astonishing sight of his father and Abi dancing together in the near-darkness, his father doing an approximation of the Twist that his generation still clung to on the dance floor, his arms gyrating like crazed chicken wings, and Abi scarcely moving, swaying and curving with the music, the sparklers she was holding making patterns in the darkness. He really did love her, so very much.

Later, they climbed the hill behind the arena and sat down, looking and listening, to the music, the laughter, the shouting, the occasional child crying: and at the little barbecue fires all over the campsite, shining in the darkness, like fairylights strung across the hill, and above them a full moon, rising most obligingly in the sky, trailing stars in its wake.

'That calf was all right, by the way,' he said. 'I forgot to tell you in all the excitement. And it was a heifer.'

'Oh, good. I think you should call her Festival.'

'Abi! You sound like a Bambi-lover. You know we don't give calves names.'

'I am a Bambi-lover. And why not? Just this once. It is a very special day. One of the best.'

'Oh, all right.' There was a silence; then, 'You're right,' he said. 'It is one of the best. And you know, I was just thinking . . .'

'I was thinking the same thing,' she said. 'That terrible, terrible day then, the awful things that happened, and now – well, look at us. Good times, in spite of it. Maybe because of it even. Very good. The best, you could almost say.'

'Yes,' he said, putting his arm round her. 'Yes, you could almost say that. Or you could actually say it. Come on, Mrs Grainger. Let's go down there and dance. And then we might go home and take those shorts off.'

Now you can buy any of these bestselling books
by **Penny Vincenzi** from your bookshop
or *direct from her publisher*.

FREE P&P AND UK DELIVERY
(Overseas and Ireland £3.50 per book)

Wicked Pleasures	£7.99
An Outrageous Affair	£7.99
Another Woman	£7.99
Forbidden Places	£7.99
The Dilemma	£7.99
Windfall	£7.99
Almost A Crime	£7.99
No Angel	£7.99
Something Dangerous	£7.99
Into Temptation	£7.99
Sheer Abandon	£7.99
An Absolute Scandal	£7.99
The Best of Times	£7.99

TO ORDER SIMPLY CALL THIS NUMBER

01235 400 414

or visit our website: www.headline.co.uk

Prices and availability subject to change without notice.